Luke Tyerman

The Oxford Methodists

Memoirs of the Rev. Messrs. Clayton, Ingham, Gambold, Hervey and Broughton

Luke Tyerman

The Oxford Methodists
Memoirs of the Rev. Messrs. Clayton, Ingham, Gambold, Hervey and Broughton

ISBN/EAN: 9783337009861

Printed in Europe, USA, Canada, Australia, Japan

Cover: Foto ©Raphael Reischuk / pixelio.de

THE
OXFORD METHODISTS:

MEMOIRS OF THE

REV. MESSRS. CLAYTON, INGHAM, GAMBOLD,

HERVEY, AND BROUGHTON,

WITH BIOGRAPHICAL NOTICES OF OTHERS.

BY THE

Rev. L. TYERMAN,

AUTHOR OF "THE LIFE AND TIMES OF THE REV. JOHN WESLEY, M.A.,
FOUNDER OF THE METHODISTS."

NEW YORK:

HARPER & BROTHERS, PUBLISHERS,

FRANKLIN SQUARE.

1873.

PREFACE.

THE present book is intended to serve as a companion volume to "The Life and Times of Wesley;" and to assist in showing the wide and gracious results of a revival of religion.

In compiling the work just mentioned, I was compelled, by want of space, to lay aside a large amount of biographical material, some portions of which are embodied in the work now submitted to the reader; and other portions of which may be published at a future time.

Memoirs of the two Wesleys and of Whitefield have been designedly omitted, on the ground, that, their Memoirs, *in extenso*, are already in existence. Still, those illustrious men are often noticed in the following pages; and, I hope, the facts concerning them will be both interesting and instructive. Of the other Oxford Methodists, no biographies have been previously written, with the exception of Hervey; and it is not censorious to say, that the two principal ones of him,— Ryland's and Brown's—are far from satisfactory.

The information concerning some of the Oxford Brotherhood is meagre. I have used all the diligence I could in obtaining materials; but brief notices, and scraps, and a few letters are all that I have to give. Fragmentary, however, though they are, I trust, they will not be regarded as useless and irrelevant. The biographical sketches of Clayton, Ingham, Gambold, Hervey, and Broughton, are more extended. It would have been a satisfaction to have left Westley Hall in the shades of oblivion ; but, in telling the story of the Oxford Methodists, it was impossible not to notice him.

A marvellous work was accomplished by the Wesley brothers and by Whitefield ; but it is a great mistake, and not a just acknowledgment of the grace of God, to regard the results of the revival of religion in the Oxford University, as confined to Methodism. Contemporaneous Reformers, raised up by Providence, are seldom all employed in the same kind of work. At the beginning of the Christian era, God "gave some, apostles, and some, prophets, and some, evangelists, and some, pastors, and teachers, for the perfecting of the saints, for the work of the ministry, for the edifying of the body of Christ" (Ephesians iv. 11, 12). Luther, Zuinglius, Melancthon, Œcolampadius, Erasmus, Calvin, Knox, Ridley, Latimer, and Cranmer were all engaged, at the same time, in the same great and glorious reformation ; but the services they rendered were as various as the dispositions and talents of the men themselves. So in regard to the movement in the Oxford University. Among the Oxford Methodists, the Wesleys and Whitefield will always be pre-eminent ; but a great work was also done by their associates. Clayton's High-Churchism was objectionable ; but it is not unreasonable to indulge the hope, that, his earnest piety exercised a useful influence upon the clergy among whom ·he lived, and especially upon the young gentlemen who were favoured with the instructions of his school. Ingham, as an evangelist, was exceedingly successful among the masses in the North. The Moravian Church owes a debt of incalculable gratitude to Gambold, for checking and correcting its early religious follies. Broughton was efficiently employed in promoting the translation of the Bible, in the work of Home and Foreign Missions, in the distribution of religious tracts, and in the education of the children of the poor, at a period when the present principal societies for such objects did not exist. Hutchins, though retaining, at least, a few of his High-Church doctrines, was a spiritually-minded, earnest Christian ; and, in the important office which, for so many years, he held in Lincoln College, could hardly fail in moulding the minds and hearts of some of the young students there. And Hervey was one of the first clergymen of the Church of England, in the last century, who turned the attention of the upper classes of society to religious matters. These were not trifling services. Do they not deserve to be recorded ?

The Oxford revival of religion was pregnant with the most momentous issues. And so are most revivals. How often in the history of Methodism, though on a smaller scale, have its revivals of the work of God resulted in consequences bearing some analogy to those of the Oxford movement of a hundred and forty years ago? Who will not pray, that such "Divine visitations" may be continued and multiplied, not only in Methodism, but, in all the Churches of the Great Redeemer?

The Oxford Methodists, up to the time of their general dispersion from that seat of learning, were all (excepting, perhaps, Whitefield) Church of England *Ritualists*. Their moral conduct was most exemplary. They were studious, devout, self-denying, charitable. Their study of the Bible gained them the nicknames of "Bible-bigots," and "Bible-moths." Every morning and every evening, they spent an hour in private prayer ; and, throughout the day, habituated themselves to the use of ejaculations, for humility, faith, hope, and love. They communicated at Christ Church once a week, and persuaded all they could to attend public prayers, sermons, and sacraments. They were constant visitors of the inmates of the parish workhouse, and of the prisoners in the Castle; and it was the practice of all of them to dispense in charity all they had, after providing for their own necessities. They also observed the discipline of the Church of England to the minutest points; and were scrupulously strict in practising the rubrics and canons. Every Wednesday and Friday, they fasted, tasting no food whatever, till three o'clock in the afternoon. Though, perhaps, they never held the doctrine of the human nature of the Divine Redeemer being present in the elements of the holy sacrament, they held something approaching this, and spoke of "an outward sacrifice offered therein." They more than approved of the mixture of water with the sacramental wine; and religiously observed saint days, holidays, and Saturdays. They maintained the doctrine of apostolical succession, and believed no one had authority to administer the sacraments who was not *episcopally* ordained. Even in Georgia, Wesley excluded Dissenters from the holy communion, on the ground, that they had not been properly baptized, and would himself baptize only by immersion, unless the child, or person, was in a weak state of health. He also enforced confession, penance, and mortification; and, as far as possible, carried into execution the Apostolic Constitutions. In short, with the exception of sacerdotal millinery, the burning of incense, the worship of the Virgin, prayers for the dead, and two or three other kindred superstitions, the Oxford Methodists were the predecessors of the present *ritualistic* party in the Church of England.

The Oxford Methodists, however, had no desire to aggrandize themselves. They had not the slightest wish to be considered superior to their fellow mortals. They were sincere, and earnest inquirers after truth, and, in the study of the Holy Bible, in prayer to God, and in other devotional exercises, were an example worthy of imitation. God rarely leaves such inquirers in the dark. Wesley, and most of his Oxford friends were brought to a knowledge of "the truth as it is in *Jesus;*" and, being so, their faith, their energy, their prayers, their toils, and their cheerfully endured sufferings resulted in one of the most glorious revivals of the work of God, recorded in the history of the Christian Church.

May we not indulge the hope, that, what God did for the Oxford Methodists, He will do for those at the present day, who, in most respects, resemble them? Ought we not to pray for this? Indeed, has it not, to some extent, been realized? Though the *leaders* of the Oxford Tractarian movement have unquestionably served the interests of the Church of Rome, far more than the interests of the Church which nurtured them; yet, is it not a fact, that some of the hard-working evangelical clergy of the Church of England, now so successfully employed in the spread of truth, began their Christian life as the Oxford Methodists began theirs? And is it wrong to prayerfully cherish the expectation, that, in mercy to mankind, others will be brought to the same convictions? The Church, the Nation, and the World need their energy, earnestness, diligence, self-denial, and devotion. Let them lay aside their popish follies and proud pretensions and embrace the truth of Christ in its simplicity and its purity, and, at least, some of them may, under God, accomplish a work as great and as blessed as was accomplished by Wesley and his "Holy Club."

I have nothing more to add, except to express my obligations to the descendants of the Oxford Methodists, for their courteous kindness in responding to my requests for information; and to other clergymen and gentlemen with whom I have been in correspondence.

The book is .not a series of written portraits. I make no pretensions to artistic skill. I have simply done my best in collecting facts, from every source within my reach; and have narrated them as truly and as lucidly as I could.

L. TYERMAN.

STANHOPE HOUSE, CLAPHAM PARK,
 April 2nd, 1873.

THE
OXFORD METHODISTS.

THE FIRST OF THE OXFORD METHODISTS.

ROBERT KIRKHAM.

1729
to
1735

WESLEY writes:—"In November, 1729, four young gentlemen of Oxford,—Mr. John Wesley, Fellow of Lincoln College; Mr. Charles Wesley, Student of Christ Church; Mr. Morgan, Commoner of Christ Church; and Mr. Kirkham, of Merton College,—began to spend some evenings in a week together in reading, chiefly, the Greek Testament."[1]

These were the first Oxford Methodists; and, though there is little to be said of Morgan, and still less of Kirkham, they must not be passed in silence. Methodism may be traced to their associating with the two Wesleys, to read the Greek Testament, in 1729.

Robert Kirkham was the son of the Rev. Lionel Kirkham, a clergyman resident at Stanton, in Gloucestershire. The family consisted of Robert and at least two sisters, Sarah and Betty.

Sarah was the intimate friend of Mary Granville, afterwards Mrs. Delany, a woman of great accomplishments, who moved in the highest society and, for more than fifty years, was honoured with the friendship and confidence of King George III. and his Queen Charlotte. Sarah Kirkham was born in 1699; and, in 1725, was married to the Rev. John Capon, or, as the name is sometimes spelt, Chapone. She was a woman of great intellect and of an intensely warm and generous nature. "Sally," wrote Mary Granville, in 1737, then Mrs.

---

[1] Wesley's Works. vol. viii., p. 334.

B

Pendarves, "would shine in an assembly composed of Tullys, Homers, and Miltons: at Gloucester, she is like a diamond set in jet,—their dulness makes her brightness brighter."[1] Mrs. Chapone died in 1764.

Her sister Betsy was probably the first of Wesley's sweethearts. As early as February 2, 1726, Robert Kirkham, writing, from home, to his "Dear Jacke," at "Lincoln College, Oxford, by the Worcester carrier," says,—

"Your most deserving, queer character, your personal accomplishments, your noble endowments of mind, your little and handsome person, and your most obliging and desirable conversation,—have often been the pleasing subject of our discourse. Often have you been in the thoughts of M. B." [Miss Betsy ?] "which I have curiously observed, when with her alone, by her inward smiles and sighs, and by her abrupt expressions concerning you Shall this suffice? I caught her this morning in an humble and devout posture on her knees. I must conclude; and subscribe myself your most affectionate friend, and *brother I wish I might write,*

"ROBERT KIRKHAM."

Twelve months after this, Wesley's sister Martha wrote to him as follows :—

"When I knew that you were just returned from Worcestershire, where, I suppose, you saw your Varenese" [the pet name of Betsy Kirkham], "I then ceased to wonder at your silence ; for the sight of such a woman might well make you forget me. I really have myself a vast respect for her, as I must necessarily have for one that is so dear to you."

For more than three years subsequent to this, Wesley kept up a correspondence with Kirkham's sister, and spoke of her in the tenderest terms. In 1731, their friendship was interrupted. Why? Did the young lady's father interfere? Or did she herself prefer another? These are questions which it is almost impossible to answer; but it is a significant fact that, though the Kirkham family seems to have consisted of only one son and two daughters, one of those daughters died about twelve months afterwards ; she, at the time of her death, bearing the name of Mrs. Wilson. Hence the following extract from a letter, written by Mrs. Pendarves, and dated " Killala, June 28th, 1732."

"Poor Mrs. Wilson! I am sorry for the shock her death must have

---

[1] Autobiography of Mrs. Delany, vol. i., p. 586.

given Sally" [Mrs. Chapone] " whose tenderness must sometimes take place of her wisdom ; but I hope when she considers the great advantage her sister, in all probability, will receive by the exchange she has lately made, that she will be reconciled to the loss of a sister that has given her more woe than happiness.   Pray, has Mrs. Wilson left any children ?"

1729
to
1735

Was Mrs. Wilson the quondam Betsy Kirkham ? It is probable she was ; for, though Mrs. Pendarves and Mrs. Chapone continued to be the warmest friends for thirty-two years after this, there is not, in the voluminous correspondence of the former, the least allusion to Betsy.

Perhaps these notices of Robert Kirkham's sisters are hardly relevant ; but it must be borne in mind that Kirkham was one of Wesley's warmest friends, and that he wished to have Wesley for a brother.

As already intimated, of Robert Kirkham himself next to nothing has been published.   In a letter to his mother, dated February 28, 1730, three months after the first Methodist meeting in Oxford, Wesley wrote :—

"I have another piece of news to acquaint you with, which, as it is more strange, will, I hope, be equally agreeable. A little while ago, Bob Kirkham took a fancy into his head, that he would lose no more time and waste no more money ; in pursuance of which, he first resolved to breakfast no longer on tea ; next, to drink no more ale in an evening, or, however, but to quench his thirst ; then to read Greek or Latin from prayers in the morning till noon, and from dinner till five at night. And how much may one imagine he executed of these resolutions ? Why, he has left off tea, struck off his drinking acquaintances to a man, given the hours above specified to the Greek Testament and Hugo Grotius, and spent the evenings either by himself or with my brother and me."

This was a brave act.   For a frank, frivolous, jovial young fellow like Robert Kirkam, who, in a letter to Wesley, four years before, had told his friend of his revelling over a dish of calves' head and bacon, and a newly-tapped barrel of excellent cider, now to resolve to live a life like that which Wesley mentions, and to have firmness enough to fulfil his resolution, was no ordinary fact, and indicated a great change in the light-hearted young collegian. Was not this the very commencement of the Methodist organization ?

In 1731, Kirkham took his leave of the Oxford brother-

1729
to
1735 hood, to become his uncle's curate. Where did he live after this? How did he live? When did he die? These are questions which we cannot answer. We have tried to obtain information concerning his subsequent career, but have failed.

WILLIAM MORGAN.

WILLIAM MORGAN was not only one of the first Oxford Methodists, but the first of them to enter heaven. The Wesleys and Kirkham were the sons of English clergymen. Morgan was the son of an Irish gentleman, resident in Dublin. As already stated, he was a Commoner of Christ Church; and Samuel Wesley, junior, who was well acquainted with him, speaks of him in the highest terms. From his childhood, he had been devout and diligent; he revered and loved his father; was a warm-hearted, faithful friend; a welcome visitor of orphans, widows, and prisoners; neither a formalist nor an enthusiast; but a man whose life was a beautiful gospel sermon, in a practical, embodied form. A short extract from Samuel Wesley's poem, on Mr. Morgan's death, will not be out of place.

> " Wise in his prime, he waited not till noon,
> Convinced that mortals ' never lived too soon.'
> As if foreboding then his little stay,
> He made his morning bear the heat of day.
> Fixed, while unfading glory he pursues,
> No ill to hazard, and no good to lose ;
> No fair occasion glides unheeded by ;
> Snatching the golden moments as they fly,
> He, by fleeting hours, ensures eternity.
> Friendship's warm beams his artless breast inspire,
> And tenderest reverence to a much-loved sire.
> He dared, for heaven, this flattering world forego ;
> Ardent to teach, as diligent to know ;
> Unwarped by sensual ends, or vulgar aims,
> By idle riches, or by idler names ;
> Fearful of sin in every close disguise ;
> Unmoved by threatening or by glozing lies ;
> Gladdening the poor where'er his steps he turned,
> Where pined the orphan, or the widow mourned ;
> Where prisoners sighed beneath guilt's horrid stain,
> The worst confinement and the heaviest chain ;

1729
to
1735

Where death's sad shade the uninstructed sight
Veil'd with thick darkness in the land of light.
Nor yet the priestly function he invades:
'Tis not his sermon, but his life, persuades.
Humble and teachable, to church he flies,
Prepared to practise, not to criticise.
Then only angry, when a wretch conveys
The Deist's poison in the Gospel phrase.
To means of grace the last respect he showed,
Nor sought new paths, as wiser than his God;
Their sacred strength preserved him from extremes
Of empty outside, or enthusiast dreams;
Whims of Molinos, lost in rapture's mist,
Or Quaker, late-reforming Quietist."[1]

It was in November, 1729, that the first four of the Oxford Methodists began their sacred meetings. Two months later, William Morgan wrote to Wesley the following, which contains a reference to the interest that the Methodists already took in prisoners, and which, being one of the very few of Morgan's letters still existing, may not be unacceptable.

"*February* 5, 1730.

"DEAR SIR,—About seven last night I reached Oxford, and, after having long rested my wearied limbs, went this morning to Bo-Cro, who have exceeded our best wishes. I have just finished my rounds, and perceive it was not for nothing that I came hither before you. Stewart's papers will not be in London till Monday. He desires you to get the rule of court for him, and let him have it as soon as possible. Coster begs you would call at Mrs. Hannah Ebbins', upholsterer, in Shadwell Street, near Tower Hill, at the sign of the Flag, and let her know his present condition. She is very rich, he says, and has often told him she would at any time do him whatever service she could.

"Fisher desires you to look into the *Gazette*, and see whether the estate of John Davies, of Goldington and Ravensden,[2] is to be sold.

"You would do well to buy a few cheap spelling-books if you can meet with any, for they are wanted much at the Castle.

"Comb's goods were seized last week, and 'tis thought he is gone to London. If he should call on you for what you owe him, put him in mind of paying you, for me, the twelve shillings he owes me. I forgot to tell you that I neglected to call at Mrs. Baxter's landlord's. I wish you would bring my picture of Queen Elizabeth to Oxford, as carefully as you can; it is in a large book in your sister's closet. There is a plan of mine in the box with your linen, which I likewise desire you would bring with

---

[1] "Poems on Several Occasions," by Samuel Wesley, A.M., 1736, p. 107.
[2] Two villages in Bedfordshire.

you.　Pray give my love to Charles, best respects to your brother and sister, and service to Mrs. Berry [1] and Miss Nancy.

"I am, dear sir,

"Your sincere friend, and affectionate humble servant,

"WILLIAM MORGAN.

"Pray don't forget to inquire for my pocket-book."

This curious letter of small commissions is not devoid of interest, inasmuch as it plainly shows,—1. The close intimacy between Morgan and the Wesley brothers.　2. Morgan's keenness in looking after his pecuniary rights.　And 3. That some, at least, of the Oxford Methodists were not, as yet, so intensely religious as they soon afterwards became.

It was not long before the young collegians evinced more earnestness.　Wesley writes :—

"In the summer of 1730, Mr. Morgan told me he had called at the gaol, to see a man who was condemned for killing his wife ; and that, from the talk he had with one of the debtors, he verily believed it would do much good, if any one would be at the pains of now and then speaking with them.　This he so frequently repeated, that, on the 24th of August, 1730, my brother and I walked with him to the Castle.　We were so well satisfied with our conversation there, that we agreed to go thither once or twice a week ; which we had not done long, before he desired me to go with him to see a poor woman in the town, who was sick.　In this employment, too, when we came to reflect upon it, we believed it would be worth while to spend an hour or two in a week ; provided the minister of the parish, in which any such person was, were not against it.　But that we might not depend wholly on our own judgments, I wrote an account to my father of our whole design ; withal begging that he, who had lived seventy years in the world, and seen as much of it as most private men have ever done, would advise us whether we had yet gone too far, and whether we should now stand still, or go forward."

Wesley's father highly approved of the project of the young Methodists, and wrote,—

"You have reason to bless God, as I do, that you have so fast a friend as Mr. Morgan, who, I see, in the most difficult service, is ready to break the ice for you.　You do not know of how much good that poor wretch, who killed his wife, has been the providential occasion.　I think I must adopt Mr. Morgan to be my son, together with you and your brother Charles ; and, when I have such a ternion to prosecute that war, wherein I am now *miles emeritus*, I shall not be ashamed when they speak with their enemies in the gate."

---

[1] Probably the mother of the wife of Wesley's brother Samuel.

The venerable Rector of Epworth then proceeds to advise them to consult with the chaplain of the prisoners, and to obtain the direction and approbation of the bishop.

This was done.   Wesley writes:—

"In pursuance of these directions, I immediately went to Mr. Gerard, the Bishop of Oxford's chaplain, who was likewise the person that took care of the prisoners when any were condemned to die (at other times they were left to their own care). I proposed to him our design of serving them as far as we could, and my own intention to preach there once a month, if the bishop approved of it. He much commended our design, and said he would answer for the bishop's approbation, to whom he would take the first opportunity of mentioning it. It was not long before he informed me that he had done so, and that his lordship not only gave his permission, but was greatly pleased with the undertaking, and hoped it would have the desired success."[1]

Methodism, in its beneficence, was now fairly started. Its first object was a condemned felon; its first visitor, William Morgan; its first approver, Wesley's father; and its next the Bishop of Oxford, with his chaplain, Mr. Gerard.

The small band of godly collegians soon became the butt of ridicule. Robert Kirkham especially was stigmatized as a member of *The Holy Club;* and his college (Merton) became immensely merry at the expense of him and his companions. On December 1st, 1730, Wesley's father addressed to them a letter to inspire them with confidence and hope :—

"Upon this encouragement," writes Wesley, "we still continued to meet together as usual; and to confirm one another, as well as we could, in our resolutions to communicate as often as we had opportunity (which is here once a week) ; and to do what service we could to our acquaintance, the prisoners, and two or three poor families in the town."

To the reading of the Greek Testament, and the visiting of prisoners and the poor, we here have weekly communion added to the programme of Oxford Methodism. What was the result?

Wesley continues :—

"The outcry daily increasing, that we might show what ground there was for it, we proposed to our friends or opponents, as we had opportunity, these or the like questions :—

1729
to
1735

---

[1] Wesley's Works, vol. i., p. 8.

1729
to
1735

"I. Whether it does not concern all men of all conditions to imitate Him, as much as they can, 'Who went about doing good'?

"Whether all Christians are not concerned in that command, 'While we have time, let us do good unto all men'?

"Whether we shall not be more happy hereafter, the more good we do now?

"Whether we can be happy at all hereafter, unless we have, according to our power, 'fed the hungry, clothed the naked, visited those that are sick, and in prison;' and made all these actions subservient to a higher purpose, even the saving of souls from death?

"Whether it be not our bounden duty always to remember, that He did more for us than we can do for Him, who assures us, 'Inasmuch as ye have done it unto one of the least of these my brethren, ye have done it unto Me'?

"II. Whether, upon these considerations, we may not try to do good to our acquaintance? Particularly, whether we may not try to convince them of the necessity of being Christians?

"Whether of the consequent necessity of being scholars?

"Whether of the necessity of method and industry, in order to either learning or virtue?

"Whether we may not try to persuade them to confirm and increase their industry, by communicating as often as they can?

"Whether we may not mention to them the authors whom we conceive to have wrote the best on those subjects?

"Whether we may not assist them, as we are able, from time to time, to form resolutions upon what they read in those authors, and to execute them with steadiness and perseverance?

"III. Whether, upon the considerations above-mentioned, we may not try to do good to those that are hungry, naked, or sick? In particular, whether, if we know any necessitous family, we may not give them a little food, clothes, or physic, as they want?

"Whether we may not give them, if they can read, a Bible, Common Prayer Book, or 'Whole Duty of Man'?

"Whether, we may not, now and then, inquire how they have used them, explain what they do not understand, and enforce what they do?

"Whether we may not enforce upon them, more especially, the necessity of private prayer, and of frequenting the church and sacrament?

"Whether we may not contribute, what little we are able, toward having their children clothed and taught to read?

"Whether we may not take care that they be taught their catechism, and short prayers for morning and evening?

"IV. Lastly: whether, upon the considerations above-mentioned, we may not try to do good to those that are in prison? In particular, whether we may not release such well-disposed persons as remain in prison for small sums?

"Whether we may not lend smaller sums to those that are of any trade, that they may procure themselves tools and materials to work with?

"Whether we may not give to them who appear to want it most, a little money, or clothes, or physic?

"Whether we may not supply as many as are serious enough to read, with a Bible and a Whole Duty of Man?

"Whether we may not, as we have opportunity, explain and enforce these upon them, especially with respect to public and private prayer, and the blessed sacrament?"[1]

Such, at the end of 1730, was the plan of benevolent action drawn up by the Oxford Methodists. Who can find fault with it? Wesley tells us, that they met with none who answered these questions in the negative, and that several helped them with quarterly subscriptions.[2]

Thus encouraged, the two Wesleys, Kirkham, and Morgan, cheerily pursued their way, "in spite of the ridicule which increased fast upon them during the winter." The men of wit, in Christ Church, called them Sacramentarians. Their allies, at Merton, styled them The Holy Club. Others stigmatized them as The Godly Club; and others the Enthusiasts, or the Reforming Club; but ridicule, though far from pleasant, failed to check them in their laborious career.

In the summer of 1731, Mr. Morgan was disabled, by an attack of sickness, and retired to Holt; but under the date of June 11th, Wesley writes :—

"The poor at the Castle, however, have still the Gospel preached to them, and some of their temporal wants supplied, our little fund rather increasing than diminishing. Nor have we yet been forced to discharge any of the children which Mr. Morgan left to our care : though I wish they too do not find the want of him; I am sure some of their parents will."[3]

Mr. Morgan's affliction excited great interest in the Wesley family. Matthew Wesley, an eminent physician in London, was on a visit to his brother Samuel, the Rector of Epworth, and from thence went to Scarborough. In a letter to her son John, dated, "Epworth, July 12, 1731," Susannah Wesley wrote :—

"Before your uncle went to Scarborough, I informed him of what I knew of Mr. Morgan's case. When he came back, he told me he had tried the spa at Scarborough, and could assure me that it far exceeded all the

---

[1] Wesley's Works, vol. i., p. 9.   [2] Ibid. p. 10.
[3] Ibid. vol. xii., p. 6.

other spas in Europe, for he had been at them all, both in Germany and elsewhere; that, at Scarborough, there were two springs, as he was informed, close together, which flowed into one basin, the one a chalybeate, the other a purgative water; and he did not believe there was the like in any other part of the world. He said, ' If that gentleman, you told me of, could by any means be got thither, though his age is the most dangerous time in life for his distemper, yet I am of opinion those waters would cure him.' I thought good to tell you this, that you might, if you please, inform Mr. Morgan of it."

Poor Morgan's work was ended.

" For more than twelve months," writes Mr. Moore, "he was so greatly reduced, that he became a burden to himself, and totally useless to others. In this stage of his disease, his understanding sometimes appeared deranged; he became more changeable in his temper than usual, and inconsistent in his conversation. But this was purely the effect of his disease; not the least symptom of the kind having ever appeared till long after his health had declined."

In the month of March, 1732, his father informed him that he should no longer be limited to a fixed allowance, but should have all the money that was necessary for his state of health; at the same time, however, strongly insisting that no part of his remittances should be spent in charity; and adding,—

" You cannot conceive what a noise that ridiculous society in which you are engaged has made here. Besides the particulars of the great follies of it at Oxford (which to my great concern I have often heard repeated), it gave me sensible trouble to hear that you were noted for going into the villages about Holt; calling their children together, and teaching them their prayers and catechism, and giving them a shilling at your departure. I could not but advise with a wise, pious, and learned clergyman. He told me that he has known the worst of consequences follow from such blind zeal; and plainly satisfied me that it was a thorough mistake of true piety and religion. I proposed writing to some prudent and good man at Oxford to reason with you on these points, and to convince you that you were in a wrong way. He said, in a generous mind, as he took yours to be, the admonition and advice of a father would make a deeper impression than all the exhortations of others. He concluded, that you were young as yet, and that your judgment was not come to its maturity; but as soon as your judgment improved, and on the advice of a true friend, you would see the error of your way, and think, as he does, that you may walk uprightly and safely, without endeavouring to outdo all the good bishops, clergy, and other pious and good men of the present and past ages: which God Almighty give you grace and sense to understand aright!"[1]

Thus had the young Methodists to encounter, not only the ridicule of the outside world, but the rebuke of their own relatives and friends. The Epworth rector encouraged them; the Dublin gentleman pronounced upon them censure.

A month after the date of Mr. Morgan's letter to his sick son, Samuel Wesley, junior, paid a visit to the Oxford Methodists, and, on his return to London, wrote a poetical epistle to his brother Charles, dated April 20, 1732. The following are some of the concluding lines :-

> "One or two questions more, before I end,
> That much concern a brother and a friend:—
> Does John beyond his strength presume to go,
> To his frail carcase literally a foe?
> Lavish of health, as if in haste to die,
> And shorten time to insure eternity?
> Does Morgan weakly think his time misspent?
> Of his best actions can he now repent?
> Others, their sins with reason just deplore,
> The guilt remaining when the pleasure's o'er;
> Shall he for virtue, first, himself upbraid,
> Since the foundation of the world was laid?
> Shall he (what most men to their sins deny)
> Show pain for alms, remorse for piety?
> Can he the sacred Eucharist decline?
> What Clement poisons here the bread and wine?
> Or does his sad disease possess him whole,
> And taint alike the body and the soul?
> If to renounce his graces he decree,
> O that he could transfer the stroke to me!
> Does earth grow fairer to his parting eye?
> Is heaven less lovely, as it seems more nigh?
> O, wondrous preparation this—to die!"

Two months subsequent to Samuel Wesley's visit, poor Morgan took his final departure from his friends at Oxford. He was sick in body and in mind. His end was near, though he knew it not. Leaving Oxford on the 5th of June, 1732, he proceeded to his father's house in Dublin. Here he spent six weeks, and again set out for Oxford. The following

---

[1] Moore's "Life of Wesley," vol. i., p. 187.

letter, addressed to Wesley by his father, will tell the brief remainder of his short history. The letter was written fifteen months after Morgan's untimely death; and, during this melancholy interval, his only surviving brother had been placed under Wesley's tuition.

"DUBLIN, *November*, 1733.

"My concern about my only son brings the misfortunes of my other son fresh into my mind, and obliges me now to impart to you, and only to you, what I have hitherto concealed from all men, as far as it could be kept secret. After he had spent about six weeks with me in Dublin, the physicians agreed that the air at Oxford was better for his health than the Irish air. I myself was obliged to take a journey with my Lord Primate into his diocese, and on the same day my dear son set out on his journey to England. He rode an easy pad, and was to make easy stages through part of this kingdom, to see some relations in the way, and to take shipping at Cork, from which there is a short passage to Bristol, and from thence the journey is not great to Oxford. He travelled twelve miles the first day, attended by that careful servant who was with him at Oxford. The servant observed him to act and talk lightly and incoherently that day. He slept little or none at night; but often cried out that the house was on fire, and used other wild expressions. The second day he grew worse; threw his bridle over the horse's head, and would neither guide him himself nor let the man guide him, but charged him to stay behind him, saying God would be his guide. The horse turned about, went in side roads, and then to a disused quarry filled with water, where my poor child fell off, and had then like to be lost, the servant not daring to do but as he bid him. The servant, finding him deprived of all understanding and also outrageous, by great art and management, brought him back to Dublin. Two of our most eminent physicians and the surgeon-general were brought to attend him. An express was sent for me, with whom I hastened back to town. He was put in a room two pairs of stairs high, yet he found an opportunity to run to one of the windows, tore it down though the sashes were nailed, and was more than half out before he could be caught. He was raging mad, and three men were set over him to watch him. By the direction of the physicians, he was threatened with ropes and chains, which were produced to him, and were rattled. In his madness, he used to say, that enthusiasm was his madness; and repeated often, 'O religious madness.' He said, they had 'hindered him being now with God,' because they had hindered him from throwing himself out of the window. But, in his greatest rage, he never cursed or swore or used any profane expressions. In seven days, God was pleased to take him to Himself; which, no doubt, the blisterings and severities used by the physicians and surgeon for his recovery precipitated."

This, in all respects, is a mournful story. No useful end would be answered by asking, whether much religion, or much unkindness, or "much learning," made poor Morgan mad. His father's letter, written in March, 1732, was, to say the least, injudicious; and the treatment of the Dublin doctors, in August following, was preposterously cruel. The man himself was a lovely character. Gambold, who seems to have made the fifth Oxford Methodist, observes concerning Morgan :—

"He was a young man of an excellent disposition, and took all opportunities to make his companions in love with a good life; to create in them a reverence for public worship; and to tell them of their faults with a sweetness and simplicity that disarmed the worst tempers. He delighted much in works of charity. He kept several children at school; and when he found beggars in the street, he would bring them into his chambers, and talk to them. Many such things he did; and, being acquainted with Messrs. John and Charles Wesley, he invited them to join with him; and proposed that they should meet frequently to encourage one another, and have some scheme to proceed by in their daily employments. About half a year, after I got among them, Mr. Morgan died. His calm and resigned behaviour, hardly curbing in a confident joy in God, wrought very much upon me; though, when I had an opportunity to observe him, he was under a lingering distemper. Some were displeased because he did not make some direct preparation for death; but to a man who has overcome the world, and feels God within him, death is no new thing."

Poor Morgan's decease occurred in Dublin, on August 26, 1732; and no sooner was the event known, than it was wickedly and cruelly alleged, that his Methodist associates had killed him. Hence the following, which Wesley addressed to Morgan's father within two months after the former's death.

"OXON, *October*, 18, 1732.

"On Sunday last, I was informed that my brother and I had killed your son; that the rigorous fasting which he had imposed upon himself, by our advice, had increased his illness and hastened his death. Now though, considering it in itself, 'it is a very small thing with me to be judged by man's judgment;' yet as the being thought guilty of so mischievous an imprudence might make me the less able to do the work I came into the world for, I am obliged to clear myself of it, by observing to you, as I have done to others, that your son left off fasting about a year and a half since; and that it is not yet half a year since I began to practise it."[1]

Apart from amply refuting the slanderous charge already

---

[1] Wesley's Works, vol. i., p. 5.

mentioned, this extract from Wesley's letter is of considerable importance, as it clearly shows that fasting was not a part of the primary programme of the Methodists; and that, if fasting is to be taken as a proof of religious earnestness, Morgan, in the first instance, was the most religious of the brotherhood. Whether Morgan was in the habit of observing the ecclesiastical fasts when the Methodist meetings were commenced in November, 1729, is not apparent; but it is quite clear that his discontinuance of fasting was occasioned by his declining health. It was about the month of May, 1731, when fasting was relinquished; and, as we have already seen, it was then that the illness commenced which issued in his death. Whether fasting induced that illness is a point which must be left undecided; but, even admitting that it did, Wesley was not to blame, for Wesley himself did not begin to fast until a year after Morgan had laid aside the practice.

Whatever others did, Morgan's father fully exonerated the two Wesleys; and, though he had censured his son for what he conceived to be excessive piety only five months before the young man's death, that piety was now a source of consolation. Replying to Wesley's letter, dated October 18, 1732, Mr. Morgan writes :—

> "*November* 25, 1732.
>
> "REV. SIR,—I give entire credit to everything and every fact you relate. It was ill-judged of my poor son to take to fasting, with regard to his health, of which I knew nothing, or I should have advised him against it. He was inclined to piety and virtue from his infancy. I must own I was much concerned at the strange accounts which were spread here, of some extraordinary practices of a religious society in which he had engaged at Oxford, lest, through his youth and immaturity of judgment, he might be hurried into zeal and enthusiastic notions that would prove pernicious. But now, indeed, the piety and holiness of life which he practised afford me some comfort in the midst of my affliction for the loss of him, having full assurance of his being for ever happy. The good account you are pleased to give of your own and your friends' conduct, in point of duty and religious offices, and the zealous approbation of them by the good old gentleman your father, reconcile and recommend that method of life to me, and make me almost wish that I were one amongst you.
>
> "I am, with respects to your brother, sir, your most obliged and most obedient humble servant,
>
> "RICHARD MORGAN."

Here the chapter on " The First of the Oxford Methodists "
ought to end ; but, perhaps, this is the most fitting place for
the following correspondence respecting William Morgan's
brother ; especially as it casts further light upon the principles
and mode of life of Wesley and his friends.   Chronologically
it is out of order, for Richard Morgan did not belong to the
quaternion brotherhood who were first branded with the
name of " Methodists;" but, still, the ensuing letters serve as
a continuation of those already given, and, viewed in such a
light, may be acceptable.

1729
to
1735

WILLIAM MORGAN'S BROTHER.

IN a letter, dated " Feb. 17, 1733," Mr. Morgan, senior,
states that he is wishful that the books of his deceased
son, William, should belong to his only surviving son; and
then adds :—

" I assure you, sir, without any dissimulation or flattery, I rejoice
sincerely at the recovery of the good old gentleman, your father.[1] And I
really am concerned that the scorners of your university continue so
malevolent. I could wish they would rather meet you at least half way in
imitation of piety and goodness. I must say that these censures have, in
a great measure, ceased here ; and I am comforted by my acquaintance
telling me that I should [not?] grieve the loss, from the assurance we
have of my dear son's happiness with God, after such a course of piety
and godliness as he had engaged in. I pray God to conduct us all to
meet together in happiness hereafter. Be assured that you shall never
want an advocate in me to defend you against any calumny that I hear
you or your friends aspersed with. Pray give my salutations to your good
father when you write to him, and to your brother of Christ Church ; for
I am, with great sincerity, theirs, and, sir, your very affectionate humble
servant,   " RICHARD MORGAN."

The Oxford Methodists were still slandered ; but the father
of the dead Morgan, so far from blaming them, was now their
faithful friend and defender. This was shown, not in words
only, but in deeds ; for, during this same year, 1733, he
sent his surviving son to Oxford, and placed him under the

---

[1] Wesley's father had been thrown out of a waggon and seriously
injured. (See " Life and Times of Rev. Samuel Wesley," pp. 416, 417.)

tuition of Wesley, one of the men who had been accused of hastening the death of William. Hence the following, extracted from a letter addressed to Wesley:—

"DUBLIN, *November 22nd,* 1733.

"REV. SIR,—I had the favour of yours, and am very thankful for your care and concern about my son, who, I am sure, will observe your advice and directions in everything. I would have .him live a sober, virtuous, and religious life, and to go to church and sacrament, according to the statutes and customs of his college; but for young people to pretend to be more pure and holy than the rest of mankind is a dangerous experiment. As to charitable subscriptions and contributions, I wholly debar him from making any; because he has not one shilling of his own, but what I give him; and this I appropriate wholly to his maintenance, education, and moderate and inoffensive recreations and pleasures. And, I believe, as a casuist, you will agree with me that it is injustice, and, consequently, sinful, rather than virtuous, to apply my money any other way than as I appropriate it. He must leave me to measure out my own charities, and to distribute them in such manner and proportion as I shall think proper. I hope you will not suspect, from anything I have said, that I intend the least reflection or disrespect to you; for if I did not think very well of you, and had not a great opinion of your conduct and abilities, I should not put my only son under your tuition, which, I think, is the best proof a man can give of his good esteem and opinion of another. I hope I may be excused for being solicitous to prevent my present son's falling into extremes, which, it is thought, were so prejudicial to my other.

"I sent a bill of £50, by the last post, to Mr. James Huey, merchant, in Aldermanbury, London, with directions to transmit the value to you, which I hope is done. I shall begrudge no money that is for my son's benefit and advantage. I would have him live as decently as other gentlemen of his station. I am very desirous that he should keep a regular account, that he may attain to a habit of it, knowing the great use and benefit of accounts to all men. I shall depend upon your letting me know when a further supply will be wanting. Pay my respects to your brother, and believe me to be your very affectionate and most humble servant,   "RICHARD MORGAN."

"To the Rev. John Wesley, Fellow of Lincoln College, Oxford."

No one can find fault with Mr. Morgan's letter. It was economical, and yet generous. For want of judicious restraint like his, hundreds of young Oxonians have been ruined. Too much money in a young man's pocket is a terrible temptation and danger. Besides, Morgan, though only nineteen years of age, had hitherto evinced none of the sobriety of his elder brother; but, on the contrary, had been a brisk, showy, gay young fellow. Hence, his father's description of him to

1729
to
1735

Charles Wesley. After stating that though he had left school at the age of sixteen, he was even then "fit for the university, and at least as good a scholar as his brother was when he went to Oxford ;" Mr. Morgan adds,—

"Three years ago, I purchased an office for him in the law; but, I fear, he has read very little of Greek or Latin since, and that he has forgotten a great deal of what he had learned at school; but I don't think his parts very bad. He was nineteen years of age last July, and is very lusty for his age. I believe he is five feet ten inches high. He has been somewhat gay, and gone to plays and balls; but addicted to no vice. He has often wished rather to be put forward in his learning, than to stick to an office; and I am now inclined to indulge him. If it be advisable to put him in this new way of life, you may be sure I can think of no other for his tutor but yourself."

Charles Wesley, however, thought that the young man would be safer with his brother than with himself; and, indeed, Morgan himself desired that he might be entered a Gentleman Commoner of Lincoln College, and be Wesley's pupil. His father complied with this request; but the youth soon became dissatisfied. Being under Wesley's care, he was branded with the name of Methodist; and, in a fit of mortified vanity, wrote to his father, saying, he would rather return to his office in Dublin, than suffer the sneers of his gay companions, in Oxford. Wesley became acquainted with this, and immediately addressed to Mr. Morgan a letter, which, though long, is too interesting and important to be omitted. We have here a glimpse of the daily life of the Oxford Methodists, a specimen of the contumely cast upon them, and a description of the collegiate wickedness surrounding them. It will be seen that Wesley's letter was written within two months after the date of Mr. Morgan's letter just given.

"*January* 14*th*, 1734.

"SIR,—Going yesterday into your son's room, I providentially cast my eyes upon a paper that lay upon the table, and, contrary to my custom, read a line or two of it, which soon determined me to read the rest. It was a copy of his last letter to you; whereby, by the signal blessing of God, I came to the knowledge of his real sentiments, both with regard to myself and to several other points of the highest importance.

"In the account he gives of me, and those friends who are as my own soul, are some things *true :*—as, that we imagine it is our bounden duty to spend our whole lives in the service of Him that gave them; or in other words, ' *Whether we eat or drink, or whatever we do, to do all to the glory of God*;' that we endeavour, as we are able, to relieve the poor, by buying books and other necessaries for them; that some of us read prayers at the prison once a day; that I administer the Sacrament once a month, and preach there as often as I am not engaged elsewhere; that we sit together five evenings in a week; and that we observe, as far as our health will permit, the fasts of the Church.

"Some things are *false*, but taken upon trust, so that I hope Mr. Morgan believed them true:—as that we almost starve ourselves; that one of us had like lately to have lost his life, by too great abstinence; that we endeavour to reform notorious whores, and to lay spirits in haunted houses; that we rise every day at five o'clock; and that I am president of the Society.

"As strange as it may appear that one present upon the spot should so far vary from the truth in his relation, I can easily account, not only for his mistake, but for his designed misrepresentation too. The company he is almost daily with (from whom indeed I should have divided him, had not your letters, coming in the article of time, tied my hands) abundantly accounts for the former; as his desire to lessen your regard for me, and thereby obviate the force of any future complaint, which he foresaw I might some time hence have occasion to make to you, does for the latter.

"And, indeed, I am not without apprehension that some such occasion may shortly come. I need not describe that apprehension to you. Is there not a cause? Is he not surrounded, even in this recess, with those who are often more pernicious than open libertines? Men who retain something of outward decency, and nothing else; who seriously idle away the whole day, and repeatedly revel till midnight, and if not drunken themselves, yet encouraging and applauding those that are so; who have no more of the form than of the power of godliness, and though they do pretty often drop in at the public prayers, coming after the most solemn part of them is over, yet expressly disown any obligation to attend them. It is true they have not yet laughed your son out of all his diligence; but how long it will be before they have, God knows. They zealously endeavour it at all convenient opportunities; and temporal views are as unable to support him under such an attack, as his slender notions of religion are; of which, he often says, he thinks he shall have enough, if he constantly says his prayers at home and in the chapel. As to my advice on this or any other head, they had secured him pretty well before; and your authority added to theirs, has supplied him with armour of proof against it.

"I now beg to know what you would have me to do? Shall I sit still, and let him swim down the stream? Or shall I plunge in, bound as I am hand and foot, and oppose myself to his company, his inclinations, and his father?

"Why, you say, I am to incite him to live a sober, virtuous, and religious life. Nay, but let me first tell you what religion is. I take

religion to be, not the bare saying over so many prayers, morning and
evening, in public or in private; not anything superadded now and then
to a careless or worldly life; but a constant ruling habit of the soul; a
renewal of our minds in the image of God; a recovery of the Divine likeness; a still increasing conformity of heart and life to the pattern of our
most Holy Redeemer.

"But if this be religion, if this be the way to life, which our blessed
Lord hath marked out for us, how can any one, while he keeps close to
this way, be charged with running into extremes? It is true, there is no
going out of it, either to the right hand or to the left, without running into
an extreme; and, to prevent this, the wisdom of the Church has, in all
ages, appointed guides for the unexperienced, lest they should wander
into bye-paths, and seek death in the error of their life. But while he is
in the right way, what fear is there of your son's going too fast in it?

"I appeal to your experience. Have you observed any such disposition
in him, as gives you ground to suspect he will love God too well, or keep
himself too '*unspotted from the world*'? Or has his past life been such,
as that you have just reason to apprehend the remainder of it should too
much resemble that of our blessed Master? I will go further. Have you
remarked in the various scenes you have gone through, that youth in
general is apt to run into the extreme of piety? Is it to *this* excess that
the fervour of their blood and the impetuosity of their passions hurry
them?

"But we may not stop here. Is there any fear, is there any possibility
that any son of Adam, of whatever age or degree, should too faithfully do
the will of his Creator, or too exactly tread in the steps of his Redeemer?
Suppose the time now come when you feel within yourself, that the silver
cord of life is loosed, that the dust is returning to the earth as it was, and
the spirit unto God who gave it. The snares of death overtake you. Nothing but pain is on the one hand, eternity on the other. The tears of the
friends that surround your bed bear witness with the pangs of your own
heart, that it has few pulses more to beat before you launch out into the
sea without a shore; before the soul shall part from the quivering lips and
stand naked before the judgment-seat of God. Will you then be content
with having served God according to the custom of the place you were
in? Will you regret your having been, even from your youth, more pure
and holy than the rest of mankind? Will you complain to the ministering
spirits who receive your new-born soul, that you have been over zealous
in the love of your Master? Ask not me, a poor, fallible, sinful mortal,
never safe either from the snares of ill example or the treachery of my
own heart; but ask *them*,—ask *Him* who died to make you and me and
your son zealous of good works,—whether you may be excused from your
solicitude, your too successful solicitude, to prevent his falling into this
extreme? How needless has he made that solicitude already! But, I
spare you. The good Lord be merciful to us both!

"Think not, sir, that interest occasions the concern I show. I abhor
the thought. From the moment my brother told me, '*Mr. Morgan will
be safer with you than me; I have desired him to be sent to you,*' I deter-

1729
to
1735

mined (though I never mentioned it to him) to restore to him whatsoever is paid me upon Mr. Morgan's account. It is, with regard to me, an accursed thing. There shall no such cleave unto me. I have sufficient motives, without this, to assist your son, so long as he will accept my assistance. He is the brother of my dear friend, the son of one that was my friend till great names warped him from his purpose, and, what is infinitely more, the creature of my God, and the redeemed and fellow-heir of my Saviour.

"That neither the cares of the world nor the fair speeches and venerable titles of any who set up their rest therein, may prevent our attaining our better inheritance, is the earnest prayer of, sir, your most obliged and most obedient servant,

"JOHN WESLEY."

"Richard Morgan, Esq."[1]

This is a noble letter, though, perhaps, somewhat hard upon Mr. Morgan, senior. The picture of collegiate life at Oxford shows the need there was for Oxford Methodism; while the definitions of real religion demonstrate that the leader of the Oxford Methodists was not the fanatic which his enemies said he was.

Unfortunately, we soon lose sight of the gay young Gentleman Commoner of Lincoln College; but Wesley's interest in his welfare was not without results. For a considerable time, no impression could be made on the airy and thoughtless youth. Wesley did his best, but failed; and, at length, he desired Hervey to undertake the task. Hervey succeeded. John Gambold writes :—

"Mr. Hervey, by his easy and engaging conversation, by letting him see a mind thoroughly serious and happy, where so many of the fine qualities he most esteemed were all gone over into the service of religion, gained Mr. Morgan's heart to the best purposes." Gambold adds, "Since Mr. Morgan became that meek, sincere Christian which he now is," [written about 1736] he has had a singular affection toward Mr. Wesley, and has run some hazard to be in his company,—a sign that those counsels and wishes, which seemed once to be given in vain, do now take place in him."

About two years after this change in the young Irishman, Wesley, and his brother, accompanied by Benjamin Ingham, set sail for Georgia; and Morgan, so far from being ashamed of their acquaintance, went to London purposely to see them

---

[1] Moore's Life of Wesley, vol. i., p. 198.

start; and expressed a willingness to go all the way to Yorkshire to do them service. Ingham writes :—[1]

"Mr. Morgan, a gentleman of Lincoln College, Oxford, came up to London to take leave of Mr. Wesley. He was a zealous and sincere Christian and was very earnest with me to go to Georgia. He promised himself to make a journey into Yorkshire to see my mother, and to do what he could towards settling the school. As to having my mother's consent, he said, If I thought it was God's will, I must obey my Master, and go wherever I could do Him service, whether my relations were willing or not."

This was the fashionable young man who, two years before, entered Lincoln College, bringing a favourite greyhound with him; choosing men "more pernicious than open libertines" for his companions; and writing to his father querulous and false complaints of the Oxford Methodists.

Now he was an Oxford Methodist himself. Hence the following letter, which was addressed to Wesley, three weeks before the two Wesleys and Ingham embarked for Georgia.

"*September* 25, 1735.

"DEAR SIR,—I hope this will find you and the rest of our friends well. This morning the Rector sent for me. He told me he had heard I had returned to my former strict way of life, and that he must acquaint my father with it. I desired, he would come to particulars, and said, that where I was wrong I should be glad to be set right. He said, I looked thin, and feared I would hurt myself by rigorous fasting. I told him, I dined in the hall on Wednesdays, and that I eat bread and butter on Friday mornings. He was pretty well satisfied with this account. He advised me to take something else instead of tea after fasting, which I promised to do. His next charge was not sitting in the common room. I said, I intended to sit there three nights every week, which he thought was sufficient. I unguardedly told him that, if it were agreeable to him, I would dine in the hall even on Fridays. He very much approved of this proposal, and said, I might observe any other day as a fast instead of it. I believe, if I would go into the hall on fast days, all my other actions would be less taken notice of, and I should put it out of the Rector's or Mr. Hutchin's power to make any complaints of me to my father. If I could be sure of not injuring religion by my example, I believe I might comply with the Rector herein, for, you are very sensible, I might notwithstanding observe the same degree of abstinence even on those days. I depend on the advice of my friends in this affair, and hope God will sanctify it to me. The Gospel tells us, that the children of God must

---

[1] MS. Journal.

suffer persecution from the world; but the Rector says, we must endeavour to have our persons in esteem, and those things wherein we differ from the world we must do privately.. We must take care our good be not evil spoken of. Though the Church enjoins fasting, yet, because the bishops, the pillars of the Church, do not observe it, it loses its force. When he finds his blood hot, he says, he fasts, but unknown to anybody. He thinks it is a relative duty, and not confined to any particular time. He looks upon it only as a remedy against unchastity, and, if we are not troubled with this passion, I suppose, not obligatory. He advised me to read such books as were genteel accomplishments. I have, through God's assistance, in some degree, seen my own weakness, by the effects of this anti-Christian doctrine, for it has quite discomposed me, though I was enabled to see the fallacy of it. I see nothing so well qualified to destroy my soul, to make me eternally miserable, as the conversation of temporizing Christians, which, I hope, by your advice and other means, God will prevent, as I am sure He will, if I am faithful to Him.

"When I desire your advice in this affair, I only desire you to prevent my eternal damnation; for it is in the greatest danger from this most subtle, deceitful, and dangerous of all enemies. Oh that I could express to you the danger I foresee from this enemy! My eyes and my heart alone could; but these you cannot see. May God enable you to comprehend it, and to do all that is in your power to prevent it! You cannot sufficiently arm me against the Rector. I suspect him of insincerity to you. I want to know whether you ever did. I believe, and Mr. Horn is of the same opinion, that my going to Ireland depends on my going into the hall on fast days. The Rector said as much as if you frightened others from religion by your example; and that you might have done a great deal of good, if you had been less strict, which I would be glad to be undeceived in, and to know whether the example of a thorough mortified Christian, though it would give the greatest offence, would not do more than that of a plausible Christian, who would give no offence at all. This is a point of great importance to me.

"It has pleased God to let me see that I can make no progress in religion till I have acquired some sense of the misery and nothingness of human nature, and of our entire dependence on Him. Though I go into the common room to avoid a greater evil,—though I would not live the life of those who spend their time there for all the world,—though I am scarcely capable of doing anything which is more disagreeable to me,—yet the poison is not removed. While I am with them, I love my sense, my judgment, my reason. It is true, I am all the time in pain; but I cannot say, at that time, they lead an un-Christian, dangerous life. I believe it is for want of faith, and for not looking upon it as a great blessing, since it is not my own choice. I want to know how to remove this delusion, and how to make an advantage of that which God no doubt intended for my good. If I do not make a use of this cross, I am satisfied it will be the ruin of me.

"Oh lay this to your heart, and make my case your own. Do not think you can spend your time better than in answering this letter. I hope you will not forget to pray to God to enable me to follow you wherever it is His will, and never to omit putting me in mind of it when you write to me.

"Mr. Robson is in a dangerous way. He is convinced of the necessity of being a Christian, but cannot leave the world. Mr. Carter, I fear, is not steady. Mr. Hervey is gone. Mr. Broughton is not yet returned. If he go to Georgia, it is best."

This is a curious letter,—not remarkable for either intelligence or scholarship; but it partly unfolds the character of its writer; reveals some of the difficulties of the collegiate life of the Oxford Methodists; shows the importance which they attached to fasts; and points to Wesley as the leader of the religious brotherhood.

The Wesleys had left Oxford; but, for a time at least, Charles Morgan and Mr. Broughton carried on the work which they and the elder Morgan had commenced. Charles Morgan undertook the care of Bocardo, which he visited three days every week. He read an hour every other day, at the house of Mr. Fox, in the Catechism of the Bishop of the Isle of Man; and, in the same place, held a meeting every Sunday night with "a cheerful number of Christians." "The Lord's kingdom," he writes, November 27, 1735, "increaseth apace; and I find more and more comfort in the holy Scriptures every day."

Our information concerning Robert Kirkham, William Morgan, and his younger brother Charles, is exhausted. As Oxford Methodists, they deserve notice; but, so far as is ascertained, they were of comparatively little use either to the Church or to the world. William Morgan had no opportunity for *public* usefulness; and Robert Kirkham and Charles Morgan drift away into the great ocean of existence, and leave no track behind them.

THE REV. JOHN CLAYTON, M.A.,

THE JACOBITE CHURCHMAN.

GOD has wisely and graciously hidden the future from us. We may form guesses concerning it ; but we have not the slightest certainty that our guesses will be realised. Who, in 1732, could have foretold the future career of the Oxford Methodists ? If the members of the Methodist fraternity could have seen beforehand the events of the next fifty years, what would have been the issue ? Would the fellowship of the Hanoverian and Jacobite, the Methodist and Moravian, the Churchman and Dissenter, the Arminian and Calvinist, the itinerant Evangelist and the parish Priest, have been continued ? That fellowship was of incalculable importance ; but its maintenance depended upon the shortsightedness of those who were united in it. The drawing aside of the veil of futurity would, in all likelihood, have converted the loving brotherhood into an Ishmaelitish band, endangering, not only its future usefulness, but its present existence, by its own internecine fights. As it was, there went forth a number of brave-hearted men, all of them the better for their godly meetings in Wesley's comfortable room in Lincoln College ; and, though their courses were divergent, yet, in the main, they continued faithful to the cause of truth, and, with few exceptions, were always loyal to their great Master, Christ. In a qualified sense, we may apply to Oxford Methodism the words of the sacred text : " A river went out of Eden to water the garden ; and from thence it was parted, and became into four heads" (Gen. ii. 10). Let us follow one of the out-flowings :—

John Clayton was the son of William Clayton, a bookseller in Manchester ;[1] was born in 1709, and was educated

---

[1] Clayton's father died in January, 1737 (The Private Journal and Literary Remains of John Byrom, vol. ii., p. 87).

by the Rev. John Richards, M.A., at the Grammar School
in that important town. He entered Brazenose College in
1726, and became Hulme's exhibitioner in 1729.[1] He was introduced to Wesley in 1732; and, by his recommendation,
the Oxford Methodists took another important step, that of
fasting twice a week. Wesley writes,—

1732
Age 23

"On April 20, 1732, Mr. Clayton meeting me in the street, and giving
Mr. Rivington's[2] service, I desired his company to my room, and then
commenced our acquaintance. At the first opportunity, I acquainted him
with our whole design, which he immediately and heartily closed with;
and, not long after, (Mr. Morgan having then left Oxford,) we fixed two
evenings in a week to meet on, partly to talk on that subject, and partly
to read something in practical divinity. The two points whereunto, by
the blessing of God, we had before attained, we endeavoured to hold fast:
I mean, the doing what good we can; and, in order thereto, communicating as often as we have opportunity. To these, by the advice of Mr.
Clayton, we added a third,—the observing the fasts of the Church; the
general neglect of which we can by no means apprehend to be a lawful
excuse for neglecting them. And in the resolution to adhere to these and
all things else, which we are convinced God requires at our hands, we
trust we shall persevere till He calls us to give an account of our steward-
ship. As for the names of Methodists, Supererogation-men, and so on,
with which some of our neighbours are pleased to compliment us, we do
not conceive ourselves to be under any obligation to regard them, much
less to take them for arguments. 'To the law and to the testimony' we
appeal, whereby we ought to be judged. If by these it can be proved we
are in error, we will immediately and gladly retract it: if not, we 'have
not so learned Christ,' as to renounce any part of His service, though men
should 'say all manner of evil against us,' with more judgment and as
little truth as hitherto. We do, indeed, use all the lawful means we
know to prevent 'the good which is in us' from being 'evil spoken of:'
but if the neglect of known duties be the one condition of securing our
reputation, why, fare it well; we know whom we have believed, and what
we thus lay out He will pay us again."[3]

These were brave Christian words; the noble utterance of
an earnest, conscientious, godly man. The Methodist brotherhood, thus portrayed, present an example which all who are
right-minded cannot but admire. There is no taking for
"doctrines the commandments of men;" no ridiculous toying with ecclesiastical or superstitious trifles; but a stout-

---

[1] The Private Journal and Literary Remains of John Byrom, 1855.
[2] Mr. Rivington, the bookseller of St. Paul's Churchyard, London.
[3] Wesley's Works, vol. i., p. 13.

hearted adherence to great, scripture principles. Wesley and his friends were not pious for the purpose of being singular, but because they felt it to be a duty. To be laughed at was far from being pleasant; but they were quite prepared to sacrifice even their reputation, rather than dishonour the religion of their great Master. Men might brand them with opprobrious epithets; but that with them was of trifling importance, if only at the day of judgment, Christ acknowledged them as friends. They knew they were not following "cunningly devised fables;" they were not flippant dabblers in "doubtful disputations;" but earnest men who knew that what they held was truth, and who, at all hazards, were resolved to practise it.

Clayton had spent six years at Oxford, and was now a college tutor.[1] The following letter was addressed to Wesley about three months after he and Clayton became acquainted. It is long, but is full of interest, and casts considerable light on the doings and difficulties of the Oxford Methodists. Wesley, at the time, seems to have been in London, where he was now made a member of "The Society for the Propagation of Christian Knowledge," and also formed a friendship with William Law.

"OXON, *August* 1, 1732.

"REV. AND DEAR SIR,—Excuse me for not interrupting you from attending to the noble work you have taken in hand, whilst I give you an account of the present state of our affairs at Oxford.

"I cannot but think it an extraordinary piece of Providence that, when we had lost our best advocate and patron, all opposition against us should immediately cease; for, since you left us, nobody has thought it worth while to attack either Mr. Smith or me,[2] or to endeavour to remove us

---

[1] Wesley's Works, vol. viii., p. 334.

[2] Mr. Smith was evidently one of the Oxford Methodists, and appears to have been a Fellow of Lincoln College. In a letter dated Aug. 17, 1733, Wesley writes,—"The thing that gives offence here, is the being singular with regard to time, expense, and company. This is evident beyond exception, from the case of Mr. Smith, one of our Fellows, who no sooner began to husband his time, to retrench unnecessary expenses, and to avoid his irreligious acquaintances, but he was set upon, by not only those acquaintance, but many others too, as if he had entered into a conspiracy to cut all their throats: though, to this day, he had not advised any single person, unless in a word or two and by accident, to act as he did in those instances" (Moore's Life of Wesley, vol. i., p. 206). We have not been able to trace Mr. Smith's subsequent career. The

from those principles wherein you, by the grace of God, have fixed us. I have gone every day to Lincoln, big with expectation to hear of some mighty attack made upon Mr. Smith; but, I thank God, I have always been disappointed; for not one of the Fellows has once so much as tried to shake him, or to convert him from the right way, wherein, I hope, he at present walks. Indeed, on Sunday, he met with a rub from Mr. Veesy, who refused to read Prayers for him in your chapel, for fear of contributing anything to his going to Christ Church. But Mr. Smith had the heart to desire that favour of the Rector which Mr. Veesy had denied him, who immediately promised to read for him, and encouraged him to proceed in the way he was in, and, if possible, to make further progress in virtue and holiness. He goes out of town to-morrow morning, and so will be entirely out of danger from the Fellows of Lincoln. We had conversation this morning, whilst we were at breakfast together, concerning the temptations which may arise from strange company and travelling; and Mr. Smith seems to be fore-armed against, and determined to oppose them to the utmost of his power. He joins with me in best respects to your brother and you, and desires you won't forget to send the bands and the poems you promised him.

"Poor Mr. Clements [1] is still recovering. He was with me last night two hours, but I doubt to no purpose.

"My little flock [2] at Brazenose are, God be praised, true to their principles, and I hope to themselves too.

"*Bocardo*, [3] I fear, grows worse upon my hands. They have done nothing but quarrel ever since you left us; and they carried matters so high on Saturday, that the bailiffs were sent for, who ordered Tomlyns to be fet-

---

following letter, however, written a few months later than the above by Wesley, will not be unacceptable.

"London, *February* 6, 1734; 4, Perpool Lane.
"My dearest Friend,—It was waiting for Mr. Greeve's coming made me not answer yours sooner. If, when I come, I don't give you a sufficient reason for my being so long absent from college, never trust me more. But, yet, alas! how lukewarm is piety become with me at the best; and fasting neglected, which I never looked for; not entirely dropped, I hope, but for a week or two, to be taken up and practised again incessantly.

"Notwithstanding, I cannot be present in body sooner than in a month's time, because I am learning shorthand, which will take up a full fortnight of it. You know, I presume, I was obliged to see my father before my return, and, therefore, we will get you to ask leave of absence, and entreat Mr. Farrer for so much longer.

"I beg my humble service to him and all friends; and accept the same yourself from, my dearest friend, your much obliged friend and servant, William Smith.
"The Rev. Mr. Wesley, Fellow of Lincoln College, Oxford."

[1] Probably another Oxford Methodist.
[2] Probably his pupils.
[3] A room over the north gate of the city, used as a common prison, principally for debtors.

tered and put in the dungeon, where he lay some hours, and then, upon promise of his good behaviour, was released again. He has been much better ever since that time, and I hope will be better for it all his life-time. Wisdom has never been to hear me read, notwithstanding his promise. I sent for him yesterday, but he would not come down; and when I had done reading, I went upstairs to him, and upbraided him with breaking his promise, upon which he very easily replied, that he had thought better of it since he had seen me, and was determined never to come near Blair, lest his indignation should rise at the sight of him.

"The *Castle* is, I thank God, in much better condition. All the felons were acquitted, except Salmon, who is referred to be tried at Warwick, to our great disappointment,—and the sheep-stealer, who is burnt in the hand, and who, I verily believe, is a great penitent. I got Mrs. Jopping a copy of her son's indictment at the assizes, which has made her mighty easy ever since; and she is now endeavouring to bring her mind into a due frame for the devout participation of the holy communion on Sunday next. Jempro is discharged, and I have appointed Harris to read to the prisoners in his stead. Two of the felons likewise have paid their fees, and are gone out, both of them able to read mighty well. There are only two in the jail who want this accomplishment,—John Clanvills, who reads but moderately, and the horse-stealer, who cannot read at all. He knows all his letters, however, and can spell most of the common monosyllables. I hear them both read three times a week, and I believe Salmon hears them so many times a day.

"One of my college scholars has left me, but the others go on mighty well. The woman, who was a perfect novice, spells tolerably, and so does one of the boys, and the others make shift to read with spelling every word that is longer than ordinary. The boys can both say their Catechism as far as the end of the Commandments, and can likewise repeat the morning and evening prayers for children in ' Ken's Manual.'

"Mrs. Tireby has been very ill this last week, so that she has made no great proficiency. I am to go down at six o'clock to hear the determination of a meeting of St. Thomas's parish, respecting separating Bossum and his wife. When I had promised to give a crown towards clothing the woman, and the overseer had determined to take her in upon that condition, the churchwarden would needs have him try to put the man upon me too, to get a crown towards clothing him; but, as he is able to work for his living, I don't think him a proper object for charity; nor can I at this time afford to do anything for him, because I am apprehensive that I must be forced to contribute to Salmon's relief, who will want near twenty shillings to subpœna proper witnesses to Warwick at his trial; and I cannot but think it a much greater act of charity to relieve a suffering innocent than to relieve an idle beggar.

"I have been twice at the school,—namely on Tuesday and Saturday last, and intend to go again as soon as I have finished this letter. The children all go on pretty well, except Jervaise's boy, who, I find, truants till eleven o'clock in a morning. I threatened the boy what we would do to him if ever he truanted any more, and he has promised (as all children do) that he will do so no more; nay, his mother assures me that she will take care for the future that he shall not. I got a shilling for her from our Vice Principal, and gave her sixpence myself, to preserve the gown that is in pawn from being sold; and the woman who has it promised not to sell it, provided Jervaise will bring her sixpence a week towards redeeming it.

"I have obtained leave to go to St. Thomas's workhouse twice a week; and, indeed, I cannot but hope it will be a noble field of improvement. I am sure the people stand much in need of instruction, for there is hardly a soul that can read in the whole house, and those that can, don't understand one word of what they read.

"I think I have nothing further to add about our affairs; only I must beg the favour of you, if you can conveniently, to pay Mr. Rivington thirty shillings for my use, and I will repay it when you come to Oxford. Pray don't forget a few Common Prayer Books for the Castle.

"You cannot imagine the pleasure it is to me to know that you are engaged every morning in prayer for me. I wish for nine o'clock more eagerly than ever I did before, and I think I begin to perceive what is meant by that union of souls which is so much talked of in Père Malebranche and Madam Bourignon, which I never understood before. Good sir, continue your prayers for me, for I feel that I am benefited by them.

"I do not envy you the happiness, which I know you will have from the conversation of so many pious men as you will meet with in London, because I assure myself that I shall have the benefit of it when I have the pleasure to see you again at Oxford.

"Mr. Hall is not yet come home, so that I am pretty much taken up amongst the poor people and the prisoners, and have not yet had time to consider of any improvements or additions to be made to the list of books for our pupils.

"I thank God that I have fully conquered my affection for a morning's nap, and rise constantly by five o'clock at the farthest, and have the pleasure to see myself imitated by the greatest part of my pupils. I have talked with Mr. Clements, and I hope have made him a proselyte to early rising, though I cannot to constant communion.

"Pray God prosper all those designs you have undertaken of doing good at London, and send you a good journey to Oxford.

"I am, rev. and dear sir, your most affectionate friend, and most obliged humble servant, "J. CLAYTON."

"I hope you will not forget to pay my due compliments to Sir John Philips, Mr. Wogan, and all my other good friends.

"To the Rev. Mr. John Wesley. To be left with Mr. Rivington, bookseller, in St. Paul's Churchyard, London."

This long epistle, besides unfolding Clayton's character, helps us to a better understanding of the position and practices of the Oxford Methodists. The debtors in Bocardo, the prisoners in the Castle, and paupers in the streets were objects of their beneficent compassion. They had their schools for the children of the poor; and, in their mission of mercy, were about to visit the workhouse of St. Thomas's. Early rising was a habit, and prayer for each other a daily practice. Constant communion was enforced; though the dogma of the *real presence* of the body and blood of Christ was, as yet at least, no article of their faith.

Wesley being absent, there was a lull in the storm of Methodist persecution; but this was of short duration. Within a month after the date of Clayton's letter, poor William Morgan died; an event which furnished an occasion for a violent attack upon the Oxford brotherhood, in what was then one of the most literary and respectable papers published,—*Fogg's Weekly Journal.* They were accused of mopishness, hypocrisy, censoriousness, enthusiasm, madness, and superstitious scruples. "Among their own party," says the writer, "they pass for religious persons and men of extraordinary parts; but they have the misfortune to be taken by all who have ever been in their company, for madmen and fools."

Hardly any evil is without a good. The virulence of *Fogg's Weekly Journal* excited the curiosity of a gentleman who had no acquaintance with the Methodists, but who now sought an interview with them, and shortly after published an octavo pamphlet of thirty pages, entitled,—"The Oxford Methodists: Being some account of a Society of young Gentlemen, in that City, so denominated: setting forth their Rise, Views, and Designs." In this first defence of Methodism ever published, the slanderous accusations cast upon Wesley and his friends were refuted; and the Methodists were described as follows :—

"There are three points to which these gentlemen think themselves obliged to adhere :—1. That of visiting and relieving the prisoners and the sick, and giving away Bibles, Common Prayer Books, and the 'Whole Duty of Man'; and of explaining the Catechism to the children of poor families, and of dropping a shilling or so to such families where they deem it needful. 2. That of weekly communion. 3. That of observing strictly the fasts of the Church, which has caused some to call them 'Supererogation Men.'"

To return to Clayton. About the time of the publication of this pamphlet (the beginning of 1733), Clayton removed to

Manchester; where, during the ensuing summer, he was visited by Wesley, who, on Sunday, June 3rd, preached thrice in three different churches, namely, the Cathedral, and Salford, and St. Anne's churches. Whether these pulpits were obtained through Clayton's influence, there is no evidence to show; but, remembering the odium connected with the name, it certainly is a curious fact, that in the populous and thriving town of Manchester, the Oxford Arch-Methodist was allowed to occupy so prominent a position.

When Clayton left Oxford, Clayton's pupils left Methodism. Ten days after his visit to Manchester, Wesley wrote,—

"1733, June 13th.

"The effects of my last journey, I believe, will make me more cautious of staying any time from Oxford for the future. One of my pupils told me at my return, that he was more and more afraid of singularity; and another, that he had read an excellent piece of Mr. Locke's, which had convinced him of the mischief of regarding authority. Our seven and twenty communicants at St. Mary's were on Monday shrunk to five; and the day before, the last of Mr. Clayton's pupils who continued with us, informed me that he did not design to meet us any more." [1]

This was somewhat discouraging. Meanwhile, besides keeping two fast days every week, Clayton, and also Wesley, began to evince other High Church proclivities. Hence the following, sent to Wesley only a month after his visit to Manchester :—

"July, 1733.

"REV. AND DEAR SIR,—I have been thinking upon the two points which you proposed to my consideration in your last, and must acknowledge myself to be utterly unable to form any judgment upon them which will be serviceable to you.

"My own rule is to spend an hour every Friday in looking over my diary,[2] and observing the difference between it and the preceding week; after which, I examine the resolutions set down in the account of my last weekly examination, and inquire how I have kept them, and then see

---

[1] Moore's "Life of Wesley," vol. i., p. 205.

[2] Where is Clayton's diary now? We wish we could find it. Wesley begun to keep a diary as early as about the year 1725 (see Wesley's Works, vol. i. p. 3), in which, he says, he noted how he "employed every hour." This practice he continued to do, wherever he was, till he left England in 1735 ; and yet not a line of these interesting journals has been published. Where are those manuscripts, and why are they not given to the public?

what others are necessary to be formed, which I write down at the end of my diary for every week, that so they may be materials for my subsequent examination.

"As to your question about Saturday,[1] I can only answer it by giving an account how I spend it. I do not look upon it as a preparation for Sunday, but as a festival itself; and, therefore, I have continued festival prayer for the three primitive hours, and for morning and evening, from the Apostolical Constitutions, which, I think, I communicated to you whilst at Oxford. I look upon Friday as my preparation for the celebration of both the Sabbath and the Lord's-day; the first of which I observe much like a common saint's day, or as one of the inferior holidays of the Church. I bless God, I have generally contrived to have the Eucharist celebrated on Saturdays as well as other holidays, for the use of myself and the sick people whom I visit.

"Dr. Deacon[2] gives his humble service to you, and lets you know that

---

[1] To use a popular designation, Clayton and Wesley were becoming Ritualists. Hitherto the Bible had been their only rule of faith and practice ; now they began to study ecclesiastical canons and decretals. One of these was to regard Saturday as the Sabbath-day, and Sunday as the Lord's-day. Christians, however, were not to "Judaize and rest on" (Saturday, or) "the Sabbath-day ; but work, and give the preference to the Lord's-day, by resting as Christians." On both days might be celebrated the Feast of the Eucharist, even during Lent. If any clergyman was found fasting on any Saturday, except Easter Eve, he was to be deposed ; and if a layman was guilty of such a peccadillo, he was to be suspended from communion. At the time of the Laodicean Council (about A.D. 363), public assemblies were held on Saturdays as well as Sundays, and it was decreed that on the former, as on the latter, "the Gospels, with the other Scriptures, ought to be read" before "the Sacrifice," or Eucharist. (Laodicean Canons, 29th, 49th, 16th ; and Apostolical Canons, 56th.)

[2] Dr. Deacon was one of the non-juring priests, or high churchmen, who refused to take the oaths to the government of King William III. They maintained :—1. The doctrine of passive obedience. 2. That the hereditary succession to the throne is of Divine institution, and, therefore, can never be interrupted, suspended, or annulled. 3. That the Church is subject to the jurisdiction, not of the civil magistrates, but of God alone, particularly in matters of a religious nature. 4. That, consequently, the bishops deposed by William III. remained, notwithstanding their deposition, true bishops to the day of their death ; and that those who were substituted in their place were the unjust possessors of other men's property. 5. That these unjust possessors of ecclesiastical dignities were rebels against the State, as well as schismatics in the Church ; and that all, therefore, who held communion with them were also chargeable with rebellion and schism ; and, 6. That this schism, which rends the Church in pieces, was a most heinous sin, whose punishment must fall heavy on all those who did not return sincerely to the true Church from which they had departed.

Dr. Deacon held such opinions and suffered for them. It was alleged by his opponents that, after the rebellion in 1715, he absolved Justice Hall and Parson Paul at the gallows, and publicly declared to them, at Tyburn, that the fact for which they were executed was meritorious. It was further the worship and discipline of the primitive Christians have taken up so much of his time, that he has never read the Fathers with a particular view to their moral doctrines, and therefore cannot furnish you with the testimonies you want out of his collection. However, if you will give me a month's time, I will try what I can do for you. I have made some progress in the earliest authors, and should have made more had I not been interrupted; first, with the public ceremony of the bishop's triennial visitation; and, secondly, with the blessing of a visit which the truly primitive Bishop of Man made to our town; with both which affairs the clergy have been almost wholly taken up for a week.

said that, on account of this, a warrant was issued against Deacon by the State Secretary, and that his friends prevented his arrest by sending him off to Holland to study physic. The principal part of this allegation was denied by Deacon. He admits that he went to Holland; but says, he lived upon his own fortune there, and did not begin his medical studies until after his return to London, where he derived great assistance from the celebrated Dr. Mead. He then removed to Manchester, where he collected a small congregation of high churchmen like himself; and, a few years later, became painfully prominent in the disturbances arising out of the Manchester visit of the Young Pretender. But more of this anon.

Dr. Deacon's publications embraced the following:—" The History of the Arians, and of the Council of Nice, written in French by Sebastian Lenain de Tillemont, and translated into English by Thomas Deacon. London, 1721." 8vo, 356 pp. " The Doctrine of the Church of Rome concerning Purgatory, proved to be contrary to Catholic Tradition, and inconsistent with the Necessary Duty of Praying for the Dead, as practised by the Ancient Church. By Thomas Deacon, Priest. London, 1718." 12mo, 143 pp. " Ecclesiastical Memoirs of the six first Centuries, made good by Citations from Original Authors, etc. Written in French by Sebastian Le Nain de Tillemont." Translated by Deacon. " London. Printed for the benefit of the Translator, and sold by J. Wilford, at the three Flower de luces, behind St. Paul's Chapter House; and W. Clayton, Bookseller in Manchester." Folio, vol. I., 1733. 667 pp. Vol. II., 1735. 593 pp. These volumes come down to the year A.D. 177. The work seems not to have been completed. The list of subscribers includes " John Byrom. A.M. F.R.S." and " Rev. John Clayton. A.M. Curate of Salford, in Lancashire." Deacon also published another work, immediately after the rebellion in 1745, entitled, " A Full, True, and Comprehensive View of Christianity: Containing a Short Historical Account of Religion from the Creation of the World to the fourth Century after our Lord Jesus Christ." 8vo, 483 pp.: a work far more Popish than Protestant. The following are some of the things which Deacon tries to elucidate and recommend:—" Public Confession and Penance;" " The Eucharist, a Sacrament and a Sacrifice;" " Unction before Baptism, and the Consecration of the Oil and Water;" " Trine Immersion, the White Garment, the Kiss of Peace, the Milk and Honey," etc.; " Prayer for the Faithful Departed;" " Infant Communion;" etc. This book excited great attention, as well it might; and several severe replies to it were published in the years 1748 and 1749.

Such was the chosen counsellor of Clayton and of Wesley. He was as much a papist as a protestant. Wesley was mercifully introduced to

1733
—
Age 24

"I was at Dr. Deacon's when your letter came to hand; and we had a deal of talk about your scheme of avowing yourselves a society, and fixing upon a set of rules. The doctor seemed to think you had better let it alone; for to what end would it serve? It would be an additional tie upon yourselves, and perhaps a snare for the consciences of those weak brethren that might chance to come among you. Observing the Stations[1] and weekly communion are duties which stand upon a much higher footing than a rule of a Society; and they, who can set aside the command of God and the authority of His Church, will hardly, I doubt, be tied by the rules of a private Society.

"As to the mixture, Mr. Colly told me he would assure me it was constantly used at Christ Church. However, if you have reason to doubt it, I would have you to inquire; but I cannot think the want of it a reason for not communicating. If I could receive where the mixture was used, I would; and, therefore, I used to prefer the Castle to Christ Church; but, if not, I should not think myself any further concerned in the matter than as it might be some way or other in my power to get it restored.[2]

"Pray be so kind as to call on Mr. Hollins, head of our college,

---

other guides. Clayton, without, perhaps, adopting all the opinions of his non-juring adviser, was doubtlessly influenced by them to the end of life. Dr. Deacon died in 1753, and was buried in St. Ann's churchyard, Manchester. The following clumsy inscription was on his tomb :—

"'Εἰ μὴ ἐν σταυρῳ.

" Here lie interred the remains (which, though mortality is at present corrupt, it shall one day most surely be raised again to immortality, and put on incorruption) of Thomas Deacon, the greatest of sinners, and the most unworthy of Primitive Bishops, who died 16th of February, 1753, in the fifty-sixth year of his age; and of Sarah, his wife, who died July 4th, 1745, in the forty-fifth year of her age. The Lord grant the faithful, here underlying, the mercy of the Lord in that day! (2 Tim. i. 18)

"'Εν τουτω νικα."

(*Gentleman's Magazine*, 1821.)

[1] The Ecclesiastical term for the Fasts of the fourth and sixth days of the week, Wednesday and Friday, in memory of the council which condemned Christ, and of His passion.

[2] Here, again, the Oxford Methodists have recourse, not to the Bible, as at the commencement of their history, but to superstitious canons. At the Council of Constantinople, A.D. 683, it was decreed against the Armenians, that wine used at the Eucharist should be mixed with water; and, in support of this, were quoted the Liturgies of St. James, and St. Basil, and the 37th Canon of the African Code. Of course, the origin of this superstition was the fact, that water, as well as blood, came out of the side of the Divine Redeemer; but Dr. Deacon, in a pamphlet, published in 1719, and entitled, "The Plaintiff's Charge Disproved," etc., took other ground. He maintained that our blessed Saviour used wine

for four pictures of mine, namely, 'Whitechapel Altar-piece,' 'Mary Magdalene,' and our two founders; and get them sent up, by any convenient opportunity, to Mr. Rivington, who will send them down to me.

"My best respects attend your brother. I must beg the favour of him to give himself the trouble of writing out the hymns to 'God the Father and God the Son,' for me. A person of quality, Lady Catherine Gray, borrowed mine, and has lost them.

"I am, dear sir, your most affectionate friend and servant,

"J. CLAYTON."

This is an important letter, not only as exhibiting the religious earnestness, but also the high churchism of the Oxford Methodists. The following, which was written two months later, is likewise full of interest. It was addressed, like the former one, "to the Rev. Mr. Wesley, Fellow of Lincoln College, Oxon."

"MANCHESTER, *September* 10, 1733.

"REV. AND DEAR SIR,—I was last week at Dr. Lever's, where I but narrowly missed of seeing Mr. Brooke, of our college, who came the evening after I left Alkrington. I saw Dr. Lever to-day, who joins with me in sincere respects to your brother and yourself. His new dignity and his being put in Commission of the Peace, have, at present, quite unfitted him for serious talk; and, therefore, I must wait for a more favourable opportunity of pressing those virtues, which you first convinced him of the necessity of.

"Dr. Deacon tells me, that, he had no view in fixing the Psalms for common days; but, after reading your letter, is convinced of the expediency of serving any of those three ends you mention. The feasts and the fasts were the days he principally regarded; but he would take it as a favour from you if you would communicate to me any improvements you may possibly make in it. He thinks your third rule would be most expedient,—namely, to put together such psalms as best explain and illustrate each other. And he knows not but that on this scheme the proper psalms for festivals and fasts may be more advantageously fixed, by transposing some from the first, second, and other Sundays, etc., to those which have psalms which better answer them. He will consider this point as soon as he has leisure, but desires, in the meantime, that you would let us know your thoughts upon the matter, because his order for reading the Psalter is likely soon to see the light, being to be published

---

and water at the Eucharist;" that He "ordained these elements to be the matter of the sacrament, and commanded His apostles and the Church to practice after His example." Deacon adds :—" How terrible the consequence may be of omitting part of our Redeemer's cup, is what I dare not determine."

with a collection of Primitive Devotions, both public and private, which is even now in the press.[1]

"Poor Miss Potter![2] I wonder not that she is fallen. Where humility is not the foundation, the superstructure cannot be good. And, yet, I am sorry to hear the tidings of her, especially that she has a great man for her confessor, who dissuades her from constant communion. I am sure, she has great occasion to use all the means of grace, which Providence provides for her, and hope that God will in time open her eyes to see the great need she has of help from above. I would not persuade you to

---

[1] This work, by Dr. Deacon, was entitled, "A Complete Collection of Devotions: taken from the Apostolical Constitutions, the Ancient Liturgies, and the Common Prayer Book of the Church of England.

"Part I. Comprehending the Public Offices of the Church. Humbly offered to the Consideration of the present Churches of Christendom, Greek, Roman, English, and all others.

"Part II. Being a Primitive Method of Daily Private Prayer, containing Devotions for the Morning and Evening, and for the Ancient Hours of Prayer, nine, twelve, and three; together with the Hymns of Thanksgivings for the Lord's Day and Sabbath; and Prayers for Fasting Days; as also Devotions for the Altar, and Graces before and after Meat; all taken from the Apostolical Constitutions, and the Ancient Liturgies, with some additions: and recommended to the practice of all private Christians of every Communion. London: Printed for the Author. 1734."

This is a curious book, showing the ritualistic proclivities of Dr. Deacon and his friends. Space forbids lengthened extracts; but, in "Morning Prayer," occurs the following; "Let us pray for those who are departed in the faith, and are at rest in Christ; that God, the lover of mankind, who hath received their souls, would forgive them all their sins voluntary and involuntary, and of His great mercy would graciously grant them perpetual peace in the region of the just."

There are public Prayers, "for the Catechumens, or unbaptized persons, who are receiving instruction in Christianity;" and "for the Energumens, or Persons possessed by Evil Spirits."

There is "The Form of admitting a Penitent to Penance," embracing a confession of his crimes to the Priest; and a prayer that God would "graciously accept the man's Penance; and that, by his continuance in a state of mournful confession and prayer, he may the sooner obtain God's merciful pardon."

In the Office of Baptism, it is ordered, that, the Priest shall "anoint the child with the Holy Oil, and make the sign of the Cross upon its forehead, breast, and palms of the hands." It was then to be "dipped in the water three times;" and then to be "clothed in White Garments;" after which, the Sponsors were to give it "the Kiss of Peace," and the Priest was to put into its mouth "a little of the Consecrated Milk and Honey."

Then there is "The Form of Consecrating the Oil for Baptism:" and "The Form of Consecrating the Milk and Honey:" and "The Form of Consecrating the Chrism for Confirmation:" and "The Form of Consecrating the Oil for the Sick." N.B. The Oil was to be "sweet oil of Olives;" and the Chrism "sweet oil of Olives and precious balsam, commonly called Balm of Gilead."

These extracts speak for themselves.

[2] Was this the daughter of Dr. Potter, Bishop of Oxford? And was she one of the Oxford Methodists?

leave off reading with her. Who knows whether you may not raise her again to the eminence from which she has fallen? At least, though she neglect the weighter matters of the law, yet keep up in her that reverend respect she bears it, even by the tithing of 'mint, anise, and cummin.'

"As to reading the ancients, I fancy 'Cotelerii[1] Biblioth. Patrum Apostol.' would be the best book to begin with; for, though I will not say, that, all the works there contained are genuine, yet I dare avow them to be very ancient, and to contain the primitive doctrine and discipline of the Church, though published under feigned names. You will find a dissertation upon every work, which contains the several testimonies of Fathers and Councils, whereby the authority is confirmed; and, according to the evidence produced, you must judge of the authenticity of the several pieces. The Epistles of St. Clement are universally owned to be his; and so are the smaller Epistles of St. Ignatius; and, indeed, I think, Whiston, in his 'Primitive Christianity,' has urged such arguments in defence of the larger as can never be answered. St. Barnabas's Epistle, and Hermas's Pastor are works of the Apostolic age, as may be proved by the internal characters both of language and doctrine, whether they be the works of the venerable authors they are ascribed to or not. The Apostolical Canons are learnedly defended by Bishop Beveridge, and they sufficiently vindicate the Constitutions.[2] The Recognitions[3] of Clement are generally reckoned the most modern piece in these two volumes, but they are really a most admirable work.

"And now for the last page of your letter. I would answer it; and, yet, for my unworthiness, I dare not,—for my ignorance, I cannot. How shall I direct my instructor in the school of Christ? Or teach you, who am but a babe in religion? However, I must be free to tell you my sentiments of what you inquire about. On Wednesday and Friday, I have, for some time, used the Office for Passion week out of 'Spinckes'[4] Devotions,' and bless God for it. I found it very useful to excite in me

---

[1] John Baptist Cotelerius was a learned French author, born in 1628. He made a collection of the writings of the Fathers, who lived in the Apostolic age, revised and corrected from several manuscripts, with a Latin translation and notes. His work was published in two volumes folio, in 1672.

[2] "The Apostolical Constitutions," a collection of regulations attributed to the Apostles, and supposed to have been collected by St. Clement, whose name they bear.

[3] "The Recognitions of Clement," a book whose authenticity has been greatly doubted, and whose chief subject is the "Travels and Acts of Peter."

[4] Mr. Spinckes was prebendary of Salisbury, and rector of St. Martin's in that town. In 1690, he was deprived of all his preferments for refusing to take the oaths to William and Mary. In 1713, he was consecrated a non-juring bishop by Dr. Hickes, and the Scotch bishops, Campbell and Gadderar. He died in 1727. The full title of the book, which Clayton mentions is, "The True Church of England-Man's Companion in the Closet; or, a Complete Manual of Private Devotions; collected from the Writings of Archbishop Laud, Bishop Andrews, Bishop Ken, Dr. Hickes, Mr. Kettlewell, Mr. Spinckes, and other eminent Divines of the Church of

that love of God, and sorrow for having offended Him, which makes up the first great branch of repentance. You know it consists of meditations on our Saviour's life, all the meditations being joined with proper devotions. I could only wish, I was provided with two such Offices, one for Wednesday, and the other for Friday.

"Refer your last question to Mr. Law. I dare not give directions for spending that time which I consume in bed, nor teach you, who rise at four, when I indulge myself in sleep till five.

"Dear Sir, pray for me that I may press forward in the paths of perfection, and, at length, attain the land of everlasting life. Adieu!

"JOHN CLAYTON."

"I believe you will see a young gentleman of my acquaintance, who is a very pious man, but who greatly stands in need of Christian prudence to direct him. In particular, with regard to his conduct towards his parents, his religion sometimes seems to savour of self. Will you instruct and save him?"

These letters are long, perhaps also dry and tedious; but they are useful in casting considerable light on Oxford Methodism. We learn, that the godly brotherhood, though unevangelical, were, in the highest degree, conscientious and devout. In this respect, they put to shame, not only the great bulk of professing Christians, but, many who, at the present day, are known by the name of Methodists. Doubtless, they sought salvation by the practice of piety and good works; but the piety and good works themselves are not to be censured, but commended. Self-examination, prayer, sacramental attendance, fasting, diligence, kindness to the poor, deep concern for the conversion of sinners, and early rising, are not things of slight importance; but deserve far more practical recognition than what they get.

As to the special religious observance of saint days and of the Jewish Sabbath; and the sacred adoption of ecclesiastical canons and decretals, opinions will differ; but most Methodists will concur in the Methodist Preachers' opinions, as stated by Wesley himself, in 1755:

"They think the Decretals are the very dregs of Popery; and that the Canons of 1603, are as grossly wicked as absurd. They think—1. That,

England. With a Preface by the Reverend Mr. Spinckes." Though deficient in its recognition of the doctrine of salvation by faith, it contains hardly anything seriously objectionable; it is intensely devotional; and could be sincerely used by none except those who made religion the supreme business of their lives.

the spirit which they breathe is, throughout, truly Popish and anti-Christian.   2. That, nothing can be more diabolical than the *ipso facto* excommunication so often denounced therein.   3. That, the whole method of executing these Canons, the process used in our Spiritual Courts, is too bad to be tolerated (not in a Christian, but) in a Mahometan or Pagan nation."[1]

Dr. Deacon, the non-juring clergyman, was Clayton's bosom friend, and Wesley's chosen counsellor.   William Law, another non-juror, was consulted as their guide.   Mr. Spinckes' volume, made up of extracts from the works of the most eminent of the high-church party, was one of their books of devotion. Under such circumstances, it is not surprising to find them plunging into the authentic and unauthentic writings of the Christian Fathers; listening to Apostolical and other Canons as to the voice of oracles; displaying ridiculous anxiety about sacramental wine being mixed with water; and assuming an arrogant willingness to become auricular confessors.   Up to the time of Clayton's admission among the Oxford Methodists, we find none of these proclivities.   The Bible had been their sole supreme authority in faith and morals; and, hence, though their views of evangelical truth were unquestionably defective, their lives were free from the practice of popish follies.   Now it began to be otherwise.   Some of the young men were priests; and priests, according to the Canons of the Church, were invested with the terrible prerogatives of enforcing auricular confession, of pronouncing divine absolution, and of administering the body and blood of the blessed Jesus!   "Poor Miss Potter" had a confessor, who, though a great man, was, evidently in Clayton's estimation, heretical. Emily Wesley indignantly and righteously refused all confessors, her brother not excepted.   Well would it be if the priests of the present day, who "creep into houses, and lead captive silly women," were answered, as this noble-minded young lady answered Wesley, the Arch-Methodist.   She writes :—

"To open the state of my soul to you, or any of our clergy, is what I have no inclination to at present ; and, I believe, I never shall.   I shall not put my conscience under the direction of mortal man, frail as myself. To my own Master I stand or fall.   Nay, I scruple not to say, that all

---

[1] Wesley's Works, vol. xiii., p. 185.

such desire in you, or any other ecclesiastic, seems to me like church tyranny, and assuming to yourselves a dominion over your fellow-creatures, which was never designed you by God. . . . I farther own, that, I do not hold frequent communion necessary to salvation, nor a means of Christian perfection. But do not mistake my meaning: I only think communing every Sunday, or very frequently, lessens our veneration for that sacred ordinance; and, consequently, our profiting by it."

This was a sensible rebuke of priestly pretensions.

Clayton was young, only twenty-four; but, besides his scholarship, he was evidently a man of extensive reading. As the son of a bookseller, he had had the opportunity of gratifying literary cravings from his earliest days. He was a man of energy; and, though he reproaches himself for his sluggishness in not rising earlier than at five o'clock, he was exemplary for his diligence. All this had already made him a man of mark. In this very year, 1733, he was appointed to preach the ordination sermon in Manchester cathedral; and was so ardent in the enforcement of the rubrics of the Church, and so successful in his ministerial and pastoral office as to bring seventy old people, all of them above sixty years of age, to be confirmed by the bishop in Salford church.[1]

Three years later, he was selected to occupy another important post. Darcy Lever, Esq., LL.D., has been already mentioned as one of the friends of Clayton and of the two Wesleys. This gentleman, being appointed, in 1736, to fill the distinguished office of High Sheriff of Lancashire, made Clayton his chaplain. In such a capacity, Clayton had to preach at the Lancaster assizes; and chose for his text, the words,—"He beareth not the sword in vain; for he is the minister of God, a revenger, to execute wrath upon him that doeth evil" (Rom. xiii. 4). This was a ticklish subject for so young a man; but the chaplain was not without courage; and gave utterance to sentiments, which, at the present day, would scarcely be popular. The discourse was printed, and the title will suggest an idea of the preacher's faithfulness. "The Necessity of duly executing the Laws against Immorality and Profaneness: Set forth in a Sermon, preached at the Assizes held at Lancaster, before the Honourable Sir Lawrence Carter, one of the Barons of his Majesty's Court

---

[1] The Private Journal and Literary Remains of John Byrom. 1855.

of Exchequer.   By John Clayton, A.M. late of Brazenose College, Oxon.   Published at the request of the High Sheriff, and the Gentlemen of the Grand Jury.   London.   1736." 8vo, 29 pp.   Two or three extracts may be useful, as serving to illustrate Clayton's views and style, and also the alarming wickedness of the nation.

1736
Age 27

"If drunkards, swearers, and debauchers were constantly brought to justice, it would doubtless lessen the number of criminals, and abate the commonness of the vices.   Many a poor family would be rescued from beggary and starving, were the drunken, idle master of it properly corrected.   Besides, this strict execution of the penal laws against these lesser crimes, would be a most probable means of preserving us from those more dreadful vices of perjury, robbery, and murder ; and would make sanguinary laws less needful, and capital punishments less frequent ; for experience teaches us that vice, as well as virtue, is of a progressive nature" (p. 15).

Again,—

"The fountain from which the Magistrate draws his power, for the punishment of wickedness and vice, is none other but God himself.   All power, whether spiritual or temporal, is originally derived from the Supreme Monarch of the world, who is King of kings, and Lord of lords.   Since, therefore, *every Power*, whether it be supreme or subordinate, does primarily and originally derive all its authority from above, surely the gift of God ought to be used to His honour and glory.   Authority is a sacred thing, of divine original, and, therefore, as it may not be resisted by subjects without danger of damnation, so neither may it be lightly neglected, nor wantonly misapplied by those entrusted with it ; lest they provoke that God to anger, *who putteth down one Ruler*, and setteth up another" (p. 17).

Again,—

"Wickedness is grown to such a head in the world,—immorality and profaneness are become so epidemical among us, that, it is much to be feared, nothing but discipline and wholesome rigour can prove a cure for it.   The infection of vice is extended so far and wide, and the contagion of sin spreads so prodigiously fast, that it seems necessary to use severe methods towards the corrupted parts, if we hope either to recover them, or to save those that are as yet untouched with the disease.   God knows, the flagrant impiety of our days, the excessive corruption of these dregs of time,—this rust of the iron age, into which we are fallen,—is such as every good man must complain of, and for which charity itself can find no sufficient excuse or extenuation " (p. 7).

Advocates of political expediency may object to these high-toned sentiments; but there are still a few who have old-fashioned hardihood enough to exclaim with the Psalmist, "Who will rise up for me against the evildoers? or who will stand up for me against the workers of iniquity?" (Psalm xciv. 16).

The friendship between Clayton and the Wesley brothers was unbroken until the latter departed from Church usages, and became out-door evangelists. In 1735, when urged by Oglethorpe and others to go to Georgia, Wesley, not only sought advice from his brother Samuel and William Law, but went to Manchester to consult with Clayton and others whose judgment he respected ; and, six weeks after his return from the Georgian colony, we find him spending several days with his old Oxford friend.   He writes :—

"1738. March 15. I set out" (from Oxford) "for Manchester, with Mr. Kinchin, Fellow of Corpus Christi, and Mr. Fox, late a prisoner in the city prison. *Friday*, the 17th, we spent entirely with Mr. Clayton, by whom, and the rest of our friends here, we were much refreshed and strengthened. Mr. Hoole, the Rector of St. Ann's church, being taken ill the next day, on Sunday, 19th, Mr. Kinchin and I officiated at Salford chapel in the morning, by which means Mr. Clayton was at liberty to perform the service of St. Ann's ; and, in the afternoon, I preached there on those words of St. Paul, ' If any man be in Christ, he is a new creature.'"[1]

Two months after the date of this extract from his journal, Wesley, ceasing to rely on the merit of his own good works, and trusting solely for salvation in the infinitely meritorious sacrifice of Christ, experienced an amazing change. His own words must be quoted. After relating that, for "above ten years," he had "dragged on heavily," "trusting to his own works and his own righteousness," " in a refined way, zealously inculcated by the mystic writers,"[2] he remarks :—

"1738. May 24. In the evening I went very unwillingly to a society in Aldersgate Street, where one was reading Luther's preface to the Epistle to the Romans. About a quarter before nine, while he was describing the change which God works in the heart through faith in Christ, I felt my heart strangely warmed. I felt I did trust in Christ, Christ alone, for salvation ; and an assurance was given me, that He had taken away my sins, even mine, and saved me from the law of sin and death."[3]

---

[1] Wesley's Works, vol. i., p. 83.   [2] Ibid. p. 94, 95.   [3] Ibid. p. 97.

This was the turning point in Wesley's history. Hitherto, like his friend Clayton, he had hoped to be saved by works; now he was saved by faith. This new experience confirmed his new conceptions of gospel truth, and he began to preach accordingly. He insisted upon good works as much as ever; but he henceforth taught, that man is saved, not by these, but by faith in Christ only. His new doctrine was the means of his being shut out of churches; and this led to his preaching in the open air; and the whole resulted in a rupture of the friendship between him and Clayton, who, so far as there is evidence to show, went on to the end of life, as he and Wesley had begun at Oxford,—a sincere, earnest, self-denying, devout, and laborious Pharisee, trusting in his own righteousness, instead of trusting solely in Christ Jesus.

After the date of Wesley's conversion, we hear of no further friendly meetings. Clayton's death did not occur till 1773, but, during this long interval of thirty-five years, though Wesley's visits to Manchester were numerous, there is no mention made of any interview between the two Oxford Methodists. No proof exists, that Clayton ever ranked himself among Wesley's opponents and slanderers; but, from this period, he ceased to be one of Wesley's friends. Coldness sprang up, and separation. In 1756, Charles Wesley spent nearly a fortnight among the Manchester Methodists, the object of his visit being to prevent their seceding from the Established Church. He himself attended the Church services, and took with him as many of the Methodists as he could. He heard Clayton preach "a good sermon on constant prayer," and, at the same service, by the senior chaplain's invitation, went "with the other clergy" present to the communion table, and received the sacrament; but even this was not enough to regain Clayton's favour; and, hence, the following entries in Charles's journal :—

"1756. Tuesday, October 26. My *former* friend, Mr. Clayton, read the prayers at the Old Church, with great solemnity." "Saturday, October 30. I dined with my candid friend and censor, Dr. Byrom. I stood close to Mr. Clayton in church (as all the week past), but not a look would he cast towards me ;

"So stiff was his parochial pride,"

 and so faithfully did he keep his covenant with his eyes, not to look upon an old friend when called a Methodist."

It has been already shown, that Clayton was an intimate friend of Dr. Deacon, the non-juror; and there can be no doubt that, substantially, the ecclesiastical and political opinions of both were identical. Hence, it is not surprising that both were implicated in the rebellious proceedings of 1745.

Charles Edward Stuart, a young man of twenty-five, with a few attendants, five or six hundred broad-swords, about two thousand muskets, and rather less than £4,000 in cash, set out from France, to overturn the government of Great Britain, and, on behalf of his father, to demand its throne. Such was his success, that, on September 16th, he entered Edinburgh. Three days afterwards, the battle of Preston Pans was fought ; and, immediately, the handsome Young Pretender began, as prince regent, to exercise various acts of sovereign authority. He appointed a council ; ordered regiments to be levied for his service ; and held drawing-rooms, which were, for the most part, brilliantly attended, and generally ended in a public supper and a ball. On the last day of October, Charles Edward quitted Edinburgh, at the head of six thousand men ; and, in a fortnight, took Carlisle. On November 29th, he and his troops reached Manchester; and then proceeded, by regular marches, to Derby, where they arrived on December 4th. This was their nearest approach to London. Before the year was ended, they were hastily retreating to Carlisle, Glasgow, Stirling, and the Highlands.

There we leave them, and return to Manchester. A local authority[1] has stated, that, previous to the rebellion of 1745, Charles Edward had passed several weeks at Ancoats Hall, the seat of Sir Oswald Moseley ; and, that, the leading inhabitants, the clergy of the Collegiate Church, together with Dr. Deacon and his followers, were all warm adherents of the cause of the exiled Stuarts, and recognised, as their political leaders, Colonel Townley, Dr. Byrom, Mr. Dickenson, and others ; who were accustomed to hold their

---

[1] " Manchester : its Political, Social, and Commercial History," by James Wheeler. 1836.

meetings in a public-house, contiguous to Jackson's Ferry, near Didsbury.

To what extent Clayton was associated with these sympathising and plotting Jacobites, it is impossible to determine; but, when the prince marched through Salford, in 1745, this high churchman, with more hardihood than prudence, fell upon his knees before him, and prayed for the blessing of God on the adventurous Chevalier.[1] Charles Edward made the "Palace" hostelry, in Market Street Lane, his residence; and hither Jacobites of both sexes flocked to welcome him. Three sons of Dr. Deacon, true to their father's principles, enlisted beneath the Pretender's banner; Charles Deacon being placed at the head of the recruiting department, and Thomas and Robert Deacon being made Lieutenants.

The results were disastrous. Charles, Thomas, and Robert Deacon fell into the hands of the Royalists, at Carlisle; were tried, condemned, and executed in London, in July, 1746; the head of the eldest, together with that of Adjutant Siddal, being sent to Manchester, and fixed on the Exchange. Townley,

---

[1] Dr. Byrom's eldest daughter has left a journal of the events of this memorable entry into Manchester. She writes :—" 1745. November 29. Friday, eleven o'clock, we went to the cross; about three o'clock, the Prince and the main body came. The Prince went straight to Mr. Dickenson's, where he lodges; the Duke of Athol at Mr. Marsden's, and the Duke of Perth at Gartside's. The bells rung, and P. Cotterel made a bonfire. All the town was illuminated,—every house, except Mr. Dickenson's. About four o'clock, the king was proclaimed. The mob shouted very cleverly.

" Saturday, November 30. An officer called on us to go and see the Prince. We went to Mr. Fletcher's, and saw him get on horseback; and a noble sight it was. I would not have missed it for a great deal of money. When he rid out of the court, he was received with as much joy and shouting almost as if he had been king without any dispute. As soon as he was gone, the officer and we went to prayers at the old church, at two o'clock. Mr. Sprigley read prayers, and prayed for the King and Prince of Wales, and named no names. We went up to Mr. Fletcher's, and stayed there till the Prince was at supper. Secretary Murray came to let us know that the Prince was at leisure; so we were all introduced, and had the honour to kiss his hand. My papa was fetched prisoner (playfully, by the ladies,) to do the same, as was Mr. Deacon; Mr. Cattell and Mr. Clayton did it without; the latter said grace for him."

Mr. Dickenson's house, in which the prince resided, was at the top of Market Street. There was a court-yard in front, shut out from the street by large iron gates. In virtue of the prince's short residence, the house was afterwards called the "Palace"; and on its becoming a hostelry, was designated the "Palace Inn."

1746
Age 37

the colonel of the Manchester Jacobinical regiment, was hanged on Kennington Common, had his bowels torn out, and his heart cast into a fire; and eight of his officers and men were treated in the same barbarous manner.[1]

Great excitement followed. People on both sides were roused. Whitworth's *Manchester Magazine*, the only newspaper published in the town, took the part of the Government; Dr. Deacon, Dr. Byrom, Clayton, and others, were obliged to send all their attacks, replies, and other Jacobite outpourings to the city of Chester, where they obtained insertion in the *Chester Courant*. For two years, this paper warfare was continued; and, in 1749, the whole of what had been printed, both in Manchester and Chester, was collected and published, in a 12mo volume of 324 pages, entitled, "Manchester Vindicated; being a complete Collection of the Papers lately published in Defence of that Town in the *Chester Courant*, together with all those on the other Side of the Question, printed in the *Manchester Magazine*, or elsewhere, which are answered in the said *Chester Courant*, Chester, 1749."

In *Whitworth's Magazine* of September 23rd, 1746, we find the following :—

"Last Thursday, about five in the morning, the heads of Thomas Siddal and Thomas Deacon were fixed upon the Exchange. Great numbers have been to view them; and yesterday, betwixt eight and nine, Dr. Deacon, a non-juring priest, and father to one of them, made a full stop near the Exchange, pulled off his hat, and made a bow to them with great reverence. He afterwards stood some time looking at them. A gentleman of the town was with him, and a considerable number of spectators were present. He and some of his flock have been seen to do so before several times."

This act, innocent and natural enough in itself, was regarded as popery—a worshipping of saints—and gave birth to not a few squibbs and verses. The following was by a Quaker :—

> "Doffing the hat I hold no sign of grace,
> Saving in prayer, which was perhaps the case;
> But yet, my friend, I hope it may be said,
> I'd rather see a hat off than a head."

---

[1] *Pictorial History of England*, vol. iv., p. 548.

Another letter, dated October 11, 1746, says :—

"The two rebel heads are revered, and almost adored, as trophies of martyrdom. The father of one of them (who is a non-juring bishop), as he passes by, frequently pulls off his hat, and looks at them above a minute, with a solemn, complacential silence. Some suppose, he offers up a prayer for them ; others, to them. His church daily increases, and he is in the highest credit and intimacy with the most of our clergy."

This was replied to in a somewhat long article. The writer says, Dr. Deacon has told him that he "never passed by his son's head but once ; and then, indeed, he did pull off his hat." In reference to Deacon's large and growing church, it is added :—

"I cannot find above a score, and those of no great figure or substance, who are partakers with him in his religious singularity. Besides, what connection is there between politics and the Doctor's restoring primitive ecclesiastical usages ? What has the mixt-cup, infant communion, trine-immersion, etc., to do with King George and the Pretender ?"

The writer continues :—

"The Doctor, I own, is respected by most of the clergy ; and, I will add, by most of the laity too ; but what then ? I could name in turn several rigid Dissenters in the *highest credit and intimacy* with *some* of our clergy ; and, if it be wrong (which is indeed a new doctrine to me) for the clergy to respect and converse with persons of different opinions in religion, I think the character of a clergyman of the Church of England in much less danger from his acquaintance with a non-juring bishop than with a Calvinistical Dissenter."

In a letter, dated December 9, 1746, Dr. Deacon writes :—

"I have not adopted the political principles of indefeasible and hereditary right into my religion, and make these an essential part of it ; and that none can become members of the Church to which I belong, that are not enemies to the present government. I do hereby declare that the same is utterly false. I adopt no political principles into my religion but what are expressed in our own Common Prayer Book, entitled, "A Compleat Collection of Devotions."

Much recrimination followed. It was broadly stated in *Whitworth's Magazine*, and absolutely denied in the *Chester Courant*, that, whilst the Rebels were at Manchester, Dr. Deacon "had the very distinguished honour paid him of being escorted by a file of musqueteers to the Pretender's lodgings ;" and one of Whitworth's poetasters favoured the public with the following :—

> " The de'il has set these heads to view,
> And put them upon poles ;
> Poor de'il, 'twas all that he could do,
> When God had ta'en their souls."

Further quotations would be useless and wearisome. Many of the poetical scraps strongly resemble the poetry of Dr. Byrom, an undoubted Jacobite and a friend of Clayton. His three poems,—" A Dialogue, occasioned by the March of the Highlanders into Lancashire, in the Year 1745 "; " A Dialogue about compelling a Person to take the Oaths to the Government"; and " A Genuine Dialogue, between a Gentle-woman at Derby and her Maid, in the beginning of December, 1745," are ample proofs of his sympathy with the non-jurors, and of his ardent attachment to the Stuarts; and, though it might be rash to assert with positiveness that he was actually the author of the Jacobite versicles in the *Chester Courant*, it is not unwarrantable to affirm that they bear a striking similitude to his well-known lines :—

> " God bless the King, and bless the Faith's Defender !
> God bless—no harm in blessing—the Pretender !
> But who Pretender is, and who is King,
> Why, bless us all, that's quite another thing."

Of Clayton's participation in this Jacobinical controversy there can be little doubt. In fact, he is said to have assisted in procuring a printing press for Joseph Harrop, who had been one of Whitworth's apprentices. Harrop began the publication of a paper, in opposition to that of his late master, and to that paper Clayton was an important contributor.[1] Clayton's Jacobite leanings were notorious. In *Whitworth's Magazine*, for November 20, 1746, he was publicly rebuked, because one of his senior scholars had recently affronted a lady at the close of public service in the church by shouting, " Down with the Rump ;" an affront, however, which was " very pardonable in the scholar, since that was a health at the master's table."

Clayton's praying for the Pretender, in the public streets of Salford, has been already mentioned. It is also said, by one who knew him personally,[2] that he visited Prince Charles at

---

[1] Everett's " Methodism in Manchester," p. 121.
[2] Mr. Samuel Barker.

the Palace Inn, paid him profound respect, and was regarded as a sort of royal chaplain. Wheeler, in his "History of Manchester," asserts that when the government sent to Manchester to search for those who had shown disloyalty to the House of Brunswick, Clayton absconded. Be that as it may, he was placed under suspension by his bishop, and was subjected to the painful penalty of a long-continued silence in the church.[1] On resuming his ministerial duties, after his inhibition was ended, he displayed considerable keenness, and, perhaps, some degree of irreverence in the selection of his text. The Bishop of Chester, having commanded him to preach before him, the bold Jacobite, who had so long been silent, but was now again allowed to speak, somewhat startled both the bishop and the congregation by reading as his text, " I became dumb, and opened not my mouth, for Thou didst it."[2]

There can be no question of the purity of Clayton's motives, but his openly avowed adherence to the cause of the Pretender involved him in serious troubles. To say nothing of his ministerial suspension, he was, for years afterwards, the target of his townsmen's malice. Some hated him, but others loved him ; and the two united turned his life into a turmoil. Hence the following, taken from a work entitled, "Jacobite and Non-Juring Principles freely examined," and published, in Manchester, against Dr. Deacon, by J. Owen, in 1748. Speaking of Clayton, Owen asks :—

" If you are the loyal people you represent yourselves to be, whence happens it that there has been such a flush of joy, discovered by your friends, for a *little, seditious priest*, by virtue of the Act of Indemnity, escaping that justice which was upon the *wing* to pursue him ? Whence was it that the bells rang on the occasion for days together ? Was it not by way of grateful *Te Deum*, for the great and undeserved deliverance ? Whence was it that this,—shall I call him *Reverend* Teacher of *Babes*,— has such numbers of his young *fry*, as I am informed he has, clad in the livery of rebellion ? Is it not to convince the world that there is no heresy in Scotch plaid, when wore only as a badge of Romish superstition ? It must be so, unless you can believe,—and believe it who can !—that plaid, politics, and popery are this gentleman's aversion."

Clayton's school has just been mentioned,—a school, per-

1748

Age 39

---

[1] Tradition says the suspension lasted three years.
[2] Everett's " Life of Clarke," vol. ii., p. 239.

haps, commenced in consequence of his clerical suspension.[1] His residence was in Greengate, Salford, and the present well-known Methodist Chapel, in Gravel Lane, stands on what was once his garden. Here he ably conducted his classical academy, not a few of his pupils becoming graduates at the Oxford University. Here he kept a favourite monkey which came to a cruel and untimely end; for his pupils, either in wanton mischief or temporary spite, seized poor Pug, and fastened him to a stake in the vicinity of a hive of bees; and then so exasperated the apiarian insects, that the excited and miserable monkey was literally stung to death. At Kersall Cell, the seat of the Byrom family at Manchester, there is a large original oil-painting representing the interior of Clayton's School in Salford, and a full-length portrait of Clayton himself, dressed in a blue velvet gown, and surrounded by his scholars.

Little more remains to be said of this sincere and earnest high church clergyman. He was stiff in his churchmanship, but was greatly respected. His Jacobite inclinations might be foolish, but they were not wicked, and were not peculiar to himself. Many of the most learned and pious and useful men then existing entertained the same sentiments and feelings. They were doubtless mistaken; but they were honest, and merited forbearance more than punishment. It is said that, in after years, Mr. Clayton's opinions were greatly modified; and that, in fact, he became a Hanoverian. Perhaps there is no absolute proof of such a politico-religious change; but a caricature (now extremely scarce) was published, in which he was represented as standing on a pedestal, with two faces looking in opposite directions; on his breast was inscribed, " The art of trimming;" in his left hand was a scroll with " God bless King James III." upon it; and in his right another, bearing the inscription of " Charles III." The remainder of the picture consisted of a view of Manchester Old Church, the initials of Prince Charles, sundry portraits, a box and dice, a schoolmaster's birchen rod, a broken punchbowl, a dog snatching at a shadow, and finally two fighting cats. At the foot of the engraving was written :—

---

[1] An excellent library was attached to Clayton's school (" Private Journal and Literary Remains of John Byrom").

> " Lye on ! while my revenge shall be
> To speak the very truth of thee."

For twenty years, Clayton was chaplain of the Collegiate Church of Manchester; and, in 1760, was elected a fellow thereof, in the place of Mr. Crouchley, deceased.[1] Nine years afterwards, in 1769, he preached the sermon at the consecration of St. John's Church, Manchester, founded by Edward Byrom, Esq., the son of his warmly attached friend, Dr. Byrom. He died September 25, 1773. His funeral sermon was preached by his intimate friend, the Rev. Thomas Aynscough, M.A., from the words, " We took sweet counsel together, and walked unto the house of God in company." His old pupils erected a monument to his memory, in the Collegiate Church, bearing the following inscription :—

> " Sacred to the Memory of the Rev. John Clayton, M.A.,
> Successively Chaplain and Fellow of this Church,
> Who died September 25th, 1773, Aged 64 Years.
> This Monument is erected by his Scholars,
> A grateful Token of their Affection and Esteem.
> He had endeared himself to them
> by his manly Cheerfulness, and strict Integrity,
> diffusive Charity, heroic Forgiveness,
> and Serenity of Temper under Disappointments ;
> his judicious Fidelity to guard against
> the Dangers of Vice, and Follies of Ignorance,
> by forming the Man, the Scholar, and the Christian,
> in every Mind submitted to his Cultivation ;
> his ardent Zeal for true Religion ;
> warm Attachment to the Church of England ;
> and unwearied Discharge of all the Labours
> of a conscientious Parish Priest ;
> by the uncommon Lustre of his declining Years,
> wherein he bore the sharpest Agonies
> of a painful and humiliating Disease,
> with the Fortitude of Faith, the Resignation of Hope, .
> and the strong Consolation of a well-spent Life."

This is high praise, but not unmerited,—given not by strangers, who never saw him, but by those who knew him best. Old Manchester Methodists used to describe him as being about five feet eight inches in stature, somewhat portly,

---

[1] *Lloyd's Evening Post,* June 30, 1760.

1773
Age 64

dignified in gait, wearing an enormous wig, always deeply serious, a rigid disciplinarian among his scholars and choristers, a pattern of canonical regularity in the performance of his ministerial duties, and very venerable in appearance at the close of life.

Though a scholar and a man of considerable mental power, he seems to have published nothing, except the Sermon already mentioned, his Jacobinical strictures in the *Chester Courant*, and a sixpenny pamphlet, with the following title, "Friendly Advice to the Poor; Written and Published, at the Request of the late and present Officers of the Town of Manchester, by John Clayton, M.A. Manchester: Printed by Joseph Harrop, opposite the Clock End of the Exchange; for Messrs. Newton's, Booksellers, 1755." 47 pp.

Clayton was a faithful and fearless friend. He had no notion of using lollipops when bitters were required. His "advice" was "friendly"; but the opposite of fulsome. In his municipal publication, he delivers himself in no measured terms. He writes :—

"If in any passage of the following Address, the Poor may seem to be treated with rigour, let it not be censured as proceeding from sourness and severity of temper; but be considered as a proof, that the author is in earnest, and desirous of recommending this Tract to the serious unprejudiced consideration of his readers. He has upon all proper occasions shown himself ready to plead the cause of the poor and needy; and, therefore, hopes he may be considered as still walking charitably, though he does, with all plainness of speech and befitting Christian liberty, rebuke that spirit of laziness, luxury, and mismanagement, which is gone out into the world, and which particularly reigns amongst the poor of this town, and to which, in a great measure, all their miseries are owing."

After this exordium, follows his castigation. He reminds his readers of the numerous charitable institutions of the town, for "lodging, clothing, and feeding the poor; for breeding up their children in useful Christian knowledge, and putting them out to proper trades; for helping young people at their first setting out in the world; for maintaining and relieving the sick and maimed; and, lastly, for succouring and supporting the impotent and aged." He tells them, that, the town abounds

"With such variety of manufactures, as, one would think, might furnish every one, that is able and willing to work, with employment and sustenance. Nay, there are many branches of business that require so little skill or labour, as that neither children nor old people need to be totally excluded from their share of them; so that a numerous family,—that common occasion of distress,—far from being a burden here, seems rather to be a blessing to its master; for most of the members of it, if properly managed, are able to get their livelihood; and, by the overplus of their gains, may contribute to maintain the impotent part of the household."

"Many of the poor, however, refuse or neglect to help themselves, and thereby disable their betters from effectually helping them. They have an abject mind, which entails their miseries upon them; a mean, sordid spirit, which prevents all attempts of bettering their condition. They are so familiarized to filth and rags, as renders them in a manner natural; and have so little sense of decency, as hardly to allow a wish for it a place in their hearts."

Clayton acknowledges, that, there are many exceptions of "edifying examples of industry, frugality, and good economy;" but he maintains, that, generally speaking, his description is painfully correct. The town swarmed with "loiterers"; and "common custom had established so many holidays, that few of the manufacturing work-folks were closely and regularly employed above two thirds of their time;" the result being "that every little accident, that prevented a single week's work, reduced them absolutely to the state of paupers." Besides this, "it frequently happened, that, the week's labour of an industrious family, were swallowed up in a day's debauch of the extravagant master." Vice is contagious, and the pestilent example of masters filled the streets of Manchester "with idle, ragged children; who were not only losing their time, but learning habits of gaming; which constantly produced lying, quarrelling, profane swearing and cursing; and frequently, led to pilfering and stealing, and every degree of wickedness and enormity." Added to this, while "the husband wasted his time and squandered his substance at the alehouse, the wife was as often wasteful at the tea-table, as the other was prodigal over his cups; for, strange as it might appear, it was a truth that even this wretched piece of luxury, this shameful devourer of time and money, had found its way into the houses of the poor; and it was no unusual thing to find a miserable family, with hardly rags to cover their nakedness, in a wretched garret, or more loathsome cellar, fooling away a precious hour, and spending more money over this confessedly

1773
Age 64

hurtful food," (beverage) "than would have furnished a good meal or two of wholesome diet." In fact, "ale, gin, and tea mainly swallowed up that slender income, which might have been turned to much better account, had it been laid out with the baker and the butcher."

Clayton adds mismanagement to his charges of idleness and luxury. There was a want of "good housewifry," of "frugal cookery," and of domestic cleanliness.

Another extract must suffice:—

"We cannot walk the streets without being annoyed with such filth as is a public nuisance; as well as seeing such objects as provoke resentment and aversion. We are grown infamous for a general want of good manners in our populace; and no wonder, because they are bred up in such habits of nastiness, as, in a manner, break through the ties of natural modesty, and set them beyond all sense of shame. The streets are no better than a common dunghill; and more sacred places are most shamefully polluted. Our very church-yards are profaned with such filth as was once intended to create a destestation and abhorrence even of idol temples;—I mean they are rendered no better than errant draught-houses. Common decency will not allow me to be more particular upon so loathsome a subject; and, if enough is said to be understood, it is to be hoped it will effect a reformation."

Clayton, besides being an able instructor of the young, and an indefatigable parish priest, wished to be a social reformer; and, certainly, his services, in this respect, were greatly needed. His picture of Manchester, a little more than a hundred years ago, is far from savoury; but there can be little doubt of its being true. Clayton's plain speaking would hardly be tolerated at the present day; but, notwithstanding that, perhaps, it might be useful. At all events, one cannot but admire the stern fidelity of this really kind and exemplary visitor of the poor and friendless, in dealing so faithfully with his fellow-townsmen, who, by their idleness and extravagance, systematically reduced themselves to rags and ruin; and, if the above extracts answer no other purpose, they will not be useless in helping to illustrate the character and principles of this Oxford Methodist.[1]

---

[1] In 1756, a 12mo pamphlet, of 34 pages, was published, with the title, "A Sequel to the Friendly Advice to the Poor of the Town of Manchester. By Joseph Stot, Cobbler." This vivaciously written *brochure* taunts Clayton with having published nothing except a solitary sermon and his " Friendly Advice," and pretends to have expected that his pen

Clayton's life was not mis-spent; but it might have been much more useful if his friendship with the Wesleys had not been broken. John Wesley, between the years 1738 and 1773, visited Manchester more than twenty times; and some of these visits were so memorable, that, Clayton must have heard of them; and, yet, there is not the slightest evidence of any renewal of that fraternal intercourse which was interrupted when Wesley began to preach salvation by faith only, and, in consequence, was excluded from the pulpits of the Established Church. This was heresy too great for a high churchman to overlook. To be saved by faith in Christ, instead of by sacraments, fasts, penances, ritualism, and good works was an unpardonable novelty, deserving of Clayton's life-long censure; and hence, after 1738, the two old Oxford friends seem to have been separated till they met in heaven. It is rather remarkable, that, Wesley's first visit to Manchester, subsequent to his conversion, was at the very time when the Jacobite controversy, already mentioned, was at its height; and that Wesley preached at Salford Cross, immediately adjoining Clayton's residence. He writes :—

"1747, May 7.—We came to Manchester between one and two. I had no thought of preaching here, till I was informed, John Nelson had given public notice, that I would preach at one o'clock. Their house would not contain a tenth part of the people; and how the unbroken spirits of so large a town would endure preaching in the street, I knew not. But after considering, that, I was not going a warfare at my own cost, I walked strait to Salford Cross. A numberless crowd of people partly ran before, partly followed after me. I thought it best not to sing, but, looking round, asked abruptly, 'Why do you look as if you had never seen me before? Many of you have seen me in the neighbouring church, both preaching and administering the sacrament.' I then began, 'Seek ye the Lord while He may be found; call upon Him while He is near.' None interrupted at all or made any disturbance, till, as I was drawing to a conclusion, a big man thrust in, with three or four more, and bade them bring out the engine. Our friends desired me to remove into a yard just by, which I did, and concluded in peace."

Clayton at the time was suspended from exercising ministerial functions by his bishop; but he was probably in Man-

would have benefitted the public during the time his tongue was silenced by his bishop. It also states that Clayton was never seen out of doors "without a great sweeping nosegay;" and accounts for this on the ground that, perhaps, the foul smells of Manchester made it necessary.

1773
Age 64

chester, and in a neighbouring house; but there was no recognition of his quondam friend. Wesley might have called upon him; but perhaps Clayton's dubious position, as a clergyman suspended for his Jacobinical leanings, prevented this. Wesley himself had been falsely accused of being a friend of the Pretender, and common prudence dictated the inexpediency of seeking the company of one who had shown Charles Edward such marks of sympathy and respect.

At his next visit but one, Wesley writes :—

"1752, March 27.—Being Good Friday, I went to the Old Church, where Mr. Clayton read Prayers; I think the most distinctly, solemnly, and gracefully of any man I ever heard; and the behaviour of the whole congregation was serious and solemn in every part of the service. But I was surprised to see such a change in the greater part of them, as soon as the sacrament was over. They were then bowing, courtesying, and talking to each other, just as if they were going from a play."

Did Wesley join in this sacramental service? Was Clayton one of the administrators? Was there any intercourse between the two?

Another of Wesley's visits was in 1755, the year in which Clayton published his "Friendly Advice to the Poor"; and Wesley's entry in his journal shows that reformation was needed not only among the working-classes, but their superiors.

"1755, April 9.—In the evening I preached at Manchester. The mob was tolerably quiet as long as I was speaking, but immediately after raged horribly. This, I find, has been their manner for some time. No wonder; since the good justices encourage them."

It was a year after this, when Charles Wesley attended the Collegiate church every day for a whole week, and every day stood close to Clayton, and yet the latter would not even look at him.

Here we must leave the Jacobite Churchman. Of his sincerity, and of his earnest purpose faithfully to fulfil his office as a minister of the Church of England, there can be no question; but, remembering the sacred associations and Methodist meetings of Oxford, this priestly superciliousness was not to be commended, even though his two former friends were now excluded from Church of England pulpits, and were so ecclesiastically irregular as to preach in the open air.

REV. BENJAMIN INGHAM,

THE YORKSHIRE EVANGELIST.

1734

Age 22

BENJAMIN INGHAM was born at Osset, in Yorkshire, June 11th, 1712. Like the Wesleys, he was a descendant of one of the ministers ejected from the Church of England by the black Bartholomew Act of 1662.[1] Having received a liberal education at the grammar-school, Batley, he was sent, when about eighteen years of age, to Queen's College, Oxford. Two years afterwards, he joined the Methodists. None of that godly brotherhood were more diligent and devout than this young Yorkshireman. Hence, the following letter addressed to his friend Wesley :—

"OSSET, *February 27th*, 1734.

"HONOURED SIR,—I meet with many cases of conscience in the country, though I can find no casuist to solve them. I did not altogether know the advantage of living at Oxford so well before as I do now. They that have it in their power to reside there, are wise if they do so. To act well in the country, requires more knowledge, prudence, and a great deal more zeal. It is scarce possible to imagine how wicked the world is. The generality are dead in trespasses and sins. Even those who would pass for good Christians, are sunk deep in a dead indifference. Sincerity is as rare as a black swan. Since I left your good brother, I have only met with one person that is in good earnest for heaven, except that poor rug-maker. God, indeed, is chief in his heart. The most wholesome discipline and best discourses have no effect upon most people. They are no more moved and concerned than a stone. Reflecting frequently on this, has confirmed my belief of an election of grace. I should be glad to know your thoughts on the subject at a convenient opportunity.

"Since my coming into the country, I have frequently been much affected with lively meetings; which has compensated me much, and made me easy and cheerful. What dejects me most is when I lie long, or am idle, or in company where I can do no good. I desire to know how I

---

[1] Calamy's "Nonconformist Memorial," vol. ii., p. 599; and *Evangelical Magazine*, 1814, p. 302.

ought to act when I am in company with superiors, who talk only about trifles. Alas! Sir, I am vastly deficient in this singularity, which is a material point; though, blessed be God! I have now a footman to call me, who visits me early, so that I hope to mend.

"I have methodized my time according to the following scheme. Suppose I rise at five, or sooner, I spend till six in devotion,—repeating a hymn, and chanting a psalm, then praying and reading the Holy Scriptures. At six, Christian treatises. At seven, we breakfast. I then get a lesson out of the New Testament, then a Collect, and most of the Common Prayer. Then forty-two poor children come to me to read. I propose to observe the three ancient hours of prayer when at home. From nine to eleven, I read in the Greek Testament, according to Frank's. At eleven, I go to teach the rug-maker's children to read. Twelve, dine; read Morris's 'Shorthand.' Two, Greek Testament. Four, walk. Five, devotion. Six, Monday, I choose the subject beforehand. Seven, supper; and read Milton and other religious books with the family. Nine, pray for myself and friends. On Wednesday and Friday, from eight to nine, meditate on my sins; twelve to one, on Christ's sufferings; two to three, read Morris. On Sunday, spend two hours in reading with the family or some poor neighbours.

"I shall readily submit to your better directions. Supposing a friend to visit me on a stationary day,[1] how must I behave myself? In eating and drinking, should I confine myself to such a quantity, when with strangers? Your directions in these cases will be very useful.

"My hearty love to your brother, and all friends. I have received a letter from Mr. Smith. He says he will acquaint his tutor with all his concerns. I design shortly to write to Mr. Ford and Watson. I earnestly desire the hearty prayers of all friends.

"From your most obliged and affectionate friend and servant,

"B. INGHAM."

Here we have another glimpse of Oxford Methodism,—intense conscientiousness, concern on account of surrounding wickedness, early rising, religious employment of every hour, devout study, care for neglected children, and observance of the weekly fasts; but not a word respecting the great truth, that sinners are saved by the alone merits of Jesus Christ, and by a penitential trust in His all-sufficient sacrifice. These were truths which the Oxford Methodists had yet to learn. Ingham, like Kirkham, the Morgans, and Clayton, looked to Wesley for guidance; but, in this respect, Wesley as yet was an incompetent instructor.

Ingham mentions his teaching forty-two children how to

---

[1] Fast-day.

read, and his Sunday meetings among the poor people at Osset. Such efforts to improve his neighbours deserve to be commended ; and it is a pleasant duty to relate, that, his benevolent endeavours were attended with great success. Numbers of persons were convinced of their lost condition as sinners : and thus was commenced a religious movement akin to that, which, eight years afterwards, seemed to up-heave a large portion of the West Riding of the county of York.

Notwithstanding his prayers, fasts, scripture reading, and diligence, Ingham was not happy ; and no wonder. He was a conscientious, earnest Pharisee, seeking to be saved by works of righteousness, rather than by penitential faith in Christ. The following letter, also addressed to Wesley, and written nine months after the former one, shows how dis-satisfied he was with his present religious state ; and reveals a scrupulousness of conscience in reference to shooting and Quakers, which is somewhat amusing :—

" Osset, *November* 30, 1734.

" Rev. Sir,—Such is the wretchedness of my station at present, that, if I durst, shame would persuade me to conceal it from my best friends. God, of His great goodness, has been pleased to chastise me, for my sins, with an ague. I am afraid, I shall make but a very indifferent use of this Fatherly correction. It may justly be expected that I should be more dead to the world, and filled with more fervent longings and thirstings after God ; that my diligence would have been quickened, and my devotion inflamed. But, alas ! sir, I am become more sensual, more indulgent, and more sub-ject to vanity. To early prayer I am now a stranger. I think it well to rise at seven. In my sickness, my thoughts, for the most part, were monstrous and trifling. I would fain make my distemper an excuse ; and, though it weakened my body, it is strange that it should disorder my soul. To give you one instance of my weakness : When I was pretty well recovered, I could not deny myself so much as to walk out for my health ; and yet, with but little persuasion, I went several times a shoot-ing. Nay, I thought it necessary, though I had renounced it. But it pleased God graciously to let my distemper relapse, which took away the power, though not the desire of going.

" At present, I keep altogether at home, scarcely stirring out of doors. My eyes are weak ; yet I am in a fair way of recovering my bodily health. The only thing in which I have not been much deficient, is in teaching the children, and conversing at night with the neighbours, when able to do it. And, indeed, this has been a means of saving myself from utterly sinking. God hath been pleased to bless my weak endeavours with pretty good success ; and, I find, that, He manifests the effects when we least expect it, hereby telling us that not our endeavours, but His Almighty arm doth the work.

"The honest rugmaker makes very slow advances in learning. I think to dissuade him from it, unless you advise me to the contrary.

"My sister proceeds excellently, and, by her example, provokes me to what otherwise I should not do.

"I desire you to resolve me : Will it be lawful to sell a thing above its worth, purely because the buyer hath a desire of it ? Also, whether it be convenient or lawful for a Christian to dwell with a Quaker when under no necessity ? Also, whether persons ought to eat, or openly declare they fast, when no necessity puts them upon it ?

"Dear Sir, let me beg your earnest prayers for your unworthy, most obliged Friend and Servant,

"B. INGHAM.

"My love to your good brother, etc.

"I have heard from Mr. Burton. Mr. Wogan joins with him in service to you and your brother. He expects to return by Oxford about Christmas. They were indifferently in health. If I recover my health perfectly, would you advise me to visit Mr. Clayton before I return to Oxford? Our family send their service.

"For the Rev. Mr. John Wesley,
"Fellow of Lincoln College, Oxon."

From the above, it is quite evident that the Oxford Methodists regarded the Quakers as not Christians; yea, as people, in whose houses, it was doubtful whether Christians, except in cases of necessity, ought to dwell. This was not surprising. Sacraments, fasts, and feast days were essentials among the Oxford Methodists; among the Quakers they were utterly neglected. The religion of the Methodists, to a great extent, consisted in the observance of outward forms; the religion of the Quakers, to an equal extent, in the neglect of them.

Ingham returned to Oxford in February, 1735 ; and was ordained in Christ Church, by Bishop Potter, on the 1st of June following. On the day of his ordination, he preached his first sermon, his congregation consisting of the prisoners in Oxford Castle. On the 4th of the same month, he proceeded, with Mr. Gambold, to London, where he was engaged as the "reader of public prayers at Christ Church, and at St. Sepulchre's," Newgate Street. Ingham's zeal was too fervent to be pent up in the reading-desks of these city churches. His age was only twenty-three ; he was full of youthful buoyancy, and longed for a wider sphere of action.

1735

Age 23

In Yorkshire, he had held conversational meetings in his mother's house ; but now, for the first time, he was allowed to mount the pulpit, and to preach. Christ Church and St. Sepulchre's had other, probably older, men than himself as preachers ; but, rather than be silent, away he went, on a sort of ecclesiastical itinerancy, far beyond the precincts of London proper, and preached in many of the surrounding villages, and with such singular success, that great numbers of the people were powerfully impressed, and had eternal cause to be grateful for his youthful and fervid ministry.[1]

The Oxford Methodists were already scattered. In consequence of his father's death, on April 25, 1735, Wesley had gone to Epworth. His brother Charles, ordained about the same time as Ingham, had also taken his departure from Oxford. Clayton was in Manchester ; Hervey at home ; Gambold in London. The following letter, addressed to Wesley, and written a fortnight after Ingham's ordination, contains interesting references to this religious brotherhood.

" Mr. Lisson's, George Yard,
Snow Hill, London,
June 17, 1735.

" Rev. Sir,—The chief intent of this is to express my respect and gratitude to you, and dear Mr. Charles, as at your departure from Oxford there might seem to be some indifference between us ; but, according to the old saying, *Amantium irae amoris redintegratio est;* my affections have the more inflamed since that, and I have often thought of writing to inform you of it, but hitherto have delayed. I have reason to believe you have met with a variety of trials at Epworth, and I have heard you evil spoken of abroad ; and, for these reasons, I do assure you I love you the more, and pray the more earnestly for you. You have heard of the fluctuating condition of some acquaintance at Oxford. London friends have much the same esteem for you : ' You are a good man, but you are too rigid,' etc. ' Master, in so saying, thou reproachest us also.'

" But to give you some good news. Mr. Salmon[2] is a sincere friend.

---

[1] " Life and Times of Lady Huntingdon," vol. i., p. 242.

[2] Salmon was one of the Oxford Methodists. In 1779, Wesley wrote : " Fifty years ago Mr. Matthew Salmon was one of our little company at Oxford, and was then, both in person, in natural temper, and in piety, one of the loveliest young men I knew." (Wesley's Journal.) Like Clayton, Mr. Salmon became alienated from the Methodists. In 1748, he published the " Foreigner's Companion through the Universities of Oxford and Cambridge," which contained the following :—" The times of

1735
—
Age 23

Mr. Whitefield is well known to you. I contracted great intimacy with him since your departure. He is zealous in a good cause. All friends at Queen's College I left in a hopeful condition. Their number is increased, and, I verily believe, will increase. Mr. Hervey fights manfully in North-amptonshire. Mr. Broughton is really a holy man. Mr. Morgan (I suppose you have heard his case, how he is forbid all conversation with you or your friends, etc.), I hope, will make a good Christian. Our friends at Osset go on very well. I baptized Piggot, and preached at the Castle the day I was ordained. I think there were thirty, save one, at the sacrament at St. Mary's the day before I came to London. Piggot and some of our friends were confirmed on Sunday. Mr. Gambold came with me to London, and is with me at Mr. Lissons's. He returns to Oxford with Mr. Hall, who has been here a considerable time, on Saturday. On Friday, I shall set forward for Matching.[1] I cannot tell how long I shall stay there. I have thoughts of visiting my friends in Yorkshire ; and, if you continue at Epworth, I think to come and see you. I have also a desire to see Mr. Clayton, at Manchester. I have been with Mr. Gambold and Hall to see Mr. Law.[2] We asked him some questions ; but he talked

---

the day the University go to this church, are ten in the morning, and two in the afternoon, on Sundays and holidays, the sermon usually lasting about half an hour. But, when I happened to be at Oxford, in 1742, Mr. Wesley, the Methodist, of Christ Church, entertained his audience two hours ; and, having insulted and abused all degrees, from the highest to the lowest, was, in a manner, hissed out of the pulpit by the lads."

The preacher on this occasion was Charles Wesley, and the two hours' sermon, was his well-known Discourse, before the University of Oxford, on "Awake thou that sleepest," etc. (Eph. v. 14). On reading Salmon's unbrotherly attack, Charles Wesley remarked : "And high time for the lads to do so, if the historian said true ; but, unfortunately for him, I measured the time by my watch, and it was within the hour ; I abused neither high nor low, as my sermon, in print, will show : neither was I hissed out of the pulpit, or treated with the least incivility, either by young or old. What, then, shall I say to my old high church friend whom I once so much admired ? I must rank him among the apocryphal writers, such as the judicious Dr. Mather, the wary Bishop Burnet, and the most modest Mr. Oldmixon." (C. Wesley's Journal, vol. ii., p. 71.)

A nephew of Mr. Salmon's, and some other branches of his family, afterwards became Methodists, at Nantwich and in the neighbourhood. Miss Salmon was an intimate friend of Elizabeth Ritchie and Hester Ann Rogers. Joseph Whittingham Salmon, the nephew, entertained Wesley at Nantwich, in 1779. In 1785, he preached, and published a sermon on the death of his wife, with the title, " The Robes of the Saints washed in the Blood of the Lamb : being the Substance of a Funeral Dscourse, preached at the Barker Street Chapel, Nantwich, on Occasion of the Death of Mrs. Salmon." 8vo, 39 pages. And, in 1796, he gave to the world a book of poetry, entitled, " Moral Reflections in Verse, begun in Hawkstone Park," etc. 8vo, 264 pages.

Matthew Salmon, the Oxford Methodist, will be occasionally mentioned in succeeding pages.

[1] A parish in Essex.
[2] The celebrated, Rev. William Law.

only about man's fall, and the one thing necessary. He is a divine man.

1735
Age 23

"I like several of the religious people in London pretty well; but I must confess they are not over zealous. I have had a great many turns and changes since I saw you. I believe I must be perfected through sufferings. Notwithstanding, by the blessing of God, I hope to press on, and persevere in the constant use of all the means of grace. I intend, at present, to read the Scriptures in English, together with Mr. Law's books.

"My hearty respects to your brother and mother. Mrs. Lissons sends her service. Pray let me hear from you shortly. When I shall have the happiness of seeing you, or your brother, I shall acquaint you with many particulars which I cannot now mention. In the meantime, I rest, dear Sir, your sincere and affectionate friend, and brother in Christ,

"B. INGHAM."

"For the Rev. Mr. John Wesley, at Epworth, to be left at the Post Office in Gainsborough, Lincolnshire."

"A man's heart deviseth his way, but the Lord directeth his steps." Within three months after this, Wesley wrote to Ingham, in substance, as follows :—"Fast and pray ; and then send me word whether you dare go with me to the Indians." Ingham's answer will be found in the following long letter, or journal, dated "Savannah, May 1st, 1736;" and which is now, for the first time, published at *full length.* The substance of it was given in the "Wesley Banner" for 1852 ; but it is here printed verbatim, and without abridgment. Perhaps, and indeed, probably, the letter was an extract from a longer journal ; but if so, the journal is unknown. The document is long, and somewhat loosely written ; but, besides illustrating Ingham's character, it contains a considerable amount of interesting information, and will serve to confirm the journals of Wesley and his brother, and to fill up gaps in them :—

"SAVANNAH, *May 1st,* 1736.

"To my much-honoured Mother, my dearly beloved Brethren and Sisters, and all my Christian Friends:—Grace, mercy and peace be multiplied from Almighty God, the Father, and from our Lord Jesus Christ, with the Holy Ghost ; to whom be glory, honour, and praise for ever and ever. Amen.

"Blessed, for ever blessed be the God and Father of our Lord Jesus Christ, the Father of all mercy, and the God of all consolation, who, of His great goodness, has been graciously pleased to conduct us safe through the terrors of the great deep ! 'They that go down to the sea in ships, and occupy their business in great waters, these men see the works of the Lord, and His wonders in the deep, for, at His word, the stormy wind ariseth, which lifteth up the waves thereof. They are carried up to the heavens, and down again to the deep. Their soul melteth away because of the trouble. They reel to and fro, and are tossed up and down, so that they are at their wit's end. Then they cry unto the Lord in their trouble, and He delivereth them out of their distress. For He maketh the storm to cease, so that the waves thereof are still. Then are they glad, because they are at rest; and so He bringeth them unto the haven where they would be! O! that men would therefore praise the Lord for His goodness, and declare the wonders that He doeth to the children of men!'

"I can now inform you that we are all arrived in safety in Georgia. But, because I believe that a relation of our voyage will not be unacceptable to you, I shall, with God's assistance, set down both the chief occurrences thereof, and also the reasons which moved me to undertake it. But, lest you should think of me, or my designs, more highly than you ought to think, I do assure you that I am a very grievous and abominable sinner, proud, sensual, and self-willed. And, oh! that I was truly sensible, and heartily sorry of being so! Oh! that it would please Almighty God, of His great grace, to make me thoroughly humble and contrite! Oh! that my sins were done away; that my nature was changed; that I was a new creature in Christ Jesus! Then, perhaps, God would make me an instrument to His glory. Oh! my dear friends, I beg of you, I entreat you, I beseech you, pray mightily to God in my behalf, that I may not be a castaway.

"About six weeks before we took shipping for Georgia, I received a letter from the Rev. Mr. John Wesley, Fellow of Lincoln College, Oxford, the substance whereof was as follows: 'Fast and pray; and then send me word whether you dare go with me to the Indians.' Having observed his directions, about three days after the receipt of this, I answered him to this effect: 'I am satisfied that God's providence has placed me in my present station. Whether He would have me go to the Indians or not, I am not as yet informed. I dare not go without being called.' I kept his letter secret for some days. I was utterly averse from going. I thought we had heathens anew at home. However, I continued to pray that God would be pleased to direct me, whether He would have me go, or not.

"About a fortnight after this, Mr. John Wesley came to London, as also his brother Charles, and Mr. Salmon, a gentleman of Brazen-Nose College, Oxon. The first time I was with them, I desired to know the reasons which moved them to leave England. They answered, they thought they could be better Christians, alleging particular advantages which they might reasonably expect would further their spiritual progress, by going amongst the Indians. Some of their reasons I approved of; to others I objected, alleging that a man might be a Christian in any place, but chiefly insisting upon this, that no one ought to go without being called of God. They told me, if I required a voice or sign from heaven, that was not now to be expected ; and that a man had no other way of knowing God's will, but by consulting his own reason, and his friends, and by observing the order of God's providence. They, therefore, thought it a sufficient call to choose that way of life which they had reason to believe would most promote their Christian welfare. Our conversation being ended, they lent me several letters, written by Mr. Oglethorpe, relating to the Indians, their manner of living, their customs, and their great expectation of having a white man come amongst them to teach them wisdom. All this moved me a little, but I had no mind to leave England. However, I now began to pray more frequently and fervently that God would be pleased to direct me to do His will.

" Besides the three gentlemen aforementioned, there was also one Mr. Hall, brother-in-law to Mr. Wesley, resolutely determined to go. When they had been in London about ten days, in which time I frequently conversed with them, I found my heart so moved one night, by being with Mr. John Wesley, that, almost without thinking it, I said to him, 'If neither Mr. Hall nor Mr. Salmon go along with you, I will go.' At that time, there seemed no probability that either of them would draw back. They were both of them ordained by the Bishop of London in order to go : Mr. Salmon, deacon ; Mr. Hall, both deacon and priest.

" But, lo ! Mr. Salmon was immediately seized upon by his relations in town, and was sent down, post haste, to his parents in Cheshire. Upon his arrival, his father left the house, furious and distracted, protesting he would not return unless his son would stay. His mother, also, was labouring under a fever. In this distress, he knew not what to do ; but he promised his parents to stay, and wrote Mr. Wesley word that he hoped to follow him next spring, though since then he has writ to him, telling him he doth not think himself as yet at liberty to leave father and mother.

" However, Mr. Hall still continued steady. Neither his wife, nor mother, nor brother, nor uncle, nor all his friends, either by prayers, tears, threats, or entreaties, could, in the least, turn him aside from his purpose.

" A few days after this, Mr. Wesley began to be more importunate with me, urging me with my promise, telling me he had now little hope of Mr. Salmon ; and, as for Mr. Hall, he could not properly be said to go with him, for his design was to go amongst the Indians, whereas Mr. Hall was only to go to Savannah, and be minister there ; and as for his brother Charles, he went over only as secretary to the trustees for the colony of Georgia.

" I still refused, telling him, ' If Mr. Hall went, I would not go.' Nevertheless, I prayed very earnestly, almost night and day revolving upon it. My heart began to be now more and more affected. It pleased God to let me see I might be a better Christian by going with Mr. Wesley. I thought, by living with him and having his example always before mine eyes, I should be enabled to rise regularly and early, and to spend all my time carefully, which are great and necessary points in Christianity, and wherein I grew very deficient by living in London. Besides these, there were three other reasons which moved me. I thought, I should not meet with so many temptations, to sensuality and indulgence, among the Indians as in England. Hereby, likewise, I saw I should be freed from the slavery of worldly interests, and the danger and drudgery of hunting for preferment, which hinders so many from being Christians, making them to betray the Church to serve the State, and to deny Jesus Christ to please worldly-minded men. The last and chief reason was the goodness of the work, and the great and glorious promises that are made to those who forsake all for the sake of the gospel.[1]

"Notwithstanding all these reasons, I was not yet fully determined to go ; but, what is very remarkable, the Psalms, the Lessons, and all that I then read suggested to me that I should go. So that, being at Morning Prayers in Westminster Abbey, on Tuesday, October 7th, 1735, the tenth chapter of St. Mark, which was then read, made so strong and vigorous an impression upon me, that, at the hearing of these words, 'And Jesus answered and said, Verily, I say unto you, there is no man that hath left house, or brethren, or sisters, or father, or mother, or wife, or children, or lands, for my sake, and the gospel's, but he shall receive an hundred-fold now in this time, houses, and brethren, and sisters, and mothers, and children, and lands, with persecutions ; and in the world to come eternal life,'—I determined in my heart that I would go. I may likewise observe that, without any intention or design, I read the same chapter the next day at St. Sepulchre's Church, which did not a little strengthen my resolution.'

"Though I was thus determined in my own mind, yet I did not make known my purpose to Mr. Wesley ; but told him there were three objections against my going. My mother and Mr. Nicolson knew nothing of the matter ; whereas I ought to have acquainted them both, and obtained their consent. To these Mr. Wesley answered, he did not doubt but God would provide better for the school in my absence than if I stayed, especially if I recommended it to His care in my prayers, which I have constantly done. Mr. Morgan, likewise, a gentleman of Lincoln College, Oxford, who came up to London to take leave of Mr. Wesley, a zealous and sincere Christian, being very earnest with me to go, promised himself to make a journey into Yorkshire to see my mother, and to do what he could towards settling the school. As to having my mother's consent, he said, if I thought it was God's will, I must obey my Master, and go wherever I could do Him service, whether my relations were willing or not. But, however, I could not go without Mr. Nicolson's knowledge and consent, because that would be leaving the parish unprovided, which would be unlawful. We therefore put the matter upon this issue,—if Mr. Nicolson consented, I might go ; if not, then there was a reasonable hindrance against my going at this time. Mr. Nicolson had been some weeks at his parish of Matching, in Essex, whereof I was

---

[1] Wesley's reasons were *substantially* the same as Ingham's. (See "Life and Times of Wesley," vol. i., p. 115, 116.)

curate. He usually came to town on Saturdays, but, by a wonderful Providence, he was now brought to town on Monday night. His intent was to have returned the next day, but he was strangely detained, by one thing or other, till Wednesday. I would gladly have met with him on Tuesday, but could not find him at home. However, I writ a letter, and ordered it to be given him as soon as he came. Next morning, he came to my lodgings at Mr. Lissons's. He told me he had received my letter, which had acquainted him with my designs. He was sorry to part with me ; my warning was short ; my departure was sudden ; yet, as I was going about a good work, he would not oppose me ; and, provided I could preach the Sunday following, he would give me his consent. I went to Mr. Oglethorpe to know if I could stay so long. He said, I might. I returned, acquainted Mr. Nicolson, and so parted with him very friendly, he going directly into the country.

"After this, I made known my designs, and got things in readiness as fast as I could. My friends in town endeavoured to persuade me; but I did not consult them, but God.

"On *Friday*, October 10, 1735, I made my will, which I sent inclosed in a letter to you at Osset.

"*Sunday*, October 12, I preached at St. Mary Somerset [1] in the morning, and at St. Sepulchre's in the afternoon. Service being ended, I took leave of my good old friend, Mrs. Lissons, and her family, who wept much—my cousin, Robert Harrap, and some other friends. Thence I went to Sir John Philips', a very worthy gentleman, and a devout Christian, who showed me a great deal of respect, and did me many favours when I was in London, where, having exhorted one another, we kneeled down to pray, and so parted. Thence I went with Mr. Morgan to Mr. Hutton's, a good family in Westminster, where we spent the next day with Messrs. Wesley, chiefly in private. But there happened such a remarkable circumstance on it, as I cannot pass over in silence. Mr. Hall, who had made great preparations for the voyage, and had now got all things ready for his departure, having this very morning hired a coach to carry himself and wife down to Gravesend, where the ship lay, at the very hour wherein they should have gone, drew back. He came unexpectedly, and told Mr. Oglethorpe, his uncle and mother would get him a living, and, therefore, he would not go. So he, whom all his friends could not dissuade before, lost himself, and dropped all his resolutions in the very last moments.

"This strange occurrence, which was so much beyond all expectation, was a strong and fresh demonstration to me, that it was God's will I should go. Because, as I observed, I had said to Mr. Wesley some time ago, ' If neither Mr. Hall nor Mr. Salmon go along with you, I will go.'— And again, ' If Mr. Hall goes, I will not go.'

"Having now no further doubt, but, that, I was intended by Providence to accompany Mr. Wesley, on *Tuesday*, October 14, he, his brother, Mr. Charles, myself, and Mr. Delamotte, son of a merchant in London,

---

[1] In Thames Street.

who had a mind to leave the world, and give himself up entirely to God, being accompanied by Mr. Morgan, Mr. Burton, (one of the trustees), and Mr. James Hutton, took boat at Westminster, for Gravesend. We arrived there about four in the afternoon, and immediately went on board the ship, called the *Symmonds.*

"We had two cabins allotted us in the forecastle; I and Mr. Delamotte having the first, and Messrs. Wesley the other. Theirs was made pretty large, so that we could all meet together to read or pray in it. This part of the ship was assigned to us by Mr. Oglethorpe, as being most convenient for privacy.

"*Wednesday* and *Thursday* we spent chiefly with Mr. Morgan and Mr. Hutton, exhorting and encouraging one another. We also received the Lord's Supper with them each day, thereby to strengthen our spiritual strength and resolutions. They were both sorry to part with us; and, I believe, Mr. Morgan would have been very glad to have gone along with us.

"*Friday*, October 17, Mr. John Wesley. began to learn the German tongue, in order to converse with the Moravians, a good, devout, peaceable, and heavenly-minded people, who were persecuted by the Papists, and driven from their native country, upon the account of their religion. They were graciously received and protected by Count Zinzendorf, of Hernhuth, a very holy man, who sent them over into Georgia, where lands will be given them. There are twenty-six of them in our ship; and almost the only time that you could know they were in the ship, was when they were harmoniously singing the praises of the Great Creator, which they constantly do in public twice a day, wherever they are. Their example was very edifying. They are more like the Primitive Christians than any other church now in the world; for they. retain both the faith, practice, and discipline delivered by the Apostles. They have regularly ordained bishops, priests, and deacons. Baptism, confirmation, and the eucharist are duly administered. Discipline is strictly exercised without respect of persons. They all submit themselves to their pastors, being guided by them in everything. They live together in perfect love and peace, having, for the present, all things in common. They are more ready to serve their neighbours than themselves. In their business, they are diligent and industrious; in all their dealings, strictly just and conscientious. In everything, they behave themselves with great meekness, sweetness, and humility.

"*Saturday*, October 18. This morning, Mr. John Wesley and I began to read the Old Testament, which we finished during our voyage. Mr. Wesley likewise baptised a man of thirty, who before only had received lay baptism.[1] I was witness.

"*Sunday*, October 19. Mr. John Wesley began to preach without notes, expounding a portion of Scripture extempore, according to the ancient usage. During our passage, he went over our Saviour's Sermon on

---

[1] Another instance of the high-churchism of these Oxford Methodists.

the Mount. Heal so constantly explained the Second Lesson, except when he catechized the children ; whereby, all that heard, with sincere hearts, were much edified. To-day, being the first time we celebrated the Lord's Supper publicly, (which we did constantly every Lord's-day afterwards,) we had but three communicants besides ourselves ;—a small number, yet God has been graciously pleased to add to them. All love, all glory, be to Thee, O Lord !

"*Monday*, October 20. I began to teach and catechize the children on board our ship, being in number about twelve. I likewise helped two or three of the Moravians[1] to learn English. This I continued to do several weeks, till we came out to sea, and then I could but do it seldom, by reason of the rolling of the ship. O that we were all like little children, willing to be instructed and guided by our Heavenly Father ! O that we were truly sensible of our own ignorance, and how very little the wisest of us knows that is worth knowing! It is God that teacheth man knowledge.

"*Tuesday*, October 21. We left Gravesend, and went down the river, though but very slowly, the wind not being favourable to us.

"We now began to be more in earnest. We resolved to rise early, and to spend our time regularly and carefully. The first hour, we allotted ourselves, was to pray for ourselves and absent friends. The next, we read the Scriptures ; and, from six to breakfast, we generally read something relating to the Primitive Church. At eight, we had public prayers. The forenoon *I* spent either in teaching and instructing the children, or reading antiquity ; *Mr. John Wesley*, in learning German ; *Mr. Charles Wesley*, mostly in writing ; *Mr. Delamotte*, in learning Greek, or Navigation. At twelve, we all met together, to join in prayer, and to exhort one another, consulting both how to profit our neighbours and ourselves. After dinner, I taught the children, or conversed religiously with some of the passengers, as also Mr. Wesley constantly did. At four, we had public prayer. From five to six, we spent in private ; then we supped. At seven, I read to as many of the passengers as were willing to hear, and instructed them in Christianity. Mr. John Wesley joined with the Moravians in their public devotions. At eight, we all met together again, to give an account of what we had done, whom we had conversed with, deliberating on the best method of proceeding with such and such persons ; what advice, direction, exhortation, or reproof was necessary for them ; and sometimes we read a little, concluding with prayer ; and so we went to bed about nine, sleeping soundly upon mats and blankets, regarding neither the noise of the sea or sailors. "The angels of the Lord are round about them that fear Him."

"*Monday*, October 27. We sailed from Margate Road to the Downs. A gentleman passenger strongly opposed our having prayers in the great cabin ; and, indeed, he half carried his point, so that we were forced to submit to the inconvenience of having them between decks in the afternoons, till it pleased God to remove him out of the ship.

---

[1] One of these was David Nitschmann, the Moravian Bishop. (See Wesley's Works, vol. i., p. 16.)

"*Sunday*, November 2. We passed the fleet at Spithead, and came into Cowes Road, off the Isle of Wight, where we lay till the 10th of December. During our stay here, we had an excellent opportunity of promoting the work of God among our fellow passengers. We met with both opposition and success, passing through evil report and good report. May it please the Almighty to give us all an abundant measure of His grace, to persevere zealously in His service to the end of our days! Every Christian must be perfected through sufferings, either inward or outward, for even the Captain of our salvation was made perfect through suffering ; and we are to be like Him.

"Mr. Charles Wesley, being known to the minister at Cowes, preached several times in the island, and read at a poor woman's house to a good number of the people there assembled. Before we came away, he left a few books among them. The poor people were very glad, expressed much thankfulness, and, I believe, were not a little edified by his admonition and exhortation.

"*Monday*, November 3. We took a walk into the Isle, where we agreed upon the following resolutions :—

"' In the name of God, Amen.

"'We whose names are here underwritten, being fully convinced, that, it is impossible, either to promote the work of God among the heathen without an entire union amongst ourselves ; or, that, such an union should subsist unless each one will give up his single judgment to that of the majority, do agree, by the help of God :—

"'*First*. That none of us will undertake anything of importance without first proposing it to the other three.

"'*Second*. That, whenever our judgments or inclinations differ, any one shall give up his single judgment or inclination to the others.

"'*Third*. That, in case of an equality, after begging God's direction, the matter shall be decided by lot,

"'John Wesley,
C. Wesley,
B. Ingham,
C. Delamotte.'

"The wind was now fair, but the man-of-war, that was to convey us over, was not yet ready. The passengers grew impatient of delay; but our Heavenly Father intended it for our good. Known unto God are all His works from everlasting. Unsearchable are Thy ways, O Lord God of hosts. Blessed art Thou for ever.

"*Saturday*, November 8. I went upon quarter-deck, after dinner, to teach the children; but, because some gentlemen were there who laughed at me for it, I was ashamed to proceed. O! what a dreadful thing is the fear of man! How does it defeat our best purposes, and stagger our stoutest courage! O! how deceitful is my heart! If Thou, O Lord, shouldest withdraw Thy grace from me but one day, I should utterly renounce Thee, and commit the most enormous crimes!

"*Sunday*, November 16. Mr. John Wesley baptized Thomas Herd and

Grace, his wife, Mark, his son, and Phœbe, his daughter, both adults, having prepared them for it by private instruction. To this, I was a witness. They were brought up Quakers; but are now serious people and constant communicants. Praised be the Lord! who has turned their hearts from error, and put them in the right way.

" *Thursday*, November 20. The man-of-war being come, we left Cowes and got down to Yarmouth, where they cast anchor. But next morning, the wind being contrary, we were forced back again into Cowes Road. During this our latter stay here, there were several storms, in one of which, two ships, that ventured out, were stranded upon the island. Notwithstanding this, several of our people murmured at the delay. If God should deal with us according to our deservings, we should be consumed in a moment.

" *Sunday*, November 23. We had, besides ourselves, eight communicants. The Tuesday following, I got a boy well whipped, by Mr. Oglethorpe's orders, for swearing and blaspheming. Private admonition had no effect upon him, so that I was forced to have recourse to public correction.

" *Sunday*, November 30. I preached on board the other ships, and read prayers, which I did several times while we lay at Cowes. We now again had prayers in the great cabin, the gentleman afore-mentioned having yesterday left the ship. Blessed be God! who delivered us from him, for he very much opposed us. I did think, and I told it my friends, that, we could not sail while he was in the ship. This, perhaps, might be one reason why we were kept so long from sailing.

" *Monday*, December 1. We agreed upon the following resolution,—' If any one upon being reproved, or upon any other occasion, shall feel any sort or degree of anger or resentment, he shall immediately, or at the next meeting, frankly and fully confess it.'

" *Saturday*, December 6. The second mate, a very insolent and ill-natured fellow, who had abused many of the passengers and also Mr. Wesley, at last affronted even Mr. Oglethorpe to his face. The next day, he was sent on board the man-of-war. The people rejoiced at this; and praised be God! who delivered them from his power. ' The fierceness of man shall turn to Thy praise; and the fierceness of them shalt Thou restrain.' This, I think, was another reason why we were kept still at Cowes.

" *Sunday*, December 7. We were fifteen communicants. This evening, we resolved to leave off eating suppers, till we found some inconvenience from it; which none of us did to the end of the voyage. Since our settling in America, Messrs. Wesley and Mr. Delamotte have resumed them. As yet, it agrees perfectly with my health, and I still continue it.

" *Monday*, December 8. A young man, very providentially, was taken into our ship. I, perceiving that he was a stranger, began to converse with him. He gave me an account of himself, and the reason of his coming. He had left his parents, he said, who were rich, (though he was their only son,) because they would not let him serve God as he had a mind. He used to spend a good part of the night in prayer, not having opportunity to do it by day. When he left home, he did not know where he should go, having no clothes with him; but he did not seek for money or worldly enjoyments; he desired only to save his soul. When he was travelling, he prayed that he might go to some place where he could have the advantage of public prayers and the Holy Sacrament. Several times he had thoughts of turning hermit; but Providence had brought him to us; and he was glad to meet with ministers with whom he could freely converse about spiritual things; and, indeed, I was glad to meet with him. This, I think, was another reason for our delay. All love, all glory be to Thee, O Lord!

"*Wednesday*, December 10. Now, at length, it pleased our Heavenly Father to send us a fair wind. We left Cowes about nine in the morning. Two gentlemen passengers of the other ship were left behind, having, the night before, gone to Portsmouth. We waited for them near two hours; but, they not coming, we made the best of our way, running between seven and eight miles an hour. Friday, in the forenoon, we left the man-of-war, he not being able to sail as fast as our ships. Most of the passengers were now sick; I was so for about half an hour; Mr. John Wesley scarce at all.

"*Friday*, December 19. Messrs. Wesley and I, with Mr. Oglethorpe's approbation, undertook to visit, each of us, a part of the ship, and daily to provide the sick people with water-gruel, and such other things as were necessary for them. At first, we met with some difficulties; but God enabled us to persevere in the constant performance to the end of the journey. Mr. Oglethorpe himself went several times about the ship to comfort and encourage the people; and, indeed, he has never been wanting in this respect. He is a pattern of fatherly care and tender compassion, being always ready, night and day, to give up his own ease and conveniences to serve the poorest body among the people. He seldom eats above once a day, and then he usually chooses salt provisions, (though not so agreeable to his health,) that, he might give the fresh to the sick. But more will appear from the following instance. One Mrs. Welch, who was believed to be at the point of death, being big with child, in a high fever, attended with a violent cough, was, by Mr. Oglethorpe's order, removed into his own cabin, which was the best in the ship, he himself lying several nights in a hammock, till another cabin was got ready for him. He also constantly supplied her with all the best things in the ship. Some of the gentlemen seemed disgusted at this; but that made him only the more resolute. Yet, notwithstanding all possible care was taken of her, human means failed; the doctor gave her up; everybody thought she would die; Mr. Oglethorpe only continued in hope. Nay, he said, he was sure God would raise her up to manifest His glory in her. She had a desire to receive the Lord's Supper before she died; and, lo! from the moment she received, she began to recover, and is now safely delivered of a daughter, and in perfect health. 'Gracious is the Lord, and merciful, long-suffering, and of great goodness; the Lord is loving to every man, and His mercy is over all His works.'

"*Sunday*, December 21. We were twenty-one communicants. This, as well as yesterday, was an exceedingly calm and pleasant day. The sky appeared to me more beautiful than ever I had observed it in England. We were likewise got so far to the southward, that, the weather was as warm now as it is in the spring at home. This being Mr. Oglethorpe's birthday, he gave a sheep and wine to the people, which, with the smoothness of the sea, and the serenity of the sky, so enlivened them, that, they perfectly recovered from their sea sickness. On Christmas-day, also, Mr. Oglethorpe gave a hog, and wine to the people.

"*Monday*, December 29. We are now past the latitude of twenty-five degrees, and are got into what they call the Trade winds, which blow much the same way all the year round. The air is balmy, soft, and sweet. The ship glides smoothly and quietly along. The clouds are finely variegated with numbers of pretty colours. The nights are mild and pleasant, being beautifully adorned with the shining hosts of stars. 'The heavens declare the glory of God, and the firmament showeth His handy-work. One day telleth another; and one night certifies another.'

> "'What, though, in solemn silence, all
> Move round this dark, terrestrial ball;
> What, though nor real voice nor sound
> Amidst their radiant orbs is found;
> In reason's ear they all rejoice,
> And utter forth a glorious voice,
> For ever singing as they shine,
> 'The Hand that made us is divine."

"1736, *Sunday*, January 4. A gentleman was very angry with me for accusing his servant, of swearing, before Mr. Oglethorpe.

"The next day, Mr. John Wesley began to catechise the children publicly, after the Second Lesson evening service, which he continued to do every day for about three weeks.

"*Monday*, January 12. I began to write out the English Dictionary, in order to learn the Indian tongue. O! 'who is sufficient for these things?'

"When the ship rolled so that we could not well go about to visit the people, we generally spent the evening in conversation with Mr. Oglethorpe, from whom we learnt many particulars concerning the Indians.

"*Saturday*, January 17. The wind was very strong. About half an hour after ten at night, we encountered such a wave as we did not meet with in all our passage besides. It shook the whole frame of the ship, from stem to stern. The water sprung through the sides of the ship, which before were tight, and, also, above the main-yard. Falling down, it covered the decks, broke into the great cabin, and filled Mrs. Welch's bed. Mr. Oglethorpe was gone to bed, and resigned his own dry cabin to the sick, betaking himself once more to his hammock. Hitherto, we had had a very fine passage; but now, approaching near land, we met with contrary winds, which kept us above a fortnight longer at sea than otherwise we should have been.

"*Tuesday*, January 20. I baptized a child, which was thought to be at the point of death; nay, some thought it was dead; but, from the moment it was baptized, it began to recover.

"*Wednesday*, January 21.   This evening, Mr. Oglethorpe called together the heads of families, as he also did at some other times, and gave them several excellent and useful instructions relating to their living in Georgia, exhorting them likewise to love God and one another.

"*Sunday*, January 25.   We were twenty communicants.   Towards evening, we had a terrible storm, which lasted several hours.   I observed it well; and, truly, I never saw anything hitherto so solemn and majestic. The sea sparkled and smoked, as if it had been on fire.   The air darted forth lightning; and the wind blew so fierce, that, you could scarcely look it in the face, and draw your breath.   The waves did not swell so high as at some other times, being pressed down by the impetuosity of the blast; neither did the ship roll much; but it quivered, jarred, and shook.   About half an hour past seven, a great sea broke in upon us, which split the main-sail, carried away the companion, filled between decks, and rushed into the great cabin.   This made most of the people tremble; and, I believe, they would then have been glad to have been Christians, how light soever they made of religion before.   I myself was made sensible, that, nothing will enable us to smile in the face of death, but a life of extraordinary holiness.   I was under some fear for a little while; but I recollected myself again, by reflecting that every thing came by the will of God; and that whatever He willed was the best for me.   If, therefore, He was pleased to take me off at this very time, so much the better:—I should be delivered from many evils, and prevented from committing many sins to come.   Betwixt eleven and twelve, I recommended myself to God, and went to bed, resting satisfied with whatever should befal me.   Towards three, the wind abated.   In the morning, we returned public thanks for our deliverance; and, before night, most of the people had forgotten, that, they were ever in a storm.   'If they hear not Moses and the prophets, neither will they be persuaded, though one rose from the dead.'[1]

"*Wednesday*, January 28.   Being a calm day, I went on board the other ship, read prayers, and visited the people.   At my return, I acquainted Mr. Oglethorpe with their state; and he sent them such things as they needed.

"*Sunday*, February 1.   Three sail appearing, we made up towards them, and got what letters we could write, in hopes some of them might be bound for England.   I writ a short one to you at Osset.   One of them, that was bound for London, made towards us, and we put our letters on board her.

"On Tuesday, we found ground; on Wednesday, we saw land; and, on Thursday afternoon, 5th of February, we got safe into Tybee-road, in the mouth of the river Savannah, in the province of Georgia, in America.

---

[1] It was during this storm, that Wesley was struck with the contrast between the Moravians and the rest of the ship's occupants.   The crew in general were in paroxysms of fear and anxiety; the Moravians were calm, and employed themselves in singing psalms (Wesley's Works, vol. i., p. 20).

Messrs. Wesley, Mr. Delamotte, and I had some discourse about our manner of living in this new country. I was struck with a deep, religious awe, considering the greatness and importance of the work I came upon, but was comforted with these words in the Psalms :—'O! tarry thou the Lord's leisure; be strong, and He shall comfort thy heart; and put thou thy trust in the Lord.' From the whole service, I was moved to think, that, the Gospel would be propagated over the whole world. May God, of His great mercy, graciously be pleased to grant it!

"*February* 6. We went on shore, and had prayers, where we were comforted by the Second Lesson. Next day, I received a letter from my brother William, one from my sister Hannah, and another from Mr. H. Washington, whereby I was very much comforted. I called to mind several things past; reflected upon the sweet happiness of true friendship; and prayed earnestly for my dear friends in England, with tears.

"*Saturday*, February 14. This morning, as well as yesterday, we met with several remarkable passages, in our course of reading the prophets, relating to the propagation of the Gospel, which not a little comforted and encouraged us. I was also strongly affected by the Second Lesson, Mark xiii.

"A little after noon, some Indians came to make us a visit. We put on our gowns and cassocks; spent some time in prayer; and then went into the great cabin to receive them. At our entrance, they all rose up; and both men and women shook hands with us. When we were all seated, Toma-Chache, their king, spoke to us to this effect. (His interpreter was one Mrs. Musgrove, who lives about five miles above Savannah. She is descended of a white man by an Indian woman. She understands both languages, being educated amongst the English. She can read and write, and is a well-civilized woman. She is likewise to teach us the Indian tongue.)

"'Ye are welcome. I am glad to see you here. I have a desire to hear the Great Word, for I am ignorant. When I was in England, I desired that some might speak the Great Word to me. Our nation was then willing to hear. Since that time, we have been in trouble. The French on one hand, the Spaniards on the other, and the Traders that are amongst us, have caused great confusion, and have set our people against hearing the Great Word. Their tongues are useless; some say one thing, and some another. But I am glad that ye are come. I will assemble the great men of our nation, and I hope, by degrees, to compose our differences; for, without their consent, I cannot hear the Great Word. However, in the meantime, I shall be glad to see you at my town; and I would have you teach our children. But we would not have them made Christians as the Spaniards make Christians; for they baptize without instruction; but we would hear and be well instructed, and then be baptized when we understood.'

"All this he spoke with much earnestness, and much action, both of his head and hands. Mr. John Wesley made him a short answer,—'God only can teach you wisdom, and, if you be sincere, perhaps, He will do it by us.' We then shook hands with them again, and withdrew.

"The Queen made us a present of a jar of milk, and another of honey; that we might feed them, she said, with milk; for they were but children; and that we might be sweet to them.

"About three next day, in the afternoon, just before they went away, we put on our surplices, at Mr. Oglethorpe's desire, and went to take leave of them.

"*Monday*, February 16. About seven this evening, I set forward with Mr. Oglethorpe, and some others, in a ten-oared boat, for the Alatamahaw river, the southernmost part of Georgia. At eleven, we arrived at a place called Skiddowa, where we went ashore into the woods, and kindled a fire under a lofty pine-tree. Having written some letters, and eaten something, we lay down to sleep upon the ground, without either bed or board, having no covering, besides our clothes, but a single blanket each, and the canopy of heaven. About eight next day, we set forward again, passing several marshes, beset on both sides with trees of various sorts, whose leaves, being gilded with the glorious rays of the sun, yielded a beautiful prospect. About twelve, the wind blew so high, that, we were driven upon an oyster bank, where we could not get a stick to make a fire. Here we dined very comfortably. Near two, we set forward again, and, with great difficulty, crossed over the mouth of the river Ogechee. The wind was exceeding high, and the water very rough. Almost every wave drove over the side of the boat; so that every moment we were in jeopardy of our lives; and, truly, if Mr. Oglethorpe had not roused up himself, and struck life into the rowers, I do not know but most of us might here have made our exit. Towards six, we got to a little place, called Boar's Island, where we encamped all right, round a roaring fire, in a bed of canes, where the wind could not reach us. Here also we came up with a large boat, called a Pettiangur,[1] loaded with people for the Alatamahaw, who had set out before us. Next morning, after prayers, Mr. Oglethorpe, considering, that, our own boat was overladen, and also that I might probably be of some service to the people, asked me if I was willing to go on board the Pettiangur, whereto I readily consented. Here, during the remainder of our passage, I read to the people, and instructed them as I had opportunity. This evening, we lay upon St. Catherine's, a very pleasant island, where we met with two Indians a-hunting. I took one of them on board the Pettiangur, and gave him some biscuit and wine, and he, in return, sent us the greatest part of a deer.

"On *Sunday* morning, February 22, we arrived at the island of St. Simons, upon the river Alatamahaw, a pleasant and fertile place, which Mr. Oglethorpe had reached the Thursday night before. Several of the people were firing guns, but, upon my landing, I asked Mr. Oglethorpe if Sunday was a proper day for sporting. He immediately put a stop to it. Having breakfasted, we joined in the Litany, and then he returned to Savannah, having already put the people in a method of proceeding.

"Next day in the forenoon, we were alarmed by a sail appearing in the river. We called all the people together; and, after consultation, we

---

[1] A sort of flat-bottomed barge (Wesley's Works, vol. i., p. 28).

threw up a trench, strengthening it with barrels of beef and pork, which we had here in abundance. We also sent a canoe down the river, and several men into the woods for scouts, to bring us intelligence. In the meantime, we got all our arms in readiness, providing for the worst. About half an hour past twelve, the canoe returned, and brought us word, it was the sloop which brought the provisions, that had returned to take in ballast.

"Two or three of the first days, the people spent in building palmetto bowers. We enclosed a little round place with myrtles, bays, and laurels, in the midst whereof we nightly kept a great fire, round which I lay several weeks in the open air, my whole bed consisting of two blankets; and I never had health better in my life. Now we had short prayers early in the morning, before they began; and at night, after they had done working. My chief business was daily to visit the people, to take care of those that were sick, and to supply them with the best things we had. For a few days at the first, I had everybody's good word; but, when they found I watched narrowly over them, and reproved them sharply for their faults, immediately the scene changed. Instead of blessing, came cursing, and my love and kindness were repaid with hatred and ill-will.

"*Sunday*, February 29. After morning prayers, which we had pretty early, I told the people that, it was the Lord's day, and, therefore, ought to be spent in His service; that, they ought not to go a-shooting, or walking up and down in the woods; and that, I would take notice of all those who did. One man answered, that, these were new laws in America! This man, as well as several others went out; but he, I think, was two days before he could find his way back again. I reproved most of them afterwards, in a friendly manner, laying before them the heinousness of the sin, and the dreadful consequences that would necessarily follow. One or two took my advice well; but the rest were hardened, and, instead of reforming, raised heavy complaints and accusations to the gentleman, that was left chief in commission, that, I had made a black list ; and that, I intended to ruin them. This caused a very sharp contest between that gentleman and me; wherein God enabled me, boldly and courageously, to vindicate the honour of His day and worship, without regarding the favour of any man. So soon as I was retired, I prayed earnestly from my heart, that, God would forgive him, and also give him a new mind; which prayer God heard (blessed be His goodness!) for, since I came away, he frankly confessed, that, he was in the wrong; that, his passions carried him to too great a height; that, I was certainly in the right, and had only done what was my duty. I mention this to show the great use of praying for our enemies. Who knows how much such prayer will avail before God? Certainly, it purifies our own heart, and is the only sure enemy to keep out hatred, malice, and revenge.

"*Tuesday*, March 2. This morning, I prayed that God would be pleased to send home the lost man, and also make him sensible of his sin. About breakfast time, he came looking very ghastly, sadly affrighted, telling me he was resolved never more to profane the Sabbath. God grant he may keep his word! This example would not make others take warning.

 Next Sunday, three more went a-shooting, who were all lost till next day. Nothing but the almighty grace of God is sufficient to turn a sinner from the error of his ways.

"*Monday*, March 8. Mr. Oglethorpe arrived, with four Pettiangurs; and, next day, my dear friend, Mr. C. Wesley, with another, wherein were all the married men and women, and children, that came over in our two ships. Mr. Oglethorpe immediately laid out the new town, Frederica, in a neat and regular method; and kept the people to strict work in building themselves palmetto houses. During the three weeks longer, which I spent here, there happened such a variety of incidents, that, it would be too tedious to relate them. Only I will add, that, Mr. C. Wesley and I had the happiness of undergoing, for the truth's sake, the most glorious trial of our whole lives, wherein God enabled us exceedingly to rejoice, and also to behave ourselves throughout with undaunted courage and constancy; for which may we ever love and adore Him! The book of God was our support, wherein, as our necessities required, we always met with direction, exhortation, and comfort—'Thy Word is a lantern to my feet, and a light unto my paths. In God's Word will I comfort me.'[1]

"*Sunday*, March 28. About seven in the evening, I left Frederica, and took boat for Savannah. We had a fair wind; and, if we had not run twice aground, I believe we should have got thither in twenty-four hours. Towards four on Tuesday morning, it began to thunder, and lighten, and rain in the most dreadful manner I ever beheld since I was born. Ours was a little open boat, without any cover. The rest of the people wrapped themselves up, head and ears, in blankets and sails, whatever they could get, and laid down in the bottom of it. I plucked up a good heart, threw

---

[1] Charles Wesley writes:—"Tuesday, March 9, 1736. The first who saluted me on my landing, was honest Mr. Ingham, and that with his usual heartiness. Never did I more rejoice at the sight of him; especially when he told me the treatment he has met with for vindicating the Lord's day." Charles had gone to be the minister of the palmetto town, Frederica; and was soon in greater trouble than Ingham had experienced. Ingham remained with his friend nineteen days; and, during this brief period, Charles encountered a difficulty about baptizing a child by immersion; got into hot water, by endeavouring to reconcile two termagant women; and was wrongfully charged by Oglethorpe with mutiny and sedition. By March 28th, things had arrived at such a pass, that Charles Wesley requested Ingham to go to Savannah for his brother. Ingham was extremely reluctant to leave his friend in such trouble and danger; but was, at last, persuaded; and, accordingly, on the day just mentioned, after preaching "an alarming sermon on the day of judgment, and joining with" Charles Wesley "in offering up the Christian sacrifice," he started. This is not the place to enter into detail respecting C. Wesley's trials at Frederica. Suffice it to give an extract from his Journal: "I hastened to the water-side, where I found Mr. Ingham just put off. O happy, happy friend! *Abiit, erupit, evasit!* But woe is me, that I am still constrained to dwell with Meshech! I languished to bear him company, followed him with my eyes till out of sight, and then sank into deeper dejection than I had known before." We must now keep company with Ingham.

my cloak over me, and stood up, as stiff as I could, in the midst of it, that
I might behold the majesty of God in thunder; and, truly, so glorious a
scene I never saw. I dare not attempt to describe. However, I passed
the time very comfortably in praising God; and, whereas, all the rest were
well wet, I was pure and dry all over, excepting only my cloak and shoes.
Betwixt seven and eight, we arrived at Savannah, where I was kindly received by Mr. John Wesley and Mr. Delamotte. The latter had began to
teach a few little orphans; and the former had brought the people to short
prayers morning and night. I now again entered upon a manner of life
more agreeable to me than what I spent at Frederica, having both time
and convenience for regular retirement.

"*Sunday*, April 4. This afternoon, Mr. Wesley and Mr. Delamotte,
took boat for Frederica. In their absence, I took care both of the church
and school.

"*Monday*, April 5. After evening prayers, I begun to catechize, at our
own house, all young persons that were willing to come, as well children as
servants, and apprentices, who would not come in the day time. I have
continued to do this every night since. On Sundays, I do it after dinner,
and also publicly in the church after the Second Lesson.

"*Sunday*, April 11. After evening service, I made a visit to a few
people, who had formed themselves into a Society,—meeting together on
Wednesday, Friday, and Sunday nights. I found their design was good.
They read, prayed, and sung psalms together. Accordingly, I exhorted
them to go on, promising myself to meet with them sometimes, and to give
them such helps and directions as I could. I have joined them every
Sunday since; and I hope it will be a means of some good. God grant
it!

"*Sunday*, April 18. This afternoon, there was an alarm made in time
of Divine service, whereupon, several people went out of church. The
cause of it was a young lad that had run away from his master. He had
broken into our house, under which, he said, he had laid a fortnight, and
stolen provisions when I was at prayers. He had taken down a pistol,
and loaded it, with a design, I suppose, to shoot in the woods; for he had
gotten the powder flask, and, as he was getting out of the window, somehow, he slipped, and fired off the pistol, which broke his arm to shivers.
He then called out aloud for help; whereupon, some people that heard,
went to see what was the matter. He begged of them to drag him out at
the window, which they did, and found him in a bad condition. They
carried him to a surgeon, who cut off his arm. In the night, not having
due attendance, he loosed it, whereby, he lost so much blood, that, he died
next morning. I was very sorry for the unfortunate wretch, for he came
to be catechized the night before he run away, and I, being informed that
he had done so several times before, talked to him a good while, to behave
himself well, and to obey his master. But, not having grace, he did the
very reverse to what I exhorted him. A sad example, whereby others
ought to take warning.

"This being the great and holy week, I dedicated it to devotion, observing the discipline of the Primitive Church.

"On Tuesday evening, Mr. John Wesley and Mr. Delamotte arrived from Frederica. Next day, Mr. Wesley gave me an account of what had passed there since my departure. O what secrets will come to pass in the last day!

"*Easter Sunday*, April 25. We were thirty-four communicants. Our constant number is about a dozen. Next day, Mr. Wesley and I went up to Cowpen, in a boat, bought for our use, to converse with Mrs. Musgrave about learning the Indian language. I agreed to teach her children to read, and to make her whatever recompence she would require more for her trouble. I am to spend three or four days a week with her, and the rest at Savannah, in communicating what I have learned to Mr. Wesley; because he intends, as yet, wholly to reside there.

"The Moravians, being informed of our design, desired me to teach one of the brethren along with Mr. Wesley. To this I consented at once, with my whole heart. And who, think ye, is the person intended to learn? Their lawful bishop.[1] 'The right hand of the Lord hath the pre-eminence; the right hand of the Lord bringeth mighty things to pass.'

"*Friday*, April 30. Mr. Wesley and I went up again to Cowpen, taking along with us, Toma-Cache and his Queen. Their town is about four miles above Savannah, in the way to Mrs. Musgrave's. We told them we were about to learn their language. I asked them, if they were willing I should teach the young prince. They consented, desiring me to check and keep him in; but not to strike him. The Indians never strike their children; neither will they suffer any one to do it. I told them, I would do my best, as far as gentleness and good advice would go. How I shall manage, God alone can direct me. The youth is sadly corrupted, and addicted to drunkenness, which he has learnt of our Christian heathen. Nay, the whole Creek nation is now generally given to this brutal sin, whereto they were utter strangers before Christians came among them.

"Oh! what a work have we before us! Who is sufficient for these things? I am nothing. I have nothing. I can do nothing. O! my dearest friends, pray for us. Pray earnestly for us; and more especially for me, your very weak, though most dutiful son, and affectionate brother,
"BENJAMIN INGHAM."

This lengthened document needs no apology. It exhibits Ingham as a sincere, earnest, self-denying, zealous servant of the Divine Redeemer. It helps to justify the suddenness of his departure from his native country, without obtaining the consent of his family and friends, and even without consulting them. It shows, that, he was a firm believer in the sacred text—" In all thy ways acknowledge Him, and He shall direct thy paths." Who can doubt that Ingham was divinely guided in embarking for America? The service that he rendered there, might be

---

[1] David Nitschmann.

comparatively small ; but, at that period, it required no ordi- 1736
nary courage, for a young man of three and twenty, to en- Age 24
counter the storms of the Atlantic, and to live with wild
Indians in the woods of Georgia.   The results of Ingham's
ministerial labours in the new colony might be few ; but the
mission there brought him into the society of a set of simple-
minded, earnest, godly men, by whom the current of the whole
of his subsequent life was changed ; and the rough experience
of the few months spent among colonial settlers and untutored
savages, was a useful training for the hard labours and hard
treatment awaiting him in his native country.   If Ingham had
not embarked for Georgia, the probability is, he would not have
been brought into fellowship with Moravians ; and, therefore,
would not have become a Moravian Evangelist among the
masses of the north of England.   The Providence, which sent
him to Georgia, separated him from the Established Church ;
but, as in the case of Wesley, it made him the Founder of a
large number of religious societies, which exercised a mighty
influence on the people of Yorkshire, and of the neighbouring
counties.

As yet, Ingham, like the Wesleys, was seeking to be saved
by works, rather than by penitent faith in Christ Jesus ; but
the very fact that he hoped to be saved thus, served as an
incentive to the practice of self-denial and other austerities,
and to the use of diligence and faithfulness in his ministerial
office which have seldom been surpassed.   The man had a
large heart, brim-full of benevolent feeling ; and regarded it
as the highest honour and happiness of his life to be of service
to the cause of God, and to the welfare of his fellow-creatures.
Without doubt, he was what would be called a high churchman when he set sail for Georgia ; but his sympathies were too
large to be ice bound with high church bigotry.   His description of the twenty-six psalm-singing Moravians is just and
generous.   He was willing to admit the fact, and to rejoice
in it, that there were as good Christians without the pale of
his own Church, as there were within it.   Like all men of noble
mind, he was not too much a man to bend to a little child.
Teaching and catechizing children was a self-imposed, but
happy task, while on the waves of the Atlantic Ocean ; and it
was equally one of his pleasant toils in Georgia.   Idleness and

G

 he were strangers to each other. Early rising, abstemious diet, and constant working, were, with him, not accidents, but principles. They were part and parcel of his religion. The Bible was his daily study; and prayer, for himself, and for others, his highest privilege and duty. The two combined inspired him with a confidence in God, which never faltered; and which kept him calm in the greatest dangers. Let us follow him.

Ingham landed in Georgia, on February 5, 1736: he re-embarked for England on February 26, 1737. Nearly three of the thirteen months he spent in Georgia, are comprehended in the Journal already given. The details of the other ten are few and scanty.

Both he and Wesley intended and wished to be, not chaplains among the English colonists, but, missionaries among the wild Indians; and, accordingly, at the end of the first three months of their Georgian residence, we find Ingham arranging to spend three days a week in learning the Indian language from a half-caste woman; and the other three in teaching what he learnt to Wesley, and to Nitschmann, the Moravian bishop. Their design was Christian and heroic; but it was not realised.

On May 16, 1736, Charles Wesley, unexpectedly, came to his brother, and Ingham, and Delamotte, at Savannah; and, for want of better accommodation, each of the four "retired to his respective corner of the room, where, without the help of a bed, they all slept soundly till the morning."[1] Charles had now left Frederica for ever; and, ten weeks later, he embarked for England.

Frederica was left without a minister; and it was agreed, that, Wesley and Ingham should take Charles's place in turns. Wesley went off at once; and remained at Frederica till June 23rd. He and Ingham now hoped to obtain permission to live among the Choctaw Indians; but Oglethorpe objected; first, on the ground, that, they would be in danger of being intercepted or killed by the French; and, secondly, because it was inexpedient to leave Savannah without a pastor. This induced them to remain where they were; but, in the meantime, they had a most interesting interview with a number of Chica-

---

[1] C. Wesley's Journal, vol. i., p. 27.

saw Indians, the details of which, Wesley has related in his Journal.

On August 4, Wesley again went to Frederica, leaving Savannah to the care of Ingham and Delamotte; and thus things continued till February, 1737; Wesley and Ingham ardently wishing to proceed as missionaries among the Indians; but not able to fulfil their wish, because there was no minister to occupy their places at Savannah and Frederica.

Ingham had been an apt and diligent pupil of Mrs. Musgrave's; and had formed a vocabulary of about one half of the words in the Indian language; but, unless Savannah and Frederica could be supplied by other ministers, all his fagging to acquire this barbarous language was likely to be useless. What was done? The following is an extract from a letter, addressed to Mr. ——, in Lincoln College, Oxon.

"SAVANNAH, *February* 16, 1737.

"DEAR SIR,—Mr. Ingham has left Savannah for some months; and lives at a house built for him a few miles off, near the Indian town.[1] So that I have now no fellow-labourer but Mr. Delamotte, who has taken charge of between thirty and forty children. There is, therefore, great need, that God should put it into the hearts of some, to come over to us and labour with us in His harvest. But I should not desire any to come unless on the same views and conditions with us,—without any temporal wages, other than food and raiment, the plain conveniences of life. And for one or more in whom was this mind, there would be full employment in the province; either in assisting Mr. Delamotte or me, while we were present here; or in supplying our places when abroad; or in visiting the poor people, in the smaller settlements, as well as at Frederica; all of whom are as sheep without a shepherd.

"By these labours of love, might any, that desired it, be trained up for the harder task of preaching the Gospel to the heathen. The difficulties he must then encounter God only knows; probably martyrdom would conclude them. But those we have hitherto met with have been small, and only terrible at a distance. Persecution, you know, is the portion of every follower of Christ, wherever his lot is cast. But it has hitherto extended no farther than words with regard to us, unless in one or two inconsiderable instances. Yet, it is sure, every man ought, if he would come hither, be willing and ready to embrace (if God should see them good) the severer kinds of it. He ought to be determined, not only to

---

[1] The Indians gave to Ingham a plot of fruitful ground, in the midst of which was a small, round hill; and, on the top of this hill, a house was built for an Indian school. The house was named Irene. (Wesley's Works, vol. i., p. 61.)

1737
—
Age 25

leave parents, sisters, friends, houses, and lands, for his Master's sake, but to take up his cross too ; cheerfully submit to the fatigue and danger of (it may be) a long voyage, and patiently to endure the continual contradiction of sinners and all the inconveniences which it often occasions.

" Would any one have a trial of himself, how he can bear this ? If he has felt what reproach is, and can bear that but a few weeks, as he ought, I shall believe he need fear nothing. Other trials will afterwards be no heavier than that little one was at first ; so that he may then have a well-grounded hope, that he will be enabled to do all things through Christ strengthening him.

" May the God of peace Himself direct you to all things conducive to His glory, whether it be by fitter instruments, or even by your own friend and servant in Christ,

" JOHN WESLEY." [1]

Wesley's standard of a Christian missionary was enough to appal ordinary men ; but who will say that the standard was too high ? He himself and also his friend Ingham answered to this description ; but it was doubtful whether others could be found, among their old associates, who were like-minded. Accordingly, ten days after the date of the above letter, another step was taken. Wesley writes :—

" 1737. February 24. It was agreed Mr. Ingham should go for England, and endeavour to bring over, if it should please God, some of our friends, to strengthen our hands in this work. February 26. He left Savannah."

The Oxford Methodists were scattered when Ingham arrived in England ; but they were still a loving and confiding brotherhood. In July, 1737, Charles Wesley and James Hutton spent some days at Oxford ; and, accompanied by Mr. Morgan and Mr. Kinchin, set out, on the 29th of that month, for London, where, at the house of Hutton's father, in College Street, Westminster, they found their " old, hearty friend, Benjamin Ingham." [2] The last mentioned also visited the Delamotte family at Blendon. Hence, under the date of September 10, 1737, C. Wesley writes :—

" I took coach for Blendon. My friend, Benjamin, had been there before me, and met with such a reception as encouraged me to follow. He had preached to them with power, and still more powerfully by his life

---

[1] *Gentleman's Magazine,* 1737, p. 575.
[2] C. Wesley's Journal, vol. i., p. 73.

and conversation. The eldest sister, and the Cambridge scholar,[1] were struck to the heart. The first evening passed in discourse of my name-sake[2] in America."

Immediately after this, Ingham was at his own home, in Yorkshire. No more faithful and honest friend existed; but, like many Yorkshiremen, he was sometimes almost blunt. The following letter, addressed to Wesley, in Georgia, supplies evidence of this, and also contains references to Wesley and the Oxford Methodists, of considerable interest :—

"OSSET, *October* 19, 1737.[3]

"DEAR BROTHER,—By your silence, one would suspect that you were offended at my last letter. Am I your enemy because I tell you the truth? But perhaps I was too severe. Forgive me then. Be lowly in your own eyes. Humble yourself before the Lord, and He will lift you up. I do assure you, it is out of pure love, and with concern that I write. I earnestly wish your soul's welfare. O pray for mine also. The Lord preserve you!

"Could you, think you, live upon the income of your fellowship? If you can, do. The trustees are, indeed, very willing to support you, and they would take it ill should anybody say that you have been too expensive. But the Bishop of London, as I have heard, and some others, have been offended at the expenses, and not altogether without reason, because you declared, at your leaving England, you should want scarce anything. I just give you these hints. Pray for direction, and then act as you judge best.[4]

---

[1] William Delamotte, who became the friend of Ingham, and joined the Moravians. For four or five years, he was one of their most ardent and useful preachers. His labours in Yorkshire were attended with great success. He died February 22, 1743, and was buried at St. Dunstan's-in-the-East, London (Holmes' "History of the Brethren," vol. i., p. 315 : Hutton's Memoirs, p. 94.)

[2] Charles Delamotte, who also became a Moravian, and, after a long life of piety and peace, died at Barrow-upon-Humber, in 1796.

[3] At this date, Wesley was in the thick of his Georgian troubles.

[4] The English bishops would have acted more justly and generously if they had helped Wesley out of their own fat incomes, instead of finding fault with his trifling expenses. On March 4, 1737, Wesley says, "I writ the trustees for Georgia an account of our year's expenses, from March 1, 1736, to March 1, 1737; which, deducting extraordinary expenses, such as repairing the parsonage house, and journeys to Frederica, amounted, for Mr. Delamotte and me, to £44 4*s*. 4*d*." Can it be correct that the bishops found fault with Wesley costing the trustees £22 2*s*. 2*d*. per year? It may be asked what Wesley received from the Society for the Propagation of the Gospel in Foreign Parts? The answer is £50 ; "which, indeed," says he, "was in a manner forced upon me, contrary both to expectation and desire" (Wesley's Unpublished Journal). Seven months later, on November 10, 1737, he writes, in the same Journal,

"Charles is so reserved; I know little about him. He neither writes to me, nor comes to see me. What he intends is best known to himself. Mr. Hutton's family go on exceedingly well. Your friend Mr. Morgan, I hear, either has, or, is about publishing a book, to prove that every one baptized with water is regenerate. All friends at Oxford go on well. Mr. Kinchin, Mr. Hutchins, Mr. Washington, Bell, Hervey, Watson, are all zealous. Mr. Atkinson labours under severe trials in Westmoreland, but is steady and sincere, and an excellent Christian. Dick Smith is weak, but not utterly gone. Mr. Robson and Grieves are but indifferent. The latter is married to a widow, and teaching a school at Northampton. Mr. Thompson, of Queen's, has declared his resolution of following Christ.

"Remember me to Mr. Wallis, Mark Hird, and the Davison family Mrs. Gilbert Mears, Mr. Campbell, Mr. and Mrs. Burnside, Mr. and Mrs Williamson.

"Yours in Christ,

"B. INGHAM."

Ingham still purposed to return to Georgia. He longed to preach the gospel of his Saviour to the heathen, and was busily employed in mastering their language. He sought spiritual fellowship among his Christian friends in Yorkshire; and, as opportunity offered, occupied the pulpit of the Established Church. His preaching created great sensation; and his private labours, among his neighbours, were not without results. A man with a soul like his,—burning with a zeal which would have led him gladly to sacrifice his life among the wild Indians of America,—could scarcely fail to be an earnest, successful evangelist in his own country. As already stated, his intention to return to Georgia was not fulfilled. Perhaps Wesley's departure from that colony, about six weeks after the date of the above letter, was one of the things which prevented it. Be that as it might, he was quite prepared for hard work, and for rough usage, in other places.

In the letter just given, he complains of the silence and reserve of Charles Wesley. At the very time, however, Charles was writing to him; and, three days afterwards, Ingham addressed to him the following reply, full of the Christian fire of the first Methodists :—

"Colonel Henderson arrived, by whom I received a benefaction of £10 sterling, after having been for several months without one shilling in the house, but not without peace, health, and contentment." This was the man at whose extravagance the bishops grumbled, and concerning whom even Ingham felt some anxiety. The Georgian trustees had no misgivings.

"OSSET, NEAR WAKEFIELD, *October* 22, 1737.

"MY DEAR BROTHER,—Your letter is just come to my hands. I rejoiced over it, because it came from you. I was afraid you had been almost lost; but, since I see you are desirous to make full proof of your ministry, I greatly rejoice. Blessed be the Lord, who, by His grace, preserves me from falling, amidst the deceitful and alluring, bewildering temptations of worldly preferment. May He still continue His loving-kindness towards you! May He thoroughly settle and establish you! May you have power to overcome the world, the flesh, and the devil, and, like a brave soldier, manfully to fight under Christ's banner! May your one desire of living be for Christ's sake, and the gospel!

"I have no other thoughts but of returning to America. When the time comes, I trust the Lord will show me. My heart's desire is, that the Indians may hear the gospel. For this I pray both night and day.

"I will transcribe the Indian words as fast as I can. I writ to Mr. William Delamotte three weeks ago. If he did not receive the letter, it miscarried. I wish you could inform me, that I might write again.

"I have just now been talking to Mr. Godly, curate of Osset. (You know, I believe, that he is misnamed.) I was all on a tremble while I talked to him, and for a good while after. He took my reproof very uneasily. But, however, he trembled as well as me. I have lent him 'The Country Parson' to read; and, since he went away, I have been praying for him in agony. I seem to be full of hope, as if God would turn his heart; and O that He may! One of the wickedest women in all Osset is turned since I came down; and, I believe, she will make a thorough convert. She says, she is sure God sent me to turn her heart. To His holy name be all the glory! There is another poor soul too here, that is under the most severe agonies of repentance. Cease not to pray for these, and the rest of your Christian friends at Osset, who pray constantly for you.

"Last Sunday, I preached such a sermon at Wakefield church as has set almost all about us in a uproar. Some say, the devil is in me; others, that I am mad. Others say, no man can live up to such doctrine; and they never heard such before. Others, again, extol me to the sky. They say, it was the best sermon they ever heard in all their life; and that I ought to be a bishop.

"I believe, indeed, it went to the hearts of several persons; for I was enabled to speak with great authority and power; and I preached almost the whole sermon without book. There was a vast large congregation, and tears fell from many eyes. To-morrow, I preach there again.

"Every day, I undergo several changes within me. Now I am under sufferings, sometimes just ready to sink; then again I am filled with joy. Indeed, I receive so much pleasure in conversing with some Christians here, that I have need of sufferings to counterbalance it. Last Saturday night, we were sixteen that sat up till after twelve. We have to meet again to-night, after the rest are gone; and we shall pray for you, and the rest of our Christian friends everywhere. You would think yourself happy to be but one night with us.

 "Give my sincere love to Mr. Hutton's family, whom I never forget. Are they all well? The Lord bless them all! Greet brother Whitefield. My heart will be with you on the seas, and everywhere. Never be discouraged.

> "Yours sincerely and affectionately,
> "B. INGHAM."[1]

On May 24, 1738, Wesley, by simple "trust in Christ alone for salvation," received "an assurance that Christ had taken away his sins." This, to him, was a new experience; but, perhaps, not to Ingham. It is a well-known fact, that, Peter Bohler, who was now on his way to the Moravians in Georgia, was of the utmost service to Wesley in teaching him the doctrine of justification by faith only. Besides this, both Wesley and Ingham had been brought into close communion with the Moravian bishop, David Nitschmann, and his Christian fraternity, during their voyage across the Atlantic. In Georgia, also, they had met with the Moravian elder, the Rev. August Gottlieb Spangenberg, a man of high position among the Brethren. The result of the whole was, that Wesley and Ingham, on June 13, 1738, embarked for Germany, principally for the purpose of becoming better acquainted with the Moravian churches in that country.

They were accompanied by John Toltschig,[2] one of the fugitives, who fled to Hernhuth, from the fierce persecution in Moravia, in 1724; who became one of Ingham's co-evangelists in the county of York; and was a man of great influence among the English Moravians. At Ysselstein, they had an interview with Baron Watteville, who had been a fellow student of Count Zinzendorf, and became a Moravian bishop. On the 4th July, they reached Marienborn, the residence of Zinzendorf, where they remained a fortnight. Whilst here, Ingham, in a letter to Sir John Thorold,[3] London, observed :—

---

[1] *Methodist Magazine*, 1848, p. 1096.
[2] Hutton's Memoirs, p. 40.
[3] Sir John Thorold belonged to one of the oldest families in Lincolnshire. He was a great friend of the first Methodists; and, as early as 1738, used to attend the Moravian meetings, in the house of James Hutton, at The Bible and Sun, a little westward of Temple Bar; and to expound among the Brethren the Holy Scriptures, and to engage in prayer. In 1742, he became dissatisfied, and brought the following charges against them. "1. Their not praying so much to the Father and

"The worthy count is occupied day and night in the work of the Lord ; and, I must confess, that the Lord is really among the Brethren. Yesterday, a boy of eleven or twelve years of age was baptized ; and such a movement of the Holy Spirit pervaded the whole assembly, as I have never seen at any baptism.   I felt that my heart burned within me, and I could not refrain from tears.   I saw that others felt as I did, and the whole congregation was moved.   The Brethren have shown me much affection; they have taken me to their conferences, and have not left me in ignorance of anything concerning their Church.   I am much pleased with my journey."

Ingham was pleased with the Moravians ; and the Moravians were pleased with him.   In fact, Ingham was preferred to Wesley, and was admitted to partake of the holy communion, while Wesley was rejected.   The reasons assigned for admitting Ingham were, (1) that he had already shown an inclination to leave the English Established Church, and to join the Brethren ; and (2), "that his heart was better than his head."   The reasons for rejecting Wesley were, (1) he was "*homo perturbatus;* (2) his head had gained an ascendency over his heart ; (3) he claimed to be a zealous English Churchman, and they were not desirous to interfere with his plan of effecting good as a clergyman of the English Church."[1]

Ingham, as well as Wesley, visited Hernhuth, where he spent a fortnight, and was "exceedingly strengthened and comforted by the services and conversation of the Brethren. Towards the end of the year, he returned to England."

It is a curious fact that Wesley and Ingham were not the only Oxford Methodists who began to associate with the Moravians.   On the first day of the year 1739, we find not fewer than seven of the Oxford brotherhood—the two Wesleys, Ingham, Whitefield, Westley Hall, Kinchin, and Hutchins,—present at a Moravian lovefeast in Fetter Lane, respecting which Wesley writes :—

the Holy Ghost as to the Son.   2. Their speaking so contemptuously of reason, which opened a door to fancy and enthusiasm.   3. Their saying, there were no duties in the New Testament.   4. Their not giving an open conscientious confession of their faith.   5. Their disowning their tenets when driven to a pinch."

Sir John Thorold died in 1748.   (Hutton's Memoirs, p. 82 ; and Life and Times of Countess of Huntingdon, vol. i., p. 77.)

[1] Hutton's Memoirs, p. 40.

"About three in the morning, as we were continuing instant in prayer, the power of God came mightily upon us, insomuch that many cried out for exceeding joy, and many fell to the ground. As soon as we were recovered a little from the awe and amazement at the presence of His Majesty, we broke out with one voice, 'We praise Thee, O God; we acknowledge Thee to be the Lord.'"[1]

This was a memorable beginning of what will ever be a memorable year in the history of the Methodistic movement.

Four days afterwards, the same clergymen, joined by Mr. Seward, had a conference at Islington, and, without effect, tried to prevail on Charles Wesley to settle at Oxford. Whitefield writes :—

"We continued in fasting and prayer till three o'clock, and then parted, with a full conviction that God was about to do great things among us. O that we may be any way instrumental to His glory! O that He would make us vessels pure and holy, meet for such a dear Master's use!"[2]

The men evidently were willing to be used in any way which Providence might appoint ; and their conviction of the coming of great events was not falsified.

On Ingham's return to Osset, his native place, he renewed his labours, and preached in most of the churches and chapels about Wakefield, Leeds, and Halifax. Private religious meetings also were greatly multiplied. Large numbers of persons were convinced of sin, and were converted. It was pre-eminently a day of divine visitation. The clergy, however, instead of rejoicing at an enlargement of the work of God, were envious and malignant; and, at a Church congress, held at Wakefield, June 6, 1739, Ingham was prohibited from preaching in any of the churches in the diocese of York ; and was thus placed in the same position as Wesley had been compelled to occupy in London. Both were ordained clergymen, and both longed to preach the gospel of God their Saviour; but both were without a church of their own, and both were now uniformly shut out of the churches of others. What Wesley began to do at Bristol, Kingswood, and elsewhere, Ingham began to do in Yorkshire. Village greens, the public streets, fields, barns, cottages, and houses of all descriptions became his preaching places ; and, such was the divine power which

---

[1] Wesley's Works, vol. i., p. 161.
[2] Whitefield's Journals, p. 115 ; and C. Wesley's Journal, vol. i., p. 139.

attended his ministry, that not fewer than forty religious societies were formed.

Ingham was reviled, but he reviled not again. The following letter illustrates his fine Christian spirit, at the period of which we are now writing. It probably was addressed to Wesley. At all events, Wesley published it in the first volume of his *Arminian Magazine* (p. 181).

"OSSET, Sept. 14, 1739.

"MY DEAR BROTHER,—Wait the Lord's leisure, and be still. His time is the best time. 'Be strong, and He shall comfort thine heart; and put thou thy trust in the Lord.'

"I shall be very glad to see you, when the Lord pleases that we shall meet together. O that we may do and suffer His will in all things ! It is following our own wills that creates us trouble and confusion.

"All your opposition will work together for good. The more the clergy oppose the truth, the more it will prevail. Their preaching against us and our doctrines excites a curiosity in the people to hear us, and to see if these things be true, whereby many have their eyes opened. If this work is of God, it cannot be overthrown : if it be of men, I wish it may speedily. We have nothing to do but to follow our Leader. O that He may direct all our ways aright !

"I say very little about the clergy in public. I preach the truth of the gospel, according to the light the Lord has given me into it, and leave it to the Lord to bless it as He pleases. I take no notice of lies and calumnies, unless I am asked whether or no they are true. It is endless to answer all that is said. Our Saviour says, 'Let them alone.' He is concerned for the welfare of His Church ; let us, therefore, depend upon Him, and let us mind what He says to us in His holy word. Let us love our enemies, and pray for them ; and let us love one another ; and thereby shall all men know that we are His true disciples. We must be hated in this world; let us, therefore, take great care to secure ourselves an inheritance in the next.

"BENJAMIN INGHAM."

While the above exhibits Ingham's spirit, the subjoined clearly shows that his ideas on the Methodist doctrines were as yet imperfect. It is a well-known fact, that Wesley himself was sorely perplexed with the doctrine of what is called "the witness of the Spirit," and that his intercourse with the Moravians rather increased his mistiness than scattered it. In 1738 he had a lengthened and very important correspondence with his brother Samuel on the subject; and now he consulted Ingham, who replied as follows :—

1739
—
Age 27

"OSSET, *February* 20, 1740.

"MY DEAR BROTHER,—The most dangerous time in the Christian race, seems to be when a person receives the forgiveness of sins, especially if he is filled with great joy, and of long continuance. Indeed, all states of great joy are dangerous, if not humbly received. If persons have not now a guide, or are not guidable, it is ten to one but they run into error and by-paths. Many souls miscarry here, and never get further in their spiritual progress. They run on till their joy and strength are spent, and then they lose themselves, and are all in confusion. I have met with several persons with whom it has been thus, and how to help them I know not. They do not get forward. I believe, indeed, that they will be saved, yet their degree in glory will be low. They are but in the first stage of the new birth.

"You ask, What are the marks of a person who is justified, and not sealed ?[1]

"I cannot give you any certain, infallible marks ; but a person to whom the Lord has given the gift of discerning will tell ; and, without the gift, we shall never be able to know surely. However, such persons are meek, simple, and childlike ; they have doubts and fears within ; they are in a wilderness state. In this state, they are to be kept still and quiet; to search more deeply into their hearts, so that they become more and more poor in spirit, or humble. They are likewise now taught to depend wholly on Christ. By all means, keep them from confusion. If they come into confusion (as they are apt to do), they receive inconceivable damage ; but, if they continue still meek and gentle, searching into their hearts, and depending upon Christ, they will find their hearts to be sweetly drawn after Christ ; they will begin to loathe and abhor sin, and to hunger and thirst after righteousness ; they will get strength daily ; Christ will begin to manifest Himself by degrees ; the darkness will vanish, and the day-star will arise in their hearts. Thus they go on from strength to strength, till they become strong, and then they will begin to see things clearly, and

---

[1] The meaning of this phraseology may, perhaps, be gathered from a letter which Wesley wrote to his brother Samuel, on October 23, 1738, five months after Wesley's conversion. The following is an extract :—" The πληροφορία πίστεως,—the seal of the Spirit, the love of God shed abroad in my heart, and producing joy in the Holy Ghost, joy which no man taketh away, joy unspeakable and full of glory,—this witness of the Spirit I have not ; but I wait patiently for it. I know many who have already received it," etc. (" Life and Times of Wesley," vol. i., p. 190). The fact is, Wesley, for a season, appeared to confound the witness of the Spirit to the justification of a Christian believer with what he afterwards meant by the attainment of Christian perfection. Soon afterwards, however, he was blessed with clearer light, and gave to the Church, perhaps, the best definition of the doctrine ever penned,—" The testimony of the Spirit is an inward impression on the soul, whereby the Spirit of God directly witnesses to my spirit that I am a child of God ; that Jesus Christ hath loved me, and given Himself for me ; and that all my sins are blotted out, and I, even I, am reconciled to God."

to understand what the Lord has done for them ; so, by degrees, they will come to have the assurance of faith.

1740

Age 28

"You ask whether, in this intermediate state, they are 'children of wrath, or heirs of the promises'?

"Without doubt, they are children of God ; they are in a state of salvation. A child may be heir to an estate before it can speak, or know what an estate is ; so we may be heirs of heaven before we know it, or are made sure of it. However, the assurance of faith is to be sought after. It may be attained ; it will be given to all who go forward. We must first be humble and poor in spirit. We must be deeply so. We must have a constant, fixed, abiding feeling,—a sense of our weakness and unworthiness, corruption, sin, and misery. This it is to be a *poor sinner.*

"If I were with you, I would explain things more largely; but I am a novice,—I am but a beginner,—a babe in Christ. If you go amongst the Brethren, they are good guides; but yet, after all, we must be taught of God, and have experience in our own hearts; or else it will not do. May the Spirit of truth lead us into all truth !

"I am your poor, unworthy brother,

"B. INGHAM."

The above is given *verbatim* from the manuscript letter, and is of great importance as revealing the views, doubts, and difficulties of the leaders of the Methodist movement.

Before proceeding further, it may be added that Ingham was not forgotten by his old friend Whitefield, who wrote to him as follows :—

"SAVANNAH, *March* 28, 1740.

"How glad I should be of a letter from dear brother Ingham. When shall my soul be refreshed, with hearing that the work of the Lord prospers in his hand ? I suppose before now you have received my letters and seen my journal. I believe God is yet preparing great things for us. Many at Charles-Town lately were brought to see their want of Jesus Christ. The Orphan House goes on bravely. I have forty children to maintain, besides workmen and their assistants. The great Householder of the world does, and will, I am persuaded, richly provide for us all. The colony itself is in a very declining way; but our extremity is God's opportunity. Our brethren, I trust, go forwards in the spiritual life. I have often great inward trials. I believe it to be God's will that I should marry. One, who may be looked upon as a superior, is absolutely necessary for the due management of affairs. However, I pray God, that I may not have a wife, till I can live as though I had none. You may communicate this to some of our intimates; for I would call Christ and His disciples to the marriage. If I am deluded, pray that God would reveal it to your most affectionate brother and servant,

"GEORGE WHITEFIELD."

In the midst of all this, a new evangelist sprang up, who,

 without the educational advantages of the Oxford Methodists, had a kindred soul.

John Nelson, the brave-hearted Yorkshire stonemason, after hearing almost all sorts of religionists,—Church of England men, Dissenters, Papists, and Quakers,—had been brought to a knowledge of the truth by Wesley. This was under the first sermon preached by Wesley in Moorfields. In 1740, Nelson returned to Yorkshire, and related to his friends his happy experience. He writes :—

"They begged I would not tell any one that my sins were forgiven, for no one would believe me, and they should be ashamed to show their faces in the street. I answered, 'I shall not be ashamed to tell what God has done for my soul, if I could speak loud enough for all the men in the world to hear me at once.' My mother said, 'Your head is turned.' I replied, 'Yes, and my heart too, I thank the Lord.'"

He went to Adwalton, to hear Ingham preach; and re-marked :—

"As soon as I got into the house, he called me into the parlour, and desired the company that was with him to go out, for he had something to say to me. When they went, he rose up, barred the door, then sat down, and asked me, 'Do you know your own heart, think you?' I answered, 'Not rightly; but I know Jesus Christ, and He knows and has taken possession of it; and though it be deceitful, yet He can subdue it to Himself; and I trust He will'. He said, 'Have you not deceived yourself with thinking that your sins are forgiven, and that you are in a state of grace? I was three years seeking before I found Him.' I replied, 'Suppose you were, do you confine God to be three years in converting every soul, because you were so long? God is able to convert a soul in three days now, as He was to convert St. Paul seventeen hundred years ago.' I then began to tell him what I had seen at London under Mr. Wesley's preaching. He said he pitied poor Mr. Wesley, for he was ignorant of his own state; and he spoke as if he believed Mr. Wesley to be an unconverted man; at which words my corrupt nature began to stir. But it came to my mind, 'The wrath of man worketh not the righteousness of God'; and I lifted up my heart to the Lord, and my mind was calmed in a moment. He said, 'You ought not to tell people that they may know their sins forgiven, for the world cannot bear it; and if such a thing were preached, it would raise persecution.' I replied, 'Let them quake that fear. By the grace of God, I love every man, but fear no man; and I will tell all I can, that there is such a prize to run for. If I hide it, mischief will come upon me. There is a famine in the land; and I see myself in the case of the lepers that were at the gate of Samaria, who found provisions in the enemy's camp; and, when they had eat and drank, and loaded themselves, said, "We do not well; for this is a day of glad tidings,

let us go and make it known to the king's household." When I found
God's wrath removed, for the sake of His dear Son, I saw provision
enough for my poor fainting soul, and for all the world if they would.
come for it. I believe it is a sin not to declare to the children of men
what God has done for my soul, that they may seek for the same mercy.'
He told me, I had nothing to do with the Old Testament, or to make
comparisons from anything in it. . I answered, ' I have as much to do with
it as with the New Testament.' He replied, ' I would not have you speak
any more to the people till you are better acquainted with your own
heârt.' I told him, I would not in his societies, unless I was desired; but
what I did in my own house, or any other person's that requested me, he
had no business with. I added, ' I do not belong to you; and though I
have heard you several times, it is no benefit to me; for I have experienced more of the grace of God than ever I heard you preach of it, or
any one else since I left London.'"

Nelson here obviously refers to his enjoyment of the Holy
Spirit's witness to the fact that his sins were pardoned ; and
hence he continues,—

"Soon after Mr. Ingham came out and began to preach; when I was
greatly surprised; for what he had forbidden me to do, he himself did
directly; for he told the people, that night, they must know their sins forgiven in this world or go to hell."[1]

Soon after this, Ingham went to London, where the Wesleys were in painful conflict with the Moravians. Philip
Henry Molther, who had been the private tutor of Zinzendorf's only son, was preaching, to large congregations, four
times every week, and was much more popular than his
talents or his misty doctrines merited. The chief controversy
between him and Wesley was concerning the use of the
means of grace. Molther recommended penitent inquirers
to "*be still;*" that is, not to search the Scriptures, not to pray,
not to communicate, not to do good ; for it was impossible to
use means, without trusting in them. Wesley, on the other
hand, recommended and enforced just the opposite. The
contention among their partisans was fierce and furious ; and
the object of Ingham's visit to the metropolis seems to have
been to reconcile the irritated disputants. Charles Wesley
writes :—

"1740. May 22.—I found our dear brother Ingham at Mr. West's. The

---

[1] Nelson's Journal.

holiday mob were very outrageous at the Foundery. God filled my mouth with threatenings and promises; and, at last, we got the victory, and the fiercest rioters were overawed into silence.

"May 25.—At the lovefeast, I was overwhelmed with the burden of our brethren, with such visible signs of dejection, that several, I was since informed, were in great hopes that I was now coming down in my pride, or unsettling, and coming into confusion. Indeed, my faith did well-nigh fail me; for in spite of the seeming reconciliation which brother Ingham *forces* them into, it is impossible we should ever be of one mind, unless they are convinced of their abrogating the law of *Christian* ordinances, and taking away the children's bread.

"May 27.—I rejoiced to find no difference betwixt my brother Ingham and me. He has honestly withstood the deluded brethren; contradicted their favourite errors, and constrained them to be *still.* That blot he easily hit: 'You say no man must speak of what he has not experienced; you, Oxley and Simpson, say that one in the Gospel-liberty can have no stirrings of sin.' 'Yes.' 'Are you in Gospel-liberty?' 'No.' 'Then out of your own mouth I judge you: you speak of things which you know not of.'

"June 2.—I *preached up* the ordinances, as they call it, from Isaiah lviii.; but first, with the prophet, I preached them *down.* Telchig" [Tolt-schig], "Ingham, etc., were present, which made me use greater plainness, that they might set me right, if I mistook.

"June 11.—I returned" [from the Delamotte family at Blendon] "to be exercised by our *still* brethren's contradiction. My brother proposed new-modelling the bands, and setting by themselves those few who were still for the ordinances. Great clamour was raised by this proposal. The noisy *still* ones well knew that they had carried their point by wearying out the sincere ones scattered among them; so that a remnant is scarcely left. They grudged us even this remnant, which would soon be all their own, unless immediately rescued out of their hands. Benjamin Ingham seconded us, and obtained that the names should be called over, and as many as were aggrieved put into new books.

"We gathered up our wreck,—*raros nantes in gurgite vasto;* for nine out of ten are swallowed up in the dead sea of *stillness.* O, why was not this done six months ago? How fatal was our delay and moderation! 'Let them alone, and they will soon be weary, and come to themselves of course,' said one,—*unus qui nobis cunctando restituet rem!* I tremble at the consequence. Will they submit themselves to every ordinance of man, who refuse subjection to the ordinances of God? I told them plainly, *I should only continue with them so long as they continued in the Church of England.* My every word was grievous to them. I am a thorn in their sides, and they cannot bear me.

"They *modestly* denied that we had any but hearsay proof of their denying the ordinances. I asked them all and every one, particularly Bray, Bell, etc., whether they would now acknowledge them to be commands or duties; whether they sinned in omitting them; whether they did not leave it to every man's fancy to use them or not; whether they did not exclude all from the Lord's table, except those whom *they* called believers. These questions I put too close to be evaded; though better dodgers never came out of the school of Loyola. Honest Bell and some others spoke out, and insisted upon their antichristian liberty. The rest put by their stillness, and delivered me over to Satan for a blasphemer, a very Saul (for to him they compare me), out of blind zeal persecuting the Church of Christ." [1]

Ingham continued among these angry people a week longer, when John Wesley wrote :—

"1740. June 18.—I went to our own society, of Fetter Lane, before whom Mr. Ingham (being to leave London on the morrow) bore a noble testimony for the ordinances of God, and the reality of weak faith.[2] But the short answer was, 'You are blind, and speak of the things you know not.' " [3]

Matters now reached a crisis. For about two years, Wesley had been a sort of member and minister of the Moravian Society in Fetter Lane. Five weeks after this, by a vote of the Brethren, Wesley was expelled ; and Molther, his rival, was left in full possession. Those who sympathised with Wesley were, in number, about twenty-five men and fifty women, all of whom seceded with him, and, on July 23rd, 1740, met, for the first time, at the Foundery, instead of at Fetter Lane ; and thus the *Methodist* Society was founded.

Whitefield was in America ; but, in the midst of these wretched squabbles, wrote to Ingham the following Calvinistic, and not too luminous epistle :—

"BOSTON, *September 26th*, 1740.

"MY DEAR BROTHER INGHAM,—I thank you for your kind letter. It is the first I have received from you since I left England. I bless God, that the work goes on in Yorkshire. May our glorious, sin-forgiving Lord, bless you and your spiritual children more and more !

"I find our friends are got into disputing one with another. O, that the God of peace may put a stop to it ! I wish many may not be building on a false foundation, and resting in a false peace. They own *free justification*, and yet seem to think that their continuance in a justified state depends on their doings and their wills. This, I think, is establishing a righteousness of our own. My dear brother, if we search the Scriptures, we shall find that the word *justified* implies, not only

---

[1] C. Wesley's Journal.

[2] One of Molther's dogmas was, that no one has any faith while he has any doubt.

[3] Wesley's Journal.

pardon of sin, but also all its consequences. ' Thus,' says St. Paul, ' those whom He justified, them He also glorified ;' so that, if a man was once justified, he remains so to all eternity. There lies the anchor of all my hopes,—our Lord having once loved me, He will love me to the end. This fills me with joy unspeakable and full of glory. I now walk by faith. I work not to keep myself in a justified state, (for men nor devils can pluck me out of Christ's hands,) but to express my love and gratitude for what Jesus hath done for my soul. This, I think, is what the apostle calls, ' faith working by love.'

" My dear brother, my heart's desire and prayer to God is, that we may all think and speak the same things ; for, if we are divided among ourselves, what an advantage will Satan get over us ! Let us love one another, excite all to come to Christ without exception, and our Lord will show us who are His.

" With difficulty, I get time to write this, but I must answer dear brother Ingham's letter. May the Lord Jesus be continually with your spirit, and make your soul brimful of peace and joy in the Holy Ghost ! I love you in the bowels of the crucified Lamb. May He unite us more and more intimately to His dear self, and to one another ! Salute all that love Him in sincerity. That you may be kept by God's power to eternal salvation, is the prayer of your most affectionate, though unworthy brother and poor weak servant in Christ,

" GEORGE WHITEFIELD."

It is needless to say, that some of the doctrines in the above letter were not held by Wesley ; but let that pass.

Ingham returned to Yorkshire with broader views and sympathies than he had when he left for London. Sending for John Nelson to one of his meetings, he said, " John, I believe God has called you to speak His word ; for I have spoken with several since I came back from London, who, I believe, have received grace since I went ; and I see God is working in a shorter manner than He did with us at the beginning ; and I should be sorry to hinder any one from doing good." Then, turning to the assembled brethren and sisters, Ingham continued, " Before you all, I give John leave to exhort in all my societies ;" and, taking the rough hand of the Yorkshire stonemason, he added, " John, God hath given you great honour, in that He hath made use of you to call sinners to the blood of our Saviour ; and I desire you to exhort in all my societies as often as you can."

Thus, in the employment of lay preachers, Ingham co-operated with his friend Wesley. Both were clergymen of the Church of England ; and both were willing to have lay helpers. Nelson's preaching was attended with great success. "Nine or ten in a week were brought to experience the love of Jesus."[1] John was no proselytizer. Those of his converts, who belonged to the Church of England, he "exhorted to keep close to the Church and sacrament;" and those who were "Dissenters, to keep to their own meetings, and to let their light shine before their own community."

In this respect, he was somewhat in advance of his reverend patron; for Ingham advised just the contrary, and several acted on his advice, which, says Nelson, "made me very uneasy." Nelson firmly adhered to the Church of England, and wished to avoid a schism. Ingham, on the other hand, had already virtually seceded, and was at the head of the Moravian sect in Yorkshire. The priest and the mason found it difficult to work in harmony. Besides, though always actuated by the best intentions, Ingham was somewhat fickle, and easily influenced by his Moravian helpers. Nelson was just the opposite; and, yet, his steadfastness was not stubbornness. He was firm, because he felt that the ground he occupied was right. As already stated, Ingham, on his return from London, publicly authorised, and even requested, Nelson to exhort in all his societies; but, shortly afterwards, the authorization was withdrawn. Why? Because Ingham was no longer the commander-in-chief of the Yorkshire converts, but a merely co-ordinate member of a common-council. He could no longer act as he liked; but must proceed in harmony with the decisions of those to whom he had allied himself. Here an explanation is necessary.

In 1740, Ingham wrote :—

"There are now upwards of fifty societies, where the people meet for edification; and of two thousand hearers of the gospel, I know, at least, three hundred on whose hearts the Spirit of God works powerfully; and one hundred who have found grace in the blood and the atonement of Jesus."

The work begun by Ingham bid fair to exceed that in London. Hitherto the rendezvous of the English Moravian

---

[1] Nelson's Journal.

ministers had been the metropolis ; now it became a farm-house in Yorkshire. About four miles east of Halifax stood a spacious dwelling, with extensive outbuildings, and a large farm attached. This the Moravians rented, that it might serve as a place of residence for those Moravian pastors to whom the spiritual affairs of the societies were committed, and as a common centre of union. They entered on the occupancy of the premises in 1741 ; and, shortly after, Ingham, who had hitherto had the chief care of the Yorkshire societies, urgently, and in writing, requested the Brethren to take the entire direction of them into their own hands, so that he might devote himself wholly to the work of preaching. To carry out his purpose, a public meeting was convened, on July 30, 1742, which was attended by about a thousand persons, belonging to these societies. Ingham's proposal was submitted to them, and was heartily accepted. A document was drawn up, which, after referring to Ingham's faithful labours, expressed a desire to be served in future by the ministers of the Brethren's Church, "whom," said the twelve hundred persons who signed it, "we not only desire to preach publicly amongst us, but also to visit us in private, put us to rights, and make such orders amongst us as they shall see useful and necessary, according to the grace the Lord shall give them."

Smith House, near Halifax, was now the head-quarters of English Moravianism. Even members in London, elected to fulfil sacred functions there, were sent all the way to York-shire to be solemnly inducted into their respective offices. The field, hitherto occupied by Ingham, Nelson, and other co-operators, was divided into six principal districts, namely, Smith House, Adwalton, Mirfield, Great Horton, Holbeck, and Osset ; and to each of these districts a Moravian minister was appointed.[1]

We now return to Ingham, and his neighbour Nelson. The latter tells us of a great Moravian meeting at Gomersal Field House, at which Ingham desired him to be present. Nelson went. The house was filled with five or six preachers, four

---

[1] See " Hutton's Memoirs," p. 100-108 ; and Holmes' " History of the Church of the Brethren," vol. i., p. 318.

exhorters, and about a hundred of the principal members of the Yorkshire societies. Not being able to gain admittance to the house, and finding a large number of people outside, the honest stonemason went into a field and preached. At length, Ingham came out, and announced the decision of the Brethren: namely, that it was not prudent to have so much preaching, for fear it should engender persecution. "I desire, therefore," said he, "that none of the young men will expound till they are desired by the Brethren; we shall meet again this day month, and then we will let you know what we are all to do." He next spoke to the young expounders, one by one, and said, "I hope you will be obedient." They all replied, "Yes, sir." He then turned to Nelson, saying, "John, I hope you will leave off till you have orders from the Church." "No, sir," replied intrepid John; "I will not leave off—I dare not; for I did not begin by the order of man, nor by my own will; therefore, I shall not leave off by your order; for, I tell you plainly, I should have left off without your bidding, but that I believed, if I did, I should be damned for disobedience." Ingham answered, "You see these young men are obedient to the elders, and they have been blessed in their labours as well as you." Nelson said, "I cannot tell how they have been blessed; but, I think, if God had sent them on His own errand, they would not stop at your bidding." At this point, one of the preachers interfered, saying, "The spirit of the prophets is subject to the prophets; therefore, they are right and you are wrong, for they are subject." John failing to be convinced by the preacher's logic, boldly answered, "You are not obedient to the prophets of God that were of old, for God saith by one of them, 'I have set watchmen upon the walls of Jerusalem that shall not cease day or night;' but you can hold your peace for a month together at man's bidding." Then turning to Ingham, Nelson continued, "You know that many have been converted by my exhorting lately, and a great many more are under convictions; what a sad thing would it be to leave them as they are." Ingham's lame reply was, "Our Saviour can convert souls without your preaching." "Yes," retorted John, "or yours either; and He can give corn without ploughing or sowing, but He does not, neither has He promised that He will." Ingham rejoined, " Be still one month, and then you will know more of your own heart." " With one proviso, I will," said Nelson : " if you can persuade the devil to be still for a month ; but if he goes about like a roaring lion, seeking whom he may devour, and God hath put a sword into my hand, I am determined to attack him wheresoever I meet him ; and wheresoever I meet sin, I meet Satan." Further conversation followed ; and, at length, Ingham "charged all the people, as they loved him and the brethren, that they should not let Nelson preach in their houses, nor encourage him by hearing him elsewhere."

This, on the part of Ingham, was painful and unworthy conduct. The preaching of the stonemason had probably been as greatly blessed and as successful as his own. The man was no irreligious, rash intruder; but a real evangelist, called and qualified by Him who, in all ages, has been wont to choose "the foolish things of the world to confound the wise ; and the weak things of the world to confound the things which are mighty ; and base things of the world, and things which are despised, and things which are not, to bring to nought things that are ; that no flesh should glory in His presence ; and that he that glorieth may glory in the Lord." Nelson was as divinely called to preach Christ's glorious gospel as Ingham was. His ministry had the seals of divine approbation in the souls it had been the means of converting; and Ingham's effort to suspend it, even for a month only, was a bold, bad act. Besides, the reason assigned for such an interference with a commission, which Nelson had received from God Himself, was a piece of cowardice unworthy of the man who had braved the storms of the Atlantic Ocean, and the hardships and miasmata of Georgia, solely for the purpose of being useful to the wild Indians and to a portion of England's outcast population. For fear of persecution, Nelson, whom God had used in saving sinners, was to be gagged and silenced. The change which had come over the naturally brave spirit of the Oxford Methodist was a painful one ; and also puzzling, except on the ground that he had changed his company.

It is a mournful duty to have to mention another incident.

Ingham interdicted Nelson, though unsuccessfully. He further renounced his old friend Wesley, and, for a season at
least, became intoxicated with the Moravian vanity, at that
time disastrously spreading. Hence, the following extract
from Nelson's Journal :—

"I was desired once more to go to Gomersal Field House to speak to
Mr. Ingham. When I got there, David Taylor was with him, and spoke
kindly to me. When Mr. Taylor was gone, Mr. Ingham began to talk to
me about making division among the Brethren. I told him, I did not
want to make division; I wanted the people to be saved. He said, 'We
cannot receive you or Mr. Wesley into our community[1] till he publicly
declares he has printed false doctrine, and you declare you have preached
false.' I said, 'Wherein?' He then burst out into laughter, and said, 'In
telling the people they may live without committing sin.'[2] I replied, 'Do
you call that false doctrine?' He answered, 'I do, I do; and Mr. Wesley
has written false doctrine, teaching the same errors.' He quoted some
words; then I said, 'They are not Mr. Wesley's, but St. John's words; it
is St. John who says, "Let no man deceive you; he that doeth righteousness is righteous, and he that committeth sin is of the devil." So, if St.
John be right, every one who preacheth contrary to what Mr. Wesley has
written here, and what I have preached, is a deceiver and betrayer of
souls.' 'If that be your opinion,' said Mr. Ingham, 'we cannot receive
you into our Church.' I replied, 'I don't want to be one of you,
for I am a member of the Church of England.' He answered, 'The
Church of England is no Church; we are the Church.' I said, 'We!
Whom do you mean?' He replied, 'I and the Moravian Brethren.' I
said, 'I have no desire to have any fellowship with you or them; it has
been better for my soul since I have been wholly separated from you, and
God has blessed my labours more since I was told, they had delivered me
up to Satan, than ever before; therefore, I think it better to have their
curse than to have communion with them.' He replied, 'If you think so,
I have no more to say to you;' and then, he turned his back on me."

Thus did Ingham fully and finally sever himself from the
Methodists. Nelson continued preaching; souls were saved;
and, in 1742, Wesley, for the first time, visited the Birstal
stonemason. After giving an account how Nelson was led to
begin to preach, and of his success, Wesley adds :—

---

[1] To say the least, this was offensively premature. Where is the
evidence that either Wesley or Nelson wished to be received into the
Moravian community?

[2] This interview probably occurred in the year 1741, though Nelson
neglects to supply the date. In 1739, Wesley had published his "Character
of a Methodist," and also his abridged "Life of Halyburton," with a preface
by himself. In both of these publications, he propounded, in strong
language, his doctrine of entire sanctification.

"Mr. Ingham hearing of this, came to Birstal, inquired into the facts, talked with John himself, and examined him in the closest manner, both touching his knowledge and spiritual experience; after which he encouraged him to proceed; and pressed him, as often as he had opportunity, to come to any of the places where himself had been, and speak to the people as God should enable him. But he soon gave offence, both by his plainness of speech, and by advising the people to go to church and sacrament. Mr. Ingham reproved him: and, finding him incorrigible, forbad any that were in his societies to hear him. But, being persuaded this is the will of God concerning him, he continues to this hour working in the day, that he may be burdensome to no man; and, in the evening, 'testifying the truth as it is in Jesus.'"[1]

This is a long account; but not without interest; inasmuch as it furnishes a glimpse of the way in which Ingham parted with the Methodists, and of the beginnings of both Moravianism and Methodism in the north of England. We only add, that, though Ingham passed through Birstal during Wesley's visit, there was no interview between them.[2] Thus was an old and close friendship severed.

It has been already stated, that, the differences between Ingham and Nelson probably occurred in 1741; and that Wesley's visit to Birstal took place in 1742. This, in some respects, was the most important period in Ingham's life.

Far away from the miserable strifes of the Moravians in London, we find him, in 1740, an humble, happy, loving, useful Christian. The following letter is simple and beautiful :—

"OSSET, *September* 20, 1740.

"MY DEAR BROTHER,—I have not heard anything of you this long time. As to myself, I am exceeding happy.[3] The Lord Jesus, my dear Redeemer, is abundantly gracious and bountiful towards me. I have, and do daily taste of His goodness. I am ashamed before Him; I am so very unworthy, and He is so very kind and merciful. My heart melts within me, at the thoughts of Him. He is all love. I am a sinful, helpless worm.

---

[1] Wesley's Works, vol. i., p. 350.
[2] Nelson's Journal.

[3] In a letter by James Hutton to Count Zinzendorf, and dated, September 17, 1740, only three days before the date of this letter by Ingham, the following occurs ;—"Ingham writes from Yorkshire, that, he also has discovered something new in his heart, and is now assured he shall not die eternally; he had never before experienced the like. He also writes, that, many souls in Yorkshire have of late found grace, and he desires that Toltschig may come to him." ("Memoirs of James Hutton," p. 63.)

"In Yorkshire, the Lord still keeps carrying on His work. Many souls are truly awakened: some have obtained mercy. The enemies are engaged against us; but the Lord is our helper. We have great peace, and love, and unity amongst ourselves. We have no differences, no divisions, no disputings. May He, who is the giver of every good and perfect gift, grant us always to be like-minded; and may we and our friends grow in grace, and increase in love towards one another, that, by this mark, all men may know that we belong to Christ!

"I remain your affectionate, though unworthy brother,

"B. INGHAM." [1]

If Ingham and John Nelson had been left to themselves, Ingham's prayer for continued unity might have been answered; but Ingham wished for Toltschig, one of the ministerial chiefs among the London Moravians; and Toltschig doubtless went.

"We, in London," writes James Hutton, "cannot spare Toltschig until Spangenberg comes to us. We here all think he will be useful to Ingham and the souls there. They must seize the opportunity presented. The souls in Yorkshire are more simple-hearted than those in London, where they are more knowing; and they do not, like those in town, quibble at every word. Toltschig is known in Yorkshire, where the souls love him, and he can speak to them with confidence. We want a thorough brother, fundamentablly correct, and of large experience, for the souls in London, able to attend our bands and conferences, and to address our meetings. Toltschig is very well in bands and conferences, but he cannot preach." [2]

Did Toltschig carry the cantankerous contagion of the London Moravians with him? We cannot tell; but there can be no question, that, the "simple-hearted" Yorkshire brethren caught it; and, that, in Yorkshire, as in London, a schism among the Moravians led to the formation of the society of Methodists.

Indeed, it is a curious fact, that, for a season, the spirit of discord, among nearly the whole of the new religionists, seemed rampant. No man ever lived who sighed for peace more ardently than Whitefield. His large and loving heart had room enough for every man. The language of the Psalmist's pen was pre-eminently the language of Whitefield's life: "Pray for the peace of Jerusalem: they shall prosper that love thee. Peace be within thy walls, and prosperity within thy palaces. For my brethren and companions' sake, I will now say, Peace be within thee." And, yet, at this very time,

---

[1] *Methodist Magazine*, 1778, p. 182. [2] "Memoirs of James Hutton," p. 64.

as if to make bad things worse, the quarrel, between the London Moravians and Methodists, was followed by the quarrel between Wesley and Whitefield, respecting Wesley's sermon on " Free Grace ;" and, to complete the whole, and to make the confusion more confounded, the Yorkshire converts, so far away from the strifeful scene, began disputing ; and the frank, warm-hearted Ingham began to regard his old friend Wesley with a suspicious eye, and presumptuously tried to annul John Nelson's divine commission to act as an evangelist among his neighbours !

Ingham's objection to Wesley's doctrine of entire sanctification has been already mentioned ; but, besides this, there were other points of difference.   Wesley writes :—

"1741. August 1.—I had a long conversation with Mr. Ingham. We both agreed,—1. That none shall finally be saved, who have not, as they had opportunity, done all good works; and, 2. That if a justified person does not do good, as he has opportunity, he will lose the grace he has received; and, if he 'repent' not, 'and do the former works,' will perish eternally. But with regard to the unjustified (if I understand him), we wholly disagreed. He believed, it is not the will of God, that, we should wait for faith in doing good. I believe, this is the will of God; and that, they will never find Him, unless they seek Him in this way."

Again :—

"1742. August 3.—I preached at Mirfield, where I found Mr. Ingham had been an hour before. Great part of the day, I spent in speaking with those who have tasted the powers of the world to come; by whose concurrent testimony I find, that, Mr. Ingham's method to this day is,—1. To endeavour to persuade them, that they are in a delusion, and have indeed no faith at all: if this cannot be done, then, 2. To make them keep it to themselves; and, 3. To prevent them going to the church or sacrament; at least to guard them from having any reverence, or expecting to find any blessing in those ordinances of God. In the evening, I preached at Adwalton, a mile from Birstal. After preaching, and the next day, I spoke with more, who had, or sought for, redemption through Christ; all of whom I perceived had been advised also, to put their light under a bushel; or to forsake the ordinances of God, in order to find Christ."[1]

Ingham's wish to prevent persecution has been noticed. On this ground, he requested Nelson and other exhorters to desist from preaching for a month. What led to this ? Perhaps, the publication, in 1740, of a furious pamphlet of eighty-four pages, with the following title : " The Imposture

---

[1] Wesley's Journal.

of Methodism displayed ; in a Letter to the Inhabitants of the Parish of Dewsbury and Occasioned by the Rise of a certain Modern Sect of Enthusiasts, (among them,) called Methodists. By William Bowman, M.A., Vicar of Dewsbury and Aldborough in Yorkshire, and Chaplain to the Right Honourable Charles Earl of Hoptoun."

This pastorly letter was avowedly written against the Methodists ; but the reverend author, like many others at the time, employed an inappropriate word ; for, at that period, there were no Methodists at all, either in Yorkshire or any other part of the north of England. His letter is dated, "Aldbrough, August 15, 1740" ; whereas, John Nelson, the beginner of northern Methodism, did not commence preaching to his neighbours for several months after this.[1] The Vicar of Dewsbury *meant* Moravians ; but, for reasons of his own, he preferred to use the word Methodists.

Terrible was the anger which Ingham and his coadjutors had excited in the Christian breast of their reverend neighbour. The pamphlet is a rarity, and, perhaps, a condensed account of it may be welcome.

It is a curious fact, that, the writer, while professing so much interest in the spiritual welfare of his flock, acknowledges, that, "for the greatest part of his time," he is "absent and remote from them." He is, however, notwithstanding this, greatly distressed on account of "the impious spirit of enthusiasm and superstition, which has of late crept in among" them, "and which sadly threatens a total ruin and destruction of all religion and virtue." Indeed, he had himself been, "in some measure, an eye-witness of this monstrous madness, and religious frenzy, which introduced nothing but a confused and ridiculous medley of nonsense and inconsistency." It was true, that, "at present, the contagion was pretty much confined to the dregs and refuse of the people,—the weak, unsteady mob ;" but, then, the mob was so numerous in the west of Yorkshire, that, the danger was greater than was apprehended. He next proceeds to review "some of the chief doctrines" of "these modern visionaries," which he will not now determine

---

[1] See Wesley's Works, vol. i., p. 349.

whether, "like the Quakers," they "are a sect hatched and fashioned in a seminary of Jesuits; or whether, like the German Anabaptists, they are a set of crazy, distempered fanatics." "The first and chief principle they inculcated was, that *they are divinely and supernaturally inspired by the Holy Ghost, to declare the will of God to mankind.*" Mr. Bowman attempts to demolish this "high and awful claim," and to demonstrate, that, its assertors are "a set of idiots or madmen," "only worthy of a dark corner in Bedlam, or the wholesome correction of Bridewell." "Another principle doctrine of these pretended pietists was, that, *for the sake of a further Reformation, it was not only lawful, but incumbent on the people, to separate from their proper ministers, and adhere to them.*" In refuting this barefaced heresy, the Dewsbury vicar, quotes, at considerable length, in the Greek and Latin languages, (which probably not half-a-dozen of his parishioners understood), the testimonies of Clemens Romanus, St. Ignatius, St. Cyprian, St. Austin, and Irenæus,—on "the necessity of Church unity." He admits, "that, all the clergymen of reputation in the neighbourhood" of Dewsbury, had "refused these Methodists the use of their pulpits;" but he was glad of this; and says "this was not done till, by their extravagant flights and buffooneries, they had made the church more like a beargarden than the house of God; and the rostrum nothing else but the trumpet of sedition, heresy, blasphemy, and everything destructive to religion and good manners." "A third mark of imposture propagated by these mad devotionalists was, *that it was lawful and expedient for mere laymen, for women, and the meanest and most ignorant mechanics, to minister in the Church of Christ, to preach and expound the word of God, and to offer up the prayers of the congregation in public assemblies.*" To refute this, Mr. Bowman favours his parishioners with a lengthy dissertation on the three orders, bishops, presbyters, and deacons; and comes to the charitable conclusion, that, the Methodists are "the most impious cheats and impostors." "*A fourth doctrine of these enthusiasts was, that, it is possible for a man to live without sin; that themselves actually do so; and that regeneration, or the new birth, necessary to salvation, consists in an absolute and entire freedom from all kind of sin whatsoever.*" Mr. Bowman asserts, that, "intolerable pride and presumption is the foundation of this unhappy delusion." "A fifth mark of imposture was, that cruel, uncharitable, and consequently unchristian doctrine, *which denounces eternal death and damnation on all*, who cannot conform to the ridiculous sentiments of these mad devotionalists." And a sixth was, "*that, in order to be true Christians, we are absolutely to abandon and renounce all worldly enjoyments and possessions whatsoever; to have all things in common amongst one another; and entirely neglect everything in this life, but prayer and meditation; to be always upon our knees, and at our devotions.*"

Such were the six charges of the Vicar of Dewsbury. They consist of a little truth enveloped in a large amount of scurrilous mendacity. After discussing them, Mr. Bowman proposes to conclude with "some general reflections;" one of which is, that, "the religion of the Methodists inculcates violence, wrath, uncharitableness, fierceness, arbitrariness, and affectation of dominion; and teaches men to hate, reproach, and ill-treat one another." Was this a dream of Mr. Bowman's? or was it a wicked invention? The reverend writer finishes with a personal attack on Ingham, which must have separate attention.

In the year 1740, bread was scarce, and prices were high. Riots occurred in various parts of England; the military were called out, and several persons killed. Yorkshire was the scene of one of these disturbances. On April 26, a mob of about five hundred people assembled at Dewsbury, broke into a mill, and took away all the meal they found. On the next day, which was Sunday, the rioters again appeared, and sacked a second mill. Sir Samuel Armitage, who filled the office of high-sheriff, and Sir John Kaye a magistrate, read the proclamation, and endeavoured to disperse them; but the mob threw stones; and, proceeding to another mill in the parish of Thornhill, captured all the meal and corn, partly pulled down the building, and stole all the miller's beef and bacon. Things were becoming desperate; and the two gentlemen, already named, desired the rioters to assemble at the house of Sir John Kaye, on

Monday, April 28th, where the neighbouring magistrates would listen to their complaints. About a thousand came, beating drums, and carrying colours. Nothing good resulted. The mob retired, shouting; they neither cared for the magistrates nor the high-sheriff. They hurried to three more mills, and decamped with all the edibles the mills contained. They next proceeded to Criggleston, and broke into the barn of Joseph Pollard, and carried away a quantity of flour. Pollard fired at them; and captured several prisoners. On Tuesday, the 29th, Pollard took his captives to Wakefield, to have them tried. The rioters assembled to release their friends; and threatened to pull down Pollard's house; to "hang himself; and to skin him like a cat." Captain Burton,[1] however, boldly advanced to meet them; "knocked down three or four of them with his stick; took six or seven prisoners;" and marched them off to the house of correction. On the same day, a detachment of soldiers were brought from York; and, though great murmurings continued; outward quiet was restored.[2]

Strangely enough, Ingham was accused as the chief promoter of this disgraceful tumult. In the *Weekly Miscellany* for June 8, 1740, the following anonymous communication, from "Yorkshire," was inserted. It was addressed to Mr. Hooker, the editor.

"You have no doubt seen an account, in the public prints, of the riot we had in this county. It took place at Dewsbury, where Mr. Ingham has propagated Methodism. Some will have him to be the author of this insurrection, by preaching up, as he certainly did, a *community of goods*, as was practised by the *Primitive Christians*. How much he may have contributed towards raising the mob, I will not pretend to say; but what I am going to tell you of this clergyman, is matter of fact. I can prove it, and you may make what use of it you think proper. A gentleman of Leeds, who was one of Mr. Ingham's followers, asked him what difference there was between the Church of England and his way of worship? To which Mr. Ingham replied, 'The Church of England is the scarlet whore, prophesied of in the Revelation; and there will be no true Christianity as long as that Church subsists.'

"Your humble Servant."[3]

---

[1] Probably the same as Mr. Justice Burton, who figured so prominently in endeavouring to obtain witnesses, that Charles Wesley was a Jacobite, in 1744. (See C. Wesley's Journal, vol. i., p. 358.)

[2] *Weekly Miscellany*, May 17, 1740.   [3] Ibid. June 8, 1740.

In the then excited state of the country, and especially of Yorkshire, it would have been unwise for Ingham to have allowed such a publication to pass in silence. Hence, he waited upon Hooker, the editor of the *Weekly Miscellany*, who, says he, "received me in a genteel manner, and gave me proof that the letter of June 8th was from Yorkshire." This is something to Mr. Hooker's credit, especially when it is borne in mind that, at that period, he was one of Methodism's bitterest opponents. The result of the interview was, Ingham wrote, and Hooker published the following lengthy letter :—

"LONDON, *June* 14, 1740.

" MR. HOOKER,—In your paper of June 8, you inserted a letter from Yorkshire concerning me. Had I followed my own inclination, I should have taken no more notice of this than of another falsity that was printed some time ago in the *News*, that the woollen manufacture in Yorkshire was likely to be ruined, implying, by me ; and of many more, spread up and down, by common report, which often contradict one another. But the advice of friends has prevailed with me to write this, in answer to what the author of that letter charges me with.

" The author of the letter charges me with two things: directly and indirectly :—

"As to the riot that was lately in Yorkshire, he does not say directly that I was the cause of it ; but he insinuates something like it, as being the consequence of my doctrine. But if this person was not sure that I was the cause of this insurrection, it is very unbecoming, either of a Christian or a gentleman, to hint at such a thing. When the riot happened, I was absent from Dewsbury parish, at the time and several days after. I neither knew nor heard anything of it till it was over. As soon as I heard of it, I spoke against it as a very wicked thing, and of dangerous consequence. I inquired particularly whether any persons that frequented the societies were in it. I heard of three. But one of them had been turned out some weeks before for misbehaviour. The other two, I ordered to be turned out directly, and publicly disowned ; though, I believe, they, as many more, were drawn to run among the rabble, through weakness and curiosity. The gentleman says, some will have me to be the author of the insurrection. It is true, *they say so.* And, indeed, everything that comes amiss is laid to my charge. *They said* I was the occasion of the wet season last summer ; of the long frost in winter ; of the present war ; and, if it blows a storm, some or other *say* I am the cause of it. But this is the talk of the vulgar ; men of sense know better. Does not every one know that, *they say*, a common report is generally false ?

" But, further, to the *second* charge. Supposing I had preached up a community of goods, as this gentleman positively asserts (which I never did), would it thence follow, that people have a liberty to plunder; that they may take away their neighbour's goods by force? If the one was a necessary consequence of the other, then the apostles and first Christians were much to blame in what they did. If all were real Christians, yet it would not be necessary to have a community of goods. None were obliged to it in the apostles' days. They entered into it willingly. But in the present state of things, it would be both absurd and impracticable to attempt such a thing. What might make some people think that I maintained this doctrine, perhaps, was this. I once preached a charity sermon at Leeds, I think, from these words : 'And the multitude of them that believed were of one heart and soul; neither said any of them that ought of the things which he possessed were his own ; but they had all things common.' But I nowhere asserted therein, that we were now obliged to do as they then did. I only exhorted my hearers to imitate the good examples of the primitive Christians, and to contribute generously to the wants of their poor brethren, according to their ability. Now, if this gentleman's mistake arose from this sermon, if he thinks it worth his while to come over to Osset, after my return into Yorkshire,—I promise to let him see the sermon, as I preached it (for it is not altered), that he may be fully satisfied ; for I neither *did*, nor *do* preach up a community of goods.

"The *third* thing which the author of the letter lays to my charge, and which he says is matter of fact, and which he can prove, is this : A gentleman of Leeds, who was one of my followers, asked what difference there was between the Church of England and my way of worship? To which, he says, I replied, 'The Church of England is the scarlet whore, prophesied of in the Revelation ; and there will be no true Christianity as long as that Church subsists.' Now, supposing any gentleman should have asked me such a question (which I do not remember), do these words look like a pertinent answer to such a question? I never pretended to set up a new way of worship. I still live in the communion of the Church of England. My neighbours can testify that I go to church constantly, and receive the sacrament. But, further, I am sure that I never *did*, nor *could* say these words ; for *they are contrary to my settled judgment*. I may have said words like these, yet quite different in their meaning.

"It has been a very common thing for people to misrepresent my sense, and to run away with half a sentence. When I have been preaching the doctrine of universal redemption, and asserting that God made no man purposely to be damned, but that He would have all to be saved, some have reported that I maintained, nobody would be damned. When I have been declaring the riches of God's love and mercy, in receiving the greatest sinners, coming to Him through Christ, some have said that I gave people liberty to live as they list. And, again, when I have been speaking of that purity of heart and holiness of life which the gospel requires, some have said (and it is the general outcry), according to my doctrine, nobody can be saved. I scarce ever preach a sermon but somebody or other misrepresents it. But, I am afraid, I have deviated too much in mentioning these things.

"To return then. I have said that Babylon and the whore, mentioned in the Revelation, relate to more Churches than one; and that the Church of England is concerned therein as well as other Churches; but I never said that she was *the scarlet whore.* I believe, indeed, that, by Babylon and the whore, the Church of Rome is chiefly and principally meant; but, yet, the Scripture saith, she sitteth upon many waters; *i.e.,* people and multitudes, and nations and tongues, all sects and parties (Rev. xvii. 15). For Babylon signifies confusion; and by the scarlet whore is meant corruption, or departing from the truth either in principle or practice (Hos. i. 2 ; ii. 5). Babylon, therefore, or the whore is in, and may be applied to, every Church and person, where there is not a perfect self-denial and entire resignation to God. And are there not multitudes of persons in every Church in Christendom, and consequently in the Church of England, who greatly depart from the truth as it is in Jesus?

"As to the latter part of this accusation,—'There will be no true Christianity as long as that Church exists,'—I absolutely deny that I could say so; because I believe there always was, always will be, and now is, a true Church of Christ, against which the gates of hell cannot prevail. I believe, likewise, that many of the Church of England, and some out of every sect and party, are members of this true Church of Christ. I have, indeed, often said that there is a glorious state of the Church to come, when the partition wall of bigotry, sect, religion, and party zeal will be broken down; and the Jews will be called; and the fulness of the Gentiles shall come in; and the whole earth shall be filled with the knowledge of the Lord, as the waters cover the sea. I do not pretend to know when this time will be; but whenever it commences there will be another face of things in Christendom. The outward pomp and grandeur of the Church will be diminished, and the inward beauty will appear the brighter. The spirit of primitive Christianity will be revived; and, probably, the last state of the Church will be more glorious than the first. It will be happy for them who live in those days; but yet, in the meantime, I believe and hope many will be saved out of all Churches or societies of Christians, and meet together in that blessed place, where there will be no difference or disputing, but all will be love and joy and peace.

"I am, sir, your humble Servant,

"B. INGHAM."[1]

Mr. Hooker, the editor, inserted Ingham's letter; but he did so with reluctance. He snarled even while pretending to be just and generous. Hence he appended an ill-tempered article of his own, from which the following is an extract. Having told his readers, that, "at Mr. Ingham's request, he had published his letter," he proceeds,—

---

[1] *Weekly Miscellany,* June 21, 1740.

"If I recollect the many instances of the great want of *simplicity,
sincerity,* and regard to *truth,* which some other *teachers* among the
Methodists have discovered, I should naturally *suspect* that Mr. Ingham
may not have given a fair account of his case. Or, if I judge of his probity
in *this* instance by his conduct in *others,* the presumption of insincerity
must lie against him. Nay, I think, there are some grounds of suspicion
in his *defence.* But what I insist upon is this,—that his *public conduct is
insincere and dishonest.* While he owns that he communicates with the
Church of England, and by communicating with her, he *subjects* himself
to her *authority,* he sets up separate meetings in *opposition to it,* in
defiance of it, nay, in *defiance* of *all* authority, both *civil and ecclesiastical.*
By this *illegal, disobedient* behaviour to the laws of that *Church* and of
that *civil society,* of which he is a member, he has given just and great
scandal to all good *Christians.* In cases of *public scandal,* the laws of
Christianity and of *common charity* require the person who gives it to ask
public pardon, to *alter his public conduct,* or *publicly to vindicate it.*"

This was hard measure. Poor Ingham had been most
unjustly accused of being the author of the Yorkshire riot,
and had defended himself; and now the editor of the *Weekly
Miscellany* charges him with insincerity, dishonesty, and
causing public scandal; and officiously prescribes that he
should ask public pardon. Hooker was too much of a
partisan to discharge his editorial duties with even-handed
justice. Ingham made no reply to the Editor's unwarrantable
attack; but the latter printed two other letters, in which the
same hostility was rampant. The first was dated, " Wakefield, July 16, 1740," and fills an entire folio page, and nearly
one third of another. In reply to Ingham's statement, that
he was not in the parish of Dewsbury when the riot commenced, nor for several days afterwards, the anonymous
letter-writer calls this "an equivocating way of talking," for
three men of veracity had declared that he was all the while
at Osset, a township in the parish. Can this be true? We
cannot but disbelieve it. Ingham was incapable of such
equivocation. The following extracts also are too manifestly
malignant to be altogether truthful :—

"There were more of Mr. Ingham's followers concerned in the riot than
he would have the world to believe. For one fellow, who had lived with him
several months under the same roof, was one of the ring-leaders of the
rioters,—a very busy man in breaking the miller's utensils, and a kind of
helper of those to wheat flour who had no right to it. This godly man
fled from justice, and has not since been heard of. Another of Mr. Ingham's admirers at Osset very carefully helped himself at the mill; and he

also absconded, till, as he thought, the danger was over, and now he appears again. A third of the Methodists concerned in this riot, was taken up by some of his Majesty's justices of the peace, and was sent to York among other criminals, where he awaits his trial at the next assizes. If Mr. Ingham had inquired as particularly as he pretends, he would have ascertained that when these outrageous men gathered from several towns to seize upon Mr. Pollard's corn at Crigglestone, there were not only two, but two hundred, perhaps many more, of his followers mixed with others in the same wicked design.

"This gentleman denies that he ever preached up a community of goods; and yet one of his former hearers at Osset, who is now returned to the Church, assured me that Mr. Ingham had often done that, and had told his auditors, 'That none of them need to labour, for God would provide for them; and that they must throw themselves upon Jesus Christ, their whole life being spent in religious exercises being no more than sufficient to save their souls; for they who were rich ought to supply the wants of the poor.' 'So,' says he, 'had I followed Mr. Ingham's advice, I should not have been worth a groat.' And even Mr. Ingham's brother declared, 'If I mind our Ben, he will preach me out of all I have.' This information I had from Mr. Glover, of Osset. I am far from thinking Mr. Ingham persuaded any to rise in this tumultuous manner, and charitably hope he did not approve of the riot; yet, when all circumstances are laid together, it is a great presumption that his preaching up a community of goods to men of low condition, was an encouragement to them in this dear season to make bold with more than their own."

"As to the charge about 'the scarlet whore,' the writer acknowledges that when the gentleman in Leeds, who had given the information, was cross-examined, 'he quibbled, gave ambiguous answers, and, in' short, could be fixed to nothing.'"

In reference to Mr. Ingham's "new way of worship," all that the correspondent of the *Weekly Miscellany* can allege, is the following :—

"Mr. Ingham has preached in a croft at Osset to a confused number of people, drawn together from several parishes, which more resembled a bear-baiting than an orderly congregation for the worship of God. When Mr. Rogers,[1] one of his fellow-itinerants, came into these parts, he accompanied him to Westgate-Moor, adjoining to Wakefield, and stood by him, while the other harangued the mob from a stool or table. Mr.

---

[1] The Rev. Jacob Rogers, of Bedford, of whom Wesley, in 1753, wrote as follows :—"Above fourteen years ago, Mr. Rogers, then curate of St. Paul's (Bedford), preached the pure gospel with general acceptance. A great awakening began, and continually increased, till the poor weather-cock turned Baptist; he then preached the absolute decrees with all his might; but in a while the wind changed again, and he turned and sank into the German whirlpool. How many souls has this unhappy man to answer for!" (Wesley's Works, vol. ii., p. 293.)

Rogers, in preaching from 'Beware of dogs,' advised his hearers to beware of the ministers of the present age; for all the ministers now-a-days preach false doctrine to tickle their carnal ears, that they may fill their coffers with money, and preach their souls to the devil. Another of Mr. Ingham's associates, Mr. Delamotte, who is still a laic, being asked by a clergyman why he did not proceed regularly for a degree, and then for orders, answered, 'If you mean episcopal ordination, I assure you I think the gospel of Jesus Christ has nothing to do with it.' Rogers also told the same clergyman, that he was 'as much inspired as St. Paul was, except the working of miracles; and that he could not commit actual sin.' Besides all this, Mr. Ingham keeps his meetings, unauthorized by law, at Dewsbury, Osset, Mirfield, and other places, particularly at Horbury, in this parish, where he prays, sings, expounds, preaches, and visits the sick, without the consent or knowledge of the minister who resides there, though he is always ready to discharge his duty, and is much superior to Mr. Ingham in every respect for the discharge of it. As to the services he uses, it is a medley of his own; for though he makes use of the Common Prayer, he disguises and spoils it by his own additions. Much more might be said about his disorderly meetings, particularly locking himself up with a select number of his hearers till midnight, or after."

The writer thus concludes :—

"Let this intruder, who pretends to act as a minister of the Established Church, say by what Canon in any General Council, by what Constitution in any National Church, he takes upon himself to wander from place to place, sometimes preaching in the fields, and sometimes creeping into private houses, to the great disturbance and disquiet of the lawfully appointed ministers, and raising schisms and distractions in a Church established upon primitive antiquity."[1]

The other letter was not dissimilar to the one already quoted. It was dated, "Dewsbury, August 18, 1740," and signed "A Layman;" and was published in the *Weekly Miscellany*, on August 30th. This charitably alarmed "Layman" brands the Methodists as "hot-headed enthusiasts;" speaks of Ingham and Delamotte as "those high pretenders to purity and holiness;" and stigmatises the latter as an "enthusiastic babbler," pouring out "effusions of nonsense." The following is the concluding paragraph :—

"Whatever sorry evasions Mr. Ingham may make to extenuate his wickedness in being instrumental to the riot at Dewsbury; yet, it is certain that he is highly culpable, and was, if not at the bottom, the sole cause of it. The principles he instils into his adherents are such as, when

---

[1] *Weekly Miscellany*, July 26, 1740.

known, no better consequences could be expected than those that have followed: and what further mischief may ensue, if he be not restrained, is shocking to consider:—no less than the introducing of Popery, or, at least, some measures of his own destructive to the tranquillity and happiness of the community."

In the same month in which this layman's letter was published, Mr. Bowman, the reverend vicar of Dewsbury, finished his furious pamphlet on "The Imposture of Methodism Displayed;" and, of course, was too zealously honest to be silent respecting the riot. Mr. Hooker's correspondents were meekness itself compared with this pamphleteering pugilist. He declares, he "never met with so much downright falsehood, such trifling evasions, and matter so foreign to the purpose" as he had met with in Ingham's letter in the *Weekly Miscellany.* He asserts, that, during the riot, Ingham "had a constant communication with several of the inhabitants, by means of his nocturnal assemblies; and, that, he had rashly given out, some little time before the riot happened, that, *in a few hours' warning, he could have ten thousand men ready for any emergency.*" Mr. Bowman writes:—

"Ingham's conduct was, at that time, so much taken notice of and suspected, that the magistrates were almost determined to apprehend him, as a disturber and incendiary; and, I believe, were only deterred from it, in consideration of what might happen from the fierceness and fury of his adherents. Were it requisite, I could name several of his great favourites and abettors, who had no small share in these disturbances. I myself heard two of his principal associates, three days before the affair happened, insinuate that such a thing was shortly to be expected, and that the people might be justified in what they did. Whence we may reasonably presume, that this horrid villany could nowhere be hatched but in these infernal assemblies." . . . "I can prove by the incontestable evidence of great numbers, both of his constant and accidental hearers, that a *community of goods* is a common topic of discourse with him, in his sermons, in his expositions, and in his private conversation also. I know, that, he has endeavoured to persuade several of his followers to sell their estates and possessions, as the first Christians did, for the relief of their poor brethren; and that he has declared over and over, *That private property was inconsistent with Christianity; and that as long as any one had anything of his own, he could not enter into the kingdom of heaven.*" . . . "It is surprising to the last degree that a set of incorrigible wretches should be thus suffered to trample with impunity on all laws, ecclesiastical and civil; to spread doctrines subversive both to religion and the state; to form secret assemblies and cabals, in order to disturb the repose of society, and throw everything into confusion and disorder. No one in the world is a heartier friend to toleration, or would make more favourable allowances to tender consciences, than myself; but, God forbid! that, under the notion of toleration, we should give opportunity to cheats and impostors to sow their hemlock and night-shade among us; to extirpate all traces of true religion and virtue; or to traitors and rebels to sap the foundation of our civil constitution; to deliver up our king and our country to ruin."

Thus, *nolens volens*, was Ingham branded as a *Communist*, and the author of the Yorkshire riots. It was far from pleasant to be pelted with such paper pellets; but there was no help for it. In every age, the inspired text has been literally fulfilled, "All that will live godly in Christ Jesus shall suffer persecution." We are not prepared to justify every-thing which Ingham said and did; but we are prepared to deny, with righteous indignation, that he was a *communist* and a *rioter*. His enemies were too bitter to be truthful. His utterances respecting the members of the primitive Church were perverted to serve a maligant purpose. They might, on some occasions, be unguarded; but they were not intended to sanction communistic politics. He himself repudiated such intention; but his adversaries persisted in their unrighteous accusation, and made it worse by charging him with men-dacity. It was hard usage; but not uncommon among the Moravians and Methodists. The newspaper controversy re-specting Ingham was ended; but, for ten months afterwards, Mr. Hooker employed almost every number of his *Weekly Miscellany* in abusing the Methodists, and Wesley and White-field in particular.

This is a long account of what some may deem a compa-ratively unimportant chapter in Ingham's life; but, we trust, it may not be altogether uninteresting and useless; first, be-cause, we believe, this was the only newspaper warfare that fell to Ingham's lot; and, secondly, and especially, because it shows the unfavourable circumstances under which John Nelson began to preach, and the difficulty there must have been in instituting Yorkshire Methodism only a few months afterwards.

Ingham's ministerial labours were not confined to his native county. John Bennett brought him into Derbyshire.[1] We

---

[1] *Memoirs of Mrs. Grace Bennett.*

have also seen, that, he paid frequent visits to the metropolis. Bedford, likewise, and the vicinity were favoured with his preaching. His Christian sympathy was world-wide. Six years before, he had crossed the Atlantic to convert the Indians. He was an active member of the Moravian "Society for the Furtherance of the Gospel"; and having, by some means, become acquainted with the great Dissenter of the day, the Rev. Dr. Doddridge, proposed him as one of its corresponding members. Hence the following letter sent to Doddridge :—

1741
Age 29

"LONDON, *August 6th*, 1741.

"DEAR SIR,—I have here sent you the letters I promised you. I am also to inform you, that you are chosen to be a corresponding member of the 'Society for the Furtherance of the Gospel.' Before you expressed your desire to me, I had already proposed you to the committee, who all approved of you; and, after the meeting was over, when I mentioned you to the society, they all unanimously chose you without balloting; so that, when you are in London, you will not only have the liberty to hear the letters and accounts read, but also to meet with the members about business,—and, further, to be in the committee. The brethren will be glad to hear from you as often as you please, and they, from time to time, will send you some accounts of the transactions of the Society. I gave what you entrusted me with to the box. Mr. Moody gave a guinea. Brother Spangenberg and all the brethren salute you.

"Your affectionate friend and brother in Christ,
"B. INGHAM."

Doddridge's answer was as follows :—

"NORTHAMPTON, *August 8th*, 1741.

"REV. AND DEAR BROTHER,—I am thankful to the 'Society for the Furtherance of the Gospel' for their readiness to admit so unworthy a member, and hope, as the Lord shall enable me, to approve myself cordially affectionate, though incapable of giving much assistance.

"I did this day, in our Church meeting, publicly report some important facts from Brother Hutton and others, as to the success of our dear Moravian Brethren and their associates. We rejoiced in the Lord at the joyful tidings, and joined in recommending them to the grace of God. I hope Providence will enable me to be a little serviceable to this good design. I shall gladly continue to correspond with the Society, and gladly hope to have some good news from these parts ere long. In the mean time, I humbly commend myself to your prayers and theirs.

"The conversation at Mr. Moody's, on Monday morning, has left a deep impression on my heart. Salute my dear brethren, Messrs. Spangenberg and Kinchin, with Mr. Hutton, etc. I shall hope to hear when that blessed herald of our Redeemer, Count Zinzendorf, arrives. We long to see you. God brought me home in peace, and I found all well here. My wife and other friends salute you in the Lord.

"I am, dear sir, your unworthy but affectionate friend in our gracious Lord,

"PHILIP DODDRIDGE.

"P.S.—I have looked over several of the letters with great pleasure, and heartily thank you for sending them. Glory be to Him, who causes His gospel to triumph, and magnifies the riches of His grace in getting Himself the victory, by soldiers, who, out of weakness, are made strong. If Christ raise to Himsel. a seed among the Negroes and Hottentots, I will honour them beyond all the politest nations upon earth that obey not His glorious gospel."[1]

This Missionary Society, of which Ingham was one of the chief members, though still in its infancy, had already accomplished a most marvellous and blessed work. Its origin was remarkable. In 1731, Count Zinzendorf visited Copenhagen, for the purpose of being present at the coronation of Christian VI., king of Denmark. Whilst there, some of the count's servants became acquainted with a negro, from the island of St. Thomas, in the West Indies. The negro told them of the ardent desire of many of the slaves in that island to be taught the way of salvation ; but added, that their labours were so incessant that they had no leisure for religious instruction ; and that the only way to reach them was for the missionary himself to become a slave, and to teach them during their daily toils. This was related to the Brethren of Herrnhut ; and the result was, two young men, Leonard Dover and Tobias Leupold publicly offered to go to St. Thomas's, and even to *sell themselves as slaves*, if they could find no other way of preaching to the negroes. Thus began the Moravian missions to the heathen ; and, within ten years, at the time when Ingham proposed Doddridge as a corresponding member of the Society for the Furtherance of the Gospel, missionaries had been sent to St. Thomas's, to St. Croix, to Greenland, to Surinam, to the Rio de Berbice, to several Indian tribes in North America, to the negroes in South Carolina, to Lapland, to Tartary, to Algiers, to Guinea, to the Cape of Good Hope, and to Ceylon.

Among others greatly benefited by Ingham's ministry, were

---

[1] Memoirs of James Hutton, p. 59 and 60.

the four daughters of the Earl of Huntingdon, Lady Anne, Lady Frances, Lady Catherine, and Lady Margaret Hastings. While on a visit at Ledstone Hall, in Yorkshire, they were induced, by motives of curiosity, to hear him preach in a neighbouring parish. He was then invited to preach in Ledsham Church; and became a frequent visitor at the Hall. When in London, the Ladies Hastings attended the preaching of the Moravians and first Methodists. Under this ministry, they were given to see the insufficiency of their own righteousness and the method of salvation on which they had been resting, and were made willing to receive the Lord Jesus Christ as the foundation of their hope and trust. Lady Margaret was the first who received the truth; and the change effected, by the Holy Spirit, on her heart soon became visible to all. Considering the obligations she was under to the grace of God, she felt herself called upon to seek the salvation of her fellow-creatures, and the promotion of their best and eternal interests. Next to her own soul, the salvation of her own family and friends became her care. She exhorted them faithfully and affectionately, one by one, to " flee from the wrath to come;" and the Lord was pleased to make her the honoured instrument of the conversion of not a few of them. Her brother, the ninth Earl of Huntingdon, had been married to Lady Selina Shirley, second daughter of Earl Ferrers; and it is a fact too interesting to be omitted, that, the conversion of this remarkable woman was, under God, the result of a casual remark which fell from Lady Margaret. The two conversing one day, on the subject of religion, Lady Margaret observed, " That since she had known and believed in the Lord Jesus Christ for life and salvation, she had been as happy as an angel." This scrap of Methodist lovefeast-experience was " a word spoken in due season." It led to self-examination, and to scriptural inquiry; and Selina, Countess of Huntingdon, never rested until she also had found peace with God through faith in Christ.

Lady Margaret Hastings was united in marriage to Mr. Ingham, on November 12th, 1741, at the residence of her brother, the Earl of Huntingdon, in London. The union was a happy one. To the last moments of his life, Ingham expressed the highest veneration and affection for his wife, and was honoured with the intimate friendship of several of her noble relatives. The marriage, in some aristocratic circles, was considered a *mésalliance*, and furnished food for scandal in the fashionable world. "The Methodists," said the Countess of Hertford, "have had the honour to convert my Lord and Lady Huntingdon, both to their doctrine and practice; and the town now says, that Lady Margaret Hastings is certainly to marry one of their teachers, whose name is Ingham." "The news I hear from London," wrote Lady Mary Wortley Montague, from Rome, "is that Lady Margaret Hastings has disposed of herself to a poor, wandering Methodist preacher." The higher classes of society indulged in ridicule; the poor Moravians gave thanks to God, and prayed for the newly-wedded couple. Ingham wrote to inform the Brethren of his marriage, and the Brethren sang for him the hymn beginning—

> "Take their poor hearts, and let them be,
> For ever closed to all but Thee," etc.

Ingham had enemies, some of them, as already shown extremely bitter; but one of them, at least, was doubtless well pleased with Ingham's marriage. By this event, the Vicar of Dewsbury got rid of a neighbour who had greatly troubled him; for Ingham now removed from Osset, the place of his nativity, to Aberford, a village about five miles from Tadcaster, and sixteen miles south-west of York; and here he continued to reside until his death.

It has been already stated that, on July 30th, 1742, nine months after his marriage, Ingham formally transferred his Yorkshire and Lancashire societies, above fifty in number, to the Moravians; and, henceforward, these societies were placed under the control of the Moravian ministerial conclave at Smith House, near Halifax.

Besides these societies, however, Ingham was connected with others. A great work had been wrought in the midland counties. The Rev. Jacob Rogers, a clergyman of the Established Church, had preached with much power and success at Bedford. Mr. Francis Okeley had assisted him; and thither Ingham repaired, and preached several times in St.

Paul's Church, to vast multitudes, who listened to him with profound attention. The number of converts increased daily, and were formed into societies, like those in Yorkshire. Being formed, the next point was how to manage them. Ingham was consulted ; and, by his advice they, also, were placed under the care of Moravian ministers. This prepared the way for the settlement of the United Brethren at Bedford, in 1745 ; and for the erection of their chapel there in 1751.

By these arrangements, Ingham freed himself from an immense amount of personal responsibility. His old friend, Wesley, was not only forming societies, but ruling them. On the contrary, Ingham formed societies, and left them to be ruled by others. By this means, Moravianism found admission to the midland counties, and instituted a flourishing and permanent Church in Yorkshire and the neighbourhood round about. Ingham was left at liberty to be what he evidently liked,—an evangelist at large. He was also helped by earnest co-adjutors. There were the Batty Brothers,—Lawrence, William, and Christopher, of Catherine Hall, Cambridge, sons of Mr. Giles Batty, a man of considerable respectability, who resided at Newby Cote, near Settle. The three brothers were all eloquent and popular preachers. Then there was John Nelson, the sturdy Methodist, whom Ingham left behind at Birstal. Also David Taylor, formerly footman to Lady Ingham, —a man who had been converted under Ingham's ministry, and who, notwithstanding certain vacillations, was a great and successful preacher, and raised societies in Derbyshire, Leicestershire, and in some parts of Lancashire and Yorkshire. Others might be mentioned, if space permitted.

Ingham had no warmer friend than Whitefield, who watched the steps taken by his old acquaintance with the utmost interest. The following letter will not be considered out of place :—

" LONDON, *May 6th*, 1743.

" MY DEAR BROTHER,—Your very kind letter I had not the pleasure of receiving till yesterday. It was very acceptable, and knits my heart closer to you than ever. I love your honest soul, and long for that time when the disciples of Christ, of different sects, shall be joined in far closer fellowship one with another. Our divisions have grieved my heart. I heartily approve of the meeting of the chief labourers together.

" I am just returned from a circuit of about four hundred miles.   I have been as far as Haverfordwest, and was enabled to preach with great power. Thousands and tens of thousands flocked to hear the word, and the souls of God's children were much refreshed.

" I am glad the Lord hath opened fresh doors for you, my dear brother. The rams' horns are sounding about Jericho ; surely the towering walls will at length fall down. But we must have patience. He that believeth doth not make haste. The rams' horns must go round seven times. Our divisions in England have the worst aspect, while they are now united in Wales ; but even this shall work for good, and cause the Redeemer's glory to shine more conspicuously. This is my comfort,—' The government is upon His shoulders,' and He is a 'wonderful counsellor.'

" But where am I running ? Pardon me. I am writing to my dear Mr. Ingham. I rejoice in the expectation of seeing you in town. I hope to be in town at the time, and to enjoy some of our former happy seasons. In the mean while, I salute you from my inmost soul ; and desire, as often as opportunity offers, a close correspondence may be kept up between you and, my dear brother, your most affectionate unworthy brother and ser-vant,   " GEORGE WHITEFIELD."

Ingham was now one of the most influential members of the Moravian Church, in England ; and, accompanied by Mr. and Mrs. James Hutton, and the Sisters, Esther Kinchin, Mary Bowes, and Martha Ireland, set out on May 20th, 1743, to attend a Moravian Synod, to be held at Hirschberg, in Germany, from the first to the twelfth of July inclusive. This important Synod seems to have supervised the Moravian operations generally ; including not only the affairs of the English Churches, but those of the Continent and Livonia, where fourteen hundred labourers of the Brethren were employed in endeavouring to bring men to a knowledge of the truth as it is in Jesus.

So far as the English community was concerned, it was determined :

" That, the London Church should be regarded as a choir of labourers (distinct from the Society and its general meetings, etc.); each member of which was to consider him or herself as in preparation, by the Lord, for future service in any station, post, or office, to which He might call them.

" That this Church, as a body of labourers, consisting of only a few souls who were wholly devoted to our Saviour, might enjoy all the privileges and discipline of a Church elsewhere, which the mere members of Society, by reason of their not dwelling together, could not enjoy.

" That this Church should be in stillness, none knowing of it but such

as were in it. (See Rev. ii. 17.) This London Church, also, should cleave
to the Pilgrim Church, as the body to its soul.

"The Pilgrim Church was described as a congregation of labourers
who go hither and thither; whom no one knows but he to whom it is
revealed.[1] Every one who has a whole mind to our Saviour, is a member
of it. It is composed of persons who indissolubly cleave together, as a
testimony in the Saviour's wounds, against all who are unfaithful; witnesses whom the Lord will preserve in the hour of trial; souls who neither
have nor desire any abiding city in this life, and who labour for the good
of others among all religions, but never form themselves into a sect.

"This Church is not the Moravian Church, but its servants, sojourn-
ing so long in it as the children and servants of God, or rather the
spiritual Church of God, has freedom of action and is acknowledged.
This relationship to the Moravian Church remains only so long as she
herself abides faithful.

"The connection between London and Yorkshire was thus defined:
That London, as a choir of labourers (a small flock hidden as yet and
acting quietly), should provide labourers for Yorkshire, and train up
souls which were to be sent from Yorkshire for the purpose; Yorkshire
being the county where our Saviour exhibited His Church openly, and
where, for the present, the congregation of the Brethren should be settled.
The London Church being private, was to have a particular connection
with Yorkshire, and be, in a measure, dependent upon it, inasmuch as the
chief elders were at this time there."

The above are extracts from the Memoirs of James Hutton,
at that period, the chief of the London Moravians. It is difficult for an outsider to understand and rightly interpret some
of the expressions; but, upon the whole, it appears, 1. That
the chief settlement of the Moravians was in Yorkshire; and,
2. That London was the training college of their ministers.

It is a well-known fact, that 1744 was a year of great
anxiety. England was threatened with a French invasion, and
with the unwelcome presence of the Jacobite Pretender. A
large number of loyal addresses were presented to the king.
Wesley wrote one on behalf of the Methodists, but his brother
Charles successfully objected to its presentation, because its
being sent, in the *name of the Methodists,* would constitute
them a sect, at least would *seem to allow* that they were a
body distinct from the Church of England. The same difficulty was felt by the Moravians; and, on April 23, a Confer-

---

[1] A pilgrim, according to Zinzendorf's definition, is "a Philadelphian
(lover of the brethren), with a Moravian coat and a Lutheran tongue."
("Hutton's Memoirs," p. 118.)

 ence of six persons met in London, respecting the Address. Ingham went all the way from Yorkshire, to be present ; and seems to have been the presiding spirit. The Conference perceived that, when so many addresses were being presented to the king, the Moravians might be regarded with suspicion, unless they also presented one ; but the perplexity was how to designate the Moravian community. The Wesleys were unwilling for the Methodists to be regarded as Dissenters from the Church of England, and so were the Moravians. Brother Neisser, one of the Conference, attempted to solve the difficulty by observing, that " the English brethren, who had joined the Moravian Church, were not, on that account, Dissenters from the English Church." They had taken such a step merely " to enjoy the blessed discipline of the Apostolic Churches, which was wanting in the English Church." This was a solution scarcely sufficient to relieve the mind from doubt ; but an address was written ; and, on April 27, Ingham Hutton, and Bell went to Court, and, being admitted to the chamber of audience, Ingham delivered into the hand of the king the document which had been prepared. His Majesty, smiling graciously, accepted the same, and Ingham kissed his hand. The following is an extract :--

To the King's Most Excellent Majesty.—The humble Address of his Majesty's Protestant subjects, the United Brethren in England, in union with the ancient Protestant Episcopal Bohemian and Moravian ·
Church :—

" Presented to his Majesty by the Rev. Mr. Ingham, Mr. Hutton, Mr. Bell, Registrar of the said Congregation in London.

" Most Gracious Sovereign,—May it please your sacred Majesty graciously to accept this Address, which, with all humility, is presented by your Majesty's most dutiful and loyal subjects, the United Brethren in England, in union with the Bohemian and Moravian Church.

" We are, though despised and hated, and few in number, a happy people, consisting of persons out of several sects and parties of Protestants, who, from an earnest concern for our own salvation, and a zeal for the good of others, are united together ; and, for the sake of her excellent discipline, are in union with the ancient Protestant Episcopal Bohemian and Moravian Church, one of the earliest witnesses against, and sufferers by, the Papists ; a sister of the Church of England ; their doctrines also, in the fundamental points, being the same."

Having thus defined themselves, they then declare affectionate loyalty to his "Majesty's sacred person, family, and government;" and their "abhorrence for Popery and Popish pretenders,"—and conclude thus :—

"We, therefore, shall stand by your Majesty to the utmost of our power, and especially by our prayers, which are our only weapons.

"May the Lord of hosts direct all your Majesty's councils and undertakings, and turn the design of all your enemies into foolishness! The Lord our God be with you. Amen.

"Presented in behalf of all the United Brethren in England, in union with the Bohemian and Moravian Church. April 27, 1744."[1]

This Address will help to define the position in which Ingham stood, with reference to the Moravian Church and the Church of England.

There is another important fact belonging to the year 1744. For some reason,—probably the disturbed state of the country,—the Brethren were prohibited preaching in the open air; and, from this period, Ingham relinquished all out-door services. In this, also, he differed from his quondam friend Wesley, who, for forty-seven years afterwards, persisted in "field-preaching."

It has been already stated that Smith House, near Halifax, had been made the head-quarters of the Moravian community in Yorkshire. This took place about the year 1741. In 1743, Mr. Holmes, the proprietor of the place, died ; and, on account of his widow not being well-disposed towards her peculiar tenants, the Brethren found it necessary to look out for another and more permanent establishment. Just at this juncture, Zinzendorf visited Yorkshire ; and, one day, when climbing a mountain on which Bank House, near Pudsey, stood, he had such a sweet feeling and deep impression of the place, that he called it *Lamb's Hill*," fully believing, that, it would become the site of a Moravian settlement. Strangely enough, the Hill soon afterwards was advertised for sale ; in 1744, Ingham, at the request of a Moravian synod, bought it ; and, on the 10th of May, 1746, the foundation stone of "Grace Hall, at Lamb's Hill," was laid amid great rejoicing. At six in the afternoon, the whole congregation came together, and sang a hymn, after which, Toltschig delivered an address.

----

[1] Hutton's Memoirs, p. 152.

A letter was read from Lady Ingham, expressing her great satisfaction in regard to the building of the Hall; the stone was to have been laid by Ingham, but, being unexpectedly detained in Lancashire, the office was performed by Toltschig, and the ceremonial was concluded with singing songs of praise. The building was completed in 1748; choir houses and schools were added; private dwellings were erected; and a Moravian settlement was established, which, in 1763, was called Fulneck, Ingham all the while being the proprietor of the soil.[1] Wesley visited the place in 1747, and wrote:—

"We walked to the new house of the Germans. It stands on the side of a hill, commanding all the vale beneath, and the opposite hill. The front is exceeding grand, though plain, being faced with fine, smooth, white stone. The Germans suppose it will cost, by the time it is finished, about three thousand pounds: it is well if it be not nearer ten. But that is no concern to the English Brethren; for they are told (and potently believe), that 'all the money will come from beyond the sea.'"

Thirty-three years after this, Wesley paid another visit. The following extract, from his Journal, will show how Fulneck had increased:—

"1780. *April* 17.—I walked to Fulneck, the German settlement. Mr. Moore showed us the house, chapel, hall, lodging-rooms, the apartments of the widows, the single men, and single women. He showed us likewise the workshops of various kinds, with the shops for grocery, drapery, mercery, hardware, etc., with which, as well as with bread from their bakehouse, they furnish the adjacent country. I see not what but the mighty power of God can hinder them from acquiring millions; as they, 1. Buy all materials with ready money at the best hand; 2. Have above a hundred young men, above fifty young women, many widows, and above a hundred married persons; all of whom are employed from morning to night, without any intermission, in various kinds of manufactures, not for journeymen's wages, but for no wages at all, save a little very plain food and raiment; as they have, 3. A quick sale for all their goods, and sell them all for ready money. But can they lay up treasure on earth, and, at the same time, lay up treasure in heaven?"

This is not the place to write a history of Fulneck; but merely to show Ingham's connection with it.

It was about this period (1746), that Ingham and Grim-

---

[1] The property is now held of Ingham's descendants, on a lease for five hundred years. (*Methodist Magazine*, 1848, p. 1,099.)

shaw, of Haworth, became acquainted; and once, and sometimes twice, a year, Grimshaw preached throughout Ingham's
circuit. The Societies increased rapidly, and spread, not only
in Yorkshire, but also in Westmoreland, Cumberland, Lancashire, Lincolnshire, Derbyshire, and Cheshire. General meetings of the preachers and exhorters were held with frequency,
several of which were attended by the Countess of Huntingdon and Lady Margaret Ingham. Grimshaw invariably
attended these meetings, and always preached, never troubling
himself to ask the consent of the minister, or caring whether
he liked it or not. Sometimes the two itinerant clergymen
met with treatment far from pleasant.

As a specimen, the following may be given. Ingham, and
Mr. Batty, one of his preachers, had been several times to
Colne, and had succeeded in establishing a small society.
Occasionally they were accompanied by Grimshaw; and, in
this instance, the three commenced a meeting by the singing
of a hymn. As soon as they begun, the Rev. George White,
the notorious vicar of Colne and Marsden, rushed into the
house, staff in hand, attended by the constable and a mob
collected from the lowest and most depraved people of the
town. White sprang towards Batty with intent to strike
him. Ingham, perceiving the danger of his friend, instantly
pulled him out of the reach of his clerical assailant, and
retired into an adjoining room. The vicar and the constable
threatened to put the master of the house into the parochial
stocks, and attempted to take him away by force. The man
demanded the constable's authority; and the official, finding
that he had none, was obliged to release his prisoner. White
and his officer of the peace then insisted, that, Ingham and
Grimshaw should sign a paper, promising not to preach in
the parish of Colne during the next twelve months, under a
penalty of fifty pounds. The demand was met by a firm
refusal; and now the "Captain-General," as White was designated, ordered the mob to lead away their captives. This
was done, and, on the way, every friend who attempted to
speak to them was abused and beaten. New proposals were
made, that, Grimshaw and Ingham should give a written promise not to preach at Colne for six months, and then two;
but without success. Magnanimously giving up the written

1748
Age 36

document, the mob asked a promise *upon their word and honour;* but this proposal also was rejected. Finding it impossible to coerce the three evangelists, the rioters let loose their vengeance. Ingham, Grimshaw, and Batty were violently dragged along the road, with clubs brandished about their heads. They were pelted with mud and dirt; and, with Ingham's coat torn and hanging on the ground, were conducted to the Swan Inn, there to receive magisterial justice at the hands of the Rev. Mr. White.[1]

In 1747, the chief labourers, Ingham, Gambold, Hutton, and Okeley, attended a Synod at Herrnhaag, in Germany. Many English affairs were carefully considered, especially the history of the English congregations since 1737, and the gradual separation of the Brethren's labours from those of the Methodists. The peculiar choir regulations were gradually introduced into England. The Discourses of Zinzendorf, the Church Litany, the Liturgies, the Common Prayers of the Brethren, and the Hymns of the Day, were translated into English; and the more intimate the acquaintance of the English Brethren became with German formularies, the more the Methodistic element was banished from among them. The Brethren and Methodists moved *alongside* of each other; and, not unfrequently, there was considerable flank-firing.

In July, 1748, Whitefield arrived in England, after an absence of nearly four years. Ingham wrote to his old friend, who sent the following affectionate reply :—

"LONDON, *August* 11, 1748.

"MY VERY DEAR MR. INGHAM,—Your kind letter, which I received but yesterday, having been taken a little tour in the country, both grieved and pleased me. Glad was I to find, that, my dear old friend had not forgotten me; and yet sorry, at it were, that, I had not written to him first. I was just going to put pen to paper, when yours was brought to my hands. I read it with joy; and now embrace the first opportunity of answering it with the greatest pleasure. These words concerning our Lord have always been weighty on my heart : 'Having loved His own, He loved them unto the end.' They, therefore, that are most like Him, will be most steady in their friendship, and not very readily given to change. O my dear sir, what has the Redeemer done for us since we used to take such sweet counsel together at Oxford ! Blessed be His name

---

[1] Life and Times of Lady Huntingdon, vol. i., p. 260.

for giving you a heart still to preach among poor sinners the unsearchable riches of Christ ! May you go on and prosper, and, maugre all opposition, see Dagon fall everywhere before the ark ! As for me, I am a poor worthless pilgrim, and thought long ere now to be with Him, who has loved and given Himself for me. But it seems, I am not yet to die, but live. Oh that it may be to declare the work of the Lord ! I think, this is the thirteenth province I have been in within this twelve-month, in each of which our Lord has been pleased to set His seal to my unworthy ministry. I came from *Bermudas* last, where I left many souls seeking after Jesus of Nazareth. In London, Bristol, Gloucester, and Wales, the glorious Emmanuel, since my arrival, has appeared to His people. In about a fortnight, I purpose leaving town again, in order to go a circuit of about five hundred miles. I need not desire you to pray for me : I need not tell you how glad I shall be, whenever opportunity offers, to see you face to face. In the meantime, let us correspond by letter. May Jesus bless it to us both ! I return cordial respects to Lady Margaret. I pray the Lord to bless her and her little nursery. For the present, Adieu !

"I am, my dear Mr. Ingham, ever yours,

" GEORGE WHITEFIELD."

In course of time, Whitefield came to Yorkshire ; and Ingham and Batty accompanied him throughout the county, and occasionally preached with him. They were also his companions into Lancashire and Cheshire. He preached four times at Aberford, the place of Ingham's residence ; and everywhere immense crowds attended him. The tour was a triumphal one ; and, moreover, the two old Oxford friends were reunited. In one place, Whitefield mounted a temporary scaffold to address the thousands who stood before him ; and, with a solemnity peculiarly his own, announced his text,—" It is appointed unto men once to die ; but after this the judgment." No sooner had the words escaped his lips, than a terrifying shriek issued from the centre of the congregation. Grimshaw hurried to the place where Whitefield stood, and shouted,—" Brother Whitefield, you stand among the dead and dying,—an immortal soul has been called into eternity,—the destroying angel is passing over the congregation,—cry aloud and spare not." A few moments elapsed, and Whitefield re-announced his text ; when another loud shriek was heard ; a shriek which, in this instance, came from the spot where the Countess of Huntingdon and Lady Margaret Ingham were standing. A *second* person had dropped down dead. Consternation was general ; but Whitefield

1750
Age 38

proceeded with the service, and, in a strain of tremendous eloquence, warned the wicked to flee from the wrath to come.[1] Who can adequately conceive, and paint the scene just mentioned? Whitefield on a platform,—thousands assembled before him,—two in the midst of them, in an instant, struck with death,—the Incumbent of Haworth rushing to the preacher with his irrepressible exclamation,—and two noble ladies, with Ingham at their side, gazing at the awful spectacle, their souls thrilled with feelings which no language can describe. And yet, if not in regard to the death occurrences, in point of solemn sublimity and religious grandeur, Whitefield's life was full of such scenic facts.

Mention has been made of Ingham and Whitefield becoming reunited. During this same evangelistic tour, efforts were used to reunite Ingham and his old friend Wesley. Seven years before, they had separated. Both were intensely conscientious, and were actuated by the purest religious motives; but their course of action was different. Ingham was a Moravian: Wesley was a Methodist. The two designations were often used synonymously; and yet their meanings were widely different. By order of Zinzendorf, an advertisement had been published, in the *Daily Advertiser*, declaring, that, the Moravians had no connection with the Wesleys. Angry pamphlets, on both sides, had been issued; and angry feelings, both among Moravians and Methodists, had been kindled. It was hardly possible for Ingham and Wesley to live on the same terms of intimate friendship as they had done at Oxford and in Georgia. There is no evidence, that, they ever *quarrelled;* but they were undoubtedly *estranged.* This was painful both to themselves and to a certain circle of their friends; and, as above stated, means were used to reunite them. Hence the following, extracted from a letter, addressed to Wesley, by the Rev. Mr. Milner, Incumbent of Chipping, in Lancashire, who accompanied Whitefield, Ingham, and Grimshaw in their glorious visits to Manchester, Stockport, and other places :—

"CHIPPING, *January* 11, 1750.
"MY MOST DEAR AND REV. BROTHER, WHOM I LOVE IN THE

---

[1] Life and Times of Lady Huntingdon, vol. i., p. 266.

TRUTH,—I have had twice the pleasure of seeing Mr. Ingham; and must say, there is a great deal of amiable sweetness in his whole behaviour. I have often and earnestly wished that he was disentangled from the Moravians, and cordially *one* with you in promoting the interests of the gospel. The last time I saw him, he was employed in reconciling two of the Brethren, who had run great hazards and suffered much hardship in the service of the gospel. He allows you incomparably the preference for prudence; but says, you have not done the count" (Zinzendorf) "justice. He adds, that, he endeavoured to prevail with you not to publish the Difference;[1] and thought he had prevailed, till he heard that it was published;—and that he would gladly have been reconciled, and got Mr. W——d" (Whitefield) "to go from his house to N——e" (Newcastle), to bring about a reconciliation; but you were not inclined to it,—'the time being not yet come.' At first, I looked upon the difference, as that betwixt Paul and Barnabas, which was a furtherance of the gospel of Christ; but since I knew more of the doctrine of the *still Brethren*, I have not had the same favourable opinion of them. Yet, I cannot help thinking, Mr. Ingham is happy. May some good Providence bring you speedily together! For, surely, such souls must glow with love at meeting, and all unkindness fly at first sight!"[2]

So far as it concerned Ingham, things were now coming to a crisis. For about a dozen years, he had been a Moravian; but Moravianism, always eccentric, was now becoming arrogant. Everything was carried on upon a higher scale, both in diet and clothing, with a view to the benevolent but impracticable design of abolishing the distinction between the different stations in life. This, however, only tended to make persons of low degree exalt themselves above their station in society, which, in more respects than one, was really injurious. Then there was also a season of trial, which is known in the Brethren's Church, under the name of '*the great sifting,*'— especially from 1745 to 1749. The Yorkshire Diary of the Brethren, 1747—1749, speaks of "the *light and trifling spirit,* which had crept into almost all the congregations, both in doctrine and practice;" and joins "in thanksgiving to the Head of the Church, who had caused a deep shame and contrition to take place in the hearts of the true Brethren and Sisters." In June, 1749, Zinzendorf addressed a pompous

---

[1] Doubtless, a Tract, of twenty-four pages, published by Wesley, in 1745, and entitled "A Short View of the Difference between the Moravian Brethren, lately in England, and the Rev. Mr. John and Charles Wesley."

[2] *Methodist Magazine*, 1797, p. 512.

 letter to the Archbishop of Canterbury, giving him a catalogue of the Moravian Bishops, Administrators of Tropuses, and Evangelics. He spoke of himself as, " Lewis, by Divine Providence, Bishop, Liturgus, and Ordinary of the Churches known by the name of the Brethren ; and, under the auspices of the same, Advocate during life, with full power over the hierarchy of the Slavonic Unity, Custos rotulorum, and Prolocutor both of the general Synod, and of the Tropus of Instruction." In a postscript, he made a characteristic attack on Sherlock, Bishop of London, as follows :—

" P.S. The Bishop of London has acted wrongfully and most injudiciously for the interest of his own Church; inasmuch, as he has not only declined intercourse with the Brethren, but likewise communicated a private decision to a certain Deacon of our Church. He has sinned against the first principles of uprightness, equity, and prudence ; and, by doing so, has done dishonour to the ecclesiastical order. It is not your part to threaten and to act insolently, but cautiously ; for your interest, and not ours, is concerned.

" LEWIS, Bishop, with his own hand."

To say the least, this was hardly modest, on the part of a foreigner, when addressed to the highest dignitary of the English Church. It is also noticeable, that, in the list of Bishops, Administrators of Tropuses, Evangelics, and Primary Ministers, sent to his Grace of Canterbury, the name of Ingham is not included. Why was this?

Further,—a new "Church Litany," of great length, and curious construction, had been published, and was now in use in the Congregations of the Brethren. Lindsey House, in Chelsea, was bought of Sir Hans Sloane ; and, at a great expense, was converted into the head-quarters of English Moravianism. Zinzendorf was the pope of the English Brotherhood. All bishops and elders were subordinate to him ; and, under the name " Papa," he was exclusively the ruler of their Church. He caused to be published a Hymn-book, in two volumes ; the second of which was filled with doggerel of the worst description. He had had the effrontery to ask the English Parliament to pass an Act, not only recognising the *Unitas Fratrum* as an ancient Protestant Episcopal Church ; but also exempting them from taking oaths ; from being summoned as jurymen ; and, in the American colonies, from being called upon to engage in military service. Marvellous to relate, all this was granted ; but one demand of the Moravian "Papa" was rejected. He asked for power to be vested in himself, to enjoin upon the bishops and ministers of the Church of England to give certificates, that, the parties holding them, were members of the *Unitas Fratrum;* and, therefore, entitled to the exemptions specified. The Lord Chancellor objected to this putting of the prelates and clergy of the Established Church beneath the power of a foreign count. "Against the will of the king," exclaimed this modest man ; "I would not like to press the matter ; but a *limitation of the Act* I will not accept. Everything or nothing. No modifications." This was German rodomontade ; for, rather than lose his Bill, he relinquished his claim to be empowered to coerce the bishops and clergy of the English Church to grant the certificates. The Act of Parliament was passed on the 12th of May, 1749. A few months afterwards, Zinzendorf published a folio volume, entitled "Acta Fratrum in Anglia," and containing, besides the Moravian public negotiations in England, an exposition of the Moravian doctrine, liturgy, etc. The book was full of repulsive jargon ; and the less that is said respecting it the better.

Besides all this, an enormous debt had been contracted. A crop of lawsuits sprung up. Zinzendorf and others were in danger of arrest. Bankruptcy was imminent ; disgrace was great ; and scandals of all kinds were rife. Henry Rimius, "Aulic Counsellor to his late Majesty the King of Prussia," published an octavo pamphlet of 177 pages, in which Zinzendorf was accused of flagrant falsehood. Wesley read the pamphlet as soon as it was printed ; and wrote, " I still think several of the inconsiderable members of that " (Moravian) "community, are upright ; but I fear their governors wax worse and worse,—having their conscience seared as with a hot iron."

Whitefield, in 1753, published "An Expostulatory Letter, addressed to Nicholas Lewis, Count Zinzendorf, and Lord Advocate of the Unitas Fratrum," in which he charges Zinzendorf and his friends with "Misguiding many honest-hearted Christians ; with distressing, if not ruining, numerous families ; and with introducing a whole farrago of superstitious, not to say idolatrous, fopperies into the English nation."

 Another pamphlet was published, at the same time, and created considerable excitement. Its long title will suggest an idea of its contents. "A true and authentic Account of Andrew Frey: containing the occasion of his coming among the Hernhutters, or Moravians; his Observations on their Conferences, Casting Lots, Marriages, Festivals, Merriments, Celebrations of Birth-Days, impious Doctrines, and fantastical Practices, Abuse of charitable Contributions, linen Images, ostentatious Profuseness, and Rancour against any who in the least differ from them; and the Reasons for which he left them; together with the Motives for publishing this Account. Faithfully transcribed from the German."

Wesley writes,—

"1753, *November 3rd*. I read over Andrew Frey's reasons for leaving the Brethren. Most of what he says, I knew before; yet, I cannot speak of them in the manner in which he does; I pity them too much to be bitter against them.

It would not be pleasant to enter into further details. Enough has been said to show that, Ingham had sufficient reasons to sever his connections with the Moravians. He had found the money for the purchase of the land about Grace Hall (Fulneck); and, in 1753, asked for the repayment; but money was not forthcoming, and he agreed to receive a yearly rental of £30 instead of it.[1]

The particulars of Ingham's separation from the Moravian community have not been published; but he now formed a circuit of his own of about five hundred miles, and had several thousand followers. Members were received by laying on of hands; they had elders; and the feast of charity; and the Lord's Supper once a month.

Ingham was the chief of the new sect in Yorkshire and the neighbouring counties. One of his principal co-workers was Mr. J. Allen; who, in 1752, and when only eighteen years of age, became a preacher in the Inghamite connexion. Allen was the eldest son of Oswald Allen, Esq., of Gayle, in the county of York. His father intended him for the ministry in the Established Church, and placed him under the care of a clergyman, whose inconsistency of conduct seems to have

---

[1] Hutton's Memoirs, pp. 221 to 280.

shocked his pupil, and to have made him doubt the propriety of entering into holy orders. In 1748, he was sent to Scorton School, near Richmond, in Yorkshire, conducted by the Rev. Mr. Noble. In the year following, he had the opportunity of hearing Ingham preach, and was converted. In 1751, he was admitted into St. John's College, Cambridge; and, a year afterwards, as already stated, began himself to preach. For many years, he was one of the most useful and popular preachers in Ingham's connexion; and his conduct throughout life was becoming a minister of Christ.[1]

Besides Allen, the three Battys, already mentioned, Lawrence, William, and Christopher,—Ingham's other coadjutors were Hunter and Brogden, both of whom had been in the British army; also James Hartley, Richard Smith, and James Crossley, all of whom had been awakened under the thundering preaching of Grimshaw, the Incumbent of Haworth; and the first and second of whom ultimately became pastors of Baptist congregations; and the third, a minister of an Independent Church at Bradford. Mr. Molesworth, likewise, of Thornhill, and Mr. Fleetwood Churchill, gentlemen descended from families of rank, and moving in the upper ranks of life, were faithful fellow-labourers. All these were earnest evangelists, and most of them suffered serious persecution for the Word of God, and the testimony which they held.[2]

Ingham's separation from the Moravians altered his relationship to the Methodists; and, at Wesley's Conference, held in 1753, it was asked, "Can we unite, if it be desired, with Mr. Ingham?—*Answer:* We may now behave to him with all tenderness and love, and unite with him when he returns to the Old Methodist doctrine."[3] Two years after this, Wesley held his yearly Conference at Leeds; and Ingham summoned several of his preachers to meet him there for the purpose of attending the Conferential sittings. Wesley admitted Ingham; but his coadjutors were excluded. Was it Ingham's wish to amalgamate his Societies and preachers with the Methodists? This is a question, we

---

[1] *Evangelical Magazine*, 1814, p. 306.
[2] Life and Times of Countess of Huntingdon, vol. i., p. 270.
[3] Minutes of Methodist Conferences, vol. i., p. 717. The 1862 edition.

cannot answer. One matter, however, was discussed in which Ingham, as an ordained Clergyman of the Church of England, must have felt interest. Wesley writes :—

> "The point on which we desired all the preachers to speak their minds at large was, 'Whether we ought to separate from the Church?' Whatever was advanced, on one side or the other, was seriously and calmly considered; and, on the third day, we were all fully agreed in that general conclusion,—that, whether it was lawful or not, it was not expedient."[1]

Supposing that Ingham wished for an amalgamation, this was a decisive answer to his proposal, for already Ingham had separated from the Church, not only by the formation of societies and the employment of lay preachers, but also, and especially, by the institution of separate sacramental services.

Some time after the Conference at Leeds, Ingham went to Derbyshire and Lincolnshire, and thence to Ashby, on a visit to Lady Huntingdon. During his stay, he preached frequently, at her ladyship's and in the neighbourhood, to large congregations. On his return to Yorkshire, the Countess accompanied him, and visited most of his northern societies.

Whilst she was in Yorkshire, a conference of his preachers was held at Winewall, when, as at Wesley's first Conference, in 1744, doctrine and discipline were discussed.

In reference to *Doctrine*, it was agreed :—1. That Justification consists in the forgiveness of sins, and an imputation of Christ's righteousness; and, that, the instrumental cause of this is faith in Christ. 2. That, sanctification consists, not in holy actions, but, in the divine life, new heart and spirit, which are given by Jesus Christ at our justification; and love, joy, and peace, and all the graces or fruits of the Spirit. 3. That, all good works spring from this, as fruit from a tree.

With regard to *Church Government*, it was resolved, That, there should be a *general overseer*, chosen and appointed by the Trustees and by the consent of the Societies.

As was natural, Ingham was set apart to this office; and he proceeded to elect one of the Batty brothers and Mr. Allen, as fellow-helpers; who, after giving an account of their conversion and call to the ministry, and, being examined respect-

---

[1] Wesley's Works, vol. ii., p. 313.

ing the doctrines they had preached, and intended to preach in future, were then and there solemnly ordained, by the laying on of Ingham's hands, and prayer.

1756
Age 44

In this respect, Ingham was far ahead of his old friend Wesley; for it was not till twenty-eight years after this, that Wesley assumed episcopal functions, by ordaining two of his preachers for America.

From this period, Lady Huntingdon used to call Ingham a *Bishop;* and, in doing so, her ladyship was not seriously wrong. There can be little doubt, that, Ingham, like Wesley, held the opinion, that, "bishops and presbyters are the same order, and consequently have the same right to ordain"; and, assuming this to be correct, there can be no question, that, he, being an acknowledged Presbyter of the Church of England, was also a Bishop.

But to let that pass. Lady Huntingdon, though on the most friendly terms with Ingham, was very far from being satisfied with several of the rules of the Inghamite Societies; and, hence, whilst a visitor at Ingham's house at Aberford, she conferred with him respecting an amalgamation with the Methodists. Whitefield proceeded to Newcastle-on-Tyne, where, it is said, he met the two Wesleys, and was commissioned by Ingham to offer them his house at Aberford, for the purpose of discussing the subject. Charles Wesley readily assented; but his brother as decidedly objected; and, from that time forth, no further steps were taken to effect a union with the Methodists.

Charles Wesley became an ardent friend and advocate of Ingham. Hence the following extracts from his journal :—

"1756, *October 1st.*—I had an opportunity of vindicating my old friend, Benjamin Ingham. It is hard a man should be hanged for his looks,—for the *appearance* of Moravianism. Their spirit and practices he has as utterly renounced as we have : their manner and phrase cannot as soon be shaken off."

Again :—

"1756, *October 7th.*—I rode on to Aberford. My old friend, Mr. Ingham, was labouring in the vineyard; but I had the happiness to find Lady Margaret at home, and their son Ignatius. She informed me, that, his round takes in about four hundred miles; that, he has six fellow-labourers, and one thousand souls in his Societies, most of them converted. I sincerely rejoiced in his success. Ignatius was hardly pacified at my not preaching. We passed an hour and a half very profitably, and set out again."

The Rev. William Romaine, also, became one of Ingham's frequent visitors, and was received by him and Lady Margaret with every mark of respect and affectionate attention. Indeed, at a period when Romaine's stipend was quite inadequate to provide sustenance for his family, his necessities were often liberally met by Lady Ingham's bounty. Ingham sometimes accompanied him in his preaching excursions into several parts of the county of Durham ; Romaine preaching wherever he obtained a church, and Ingham in the Methodist Chapels and private houses. Long after this, Romaine remarked in reference to Ingham's societies,—

" If ever there was a Church of Christ upon earth, that was one. I paid them a visit, and had a great mind to join them. There was a blessed work of God among that people, till that horrid blast from the north came upon them and destroyed all.

This horrid northern blast must be explained. In 1755, Hervey published his "Theron and Aspasio," in three octavo volumes. In 1757, Robert Sandeman issued an elaborate reply, in two volumes octavo, entitled, "Letters on Theron and Aspasio, addressed to the Author of that Work." Very erroneous were some of the views of Sandeman, but, all who have read his publication must admit that he was a man of considerable ability. His work, however, was blemished, not only by heterodox expositions of holy Scripture, but by severe attacks on the chief evangelical preachers and authors of the day. A furious controversy succeeded ; and a large number of pamphlets and tracts bearing on the subject were printed. Sandeman's volumes themselves were in great demand, and, in less than five years, three editions of them were published. His principal doctrine, from which all his other erroneous teachings sprang, was his doctrine of Christian faith. Hervey, Whitefield, Erskine, and others, substantially acquiesced in Wesley's definition, namely, " Christian faith is not only an assent to the whole gospel of Christ, but also a full reliance on the blood of Christ ; a trust in the merits of His life, death, and resurrection ; a recumbency on Him as our atonement and our life, *as given for us, and living in us."* Perhaps it would sound less sectarian to say, that the whole of these distinguished men held the doctrine of the Homilies of the Church of England : " The right and true Christian faith is, not only to believe, that holy Scripture and the articles of our faith are true, but also, to have a sure trust and confidence, to be saved from everlasting damnation by Christ; whereof doth follow a loving heart to obey His commandments." Or, again; a man's "sure trust and confidence in God, that, by the merits of Christ, his sins are forgiven, and he reconciled to the favour of God." " Three things must go together in our justification. Upon God's part, His great mercy and grace ; upon Christ's part, the satisfaction of God's justice, by the offering His body and shedding His blood, with fulfilling the law perfectly and thoroughly ; and upon our part, true and lively faith in the merits of Jesus Christ. So that, in our justification, there is not only God's mercy and grace, but His justice also. And so the grace of God doth not shut out the righteousness of God in our justification ; but only shutteth out the righteousness of man ; that is to say, the righteousness of our works. And, therefore, St. Paul declareth nothing on the behalf of man concerning his justification, but only a true and living faith, which itself is the gift of God. And yet that faith doth not shut out repentance, hope, love, and the fear of God, to be joined with faith in every man that is justified. But it shutteth them out from the office of justifying. So that although they be all present together in him that is justified ; yet they justify not altogether." (*Homilies of the Church of England.*)

Sandeman's views were widely different, as a few extracts from his book will show :—

" Every doctrine which teaches us to do, or endeavour any thing toward our acceptance with God, stands opposed to the doctrine of the Apostles ; which, instead of directing us what to do, sets before us all that the most disquieted conscience can require, in order to acceptance with God, as already done and finished by Jesus Christ. What Christ has done, is that which pleases God ; what He hath done, is that which quiets the guilty conscience of man as soon as he knows it ; so that, whenever he hears of it, he has no occasion for any other question but this, ' Is it true or not ?' If he finds it true, he is happy ; if not, he can reap no comfort by it. If, then, we slight the comfort arising from the bare persuasion of this, it must be owing, at bottom, to our slighting this bare truth, and to our slighting the bare work of Christ, and our considering it as too narrow a foundation whereon to rest the whole of our acceptance with God." (Vol. i., p. 17.)

" Whatever doctrine teaches us to think, that our acceptance with God is begun by our own good endeavours, seconded by Divine aid, or even first prompted by the Divine influence, leads us to look for acceptance with God by our own righteousness; for whatever I do, however assisted or prompted, is still my own work. Aspasio tells us, ' Faith is a real persuasion that Christ died *for me.*' This account of faith somewhat resembles the arch of a bridge thrown over a river, having the one end settled on a rock, and the other on sand or mud. That Christ died, is indeed a truth fully ascertained in the Scriptures; that Christ died *for me,* is a point not so easily settled. This is a point which the Scripture nowhere ascertains; so far from it, that it often affirms the final perdition of many, not merely hearers of the gospel, but who have heard and received it with joy; yea of those who have made such progress, that their only deficiency is, that their fruit came not to perfection." (Ibid. p. 20.)

" Men are justified by the knowledge of a righteousness finished in the days of Tiberius; and this knowledge operates upon them, and leads them to work righteousness." (Vol. ii., p. 190.)

" The change made upon a man by the gospel, is called *repentance unto life,*—a change of a man's mind to love the truth, which always carries in it a sense of shame and regret at his former opposition to it." (Ibid. p. 193.)

" No man can be assured, that his sins are forgiven him, but in as far as he is freed from the service of sin, and led to work righteousness; for the favour of God can only be enjoyed in studying to do those things which are well pleasing in His sight." (Ibid. p. 194.)

" When once the saving truth is admitted in the conscience of any man, it becomes, as it were, a new *instinct* in him, encouraging him to draw near to God, providing him with an answer to the condemning voice of the law, which haunted his conscience before, and opposing the natural pride of his heart, in the exercise of which he formerly lived. By this instinct, he is led to desire 'the sincere milk of the word, that he may grow thereby.' And he arrives at the proper consciousness and enjoyment of life, when he comes to full age, and, *by reason of use, has his senses exercised to discern both good and evil.*" (Ibid. p. 200.)

" If, notwithstanding our natural bias against the gospel, our heart condemn us not, as destitute of love to that truth which the world hates, then have we confidence toward God, even as much confidence as the testimony of our own conscience can give us. Yet this is but one witness, and needs to be supported. Here then the Spirit of the truth gives His testimony, as a second witness supporting the former. And this He does, by shedding abroad in the heart, such an abundant sense of the divine love as casts out the anxious fear of coming short of life everlasting. Thus, that love to the truth, which formerly wrought in the way of painful desire, attended with many fears, is perfected, by being crowned with the highest enjoyment it is capable of in this mortal state." (Ibid. p. 203.)

"Perhaps it may be thought needful, that I should define what I mean by the *popular doctrine*; especially as I have considered many as preachers thereof, who differ remarkably from each other ; and particularly as I have ranked amongst them Mr. Wesley, who may justly be reckoned one of the most virulent reproachers of God that this island has produced. I consider all those as teachers of the *popular doctrine*, who seek to have credit and influence among the people, by resting our acceptance with God, not simply on *what Christ hath done*, but more or less on *the use we make of Him*, and the advance we make toward Him, or some secret desire, wish, or sigh to do so; or on something we feel or do concerning Him, by the assistance of some kind of grace or spirit; or, lastly, on something we employ Him to do, or suppose He is yet to do for us. In sum, all who would have us to be conscious of something else than the bare truth of the gospel; all who would have us to be conscious of some beginning of a change to the better ; or some desire, however faint, toward such change, in order to our acceptance with God." (Ibid. p. 300.)

Perhaps, the reader has had enough of the misty dogmas of Robert Sandeman. The foregoing extracts contain the kernel of his heresy. By the obedience and sufferings of Christ, a number of persons, the elect, are accepted or justified of God. The gospel declares this. It is the sinner's privilege and duty to believe this general statement ;—not to *believe on* Christ as *his* Saviour (for he has no authority to do that), but simply to become persuaded of the truthfulness of the gospel's general declaration, that a select number are accepted of God, solely and entirely, because of the finished work of Christ. This persuasion, in the course of time, and in the case of the accepted persons, produces what Sandeman calls *repentance unto life*. For a season, they have "anxious fears of coming short of everlasting life." Their love to the truth works "in the way of painful desire, attended with many fears." At length, however, they attain to such a state, that their conscience testifies, they are "not destitute of love to that truth which the world hates ;" and now "the Spirit of the truth gives His testimony, as a second witness, by shedding abroad in the heart such an abundant sense of the divine love, as perfects their love to the truth, and crowns it with the highest enjoyment it is capable of in this mortal state."

This, in brief, was Sandeman's way of salvation—a huge heresy tagged to the glorious truth, that man is accepted of

God solely through the meritorious work and sufferings of Christ. This is not the place for its refutation. Suffice it to remark, that, in 1759, Ingham read Sandeman's " Letters on Theron and Aspasio," and also Glass's " Testimony of the King of Martyrs ; " and that this was the means of bringing upon Ingham's societies the " horrid blast from the north," so strongly deprecated by the Rev. William Romaine.

The Rev. John Glass, about the year 1728, had been expelled from the established Church of Scotland, and had formed a number of Churches conformable, in their institution and discipline, to what he apprehended to be the plan of the first Churches of Christianity. Sandeman was an elder in one of these Churches. The chief practices in which they differed from others were :—their weekly administration of the Lord's Supper ; their love feasts, of which every member was not only allowed, but required to partake, and which consisted in their dining together at each other's houses in the interval between the morning and afternoon services ; their kiss of charity, used on this occasion, at the admission of a new member, and at other times, when they deemed it to be necessary or proper ; their weekly collection before the Lord's Supper, for the support of the poor, and defraying other expenses ; mutual exhortation ; abstinence from blood and things strangled ; washing each other's feet, the precept concerning which, as well as other precepts, they understood literally ; community of goods, so far as that every one was to consider all that he had in his possession and power as liable to the calls of the poor and the Church ; and unlawfulness of laying up treasures on earth, by setting them apart for any distant future, or uncertain use ; the allowing of public and private diversions so far as they were not connected with circumstances really sinful ; and the employment of a plurality of elders, pastors, or bishops, in each Church, and the necessity of the presence of two elders in every act of discipline, but the administration of the Lord's Supper. In the choice of these elders, want of learning, and engagements in trade, were not regarded as disqualifications for office, but a second marriage was. The elders were ordained by prayer and fasting, imposition of hands, and giving the right hand of fellowship. In their discipline, they were strict and severe,

and thought themselves obliged to separate from the com- 1759
Age 47
munion of all such religious societies as appeared to them not
to profess the simple truth to be their only ground of hope,
and who did not walk in obedience to it. In every Church
transaction, also, they esteemed unanimity to be absolutely
necessary.

Such were the Glassites or Sandemanians more than a
hundred years ago. In an evil hour, after reading the publications of Glass and Sandeman, Ingham sent his fellow-helpers,
Mr. Batty and Mr. Allen, *privately* to Scotland, for the purpose of acquiring more distinct and detailed information
respecting this Scottish sect. At Edinburgh, they were introduced to Sandeman ; and at Dundee, to Glass ; and returned
to Yorkshire thoroughly converted to the Sandemanian
theology and discipline. Warm debates took place in
Ingham's societies respecting the nature of a *true* Church.
and respecting their former views of religious experience.
Many became jealous of the authority which Ingham exercised ; but he steadfastly adhered to the validity of his commission as general overseer, and wished the dissatisfied to
withdraw. Frequent attempts were made to reconcile the
two contending parties : the Countess of Huntingdon wrote
letters ; Romaine paid a personal visit ; and Whitefield
prayed and wept ; but all was ineffectual. Disputes without
end arose ; excommunications followed ; and thus the great
work over which Ingham had most religiously watched,
was nearly wrecked. Out of upwards of eighty flourishing
Churches, only thirteen remained under Ingham's care. This
was probably the severest trial of his life, and was one
from the effects of which he never afterwards recovered.[1] It
would be incorrect and uncharitable to assert, that, all who
were excommunicated or seceded, ceased to be Christians.
Dr. Stevens says, "many of them were merged in the
Wesleyan or Dissenting bodies, especially in the class of
Scotch Presbyterians called Daleites."[2] Mr. Allen formed a

---

[1] Sandemanianism was afterwards introduced into New England, but
failed by its own distractions. Sandeman died in Danbury, Connecticut.
His tomb is still preserved there, and slight traces of his system linger in
the vicinity. (Stevens' History of Methodism, vol. i., p. 393.)

[2] Stevens' History of Methodism, vol. i., p. 392.

[3] The Daleites derived their name from David Dale, Esq., a successful

1760

Age 48

number of them into a separate Church, and officiated as their pastor until his death, in 1804. The Messrs. Batty also continued to preach; and, in 1761, published, at Kendal, a Hymn Book of 136 pp., entitled, "A Collection of Hymns for the Use of those that seek, and those that have, Redemption in the Blood of Christ." Many of the hymns are thorough doggerel. Some other of the seceding preachers also "remained useful men; and the disaster was much relieved by the consideration that Wesleyan Methodism took general possession of Yorkshire, and by the fact, that two Methodist orders were hardly necessary at the time of Ingham's failure."

Efforts were not wanting to conserve and perpetuate the work. In September, 1760, Lady Huntingdon and the Rev. William Romaine joined Ingham, at a general meeting of his societies, held at Wheatley, when the choice of Church officers was determined by lot. They also visited, in company, several of the brotherhoods in Yorkshire and Lancashire, Ingham and Romaine preaching alternately, almost every day. At Thinoaks, in Craven, where they remained several days, there was a large assemblage of people, and two elders were ordained. There, also, it was agreed to recommend to the different societies in the connexion to make collections every Sabbath; and the following circular was issued :—

"DEAR BRETHREN,—Being mindful of the words of the Apostle Paul, we have determined to recommend to our Societies to have voluntary collections on the first day of the week, to defray all expenses relative to the preachers, meetings, etc., etc. Farewell !"

Nothing more need be said of this unhappy schism, except quoting a sentence from Wesley's sermon, preached at the laying of the foundation stone of City Road Chapel, in 1777. With an undoubted reference to Ingham, he remarked :—

"Nearly twenty years ago, immediately after solemn consultation on

---

man of business, who, after being agent for the sale of the cotton yarn of Sir R. Arkwright, became, in 1785, the proprietor of the cotton mills at Lanark. A lawsuit, between the magistrates of Glasgow and the General Session, led Mr. Dale to secede from the established kirk. Having began to preach, he was the means of founding several Independent Churches in Scotland; and, after an active and useful life, died, greatly lamented, in 1806, aged sixty-seven. (*Evangelical Magazine*, 1807, p. 49.)

the subject, a clergyman, who had heard the whole, said, with great
earnestness, ' In the name of God, let nothing move you to recede from
this resolution. God is with you for a truth ; and so He will be, while
you continue in the Church ; but whenever the .Methodists leave the
Church, God will leave them.' Lord, what is man ! In a few months
after, Mr. Ingham himself left the Church, and turned all the societies
under his care into congregations of Independents. And what was the
event? The same that he had foretold ! They swiftly mouldered into
nothing."

Unlike his friend Wesley, Ingham made but little use of
the printing-press.   In 1748, he published a Hymn Book, of
96 pp., 12mo, with the title, " A Collection of Hymns for
Societies.   Leeds : Printed by James Lister, 1748."   The
book, now extremely scarce, contains eighty-eight hymns ;
five of which are translations from the German, by John
Wesley; fifteen are by Watts ; five by Cennick ; and three by
Charles Wesley.   How many Ingham himself contributed is
not known.   The following serves as a sort of Preface :—

" In singing, two things ought to be regarded. The one is to sing in
outward harmony, keeping the tune ; and, if we do not understand it, 'tis
better to be silent and hear others, or to sing low and after others, that
we may not make a discord, which is disagreeable, and causes confusion ;
and, in general, it is not well to sing so very high and loud. But the other
and more material thing to be regarded is, seriously to mind what we are
about,—to be present with our thoughts,—to meditate upon the matter ;
and, above all, to sing with grace in the heart to the Lord. This makes
singing sweet and heavenly ; and, without this, our singing can neither be
edifying to ourselves nor to others."

Ingham's only other publication was a small volume,
entitled, " A Discourse on the Faith and Hope of the
Gospel. Leedes : Printed for the Author, by Griffith Wright,
1763." 12mo, 207 pp.
This, though a small, was an important book, for it contained
the views of Ingham, on the chief doctrines of the Christian
religion, immediately after he had read the works of Glass
and Sandeman. There can be no question, that, he substantially embraced the dogmas which they had so boldly
propounded. The following extracts are confirmative of this.
The reader will excuse the length of them, on the ground, that
they exhibit the principal articles of Ingham's creed towards

1763
Age 51

the close of life. The book is pervaded by a fine Christian spirit ; and, here and there, almost waxes eloquent.

> "Every true and real minister of Jesus Christ hath a divine commission, or is sent of God." (Preface.)
>
> "I believe, that the whole counsel of God to the Church is faithfully recorded in the holy Scriptures." (Ibid.)
>
> "I believe no servant of Christ hath now any new revelation to deliver ; but, I also believe, that no man can clearly comprehend or truly understand the holy Scriptures without the illumination of the Holy Ghost. Yet, the Holy Ghost neither revealeth, teacheth, impresseth, or applieth anything to any person now, but what is either expressly written, or is agreeable to the analogy of faith delivered, in the holy Scriptures." (Ibid.)
>
> "It is my opinion, that, both the doctrine and also the very words of Scripture, in the languages wherein they were originally written, were inspired by the Holy Ghost. The translation of the Holy Scriptures into the modern tongues hath been a great blessing, and of very great use to the cause of Christianity. Yet, men of learning, who have studied the originals, know that some places are falsely translated, and others weakly and lamely. It would be well worth the labour of all the learned men in every nation to conspire together to publish an accurate translation." (p. 5.)
>
> "To believe a thing meaneth to assent to, and credit it as true. To believe *in* a thing meaneth to confide or trust in it, to rely or depend on it." (p. 6.)
>
> "The faith of the Gospel is the believing of God's testimony concerning Christ and His righteousness, and believing in Jesus Christ and His most perfect and Divine righteousness, as the only sure ground of the hope of eternal life." (p. 9.)
>
> "Sinners are neither justified for their own believing, nor their own obeying, nor for both together ; neither for the truth or sincerity of their believing, or any act of faith, nor anything they have done, can do, or ever will do. Neither are they justified for anything wherein they differ from others, or excel others, nor for anything done or wrought in them, or received by them ; for the whole and sole cause of the justification of sinners is the active and passive obedience of Jesus Christ, called the righteousness of God, 'which is unto all and upon all them that that believe.'" (p. 13.)
>
> "This work of Christ,—His most perfect and divine righteousness,—His obedience in all things, and even unto death, is the whole and sole cause of the salvation of sinners. There needeth no other requisite, neither less nor more, neither little nor great. This alone is complete and all-sufficient." (p. 35.)
>
> "Yet, the generality of men lay the greatest stress upon something else. And even those who lay some stress upon it more or less connect something else with it, whereon they also lay some stress, more or less. So that they do

not believe that God is well and fully pleased with the work of Christ, as alone sufficient for salvation without anything else at all ; but that God is placable, or willing to come to terms with them, upon condition that they themselves first perform those other things which they think necessary, either in whole or in part, as preliminaries to make peace with God." (p. 39.)

1763
—
Age 51

" If any should object, and say, that the Lord Jesus and the apostles connected repentance with faith and remission of sins, I allow it. Repentance and faith are duties required by the gospel, because God commandeth all men everywhere to repent and believe the gospel. It is man's duty to do whatever God commandeth." (p. 40.)

" Repentance to life is the change made upon the mind by the gospel, when a man is turned from darkness to light, and from the power of Satan unto God. His understanding being enlightened, he ceases to work for acceptance ; he turns to God, believing that He is well pleased in His beloved Son. This repentance, as well as faith, is the gift of God. And they are both given at the same time." (p. 40.)

" Some modern divines have defined faith to be *a confidence that Christ loved me and gave Himself for me;* but this is not the faith of the gospel, though it hath passed current for it with many for a long time. It must indeed be granted that, if a person can say that Christ hath loved him and given Himself for him, upon as good ground as the Apostle Paul said it of himself, he is a true believer. Yet it is presumed that many believe the gospel and will be saved, who neither can, in truth, nor dare say this." (p. 42.)

" No one hath the assurance of his eternal salvation upon his first believing the gospel, or can have it, till his faith hath wrought some time, more or less, by love. No man can be assured that he shall be eternally saved without any possibility of falling away, but by the sealing, witness, or testimony of the Holy Ghost. But that no one is sealed by the Spirit upon his first believing the gospel is proved by Ephesians i. 13." (p. 43.)

" Those, who have the faith of the gospel, have not obtained it by their own labour, or by any acts exerted by their own minds ; but it hath been freely given to them from above, by Him who of His own will begetteth His people with the word of truth. So that it is as easy to believe in the gospel, when Christ is revealed to any person, as it is to see or hear, when a man hath eyes and ears." (p. 60.)

" The faith of the gospel is a working faith. Justification and sanctification are inseparably connected together." (p. 90.)

" All true believers are sanctified, but they are not equally sanctified ; for there are children, young men, and fathers in Christ. They are sanctified in all the faculties of their souls, but not completely sanctified as yet in any one of them." (p. 138.)

" Some argue, *that God, in the word of the gospel, maketh an offer of Christ and His righteousness, as a free gift, to all indefinitely who hear the gospel; and also promiseth remission of sins and eternal life; and, further, that God's word is a sufficient warrant to every one to lay claim to the gift, and that Faith is a receiving of the gift;*

but then it must be an appropriating and applying faith. For no man is possessed of a gift till he receives it; but, in receiving it, he obtains a special interest in it, which he had not before. That God, by the word of the gospel, maketh known to all indefinitely who hear it, that He is well pleased in His beloved Son, and that He giveth His Son and remission of sins and eternal life to all who unfeignedly believe the gospel with understanding, is as surely true as God's word is true. And, that no man is possessed of a gift till he receives it, and that in receiving it he obtains a special interest in it, is also true. It is also granted that no man hath Christ, or a special interest in Him, but he that receiveth Him. But, then, doth any man receive Christ before he believeth the gospel? Coming to Christ, receiving or embracing Him, looking to Him, trusting or confiding in, relying or depending upon Him and His divine righteousness, belong to faith, and always accompany it ; although they may be deemed immediate consequent effects of it " (p. 142).

" I cannot approve the doctrine, which some teach, that a man may become perfect at once, or assured of his salvation, by putting forth some sort of an act of faith." (p. 155.) " God generally worketh gradually both in nature and in grace." (p. 156.)

" Believers, by keeping the Father's commandment to believe on the name of Jesus Christ ; and by obeying the new commandment, not in word, but in works,—attain the testimony of their own heart and conscience, that they are of the truth. Herein, also, they have the sure testimony of the word of God, whereby they are to try and judge themselves. And the Holy Ghost, as the Comforter, will be given to them, by whose testimony they will know and be satisfied that they are the children of God." (p. 171.)

" Be it observed that I have limited no time, how long it is, or how long it must be, before any man is sealed by the Holy Ghost after he believeth the gospel. This dependeth upon the good pleasure of Almighty God." (p. 175.)

" Those writers and preachers, who maintain that the assurance of salvation cometh by a direct act of faith, or by the appropriating act of faith, or by any other sort of an act of faith, are mistaken ; for it cometh by no act of faith, but by the testimony of a believer's own conscience, and by the testimony of the word and Spirit of God." (p. 179.)

" Some writers and preachers lay down so many steps and stages of conviction, and speak of so many different sorts of faith that they greatly perplex the minds of serious people. But this is not the worst of it. Such doctrine hath a tendency to teach people to establish their own righteousness, and to turn away their minds from the atonement made by the blood of Christ ; for, when they hear such doctrine, they are very apt to examine whether they have gone through such exercises of soul, and whether they have put forth such acts of faith ; and, if they think that they have not, they are perplexed and distressed to no purpose ; but, if they think that they have, they are ready to build upon such things, which may be nothing but their own workings and fancies, and so get into a good conceit of themselves to their own loss and damage." (p. 181.)

"True believers are too apt to live by other things than by Christ alone. It is the duty of every believer to keep the faith, and constantly to live by believing in Christ. This is a lesson not soon or easily learned. To keep the faith, in opposition to the natural propensity which is in us all, to live by our own righteousness, or something of our own, is the principal part of the Christian warfare. It is like the pendulum in a clock, which moves all the wheels. If the pendulum stops, then the whole clock stands. All our strength to obey flows from believing in Christ." (p. 185.)

"All the heavenly frames, sweet sensations, manifestations of God's love, all the joys and comforts, are all and each of them valuable blessings, for which God's people should be thankful; but they should not live by them, but by Christ. All the works and duties of believers, which are done in faith and love, which is in Christ Jesus, are pleasing to God; all the doctrines revealed in the book of God ought to be regarded and believed; the promises, threatenings, and precepts of the word of God should be used as the Lord Jesus used them when He was on earth; all the ordinances and means of grace should be conscientiously observed; but believers are not to make a Christ of any of these things, nor to live by them, but by Christ Himself." (p. 188.)

These extracts are long, but they serve to exhibit Ingham's views of the way of a sinner's salvation. Substantially, they are the same as Sandeman's, and were doubtless derived from him. One cannot but regret that Ingham suffered himself to be led astray by the hazy dogmatisms of the new Scottish sect, instead of adhering to the Scriptural views of his friend Wesley.[1] Of his sincerity there cannot be a doubt; but, in trying to make the salvation of a sinner more simple, he made it vastly more dubious and difficult. How different were these misty speculations to the plain, straightforward teachings of the Methodists! Their adoption by the truly converted and godly societies, raised up by Ingham and his friends, was a fatal error, and renders it no matter of regret, that, societies espousing and propagating such principles gradually dwindled, and nearly became extinct.

Before taking our leave of Ingham's book, a few lines may be added concerning its general merits, apart from its doctrinal heresies; and these shall be given as an extract from a review,

---

[1] Wesley writes: "1765. January 20, I looked over Mr. Romaine's strange book on the 'Life of Faith.' I thought nothing could ever exceed Mr. Ingham's, but really this does; although they differ not an hair's breadth from each other, any more than from Mr. Sandeman." (Wesley's Works, vol. iii., p. 193.)

1763
Age 51

written by Samuel Drew, the able and honest editor of the *Imperial Magazine*, for 1823. After adverting to Ingham's doctrinal peculiarities, Mr. Drew proceeds :—

"Notwithstanding these blemishes, Mr. Ingham's treatise contains innumerable excellencies, fully entitling it to the patronage which has carried it through four editions. Though Faith and Hope form its distinguishing characteristics, the practical part of religion is not forgotten. This the author enforces by a variety of motives, and warns his readers against the rock of Antinomianism on which thousands have struck to rise no more. The language is simple and unadorned; it discovers spirit without acrimony, and never degenerates into reproaches when he reprehends the sentiments of others. On all occasions, he seems far more intent upon what he says, than upon the manner in which it is said, invariably paying a greater regard to truth, than to any fame which might be purchased, by disregarding this jewel, while hunting after the flowers of diction."

Ingham's active and useful work was now nearly ended. In 1762, on the re-settlement of affairs, he was chosen elder of the Church at Tadcaster, which office, in addition to that of general overseer, he sustained to the end of life ; but the labours of himself and his coadjutors resulted in small success. On July 23rd, 1766, Wesley wrote :—

"I went to Tadcaster. Here Mr. Ingham had once a far larger society than ours ; but it has now shrunk into nothing; ours, meantime, is continually increasing."

The state of his societies greatly affected poor Ingham's mind. The well-informed author of the "Life and Times of the Countess of Huntingdon," remarks, "The almost total dispersion of the Yorkshire Churches, caused by the introduction of the Sandemanian principles, had a sad effect on Mr. Ingham's mind. He was liable to sudden transitions from the highest flow of spirits to the utmost depression, and the peculiar character of his temperament was an extreme accessibility to sudden attacks of melancholy." The thing which he had "greatly feared had come upon him." He was deserted by his spiritual children, and the thought distressed him. "I am lost! I am lost! was his despairing cry." It is true, that, there were gleams of comfort. Lady Huntingdon's letters were soothing to his anguished spirit. "A thousand and a thousand times," he tells her, "do I bless and praise my

God, for the words of comfort and consolation which your ladyship's letters conveyed to my mournful heart, dismayed and overwhelmed as it was by the pressure of my calamities. ' Righteous art Thou, O Lord, and just are Thy judgments.' "

This was but the beginning of his sorrows. One of his beloved and faithful friends was the laborious and devoted Grimshaw. In the early part of the year 1763, Haworth was visited with a malignant putrid fever, and, among its many victims, Grimshaw was one. At great risk, Ingham repeatedly visited the Christian veteran in his fatal illness; and, afterwards, gave to Lady Huntingdon, the following account of his several interviews :—

"From the moment he was seized with the fever, he felt the sentence of death in himself. When I first saw him, he said, ' My last enemy is come ! the signs of death are upon me, but I am not afraid. No! No! Blessed be God, my hope is sure, and I am in His hands.' When I was pouring out my soul in prayer to the Lord, I mentioned the further prolongation of his life, that he might have more opportunities of being useful; and when I had concluded, he said, 'My dear brother Ingham, if the Lord should raise me up, I think I could do more for His glory than I have hitherto done. Alas ! what have my wretched services been ? and I have now need to cry, at the close of my unprofitable course—*God be merciful to me a sinner !*' At my next visit, I found him much worse, and evidently sinking. I mentioned having received a letter from your ladyship, and delivered your message. He seemed much affected, but, after a few moments, revived a little. When I had prayed with him, he said, ' I harbour no desire of life,—my time is come,—and I am entirely resigned to God.' Then, lifting up his hands and eyes to heaven, he added, ' Thy will be done !' At another time, he said, laying his hand upon his breast, ' I am quite exhausted, but I shall soon be at home for ever with the Lord—a poor miserable sinner redeemed by His blood.' Mr. Venn having arrived, I shortly after took my leave, but never after saw my dear brother Grimshaw alive."

Not long after this, Ingham had to mourn the death of another and dearer friend. After twenty-seven years of connubial happiness, his noble and Christian wife was taken from him. During her fatal sickness,

"She continued to exercise those Christian graces for which she had been long distinguished. Of herself and her efforts, her view was ever humble, and every reference to her usefulness she met with grateful acknowledgment of the sovereignity of that grace, that made her the instrument of good to others. Her end, though painful, was triumphant. She welcomed the hour—she longed to receive the prize of her high calling. 'Thanks be to God! thanks be to God!' she exclaimed, 'The moment's come! the day is dawning!' and thus, in holy ecstasy, she winged her way to glory." "When she had no longer strength to speak to me," (wrote Ingham), "she looked most sweetly at me and smiled. On the Tuesday before she died, when she had opened her heart to me, and declared the ground of her hope, her eyes sparkled with divine joy, her countenance shone, her cheeks were ruddy: I never saw her look so sweet and lively in my life. All about her were affected; no one could refrain from tears, and yet it was a delight to be with her.

Lady Margaret Ingham died on the 30th of April, 1768, in the sixty-eighth year of her age.

Her sorrowing partner did not long survive. He, also, four years afterwards, in 1772, passed away to that "rest which remains to the people of God," leaving behind him a son, who, for a time at least, united himself with Wesley's societies, and officiated as a local preacher.[1]

"In person, Ingham is said to have been extremely handsome—'too handsome for a man'—and the habitual expression of his countenance was most prepossessing. He was a gentleman; temperate, and irreproachable in his morals; as a public speaker, animated and agreeable rather than eloquent; studious of the good conversation of his people, and delicately fearful of reproach to the cause of Christ."[2]

His societies, once so flourishing, gradually dwindled. In 1813, when they became united to the Daleites, or Scotch Independents, they were thirteen in number, assembling in the following places—Wheatley, 56 members; Winewall, 41; Kendal, 27; Nottingham, 25; Salterforth, 21; Bulwel, 17; Tadcaster, 14; Howden, 11; Wibsey, 10; Leeds, 9; Rothwell, 8; Haslingden, 8; Todmorden, 5. So far as has been ascertained, these, at the present moment, are reduced to six,— Winewall, (the largest and most flourishing,) Wheatley, Todmorden, Kendal, Tadcaster, and Leeds.[3]

---

[1] *Evangelical Magazine*, 1814, p. 308.
[2] Life and Times of Countess of Huntingdon, vol. i., p. 303.
[3] *Wesleyan Times*, December 14th, 1863.

REV. JOHN GAMBOLD, M.A.,

THE MORAVIAN BISHOP.

THE whole of the Oxford Methodists intended to devote their lives to the service of the Church of England. This, at Oxford, was their highest wish and holiest ambition. The future was hidden from them,—fortunately so. Without this, their brotherhood would not have lasted for a single week; and many of the results of their godly intercourse would never have been realized. How different from the course of Clayton was that of Ingham; and how different again was that of Gambold from that of Whitefield and the Wesley brothers; and again, how different was that of Hervey and Broughton from any of the others! Men would have ordered it otherwise; but who will say that the way of Providence was not infinitely better? There may be much in the lives of men that is mysterious and perplexing; but of all the sincerely pious it may be confidently asserted,—"A man's heart deviseth his ways, but the Lord directeth his steps." The subject of the following memoir is no exception.

John Gambold was born April 10th, 1711, at Puncheston, in Pembrokeshire, South Wales. His father, a clergyman of the Church of England, lived an ornament to his profession, and was greatly respected, for his unaffected piety and purity of manners. The children of this devout minister were educated with the utmost care and attention, and no pains were spared to instil into their minds the principles and precepts of the Christian religion.

. Nothing is known of the early life of young Gambold, except, that he was greatly benefited by his father's instructions; and, at the early age of fifteen, went to the University of Oxford, where he entered as servitor in Christ Church College, and soon became eminent for his diligent devotion to reading and study. He was naturally of a vivacious and active spirit; and, besides his attention to his collegiate exercises, employed himself in an extensive perusal of the most approved dramatists and poets in the English language.[1]

Two years after he went to Oxford, his father died; and this event, together with the exhortations and counsels he received from the dying minister in his last moments, so affected him, that he at once abandoned poetry and plays, lost his liveliness of disposition, sunk into a state of melancholy, and made the salvation of his soul the chief business of life. Painful experience was the inspirer of a short poem of his, afterwards published in his collected works :—

> " In nature's ebbs, which lay the soul in chains,
> Beneath weak nerves and ill-sufficing veins,
> Who can support bare being, unendow'd
> With gust voluptuous, or reflection proud?
> No more bright images the brain commands,—
> No great design the glowing heart expands,—
> No longer shines the animated face,—
> Motion and speech forget their conscious grace.
> How can the brave, the witty, and the gay
> Survive, when mirth, wit, courage die away?
> None but the Christian's all-comprising power
> Subdues each chance, and lives through every hour :
> Watchful, he suffers all, and feels within
> All smart proportion'd to some root of sin ;
> He strikes each error with his Maker's rod,
> And, by self-knowledge, penetrates to God."

Gambold entered Christ Church College in the same year that Charles Wesley did, the latter being more than two years older than the former. John Wesley also was a member of the same college, and twelve months before, on September 19, 1725, had been ordained a deacon. In 1729, the society of Oxford Methodists was formed by Charles Wesley; and, a year afterwards, Gambold, still only in his teens, became one of them. He shall narrate his own story, written when Wesley was in Georgia. The account is long; but, containing as it does a full description of the rise and peculiarities of the " Holy Club," and a faithful delineation

---

[1] It is a noticeable fact, that Whitefield also was extremely fond of reading plays, not only when at school in Gloucester, but, even after he went to Oxford.

of the character and influence of their confessed "curator," it is too important to be omitted. Gambold writes :—

1730
Age 19

"Mr. Wesley, late of Lincoln College, has been the instrument of so much good to me, that, I shall never forget him. Could I remember him as I ought, it would have very near the same effect as if he was still present ; for a conversation so unreserved as was his, so zealous in engaging his friends to every instance of Christian piety, has left nothing now to be said, nothing but what occurs to us as often as we are disposed to remember him impartially.

"About the middle of March, 1730, I became acquainted with Mr. Charles Wesley, of Christ Church. I was just then come up from the country, and had made a resolution to find out some pious persons of religion to keep company with, or else to instil something of it into those I knew already. I had been, for two years before, in deep melancholy : so God was pleased to order it, to disappoint and break a proud spirit, and to embitter the world to me ; as I was inclining to relish its vanities. During this time, I had no friend to whom I could open my mind, to any purpose. No man did care for my soul ; or none, at least, understood its paths. They, that were at ease, could not guess what my sorrow was for. The learned endeavoured to give me right notions, and the friendly to divert me. But I had a weight upon my heart, which only prayer could in some degree remove. I prepared myself to make trial of the value and comfort of society, being a little recovered. One day, an old acquaintance entertained me with some reflections on the whimsical Mr. Wesley, his preciseness and pious extravagancies. Though I had lived with him four years in the same college, yet, so unable was I to take notice of anything that passed, that I knew nothing of his character ; but, upon hearing this, I suspected he might be a good Christian. I therefore went to his room, and, without any ceremony, desired the benefit of his conversation. I had so large a share of it henceforth, that hardly a day passed, while I was at college, but we were together once, if not oftener.

"After some time, he introduced me to his brother John, of Lincoln College. ' For,' said he, ' he is somewhat older than I, and can resolve your doubts better.' This, as I found afterwards, was a thing which he was deeply sensible of ; for I never observed any person have a more real deference for another, than he constantly had for his brother. Indeed, he followed his brother entirely. Could I describe one of them, I should describe both. And therefore I shall say no more of Charles, but that he was a man made for friendship ; who, by his cheerfulness and vivacity, would refresh his friend's heart ; with attentive consideration, would enter into and settle all his concerns ; so far as he was able, would do anything for him, great or small ; and, by a habit of openness and freedom, leave no room for misunderstanding.

"The Wesleys were already talked of for some religious practices, which were first occasioned by Mr. Morgan, of Christ Church. From these combined friends, began a little society; for several others, from time to time, fell in; most of them only to be improved by their serious and useful discourse; and some few espousing all their resolutions and their whole way of life.

"Mr. John Wesley was always the chief manager, for which he was very fit; for he not only had more learning and experience than the rest, but he was blest with such activity as to be always gaining ground, and such steadiness that he lost none. What proposals he made to any was sure to charm them, because he was so much in earnest; nor could they afterwards slight them, because they saw him always the same. What supported this uniform vigour, was the care he took to consider well of every affair before he engaged in it, making all his decisions in the fear of God, without passion, humour, or self-confidence: for, though he had naturally a very clear apprehension, yet, his exact prudence depended more on humanity and singleness of heart. To this I may add, that he had, I think, something of authority in his countenance; though, as he did not want address, he could soften his manner, and point it as occasion required. Yet, he never assumed anything to himself above his companions. Any of them might speak their mind, and their words were as strictly regarded by him as his were by them.

"It was their custom to meet most evenings, either at his chamber or one of the others, where, after some prayers, (the chief subject of which was charity,) they ate their supper together, and he read some book. But the chief business was to review what each had done that day, in pursuance of their common design, and to consult what steps were to be taken the next.

"Their undertaking included these several particulars:—to converse with young students; to visit the prisons; to instruct some poor families; and to take care of a school, and a parish workhouse.

"They took great pains with the younger members of the University, to rescue them from bad company, and encourage them in a sober, studious life. If they had some interest with any such, they would get them to breakfast; and, over a dish of tea, endeavour to fasten some good hint upon them. They would bring them acquainted with other well disposed young men. They would help them in those parts of learning which they stuck at. They would close with their best sentiments, drive on their convictions, give them rules of piety, when they would receive them, and watch over them with great tenderness.

"Some or other of them went to the Castle every day; and another most commonly to Bocardo. Whoever came to the Castle was to read in the chapel to as many prisoners as would attend, and to talk to the man or men whom he had taken particularly in charge. Before reading, he asked: Whether they had prayers yesterday? (For some serious men among the prisoners read family prayers with the rest.) Whether they had read over again what was read last, and what they remembered of it? Then he went over the heads of it to them; and afterwards went on in the same book for a quarter of an hour. The books they used were the 'Christian Monitor,' the 'Country Parson's Advice to his Parishioners,'

and such-like. When he had done, he summed up the several particulars
that had been insisted on, enforced the advice given, and reduced it at
last to two or three sentences, which they might easily remember. Then
he took his man aside, and asked him, Whether he was in the chapel
yesterday? and other questions concerning his care to serve God, and
learn his duty.

" When a new prisoner came, their conversation with him, for four or
five times, was particularly close and searching. Whether he bore no
malice towards those that did prosecute him, or any others? The first
time, after professions of good-will, they only inquired of his circumstances
in the world. Such questions imported friendship, and engaged the man
to open his heart. Afterwards, they entered upon such enquiries as most
concern a prisoner. Whether he submitted to this disposal of Providence?
Whether he repented of his past life? Last of all, they asked him,
Whether he constantly used private prayer, and whether he had ever
communicated? Thus, most or all of the prisoners were spoken to in
their turns. But, if any one was either under sentence of death, or appeared to have some intentions of a new life, they came every day to his
assistance; and partook in the conflict and suspense of those who should
now be found able, or not able, to lay hold on salvation. In order to
release those who were confined for small debts, and were bettered by
their affliction, and likewise to purchase books, physic, and other necessaries,—they raised a small fund, to which many of their acquaintance
contributed quarterly. They had prayers at the Castle most Wednesdays
and Fridays, a sermon on Sundays, and the Sacrament once a month.

" When they undertook any poor family, they saw them, at least, once a
week; sometimes gave them money; admonished them of their vices;
read to them, and examined their children.

" The school was, I think, of Mr. Wesley's own setting up. At all
events, he paid the mistress, and clothed some, if not all, of the children.
When they went thither, they enquired how each child behaved; saw their
work (for some could knit and spin); heard them read; heard them their
prayers and catechism; and explained part of it.

" In the same manner, they taught the children in the workhouse; and
read to the old people as they did to the prisoners.

" Though some practices of Mr. Wesley and his friends were much
blamed,—as their fasting on Wednesday and Friday, after the custom of
the Primitive Church,—their coming on those Sundays, when there was
no sacrament in their own colleges, to receive it at Christ Church,—yet
nothing was so much disliked as these charitable employments. They
seldom took any notice of the accusations brought against them; but, if
they made any reply, it was commonly such a plain and simple one, as if
there was nothing more in the case, but that they had heard such doctrines of their Saviour, and believed and done accordingly,—' Shall we be
the more happy in another life, the more virtuous we are in this? Are we
the more virtuous, the more intensely we love God and man? Is love, as
all habits, the more intense, the more we exercise it? Is either helping,
or trying to help man, for God's sake, an exercise of love to God or man?

Particularly, Is the feeding the hungry, the giving drink to the thirsty, the clothing the naked, the visiting sick persons, or prisoners, an exercise of love to God or man? Is the endeavouring to teach the ignorant, to admonish sinners, to encourage the good, to comfort the afflicted, to confirm the wavering, and to reconcile enemies, an exercise of love to God or man? Shall we be the more happy in another life, if we do the former of these things, and try to do the latter? Or if we do not the one, nor try to do the other?"

In the above extracts, the reader has the practices which principally distinguished the Oxford Methodists from their fellows. The account is full of interest, and of great importance, being written by one of the members of this godly brotherhood, and immediately after that brotherhood was broken up. The remainder of Gambold's narrative is chiefly a defence and eulogy of Wesley, their "Curator;" and only such parts of it will be given as affect the whole of these earnest students. Gambold continues:—

"What I would chiefly remark upon, is the manner in which Mr. Wesley directed his friends.

"Because he required such a regulation of our studies, as might devote them all to God, he has been cried out upon as one that discouraged learning. Far from that;—the first thing he struck at in young men, was that indolence which would not submit to close thinking. Nor was he against reading much, especially at first; because then the mind ought to fill itself with materials, and try every thing that looks bright and perfect.

"He earnestly recommended to them a method and order in all their actions. After their morning devotions (which were at a fixed and early hour, from five to six being the time, morning as well as evening), he advised them to determine with themselves what they were to do all the parts of the day. By such foresight, they would, at every hour's end, not be in doubt how to dispose of themselves; and, by bringing themselves under the necessity of such a plan, they might correct the impotence of a mind that had been used to live by humour and chance, and prepare it by degrees to bear the other restraints of a holy life.

"The next thing was to put them upon keeping the fasts, visiting poor people, and coming to the weekly Sacrament: not only to subdue the body, increase charity, and obtain Divine grace; but (as he expressed it) to cut off their retreat to the world. He judged, that, if they did these things, men would cast out their name as evil, and, by the impossibility of keeping fair any longer with the world, oblige them to take their whole refuge in Christianity. But those, whose resolutions he thought would not bear this test, he left to gather strength by their secret exercises.

"It was his earnest care to introduce them to the treasures of wisdom

and hope in the Holy Scriptures: to teach them not only to endure that
book, but to form themselves by it, and to fly to it as the great antidote
against the darkness of this world. For some years past, he and his
friends read the New Testament together at evening. After every portion of it, having heard the conjectures the rest had to offer, he made his
observations on the phrase, design, and difficult places. One or two
wrote these down from his mouth.

"He laid much stress upon self-examination. He taught them (besides
what occurs in his Collection of Prayers) to take account of their actions
in a very exact manner, by writing a constant diary. In this, they noted
down in cipher, once if not oftener in the day, what chiefly their employments had been in the several parts of it, and how they had performed
each. Mr. Wesley had these records of his life by him for many years
past. And some I have known, who, to seal their convictions and make
their repentance more solemn, would write down such reflections upon
themselves as the anguish of their soul at that time suggested, adding any
spiritual maxim which some experience of their own had confirmed to
them.

"Then, to keep in their minds an awful sense of God's presence, with a
constant dependence on His help, he advised them to ejaculatory prayers.
They had a book of Ejaculations relating to the chief virtues, and, lying
by them as they stood at their studies, they at intervals snatched a short
petition out of it. But at last, instead of that variety, they contented
themselves with the following aspirations (containing acts of faith, hope,
love, and self-resignation at the end of every hour)—'Consider and hear
me,' etc.

"The last means he recommended was meditation. Their usual time
for this was the hour next before dinner.

"After this, he committed them to God. What remained for him to
do, was to encourage them in the discomforts and temptations they might
feel, and to guard them against all spiritual delusions. In this spiritual
care of his acquaintance, Mr. Wesley persisted amidst all discourage-
ments. He overlooked not only one's absurd or disagreeable qualities,
but even his coldness and neglect of him, if he thought it might be conquered. He helped one in things out of religion, that he might be more
welcome to help him in that. His knowledge of the world, and his insight
into physic, were often of use to us.

"If any one could have provoked him, I should; for I was slow in
coming into his measures, and very remiss in doing my part. I frequently contradicted his assertions; or, which is much the same, distinguished upon them. I hardly ever submitted to his advice at the time
he gave it, though I relented afterwards. One time he was in fear, that, I
had taken up notions that were not safe, and pursued my spiritual improvement in an erroneous, because inactive, way. So he came over and
stayed with me near a week. He accosted me with the utmost softness,
condoled with me the incumbrances of my constitution, heard all I had to
say, endeavoured to pick out my meaning, and yielded to me as far as
he could. I never saw more humility in him than at this time. It was

M

enough to cool the warmest imaginations that swell an overweening heart. It was, indeed, his custom to humble himself most before the proud,—not to reproach them; but, in a way of secret intercession, to procure their pardon.

"He had not only friends in Oxford to assist, but a great many correspondents. He set apart one day at least in the week (and he was no slow composer) for writing letters; in which, without levity or affectation, but with plainness and fervour, he gave his advice in particular cases, and vindicated the strict original sense of the Gospel precepts."[1]

This long account does something more than give a general idea of the Oxford Methodists and of their distinguished leader. It exhibits the course of life adopted by Gambold in his twentieth year. Like the rest of his youthful friends, he became an earnest religionist; but he was not happy. "He gave way to desponding thoughts; neglected his person and apparel; confined himself as much as possible to his room; and applied, in search of information and comfort, to the works of such authors as he supposed could satisfy his inquiries, namely, the fathers of the first ages of the Christian Church. Of these, the most abstruse were his greatest favourites, and particularly those which are called mystics. Being well versed in the Greek language, he was much pleased with that energy of expression in which it excels. The deep speculations of these ancient writers, their beautiful allusions, the richness of style with which they clothed their ideas, and the strain of piety running through the whole, suited his taste, and so far influenced his understanding, that he adopted their sentiments, went the same lengths with them in the scenes of imagination, and, by degrees, became so much like one of them, that his cast of mind bore a nearer resemblance to that which was peculiar in them, than to any that appeared among the modern. By a close attention to writers of this stamp, he contracted such a turn of mind, and imbibed such an exalted notion of internal purity, that he could not be satisfied with himself, unless he became such a refined being as those philosophical Christians portrayed. This being the state to which his aim was directed, he spared no pains to model himself according to the idea which he had formed of it. His exertions were abortive. Disappointment

---

[1] *Methodist Magazine,* 1798, p. 172

occasioned great concern ;" and it was not until after years of laborious endeavour to form and establish a righteousness of his own, that he was led to submit to "the righteousness of God, by faith of Jesus Christ."

In September, 1733, he was ordained, by Dr. Potter, Bishop of Oxford ; and, as soon as he was capable of holding a living, was instituted to that of Stanton-Harcourt. In this sequestered village, where his parochial duties were not numerous, he had more leisure than was desirable to pursue his philosophical inquiries. He loved retirement, and seldom went abroad., But whenever he could prevail upon himself to visit any of his friends, and, among the rest, Lord Harcourt, he was received with much respect. His abilities, both natural and acquired, were great, but his unfeigned humility was so apparent to every one with whom he conversed, that, his superior powers excited no dislike in any. Indeed, his whole conduct was so inoffensive, that he very rarely, if ever, made himself an enemy. Still, his philosophical and platonic kind of religion failed to make him happy, and was of little use to his rustic parishioners. Four years were spent, —almost wasted,—in those high flights of imagination, deep speculation, intense reflection, and metaphysical reasoning, to which his natural disposition inclined him.

Meanwhile, his friendship with the Wesleys was continued. Charles returned from Georgia in the month of December, 1736; and, in the following February, speaks of meeting his "good friend Mr. Gambold," at Oxford, who was " right glad to see" him. In fact, at this period and more or less for at least a year and a half afterwards, Kezziah Wesley, the youngest surviving sister of John and Charles, was domiciled with Gambold and his sister (who kept his house,) at Stanton-Harcourt. Poor Kezziah, from childhood, had been delicate, and her health had not been bettered by her residence at Lincoln, where, at nineteen years of age, she became a teacher in a boarding-school, and was painfully in want of both clothes and money. Her life was a wandering one. For a time, she lived in the house of the Vicar of Bexley, the Rev. Mr. Piers, and, afterwards, she resided with an aunt at Islington. It was not long that she needed the kindness of her friends, for, at the age of thirty-one, nearly a year and a half before the decease of her Christian mother, she peacefully expired, on the 9th of March, 1741.[1]

John Wesley landed in England on February 1, 1738 ; and, a week afterwards, met with Peter Bohler, just arrived from Germany. Within a fortnight, the two Wesleys, accompanied by Bohler, set out for Oxford, whence all the first brotherhood of Oxford Methodists were now dispersed. The elder Wesley writes :—

> " I found not one of those who had formerly joined with me ; and only three gentlemen who trod in their steps, building up one another in the faith."

The nearest to Oxford was Gambold ; and, accordingly, on February 18th, Wesley says :—

> " We went to Stanton-Harcourt, to Mr. Gambold, and found my old friend recovered from his mystic delusion, and convinced that St. Paul was a better writer than either Tauler or Jacob Behmen."

Gambold was already returning to gospel simplicity ; and his acquaintance with Bohler rendered him service of the highest importance. Bohler held meetings in Oxford, attended both by members of the university and citizens. He delivered discourses in Latin, and Gambold interpreted them for the benefit of those of his audiences who were unfamiliar with that language. This friendship with the newly arrived German, proved the means, not only of the conversion of the two Wesleys, but, ultimately of Gambold also.

> " After many struggles and conflicting thoughts, arising from repeated attempts to combine philosophy with the simplicity of the gospel ; he, at length, by the grace of God, yielded to the power of the latter. He saw and lamented his natural depravity and consequent alienation from God, and also the insufficiency of his best works to merit heaven. He rejoiced in the sufficiency of the atonement of Jesus to sanctify and justify every true believer in Him. His former melancholy was dissipated ; his spirit was made joyful in God his Saviour ; and he became, in the fullest sense of the term, a new man."[2]

The following letters will show the change which took place in Gambold's views and feelings. The first was addressed to

---

[1] For further particulars of Kezziah Westley, see Memoir of Westley Hall.
[2] Holmes's " History of the United Brethren," vol. ii., p. 38.

Wesley, and has never before been published. As will be
seen, it was written three days before Wesley's return from
Georgia, and, consequently, before Wesley and Gambold
became acquainted with Bohler. It is given here without
abridgment, and verbatim.

1738

Age 27

"*January* 27, 1737-8.

"DEAR SIR,—The point you mention has long been a difficulty to me ;
of which I could find no end, but that general solution of all doubt, and
cure of all anxieties, resignation to eternal Providence. Can I offer a
more particular solution now? No ; but I will let you see, that I, and
doubtless many more, labour under the same perplexity; which will incline one to believe, that, as God has a fire of grace to cleanse us from
our common pollutions, so he has also a light in reserve, (and the needs
of so many strongly call for it,) that would give a comfortable turn to our
common speculations.

"O, what is regeneration? And what doth baptism? How shall we
reconcile faith and fact? Is Christianity become effete, and sunk again
into the bosom of nature? Was the short triumph of it over flesh and
blood designed as the standing enjoyment, or standing humiliation of
succeeding ages? Was the Church to condemn the world as God does,
in order to meet and embrace it at last?

"What advantage would a deist make of the present appearance of
things? He would say, that, when the gospel, by setting up some particular institutions, made a separation from natural religion, it was only
an economical enmity ;—the new dispensation did operate upon the old,
as plaisters do upon the body, which, when they have spent their strength
in expelling its diseases, drop off, and leave it sound, clean, and beautiful.
That, the distance it stood in from it, was only a means to correct the
prejudices, and manage the affections of mankind ; and, as these ends
were served, Christianity and natural religion were to come closer. That,
the former was to lose its name in the latter, when its whole light was
kindled up,—when the grace of a Redeemer, the inward touches of divine
power, and the obligations of penance and self-denial, which were received for a while as extraneous appendages to natural religion, were
found to be involved in the very bowels of it. That, the restitution of all
things is the time when they shall fully be reconciled ; when nature and
grace shall be at their height, and the perfection of both be the same
thing. That, this conclusion seems to be nigh us in the present age,
when evangelical and moral virtue, which formerly stood in points so
remote from each other, are so near falling into coincident lines, that,
men have much ado to make any distinction that will hold in fact.

"But to come to the point. That regeneration is the beginning of a
life which is not fully enjoyed but in another world, we all know. But
how much of it may be enjoyed at present? What degree of it does the
experience of mankind encourage us to expect? And by what symptoms
shall we know it?

"Let us consult our observation as to the gradual progress of a religious life. At first, men are solicited with strong convictions of conscience : the pain of these and the sensible pleasure they feel as rewarding their acts of duty, are their bias to religion ; while an overwhelming admiration of divine things, and a view to the issues of eternity, check their natural boldness and levity ; at once abase and enlarge the understanding ; and, from the anguish of hope and fear, produce zeal. Then, having reformed all crying disorders, and being prompt and expert in exercises of devotion, there is less matter for vehement remorse or fear ; and the peace and congratulation of conscience hereupon being comfort sufficient, the more transporting flashes of joy are withdrawn ; and thus, the man, having no religious passions, and being in war with corrupt passions, acquaints himself with the measures, motives, and fitness of virtues, and acts them in the strength of rational consideration.

"Here he labours long, and seems perhaps to have overcome all his vicious inclinations ; (unless some one may show itself, more to his secret confusion and pain, than guilt,) being always in a posture of religious care, severity of thought, and habitual regularity of life. But then he complains of a general lukewarmness,—his intercourse with God is not enlivened with any particular successes, tender affections, or noble discoveries. For this he is much afflicted ; yet, in the multitude of his thoughts within him, there is a good hope towards God at the bottom, which becomes more explicit by listening to the gospel. The redemption through Christ drops like balm into his soul, and he scruples not now to confess that his religious actions were but formal and worthless ; yet, through gratitude to his Saviour and joy in Him, he is more ready than ever to continue the practice of them.

"Yet, he frequently falls into faintings and desolations. He is chiefly troubled at the opposition which self-love and pride make to the spirit of Christ within him. These make him unfaithful in the happy moments of grace, and infest him continually in his weaker intervals. Yea, he can trace them through every action of his life, and begin to see the depth and extent of his depravity. Hereupon, he keeps himself in constant recollection, to watch and resist it. He rejoices that, upon applying to God, a temptation vanishes ; yet, very often it dwells so obstinately upon his mind, that his thoughts are shut up within the circle of their own folly and baseness, and he can only send groanings that cannot be uttered after the divine gift he once enjoyed. That gift, however, returns, and sometimes so long together, that he is able to form some idea of a spiritual life,—of the purity and long-suffering, the humility and charity, the magnanimity and singleness of heart, that are suitable for one in whom the Holy Spirit dwells. His desire insensibly sets him on work to procure those dispositions, which follow upon his wish ; for the soul no sooner conceives the temper it would be in, but the body (being taught that obsequiousness by the strong recollection lately used, which suspends, clarifies, and determines the animal spirit) immediately furnishes the sensation, air, and whole energy of that temper.

"These smooth and ready emotions of virtue, which seem to give a man a more real and genuine possession of it than ever, do also encourage the mind to launch out in sublime theories; wherein it is much assisted by the repose and security it enjoys towards God, and by the delicate philosophic joy overflowing all the faculties, which raises the imagination to greater magnificence and sagacity. Here the grand system of Providence and all its various dispensations; the correspondencies of heaven and earth, of time and eternity; the gaiety and mournings of nature, and the greatness and abjectness of man; the saving mystery of human life, and the saving mystery of Christianity inserted into it;—all these are inquired into, not out of vain curiosity, but at the instigation of love, to salute the divine goodness in all its works. This is the meridian of the religious man. His notions and his virtues are at the height, in their full clearness and fervour. The love of holiness shines through him, and unites under it all the movements of nature. It commands and pierces all that converse with him. All, after this, is, to the eye of man, a decline and a fall; but a decline by a regular appointed path, and a fall into the arms of secret and infinite mercy. I need not explain to you what I mean; so I will shut up the description.

"Now, where in all these stages shall we place our regeneration? And what shall we say it is? There is reason to think, that, we have no more real goodness (except experience) in one of these states than another,—in the last than the first; we only fill our minds with new sets of ideas, and, by a temporary force, drive our constitution into something that seems answerable to them. Let this force cease, and we are the same as before; when we are in the most plausible posture of virtue, let us but sleep upon it, or otherwise remit the contention of the mind, and 'tis no more; affectation gives place to nature.

"But, you will say, the operation of grace is a real thing. It is so; but, for all the indications we commonly go by to prove the peculiar presence of it, it may· be nowhere or everywhere to be found. Most people measure it by the relish they have for some particular schemes and draughts of religion. Little do they think, that, the persons whom they most condemn as unspiritual and deluded, abating for what is merely accidental, are in the same state of heart as themselves. It may be the same complexional turn of the soul, (God also speaking peace to it, and to every man in his own language,) that makes the mystic happy in his prayer and quietness, the solifidian in his imputed righteousness, and the moral man in a good conscience. Nay, perhaps, what many a man calls divine love and joy in the Holy Ghost, has nothing in it, beyond the alacrity of youth or good blood in other people, but a set of phrases and notions from the last book he read; which has given a determination to that natural vigour and sweetness of temper, that were indifferent to any other issue or exercise.

"I do not doubt but there is goodness in mankind, and a goodness of God's inspiring too; but, I believe it more evenly distributed among them, and less annexed to particular ways of thinking and behaviour. Nay, that it is not so annexed even to Christianity, (though it does essentially depend on Christ, the universal Redeemer,) but, that, as it was in being before this particular institution, so it might be obtained if the initiating rite should happen to be wanting. Yet, this rite must always be used, for the same reason as it was at first appointed, to be memorial to mankind of what is continually done for them in their hearts. Therefore, it was attended with such extraordinary effects at first, that, by these manifestations of the divine life, the reality of it might be firmly believed and depended on in succeeding times, as well as sacramentally acknowledged. The same would still continue, if we had more faith in, and zeal for, the Christian institution; for, according as men believe and expect, God does unto them. But, at present, He seems to have let the Church drop into the world, and does not so much distinguish some from the rest, in righteousness and salvation.

"Whether this be a right state of things, I cannot tell; but it seems unavoidable when every one that is born, is, of course, a member of the Church. If the safety and tolerable piety of whole nations is thereby better provided for, the exemplariness and instruction of an elect city set upon a hill cease. It seems to be the order of Providence now, that none should have much holiness, that all may have a little.

"Dear sir, I have given no particular answer to your questions; but I have said something hastily, perhaps very wrong; but I know to whom Miss Wesley[1] gives her love, and would have written, but she is somewhat indisposed.

> "Your affectionate brother and servant,
>
> "J. GAMBOLD."

Such was Gambold's philosophical religion, previous to his acquaintance with Peter Bohler. He was sincere and in earnest; but he was enveloped in a mystic fog. His was a grand attempt to save himself, but how the thing was to be accomplished he hardly knew. It was greatly to his credit, as it was also to that of Wesley, that he was willing to be taught, even by a German stranger. Twelve months after the date of the foregoing letter, Gambold wrote another equally important. In the interval, both he and the two Wesley's had been "brought out of" Pharisaic and Philosophic "darkness into marvellous light." The two letters have only to be compared to see the surprising change in the writer's views. The following was addressed to Wesley's brother Charles :—.

> "*January* 23rd, 1738–9.

DEAR SIR,—I understand that you have written to me, but the letter happened to be lost, and I did not receive it. Your brother desired me to read his sermon for him; which, God willing, I shall do next Sunday.

---

[1] Wesley's sister, Kezziah, now Gambold's guest.

"I have seen upon this occasion, more than ever I could have imagined, how intolerable the doctrine of faith is to the mind of man ; how peculiarly intolerable, even to most religious men. One may say the most unchristian things, even down to deism ; the most enthusiastic things, so they proceed but upon mental raptures, lights, and unions; the most severe things, even the whole rigour of ascetic mortification ; and all this will be forgiven. But if you speak of faith, in such a manner as makes Christ a Saviour to the utmost,—a most universal help and refuge,—in such a manner as takes away glorying, but adds happiness to wretched man; as discovers greater pollution in the best of us than we could before acknowledge, but brings a greater deliverance from it, than we could before expect. If any one offers to talk at this rate, he shall be heard with the same abhorrence as if he were going to rob mankind of their salvation, their Mediator, and their hopes of forgiveness.

"I am persuaded that a Montanist, or a Novatian, who, from the height of his purity, should look down with contempt upon poor sinners, and exclude them from all mercy, would not be thought such an overthrower of the Gospel, as he who should learn, from the Author of it, to be a friend of publicans and sinners, and to sit down upon a level with them as soon as they begin to repent. But this is not to be wondered at. For all religious people have such a quantity of righteousness acquired by such painful exercise, and formed at last into current habits, which is their wealth both for this world and the next ! Now all other schemes of religion are either so complaisant, as to tell them they are very rich, and have enough to triumph in ; or else, only a little rough, but friendly in the main, by telling them their riches are not yet sufficient, but by such arts of self-denial and mental refinement, they may enlarge the stock. But the doctrine of faith is a downright robber. It takes away all this wealth, and only tells us it is deposited for us with some one else, upon whose bounty we must live like mere beggars, Indeed, they who are truly beggars, vile and filthy sinners till very lately, may stoop to live in this dependent condition ; it suits them well enough ; but those who have long distinguished themselves from the herd of vicious wretches, or have even gone beyond moral men,—for them to be told, that they are either not so well, or but the same needy, impotent, insignificant vessels of mercy with the others,—this is more shocking to reason than transubstantiation ; for reason had rather resign its pretentions to judge what is bread or flesh, than have this honour wrested from it, to be the architect of virtue and righteousness.

"But whither am I running? My design was only to give you warning, that, wherever you go, this foolishness of preaching will alienate hearts from you, and open mouths against you. What are you then to do, my dear friend? I will not exhort you to courage; we need not talk of that, for nothing that is approaching is evil. I will only mention the prejudice we shall be under if we seem in the least to lay aside universal charity and modesty of expression. Though we love some persons more than we did, let us love none less ; and the rather, because we cannot say any one is bad, or destitute of divine grace, for not thinking as we do. He only less apprehends, less enjoys that in Christianity, which is the refuge of the weak and miserable, and will be his when he finds himself so. Indignation at mankind is a temper unsuitable to this cause. If we are indeed at peace with God in Christ, let it soften our demeanour still more, even towards gainsayers. Let them reject us: till then, and (as far as it will be admitted,) afterwards, let our friendship with them continue inviolate.

"Then as to expressions. What has given most offence hitherto, is what, perhaps, may be best spared,—as some people's confident and hasty triumphs in the grace of God; not by way of humble thankfulness to Him for looking upon them, or acknowledgment of some peace and strength unknown before; but insisting on the completeness of their justification, the completeness of their deliverance already from all sin, and taking to them every apostolical boast in the strongest terms. I do not deny but power over sin, and every Gospel privilege, are bestowed, perhaps, in as large a degree, in the beginning of grace, as at any time afterwards; for it depends upon the actual operation of the Spirit that moment upon the heart, not on a mere federal or habitual union with Him; and his operation is particularly strong at the first entrance upon a new life. Yet, as such converts must remember, that, as this absolute degree of innocence, excluding for the most part even the first motions of sin, may soon depart from them, and be given them but sometimes; though till they fall from God, they will still be free from wilful sins; so while it continues, it is the most slippery and dangerous thing, among all the blessings they receive, for themselves to reflect much upon, and the most exceptionable that they can talk of to other men. Let us speak of everything in such a manner, as may convey glory to Christ, without letting it glance on ourselves by the way.

"JOHN GAMBOLD."[1]

Though exception may be taken to some of the expressions, yet the above is a most admirable letter; and shows that Gambold had embraced the same faith as Wesley,—sinners are saved solely through the merits of Christ Jesus; and on the simple exercise of faith in Him. It was not without a struggle that he was brought to this conviction. Peter Bohler said to Wesley, "My brother, my brother, that philosophy of yours must be purged away." The same might have been said to Gambold. His learning had to give place to the simple teaching of the Word of God. He had to relinquish philosophical theories; and submit to the authoritative utterances of Christ and of His Apostles. Reason had to bend to revelation. In the case of a sincere

---

[1] The Works of Rev. John Gambold. p. 260.

and earnest man, like Gambold, this mental transformation was not a trifle. He himself, in a letter without date, and apparently addressed to Wesley, refers to the difficulties, and obstacles he encountered. His very learning was a hindrance in the way of his being saved; and he was reluctantly convinced, that, when "the aphorisms of learning pretend to describe and circumscribe the process of salvation, then the words of any one who has but a good heart and common sense, are generally more complete than those of a finished divine; and tally better with the unsearchable divine economy." He continues :—

1739
—
Age 28

"These obstacles of nature's education, I have often sighed under; and, imagining I knew where the shoe pinched in your case also, I advised the most artless, direct, and confident laying hold of the Scripture declaration, without the ceremony and circuitions of a man of learning, and a man of prudence, or a man of decorum, but simply as a *plain man*, who wants for his own soul to experience the manifestation of redeeming grace. The words of our Saviour and His apostles, which I said we are to take quite simply, are such as these,—'Come unto Me, all ye that labour and are heavy laden, and I will give you rest.' 'Him that cometh unto Me, I will in no wise cast out.' 'He that believeth, shall not come into condemnation; but is passed from death unto life.' 'If thou canst believe, all things are possible to him that believeth.' 'My grace is sufficient for thee; for My strength is made perfect in thy weakness.' 'This is a faithful saying, that Jesus Christ came into the world to save sinners,' etc., etc."

There is another letter, written by Gambold, during his transition state, which further illustrates his views and feelings at this important crisis. It was addressed "to a studious young lady,"—probably Kezziah Wesley,—and concerning it Wesley himself remarks :—"It well deserves the attention of the serious and sensible reader. Indeed, unless read with a good deal of attention, it will scarce be understood, the thoughts are so deep, and so concisely expressed." The following are brief extracts :—

"I will no more speak against reading, since, as you say, you 'take pleasure in nothing else in the world.' For, I cannot deny, but I should be glad myself to have some object of pleasure in the world; something, whether great or mean, I do not care, so it be innocent, that might be a relief to my weary mind. In the situation I am in, not yet admitted to the glorious comforts of faith, and yet sick of the burden of corrupt nature, it seems necessary sometimes to set aside the dejecting prospect, by some amusement, however low. The lower it is, the fitter for me, till faith in Christ raises me from spiritual darkness and death. Then I would hope for such solid consolation, as may well supersede the poor amusements and delights of the natural man."

"There is no such lumber in the world, as our last year's notions, which yet, in their day, were wonderfully fine and delightful. The fruit of the Tree of Knowledge will not keep: it is pleasant enough when you first pluck it; but, if you pretend to lay it up, it will rot. The man who has discovered, as far as human thought can go, the manner how the world was created, and how it shall be restored, the nature of the human soul, and its state after death,—when he has done, what is he the better? When the heat of thinking is over, will his heart be found in any better or nobler condition, than other men's? Unless some bye-reasons engage him still to his old speculations (as the respect paid him upon that account by the world and by his juniors), will not he confess, that he is now never the happier for them? Will not he prefer plain common-sense before all such subtleties? Alas, alas! Under the greatest accomplishments of the head, the heart remains just the same as it was. This is very true, though it does not presently appear to us. I cannot, therefore, agree to that fine Platonical insinuation, that, 'so much as we have of truth, so much we have of God.'

"I heartily condole with you under the troubles of this life: I am ready to sink under them myself. You suffered severely, while you lived with us, from sickness and pain, bodily hardships, etc. It grieves me to think, that ever it should be your lot to struggle with these. Yet, while you continue in this world, you must expect to bear your cross. Comfort yourself under it as well as you can, by applying arguments for patience; and if at any time you should not have strength of mind to do this, God Himself will either support and comfort you, or pity and accept you amidst your weakness."

"Now, after all this long talk, the chief thing, that, by my calling and my conscience, I ought to have spoken of, and recommended to you, I have passed over; and that is faith in Christ. This is the thing that I ought to speak of with zeal and delight;—that ought to be the brightest in my imagination, and nearest to my heart. How little do any other speculations or reasonings conduce to this faith; and how insignificant are they, if they do not conduce to it! I know, and actually make the reflection upon myself, that, whatever I read, or write, or speak, upon any other subject but this, I am a miserable trifler. Perhaps then I do very ill, to trifle with you. It may be, you have felt the great work of faith, cleansing you from all sin in the blood of Christ;—that, being righteous before God, you have peace therefrom, which passes all understanding;— that, all things are become new with you; and you have a new judgment and taste, as well as new satisfactions and employments suggested to you by the Spirit of wisdom and consolation. You seem to hint in the beginning of your letter, that, either you are in this state, or the desire of your heart is towards it; for you say, you now acquiesce in that, which (by the description I could make of it), is the righteousness of faith. If so, then you have cause to rejoice; and your joy no man taketh from you."

Some may think, that, in these quotations, the importance of human learning is unduly lowered ; but all will admit that the learned recluse at Stanton-Harcourt, had embraced the simple method of human salvation, by a simple and sole reliance on the sacrifice and merits of Christ Jesus. This is the point which we are wishful to enforce ; inasmuch as it, not only is " the truth as it is in Jesus ;" but, was the origin of the great Methodist movement of the eighteenth century. Without this, England would have been without its latest religious reformation. On this ground, some other extracts from the works of Gambold, may be useful.

It is a fact, not generally noticed, that, though Gambold's Tragedy,—the Martyrdom of Ignatius, was not published until after the author's death,[1] it was written as early as the year 1740 ; and, hence, may be taken as an exposition of Gambold's views and feelings, at this early period of his life.

It certainly seems somewhat strange, that an earnest young clergyman, twenty-nine years of age, and only recently brought to the enjoyment of personal salvation, by penitent faith in Christ, should employ his time and pen upon a dramatical production ; but it must be borne in mind,—(1) that, from his youth, Gambold had had a great fondness for dramatic pieces, both ancient and modern, (2) that, Gambold's Tragedy was never intended for the stage, (3) that, its sentiments are unexceptionably pure and good ; and (4) that, he was not the first who had attempted to represent the principles and practices of the Christian religion in such a form.

Gambold's work may be a defective drama ; but it is a thoughtful poem, and deserves attention. Take the following extracts, all bearing upon faith in Christ and its immediate results.

> " This is the sum, my brethren ! Christ is all:
> If e'er we lean to other things we fall.
> Spirit, and rites, and reason too, are good,
> If planted and if glorying in His blood.

---

[1] The first edition was published in 1773, with the following title : " The Martyrdom of Ignatius ; a Tragedy. Written in the year 1740. . By the late John Gambold, at that time Minister of Stanton-Harcourt, Oxfordshire," 8vo. Cadell, etc.

Faith is so simple, whence all good doth spring,
Mankind can't think it is so great a thing ;
Still o'er this pearl steps their ambitious pride,
Pursuing gladly any form beside."

" Come hither, ye, whom from an evil world
The name of Jesus draws !   You count Him sweet,
And great, and mighty, by that glimm'ring light
Your novice minds have gained.   You venerate
That full acquaintance, and that vital union
Whereby the faithful know Him ; and to this
You now aspire.   But can you then let go
Your manly wisdom, and become as babes,
To learn new maxims and the mind of Christ ?
Can you forsake your former ease and sunshine,
T' associate with a poor afflicted people,
The scorn of all mankind ?   Can you the weight
Of your whole souls, with all your hopes of God,
Rest on a long-past action ; and that, such
As your Lord's mystic but opprobrious death ?"

                    " The friends of Christ
Don't strive with sin, but trample under foot
Its poor, exploded, antiquated strength ;
They don't rely on some benign event
From the wide wheel of things ; but pierce directly
Where Jesus now admits them, and ordains
Their thrones in bliss : hence they in spirit stand
Free from all spot, amidst the train of heaven,
And see God's face, whose full and constant smile
Doth so attend them through the wilds of life,
That natural dejection, flitting fears,
And all vicissitude, are swallowed up
In one still dawn of that eternal day."

                    " Are there not here
Men who can say, in soberness and truth,
That guilt is done away, and innocence,
Fearless and free, restored within their breasts ?
That vice, with dark inextricable bands,
No more detains, nor drives to acts of shame
The blushing, reasoning, reluctant mind ?
That, for the passions, which by turns inspire
The worthless life of nature,—anger, sloth,
And avarice, and pride,—pure love prevails,
Kindled by heaven, nor by a bad world quenched ?
That, they have inwardly exchanged their climate,
And passed from death to life ; so that their heart,
Healed and exulting, from its deep recess,

> Returns this answer : That the power of evil,
> The sting of pain, and terrors of the grave,
> Are now no more, or but at distance rage
> In faithless minds ; while not a dart can reach
> Their citadel of peace in Jesu's love?
> That they, in short, to God's paternal face
> And firm affection can appeal and look,
> Nor earthly griefs dare intercept the prospect;
> But still to every want they feel as men,—
> To every priestly, charitable prayer
> They breathe as saints of God ; His ear and power
> Are nigh ; till, thus, by constant use and proof
> Of aid celestial, heaven is, more than earth,
> Their home, the country of their heart and commerce ?"

More extracts are not needed. John Gambold, the learned, moping, gloomy, philosophic Mystic, became an humble, happy, trustful believer in Christ Jesus. He shall tell his own story. Though he was introduced to Bohler in January, 1738, and became his interpreter when he preached, yet, for two years after this, his state of mind was very painful. In a letter dated April 3, 1740, he describes himself as being "mostly pensive and dejected, surrounded with solitude, sickness, and silence ; not gathering strength, like the heroes, from rich circumstances, but, like vulgar minds, contracting an abjectness that blunts every finer sentiment, and damps every nobler ardour of the soul." The day of his deliverance, however, was drawing nigh. Speaking of the Moravians, he writes :—

"I looked upon them as a happy people, and their doctrine as fundamentally true, but could not apply the comforts thereof to myself, being discouraged from so doing by the deep sense I had of my own guilt and depravity, and by being defeated in the hopes of being happy in the notions which I had formerly imbibed. Therefore, I despaired of being in a condition better than the generality of mankind, or different from them. But, in December, 1740, my younger brother, having been with the Brethren in London, came to see me. The account which he gave of the happy course he observed amongst them, struck me with such an agreeable surprise, that I could not but return with him thither. My design was to see the order established, and to feel the spirit which prevailed amongst them where several of them dwelt together. The purpose of my visit was answered to my great satisfaction, and I could believe, not only that they were right both in principle and practice, but that I might have a share of the same grace which they enjoyed. After having been again in their company, I perceived an impulse upon my mind to devote myself entirely to Him who died for me, and to live wholly for Him and to His service."

It is a curious fact, that, in the same year in which Wesley seceded from the London Moravians, Gambold became enamoured with them. Philip Henry Molther had created immense confusion and bitterness, by preaching the unscriptural doctrine, that, " to search the Scriptures, to pray, or to communicate, before we have faith, is to seek salvation by works ; and such works must be laid aside before faith can be received." Strangely enough, Gambold, and also Westley Hall (another of the Oxford Methodists), adopted this dangerous delusion. Hence the following from Wesley's Journal :—

" 1741, January 28. Our old friends, Mr. Gambold and Mr. Hall, came to see my brother and me. The conversation turned wholly on silent prayer, and quiet waiting for God; which, they said, was the only possible way to attain living, saving faith.

" Sirenum voces, et Circes pocula nosti ?

" Was there ever so pleasing a scheme ? But where is it written ? Not in any of those books which I account the oracles of God. I allow, if there is a better way to God than the scriptural way, this is it. But the prejudice of education so hangs upon me, that I cannot think there is. I must, therefore, still wait in the Bible-way, from which this differs as light from darkness."

The reader has here a characteristic specimen of Wesley's refined irony, and determined adherence to the word of God. In the latter, Gambold sometimes failed. He was still a young man of only thirty ; and yet not a few of the years of his past life had been worse than wasted, by his indulging in the philosophical speculations of the ancients, instead of taking the Scriptures for his guide ; and now, when he had emerged from the mists of the early ages of the Christian Church, he suddenly plunged into the delusive fog of the newly-arrived Philip Henry Molther. How long he continued there we have no means of knowing ; but one thing is certain, that, the above-named heresy occasioned contentions which created a partial estrangement between him and his old friend Wesley. In July, 1741, Wesley had to preach before the Oxford University, in the church of St. Mary's ;

and, being in doubt as to the subject of his sermon, whether it should be from the text, " Almost thou persuadest me to be a Christian," or from, " How is the faithful city become an harlot ! " he went to Oxford, a month before the time of its delivery, to advise with Gambold concerning it, but met with a response far from friendly. Wesley writes :—

" He seemed to think it of no moment ; ' For,' said he, ' all here are so prejudiced, that they will mind nothing you say.' "

Wesley adds :—

"I know not that. However, I am to deliver my own soul, whether they will hear, or whether they will forbear."

Even this was not all. Only a fortnight later, Wesley wrote :—

" 1741, July 2. I met Mr. Gambold again, who honestly told me he was ashamed of my company, and, therefore, must be excused from going to the society with me. This is plain dealing at last."

Such was another of the disastrous results of Molther's visit to the London Moravians : Wesley and Gambold, bound together by hundreds of endearing facts, were parted ; and, though not converted into foes, were no longer friends.

It is a melancholy fact, that this estrangement was not temporary. Twelve months before, the friendship between Whitefield and Wesley had been ruptured ; but, in 1742, there was a sincere and hearty reunion, which lasted until death. In the case of Gambold, it was otherwise, but through no fault of Wesley's. On December 23, 1745, Charles Wesley wrote as follows :—

" I met my old friend, John Gambold, at my printer's, and appointed to meet him to-morrow at Dr. Newton's. I brought my brother with me. I found the Germans had quite estranged and stole away his heart, which nevertheless relented, while we talked over the passages of our former friendship ; but he hardened himself against the weakness of gratitude. We could not prevail upon him to meet us again."

Yea, more than this. Eighteen years afterwards, Wesley himself made the following entries in his journal :—

" 1763, November 5. I spent some time with my old friend, John,

Gambold. Who but Count Zinzendorf could have separated such friends as we were? Shall we never unite again?

"December 16. I spent an agreeable hour, and not unprofitably, with my old friend, John Gambold. O how gladly could I join heart and hand again! But, alas! thy heart is not as my heart!"

Gambold would not resume the friendship; but, to the very last, Wesley held him in high esteem. Only twelve months before Gambold's death, he spoke of him as being one of the most "sensible men in England."[1] But to return to Oxford, where the breach first occurred.

Wesley's sermon, before the University, was preached and published; and it is a curious fact, that, of all the sermons Gambold ever preached, only two have appeared in print, and, that, one of the two was delivered in the same year, in the same church, and before the same audience, as this of Wesley's was. Gambold's sermon was founded upon the text, "And the angel said unto them, Fear not: for behold I bring you good tidings of great joy, which shall be to all people;" and was entitled: "Christianity Tidings of Joy. A Sermon preached before the University of Oxford, at St. Mary's, on Sunday, December 27, 1741. Published at the request of Mr. Vice-Chancellor."

The two sermons were widely different. Wesley's was intensely practical and faithful; an earnest and comprehensive enforcement of experimental and practical religion, with a direct, searching, personal application, which, under the circumstances, was much more likely to be censured than applauded. Gambold's was much more than twice the length of Wesley's; but not half so simple and useful. Wesley's was full of the Methodist doctrine of the day; Gambold's was a metaphysical disquisition, which might, with consistency, have been uttered by any of the Oxford divines opposed to the Methodist movement. It would not be true to say, that, his remarks were not pertinent; but they were not what such an audience might have expected from a newly converted Methodist. How to account for this we know not. His sermon is long, learned, and able; but it fails to reach the heart and conscience as Wesley's does. Besides,

---

[1] Wesley's Works, vol. iii., p. 388.

there is one sentence in it which, as coming from such a man, is perfectly perplexing. He expressly asserts that "a man's sins are forgiven in baptism ;" and that baptism, "the channel of remission, is qualification enough for heaven, to those who die upon it." To reconcile the discrepancy between this and Gambold's own statements as already quoted, is difficult, if not impossible. The fact seems to be, that, though he had embraced the doctrine of salvation by faith only, he was still infected with some of the High Church principles of the Oxford Methodists ; and his evangelical and able ministry was marred and made misty by the philosophical speculations and reasonings in which he had so long indulged. That he was a trustful and saved believer in Jesus Christ, there cannot be a doubt ; but he failed to announce the great doctrines, which he had been taught by Bohler, with the simplicity, clearness, earnestness, and pathos that Wesley did. Wesley's heart was full of them ; and, in all his wanderings, they were almost the only theme of his daily ministry. Gambold held, and also preached them ; but, perhaps, from his metaphysical cast of mind, they were not so clearly and forcibly presented as by his quondam friend.

Nine months after the delivery of his sermon before the University, Gambold formally severed himself from the Established Church, and united with the Moravians. He was the fifth of the Oxford Methodists who had joined the Brethren. Of these, the two Wesleys had seceded,—or, it might almost be said,—had been virtually expelled. The third, Benjamin Ingham, in this very year, 1742, transferred to the Moravians more than fifty societies, which he had been the instrument of raising in two of the northern counties. Westley Hall, the fourth, need not here be further mentioned. Gambold, the fifth, was the only one who died in the Moravian communion. The step he took was well-considered. He might seem odd ; but he was unquestionably sincere. The Moravians in England were only of a few years' standing, and had many faults ; but there was one thing in existence among them, and practised by them, after which Gambold, newly converted, longed with the utmost earnestness,—Christian fellowship. Of this, there was none at Stanton-Harcourt ; and it was only now, in 1742, that his old friend Wesley thoroughly succeeded in making such a provision for the Methodists, by dividing their Societies into Classes. This was the thing for which Gambold pined. It could be enjoyed nowhere except among either Wesley's people or the Moravians. Gambold and Wesley were no longer friends; and, hence, the union of Gambold with the Brethren. With this view, he applied to them for admission, committing himself to their direction, and having no choice with regard to any station or office to be held by him in the future. In the beginning of October, 1742, he simply writes :—

"Having had assurance that such a favour might be granted, I left my parish with a view to live wholly with the Brethren."

Of course he had previously communicated his intention to the Bishop of Oxford, and also to his patron, Lord Harcourt; and both had strongly urged him to change his purpose : but his resolution was fixed. In due form he resigned his living, and issued an address to his parishioners, of which the following is the substance :—

"It is not in consequence of any resentment, or of any worldly motive that I give up my parish. I have not so implicitly given up my judgment to others as to be prevailed upon, by their persuasion, to take this step. The reason for my so doing is well grounded, and to my own satisfaction. It does not, I assure you, proceed from any dislike that I have to the worship of God in the Church of England. I find no fault with any passage or clause in the Common Prayer Book. Nor can I, in justice, be considered in the same light with such persons as slight and forsake one party of Christians and go over to another without sufficient cause. But that which has determined the choice I have made, was the earnest desire I found in myself of that improvement in the knowledge of the Gospel, and in the experience of the grace of Jesus Christ, which I stood in need of. The blessings purchased by the blood of the Shepherd of our souls, I longed to enjoy in fellowship with a little flock of His sheep, who daily feed on the merits of His passion, and whose great concern is to build up one another in their most holy faith, and to propagate the truth, as it is in Jesus, for the good of others. His gracious presence, the power of His Word, and the virtue of His blood, I wanted to have a more lively sense of, for my own comfort and support in the Christian warfare; and I had reason to hope for those means of happiness, especially where brethren dwell together in unity, for there the Lord commandeth His blessing and life for evermore. This is all I aim at in withdrawing myself from you; and may this departure give no offence to any one.

"I now take my last adieu, and earnestly pray for you and for myself. For myself, that I may be faithful to the grace of our Lord Jesus Christ,

and prove His servant, truly devoted to Him, where I am going; and
may you, where you remain, be as obedient to the influence of His Spirit
and the dictates of His word as I wish to be; so shall we one day rejoice
before the Great Shepherd of our souls, that merciful and compassionate
Saviour, in whom there is, in the meantime, life, peace, and joy for all
believers. I do not go from you because I cannot live in the Church of
England, as an outward profession, or because I prefer any other form of
ecclesiastical government before that which is by. law established in this
kingdom; but the inducement which leads me to this change, is the great
concern I have for the attainment of a happy state of mind; 'and, 'to com-
pass this end, no means, through the blessing of God, appear to me so
proper as a free intercourse with those who are of the same principles
with my own, to whom I may communicate without reserve; and from
whom I can receive that assistance of advice and comfort, which is necessary for a person encompassed with such infirmities as I am. I heartily
wish you may derive more benefit from the instructions of my successor,
than you have, or could have done, from mine; and I trust this will be
the case."

Nothing need be added to this, except the remark that, in
these days, when the utility and necessity of meetings for
religious fellowship are so boldly called in question, an argument in their favour may be taken from the yearning experience of this Oxford Methodist.

Gambold spent twenty-nine years in close and active connection with the Moravians; but his life, compared with the
career of Wesley and of Whitefield, was uneventful.

At the time of his admission, "the congregation of the
Lamb, with its officers and servants as settled in London,"
consisted of twenty-one married men, thirteen married women,
three widowers, five widows, sixteen single men, and fourteen
single women, a total of seventy-two persons. This was a
small affair. The Moravians had the start of Wesley's society
in London; and yet that Society, in February, 1743, numbered not fewer than 1950 members.[1] It is also a curious
fact, that, nearly one half of the Moravian Society were
office-bearers; that is, "Congregation Elders, Vice Elders,
Eldresses, Waiters, Choristers, Admonitors, Censors, Servants, and Sick Waiters." Excepting Gambold and James
Hutton, none seem to have had the advantages of education;
and, probably, all the men were tradesmen, journeymen, or

---

[1] Stevenson's " City Road Chapel," p. 28.

1742
—
Age 31

mechanics.[1] This was the society Gambold joined, for the sake of Christian fellowship.

His stay in London was not long. On the 14th of May, 1743, he married, and, for eighteen months afterwards, abode in Wales, chiefly at Haverfordwest, where he kept a school, and preached occasionally.

Gambold returned to London in November, 1744; and here, with trifling exceptions, he seems to have resided until his death, in 1771. Here, at Fetter Lane, he preached with power, eloquence, and sacred unction; and numbers were benefited by his ministry. His views of baptism, and his mode of administering it, may be gathered from a paragraph in the "Memoirs of James Hutton," where, under date of September 13, 1745, it is said,—

"Gambold baptized Brother Fell's little boy. He spoke on baptism, and said, 'it was a delivering a child over into the death of our Saviour.' After prayer, he took the child into his arms, and, taking water three times, he baptized him in the name of the Father, and of the Son, and of the Holy Ghost; then, singing some verses, he carried the child round to the labourers who were present, who blessed him by laying on of hands."

As already stated, the Moravian Society in London was small; but its meetings were numerous. From a list of the "public and private opportunities of the Brethren at London, throughout the whole week," in February, 1747, we learn that they had four sermons every Sunday, two in English and two in German; also German preaching every Tuesday, and English every Tuesday and Thursday. Besides these services, however, there were twenty-two others on Sunday, six on Monday, five on Tuesday, thirteen on Wednesday, nine on Thursday, five on Friday, and five on Saturday, making seventy-two religious services every week, exclusive of monthly general meetings, prayer days, children's prayer days, and sacraments. To what extent Gambold took part in these Moravian meetings, it is impossible to say; but, numerically considered, there was, beyond a doubt, sufficient scope to gratify his longings for religious fellowship.

In 1747, Gambold, accompanied by Ingham, Okeley, Hut-

---

[1] Hutton's Memoirs, p. 97.

ton, and Cennick, paid a visit to Hernhaag, where he continued for several months, and gained the respect and love of
all who knew him. His visit was at an important crisis in
the Brethren's history ; and, probably, was occasioned by the
disastrous fanaticism which had broken out in that important
settlement. In 1738, a building was begun at Hernhaag,
designed to serve as an asylum for persons educated in the
German Calvinistic Church, and persecuted on account of
their connection with the Brethren. In 1740, a congregation
was regularly organized ; and, in a few years, Hernhaag contained a greater number of inhabitants than Herrnhut. Here
boarding-schools were established for the education of the
children of the Moravian ministers, whether employed in the
service of the church at home or in foreign lands ; and the
place altogether was one of great importance. In 1746, however, there was the utmost danger of this Christian settlement
being ruined. Here began an evil, which soon became wide-
spread, and which required vigorous and long-continued efforts
to annihilate. The following is extracted from Holmes' " History of the Protestant Church of the United Brethren " (Vol.
i., p. 399).

" In their zeal to root out self-righteousness, the Brethren were not
sufficiently on their guard against levity of expression. The delight they
took in speaking of the sufferings of Christ, which arose from the penetrating sense they had of their infinite value, by degrees degenerated into
fanciful representations of the various scenes of His passion. Their style,
in speaking and writing, lost its former plainness and simplicity, and
became turgid, puerile, and fanatical, abounding in playful allusions to
Christ as the Lamb, the Bridegroom, etc., by which He is described in
holy writ, and in fanciful representations of the wound in His side. In
describing the spiritual relation between Christ and His Church, the
highly figurative language of the Canticles was substituted in the place
of the dignified simplicity, used by our Saviour and His apostles, when
speaking on this subject. Some less-experienced preachers even seemed
to vie with each other in introducing, into their discourses, the most
extravagant, and often wholly unintelligible, expressions. This kept the
hearers in a state of constant excitement, but was not calculated to subject every thought of the heart to the obedience of Christ. Religion,
instead of enlightening the understanding, governing the affections, and
regulating the general conduct, became a play of the imagination.
" This species of fanaticism first broke out at Hermhaag, in the year
1746, and, from thence, spread into several other congregations. Many
were carried away by it, for it seemed to promise a certain joyous perfec-

 tion, representing believers as innocent, playful children, who might be quite at their ease amidst all the trials and difficulties incident to the present life. The effect produced was such as might be expected. The more serious members of the church (and these after all formed the major part) bitterly lamented an evil, which they could not at once eradicate. Others, considering the malady as incurable, withdrew from its communion. The behaviour of such as were most infected with this error, though not immoral and criminal, was yet highly disgraceful to their Christian profession. Had not God in mercy averted the impending danger, a spirit of religious levity and antinomianism might, by degrees, have sapped the very foundation of the Brethren's Church, and completed her ruin."

What part Gambold took in this affair at Herrnhaag, and with what results, we have no means of knowing ; but certain it is, that, this pestiferous lusciousness spread to England, and, for many a long year afterwards, disgraced the Moravian hymns, and justly exposed the Moravians themselves to the censures and taunts of both friends and foes. It would be easy to quote instances illustrative of this, from the English Moravian Hymn Book, " published chiefly for the Use of the Congregations in Union with the Brethren's Church," in 1754; but the reader would not be edified by such quotations.

The Moravians in England, when compared with the Methodists, could hardly be considered a prosperous community. From the first, a considerable number of their members belonged to other churches; and, in 1749, an effort was made to multiply such extra-ecclesiastical adherents, by instituting what was called an English Tropus, the object being to provide a means whereby the members of other communities, and, notably, of the Church of England, might be enrolled in the Moravian Brotherhood, without severing themselves from the churches of which they already formed a part. This was one of the subjects discussed at a synod held in London in the above-mentioned year ; and, to facilitate the matter, Gambold addressed the following letter." To Papa, *i.e.* Count Zinzendorf," the beginning of which, to mention nothing else, shows how far even Gambold had fallen into the offensive use of the adulatory language of Moravian sycophants.

"MOST DEAR AND PATERNAL HEART,—A certain reflection has this

day arisen in my mind, which, such as it is, I wish to communicate to you.
I perceive that you and your faithful colleagues are earnestly labouring to
bring it about, that, those, who flee from the fold of the Anglican religion,
may not be completely cut off from the said religion ; but still continue
in ecclesiastical bond with it ; and, therefore, you propose to constitute
an Anglican tropus among the Brethren,—an object most dear to us, and
with the greatest propriety recommended ; inasmuch as it is beginning,
as I imagine, to be thought desirable by the clergy of this country also. I
greatly fear, however, that there are, in their hierarchy, certain deficiencies
which may occasion some obstruction to the consent of the majority ;
moreover, other considerations may oppose the arrangement, that one
prelate (the others being unconsulted, except, perhaps, synodically),
should be able to concede this privilege.

" Two special means, or symbols of union, are contained, as I understand, under the word Tropus. ONE REQUISITE is, that some prelate of
the Anglican Church should be invested with the office of examining into
such matters as the Brethren agitate, and, on the part of his Church, and
with the seal of the same, assisting at their ordinations. The *other
requisite* is, that the Liturgy, or Prayers of the Anglican Church should be
admitted in our assembly. The *former* involves the appointment of prudent political men ; the *latter* provides for the security of religious, pious
persons sustaining any injury from us ; tending, moreover, to the abate-
ment of disaffection as respects both communities, and to their mutual
benefit and salvation. I, therefore, earnestly desire the accomplishment of
the design.

" What evil, in the mean time, could ensue if the whole Book of Prayers
of the Anglican Church should occasionally be used in public ; not at this
time as prayers, but as text ; and an explanation occasionally given as to
the passages which, with us, may seem to require some explanation ? Certain exceedingly grand portions of sacred Scripture which are intermingled
with these may, in this service, be omitted as being beyond all dispute ;
and so, in six or eight prelections, or short discourses, the whole may be
finished. The service may, with propriety, be preceded by some such
introduction as the following :

" ' Inasmuch as we and some other nurslings of the Anglican Church,
who have embraced the spiritual aid of the Moravian Brethren, yet certainly with no design, by so doing, of departing from our own proper
religion ; being, however, in such situation, it manifestly follows that we
constitute an assembly which is extraordinary and extra-parochial, being
ecclesiastically made up out of various parishes ; and that we, moreover,
have a sacred place of meeting, which certainly is not a parish church ;
consequently many will immediately conclude that we are now of a
different mind, and that we have altogether forsaken the Anglican
Church. Such, however, would be an erroneous opinion. That we constitute such a society or assembly as we have mentioned, arises from our
desire to exercise that salutary and vigorous discipline which the Anglican
Church pants for ; but, by reason of its exceeding magnitude, cannot
maintain ; that we have a place in which we assemble, and a pulpit,

arises from our delight in hearing the principal doctrine respecting the death and grace of our Redeemer more clearly and more fully enunciated there than can in these times be expected elsewhere, notwithstanding the same doctrine is maintained in the primary article of the Anglican Church. There is, therefore, no reason why we should be offended with the Church of our fatherland ; and let it not so tenaciously disallow to us those superadded aids for our benefit and edification which we now enjoy, and nothing will be more agreeable to us than (provided these be preserved with a good conscience) henceforward still to preserve with it the bond of unity. For we are able to do so both openly and sincerely. In testimony of this, we are prepared to adopt in our assemblies the Liturgy or Common Prayers of the Anglican Church. But, because, as we are informed, the use of the Anglican Liturgy, beyond the ordinary churches, will either be unlawful, or, at least, exceedingly offensive ; and as a kind of secret disaffection, rather than amity, might arise therefrom with those whom, from the most sincere respect, we would not injure even in the least, we must therefore defer the adoption of this Liturgy, in our *proseucha* or house of prayer, until full liberty of using it be granted to us by those who have the authority. In the meantime, however, in order to its being made manifest that what we have asserted is true, that union with the Church of our fatherland is possible, since no violence is thereby done to our conscience (providing there be left to us discipline and evangelization, neither one nor the other of which being opposed to the Anglican Church ; nay, perhaps, more closely allied to it than some imagine),—let us proceed to examine in due order the whole liturgy of the Anglican Church. As to what others, who, diverging into sects, have departed from the Anglican fold, may have to object to this Liturgy I shall take no notice, for they and we are neither affected nor aggrieved by the same things. But, throughout this examination I shall make it my special care to omit nothing which can, in accordance with our light and principles, or indeed ever can, occasion any obstacle to any one of us. To such passages I shall assign that sense and exposition which I judge to have been, and to be, the true meaning ; and, unless I am deceived, such will be found neither grievous nor unreasonable to the mind which is imbued with the clearer knowledge and love of the Saviour.'

"I have run out further than is suitable for an introduction ; but, as if carefully reviewing the whole matter in question, I have been imagining what effect would result from the procedure: the same that you also desire through the means of a *Tropus*, only more feebly and less constant. But why, in any degree, less constant? Because it is sufficiently constant, considering the novelty of the measure. Such a declaration would sink into the memory, and would be preserved by all as a memorial of the true mind and will of the Brethren.

"Your most respectful son, and desiring to be excused, though some should prate beyond their measure,

"JOHN GAMBOLD."[1]

---

[1] Hutton's Memoirs, p. 245.

This long and tiresome letter is not without its use. For eight years, Gambold had been a Moravian; he was in the vigour of his manhood; but his mode of thinking and style of writing were not improved; nay, had become as murky as the religious clouds in which he lived. Besides, he was only eleven years the junior of Zinzendorf, and was naturally and scholastically his equal, if not his superior; and, yet, contaminated by the sycophancy of his associates, Gambold, the Oxford student, the learned mystic, the dramatic poet, condescends to use the offensive twaddle then so common, and must needs address the ambitious foreigner as "Papa," and "Most dear and paternal Heart." Think of Wesley, or even of Ingham, employing such epithets as these! The manliness of the man was being dwarfed by the fooleries of his friends.

But, apart from this, Gambold's letter is a curious production, and not without interest at the present day, as containing a scheme for a kind of amalgamation of some of the Moravians with the Established Church. The Moravians differed from the Methodists; for Zinzendorf, at the very Synod held immediately after the date of Gambold's letter, formally announced that the English Moravians were "now openly in the eye of the world acknowledged to be a Church;" whereas Wesley, to the day of his death, denied this distinction to the Methodists, affirming, in the strongest terms, that the Methodists were not a Church, but only *Societies within a Church.* Thus, the position' of the two communities was different. To be consistent, the Methodists, might have claimed, and, indeed, ought to have claimed, membership with some existing Church, beyond the circle of the Society enclosure; but, according to Zinzendorf and the London Synod of 1749, the Moravians were themselves a Church; and, hence, for any Moravian, like Gambold, to profess himself a member of the Anglican Church, was, in point of fact, to claim to be a member of two Churches instead of one. This was a grave inconsistency; but, in accordance with Gambold's suggestions, an attempt was made to carry it into effect.

The proposed Synod met in London, in September, 1749; and "the Most Reverend Thomas Wilson, Bishop of Sodor and Man," already in the eighty-sixth year of his age, with great formality, and with a pomp of language almost startling, was "chosen into the order and number of the Anetecessors of the General Synod of the Brethren of the Anatolic Unity." It was also decreed further, "that, the aforesaid Most Reverend Prelate ought to be offered the administration of the Reformed tropus in our hierarchy for life, with full liberty, in case of *emergency*, to employ, as his substitute, the Rev. Thomas Wilson, Royal Almoner, Doctor of Theology, and Prebendary of St. Peter's, Westminster."

The good old Bishop, with joy and thankfulness, accepted the office to which the Moravians had elected him;[1] and, thus, Gambold and Zinzendorf succeeded in securing the patronage of an English Prelate. Practically, the arrangement was of little use, perhaps of none at all. Five years afterwards, the venerable and pious Bishop was gathered to his fathers, at the age of ninety-one.

Moravianism and its illustrious "Papa" had now arrived at the zenith of their offensive ambition. It would be useless, and also far from pleasant, to disinter the history of the Moravian Brotherhood at this important crisis. A few of the facts have been mentioned in Ingham's Memoir; and nothing more need now be added, except, that, while Zinzendorf was almost idolatrously honoured by the Moravians themselves, he was the subject of severe but just attacks outside the pale of his own community. Prudently, though perhaps somewhat arrogantly, he generally declined to defend himself, partly on the ground that royalty always acted thus; but he found it desirable to do something else which was almost tantamount to this. In this same year, 1749, he published, in his own private printing-office, a folio volume of 184 pages, entitled, "Acta Fratrum Unitatis in Angliâ, 1749;" the whole of which, with the exception of the sixth section of the second part, was translated or edited by Gambold. The first part of this curious work consists entirely of Acts of Parliament and Reports of Parliamentary Committees in reference to the Brethren, together with original documents adduced as proofs of the propositions which had been made.

---

[1] Hutton's Memoirs, p. 246.

The second part embraces :—1. A paraphrase of the twenty-one Articles of the Confession of Augsburg; 2. The Brethren's method of preaching the Gospel according to the Synod of Berne; 3. The Moravian Litany; 4. Extracts from the Minutes of Moravian Synods; 5. Zinzendorf's *Rationale* of the Brethren's Liturgies; 6. Original passages from the writings of the early fathers of the Church, and of theologians of the middle ages.

This was not the only service which Gambold rendered to Zinzendorf and the Moravians. On June 4, 1750, he sent to Spangenberg a long letter, which was afterwards published in a pamphlet, with the title, "An Essay towards giving some just ideas of the personal character of Count Zinzendorf, the present Advocate and Ordinary of the Brethren's Church : In several Letters wrote by Eye-Witnesses. Published by James Hutton, late of Westminster, and now of Chelsea. London, 1755." 8vo. Gambold's letter is too long for insertion here ; but throughout it is a vindication of the Count,—the best doubtless that Gambold could supply,—and a few extracts may be useful :—

"There are a great number of thinking persons, who, if the bear-skin could be taken off from the Brethren, would directly be well satisfied with that somewhat extraordinary, but yet reasonable, zeal for the fundamentals of Christianity, which, after all, is the Brethren's whole mystery and peculiarity."

"The Brethren's Church has, at present, an illustrious nobleman both for her Advocate and Ordinary; and most of the hard imputations cast upon her by her antagonists are levelled against him, and either arise from or imply a misunderstanding of his true character. He is an *extraordinary* person or genius, and, as such, requires to be looked at in a particular point of view, if one will avoid error. I will, therefore, do nothing else but set down to that end some remarks which occur to me, from ten or eleven years' acquaintance with him."

"Count Zinzendorf has in him something unlike other people. But what is it? A very tender and deep-rooted *love to our blessed Redeemer*, and the highest and most *honourable conceptions of His atonement.* He willingly believes, as the New Testament supposes, that the bitter sufferings of the Saviour are alone able to *enervate*, as well as atone for sin; and the contemplation and influence of His tormented person, to effect our *sanctification* in all its branches. And all the hearty expressions to the honour of Jesus, that are found in ancient Hymns, or Meditations of pious Divines, (which, because mankind do not always keep up to the same strain of truth, are unjustly looked upon as flights and raptures), are with him serious principles."

"Some have censured him for introducing, or suffering to be introduced, some new *Phrases*, and delivering assertions which have the look of *Paradoxes;* but these Phrases and Paradoxes, when examined to the bottom, are orthodox; and, if not *verbatim* used in former ages, are, at least, parallel to the always received theological language; and, upon some occasions, are necessary, and happily effectual, to set people a-thinking, and to recover in their minds the full idea belonging to many terms and sayings over which they, by frequent repetition, have fallen asleep, and forgot the force and import of them. In the same view, he also likes very much to translate the Scriptures in a free, round manner, and in modern words."

"The same jealousy to keep the word of God from being robbed of its energy, has led him to oppose another abuse. Many pious people, though not sleepy and unmoved by the words they repeat, yet amidst their best emotion, have only vague and indeterminate ideas, nor can it be known precisely what they mean. Now, though a dealer in mere metaphors and allegories may be a very good soul, yet, it is not for the honour of God, that its doctrine should rest upon such a foundation; but all its assertions must rather be literally ascertainable realities, in the same manner as physical ones are, upon a nearer experience; and this is the motive of his bringing spiritual matters to a point, under a clothing and illustration somewhat *philosophical*, for a season, until the supposition that those matters are only something *shadowy*, and not substance, is exploded."

" His original design was purely to preach and recommend his Saviour to mankind at large, wherever he could find audience. It was wholly accidental, and by him unsought, that he has been entrusted with the direction of a particular Church. However others may look upon the occurrences in the Brethren's congregation, *he* is always deeply struck with *reverence* for our Saviour's immediate guidance of, and benediction over the whole, which occasions his using, sometimes about things which others may account small or common, that *magnificence* of expression which is observable in him. The same tender attention to his Master's mind and order, renders him sometimes, when he apprehends any deviation therefrom, more *vehement* in his manner, than is incident to those who have not zeal enough ever to be constrained in spirit. Upon this account, he has been thought magisterial; but very unjustly, for, abstracting from the fervour, which, in an agony of faithfulness, he may at such times discover, he is ready to be informed by any one, distrustful of himself, extremely moderate towards those against whom he may be expected to be sharp, and not at all fond of power.

" Further, from a long experience in regard to congregations, he sometimes delivers his opinion about the method of carrying on the Gospel work in a very systematical manner, implying, one might think, a great deal of *policy;* but, when his counsels are traced to their first idea, they are always an inculcation of one or other of the known maxims of our Saviour, with only a more direct application to special and present cases than is common.

"He is deeply persuaded of the blessed ends attained by gathering some of the children of God together into such little *congregations* as he has the care of; but he is also fully convinced, not only that there are many more of God's children remaining scattered in the several *Christian parties* and societies; but even that the establishments, confessions, forms of worship, etc., in those societies, have a blessed effect for the salvation of such. For which reason, if the hearts on all sides did but permit things to go according to his mind, the souls who are quickened to spiritual life, even through the necessity of the Brethren, should, notwithstanding, remain generally in the communion and way they had been brought up in, without the least affront or infringement offered thereto.

"His *noble* way of thinking, in several other particulars, will not so much recommend him at first sight, as expose him to censure; but noble it is, however, and will be found best in the end. He is against using any *compulsion* with hearts, who ought to be led by the love of the Saviour, and by a new nature; and is endeavouring to bring the discipline of the congregation to such a temperature, as that it may assist a work of grace where it is, but not mimic it where it is not. In pursuance of which principle, he rather tolerates (with secret grief and employing only distant hints), several unessential faults' of those about him, than correct them with detriment to the ingenuity of spirit. These faults are charged upon him; as for instance, a few ill-judged flights of spiritual joy and cheerfulness, which he discerned to be such from the beginning, but would not retrench them, because they would not subside of themselves; and the *true* Christian gaiety of spirit is too valuable a jewel to hazard the breaking of it, by a rough blow in the polishing. So far goes the generosity of his conceptions, that he is resolved to drop the whole fabric of the congregation, if ever the life and spirit should be found to have left it. No wonder, then, that he insists upon adapting the outward worship, from time to time, to the inward state of the members; so that the Liturgy, from honesty and not from fickleness, is capable of many *progressive gradations*, and even of *retrogradations*, rather than fall into hypocrisy.

"In short, the person I have been speaking of is a plain man, who proceeds straight forward; and, amidst all the richness of his active and extensive genius, will always be serving and inculcating *one* only point, namely, the *meritorious sufferings of our Creator,*—a point by which alone Christians are distinguished from Deists."

How far this serves as a vindication or apology, the reader must form his own opinion; but it exhibits the fidelity of Gambold to his German leader, and also indicates some of the principles which Gambold himself entertained at this period of his history.

Gambold did more than this for the censured Zinzendorf. In 1751, a five shillings volume was published, with the title, "Maxims, Theological Ideas, and Sentences, out of the

  present Ordinary of the Brethren's Dissertations and Discourses, from the year 1738 to 1747. Extracted by John
Gambold, M.A. 8vo. In his Preface, Gambold writes :—

" Every one has heard, in some light or other, this *noble person's* name
mentioned. To judge *impartially* of him, we are to look back at what he
has preached in a course of several years, especially since the *discourses*,
by their nature and circumstances, were such a *free out-pouring of his
heart.*"

To this there could be no objection; but it may be doubted
whether Gambold's extracts were as *impartial* as he wished
them to be regarded.

In 1753, Gambold rendered another service to the Count,
by the publication of "The Ordinary's Remarks upon the
manner of his being treated in Controversy. Translated from
the High-Dutch, with a Preface, by John Gambold, Minister
of the Moravian Chapel in Fetter Lane."

And shortly after this, in 1754, Gambold issued, "A
Modest Plea for the Church of the Brethren," of which
publication, Lavington, Bishop of Exeter, wrote :—

" The whole drift of this pamphlet is to commend their sect in *general*
terms, without answering any one *accusation* brought against them." [1]

Lavington was a bitter antagonist, and what he says must
be received with caution ; but still, the very title of Gambold's
production indicates that the Brethren's Church was hardly
perfect.

More than this. In 1754, was published the largest hymn-
book in the English language : "A Collection of Hymns of
the Children of God in all Ages, from the Beginning till now.
In two Parts. Designed chiefly for the Use of the Congregations in Union with the Brethren's Church." Two Volumes,
pp. 380, and 390. [2] 8vo. Zinzendorf projected this ; but

---

[1] " The Moravians Compared and Detected," 1775, p. 150.

[2] It is said, on what authority we know not, that Gambold's contributions to this hymn-book consisted of twenty-eight original hymns, and
eleven translations from the Greek, Latin, or German. (*Wesleyan Times*,
January 23, 1865.)
The following are the first lines of both, the numbers being those of
the hymns as they are placed in the respective volumes :—

TRANSLATIONS.

Vol. I.   182. Ye elect, who peace possess unshaken.
   „   183. I'm bound fast, with Jesus' grave clothes platted.

Gambold was his chief editor.[1] The Preface, which probably was Gambold's production, contains the following description of the Brotherhood :—

1754

Age 43

"The Brethren's grand topic, in their hymns, as every one may see, is the Person and Propitiation of Jesus Christ. They collect, as in the *focus* of a burning glass, what has descended to them from past ages, or

Vol. I.   184. In this sense we're a body.
  „   191. Jesu, Saviour of man's nature.
  „   192. Be propitious.
  „   193. O thou eternal Saviour.
  „   208. Majestic Father ! whose pity gave.
  „   211. Saviour of the nations, come.
  „   221. Thousand times by me be greeted.
  „   222. O head so full of bruises.
  „   442. O World ! attention lend it.

ORIGINAL COMPOSITIONS.

Vol. II.   1. God we praise, that in these days.
  „   17. What says a soul, that now doth taste.
  „   34. No more with trembling heart I try.
  „   42. O tell me no more.
  „   50. Ye who have known th' atoning blood.
  „   51. Jesu, that gentle touch of thine.
  „   55. How happy is the heart.
  „   56. Jesu, each blind and trembling soul.
  „   58. How is it, Lamb ?
  „   66. How happy we, when guilt is gone.
  „   67. How Christ his souls doth bless.
  „   71. Grant Lord, I ne'er may doubt again.
  „   89. Hear what of him and me this day.
  „   127. After the labours of thy life.
  „   138. Attend, O Saviour, to our prayer.
  „   167. Few in former times could venture.
  „   168. For us no night can be happier styled.
  „   169. Whene'er him I can eat.
  „   170. The man from Nazaret.
  „   185. They who now God's children are.
  „   199. O my Lamb ! thou slaughter'd Prince !"
  „   230. That I am thine, my Lord and God.
  „   303. Should an historiographer.
  „   304. Of this point so divine.
  „   431. Since I, a worm unworthy.
  „   451. Look on me, Lamb, a child of thine.

Can these hymns be Gambold's ? We doubt it. Nay, we hope that they are not. It is scarcely possible to conceive, that a man of such culture could write such doggerel. With two or three poor exceptions, they ought never to have been printed. To say nothing of their horribly limping rhythm, they have far too much of the irreverent familiarity with the Divine Redeemer, which was so offensively employed in the hymns at that time sung by the Moravian Brotherhood. The two best are republished in Gambold's Works.

Hutton's Memoirs, p. 303.

O.

properly from the Bible itself, upon this head ; and, that it may not be evaded under the notion of *dicta ardentia*, they present it in a system, and apply that system to practice. They affirm our free acceptance with God as sinners, and through pure grace, and yet the necessity of, and powerful assistances for, a most real holiness of life afterwards, with such a warmth, upon each of these subjects successively, that many a reader runs away with the supposition of their over-doing on that side he happened to take notice of, for want of waiting the balance. They cherish, as an hereditary platform from their ancestors, a very high persuasion of, and very strict rules concerning, a New Testament Church. To mention but one peculiarity more, they continually betray a burning propensity to the work of propagating the Gospel of peace. If any one finds more things uttered in this spirit, than he can make application of in his sphere, let him remember that these are a people, very many of whose members have such a call. Above a hundred of them have already consumed and laid down their mortal tabernacles in ministering the Gospel to the heathen."

The last statement is remarkable, and greatly to the honour of the Brethren's Church, especially when it is remembered · that only thirty years had elapsed since the Church was founded at Herrnhuth, in Germany.

From these brief notices of his literary labours, it will be seen, that, Gambold was a faithful, unflinching friend of the illustrious Count. The English Moravians were passing through the terrible crisis already mentioned in the Memoir of Ingham. They were nearly wrecked; and not undeservedly. Ingham left them; but Gambold did his utmost to defend. them; and, as the chief English member of their community, was ordained a "*Chor-Episcopus*," in other words, an Assistant Bishop. The ceremony took place at a Synod, held at Lindsey House, London, in November, 1754; and was performed by Bishops Watteville, and John and David Nitschmann.[1]

Little more remains to be told of this sincere and devoted man. For seventeen years, he wore the honours of his office "with humility and diffidence." The writer of the Memoir, prefixed to Gambold's works, remarks :—

"Such a Bishop would have justly been esteemed an honour to any Church, whether ancient or modern, if disinterestedness of spirit, humility of mind, devotion of heart, a benevolent disposition towards all men, and

---

[1] Hutton's Memoirs, p. 294, and Holmes' History of the United Brethren, vol. ii., p. 41.

a voluntary submission to the service, not only of the Church in general, but of every member thereof, though in the most inferior situation, be the proper qualifications and distinguished ornaments of the Christian Episcopacy."

It has been already stated, that, of the thousands of sermons which Gambold preached, during the thirty-eight years of his Christian ministry, only two were printed. One of these was delivered, before the University of Oxford, in 1741; the other, in Fetter Lane Chapel, London, on a National Fast Day, in 1756.

At the latter period, the nation was in a state of great excitement and alarm. War with France was inevitable. February 6, 1756, was observed as a day of humiliation and prayer. Such a fast in London had not been seen since the Restoration. Business was suspended; and churches and chapels everywhere were crowded. Gambold's sermon was founded upon the text, "Tremble, thou Earth, at the presence of the Lord;" and, when published, was entitled, "The Reasonableness and Extent of Religious Reverence." Though somewhat metaphysical in its style, and mode of reasoning, it displays ability, and is worth perusing.

So far as is known, there are only two other works with the publication of which Gambold was connected.[1] One was a beautiful and comprehensive Catechism, of about sixty pages, 12mo, published in the year 1765, with the title, "A Short Summary of Christian Doctrine, in the Way of Question and Answer: The Answers being all made in the sound and venerable Words of the Common Prayer Book of the Church of England. To which are added, Some Extracts out of the Homilies. Collected for the Service of a few Persons, Members of the *Established Church;* but imagined not to be unuseful to others." Two facts are made manifest by this publication; namely, that, Gambold's creed was orthodox; and that, notwithstanding his Moravian bishopric, he had still a warm affection for the Church of England.

---

[1] It is said, however, that he translated the "Divine Poems" of Rees Pritchard, from Welsh into English; (*Wesleyan Times*, January 23, 1865), a work which we have never seen.

1765
Age 54   The other book, referred to above, was Cranz's History of
Greenland.   This was, in the first instance, published in
Germany; but the General Synod of 1765, directed that it
should be translated into English; and a great part of the
translation, and the whole of the editing was devolved upon
Gambold.   The work was published, in London, in 1767,
with the following title: "The History of Greenland: containing a Description of the Country and its Inhabitants;
and particularly a Relation of the Mission carried on, for
above thirty years, by the Unitas Fratrum at New Herrnhuth and Lichtenfels, in that Country.   By David Cranz.
Translated from the High Dutch; and illustrated with Maps
and other Copperplates.   London, 1767.   Printed for the
Brethren's Society for the Furtherance of the Gospel among
the Heathen."   8vo; vol. i., pp. 405; vol. ii., pp. 497.

About eighty copies were distributed among the nobility
and gentry, for the purpose of enlightening them respecting
the Moravian Mission; and the writer of the Memoirs of
James Hutton, says:—

> "Although the work, in a pecuniary sense, was by no means profitable;
> yet, the distribution of the copies among the higher ranks, produced the
> happiest effects, by removing the prejudice which had been excited in the
> public mind, through the writings of the Bishop of Exeter, and others."

For ten years after his episcopal ordination, Gambold
resided chiefly in London, employing himself in every
branch of service for the congregation settled there, and
in regular correspondence with all his fellow-labourers of the
same communion throughout England.

In 1760, the death of Zinzendorf occurred; and four
years later, a General Synod was held at Marienborn, which
Gambold attended.   Besides himself, there were present,
eleven bishops, forty-six presbyters, deacons, and lay-elders,
and thirty-seven deputies from different congregations.   It
was opened, with great solemnity, on the 1st of July, and
continued its deliberations, by several adjournments, in forty-
four sessions, till the 29th of August.

Ten years had elapsed since the last General Synod;
and, hence, many and momentous were the questions that
had to be considered.   Their sphere of labour had been

considerably enlarged, especially in heathen countries. There had been the long and embittered controversy in England. Some of their Settlements had been disturbed and injured by the existing war. Zinzendorf, their chief, had died; and the debt of the Brethren's Church amounted to the alarming sum of £150,000.[1] It is unnecessary to enter into the details of this important Conference. Suffice it to say, that, from this period, Moravianism became a purer, healthier, and more scriptural thing than it had been before.

Gambold secured the respect and love of the Brethren composing this General Synod; and was in a position to be of greater service to his community than ever. His work, however, was nearly ended. After the sessions of the Synod were concluded, he returned to London, where he continued to reside till 1768, when he was seized with "a dropsical asthma," from which his sufferings were such, that his friends, who were about him, apprehended that every day would be his last. Hoping to be benefited by the change, he removed to his native air; and, for a time, there were flickering hopes of amended health. Wishing to render himself useful to the Brethren's Church at Haverfordwest, he exerted his failing energies to the utmost. As far as he was able, he visited the sick, and poor, and tried to comfort them in their distresses. When he could, he preached; his last text being "Set your affections on things above." When not able to preach in public, he explained the Scriptures in private, and held fellowship with his Christian friends. His work was done; and it only remains to see how the Oxford Methodist, and Moravian Bishop died.

In a letter dated October 11, 1770, after stating that his asthma was so relieved that he could now lie down in bed, and obtain a little sleep, he continued:—

"I ought to be thankful for every mitigation of pain; but it becomes, I think, plainer than ever, that I have a real attack of the dropsy, which whether I shall get the better of it, or it, by and by, get the better of me, is a question. I totter on my legs, and, though I look pretty well, yet there are few intervals in the day wherein I have anything like strength either of body or mind However, I set no bounds to my Sav-

---

[1] Holmes' History of the United Brethren, vol. ii., p. 2, etc.

iour's power, if He sees it good to continue me here a little longer; but it is hardly to be any more expected in my case. I really do all I can to support my impaired constitution, and walk, most days, a little in the chapel or burying-ground, till I am ready to drop down. All that I can properly desire of my gracious Lord is, that, He would be merciful to me an unworthy sinner, wash me from all my unfaithfulness and transgressions in His blood, keep me in communion with Himself and His people, help me to behave rightly, at least not offensively, in my sickness, and be perceptibly near to me in my last hour, whenever it is to be."

In another letter, dated July 28, 1771, he wrote :—

" The writing of the few lines before the present, was the work of several days, attended with more difficulty and pain than any one is able to conceive, who does not feel what I have suffered. But to complain is disagreeable to me. The constant prayer of my heart, most tenderly united with yours, is for the welfare and prosperity of the Church of God, and especially that part of it which is the immediate object of our care. May our faithful and best Friend, who purchased it with His blood, and is the supreme Head thereof, so defend His people amidst all opposition, and support His servants who labour in the word and doctrine, and have the general charge over His house, that the several members of it may increase in faith, hope, and love, to their comfort and joy.

" With respect to myself, if I may judge from what I feel, I can think no otherwise than that I am very near the end of my course. Therefore, all my prayers are centred in this, that my gracious Lord may wash me, a sinner, in His blood, and abide always near me, especially in my last extremity."

The last time that he attended the public celebration of the Lord's Supper, was only five days before his death. At the conclusion of it, weak and wasted as he was, he commenced singing a verse of praise and thanksgiving, and the impression produced was such, that the whole congregation began to weep.

From the nature of his disease, it was seldom he could sleep ; but he was always patient and confiding. " All He does is well done," said he ; "let us only look to Him, and the end will be blessed." He was deeply thankful for the kind offices of his friends, and especially for those of his loving wife, who nursed him, in every stage of his illness, with the greatest tenderness. Just before the close of all his sufferings, he was heard to pray : "Dear Saviour ! remember my poor name, and come, come soon !" His prayer was answered. Shortly after these words were uttered, he peacefully expired, on September 13, 1771, leaving behind him, besides his widow, two children, a son and a daughter, to lament their loss. [1]

Gambold, like Wesley, wrote an epitaph on himself; and, as it is a fair specimen of the better class of his poetical productions, it is here subjoined :—

> " Ask not, who ended here his span ?
> His name, reproach, and praise, was—Man.
> Did no great deeds adorn his course
> No deed of his, but show'd him worse !
> One thing was great, which God supplied,
> He suffered human life,—and died.
> What points of knowledge did he gain ?
> That life was sacred all,—and vain ;
> Sacred, how high ? and vain, how low ?
> He knew not here, but died to know."

Though Bishop Gambold was a man of great learning, and of extensive reading, especially in the early writings of the Christian Church, he himself was not a voluminous author. Excepting his translations, and the works he merely edited, all that he published of his own were two sermons ; his Short Summary of Christian Doctrine; a few Prefaces : and some brief Hymns and Poems. In this respect, he differed widely from his old friend Wesley. Then again, though an able and effective preacher, his pulpit exercises were almost entirely confined to the small village of Stanton-Harcourt, and the Brethren's Chapel in Fetter Lane, London. In this also, he differed, not only from Wesley, but from Whitefield. Still, it would be incorrect to say, that his life, to a great extent, was a useless one. Wesley, after publishing one of Gambold's poetic pieces, is reported to have said: " And this light was buried *under a bushel !* How might he have enlightened all Christendom !"[2] We scarcely concur in this. Gambold, notwithstanding his learning and his piety, was con-stitutionally too timorous and retiring to be the man to en-

---

[1] It is a somewhat curious coincidence, that of the Oxford Methodists, Whitefield died in 1770, Gambold in 1771, Ingham in 1772, and Clayton in 1773. At least three of these also died in the month of September. The two Wesleys were in the midst of the Calvinian controversy,— the hottest of their lives.

[2] Methodist Magazine, 1814, p. 92.

 lighten all Christendom ; but, at the same time, he was of such
service to the Moravian Church, that, it is an extravagance
to say, "his light was buried under a bushel." With all
its weaknesses, follies, and faults, at the beginning of its
history, the Moravian Brotherhood set a Christian and heroic
example to other Churches, in its missions to the heathen ;
and the man who chiefly helped to edify, purify, improve, and
perpetuate such a community, did no mean service to the
cause of the Divine Redeemer. Gambold's poetry has been
over-estimated by Methodist and Moravian writers ; and,
perhaps also, his natural ability and learning ; but all must
admit, that he was an exceedingly devout and earnest Christian ; and that, though he might, for a season, be somewhat
tainted with the religious lusciousness of the early Moravian
society, his moral character, from first to last, was without a
speck.

Perhaps it ought to be added, that, a beautiful portrait
of Gambold was painted by Abraham Louis Brandt, an
earnest and laborious Moravian minister, and that an exquisite engraving from the original picture was prefixed to
Gambold's works, when first published in 1789.

REV. JAMES HERVEY, M.A.,

THE LITERARY PARISH-PRIEST.

JAMES HERVEY, with great appropriateness, was designated by Charles Wesley, the "Isocrates" of the Oxford Methodists.[1] The old Greek rhetorician was not an orator; the weakness of his voice and his natural timidity prevented that; but the polish of his style in writing and the harmonious construction of his sentences obtained for him a fame which seems to be undying. And so in regard to Hervey. He lacked Whitefield's eloquence, and Wesley's constructive faculty; but he had a peculiar mental quality, which invested his productions with an air of gracefulness beyond the power of either of his friends to imitate. Critics, great and small, genuine and pretentious, have condemned Hervey's style; and yet, notwithstanding this, few books have passed through more editions than his have done; and, after the lapse of a hundred years since their author's death, few are greater favourites at the present day. Why is this? Perhaps some of his censors can answer the question.

James Hervey, like the Wesleys and Gambold, was the son of a country clergyman. He was born at Hardingstone, near Northampton, on the 26th of February, 1714; his father holding the two neighbouring livings of Weston-Favel and Collingtree. His ancestors appear to have been highly respectable. One of them was a judge; another had been member of Parliament for the town of Northampton; and the patronage of the above-mentioned livings had been, for many years, in the possession of the family.

Until the age of seven, Hervey was under the tuition of his mother. He then became a day-scholar in the free grammar school at Northampton, where he displayed great dexterity in

---

[1] Charles Wesley's Journal, vol. ii., p. 393.

1733
———
Age 19

the usual gymnastic exercises of boys like himself; and where, in the course of ten years, he learned enough of the Latin and Greek languages, to enable him to matriculate at the Oxford University. His progress, however, would probably have been greater than what it was, had it not been for the execrable conduct of his master, who determined that no one in the school should learn faster than his own stupid son. "Hervey himself told me," says Mr. Ryland, "that his master never made but one remark in reading the Greek Testament, and that was a very foolish one."

When only a boy, seventeen years of age, Hervey, full of youthful frolic, left the quietude of his father's house for the animated scenes, the high advantages, and peculiar dangers of collegiate life. It was something infinitely more sacred than an accident which led to his admission into Lincoln College, where Wesley was a fellow and a tutor, and where, for the last two years, the Methodists had frequently held their meetings.[1]

The effects of the idleness enforced upon him at the Northampton free grammar school, were felt at Oxford. It was difficult for a sprightly and clever boy, like Hervey, to lay aside, all at once, the unstudious habits of the last ten years, and to devote himself, with unflagging earnestness, to the academical pursuits which now demanded his attention. For two years, from 1731 to 1733, he was idle at Oxford, as he had been obliged to be idle at Northampton. At the end of that time, he became acquainted with the Methodists, and distinguished himself, as they also did, by his devotion to the duties of religion, and to his collegiate studies. Wesley rendered him considerable assistance, especially by giving him instructions in the Hebrew language.

"Oxon, Sept. 2, 1736. I hereby thank you, as for all other favours, so especially for teaching me Hebrew."

Thus wrote Hervey, at the age of twenty-two, when he had taken his degree of Bachelor of Arts, and was leaving the

---

[1] Mr. Hutchins, one of the Oxford Methodists, and afterwards doctor, and rector of Lincoln College, was Hervey's tutor (*Gospel Magazine,* 1769, p. 12).

university to enter upon the duties of the Christian ministry. Eleven years afterwards, when in the midst of the fame arising from the recent publication of his " Meditations among the Tombs," etc., he wrote to Wesley another letter :—

1733
——
Age 19

"WESTON, NEAR NORTHAMPTON, *December* 30, 1747.

" Assure yourself, dear sir, that I can never forget the tender-hearted and generous Fellow of Lincoln, who condescended to take such compassionate notice of a poor under-graduate, whom almost everybody condemned ; and when no man cared for my soul."[1]

Here we pause, to take a glance at Hervey during his five years' residence at Oxford. John Gambold, writing of him, while he was still at college, says :—

" He is a man of surprising greatness of soul ; and, if you look for his virtues, you will not be able to discover them one by one, but you will see that he walks before God with a reverence and alacrity which includes them all."[2]

Hervey became one of the Oxford Methodists in 1733, when he was only nineteen years of age. In the same year, he wrote as follows to his sister :—

"LINCOLN COLLEGE, OXON, *Sept.* 16, 1733.

" DEAR SISTER,—Was there any occasion to apologize for the serious purport of this, it would be sufficient to direct you to the date,[3] and the time of its inditing, but I promise myself, that, to you anything of this nature will be unnecessary ; for, though we are in the very prime and spring of our years, strongly disposed to admire, and perfectly capacitated to relish the gaieties of youth, yet we have been inured to moderate the warmth of our appetites, accustomed to anticipate in our minds the days of darkness, and incessantly disciplined into a remembrance of our Creator. For my part, I find no season so proper to address one of the principal sharers of my heart, one of my nearest and dearest relations, as that I have at present chose and made use of, when either an universal silence composes the soul, and calms every turbulent emotion, or the voice of joy and gladness, speaking through celestial music, invites to adore the wonders of our Redeemer's love, touches upon the strings of the softest passions, and inspires the most sweet, most tender sentiments.

"As I was the other day traversing the fields in quest of health, I observed that they had lost that profusion of fragrant odours which once perfumed the air, and were disrobed of that rich variety of curious dyes which surpassed even Solomon in all his glory. Not a single flower

---

[1] Coke and Moore's " Life of Wesley," p. 51.
[2] *Arminian Magazine*, 1798, p. 171.
[3] The letter was written on the Sabbath.

appears to gladden the sight, to bespangle the ground, or enamel the barren landscape. The clouds, that recently distilled in dews of honey, or poured themselves forth in showers of fatness, now combine in torrents to overflow the lifeless earth, and to bury or sweep away all the faint footsteps of ancient beauty. The hills, that were crowned with corn, the valleys that laughed and sung under loads of golden grain, in a word, the whole face of nature, that so lately rejoiced for the abundance of her plenty, is become bare, naked, and disconsolate. As I was continuing my walk, and musing on this joyless scene, methought, the sudden change exhibited a lively picture of our frail and transitory state; methought, every object that occurred seemed silently to forewarn me of my own future condition.

"I dwelt on these considerations till they fermented in my fancy, and worked themselves out in such-like expressions: 'What! must we undergo so grievous an alteration? We, whose sprightly blood circulates in brightest tides? We, who are the favourites of time, on whom youth, and health, and strength, shed their selectest influence? We, who are so apt to look upon ourselves as exempt from cares, or pains, or troubles, and privileged to drink in the sweets of life without restraint, without alloy? Must we forego the sunshine of our enjoyments for anything resembling this melancholy gloom? Must the sparkling eye set in haggard dimness? the lovely features and glowing cheeks be obscured by pale deformity? Must soft and gay desires be banished from our breasts, or mirth and jollity from our conversation? Must the vigour of our age fall away like water that runneth apace, and the blissful minutes of the prime of our years vanish like a dream? If this be our case, in vain do we boast of our superior felicity. In vain do we glory in being the darlings of heaven. The inanimate creation droop indeed, sicken and languish, for a time; but quickly revive, rejoice, and again shine forth in their brightest lustre. It is true, they relinquish, at the approach of winter, their verdant honours; but rest fully assured of receiving them with interest from the succeeding spring. But man, when he has passed the autumn of his maturity,—when he has once resigned himself into the cold embraces of age,—bids a long, an eternal adieu to all that is entertaining, amiable, or endearing. No pleasing expectations refresh his mind; not the least dawnings of hope glimmer in to qualify the darksome looking-for of Death.'

"I had not long indulged these bitter reflections before I espied a remedy for those sore evils which occasioned them. Though I perceived all our passionate delights to be vanity, and the issue of them vexation of spirit; yet I saw, likewise, that virtue was substantial, and her fruits joy and peace;—that, though all things come to an end, the ways of wisdom were exceeding broad. The seeds of piety, if implanted in our tender breasts, duly cherished, and constantly cultivated, will bud and blossom even in the winter of our days; and, when white and red shall be no more,—when all the outward embellishments of our little fabric shall disappear,—this will still flourish in immortal bloom.

"To walk humbly with our God, dutifully with our parents, and

charitably with all, will be an inexhaustible source of never-ceasing com-
forts. What, though we shall sometimes be unable to hear the voice of
singing men and singing women,—though all the senses prove false to
their trust, and refuse to be any longer inlets of pleasure,—it is now, dear
sister, it is now in our power to make such happy provisions as even
then, in those forlorn circumstances, may charm our memories with
ravishing recollections, and regale all our faculties with the continual
feast of an applauding conscience. What sweet complacency, what
unspeakable satisfaction shall we reap from the contemplation of an
uninterrupted series of spotless actions! No present uneasiness will
prompt us impatiently to wish for our dissolution, nor anxious fears for
futurity make us immoderately dread the impending stroke. All will be
calm, easy, and serene. All will be soothed by this precious, this invaluable thought, that, by reason of the meekness, the innocence, the purity,
and other Christian graces which adorned the several stages of our progress through the world, our names and our ashes will be embalmed; the
chambers of our tomb consecrated into a paradise of rest; and our souls,
white as our locks, by an easy transition, become angels of light.

"I am, with love to my brother, dear sister, your most affectionate
brother,

"JAMES HERVEY."

This letter has been inserted without abridgment, 1. Because, it evinces, that, even while in his teens, Hervey cultivated that flowingly harmonious style, which was one of the
chief characteristics of all his publications. And, 2. Because,
it is thoroughly unevangelical, and, in spirit, such as might be
naturally expected from an Oxford Methodist seeking salvation by his own good works. 3. It was written at the time
when Hervey first united himself with Wesley and his
Pharisaic friends.

There are several other letters, written during the years
of Hervey's collegiate life; but, for want of space, they can
be only sparingly employed :—

(To his sister.)
"LINCOLN COLLEGE, OXON, *March* 28, 1734.
"DEAR SISTER,—My fancy has often took its flight to Hardingstone,
and delighted itself with the imaginary conversation of you and my other
dear relatives. I have frequently recollected, and, as it were, acted over
again in my mind the many pleasing hours we have spent together in
reading holy and edifying books, or discoursing on pious and useful subjects.

"There is great reason for congratulation, on account of your being so
choice a favourite of heaven, as your frequent sicknesses, and often infirmities speak you to be. How does the goodness of our gracious Father

endeavour, by the repeated, though lightest, strokes of His rod, to cure whatever is disordered, to rectify whatever is amiss in you ! Do not then hold out against these kind calls to repentance; but suffer yourself, by this loving correction, to be made great;—great in humility, holiness, and happiness. Humble yourself under the mighty hand of God; and, by a hearty sorrow for your past faults, and a firm resolution of obedience for the future, let this fatherly chastisement bring forth in you the peaceable fruits of righteousness."

All good, so far as it goes, especially from a youth of twenty; but not a word of Christ, or of being saved by His mediatorial merits, and by the exercise of faith in Him.

His sister wished him to turn poet; but, instead of writing poetry himself, he sent her "The Last Day," by Dr. Young; and wrote as follow :—

"LINCOLN COLLEGE, OXON, *May* 2, 1734.

"DEAR SISTER,—I scarcely know any human composition more likely to improve and edify, at the same time that it diverts and delights, than this poem of "The Last Day." If you would please yourself, refine your taste, or have the practice of religion pleasing, instead of plays, ballads, and other corrupt writings, read this almost Divine piece of poetry ;— read it (as I have done), over and over; think upon it; endeavour to digest it thoroughly; and even to get by heart the most moving passages: and then, I trust, you will find it answer the ends I purpose in sending it.

" You will excuse me from exercising my poetical talent; because, I perceive, such an attempt will be either very absurd, or very dangerous. For, should I tack together a few doggerel rhymes, this would be an affront to you; whereas, should I succeed so well as to gain the applause of my reader, this, I am sure, would portend very great harm, if not to you, yet, most certainly, to me. For what can portend greater harm than the words of praise, which, though smoother than oil, yet, are very swords? What can be more destructive of that humble mind which was in Christ Jesus,—that meek and lowly spirit which is in the sight of God of great price? I am so far from carrying on my versifying designs, that, I heartily wish I had never conceived any; and that those lines I sent to my cousin had either never been made, or that I had never heard them commended. Pride and vanity are foolish and unreasonable in dust and ashes; and, which is worse, odious and detestable before infinite perfection and infinite power."

The next are extracts from a long letter, of six octavo pages, entirely on the Christian eucharist, and addressed to Whitefield :—

"OXON, *July* 29, 1735.

"DEAR SIR,—Is the sacrament indeed administered at one or other of your churches every Sunday? Sure then the lot is fallen to you in a fair ground; sure you have a goodly heritage. The holy eucharist is a communion of the body and blood of Christ;—a participation of all the benefits procured for us by His most meritorious passion. In this most comfortable sacrament, pardon is freely offered to all. Has any one been an enemy to God by wicked works? By this body shall he be reconciled. By this blood shall his peace be made.

"Let me put this one question, and I have done. In the last great day, on what will you rely for salvation? Will you seek to your good thoughts and pious discourses? Alas! they are full of imperfection, and cannot bear the severe trial. All your own righteousnesses are as filthy rags, and will be utterly unable to gain your acceptance. To what then will you have recourse? To whom will you fly in this great extremity? Surely, to the sufferings of Jesus Christ. There is nothing else under heaven whereby you can be saved, but His meritorious passion. Unless His body plead in your behalf, you are covered with shame, and everlasting confusion. Unless His blood make your peace, you are cast, you perish, you are eternally undone. Think, oh, do but think deeply on this, and then you will gladly embrace every occasion of partaking of the holy communion.

"By exhibiting such benefits, by urging such motives, may we prevail on all our neighbours to secure to themselves a resting place for their souls, an anchor of their hopes, sure and stedfast.

"Yours in the Lord,
"JAMES HERVEY."[1]

This was a letter widely different from those which Hervey had written to his sister. In them, he wrote as a man trusting for salvation solely in his own good works. In this, he propounds the doctrine, that, salvation is entirely owing to the sacrifice of Christ; and, that its blessings are obtained (not by the exercise of faith, but,) in the participation of the Christian sacrament. It need not be added, that, this was one of the chief doctrines of the Oxford Methodists.

The two Wesleys and Ingham left Oxford in 1735, and the time was now approaching for Hervey's departure. Hence, the following letter to his father:—

"*April* 8, 1736.

"HONOURED SIR,—You reprove me for my dilatory way of proceeding,—very justly I own. I hope, I shall, from this time, amend. I was

---

[1] *Evangelical Magazine*, 1794, p. 295.

examined yesterday.   I must do my juraments five times on Friday, and be admitted to my degree on Monday.   Mr. H—— tells me, I must wear a bachelor's gown.

"Mr. Farrer, a little while ago, asked me to resign my room to a pupil of his, who is to come the middle of this month.   To which proposal, I have agreed, because I can live much cheaper out of college.   I shall, by this means, save the expense of calling up, of bed-making, etc., as well as have a room at a cheaper rate, and pay for it only when I am resident : on which account, I assure myself, this step, I have taken, will be approved of by you and my mother.

"I am sorry to hear of your being obliged to go on with farming.   I could wish you would let it, though at some disadvantage, and though we should suffer thereby something in our fortunes.

"As to the curacy near Bath, I can give you no determinate answer. My friend, I believe, is a very sincere one, and will do me what service he can.   There is one person who has had the offer of it before me: whether he will accept of it is not known.   As soon as *I* know, *you* shall know.

"I hope you will send me a letter next week, to wish me joy on being a graduate.

" JAMES HERVEY."

Though not ordained, when Hervey left Oxford, in June, 1736, and returned to his father's house at Hardingstone, he, at once, commenced holding meetings among his neighbours. The following letter, addressed to Mr. Chapman, one of the Oxford Methodists, refers to this, and contains Hervey's views on what ought to be Chapman's behaviour among the polite inhabitants of Bath, whither he was going :—

" HARDINGSTONE, *June* 12, 1736.

"I humbly thank you for sending me the Journal," (probably Wesley's, who was now in Georgia.) "Blessed be God, for His unspeakable love to the poor Indians, and for His watchful care of our dear friends ! With what zeal and ardour do those glorious combatants run the race that is set before them.   May we, dear Mr. Chapman, may we go and do likewise ! go and improve our little stock of knowledge and holiness, by imparting them to as many as want and are willing to receive !

"I hope my evening assemblies are, and will be, prospered.   I heartily thank you for advising me to resume those means of instructing my neighbours.   I have had some comforting assurances that the sanctifying Spirit has been among us, and blessed my discourses to the edifying of the hearers.   I have some from two parishes besides this, that attend upon my little catechetical lectures, and am likely to have a young gentleman from the academy at Northampton.

"If you are going to Bath, how must you behave yourself in such a situation? I wish I could advise you aright; but, I fear, I am one of those whom the apostle styles μυωπα ζοντες. Nevertheless, my opinion, such as it is, I will freely give you.

"I think then, sir, great regard is to be had to the genius and temper of the city. Since that is light and gay, I would accommodate myself to it as much as possible, so it be consistently with innocence. I would, at all times, endeavour to be perfectly cheerful and obliging and complaisant, to the utmost of my power. I would be earnest with God to make my countenance shine with a smiling serenity; that there might sit something on my cheeks, which would declare the peace and joy of my heart. The world has strange apprehensions of the Methodists. They imagine them to be so many walking mopes, more like the ghost in a play, than sociable creatures. To obviate this sad prejudice, be always sprightly and agreeable. If a pretty turn of wit, or a diverting story offer itself to your mind, do not scruple to entertain the company therewith. Everything that borders upon sourness, moroseness, or ill-breeding, I would cautiously avoid. . And everything that may give a beautiful or amiable idea of holiness, I would study to show forth. I see no manner of harm in bowing at church, provided it be not in divine service, so as to interrupt our devotions. I think Mr. Wilson disapproved of this; but I cannot bring myself to believe, that, a modest and decent respect to our neighbours is disparaging to God, but rather acceptable to Him. I do not mean, by what I have said, that you should make all sorts of compliances. A solicitation to join with your acquaintance in billiards, dice, cards, dancing, etc., should be rejected.

"If Mr. Morgan is at Bath, pray present my thanks and love to him. God Almighty make him and you bold as lions, wise as serpents, and harmless as doves! If I had not heard you were at Oxon, this had been sent by the post to Bath.

"JAMES HERVEY."

Hervey was a churchman; but he was not a bigot. At this period of his history, one of the students in Doctor Doddridge's Academy, at Northampton, was the celebrated Rev. Risdon Darracott, then a youth, nineteen years of age. Hervey and young Darracott had had an interview in the house of a member of Dr. Doddridge's church. Darracott was endeavouring to form a religious society among Doddridge's students, somewhat similar to the society of Methodists at Oxford; and the interview, just mentioned, led him to write to Hervey for advice. The latter had recently left Oxford, and the following is an extract from his answer:—

"HARDINGSTONE, *June* 3, 1736.

"DEAR SIR,—I think your proposal, as far as I can see into it, is very

P

proper; and if discreetly managed, and steadily persisted in, cannot fail to be advantageous to yourself and others. This seems to be evident for several reasons ; four of which at present occur to my mind.

"1. Because we are ignorant and short-sighted, and oftentimes unable to discern the things that are excellent. But God is pleased to reveal to one what is concealed from another; so that, in a multitude of counsellors, there is wisdom.

"2. Because we are lovers and admirers of ourselves, unwilling to see our own errors, and, therefore, unlikely to amend them. Whereas, our friends will, with a meek and impartial spirit, show us our faults.

"3. Because we are weak and irresolute ; easily shaken from the most laudable purposes, and apt to let go our integrity upon any opposition. But a band of friends, who are like minded, inspires us with courage and constancy. ·

"4. Because we are slothful and lukewarm in religious duties. But a holy fellowship will kindle and keep alive a holy fervour. How often have I gone into the company of my dear friends, listless and spiritless ; yet, when I came home, I have found myself quite another person; vigorous and active, sanguine and zealously affected in good matters."[1]

Hervey, as an Oxford Methodist, was doubtless speaking from experience ; and his reasons for religious fellowship are well worth weighing.

A few weeks after the date of the above, Hervey proceeded to Oxford to be ordained ; and, whilst there, wrote again, to this young Dissenter, as follows :—

"LINCOLN COLLEGE, OXON, *Sept.* 1, 1736. •

"DEAR MR. DARRACOTT,—I wish you would suggest to me what I must do to further the Gospel of God my Saviour. I employ, every day, an hour or more with some well-inclined people of the poorer sort. We read Mr. Henry on the Holy Scriptures, and pray together. There is one set in one part of the city, and another in another. I meet them at a neighbour's house. Oh! that I could also open my mouth as he did; so boldly, so powerfully !

"I am preparing to enter into holy orders, and to take upon me the work of the ministry. That great, wonderful, and important work ! Help me with your prayers to the Lord God my Saviour, that I 'may receive the Holy Ghost not many days hence,' by the laying on of hands ; even 'the spirit of wisdom and understanding, the spirit of counsel and might, the spirit of knowledge and of the fear of the Lord.'

"Dear sir, pray give my humble service, and best thanks to Dr. Doddridge, and beg of him, when he is in the acceptable time, to re-member me, who am in the time of need. If he has any word of exhortation ; but, especially, if he has any treasures of instruction, proper for

---

[1] Memoirs of Risdon Darracott, p. 24.

a candidate of the ministerial office, how glad should I be if he would please to impart them, and how gratefully should such a favour be always acknowledged by his and your affectionate servant and brother in Jesus Christ,

"J. HERVEY."[1]

1736
——
Age 22

Another letter, written previous to his ordination, shall be given, at full length. Wesley was now in Georgia; and Hervey addressed to him the following :—

"OXON, *Sept.* 2, 1736.

"REV. AND DEAR SIR,—I have read your Journal, and find that the Lord hath done great things for you already, whereof we rejoice. Surely, He will continue His loving-kindness to you, and show you greater things than these. Methinks, when you and dear Mr. Ingham go forth upon the great and good enterprise of converting the Indians, you will, in some respects, resemble Noah and his little household going forth of the ark. Wherever you go, you must walk among dry bones or carcasses, among a people that are aliens from the life of God, buried in ignorance, dead in trespasses and sins. Oh, may the blessing of that illustrious progenitor of ours, and of that favourite with the Most High, be upon your heads ! May you be ' fruitful and multiply,' may you bring forth abundantly in that barren land and multiply therein !

"As for me, I am still a most weak, corrupt creature. But blessed be the unmerited mercy of God, and thanks be to your never to be forgotten example, that I am what I am. As to my strength, and activity with regard to others, I fear it may be too truly said, ' It is to sit still.' I am at present one of the multitude; but I expect, before this reaches you, to receive the office of a Deacon, and become a minister of the New Testament. Oh, may I also ' receive the Holy Ghost not many days hence;' and be made a faithful minister of those saving mysteries, from that time forth and for ever ! I hope, I shall then hear a voice behind me, saying, ' Awake thou that sleepest, from thy slumber, and Christ shall give thee light.' Christ shall be thy sanctification, Christ shall be thy illumination. He shall stand by thee, and strengthen thee. He shall give thee both to will and to do. Through the power of His grace, thou shalt run and not faint; thou shalt be fervent in the business and propagation of righteousness, nor ever give over, till thou givest up thy soul to God, its Maker, and thy body return unto the dust, as it was.

"That I may be obedient to such a heavenly call, is, I hope, ' all my wish and all my desire.' This is, indeed, the treasure I value, the thing that I long for. Do you, dear sir, put up your incessant prayers; and, oh, let the mighty God set to His seal, that the thing may be established, that it may be unto me according to my heart's desire ! Then, will I invite

---

[1] Memoirs of Risdon Darracott, p. 155.

you (my *father*, shall I call you, or my *friend?* For, indeed, you have been both unto me), to meet me among the spirits of just men made perfect; since I am not like to see your face in the flesh any more for ever! Then, will I bid you welcome, yea, I will tell of your love, before the universal assembly, and at the tremendous tribunal. I will hear with joy the Man Christ Jesus say of you, 'Oh, ye that are greatly beloved. Well done, good and faithful servants; ye have served your Lord and your generation with your might; ye have finished the work, which the eternal foreknowledge of my Father gave you to do. If others have turned their thousands, ye have turned your tens of thousands from the power of Satan unto God. Receive, therefore, a glorious kingdom,—a beautiful and immortal crown from my hand. Enter, with the children I have given you,—with the souls that you have won. Oh ye blessed ones, ye heirs of glory, enter in at those everlasting doors, and receive there the reward of your labours, even the fulness of joy for ever and ever.'

"I am, and may I always be, dear sir, your son in the Lord Jesus Christ,

"J. HERVEY.

"P. S. I heartily thank you, as for all other favours, so especially for teaching me Hebrew.[1] I have cultivated (according to your advice) this study, and am, blessed be God, the giver of knowledge! somewhat improved in this language. My prayers accompany you, and all that are engaged with you in the same glorious design. Let me also have yours and theirs for Jerusalem's, for Christ's sake."[2]

Seventeen days, after the date of the above letter, Hervey was ordained a deacon at Christ Church, by Dr. Potter, Bishop of Oxford.[3]

One of the Oxford Methodists was Charles Kinchin, Fellow

---

[1] Mr. Ryland writes,—"Mr. Hervey began the study of the Hebrew about the ninteenth year of his age, by the instigation of an acquaintance, who gave him no manner of assistance. The only book he took up was the Westminster Hebrew Grammar. That book seems to be contrived by the devil to prevent the learning of the Hebrew language : it is dark and obscure, harsh and unpleasant, ugly and disgustful, dull and listless ; and Hervey threw it by in despair. After a long time and much perplexity, by a happy Providence, there was another Fellow of Lincoln College, who, seeing Hervey in his painful embarrassment, pitied him, and took him into his bosom. He conducted him to the first chapter of Genesis, and analysed every word; he taught him to reduce every noun to its proper pattern ; he instructed him to trace every verb to its proper root, and to work every verb through the active and passive conjugations. If the devil could have had his way, we should have lost one of the finest Hebrew scholars in the world ; but, after Mr. Hervey had learnt to analyse the first chapter of Genesis, he went on like a giant, and, to my certain knowledge, became one of the first scholars in Europe for a familiar knowledge of the Hebrew Bible."

[2] *Arminian Magazine,* 1778, p. 132.

[3] He was ordained a priest, at Exeter, in the month of December, 1739

of Corpus Christi College.[1] On leaving Oxford, he was presented with the rectory of Dummer, near Basingstoke; and now, in 1736, Hervey became his curate. This is not the place to describe his curacy; but further extracts from his letters, during the time he held it, will serve to illustrate his character.

His brother, being desirous to be apprenticed in London, received from him the following :—

"DUMMER, *June* 27, 1737.

"DEAR BROTHER,—I find you are at London looking out for a trade, and a master to set yourself to. I hope, you pray earnestly to God to guide you in your choice. Desire also your honoured mother, and mine, to have a great regard to your soul. Let it be inquired, not only whether such a tradesman be a man of substance and credit, but also, whether he be a man of religion and godliness? Whether he be a lover of good people, a careful frequenter of the Church? Whether his children be well nurtured and educated in the fear of the Lord? Whether family prayer be daily offered up in his house? Whether he believes that the souls of his servants are committed to his trust, and that he will be answerable for the neglect of them at the judgment-seat? It will be sadly hazardous to venture yourself under the roof of any person, who is not furnished with these principles, or is a stranger to these practices. But, if he be contrary to all these, a despiser of God and goodness, wholly devoted to carnal pleasure and worldly gain; if he not only omit the religious care and oversight of his household, but also set them a wicked and corrupt example, let nothing induce you to enter into his service."

At the time when this letter was addressed to his brother, he received a sort of petition, signed by the inhabitants of Collingtree, one of his father's parishes, praying him to become their minister. In his long reply, dated June 29, 1737, he did not absolutely refuse to accede to their request; but sketched what a minister of Christ ought to be, and exhorted them to ask the great Head of the Church, to supply them with such an one. The letter is too long for insertion here; but, it shows, that, this young man of twenty-three had correct and exalted notions of ministerial duty. The standard of excellence was high, and but seldom reached; but it was not higher than it ought to be.

Meanwhile, the services of Hervey were not confined to Dummer. Even the *Oxford* Methodists, to some extent,

---

[1] Wesley's Works, vol. i., p. 81.

 were itinerant ministers, and, by interchange, occupied each other's pulpits. Hence the following :—

> "DUMMER, *October* 26, 1737.
>
> "DEAR MR. ——,—I received your last at Oxford. After that, I removed to Stanton-Harcourt ; and now am replaced at Dummer. These frequent removals and changes of situation, I hope, will be some small excuse for my dilatoriness in writing ; for, you know, they occasion trouble and take up time.
>
> "Mr. Broughton, Mr. Gambold, and Mr. Kinchin, have been exercising their ministry here. O may I not pull down, by my indiscretion or in-activity, what they have begun to build !
>
> "As to the making of sermons, I am deterred from writing them, not because I look upon it as a useless employment ; but because I feel, and cannot help confessing, my absolute inequality to a task so important. I entreat your intense and persevering prayers on my behalf, that the great and good God, the dispenser of all wisdom, would vouchsafe to be a light to my darkness, and strength to my weakness. Should these supplications be graciously answered, my heart will then teem both with abundance of matter, and propriety of expression ; my pen too will be that of a ready writer.
>
> "I am, dear sir, your obliged and affectionate, but unworthy friend,
>
>   "J. HERVEY."[1]

In the early part of the year 1738, Hervey suffered from enfeebled health ; and accepted the invitation of Paul Orchard, Esq., who resided at Stoke Abbey,[2] a beautifully situated old mansion in Devonshire.

Taking Bristol on his way, he wrote as follows to Mr. Orchard :—

> "BRISTOL, *February* 3, 1738.
>
> "WORTHY SIR,—I have been at Bristol little less than a fortnight, waiting of an opportunity of coming to Cornwall by water ; but, the wind still continuing contrary, I intend, this day, to set out for Exeter, on horse-back. I hope, by three or four easy stages, to reach it on Monday or Tuesday next. Here I propose to rest, till I have the satisfaction of hearing from my much-esteemed, though unknown patron. I expect, sir, to be sorely fatigued, not being accustomed to travelling ; and, if you please to permit your man and horse (for I dare not presume to ask for your chariot) to give me the meeting at Exeter, by the time he arrives, I hope to have worn off my weariness. I beg my humblest service may be accepted by your lady, and am, good sir, your obliged humble servant,
>
>   "JAMES HERVEY."

---

[1] *Gospel Magazine*, 1771, p. 174.
[2] In after-years, called Hartland Abbey.

The foregoing, to Mr. Orchard, was written three days after Whitefield embarked for Georgia, and Wesley returned to England. No sooner did Hervey hear of his friend Wesley's safe arrival, than he wrote him the following loving and interesting letter :—

"STOKE ABBEY, March 21, 1738.

"REV. AND HONOURED SIR,—How agreeably surprising was the news, which a letter of Mr. Chapman's lately brought me. I am at a loss to say, whether it was more unexpected or more grateful. It assured me that Mr. Wesley was arrived in England; had visited Oxon; and was coming to Bath : and shall I not hasten a congratulatory address, to welcome the friend of my studies, the friend of my soul, the friend of all my valuable and eternal interests? To do it cannot be deemed impertinency; but not to do it would justly bring upon me the imputation of ingratitude.

"I hope, sir, your health is not impaired by your travels. I dare say, your experience is increased, and your knowledge enlarged; your faith strengthened, and your zeal quickened. I do not doubt but the God whom you serve, has shown you wonderful things in His righteousness; His Almighty wisdom and goodness have dealt graciously with you, and wrought marvellously by you. O! how greatly pleasing, and, perhaps, not unprofitable would a relation of them be.

"I believe you had the pleasure of finding some of the Oxonians grown considerably in grace. They have made haste, since your departure, to improve their talents; and to edify their neighbours, as though they were earnestly and resolvedly desirous to enjoy their company in a better world.

"You cannot but have heard, and, hearing, you cannot but rejoice at, the successful zeal of our friend Whitefield. All London, and the whole nation ring of μεγαλια του Θεου done by his ministry. But, alas! it will damp your rising satisfaction to receive an account of useless, worthless Hervey's having run a round of sin and vanity; and, at length, weary and giddy, being almost ready to drop into hell. Oh! it is not fit to be mentioned; worthy of nothing but oblivion. Spare the narrative, and cure the wretch. Send a line, and accompany it with a prayer, to warm my frozen and benumbed soul; that, if there be any seeds of goodness latent, any sparks of piety dormant in my breast, they may break forth to life, and kindle into a flame.

"I am retired from the scene of action into a worthy and wealthy gentleman's family. Mr. Chapman will inform you, how much he deserves your prayers, and the prayers of all who are mighty with God and prevail.

"Dear sir, if other business,—if other charitable employments will allow you leisure, pray favour me with a letter. To none will it be more acceptable ; by none is it more needed, than by your most obliged humble servant,

"JAMES HERVEY."

Hervey's health did not improve at the beautiful residence of his friend, Orchard. Hence, four months after his settlement at Stoke Abbey, he wrote to his sister as follows :—

"1738. June 19. My disorder is a languor and faintness, a feebleness and inability for action, which is increased or lessened according to the various temperature of the weather. I bless God Almighty! I am not deprived of my appetite for food, neither are my bones chastened with pain ; so that, many impute all my complaints to a hippish and over-timorous turn of mind,—to a distempered imagination, rather than a disordered body.

"I have been about twenty or twenty-six miles into Cornwall, and seen wondrous workmanship of the all-creating God. At Bideford, about fourteen miles off, I am pretty well known, and am a little esteemed. It is strange to tell, but let it be to the glory of God's free and undeserved goodness, though I am worthy of shame and universal contempt, that, I find favour almost wherever I go."

For upwards of two years, Hervey was the cherished guest of Mr. Orchard and his family. David and Jonathan were not warmer or more faithful friends than these. Hence the following remarkable agreement :—

"We, the underwritten, whom God's providence has wonderfully brought acquainted with each other, for purposes, no doubt, of piety and everlasting salvation, sensible how blind and corrupt our nature is, how forward to fall into errors and iniquities, but how backward to discern or amend them ; —knowing also the great advantage of kind and affectionate, but, at the same time, sincere and impartial reproof and admonition ;—do oblige ourselves to watch over each other's conduct, conversation, and tempers ; and, whenever we perceive anything amiss therein,—any duty ill done, or not done so well as it ought,—anything omitted which might be for our spiritual good, or practised which will tend to our spiritual hurt,—in fine, any thing practised or neglected, which we shall wish to have been otherwise in a dying hour :—All this we will watch to observe, never fail to reprove, and earnestly endeavour to correct in each other, that so, we may have nothing to upbraid one another with when we meet in the eternal state. We resolve to do all this with the utmost plainness, and all honest freedom ; and, provided it be done with tenderness, with apparent good-will, and in private, we will esteem it as the greatest kindness we can show,— the truest interest of sincere friendship that we can exercise, and the only way of answering the gracious ends of Almighty wisdom in bringing us together. In witness and confirmation of which resolution, we here subscribe our names.

"PAUL ORCHARD,
"JAMES HERVEY."

"*November* 28, 1738."

While Hervey was thus resting, and recruiting his health, in Devonshire, Wesley and his brother Charles became acquainted with Peter Bohler, found peace with God, associated with the Moravians, and began to preach the doctrine of salvation by faith only, with a fervour and earnestness, which excited almost national attention, and brought upon them, in varied forms, the malice of their enemies. Hervey, in his beautiful retirement, heard of this, and wrote to Wesley as follows[1] :—

"STOKE ABBEY, *December* 1, 1738.

"MOST DEAR AND REVEREND SIR,—Whom I love and honour in the Lord : indeed, it is not through any forgetfulness of your favours, or unconcernedness for your welfare, that, you have not heard from me, but through the miscarriage of my letter. Immediately on the news of your first arrival in England, I made haste to salute you, and wondered why your answer was so long in coming ; but wondered more when I heard you had left the nation a second time,[2] without being so condescending as to own me, or so kind as to vouchsafe me a single line. But, now, sir, that, I am assured under your own hand, that, you have escaped the perils of the sea, the perils of foreign countries, the perils of those that oppose the truth ; and, that, you, restored in safety to your native country, are re-settled at Oxon, and both have been doing, and still are doing spiritual and everlasting good to men,—I may truly say 'my heart rejoiceth, even mine.'

"O that I could give you a comfortable account of myself, and of my zeal for God ! Alas! I must confess, with shame and sorrow, 'my zeal has been to sit still.' I am not strong in body, and am lamentably weak in spirit. Sometimes, my bodily disorders clog the willing mind, and are a grievous weight upon its wheels. At other times, the mind is oppressed with sloth, and thereby rendered listless and indisposed for labouring in the Lord. Pray for me, dearest sir, and engage all my friends to cry mightily to Heaven in my behalf, if so be, this dry rod may bud and blossom ; this barren tree may bring forth much fruit.

"I live in the family of a worthy gentleman, who is a hearty well-wisher to the cause of pure and undefiled religion ; who desires no greater happiness than to love the Lord Jesus Christ in sincerity ; and who would be glad of a place for himself and household in your prayers.

"Dear sir, will you permit me to inform you what is said, though I verily believe slanderously said, of you ? It is reported, that, the dearest friends I have in the world are setters forth of strange doctrines, that are contrary to Scripture, and repugnant to the Articles of our Church. This cannot but give me uneasiness ; and I should be glad to have my fears removed by yourself. It is said, that, you inculcate faith, without laying

---

[1] *Arminian Magazine,* 1778, p. 132.
[2] This refers to Wesley's visit to Herrnhut in 1738.

stress upon good works ; and, that, you endeavour to dissuade honest tradesmen from following their occupations, and persuade them to turn preachers. Now, these calumnies I wish you would give me power to confute, who am,

"Dear sir, your ever obliged and grateful friend,

"J. HERVEY."

The first of these rumours was a calumny ; for, while Wesley inculcated faith, he also strenuously enforced good works. The second was not without foundation ; for Wesley himself writes :—

"Joseph Humphrey was the first lay preacher that assisted me in England, in the year 1738." [1]

The two Wesleys and Whitefield, full of the love of God, and with faces beaming with peace and joy through believing in Christ Jesus, were now about the most abused men in England. All the churches were closed against them ; and fields, streets, and village greens were their chief preaching places. The mob treated them with violence. The clergy used the pulpit in denouncing them. The press was employed in spreading scandalous reports concerning them. Some of their old friends were puzzled, and began to stand aloof from them. But, in the midst of all, they themselves were happy ; and were honoured, almost every day, in being made the instruments of turning men from sin to holiness, and from the power of Satan unto God.

Hervey's health was such, that, even had he wished, he was utterly unable to join his friends in this their bold and marvellously successful out-door mission to the unconverted masses. While they were preaching to assembled thousands on Hannam Mount, Kennington Common, and Blackheath, he was being nursed, with the greatest tenderness, amid the comforts and beauties of Stoke Abbey ; and was preaching, as opportunity permitted, and as his strength allowed, in some of the neighbouring churches, and especially in Mr. Thompson's, of St. Gennys, Cornwall. Though absent, however, he was not forgotten. Whitefield, full of faith and of the Holy Ghost, wrote to him, inquiring whether he had found the same blessings, which he and the Wesleys had.

---

[1] Wesley's Works, vol. iv., p. 473.

Hervey's answer was so beautifully ingenuous; and, moreover, is so important as bearing upon the subject of his conversion, that, it is given here without curtailment.

"STOKE ABBEY, *April* 4, 1739.

"DEAR MR. WHITEFIELD,—Your kind favour, dated March 6, I
received not till yesterday, not returning sooner from worthy Mr. Thompson's charge. O that he may not find his dear flock gone back ; but
adorned in Christian knowledge, during his absence from them !

"I thank you for the good news you sent me. Christ enable me to
praise, rejoice, and give thanks on this behalf !

"I am obliged for the searching questions you put to me. Before I
answer them, give me leave to exhort you in the words of the Psalmist,
'Try me, my dear and faithful friend, try me, and seek the ground of my
heart, and examine my thoughts; look well if there be any way of wickedness in me, and lead me in the way everlasting.'

First question, Does the Spirit of God witness with your spirit that you
are a child of God? In truth, I cannot tell. I have sometimes a comforting hope, that I am a child, and not an outcast ; a true son, and no
bastard ; but whether this persuasion cometh of Him that has called men
to salvation, I know not. Whether it be the testimony of the Holy Spirit
witnessing within me, or the whisper of a vain presumption speaking
peace where there is no peace, I am at a loss to determine. Tell me,
dear sir, by what touchstone I shall distinguish them.

"Second question, Have you peace and joy in the Holy Ghost? I sometimes do rejoice, and not in carnal satisfactions, but in hope of the glory
which shall be revealed. But the bright prospect is quickly intercepted ;
dark clouds of fear intervene ; and sad misgivings of mind throw a damp
upon the rising joy. Sometimes I am blessed with inward peace, and
possess my soul in tranquility ; but this also is like our April sun,—very
changeable and short-lived. The sweet calm is broken, and ruffling gusts
of peevishness and uneasiness discompose the tenour of my mind. I
must confess, that, I feel touches of envy (oh that I could mingle my tears .
with my ink, as I write !), motions of pride, hankering after unnecessary
sensual delights ; that, I too frequently am destitute of love to my
brethren, of a compassionate long-suffering zeal for their welfare, and
cannot perceive one spark of devotion kindled in my cold heart. For
these things, my soul is, at some intervals, disquieted within me. Such
sad experiences turn my peace into pain ; they destroy my gladness, and
fill me with grief.

"Third question, Are we justified by faith only? I answer, By faith
only. Works can have no share in our justification, because there is
iniquity in our holy things. They are done after an imperfect manner, or
from improper views, or sullied with some secret self-glorying ; and, therefore, cannot recommend *themselves,* much less the *sinful doers* of them,
to infinite purity. .Nay, if God should enter into strict and rigorous
judgment, I fear our best works would deserve punishment. And to

think, that, those performances, which deserve punishment, can merit, either in whole or in part, in any measure or degree, an eternal reward, is surely to misjudge the case. It seems to be as false as to fancy, that, the addition of some dross would enhance the value, or increase the lustre, of refined gold. Yet still I believe, that, these works, poor and mean and imperfect as they are, are absolutely necessary, and that there is no justification without them. A tenant upon lease must duly and punctually pay his pepper-corn, though it be not considered, by the payer or receiver, as of any worth at all. So, a Christian must exercise himself in all good works, if he would obtain salvation, though that can add no worth to the perfect, sufficient, and alone meritorious sacrifice of Jesus Christ. We must be as careful to maintain good works, as if our salvation was the purchase of them alone, and yet renounce them utterly, and rely upon the merits, death, and intercession of our blessed Saviour, who is made unto them that believe, not only wisdom, but righteousness, sanctification, and redemption.

"If I am wrong, be pleased to inform me; and God Almighty give me a child-like, unprejudiced, teachable spirit! Pray for me, dear sir, that, my sins, which blind my understanding, may be subdued; and that, together with a right spirit, I may have a right judgment in all things. That text, James ii. 24, I dare not blot out of my Bible, and I cannot put out of my mind. Indeed, it perplexes me. It makes me unsettled and wavering. When I think of it, I am ready (ready! nay, ought I not to be resolved, since the Apostle has put the words into my mouth?) to alter my reply, and say, not by faith *only*, but by works (in conjunction with it) a man is justified. Give me leave, henceforward, to become your pupil in this important doctrine of Christianity, as I have long been, and ever shall be,

"Your most affectionate friend,

"J. HERVEY."[1]

The friendship of these Oxford Methodists was most sincere and cordial; but was not unruffled. All was not plain sailing. Breakers were a-head. It is a well-known fact, that, early in the year 1739, Whitefield and Wesley, being shut out of the pulpits of the Established Church, commenced their marvellous career of out-door preaching. Astonishing effects followed. All sorts of rumours were current. Enemies were active, and, as already stated, even friends were staggered. In his Devonshire retreat, Hervey was excited, and wrote to the Rev. Mr. Kinchin, of Dummer, an immensely long letter from which the following is an extract :—

"STOKE ABBEY, *April* 18, 1739.

"DEAR MR. KINCHIN,—This day, a letter informs me, that, my worthy

---

[1] *Evangelical Magazine,* 1794, p. 373.

and ever-esteemed Rector has hearkened to men of unsound opinions, and is turning aside to their errors ;—that, he is inclined to throw off his gown, renounce the Church of England, relinquish his Fellowship and living, and become itinerant preacher. And can I see a friend, who has been kind to me as a father, is dear to me as a brother,—can I see such a friend run away with such erroneous and pernicious notions, and sit silent and unconcerned? No; my affections constrain me; and I cannot hold my peace. I love him, and, therefore, must speak. I love him tenderly, and, therefore, must speak freely."

1739

Age 25

Here follow twelve printed octavo pages of remonstrance. Hervey then adds :—

"There is no man living that I more sincerely love and honour than Mr. Wesley. His memory is most dear and deservedly precious to me; but, yet, I must frankly own, he is liable to mistakes,—mistakes in religion, and dangerous ones too. I remember the time when he was fond of the mystic writers; read one of their leading authors over and over again; and commended what he read as the best book, next to those that were given by inspiration. But, within the space of a few months, he saw his error; retracted his opinions; and inveighed against them as studiously as he ever extolled them. This I mention only to show, that, the best designing men,—men of eminent learning and exemplary devotions,—may be led into false apprehensions of things. He has arguments, I do not doubt, to support his tenets, as he had in the former case, and can manage them with a masterly skill; but, yet, he may be deceived, though he means only the glory of Christ. Therefore, dear sir, withhold your assent a little, and do not too easily fall in with his principles. At least, suspend your determination for awhile; wait the event; and let that speak for the attempt.

"You see how moderate I am in the matter. I do not exclaim against the gentlemen who have brought these new doctrines to our ears. If truth and purer Christianity be on their side, God forbid, but that I myself and every true-hearted disciple should go over to their party! Only have a little patience; tarry thou the issue of things; and let *excitus acta probet.*

"I wonder why they dissuade you from cleaving to the Establishment. Why do they find fault with our excellent Church? And why should they entice you from your parish? Sure we are, that, the Holy Ghost made you overseer over that little flock; but, that, He has released you from the charge and called you to another sphere of labour, is not so evident. There was a time when Mr. Wesley was a warm and able advocate of the primitive institutions. I marvel, that, he is so soon removed to another opinion. This is a fresh conviction how variable his mind is, and, though burning with zeal for God, yet, given to change. And, having altered so often already, why may he not alter again, and new-mould his present sentiments as well as his former?

"They advise you to become an itinerant preacher. But why? I would gladly know. Is greater perfection to be attained by wandering into the wide world, and preaching in variety of places? Or will this way of preaching be more successful and efficacious? I cannot bring myself to believe this.   "Etc., etc.,

"JAMES HERVEY."

To some extent, Hervey was evidently misinformed. It is possible, it is not unlikely, that, Wesley and Whitefield had advised their brother Methodist, Mr. Kinchin, to become an itinerant preacher; but there is no evidence, that, they ever wished either him or any of their friends to leave the Established Church, or, that, they ever entertained the idea of leaving the Church themselves. Still, there can be no doubt, that Hervey had heard such reports as these, and was intensely anxious on this account. Hervey refers to the diffusion of "erroneous and pernicious notions." These were, probably, not so much the doctrines of justification by faith, the witness of the Spirit, and cognate truths, as the things mentioned in the following letter, addressed to Whitefield, three weeks after the foregoing letter was sent to Mr. Kinchin :—

"STOKE ABBEY, *May* 10, 1739.

"DEAR MR. WHITEFIELD,—I sincerely thank you for your last letter. I can hardly bring myself to assent to your whole account of justification by faith. This, perhaps, may proceed from some obstinate prejudices, rather than from reasonable and weighty scruple. However, I waive the mention of my objections, and make the care of my own right faith give place to a concern for the principles and practices of my dear friends.

"It is reported, and creditably reported, from Oxon, that, several strange notions have been lately broached there, and have gained proselytes and espousers among the most hopeful and promising part of the University. They, who bravely stood their ground against sin, are become an unhappy prey to error and delusion. I hope you are not fallen from your once avowed steadfastness to the truth as it is in Jesus, and as it is in our excellent Church. It is whispered, indeed, that, the seducers are practising their arts upon you, and trying to subvert my dear Mr. Whitefield's orthodoxy.

"In a late letter, I gave an answer to some queries you were pleased to put to me. Now, I beg the favour of your opinions concerning the following doctrines: 'That, the Distinction, Order, Degrees, even Robes and Habits of the University are all Anti-Christian; that, nothing is taught in it, but that learning and wisdom, which opposes the power of God; that, whoso is born of God is also taught of God, not in any limited sense, but, so as to make the use of natural means of no effect; that, all human learning (however said to be sanctified of God) entirely disqualifies us for preaching the true Gospel of Jesus Christ; that, an Established ministry is a mere invention of men; that, our whole Church and all its authority, are founded on, and supported by a lie; and, that, all who receive power of preaching from it, are in a state of slavery, and must throw off all obedience to it, before they can enjoy the freedom of the Gospel.

"These tenets, extravagant and pernicious as they are, have been, I find, studiously advanced; but let them not have the sanction of your approbation. If they will get abroad into the world, let them go branded with your dislike and censure.

"JAMES HERVEY."

1739
—
Age 25

Remembering the rumours of the day, such a letter as the above is not surprising. Falsehoods concerning Wesley and his friends were rife. No report was too extravagant to be believed. Unfortunately, Whitefield's answer to Hervey is not forthcoming; but the invalided recluse was soon led into the way of truth. Hence, the following, also addressed to Whitefield, pointing out the means by which Hervey had been induced to renounce his Oxford Pharisaism, and to embrace the doctrine of salvation by faith in Christ only. The letter is too valuable to be abridged :—

"Yes, dear sir, with pleasure, I send another letter. I rejoice to find, that, you remember me. I am thankful, that, you have not renounced a correspondent, made odious by so much ingratitude.

"You are pleased to ask, How the Holy Ghost convinced me of self-righteousness, and drove me out of my false rests? Indeed, sir, I cannot precisely tell. The light was not instantaneous, but gradual. It did not flash upon my soul, but arose like the dawning day. A little book, wrote by *Jenks*, upon Submission to the Righteousness of God, was made serviceable to me. Your Journals, dear sir, and Sermons, especially that sweet Sermon upon 'What think ye of Christ?' were a means of bringing me to a knowledge of the truth. And another excellent piece has been, and I hope will be, as so much precious eye-salve to my dim and clouded understanding,—I mean '*Marshall's* Gospel Mystery of Sanctification.'

"These,—blessed be He, who is a light to them that sit in darkness!—have, in some degree, convinced me of my former errors. I now begin to see, that, I have been labouring in the fire, and wearying myself for very vanity, while I have attempted to establish my own righteousness. I trusted I knew not what, while I trusted in some imaginary good deeds of my own. These are no hiding-place from the storm. They are a refuge of lies. If I had the meekness of Moses, and the patience of Job, the zeal of Paul, and the love of John, I durst not advance the least plea to everlasting life on this footing. But as for my own beggarly performances,—wretched righteousness,—gracious, adorable Emmanuel!—I am ashamed; I am grieved, that I should thrust them into the place of Thy Divine, Thy inconceivable precious obedience!

"My schemes are altered. I now desire to work in my blessed Master's service, not *for*, but, *from* salvation. I believe, that, Jesus Christ, the Incarnate God, is my Saviour; that, He has done all which I was bound to perform; and suffered all that I was condemned to sustain; and, so, has procured a full, final, and everlasting salvation for a poor damnable sinner. I would now fain *serve* Him who has *saved* me. I would glorify Him before *men*, who has justified me before *God.* I would study to please Him in holiness and righteousness all the days of my life. I seek this blessing, not as a *condition*, but, as a *part*,—a choice and inestimable *part* of that complete salvation, which Jesus has purchased for me.

"Now, if at any time, I am fervent in devotion,—seem to be in a gracious frame,—or am enabled to abound in the works of the Lord,—I endeavour to put no confidence in these bruised reeds, but to rest upon the Rock of Ages. Not in these, most blessed Jesus, but in Thy robes of righteousness, let me be found, when ' God shall call the heavens from above, and the earth, that, He may judge His people.'

"When, on the other hand, I feel myself most deplorably dead and deficient,—when I am apt to sigh for my unprofitableness, and cry out with the prophet, ' My leanness, my leanness!' I no longer comfort myself with saying, ' Be of good cheer, soul, thy God requires only *sincere* obedience, and, perhaps, to-morrow may be better than this day, and more abundant in acts of holiness.' Jesus is now become my salvation, and this is my song in the house of my pilgrimage,—' Why art thou cast down, O my soul?' Though imperfect in thyself, thou art complete in thy Head. Though poor in thyself, thou hast unsearchable riches in thy Divine Surety. The righteousness of Thy obedience, O Lord Redeemer, is everlasting. O grant me an interest in this, and I shall live.

"If overtaken by sin, or overcome by temptation, I dare not, as formerly, call to mind my righteous deeds, and so think to commute with Divine justice ; or quit scores for my offences, by my duties. I do not, to ease my conscience, or be reconciled to God, promise stricter watchfulness, more alms, and renewed fastings. No ; in such unhappy circumstances, turn, O my soul ! neither to the right hand nor to the left; but fly instantly to Him, whom God has set forth for a propitiation. Hide thyself in His wounded side, and be safe. Wash in His streaming blood, and be clean.

"If in these, or in other points, I am otherwise minded, than corresponds with the gospel of truth, cease not, dear sir, to pray, that, ' God may reveal even this unto me.'

"But why will not my dear friend come amongst us ? Why won't he drop his word towards the west? Many, in these parts, long for your arrival. Many long to hear the joyful sound from your lips. Many, I am assured, would hail my dear brother with that acclamation, ' How beautiful are the feet of him that bringeth glad tidings ; that bringeth glad

tidings of good things!' O that it would please the Divine Providence
to direct your way unto us! Come, dear sir, come with the fulness of the
blessings of the gospel of peace. Come amongst living multitudes, who
will be attentive to hear you; and come, once more, into the arms of him
who dearly loves you.

"J. HERVEY."[1]

Hervey and Whitefield were young men, both twenty-five
years of age; but they were not novices in religious knowledge. By extensive reading, by conversation, by docility,
above all, by the blessed Bible, and by the Spirit's teaching,
they had, at this early period of their history, arrived at
theological conclusions, from which they never wavered to
the end of life. Exception may be taken to some of the
expressions of Hervey in the foregoing letter; and to the
Calvinistic views of both; but they *believed* what they
preached; and they undoubtedly thought and felt that their
doctrines were founded upon the Divine authority of the
sacred Scriptures. It is no part of the plan of the present
work to defend or to attack the doctrines taught by the men
whose histories are sketched; but simply to furnish honest
information respecting their manner of life, their teaching,
their religious experience, their success, and the termination
of their toil and suffering.

In 1740, Hervey's health was sufficiently restored to justify
his undertaking the curacy of Bideford, where he continued
till about the month of July, 1743. His congregation was
large, but his stipend small, amounting to not more than £60
a year. Here he planned and partly executed his "Meditations among the Tombs," and his "Reflections on a Flower
Garden." A ride from Bideford to Kilhampton suggested
the former; and the latter were, in part, composed in the
summer-house of a pleasant garden, belonging to the family
with whom he lodged. At his entrance upon his ministry at
Bideford, he wrote as follows to his friend, Mr. Orchard, in
whose hospitable mansion he had been so long a guest :—

"Your excellent proposal is not yet put into execution; we have no
evening prayers in public as yet; nay, I have not so much as communicated the design to my rector. I am shamefully timorous: lions,

---

[1] *Evangelical Magazine*, 1794, p. 503; and A Selection of Letters,
partly Original, by J. Hervey, 1816, p. 261.

giants, and the sons of Anak are much in my thoughts. I dream (and may it be no more than a dream, and not too real a presage,) of difficulties, both in getting leave to attempt, and in getting strength to perform, this spiritual service, which I owe to my little flock. Your zeal will reproach me with cowardice; your faith upbraid me with unbelief; but, O, let your charity and pity pray against both. I hope ere long to disclose the matter to Mr. Nichols."

Another letter, written at Bideford, and addressed to Whitefield, will be welcome. It strikingly exhibits the change in Hervey's views and religious character :—

"BIDEFORD, 1741.

"DEAR MR. WHITEFIELD,—Your favour struck me with an agreeable surprise. I verily thought my stubborn silence had razed me from your remembrance; but, since you still have an affection for an ungrateful friend, I take this opportunity of returning my grateful acknowledgments.

"I rejoice to hear the Redeemer's cause revives. Set up Thyself, O Incarnate God! above the heavens, and diffuse Thy glory through all the earth! Let Thy enemies perish, O Lord! Let disappointments attend the attempts of Thy foes and the devices of hell; but let Thy servants be prosperous, and their message crowned with success!

"Dear sir, I cannot boast of trophies erected here by the Captain of our salvation; but, I hope, the arm of the Lord will be revealed more and more among us. I hope, the triumphs of free grace will have wider spread and free course, and will prevail mightily over our unbelief. I own, with shame and sorrow, that, I have been too long a blind leader of the blind. I have perverted the good ways of God, and have darkened the glory of redeeming merit and sovereign grace. I have dared to invade the prerogatives of an all-sufficient Saviour, and to pluck the crown off His head. I have derogated from the honours, the everlasting and incommunicable honours of Jesus. I have presumed to give works a share in the redemption and recovery of a lost sinner; and have placed those filthy rags upon the throne of the Lamb; and, by that means, debased the Saviour, and exalted the sinner.

"But, I trust, the Divine truth begins to dawn upon my soul. Was I possest of all the righteous acts that have made saints and martyrs famous in all generations,—could they all be transferred to me, and might I call them all my own,—I would renounce them all that I might win Christ. I would not dare to appear before the bright and burning eye of God with such hay, straw, and stubble. No, dear sir, I would long to be clothed in a Mediator's righteousness, and ascribe all my salvation to the most unmerited and freest grace.

"Dear sir, cease not to pray for me ; desist not to counsel me ; since, I perceive, you cannot forbear to love me.

"I am," etc.,

"J. HERVEY."

In the discharge of his ministerial duties at Bideford
Hervey was exemplary. He preached twice every Sunday;
and, on Tuesdays and Fridays, expounded part of one of
the Lessons for the day; except when he examined the
children, and gave explanations of the Church's Catechism.
Like his friends Wesley and Whitefield, he also formed a
religious society, which continued to meet above forty years.
This brought upon him considerable reproach; but, "so far
from being ashamed" of what he had done, he wrote,—

"I am only ashamed of the inconsiderable assistance which I am able
to contribute to so worthy an attempt. Ashamed! no; but if it were
lawful for a Christian to glory in anything beside the cross of Christ, this
should be matter of glory and triumph to me. Their scorns, derision,
and mockery, I would bind on my head as a beautiful crown, and be
better pleased with such a character, than with an ornament of gold
about my neck." [1]

Brave words were these! The Wesleys and Whitefield
were encountering murderous mobs in all directions; and, so
far from complaining, were "rejoicing, that, they were counted
worthy to suffer shame for the name of Jesus Christ." The
feebleness of Hervey's body rendered it impossible for him
to undertake the rough mission work, which was so zealously
undertaken by his friends; but, the Christian heroism of his
soul, rendered him not unworthy of their brotherhood. The
men, one and all, were animated with the spirit of " the noble
army of martyrs;" and, at any moment, were prepared to die
for the sake of the Lord Jesus. No wonder, that, such men
were successful, and, that, their memories are wreathed with

---

[1] From a long printed letter, of twenty-four octavo pages, we learn,
that, this society was formed, as early as May 21, 1739, before the
Methodist Societies were formed. Hervey refers to the "*scaring* reports,
that had lately been raised concerning religious societies," and proceeds
to state their object, and their practices. The society at Bideford was,
"by no means, in contradistinction to the Established Church, but in
dutiful conformity to her." He says, "Woodward's rules we purpose
punctually to observe, reading his exhortations distinctly and solemnly;
offering up his prayers humbly and reverently; only with this difference,
that some edifying book be substituted in the room of religious talk, not
because we disapprove of religious conference, but because we think ourselves scarcely capable of managing it with regularity, propriety, and
order. We set up no examination, nor require any confession before
others; but hope to be constant, careful, and strict, in searching our hearts,
and acknowledging our iniquities before the all-seeing God."

1741
——
Age 27

unfading laurels; while the names of their "enemies, persecutors, and slanderers," are either forgotten, or only remembered with contempt.

The Rev. Mr. Nichols, the Rector of Bideford, died early in the year 1741, only a few months after Hervey had entered upon his labours there; and, as the Bideford living was a valuable one, there were a considerable number of aspirants after it. On March 2, 1741, Hervey wrote to a friend as follows:—

"You have heard, I do not doubt, that, Mr. Nichols, my rector, is no more: who will succeed him is yet a secret. Many, I believe, are eagerly wishing for it, as a place of considerable profit, but few, perhaps, are solicitously considering whether they are equal to the discharge of so difficult and important a service. But hold, my pen: what have I to do to judge others? Let it be all my care to approve myself faithful in my appointed station.

Shortly after this, Hervey was summoned home, on account of the serious illness of his father. Hence the following:—

"WESTON, *May* 30, 1741.

"DEAR MR. W.——,—'Tis late, midnight drawing on, and the Sabbath approaches; but I must snatch a few minutes to tell my dear friend the good news. My father is made whole; quite freed from his pains; quite cured of his disorders; and almost in a new world. Deep, indeed, was his distress; grievous his affliction; but now the clouds are over and gone, and the voice of joy and health is restored to his dwelling.

"Now, therefore, I am free: I have no engagement here. My father, it is true, offers me a curacy; but, if Mr. —— chooses it, and my dear people think it may contribute in any measure to their spiritual benefit, nothing hinders but I may return to Bideford: Return, and address them much in the same strain as Peter bespoke the impotent man: 'Eloquence and oratory, learning and accomplishments have I none; but such as I have, in the name of Jesus, give I you.'

"From your affectionate friend,

"J. HERVEY."[1]

Hervey did return to Bideford; but, at the end of about two years, the new rector dismissed him, against the united request of his parishioners, who offered to maintain him at their own expense. This, to a man of Hervey's exquisite sensitiveness of feeling, was no trivial trial. To the people

---

[1] *Evangelical Magazine,* 1806, p. 28.

of Bideford he was devotedly attached. He writes, while still among them :—

"I live in the very heart of the town. O that the immortal interests of its inhabitants may be ever on my heart ! May I covet no other prosperity, and pursue no other happiness, than to be an instrument of doing them some spiritual good ! I hope, I shall never forget my dear people of Bideford. I shall bear them upon my heart, when I retire into my study for reading, when I walk solitary in the fields for exercise, and when I bend my knees before the God and Father of our Lord Jesus Christ."

And again, after he had left them :—

"I rejoice to hear that dear Mr. Thompson[2] proposes to make you a monthly visit. O that his doctrine may distil as the dew ! He will teach you the way of God more perfectly, for he has the unction of the Holy One, and knows the truth as it is in Jesus. There will not be wanting those who will censure his righteous dealings, and ridicule his zeal for the glorious Redeemer ; but all those who have Jesus and His salvation, will say, 'The Lord prosper you !' If any of my acquaintances think it worth their while to hear from me, I. shall, with as much pleasure, go to my desk and write to them, as I formerly went to their houses and conversed with them. I assure you, I would still seek to please my people for their good to edification."

Before following Hervey to his next sphere of labour, further extracts from his correspondence, at and about this period, will help to illustrate his character.

Hervey was an earnestly religious man, a devout student of the holy Bible, and an extensive reader of pious authors, but he was also a lover of at least some of the light and popular literature of the age. Hence the following to his sister :—

"BIDEFORD, *October* 12, 1742.

"See how our judgments and inclinations alter in process of time ! I once thought, I should make less use of the *Spectator* than you ; but now, I believe, the reverse of this is true ; for we read one or more of these elegant and instructive papers every morning at breakfast, and they are served up with our tea, according to their original design. We reckon our repast imperfect without a little of Mr. Addison's or Mr. Steele's company."

Such a confession is not surprising in a man who was now employed in writing "Meditations among the Tombs," and "Reflections on a Flower Garden."

The Rev. Mr. Thompson, Rector of St. Gennys, a warm friend of the Oxford Methodists.

 Hervey seems to have left Bideford in the month of July, 1743 ; but, on his way to Northamptonshire, he halted at Bath, where he resided several weeks, and wrote a number of his most interesting letters. The following are extracts from some of them :—

" DEAR MRS. A——,—I am got as far as Bath, in my way homeward ; and here I am likely to make a considerable stay. My friend, Mr. C——,[1] has taken a trip into Devon, and left me entrusted with his flock : so that, here is my abode till his return releases me.

Sunday last[2] I spent at Bristol, attending Mr. Whitefield's preaching. Never have I seen, never have I read, so remarkable an accomplishment of our Lord's promise, as is evident in that indefatigable, powerful preacher. He does indeed believe in his Divine Master, and *out of his heart flow rivers of living waters.*

" This afternoon, some hopeful young persons came to visit me. They seemed to be in the number of those who are pressing forward unto the prize of their high calling in Christ Jesus. Perceiving them to be thus minded, I introduced a discourse concerning growth in grace," etc.[3]

The next furnishes a glimpse of Bath a hundred and thirty years ago.

To MRS. ORCHARD.

BATH, *August* 10, 1743.

" MADAM,—I expected to have been at home before this time ; but, as I have dropped short at Bath, and am likely to continue here awhile, you will give me leave to transmit my best wishes from hence.

" There is a good deal of company at Bath. A new mineral water is found out, about a mile distant from the city. It is grown into considerable repute, and is much frequented. Several of the nobility and gentry drink it constantly. It will not bear bottling, and, for that reason, must be used on the spot. It is called the Lincomb Spa.

" The latter season is approaching, which, you know, madam, brings

---

[1] Most likely William Chapman, the Oxford Methodist.

[2] This was probably July 17, 1743, for Whitefield writes on Tuesday, July 19th, " I came here " (Bristol) " to preach at the fair, because people from all parts flock hither at that season. Yesterday I preached four times. Last night was such a time as I never saw in Bristol society before. To-morrow, God willing, I set out for Hampton, to see what can be done for the poor persecuted sheep there. I hear I am threatened, but Jesus will stand by me."
It may be added, that, a few days before, Whitefield had been almost murdered at this self-same Hampton. First of all, the mob threw him into a lime-pit, and then twice over into a deep brook of water (Whitefield's Letters, Nos. 527 and 528).

[3] *Gospel Magazine,* 1777, p. 260.

abundance of strangers with it. Some invalids resort to the English Bethesda; some, as lovers of pleasure, to this mart for all manner of diversions. Every one seems studious of making a gay and grand appearance. It is, I think, one of the most glittering places I ever beheld. 'Anointed with oil, crowned with rose-buds, and decked with purple and fine linen,' they sport away their days, chanting to the sound of the viol, drinking wine in bowls, and stretching themselves on couches of ivory; and, perhaps, never remembering the afflictions of Jesus, nor His love, 'which is better than wine,' nor His name, 'which is as ointment poured forth.'

"While they are contriving every art to embellish their persons, let us, dear madam, give all diligence to be all-glorious within. While they are studying to outvie the butterfly and the tulip, let us be animated by higher views, and put on the Lord Jesus Christ," etc.

* * * * * * *

"And now, madam, will you permit me to anticipate a remark which you will naturally make. Shall I spare you the necessity of saying, Why here is a sermon instead of a letter.

"Indeed, madam, if it be a sermon, the Bath finery has furnished me with a text.

"And why, good madam, should not the world expect such sermon-like epistles from us ministers? Why will not they let us be comformable to ourselves, and act in character? Would you not expect to hear of engagements and victories from a soldier just come from making a campaign? Would any one be surprised to find a merchant discoursing of foreign affairs, or canvassing the state of trade? Nay, is it not allowable even for our tailor and milliner to talk of the newest fashions and most modish colour? Why, then, should not the agents for the court of heaven treat of heavenly things? Why should not their whole conversation savour of their calling? Why should they be one thing when they bend the knee, and another when they put pen to paper? Why act one part when they speak from the pulpit, and quite a different one when they converse in the parlour? To say the truth, madam, if you do not allow me this liberty, I may pretend, indeed, but can never act the grateful, the affectionate, the faithful, humble servant."

The following is an extract from an enormously long letter, of eighteen printed pages, addressed to a clergyman, who had been preaching in the Abbey Church.

"BATH, *August* 27, 1743.

"REVEREND SIR,—Sunday last, I happened not to be at the Abbey Church in the afternoon; but, conversing with a gentleman who was one of your auditors, I desired to have a summary account of your sermon. And, truly, he gave me such an account as both astonished and grieved me. You dignified worldly prosperity at so extraordinary a rate, and almost canonized the prosperous man. On the other hand, you vilified the glorious Jesus in so scandalous a manner, and set the Incarnate Godhead to one of the most ignoble and abominable offices. This made me encourage my friend to send you a word of admonition; and, when he declined, I could not forbear undertaking it myself. For, it would be unkind to you, sir, to perceive you under such grievous mistakes, and not to warn you of the error of your ways. Nor would it be less unfaithful to your Master, and my Master, to be informed of such preaching, and suffer it to pass current, without any animadversion.

" I understand, you first exhorted people to rejoice, when their circumstances were affluent and their worldly affairs prosperous. You enforced this palatable advice by the precepts of Scripture; and, lest it should not be received with a proper welcome, you further urged it on your hearers by the example of our blessed Saviour.

"In opposition to this strain of teaching, permit me to observe, 1. That, worldly prosperity is no sufficient cause for a Christian to rejoice. 2. That, it is often one of the sorest evils that can befal a person. And 3. Allow me to sketch out the true nature of spiritual prosperity; or discover what is that solid ground for rejoicing, which the oracles of God recommend."

These were the three points explained and enforced in Hervey's pungent and scorching letter, sent to the clerical sycophant, who, because the sinners, in his crowded church, were fashionable ones, imitated, not the honest Baptist of Scripture history, but the dangerous Syren of ancient mythology, and flattered the rich and elegantly dressed "children of wrath" who sat before him, instead of reproving their sins, and proclaiming their danger. Hervey was still young in years; but the unfaithful preacher deserved all he got.

This was not the only rebuke which Hervey administered during his brief residence in the gay city of the west. At this period, Bath was, perhaps, the most fashionable place in Great Britain; and the most renowned man in Bath was Richard, commonly called "Beau," Nash. Four years before, this accomplished rake had endeavoured to prevent Wesley preaching in the city where, by a sort of general consent, he acted as the king of all the fops and fashionables there assembled; but Nash was not a match for the poor, persecuted Methodist; and, smarting from Wesley's keen retort, and stung by an old woman's taunts, was glad to sneak away from a scene of conflict of his own creating. Beau Nash was still in power; and now young Hervey addressed to him the following faithful, and caustic letter,—

"SIR,—This comes from your sincere friend, and one, who has your best interest deeply at heart. It comes on a design altogether important, and of no less consequence than your everlasting happiness; so that, it may justly challenge your careful regard. It is not to upbraid or reproach, much less to triumph and insult over your misconduct. No; it is pure benevolence,—it is disinterested good-will which prompts me to write; so that, I hope, I will not raise your resentment. However, be the issue what it will, I cannot bear to see you walk in the paths that lead to death, without warning you of your danger,—without sounding in your ears the awful admonition, 'Return and live;—for why will you die?' I beg of you to consider, whether you do not, in some measure, resemble those accursed children of Eli, whom, though they were famous in their generation, and men of renown, yet, vengeance suffered not to live. For my part, I may safely use the expostulation of the old priest,—'Why do you such things? For I hear of your evil dealings by all this people; nay, my brother, for it is no good report I hear; you make the Lord's people to transgress.'

"I have long observed and pitied you: and a most melancholy spectacle, I lately beheld, made me resolve to caution you, lest you also come into the same condemnation.

"I was, not long since, called to visit a poor gentleman, erewhile of the most robust body and gayest temper I ever knew; but, when I visited him, oh! how was the glory departed from him! I found him no more that sprightly and vivacious son of joy which he used to be; but languishing, pining away, and withering under the chastising hand of God: his limbs feeble and trembling; his countenance forlorn and ghastly; and the little breath he had left sobbed out in sorrowful sighs; his body hastening apace to the dust, to lodge in the silent grave, the land of darkness and desolation; his soul just going to God who gave it, preparing itself to wing its way to its long home, to enter upon an unchangeable and eternal state. When I was come up into his chamber, and had seated myself on his bed, he first cast a most wishful look upon me, and then began, as well as he was able, to speak. 'Oh! that I had been wise, that I had known this, that I had considered my latter end! Ah! Mr. H——y, death is knocking at my doors; in a few hours more, I shall draw my last gasp, and, then, judgment, the tremendous judgment! How shall I appear, unprepared as I am, before the all-knowing and Omnipotent God? How shall I endure the day of His coming?' When I mentioned, among other things, that *strict holiness* which he had formerly so lightly esteemed, he replied, with a hasty eagerness, 'Oh! that *holiness* is the only thing I now long for. I have not words to tell you how highly I value it. I would gladly part with all my estate, large as it is, or a world, to obtain it. Now my benighted eyes are enlightened. I clearly discern the things that are excellent. What is there in the place whither I am going but God? Or what is there to be desired on earth but religion?' But, if this God should restore you to health, said I, think you that you would alter your former course? 'I call heaven and earth to witness,' said he, 'I would labour for holiness as I shall soon labour for life. As for riches and pleasures and the applauses of men, I account

1743
—
Age 29

them as dross and dung; no more to my happiness than the feathers that lie on the floor.   Oh! if the righteous Judge would try me once more; if He would but reprieve and spare me a little longer;—in what a spirit would I spend the remainder of my days!   I would know no other business, aim at no other end, than perfecting myself in holiness.   Whatever contributed to that,—every means of grace,—every opportunity of spiritual improvement,—should be dearer to me than thousands of gold and silver.   But alas! why do I amuse myself with fond imaginations? The best resolutions are now insignificant, because they are too late. The day in which I should have worked is over and gone; and I see a sad horrible night approaching, bringing with it the blackness of darkness for ever.   Heretofore, (woe is me!) when God called, I refused; when He invited, I was one of them that made excuse; now, therefore, I receive the reward of my deeds.   Fearfulness and trembling are come upon me. I smart; I am in anguish already; and yet this is but the beginning of sorrows!   It doth not yet appear what I shall be;—but sure I shall be ruined, undone, and destroyed with an everlasting destruction.'

"This sad scene I saw with my eyes; these words, and many more equally affecting, I heard with my ears; and soon after attended the unhappy gentleman to his tomb.   The poor breathless skeleton spoke in such an accent, and with so much earnestness, that I could not easily forget him or his words; and, as I was musing upon this sorrowful subject, I remembered Mr. Nash;—I remembered you, sir;—for I discerned too near an agreement and correspondence between the deceased and yourself.   They are alike, said I, in their ways; and what shall hinder them from being alike in their end?   The course of their actions was equally full of sin and folly; and why should not the period of them be equally full of horror and distress?   I am grievously afraid for the survivor, least, as he lives the life, so he should die the death of this wretched man, and his latter end should be like his.

"For this cause, therefore, I take my pen, to advise,—to admonish,— nay, to request of you to repent while you have opportunity, if happily you may find grace and forgiveness.   Yet a moment, and you *may* die: yet a little while, and you *must* die; and will you go down with infamy and despair to the grave, rather than depart in peace, and with hopes full of immortality?

"But I must tell you plainly, sir, with the utmost freedom, that, your present behaviour is not the way to reconcile yourself to God.   You are so far from making atonement to offended justice, that you are aggravating the former account, and heaping up an increase of wrath against the day of wrath.   For what say the Scriptures?   Those books which, at the consummation of all things, the Ancient of days shall open, and judge you by every jot and tittle therein—what say these sacred volumes? Why, they testify and declare to every soul of man, 'That, whosoever liveth in pleasure is dead while he liveth'; so that, so long as you roll on in a continued circle of sensual delights and vain entertainments, you are dead to all the purposes of piety and virtue; you are odious to God, as a corrupt carcass putrifying in the church-yard; you are as far from doing your duty, or working out your salvation, or restoring yourself to the divine favour, as a heap of dry bones nailed up in a coffin is from vigour and activity.

" Think, sir, I conjure you, think upon this, if you have any inclination to escape the fire that never will be quenched. Would you be rescued from the fury and fierce anger of Almighty God? Would you be delivered from weeping, and wailing, and incessant gnashing of teeth? Sure you would! Then, I exhort you as a friend ; I beseech you as a brother ; I charge you as a messenger from the great God, in His own most solemn words : ' Cast away from you your transgressions ; make you a new heart and a new spirit ; so iniquity shall not be your ruin.'

" Perhaps you may be disposed to contemn this and its serious import, or to recommend it to your companions as a fit subject for raillery; but, let me tell you beforehand, that for this, as well as for other things, God will bring you into judgment. He sees me now write. He will observe you while you read. He notes down my words in His book. He will note down your consequent procedure. So that, not upon me, but, upon your own self, will the neglecting or despising of my sayings turn. ' If thou be wise, thou shalt be wise for thyself ; if thou scornest, thou alone shalt bear it.'

"Be not concerned, sir, to know my name. It is enough that you will know this hereafter. Tarry but a little, till the Lord, even the most mighty God, shall call the heaven from above, and the earth, that He may judge His people, and then you will see me face to face. There shall I be ready, at the dread tribunal, to joy and rejoice with you, if you regard my admonitions, and live ; or to be—what God prevent—by not inclining your heart to receive this friendly admonition."

This was plain dealing ; but was greatly needed. To write such a letter, to such a man,—an accomplished gallant, exercising sovereignty over nearly all the fashionable residents of a gambling, dissipated city,—required no ordinary courage in a young clergyman, who had not yet attained his thirtieth year. How it was received, and what were its effects, we are left to guess ; but it is a curious fact, that, it was not destroyed, but was found among Nash's papers after his decease.

Leaving Bath, Hervey, in October, 1743, became curate to his father, at Weston-Favel, a small village of three or four hundred inhabitants, near Northampton ; and here, in this rural seclusion, he continued to reside (with the exception of a short interval) until his death, in 1758.

His pastoral duties were comparatively light ; but his time was not unoccupied. Compared with the career of Wesley and Whitefield, who were living a rough, itinerant life, this settlement of Hervey was a perfect contrast ; but, it must be borne in mind, that, Hervey was physically unfit for the out-door preaching, which his two old Oxford friends were practising. His voice was unsuitable for such exercises. The exposure to rain, frost, and snow, would have made his brief life briefer still. Besides, the delicate gentleness of his nature totally disqualified him for encountering the hardships, privations, and persecutions of Wesley and Whitefield's wandering life. It would be hasty to say, that, he was lacking in faith, love, zeal, prayer, and religious energy. He possessed all these in a far more than ordinary degree. In this respect he had but few equals, and scarcely any superiors. The spirit was willing, but the flesh was weak. To imitate Wesley, Whitefield, Grimshaw, Berridge, was simply impossible ; but Hervey did all he could. He most conscientiously cared for the souls of his handful of parishioners ; and as conscientiously employed his leisure, not only in writing long religious letters to his absent friends, but, in composing books, which, as every one admits, breathe the devoutest piety, and which have been read, with pleasure and with profit, by thousands belonging to each successive generation during the last hundred and twenty years. Hervey's life was not a failure, because the last fifteen years of it were spent in a secluded country village.

Apart from his ministerial duties, the first labour to which his attention was devoted, after his settlement at Weston-Favel, was the finishing and the publication of the well-known works begun in Devonshire, namely, "Meditations among the Tombs," and "Reflections on a Flower Garden." Hence the following :—

"AT MR. THOMAS HERVEY'S, IN BASINGHALL STREET,
"LONDON, *May* 23, 1745.

"DEAR MR. ——,—You will be surprised when you observe the place from whence this letter is dated. Prevailed on by the kind solicitations of my friends, I have taken a trip to London, where I propose to continue about a fortnight.

"Your last two favours I received together. I thank you for the specimen of types. I hope better paper is intended to be used, than that whereon the types were printed ; which I think coarse and slovenly. I am most inclined to send abroad the pieces in a matrimonial state : I mean, not in separate pamphlets, but united in a volume. They seem to be a contrast to each other, and may, perhaps, mutually recommend one another. Probably the ' Meditations among the Tombs' may carry too doleful an aspect ; and, if not enlivened a little with the brighter scenes of ' The Garden,' may terrify the reader, and create disgust. I shall take an opportunity of talking with Mr. Richardson on this affair ; and shall, if he takes the trouble of perusing it, put one of the letters into his hands: though it must be the mourning piece, because I have no copy of the gayer essay, but what is in shorthand. What you hint at, with regard to the largeness of the character, that old and enfeebled eyes may be able to read it, is perfectly right. I shall desire that this suggestion may be observed.

" I hope your ingenious friend has examined the piece, with a kind severity, by this time. It will be a favour if you will give me a line while I abide in the city ; and a greater, if you will inform me of Mr. S—h—m's opinion, and transmit me some of his remarks. Before I sent the ' Reflections' to Bath, Mr. Payne, brother to our old acquaintance, gave them a reading. He frankly acquainted me, in a letter, both with what he liked, and what he disapproved of. He advised me to expunge the long note relating to Mr. Pope's opinion.[1] He is a Fellow of King's College, and a very ingenious scholar. Upon the whole, he declared himself pleased with the performance, and marked out several places that struck his fancy in a peculiar manner.

" My heart's desire and prayer to God is, that it may be, in some degree, serviceable to the interests of religion : which end, of all others most desirable and important, if it may be so happy as to promote, I shall rejoice in the publication. Otherwise, may Providence, which discerns the remotest consequences of every transaction, not give it an imprimatur.

" I have no motto for the thoughts among the tombs.[2] Does any fine passage, from the ancients or moderns, proper to introduce and give credit to such serious remarks, occur to your mind ?

" Now, perhaps, you will expect to hear how I proceed in London. I intend, sir, to see and hear as much as I possibly can, in the space allotted for my stay. I have thoughts of going, incog., to the places of teaching and worship, frequented by persons of every denomination. ' Try all things,' is the Apostle's permission ; ' Hold fast that which is good,' is his direction. I shall indulge myself in the one ; may I be enabled to put in practice the other !

" I believe it will be my most prudent course not to visit a certain lady. If I debar myself that pleasure, it will be entirely owing to an appre-

---

[1] This was left out in the first edition, but inserted in subsequent ones. It was a long, but irrelevant comment, on a verse by Pope, inscribed on the monument of Dr. Stonehouse's wife, in Northampton church.

[2] The motto afterwards selected was : " Every stone that we look upon, in this repository of past ages, is both an entertainment and a monitor." (" Plain Dealer," vol. i., No. 42.)

hension of wounding my own ease and tranquility. Who knows what impressions may be made by an amiable person and engaging behaviour, heightened by the exercise of good sense, and completed by an apparent regard for religion and eternity? Indeed, sir, I must own, my heart is not proof against such charms.

"Since I wrote the preceding, I have heard our old acquaintance.[1] He preached upon, 'The gift of the Holy Ghost:' showed what fruits it produced in the heart and life; then applied the whole by way of examination, in a searching and very forcible manner. May I never forget what was uttered this night! Might I but experience it, I should bless the day in which I was born. I have room to add no more, than my service to Mrs. ——; and that the favour must be speedy, if you intend me a letter while in London.

"Yours affectionately,
"J. HERVEY."[1]

An extract from another letter, on the same subject, may not be unacceptable. Probably it was addressed to Dr. Doddridge.

"WESTON-FAVEL, *Nov.* 16, 1745.

SIR,—It is not easy to express the satisfaction, I received from your agreeable and useful conversation this afternoon. I rejoice to find that there are gentlemen of genius, learning, and politeness, who dare profess a supreme value for the Scriptures, and are not ashamed of the cross of Christ.

"This brings the dedication and the preface, which are to introduce a little essay, entitled, 'Meditations among the Tombs,' and 'Reflections on a Flower Garden,' in two letters to a lady. I hope, sir, in consequence of your kind promise, you will please to peruse them with the file in your hand. The severity of the critic, and the kindness of the friend, in this case, will be inseparable. The evangelical strain, I believe, must be preserved; because, otherwise, the introductory thoughts will not harmonize with the subsequent, the porch will be unsuitable to the building. But, if you perceive any meanness of expression, any quaintness of sentiment, or any other impropriety and inelegance, I shall acknowledge it as a very singular favour, if you will be so good as to discover and correct such blemishes.

"I hope, sir, my end in venturing to publish is a hearty desire to serve, in some little degree, the interests of Christianity, by endeavouring to set some of its most important truths in a light that may both entertain and edify. As I profess this view, I am certain, your affectionate regard for the most excellent religion imaginable, will incline you to be concerned for the issue of such an attempt; and, therefore, to contribute to its success, both by bestowing your animadversions upon these small parts,

---

[1] Probably Wesley, who was now in London. Whitefield was in America.

[1] *Gospel Magazine,* 1771, p. 176.

and by speaking of the whole (when it shall come abroad) with all that candour which is natural to the Christian, and will be so greatly needed by this new adventurer in letters, who is, etc.,

> " J. HERVEY."

Hervey's book, referred to in these letters, was published in 1746, the size, 8vo., the pages, 216. The lady to whom it was dedicated was the daughter of his friend, the Rev. Mr. Thompson, Vicar of St. Gennys, Cornwall. The book is too well known to render an account of its contents necessary ; but a brief extract from the preface will show the objects at which he aimed.

" The first of these occasional Meditations begs leave to remind my readers of their latter end; and would invite them to set, not their houses only, but, which is inexpressibly more needful, their souls in order ; that they may be able, through all the intermediate stages, to look forward upon their approaching exit, without any anxious apprehension.

" The other attempts to sketch out some little traces of the All-sufficiency of our Redeemer, for the grand and gracious purposes of our everlasting salvation; that a sense of His unutterable dignity and infinite perfections may incite us to regard Him with sentiments of the most profound veneration, to long for an assured interest in His merits, and to trust in His powerful mediation, with an affiance not to be shaken by any temptation, not to be shared with any performances of our own."

During the year 1746, Hervey wrote to a friend several long and very valuable letters on the doctrine of the Trinity. These may be found in his collected works, and are well worth reading. He also, as was his usage, carried on an extensive correspondence concerning experimental and practical religion ; and his letters, belonging to this class, though occasionally verbose and fanciful, are characterized by the devoutest piety. None but a godly man could have written them ; and none but godly people will peruse them. Many of them are almost little sermons, and all of them are rich in religious truth. In the days of penny postage, letters like these are rarely written ; and it is greatly to be feared, that, English biographers in future centuries, will find a vexatious lack of biographical material belonging to this. People are too busy to write long letters ; and, were it otherwise, the removal of the heavy postage of olden times has taken away one of the chief stimulants to make a letter longer than the pressing necessities of the case demand.. Besides, locomotion is now so easy, cheap, and rapid, that friends, instead of sending their secrets to each other, in a written form, prefer to make a railway trip, and to tell them *viva voce.* Things were widely different a hundred years ago ; and, hence, the extensiveness, richness, the fulness, and detail, the confidential gossip, and the heart-outpourings found in the correspondence of our English ancestors. They wrote letters : their grandsons send telegrams. The letters are of the greatest use to those who wish to become biographers. The telegrams are usually burnt as soon as they are read. In former days, letters were too long, interesting, and valuable to be destroyed. At the present day, they are too brief and common-place, to be worth preserving. The results of such a change in the epistolary habits of the people, are not felt at present ; but they will be bitterly lamented in the approaching future.

Not to mention other distinguished men belonging to the past, the most eminent of the Oxford Methodists all excelled in epistolary correspondence. Wesley's collected works alone contain nine hundred and twenty-three of his private letters ; Whitefield's works, when published, even more than a hundred years ago, contained one thousand four hundred and sixty-five ; while the works of short-lived Hervey, by far the *longest* letter writer of the three, contain two hundred and nine, to all of which must be added hundreds more, published in other forms.

In a book like this, it is impracticable to do more than very sparingly employ such copious materials ; and nearly all that is attempted, in the case of Hervey, is to give only extracts containing incidents. These, however, shall be as exhaustive as possible. Proceeding on this plan, the following belong to the year when Hervey first became an author.

Hervey's charity to the poor was only limited by his means, and even such a limit was sometimes overstepped. At Bideford, for instance, such was his unbounded benevolence, that, to prevent embarrassment, his friends practised upon him the innocent deception of borrowing his money when he received his salary, lest he should disperse it all in benefactions ; and then repaying it as his necessities required. All the profits of his ' Meditations,' amounting to £700 pounds, he distributed in charitable donations ; and directed that any profit, arising from the sale of his books after his decease, should be used in the same manner.

1746

Age 32

"This," said he, "I have devoted to God. I will, on no account, apply it to any worldly uses. I write, not for profit, nor fame, but, to serve the cause of God; and as He hath blessed my attempt, I think myself bound to relieve the distresses of my fellow-creatures with the profits that come from this quarter."

The following extract is in harmony with this:—

"WESTON-FAVEL, *Feb.* 2, 1746.

"DEAR Mr. W——,—Your spouse informed me, you were concerned, that the little money, I left in your hands, had not been remitted to me; but, dear sir, I am glad on this account. If it may be the means of cherishing one of the least of our Redeemer's brethren, I rejoice that it has not been returned.

"You did right in delivering a guinea to Mrs. Williams, for the benefit of poor widow Cole. If Molly Lake, or Betty Peak, are in want, by all means, let them be relieved. Tell them, I present them each with a crown; and bid them think, if a poor mortal, a wretched sinner, is so ready to help them, according to his ability, how much more ready is the infinitely compassionate Saviour of the world to pity all their miseries, and comfort them in all their troubles. Were it in my power, I would willingly do more for them; but let them remember that the power of the blessed Jesus knows no limits. Oh, it is impossible to imagine how rich our Divine Master is in goodness, and how mighty in power!"[1]

Every one knows that, in 1745, England was thrown into a state of the utmost excitement, by the landing of Charles Edward Stuart, and his Scotch and Irish adherents, and by the futile march to Manchester, and subsequent retreat to Culloden. The following refers to this and other matters:—

"WESTON-FAVEL, *Feb.* 9, 1746.

"Thanks to you, dear sir, for your kind wishes. Blessed be the Divine Providence! I am now able to inform you, that what you wished is accomplished. I have had one of the most agreeable losses I ever met with. I have lost my indisposition, and am, in a manner, quite well.

"I congratulate you, sir, and my country, on the good news received from the north.

"How do you like Stackhouse's History of the Bible? I am sure, he has one advantage superior to all the historians of the world, namely, that, the facts, which he relates, are more venerable for their antiquity, more admirable for their grandeur, and more important on account of their universal

---

[1] *Evangelical Magazine*, 1802, p. 393.

R

usefulness. The Scriptures are finely calculated to furnish the most exquisite entertainment to the imagination, from those three principal sources, mentioned by Mr. Addison,—the great, the beautiful, and the new."

The next was written to his Cornish friend, the Rev. Mr. Thompson, of St. Gennys,—a gentleman possessed of considerable property, and whose family seat was at Brynsworthy, near Barnstaple, in Devonshire.

"WESTON, *June* 28, 1746.

"DEAR MR. THOMPSON,—Your last gave me hopes of the speedy receipt of another letter ; in pleasing expectation of which, I have waited thus long. But now my pen refuses to be restrained, and, therefore, writes to the friend whom its master honours, and loves from his very soul.

" I presume, this will find you at Brynsworthy, that agreeable seat, where, three years ago, I passed several delightful weeks. Oh ! when shall I spend my hours of conversation so much to my improvement !

"I very much want to know something relating to the condition and conduct of my old acquaintance. When were you at the Abbey?[1] When did you favour Bideford with your company? How goes on the good cause among the people lately committed to my care? How are your lectures prospered at your own and Mr. B——'s Churches?[2] Have you heard of Mr. S——? Where is he settled, and how does he proceed? Is Mr. W——'s abode in your parts? I hope, his manner of life answers your expectations of him ; and, I hope, your acts of kindness and words of exhortation have not been in vain. Have you received any tidings of, or from, Mr. Walker?

" One more question permit me to ask, and I have done with my interrogatories. Did not a certain Cornish clergyman take a journey to Exeter some time ago, on a very particular occasion? Was he not summoned to appear before the bishop of the diocese, in order to give an account of his behaviour and zeal?

" If you have any knowledge of this remarkable affair, (and I believe it will be impossible to apply to one who knows it more perfectly), be pleased to favour me with a narrative of its occasion, its circumstances, and its issue. I imagine an answer to this one query, will furnish materials for a very long letter.[3]

---

[1] The seat of Hervey's friend, Mr. Orchard.
[2] Doubtless, the Rev. Mr. Bennet, of Tresmere.
[3] Mr. Thompson, though not an Oxford Methodist, had begun to preach the Methodist doctrine of salvation by faith, and had received Charles Wesley, with open arms, at St. Gennys. He had allowed the branded itinerant to preach twice in his parish church, and had kept him company on a preaching excursion to Penryn, Gwennap "Pit," and other places. In Mr. Bennet's Church, at Tresmere, a strange scene had been witnessed. Charles Wesley was the preacher, and, on his declaring, that, by " harmless diversions," he had been " kept dead to God, asleep in the devil's

"We had this week a very heavy storm of rain, attended with a surprising darkness, awful thunders, and fierce lightnings. At a celebrated fair, that was held upon a spacious common in this neighbourhood, several persons were struck down with the flashes, and one poor man, with two horses, killed upon the spot.

"I congratulate you, dear sir, and my country in general, on the late most important and happy victory obtained by the gallant Duke of Cumberland. We can never be sufficiently thankful to the God of the armies of Israel for turning the scale of war in our favour at that ever-memorable event.[1]

"My little piece, entitled 'Meditations among the Tombs' and 'Reflections on a Flower Garden,' has been published a considerable time.[2] I have taken the liberty to dedicate it to Miss R. Thompson; and, was I near, or had I the opportunity of conveyance, would desire Miss C. Thompson to accept one of the books. The thing, I am told, finds acceptance with the public, greater indeed than I durst expect. Mr. Richardson, the author of 'Pamela,' is my printer. Seven hundred and fifty copies are struck off; the printer and writer are joint adventurers with regard to pecuniary advantages, if any such should accrue from the sale. If, at some leisure moment, you should happen to cast a glance upon the lines, mark, dear sir, their blemishes, correct their improprieties, and improve them into a greater neatness, in case a second edition should be demanded. O may they tend, in some small degree, to awaken my readers into a serious concern for their eternal state, and lead their minds unto the Rock of ages, the Hope of all the ends of the earth, Jesus Christ! May they, under the propitious influence of grace, answer this desirable end; or else let them share the fate of literary rubbish, and be swept away into utter oblivion!

"Be pleased to make my most respectful and affectionate compliments acceptable to Mrs. Thompson. I wish Miss Thompson may be a living picture of that amiable and virtuous woman, whose price is above rubies. If your trusty friend, Mr. B (ennet) is with you, pray tell him I love him, because he loves Mr. Thompson.

"Should you inquire after my state, you will find a description of it, Judges viii. 4—'Faint, yet pursuing.' Cease not, dear sir, to pray, that, the hands which hang down may be lifted up, and the feeble knees strengthened, to walk in the way everlasting.

"In your last, you inquired after a very holy woman, whose name is Mary. I have asked Dr. Doddridge about her. He declined giving me

1746
——
Age 32

---

arms, secure in a state of damnation for eighteen years," Mr. Merriton, one of his travelling companions, added aloud, "And I for twenty-five;" "And I," cried Mr. Thompson, "for thirty-five;" "And I," said Mr. Bennet, "for above seventy." This was quite enough to expose Thompson to the ecclesiastical anger of the bishop of the diocese.

[1] The battle at Culloden.

[2] His "Descant on Creation," also was published in 1746. It is so well known as not to need further notice.

a particular account of her intercourse with heaven, and only said, that, she was a very sincere and devout soul, but somewhat addicted to chimerical and extravagant imaginations. The Doctor desired me to transmit his cordial good wishes and service to yourself and spouse.

"Let it not be long before dear Mr. Thompson, with a letter, delights, animates, and comforts, his most obliged and affectionate friend,

"JAMES HERVEY."

The success of the "Meditations and Reflections" was such, as to encourage Hervey to attempt another work of the same description. Hence, the following letter, probably addressed either to his friend Dr. Doddridge or Dr. Stonehouse :—

"WESTON-FAVEL, *Nov.* 1, 1746.

"DEAR SIR,—This morning, I received your favour. The day lowers, and threatens rain, which debars me from the pleasure of paying you my thanks in person.

"Mr. Huygens[1] I hope to read very carefully; but, I believe, it will be proper to take heed of adopting into my plans any notions that are difficult and abstruse. I would have everything so perspicuous, that, the dimmest understanding may apprehend my meaning ; so obvious, that, he who runs may read. Let me lay before you a little sketch of my design, with a request, that, you would alter the general order, and make retrenchments, or additions of particular incidents, as you shall think most expedient.

"A contemplative walk. The approach of evening, and gradual extinction of light. The advantages of solitude. The stillness of the universe. The coolness of the atmosphere. Darkness, and its usefulness to mankind. Sleep, and its beneficial effects. Dreams, and their extravagance. A glow-worm glimmering. An owl shrieking. A nightingale singing. The very different circumstances of mankind; some revelling and carousing ; some agonizing and dying ; A knell sounding ; The notion of ghosts walking ; The moon, with its various appearances, and serviceableness to our globe ;—the heavenly bodies—their number, size, courses, distances, —display many of the glorious attributes of their Creator ; some of which are specified. They teach nothing of redemption ; this, the peculiar prerogative of revelation—Christ, the day-star from on high, that points out, and makes clear the way of salvation.

"These are some of the subjects which, I imagined, might be admitted into the composition of a Night-piece. If others occur to your mind more pleasing, or more striking, be pleased to suggest them.

"I am glad to find, by the quotation from Mr. Locke, that your esteem and veneration for the Scriptures are on the increasing hand. May we be persuaded, even more and more, of the incomparable excellency of those sacred volumes ! This one consideration, that they are the Book of God,

---

[1] The eminent mathematician and astronomer.

is a higher recommendation of them, than could be displayed in ten thousand panegyric orations. For my part, I purpose to addict myself, with more incessant assiduity, to this delightful and Divine study. Away, my Homer ! I have no more need of being entertained by you, since Job and the prophets furnish me with images much more magnificent, and lessons infinitely more important. Away, my Horace ! Nor shall I suffer any loss by your absence, while the sweet singer of Israel tunes his lyre, and charms me with the finest flights of fancy, and inspirits me with the noblest strains of devotion. And even my prime favourite, my Virgil, may withdraw ; since, in Isaiah, I enjoy all his majesty of sentiment, all his correctness of judgment, all his beautiful propriety of diction, and——But I must have done. The messenger waits ; he can stay no longer, than barely to allow me leisure to subscribe myself, dear sir, etc.,

" J. HERVEY."

While Hervey was thus occupied in literary pursuits, he was neither unmindful of his flock, nor of the general claims of Christian charity. Among other public institutions in which he felt deeply interested, the county hospital of Northampton was not the least important. In a letter, apparently to Dr. Stonehouse, he writes :—

" WESTON-FAVEL, November 22, 1746.

"DEAR SIR,—I heartily applaud the zeal you show for the spiritual welfare of the patients. The infirmary would be an inestimable blessing, if it might be productive of a reformation in the persons whom it admits and discharges. As distressed objects will, in all probability, resort to it from all parts of the county, a change wrought in their hearts, and a renewal begun in their lives, might be a happy means of diffusing religion far and near. I hope the clergy, concerned in the management, will concur in the prosecution of so desirable an end. I wish some proper scheme was contrived for this, in which I might bear some little part, without giving umbrage to my brethren, or alarming their jealousy. I have thought of offering to give the patients a kind of lecture or exhortation once a week ; but, sometimes doubtful whether such a proposal would meet with acceptance, and sometimes checked by the infirmities of my constitution, I have hitherto neglected to mention the affair. However, I now venture to submit it to your consideration. To this, or any other more advisable method, I should very readily contribute the best of my assistance."

In 1747, Hervey joined himself to a society, whose object was that of reading together the Old Testament in English, and the New Testament in Greek. This assembly, which was not to "consist of more than ten or twelve individuals, lest an increased number should produce confusion or dissensions," met on the first Tuesday morning in every month, and, oddly enough, in different inns, agreed upon, from time to time, by the majority. Each member was chairman of the meetings, in alphabetical succession, and read a chapter out of each of the two Testaments, pausing at the end of every verse for inquiries and reflections. Every one also was expected to give an account of some religious book, which had been read by him since the last time of meeting; all dined together, at the expense of eighteen-pence a head; and each one subscribed half a crown a month for charitable uses. The meetings, including an hour for dinner, lasted seven hours in the summer season, and six in winter. Hervey drew up two beautiful forms of prayer, to be used by the respective members, before and after they came together. The society was unique, but useful. None but gentlemen of social position and of good education were qualified for admission; and it was certainly to the honour of the neighbourhood in which Hervey lived, that, in that age of fox-hunting, carousing, and roistering, such an assembly was formed.

Meanwhile, Hervey was busily occupied in completing his "Contemplations on the Night"; and also in publishing a second edition of the volume which he had issued in 1746. References to these and other matters will be found in the following extracts from his letters.

"WESTON-FAVEL, *February*, 1747.

"DEAR SIR,—I have heard nothing from my printer during all this interval. What can be the reason of his long silence and great negligence I cannot imagine. But, this week, it occurred to my mind, that, if he delays the second edition at this rate, I may possibly be able to prepare the third letter [1] to accompany it. Accordingly, I have postponed other business, and applied myself wholly to this work. I have transcribed some part of the intended piece, and sent it for your perusal. Pray be so good as to examine it narrowly, and favour me with your remarks and improvements, on a separate paper. There are, I fear, besides more material faults, several mistakes in the copy, owing to my want of leisure to review it. I suppose the remainder of my design, when completed, will consist of about the same number of pages.

"If I live till Monday, I propose to visit my patient at the infirmary; and, if company happens to be agreeable, will take the pleasure of spending an hour with a certain valuable and very much esteemed friend at

---

[1] "Contemplations on the Night."

Northampton. If you are not able to guess the person I mean, you shall soon be informed by,

1747
—
Age 33

Dear sir, yours, etc.,

" J. HERVEY."

"WESTON-FAVEL, *April* 12, 1747.

" DEAR SIR,—I have folded down a corner of the leaf at the place where your perusal left off. There is a note or two subjoined to the preceding pages, which I wish you would please to examine. My humble service to Dr. ——. I desire He will write his remarks and corrections on a separate paper. What think you of the following lines for a motto ?—

> " ' Night opes the noblest scenes, and sheds an awe,
>   Which gives these venerable scenes full weight,
>   And deep impression on th' intender'd heart.'[1]

" Your plan for forming a Christian society,[2] and regulating our interviews, I greatly approve. It seems to me to be complete. I heartily wish to have it carried into execution, and hope it will be productive of considerable comfort and advantage to the members ; and not to them only, but, by rendering them more useful in their respective stations, to many others.

" I hope you have perused the remainder of the manuscript : and cannot but wish you would give the whole a second reading. The unknown importance of what we print, inclines me to urge this request. Who can tell how long it may continue, and into what hands it may come ? I almost tremble at such a thought, lest I should write unadvisedly with my pen; and injure, instead of serve, the best of causes.

" I shall soon create you a second task, by transmitting for your correction, twenty folio pages of the Remarks on the Stars, and Serious Improvements.

" Yours, etc.,

" J. HERVEY."

" *June* 2, 1747.

" REV. AND DEAR SIR,—My father is wonderfully recovered. Had he lived in the times of superstition, for ought I know, his uncommon disorder might have been ascribed to witchcraft, and his speedy recovery passed current for a miracle. We thought him to be on the very brink of death; but now he lives, and regains his strength daily. Last Sunday, he read prayers in his church ; and intends next Sunday to fill the pulpit.

" I am just now going to our visitation, held at Northampton. I shall

---

[1] The motto really used was the following :—
" Night is fair Virtue's immemorial friend :
   The conscious Moon, through every distant age,
   Has held a lamp to Wisdom."
[2] The society mentioned on a previous page.

 appear as a stranger in our Jerusalem! knowing few, and known by fewer. Methinks, there is something august and venerable in a meeting of the clergy; especially if one looks upon them as so many agents for the invisible God, and envoys from the court of heaven. I hope to be put in mind of that awful day, when the Lord Jesus Christ, that great Shepherd of the sheep, and Bishop of souls, will make His entrance in the clouds of heaven." Etc.

"J. HERVEY."

From the above, it is evident, that, though Hervey had now spent several years at Weston-Favel, his acquaintance with the clergy of the diocese was extremely limited. Why was this? Was it because he lived, to a great extent, the life of a literary recluse? Or was it because he had been a Methodist? Or was it because of his known friendship with Dr. Doddridge, the great and good Dissenter of Northampton? Whatever the reason, the fact existed; and, in this respect, he was in the same position as his old friends Wesley, Whitefield, and Ingham.

The next extract is valuable, and ought to be seriously considered by all who are chargeable with the same criminal inadvertencies. It is also a beautiful instance of Hervey's extreme delicacy in administering reproof.

"WESTON-FAVEL, *June* 27, 1747.

"MY DEAR FRIEND,—Was it you, dear sir, or I, that, when a certain passage in Scripture happened to be mentioned, treated it, not indeed with contemptuous disdain, but, with too ludicrous an air? descanted on it, in a sportive and frolicsome manner, in order to create a little pleasantry? If I was the person that indulged this improper levity, I beseech you to rebuke me, and severely too. Though my design might be innocent, my conduct was apparently wrong. That infinitely precious and important book, should be always held in the highest veneration. Whatever the Divine Spirit vouchsafes to dictate, should be thought and spoke of by mortals, with gratitude, dutifulness, and awe. It is the character of a religious man, that, he trembles at God's Word; and it is said of the great Jehovah, that, He has magnified His name and His Word above all things.

"Who was it, dear sir, that lent to our valuable friend, that vile book, 'Le Sopha,' and yet wrote by Crebillon,[1] with an enchanting spirit of elegance, which must render the mischief palatable, and the bane even delicious? I wonder, that, your kind and benevolent heart could recommend arsenic for a regale. It puts me in mind of the empoisoned shirt

---

[1] The famous French novelist, who died in 1777.

presented to Hercules. I am sure, you did not think on it, or else you would no more have transmitted such a pestilent treatise to the perusal of a friend, than you would transmit to him a packet of goods from a country depopulated by the plague. If that polluting French book still remains in your study, let me beg of you to make it perform quarantine in the flames.

"Dear sir, bestow a thought on these things. If the remonstrances are wrong, I willingly retract them; if right, you will not pronounce me impertinent. Love and friendship dictate what I write; and the only end I have in view, is the holiness, the usefulness, the happiness, the final salvation of my much esteemed friend."

In July, 1747, Hervey completed his "Contemplations on the Night," which he dedicated to the youthful son of his deceased friend, Mr. Orchard, of Stoke Abbey. He was also diligently occupied in the preparation of his "Contemplations on the Starry Heavens," and his "Winter Piece"; hence the following, from a letter by Dr. Doddridge, dated,

"July 6, 1747.

"I have just been writing to my good friend, Mr. Hervey; whose manuscript on The Stars, I have reviewed with pleasure. I hope it will be means of raising the hearts of many *above* the stars; and of fixing them on Him, who is, so much more than anything material, 'The bright and morning Star.' I see, in Mr. Hervey, an example of diligence, humility, candour, and universal goodness, which I am sure ought to keep *me* humble, and, I hope, in some measure, does so."[1]

The next, which appears to have been sent to some friend in the neighbourhood of Stoke Abbey, refers to the same subject; and also shows, that the state of Hervey's health was becoming serious :—

"WESTON-FAVEL, August 8, 1747.

"DEAREST MR. ——,—"I ought to take shame to myself, for suffering so kind a letter, received from so valuable a friend, to remain so long unanswered. Upon no other consideration than that of my enfeebled and languishing constitution, can I excuse myself, or hope for your pardon. My health is continually upon the decline, and the springs of life are all relaxing. Medicine is baffled, and my physician, Dr. Stonehouse, who is a dear friend to his patient, and a lover of the Lord Jesus, pities, but cannot succour me. This blessing, however, together with a multitude of others, the Divine goodness vouchsafes, to gild the gloom of decaying nature, that, I am racked with no pain, and enjoy the free, undisturbed exercise of my understanding.

---

[1] *Gospel Magazine*, 1771, p. 179.

1747

Age 33

"I am much obliged to you for carrying my message to Stoke Abbey, with so much speed, and conveying to me, with equal despatch, a satisfactory answer. When you visit the worthy family again, be pleased to inform Mr. Orchard, that the piece is sent to the press, and, after some corrections made in the dedication, addressed to my godson.[1] It is my humble request to him, and my earnest prayer to God, that, he may regard it, not merely as a complimentary form, but as the serious and pathetic advice of his father's intimate acquaintance, and his soul's sincere friend; who, in all probability, will be cut off from every other opportunity of fulfilling his sacred engagements, and admonishing him of whatever a Christian ought to know and believe to his soul's health.

"I forget whether I told you, that, the last work will be divided into two parts; will be full as large as the first two letters; and, therefore, the whole will be disposed into two small pocket volumes, on a very neat paper, with an elegant type, in duodecimo. But a convenient number of the new essays will be printed in the octavo size and character, for the satisfaction of those who purchased the former edition, and may possibly be willing to complete their book. It was a considerable time before I could think of a title for the last pieces, that suited their nature, and expressed their design. At length, I have determined to style them, 'Contemplations on the Night,' and 'Contemplations on the Starry Heavens.'

"Now I apprehend myself to be so near the close of life, with eternity full in my view, perhaps, my dear friend would be glad to know my sentiments of things in this awful situation.

"I think, then, dear sir, that, we are extremely mistaken, and sustain a mighty loss in our most important interests, by reading so much, and praying so little. I think also, we fail in our duty, and thwart our comfort, by studying God's Holy Word no more. I have, for my part, been too fond of reading everything elegant and valuable, that has been penned in our own language; and been particularly charmed with the historians, orators, and poets of antiquity. But were I to renew my studies, I would take my leave of these accomplished trifles. I would resign the delights of modern wit, amusement, and eloquence, and devote my attention to the Scriptures of truth. I would adopt the Apostles' resolution, and give myself to prayer and to the Word.

"With regard to my public ministry, my chief aim should be, to beget in my people's minds a deep sense of their depraved, guilty, undone, condition; and a clear believing conviction of the all-sufficiency of Christ, by His blood, His righteousness, His intercession, and His Spirit, to save them to the uttermost. I would always observe, to labour for them in my closet, as well as in the pulpit; and wrestle in secret supplication for their spiritual and eternal welfare. For, unless God take this work into His own hand, what mortal is sufficient for these things?

"My hope, my whole hope, with regard to my future and immortal state, is in the Lord Redeemer. Jesus is all my trust. His merits are my

---

[1] Hervey was godfather to the son of his friend, Mr. Orchard.

staff, when I pass through the valley of the shadow of death. His merits
are my anchor, when I launch into the boundless ocean of eternity.

"Though the days are come upon me, in which I have reason to say of
worldly things, I have no pleasure in them; yet, I find a secret satisfaction in
this consideration, that, to you and to others, I may be permitted, even when
dead, to speak in my little treatises. May they, when the author is gone
hence, testify, with some small degree of efficacy, concerning Jesus! May
they fan the flame of love to His person, and strengthen the principle of
faith in His merits! Once more, dear sir, adieu!

"J. HERVEY."

Hervey was afflicted in person; he was also afflicted in the
sufferings of his friends. Hence the following, written in the
month of December, 1747.

"Your last found me on the recovering hand, getting strength and
spirits, though by slow degrees. Soon after I received your favour, a
messenger came from London, bringing us the alarming news, that my
youngest brother was extremely ill. My father's bowels yearned, and his
heart bled; but the infirmities of age, and an unwieldy constitution,
hindered him from taking the journey. Upon me, therefore, the office
fell. Feeble and languid as I was, there was no rejecting such a call.
Accordingly, I took coach, and, in two days, arrived safe in London,
where I found my poor brother (the packer) seized with a most violent
fever. He was attended by two eminent physicians; but they proved
vain helpers. For a considerable time, his stout constitution struggled
with the disease; but, at last, was forced to yield. After attending his
sick-bed for several days, I had the melancholy task of closing his dear
eyes, and resigning him up to death. Oh, the uncertainty of mortal
things! Who could have thought that I should survive my brother? I,
sickly and enervated; he, always lively and vigorous. In flourishing
circumstances, and blessed with prosperity in his business; but now
removed to the dark, inactive, silent tomb! Lately married to a beautiful
and blooming bride, but now a companion for creeping things!

"Scarce was I returned to Weston, but another awful Providence
fetched me from home. My very worthy physician, Dr. Stonehouse, who
lives and practises in Northampton, had the misfortune to lose an
amiable and excellent wife. She also was snatched away in the morning
of life (aged twenty-five), and dead before I so much as heard of her
being disordered. At this valuable friend's house, I was desired to abide
some time, in order to assist in writing letters for him, and dispatching
his necessary affairs; in comforting him concerning the deceased, and
in endeavouring to improve the awakening visitation to our mutual
good.[1]

---

[1] Dr. Stonehouse was one of Hervey's most intimate and confidential
friends. For seven years, he was an infidel, and even wrote a pamphlet
against the Christian religion. He was brought to the obedience of the

" You will surely say, when you read this account, that, I have been in deaths oft : once upon the borders of it myself, and more than once a spectator of its victory over others.

" The ' Contemplations,' you are pleased to inquire after, are, after long delays, or a very slow procedure of the press, launched into the world. What may be their fate, I dare not conjecture.

" J. HERVEY."

Two more letters, belonging to the year 1747, must be added.

The venerable Dr. Watts, in 1746, had published his speculative and dangerous book, entitled, " The Glory of Christ as God-Man Displayed," and had presented Hervey with a copy. He was now in the last year of his life, and died November 25, 1748. Hervey wrote to him as follows :—

" WESTON-FAVEL, *December* 10, 1747.

" REV. AND DEAR SIR,—Pardon me if I take leave to interrupt your important studies for the good of mankind, or suspend for one moment your delightful communion with the blessed God. I cannot excuse myself without expressing my gratitude for the present, by your order, lately transmitted from your bookseller, which I shall always value, not only for its instructive contents, but, in a very peculiar manner, for the sake of the author and giver.

" To tell you, worthy doctor, that your works have long been my delight and study, the favourite pattern by which I would form my conduct and model my style, would be only to echo back, in the faintest accents, what sounds in the general voice of the nation. Among other of your edifying compositions, I have reason to thank you for your ' Sacred Songs,' which I have introduced into the service of my church ; so that, in the solemnities of the Sabbath and in a lecture on the week-day, your muse lights up the incense of our praise, and furnishes our devotions with harmony.

" Our excellent friend, Dr. Doddridge, informs me of the infirm condition of your health ; for which reason, I humbly beseech the Father of spirits, and the God of our life, to renew your strength as the eagle's, and to recruit a lamp that has shone with distinguished lustre in His sanctuary : or, if this may not consist with the counsels of unerring wisdom, to make all your bed in your languishing, softly to untie the cords of animal existence, and enable your dislodging soul to pass triumphantly through

---

faith by the labours of Dr. Doddridge and Hervey. After the death of his wife, he entered into holy orders ; and, for many years, officiated as minister in St. James's Church, Bristol. He was a man of great ability, was no mean poet, published many religious treatises, and died in 1795, full of years and honour.

the valley of death, leaning on your beloved Jesus, and rejoicing in the greatness of His salvation. ,

"You have a multitude of names to bear on your breast, and mention with your lips, when you approach the throne of grace in the beneficent exercise of intercession ; but none, I am sure, has more need of such an interest in your supplications, none can more highly esteem it, or more earnestly desire it, than, dear sir, your obliged and affectionate humble servant,

"JAMES HERVEY."[1]

It is a curious fact, that, Hervey possessed and cherished the friendship of the two greatest Dissenters of the age, Doctor Doddridge and Dr. Watts ; and, that, the hymns of the latter, even in his lifetime, were sung in the service of an established church.

For eight years, Wesley had been an itinerant preacher, and had encountered an unparalleled amount of violent opposition. There had been a temporary estrangement between him and Whitefield, on Calvinistic doctrines ; but the two were now as warmly attached to each other as ever. Methodism, meanwhile, had been established in all directions ; and, in this very year, 1747, had been introduced into Ireland. Brutal were the persecutions from which the poor Methodists still had to suffer ; but their truth was mighty and triumphant. Hervey had taken no part in the great movement of the Wesleys and Whitefield ; but he had not opposed it. Indeed, it had his sympathy and prayers. His old friends occupied one sphere of Christian usefulness ; he, according to his ability, occupied another. Hence the following, addressed to Wesley :—

"WESTON, NEAR NORTHAMPTON,
"*December* 30, 1747.

"DEAR SIR,—With pleasure I received,and with gratitude acknowledge, the favour of your two letters. That which bears the date of November 21, I should have answered long ago, had I not been retarded by the following reason :

"I was desirous to give a proof of my love for your person and of my reverence for your conduct, somewhat more substantial than the bare profession of my pen. My bookseller is, this week, to pay a sum of money for a second impression of my two little pieces of devotional

---

[1] *Evangelical Magazine*, 1811, p. 338.

1747

Age 33

meditation, which I lately ventured to publish, and which God has vouchsafed to honour with acceptance. This is to be received by my brother, in Miles's Lane, at whose house, if you please to call, he will, in my name, present you with five guineas, which I beg of you to accept, as a token of that affectionate and grateful esteem which I bear to my ever-valued friend ; and distribute among the indigent or distressed members of that Divine Benefactor, who died for us both.[1]

"Assure yourself, dear sir, that I can never forget that tender-hearted and generous Fellow of Lincoln, who condescended to take such compassionate notice of a poor undergraduate, whom almost everybody condemned, and for whose soul no man cared.

"If you ask, Why I have withdrawn into a corner, and lain hid in obscurity, while God seems to be shaking the heavens and the earth, and to be doing His work, His great and glorious work, of bringing sinners to Christ, as the doves to their windows ? I will tell you freely. It is because of an infirm constitution, a languid flow of spirits, and an enervated state of body, which render even that small share of business, which lies within my narrow sphere, too often burdensome to me, and but very poorly performed by me.

"As for points of doubtful disputation,—those especially which relate to *particular* or *universal* redemption,—I profess myself attached neither to the one nor the other. I neither think of them myself, nor preach of them to others. If they happen to be started in conversation, I always endeavour to divert the discourse to some more edifying topic. I have often observed them to breed animosity and division, but never knew them to be productive of love and unanimity. I have further remarked, that, in forming their sentiments on these doctrines, persons may be diametrically opposite, and yet be high in the favour of God, and eminently owned by Him in their ministry. Therefore, I rest satisfied in this general and indisputable truth, that, the Judge of all the earth will assuredly do right ; and whosoever cometh to Him, under the gracious character of a Saviour, will in no wise be cast out.

"I embrace—readily embrace—your offer. Let me ever be reckoned in the number of your friends, and often remembered in the earnestness of your prayers. Though it is your distinguished province, to lift your voice on high, and make the world resound with the Redeemer's name ; though my employ is to catch the pleasing accents, and echo, or rather whisper, them among a little circle of acquaintance, yet, I hope, we may be united in the same cordial affection here, and united in the same kingdom of our common Master hereafter.

"Your correspondence will be greatly esteemed, and, I hope, will prove

---

[1] Not to mention other places, Wesley already had, in connection with his Old Foundery, in London, a dispensary, a poor-house, a day-school, and a lending society, to which must be added an efficient organization for visiting and relieving the afflicted poor in their own houses.

a blessing to, dear sir, your very unworthy, but truly affectionate brother and servant,

" J. HERVEY."[1]

1748
—
Age 34

Affliction was still the heritage of Hervey; but, in the midst of all, his full heart overflowed with pure benevolence, and his pen was not unemployed. Having completed his " Contemplations," he now devoted what health he had to the revision and enlargement of his " Descant on Creation." The following are extracts from letters written in the months of March and April, 1748.

" If you have not so much as you wish to relieve the necessities of the poor, distribute from my stock. I am cloistered up in my chamber, and unacquainted with the distresses of my brethren. Lend me, therefore, your eyes to discover proper objects, and your hand to deal about my little fund for charity. Do not forbid me to send a guinea in my next for this purpose. Do not deny me the pleasure of becoming, through your means, an instrument of some little comfort to my afflicted fellow-creatures.

" Herewith comes the ' Descant ' enlarged. I hope you will be able to read it, and not a little to improve it. Can you engage Dr. —— to run it over? I must write it over again, so fear not to erase and blot.

" A letter from my father is enough to cast contempt on created things. It informs me, that, my poor sister is reduced very low, so low that my father cannot hear her speak. He seems to look upon her life to be in very great danger. May the Father of compassion restore her health, that she may live to the honour of her dying Master, and be a comfort to her afflicted parents ! "

For months after this, Hervey's health was very feeble, but his soul as large as ever; hence the following :—

WESTON-FAVEL, *Aug.* 18, 1748.

" MY VERY DEAR FRIEND,—I received your letter, full of tenderness, and full of piety, last night. The very first thing I apply myself to this morning, is to acknowledge your favour, and confess my own negligence. But your affectionate heart will pity rather than blame me, when I inform you, that, a relapse into the disorder, of which I was never thoroughly cured, has brought me very low, insomuch that I am unable either to discharge the duties of life, or to answer the demands of friendship. I have not been capable of preaching for several Sundays. Pyrmont water, ass's milk, and such kind of restoratives I try, but try in vain.

You are not ignorant of my sentiment with regard to our Dissenting brethren. Are we not all devoted to the same supreme Lord? Do we not

---

[1] *Arminian Magazine,* 1778, p. 34.

 all rely on the merits of the same glorious Redeemer? By professing the same faith, the same doctrine which is according to godliness, we are incorporated into the same mystical body. And how strange, how unnatural it would be, if the head should be averse to the breast, or the hands inveterately prejudiced against the feet, only because the one is habited somewhat differently from the other? Though I am steady in my attachment to the Established Church, I would have a right hand of fellowship, and a heart of love, ever ready, ever open for all the upright, evangelical Dissenters."

To a great extent, Hervey was now an invalid. Sometimes he catechised the children on the Apostles' Creed, the Lord's Prayer, and the Ten Commandments; but confesses his want of aptitude for this, and that he rarely did it so as to satisfy himself. His public work, however, was extremely limited. By preaching, he could do but little; but, by his treatises, he was reaching the hearts and consciences of thousands who never heard his voice. In 1749, a sixth edition of his "Meditations and Contemplations," in two volumes,[1] was published; and Whitefield wrote as follows :—[2]

"July 10, 1749. Your sentiments concerning Mr. Hervey's book are very just. It has gone through six editions. The author of it is my old friend, a most heavenly-minded creature, one of the first of the Methodists, who is contented with a small cure, and gives all that he has to the poor. He is very weak, and daily waits for his dissolution. We correspond with, though we cannot see, one another. We shall, ere long, meet in heaven."

In another letter, to Hervey himself, Whitefield says :— .

"Blessed be God, for causing you to write so as to suit the taste of the polite world! O that they may be won over to admire Him, who is indeed altogether lovely! O when shall we get within the veil! Thanks be to God, it cannot be long. We are both sickly. Lord, give us patience to wait till our blessed change come!"

---

[1] *London Magazine*, 1749, p. 436.

[2] Hervey's book became so popular, that, in more instances than one, some parts of it were turned into poetry. The most notable instance was that of Mr. T. Newcomb, M.A., who, in 1757, published "Mr. Hervey's Contemplations on the Night, done into blank verse, after the manner of Dr. Young." In 1764, the same gentleman published the whole of the "Meditations and Contemplations," in the same form. It may be added, that, the demand for the "Meditations and Contemplations" was such, that, in 1764, not fewer than seventeen *authorized* editions of the work had been published, or about one a year from the time when the work was first printed.

On November 8, 1749, Whitefield wrote :—

"Your present circumstances almost distress me. I think it requires more grace heartily to say, 'Father, Thy will be done,' in such a situation, than to die a martyr forty times. But, my dear friend, though your body is weak and confined at home, your pen hath been active, and your works walk abroad. I hear of them from all quarters. God hath blessed, and will bless them. Let that comfort you, and, if health any way permits, pray write again. Fear not, my dear, dear man ; let faith and patience hold out a little longer, and then the struggle shall be over. Yet a little while, and you shall join with that sweet singer, Dr. Watts, who, whilst on earth, dragged a crazy load along, as well as you, for many years. I am now at Ashby, with good Lady Huntingdon. Her ladyship has a great regard for you, and begs you would come and stay a week at her house. She will take great care of you."

Hervey was ill, and the warm-hearted Whitefield never loved him so much as now. Hitherto, Lady Huntingdon had not corresponded with Hervey, though she had long entertained a great regard for him. One or two letters had passed between them, but no regular correspondence took place till the beginning of the year 1750. Again and again, had Whitefield conveyed her ladyship's request that he would write to her ; and, at length, on February 2, 1750, Hervey yielded, and commenced a correspondence, which was continued, without interruption, until his death. Whitefield was delighted, and wrote :—"I am glad you have opened a correspondence with our elect lady. Keep it open, I entreat you, my dear friend."

An extract from another letter, by Whitefield, will be welcome :—

PLYMOUTH, *Feb.* 25, 1750.

"REVEREND AND DEAR SIR,—Your letters always fill me with sympathy. Your last I have just been reading, and in reading breathed out the ejaculation, 'Lord, when will the days of his mourning be ended?' Surely, you are not always thus to stick fast in the mire and clay. Look up then, my dear Mr. Hervey ; you shall find grace to help in time of need.

> "'Leave to His sovereign sway,
>   To choose and to command ;
>   So shalt thou, wondering, own His way,
>   How wise, how strong His hand.
>   Far, far above thy thought
>   His counsel shall appear,
>   When fully He the work hath wrought,
>   That caused Thy needless fear.'

"This is the advice I give you. I sent your hymn to good Lady Huntingdon, who has been ill, but is now, I hope, recovered. Pray write to me often. Sorrows grow less, joys grow greater, by being communicated. Load me as much as you will with all your grievances, and I will lay them before Him, who came to bear our sicknesses and heal our infirmities."

Two months later Whitefield wrote aga'n:—

"PORTSMOUTH, *April* 28, 1750.

"MY VERY DEAR FRIEND AND BROTHER,—Your letter should have had an immediate answer, if the least leisure had offered when in town. But there I am continually hurried, and had scarce time to eat bread. However, our Lord gave me meat which the world knows not of, and enabled me to preach three or four times a day to great multitudes, and, I trust, with great blessings.

"Fear not your weak body. We are immortal till our work is done. Christ's labourers must live by miracle; if not, I must not live at all; for God only knows what I daily endure. My continual vomitings almost kill me, and yet the pulpit is my cure. I speak this to encourage you. Persons whose writings are to be blessings must have some thorns in the flesh. Your disorders, like mine, I believe, are, as yet, only to humble, not to kill us. Though I long to go to heaven, yet I am apt to think we are not to die presently, but live and declare the works of the Lord—you by your pen; I by my tongue. Courage, my dear, very dear Mr. Hervey; courage! When we are weak, then are we strong.

"But to your letter. How shall we contrive to meet? I purpose being at Olney next Sunday seven-night, and in a day or two after at Northampton. I wish I could have a line from you. Your 'Meditations' are now printing at Philadelphia. Why do you not sit for your picture? The Lord· be with you. I love you most tenderly. I thank you ten thousand times for all favours, and am, very dear friend, yours most affectionately, and eternally, in our Lord Jesus,

"G. WHITEFIELD."

The programme was carried out; and the old friends met. Whitefield writes:—

"ASHLEY, *May*, 11, 1750.

"I preached last Lord's-day at Olney.[1] We had two sweet seasons. A

---

[1] To some, it may seem strange, that, Whitefield did not occupy Hervey's pulpit; but it must be remembered, that, as yet, Hervey was only his father's *curate*. Notwithstanding this, however, Hervey, in 1749, took the liberty of inviting Whitefield to occupy his church. Whitefield's reply was characterized by greater prudence then he sometimes manifested. In a letter dated, "Chelsea, January 13, 1749," he writes,—

"You will not be offended if I tell you that good Lady Huntingdon saw your letter. She was much pleased with it, and has a great regard for you. The prospect of doing good to the rich that attend her ladyship's house, is great multitude attended. On the Monday, about six miles from Northampton, I had a private interview with Dr. Stonehouse, Dr. Doddridge, Messrs. Hervey and Hartley. On the Tuesday, I preached, in the morning, to Dr. Doddridge's family, and, in the afternoon, to about two thousand in the field. Dr. Stonehouse, Mr. Hervey, etc., attended me, and walked with me along the street ; so that, I hope, the physician will now turn his back upon the world. I expounded at his house in the evening, and am, hereafter, to come to it as my own. On Tuesday, I preached twice at Kettering to several thousands. On Wednesday, I came hither, and found good Lady Huntingdon, though very weak, yet, better than I expected."

Concerning this visit by the great evangelist, Hervey wrote :—

"WESTON, *May* 12, 1750.

" This week, we had another visit by that indefatigable preacher of the everlasting gospel, Mr. Whitefield. He delivered his message under the canopy of the skies, and in the midst of a numerous and attentive audience. Dr. Doddridge, Dr. Stonehouse, another doctor of physic, Mr. Hartley, a worthy clergyman, and myself, were on his right hand, and on his left. His text was, ' Ye are the temples of the living God.' He showed himself a workman that need not be ashamed, rightly dividing the word of truth. He dealt out to saints and sinners their portion in due season. All the hearers hung on his lips, and many were visibly impressed by the power of his doctrine. I hope, I am the only one who suffered by attending. I was obliged, as soon as the sacred service was over, to lie upon the bed for a little refreshment, and took such a cold as I have not yet got rid of.

" I dined, supped, and spent the evening with Mr. Whitefield, at Northampton, in company with Dr. Doddridge, and two pious, ingenious clergymen of the Church of England. And, surely, I never spent a more delightful evening, or saw one who seemed to make nearer approaches to the felicity of heaven. A gentleman of great worth and rank in the town invited us to his house, and gave us an elegant treat ; but how mean was his provision, how coarse his delicacies, compared with the fruit of my friend's lips ! They dropped as the honey-comb, and were a well of life. Surely, people do not know that amiable and exemplary man ; or else, I cannot but think, instead of depreciating, they would applaud and love him.

---

very encouraging. I preach twice a week, and, yesterday, Lord Bolingbroke was one of my auditors. His lordship was pleased to express very great satisfaction. I thank you for your kind invitation to your house and pulpit. I would not bring you, or any of my friends, into difficulties, for owning poor, unworthy, ill and hell-deserving me. But, if Providence should give me a fair call, I should be glad to come your way. I rejoice in the prospect of having some ministers in our church pulpits that own a crucified Redeemer."—*Whitefield's Letters,* No. 726.

For my part, I never beheld so fair a copy of our Lord,—such a living image of the Saviour,—such exalted delight in God,—such enlarged benevolence to man,—such a steady faith in the Divine promises,—and such a fervent zeal for the Divine glory; and all this without the least moroseness of humour, or extravagances of behaviour; sweetened with the most engaging cheerfulness of temper, and regulated by all the sobriety of reason, and wisdom of Scripture; insomuch, that I cannot forbear applying the wise man's encomium of an illustrious woman to this eminent minister of Christ, ' Many sons have done virtuously, but thou excellest them all.'

A few weeks after this, Hervey was prevailed on, by the repeated importunity of Whitefield and Lady Huntingdon, to visit London, for the benefit of his enfeebled health.[1] He arrived in June, 1750, and remained until the death of his father, in May, 1752. One of the winters was spent in the house of Whitefield; and, for some time, he lodged with his brother William, in Miles Lane. By means of Lady Huntingdon, he became acquainted with Lady Gertrude Hotham, Lady Chesterfield, the Countess Delitz, Lady Fanny Shirley, and many other distinguished and pious persons. Here he met with Charles Wesley; was visited by Dr. Gill, Mr. Cudworth, and John Cennick; and, for the first time, heard Romaine. Here, also, he enlarged and corrected his ' Meditations,' composed his ' Remarks on Bolingbroke's Letters,' and wrote part of his ' Theron and Aspasio.' He could rarely attempt to preach ; but his time was fully occupied. How his two years in London were employed will be best exhibited by extracts from his voluminous correspondence.

---

[1] Hervey's removal to London was a sort of abduction, accomplished by Whitefield, Dr. Stonehouse, and the Rev. Thomas Hartley. The particulars need not be given. Suffice it to say, on his arrival, he wrote his father as follows :—

" I am now at Mr. Whitefield's house, where everything is neat and convenient; great care is taken of me, and a hearty welcome given me. The house is very open and airy, and has no bug, a sort of city gentry for whom I have no fondness. I hope my mother has taken care to get my parish supplied. I desire her to send me some shirts, a silk handkerchief or two, a pair of shoes, and anything that she may think necessary. I have already bespoken a new suit of clothes, and a wig. Dr. Stonehouse, when he pressed me into this expedition, put five guineas into my hand, for which I am accountable. I would not have Mary clean my study, lest she should displace or lose any papers, of more importance than they appear to be. I conclude myself, with duty to my mother and love to sisters, honoured sir, your dutiful son,

" JAMES HERVEY."

At the time of Hervey's arrival in the metropolis, Whitefield was in the north of England, and the two friends did not again see each other till about the beginning of September.

1750

Age 36

" *September* 11, 1750.

" MY DEAR FRIEND,—Thanks for your subscription; I have procured more of another friend. I shall soon be a poor man, here are so many necessitous objects. And who can bear to be in affluence, while so many fellow-creatures are in deplorable want?

"This night, dear Mr. Whitefield is with us, returned from his expedition, full of life, and rich with spoils,—spoils won from the kingdom of darkness, and consecrated to the Captain of our salvation.

"I have been prevailed upon to sit for my picture. If ever portrait was the shadow of a shadow, mine is such. Oh, that I may be renewed after the image of the blessed Jesus! When I awake up after His likeness, I shall be satisfied with it."

Three days after this, Hervey, Whitefield, and Charles Wesley,—a happy trio,—met at Whitefield's house. C. Wesley writes :—"1750. September 14. I met James Hervey at the Tabernacle, and in the fellowship of the spirit of love ;"[1] and, on the same day, Whitefield, as follows :—

"At my return to town, I was received, though utterly unworthy, with great joy ; and our Lord has manifested forth His glory in the great congregation. I have preached in Mr. Wesley's chapel several times; and I trust, a young lady of high rank was truly awakened about a fortnight ago, and is since gone triumphantly to heaven. Mr. Charles Wesley breakfasted and prayed with me this morning, and Mr. Hervey was so kind as to come up to be with me in my house. He is a dear man, and, I trust, will yet be spared to write much for the Redeemer's glory. I have prevailed on him to sit for his picture, and it will be published in a short time."[2]

The young lady referred to in this extract, was the daughter of Lady Gertrude Hotham. Hervey had frequently visited her in her last sickness, and, on one occasion, had administered to her the Lord's supper. Hence the following to the Countess of Huntingdon :—

"I had the pleasure of perusing your ladyship's letter to Mr. Whitefield, and return my grateful acknowledgments for your condescension in inquiring after me. My kind patroness, Lady Chesterfield, and many honourable persons, whose names, I trust, are written in the book of life, are very desirous for your ladyship's return to the great city. I have

---

[1] C. Wesley's Journal, vol. 2, p. 75.
[2] Whitefield's Letters, No. 860.

lately expounded, and administered the ordinance, at good Lady Gertrude Hotham's. Her daughter is ripening fast for glory. I had but little conversation with her, for she is too weak to endure much fatigue. When speaking of God's stupendous love, in giving His only Son for our salvation, and of our interest in the all-sufficient propitiation of His death, I quoted these portions of Scripture.—'He came into the world to save sinners;' 'He poured out His soul for transgressors.' 'Yes,' said Miss Hotham, who had been listening with singular attention; 'He died, the just for the unjust; He suffered death upon the cross, that we might reign with Him in glory.' On a subsequent visit, I found her much altered for the worse, as respected her bodily health. Mr. Whitefield had been to see her the preceding day, and has since gone to erect the joyful standard at Portsmouth. Blessed be God, she enjoyed much peace and tranquillity of mind, and a firm persuasion, that God was her reconciled Father, and the blessed Redeemer her all-sufficient portion. I expect to hear every day of her abundant entrance into the joy of her Lord. Good Lady Gertrude, and all her noble relatives and friends, are wonderfully supported in this trying affair."

Hervey was already employed in writing another book. He was slowly dying, but to be idle was impossible. Hence, the following :—

"*December* 20, 1750.

" MY VERY DEAR FRIEND,—Your letter found me, after a considerable delay in its passage, where do you think? Where I never expected to go any more,—found me at London! Prevailed on by the repeated importunity of my friends, I came by easy stages to town, in order to try whether change of air may be of any service to my decayed constitution: for my worthy physician, Dr. Stonehouse, has declared that nothing which he can prescribe, is likely to administer any relief.

" You inquire about my new work, intended for the press. It is a great uncertainty whether my languid spirits and enfeebled constitution will permit me to execute my design. It is a pleasure, however, to hear that I am sometimes admitted to converse with you by my book."

The sale of the works which Hervey had already published was extraordinary. The ensuing letter to his father is evidence of this, and also unfolds a feature of Hervey's domestic character not heretofore noticed.

"LONDON, *January* 23, 1751.

" HONOURED SIR—Mr. Rivington has advertised the next edition of my books, and has fixed upon the 31st for publication. Then there will be five thousand volumes ready for sale. Oh may they be five thousand trumpets to proclaim far and near the glories of Him, who died for our sins, and rose again for our justification!

" If you inquire about my picture, Mr. Willis will be so kind as to inform you. I am quite tired of sitting to the painters.

"If mother and you think Mr. Thayer would accept a couple of gallons of rum, brandy, or shrub, I would very gladly make him a present; and, when my mother's stock of shrub is out, she may command a fresh supply from your and her dutiful son,

"JAMES HERVEY."

When Hervey first came to London, he had no intention of staying the length of time he did. On September 11, 1750, in a letter to his father, he wrote :—

"I have entertained thoughts of returning home very soon ; but, if you choose that I should stay and make trial a little longer, I should be glad to have my MSS. here. Some of them, I think, lie on the chair at the right hand of my desk. There are others, but I forget where they are laid. If my sister can find any, containing dialogues or letters between Theron, and Aspasio, I desire she will pack them up, and send them carefully by coach."

During the whole of the year 1751, Hervey continued in the same debilitated state. It was now, that, he began his long series of letters to Lady Frances Shirley, one hundred and eighteen of which were subsequently published by her ladyship's executors. Early in the year, he tells his noble correspondent, that, he had put on his "coat but once during all the winter," and, even then, he "returned home with a cold, and was obliged to take to his bed." There is something painfully affecting in extracts like the following :—

"Should I attempt to speak roundly to Mr. ——, my cheeks, pale as they are, would be encrimsoned. Instead of working conviction in a brother, I should suffer disorder in myself. So tender are my spirits! As, I am sure, your ladyship must perceive, by a certain confusedness and precipitancy in my behaviour; quite contrary to that ease and serenity which every one must observe in your ladyship. I know not how it is, but I cannot, either by the exercise of my reason, or even by an advertence to God, rectify this weakness. I trouble you with this complaint, only with a view of demonstrating that nothing considerable can be expected from a person, to whom 'the grasshopper is a burden.'"

Again,—"*April* 14, 1751. My health is so very precarious, and my constitution so enervated, that, I scarce ever am able, and am always unfit, to wait upon your ladyship. I have often found pleasure in visiting the poor tenants of the meanest hut, where I had an opportunity of talking on heavenly things. How much more should I be delighted, in an admission to your ladyship's company, where I should hear the same favourite topics discoursed on, with all the refinements of politeness and superior sense! But extreme weakness, and great languor, disqualify me for the enjoyment of this satisfaction."

Again,—" My poor heart, that is naturally fond of activity, and would fain exert itself for the blessed Redeemer's glory,—that is peculiarly charmed with the works of creation, and knows no higher entertainment than a contemplative rural excursion,—is sometimes apt to repine at being cut off from its favourite gratifications. But I desire to check such unsubmissive emotions; and rest satisfied, that, whatever the all-gracious God ordains, is incomparably better than I could choose for myself. Let the voice of murmuring, therefore, be entirely suppressed. Let the praises of God be upon my tongue, and let all that is within me bless His holy name."

Again,—" *September* 23, 1751. Though my hand is able to hold a pen, my feet are not able to carry me across the room, without some borrowed support. I have been extremely ill: hovering upon the very brink of eternity. The doctor was twice sent for, by a special messenger, from an apprehension, that, my dissolution was approaching. You will probably be desirous to know how my mind was affected, amidst such circumstances of peril and pain. I humbly bless the Divine goodness, I was under no terrifying fears with regard to death. It was desirable, rather than dreadful; the thing I longed for, rather than deprecated. You are pleased to ask, What I am going to publish? I was writing a little Treatise[1] upon some of the most important doctrines of Christianity: to be disposed partly into dialogues, partly into letters; and rendered entertaining by several descriptive pictures in nature and its ever-pleasing scenes. I have sketched out the greatest part, in a rough un-connected manner; but a considerable time will be requisite, to dispose it properly, and polish it for the nice taste of the present age. This time, whether it will please the Sovereign Disposer of all things to allow; or whether my constitution, always very inferior, but now more exceedingly enervated, will yield a sufficient supply of animal strength,—is a great uncertainty. But of this, my lady, we are absolutely certain, that, whatever is ordered, by unerring wisdom and infinite mercy, must be good,—must be best."

One cannot but experience a feeling of surprise, that, a man in such physical debility was able to evince such activity of mind. Hervey could not be idle. To have been totally unemployed would not have retarded, but probably have hastened his decease. To some men, at least, a certain amount of work is a solace. It braces the mind; and enables the sufferer to better bear the afflictions of the body. So it was with Hervey. In the house of his brother, he had a comfortable home; and his father and friends were able and willing to afford him all the help he needed. No man was

---

[1] This refers to his greatest work, " Theron and Aspasio," published, in three octavo volumes, in 1755.

more free from the love of money. His wants were few, and his earthly longings were quite as limited. He had no need to work; but work was what he liked. His brain teemed with thought; and it was no inconsiderable relief to put some of his conceptions and conceits on paper. Besides, as he himself was wont to solicit the critical kindness of his friends, in the revision of his writings; so he sometimes rendered the same assistance to others. The following was written to the Rev. Mr. Pearsall, of Taunton, and is somewhat amusing as coming from one of the most florid writers of the period,—

"*May* 29, 1751.

"REV. AND DEAR SIR,—Give me leave to return my best thanks for your obliging letters and very valuable manuscripts: those, I mean, which you were so kind as to transmit for my use. I look upon them as a detachment of auxiliary forces, seconding and supporting a feeble attempt to oppose the enemies, and to spread the conquests, of *Free Grace*. I wish they had fallen into abler hands : for mine, weak, always weak by nature, are now enervated to the last degree by sickness. For several hours, I have been unable to take up my pen; and could only endeavour, by resting myself in some easy posture, to sustain a being, whose *strength is become labour and sorrow*.

"I now return, after a long delay, your truly pleasing and profitable letters. I have read them with singular pleasure; and, I hope, with some improvement. Many parts I perused several times; and the warm piety, garnished by an elegant fancy, made them as delightful as if they were new. I cannot pretend to the merit of doing your compositions any service; unless it be in this one circumstance, that, I have detained them from you for a considerable time; by which means, they will be, in a manner, new to your own eye: and you will be much more capable of judging maturely, concerning each sentiment, and every expression.

"One thing, in general, let me remark : That, my worthy friend's genius is too rich; his invention quite luxuriant. He must use the pruning knife, and cut off several of the shoots. Yes, though they are perfectly beautiful, they must be sacrificed; that, the fruit may acquire the finer flavour. There is a certain prettiness in some periods, that betrays us all into an ill-judged redundancy; which, though its neatness should secure it from being tiresome, yet, weakens the force of the principal thought.

"I wish you would introduce some suitable *descriptions* to beautify the last letters. As they all turn upon the same subject, and have no pieces of entertaining *scenery* to enliven them, I fear, they will read a little flat and heavy; especially when compared with the preceding ornamented pages.

"A few alterations I have proposed, and only proposed. Admit, or reject them, as shall appear, on your own examination, most expedient. Don't, dear sir, be *hasty* in publication. Compositions, that would spread far and continue long, in an age of so much refinement, should be touched and re-touched.

"I remain, dear sir, your obliged friend, and affectionate brother,

"JAMES HERVEY."[1]

The sick man used his utmost endeavours to be useful. Writing to another friend, towards the close of the year 1751, he says,—

"If I mistake not, you are a subscribing member of the Society for Promoting Christian Knowledge. Will you be so kind as to procure for me a dozen Bibles, and a dozen of the Bishop of Man on the Lord's Supper. I give away this to communicants, because it has the Communion Service in it; and because it is more evangelical, and less exceptionable than the generality of what are called preparations for, or companions at, the Sacrament. Too many of these books, by long prayers for each day of the week, and by injudicious representations, have sometimes, I fear, the contrary effect to what is intended. I had once a design, nor have I wholly laid it aside, of extracting from "Jenks' Office of Devotion," the few leaves, he has there wrote so pathetically on the Sacrament, and of printing them with the Communion Service; adding suitable observations of my own, to supply Jenks' deficiencies. I propose likewise to add what Marshall says on the subject; and insert, from the Bishop of Man, his short, yet striking meditations on some well-chosen texts of Scripture? What says my *fidus Achates* to this? Give it a place in your thoughts; and, however we may determine on this, let us determine to cleave more closely to the Lord, and wait upon our God continually.

It is a curious fact, that, there is no evidence of any interview between Hervey and the Wesleys, during 1751. At the beginning of the year, John Wesley was married, in London, to Mrs. Vazeille; and his brother Charles also spent several months in the metropolis; but neither their Journals nor their Letters contain the least allusion to their valetudinarian friend Hervey. With the exception of the month of January, Whitefield was scarcely at all in London; but he wrote to Hervey, from Bristol, as follows :—

"BRISTOL, *March* 17, 1751.

"MY VERY DEAR FRIEND,—This comes with a summons from good Lady Huntingdon, for you to appear in Bristol, and abide for a month or two at my brother's house. You must not refuse. The God, who has carried that elect Lady through such bad roads from Ashby hither, will take care of you, and, I am persuaded, you will not repent your journey.

---

[1] *Gospel Magazine,* 1777, p. 298.

Her Ladyship made the motion to me, and intends writing herself. Blessed be God! she is much better, and I trust will do well. She will have nobody to give her the Sacrament unless you come. I hope this will find you at the Tabernacle House. I ventured, the other day, to put out a guinea to interest for you. It was to release an excellent Christian, who, by living very hard, and working near twenty hours out of four-and-twenty, had brought himself very low. He has a wife and four children, and was above two guineas in debt. I gave one for myself and one for you. We shall have good interest for our money in another world."

Hervey's health was such that he declined yielding to this request;[1] and Whitefield wrote him another of his great-hearted letters:—

"EXETER, *April* 11, 1751.

"MY VERY DEAR MR. HERVEY,—I was pleased last night to find, by my wife's letters, that, your sister was delivered, and, more so, because my wife wrote as though you were again under my roof. This I count a great honour, and such a privilege, that, I wish to have the favour conferred upon me as long as I live. These my hands (could they work, and was there occasion for it) should readily minister to your necessities. If my wife should come down to Bristol, pray let not my dear Mr. Hervey move. If Molly stays in London, she will take care of you; if not, Polly and Mr. D—— will gladly wait upon you. I have preached about forty times since I left London, and have been enabled several times to ride forty miles in a day. I find, that, this sensibly refreshes me. I wish you could say so too : your Bideford friends would then see you. They hold on their way, and long to have a line from you. I hope Jesus gives you strength to proceed in your book. It is inquired much after. The Lord be with you, and bless your pen, and your heart !"

Hervey was very happy in the house of his friend, and wrote to Mrs. Whitefield, at Bristol, with a playfulness which was unusual in him :—

"This leaves your family in good health, and me, whom you appoint steward, like Gideon's soldiers,—*faint, but pursuing;* faint with bodily languors, but following after that amiable, adorable God, whose loving-kindness is better than life. We go on comfortably, and want for nothing, but your company. Mr. Cruttenden says, I live like a king, and dine every day in state. I tell him, No, I am nothing more than lord high-steward of your majesty's household ; but, since he will have it that I am a monarch, I this day began to act in character, and commanded and charged our trusty and well-beloved Robert Cruttenden, Esq., not to be awanting in his attendance on our royal person. I hope my friend's jest is a good omen.

---

[1] Charles Wesley partly supplied his lack of service (see C. Wesley's Journal, from June 1 to June 27, 1751).

long been struck out of her list ; and bestows her caresses upon a mean creature, who has been used to sit on the dung-hill ? O ! that it may be for the glory of Christ's grace, Christ's wisdom, Christ's power ! May I serve to the Sun of Righteousness, as a cloud is subservient in the firmament ; which, though all-gloomy in itself, exhibits a rainbow ; and, thereby, shows the world what beautiful colours are combined in that magnificent luminary.

"You are pleased to inquire after my little work. Dear Sir, add, to your kind inquiries, a prayer to God, that, it may be executed under the anointings of His Spirit, and appear (if it ever appears) under the influence of His blessing. My late sickness laid an absolute embargo upon it, for a considerable time ; and has so shattered my feeble constitution, that, I proceed like a vessel which has lost its rigging, and is full of leaks."

Hervey was, in part at least, a Calvinist. Wesley, on the other hand, was an Arminian ; and, in 1751 and 1752, published two of his most convincing and cogent pamphlets, namely, "Serious Thoughts upon the Perseverance of the Saints," and "Predestination Calmly Considered." It would not be rash to say, that, both were unanswerable, though Hervey thought differently. On the first, he was thoroughly opposed to his friend Wesley ; on the second he was dubious. Hence the following :—

"MILES'S LANE, *March* 24, 1752.

" Mr. Wesley's last piece I have not read through. I can't say, I am fond of that controversy. The doctrine of the perseverance of Christ's servants, Christ's children, Christ's spouse, and Christ's members, I am thoroughly persuaded of. Predestination and reprobation I think of with fear and trembling. And, if I should attempt to study them, I would study them on my knees."

Hervey was now employed in writing his able and beautiful controversial pamphlet, entitled, " Remarks on Lord Bolingbroke's Letters on the Study and Use of History ; so far as they relate to the History of the Old Testament, and especially to the case of Noah, denouncing a Curse upon Canaan ; in a Letter to a Lady of Quality." The great infidel had died on November 15th, 1751 ; and his book, which had been published posthumously, had created a painful sensation. Hervey completed his " Remarks " on April 22, 1752 ; though they were not published for some time after : indeed, originally, they were not intended for publication at all. Lady Frances Shirley, having read Bolingbroke's bad book,

wrote to Hervey, asking his opinion concerning it; and the
"Remarks" were, in the first instance, nothing more than a
private letter to the "Lady of Quality" just mentioned.[1]
The pamphlet is a successful attempt to refute a few of
Bolingbroke's bold and unauthorized assertions, namely:
1. That, "the Old Testament is no sufficient authority for
chronology from the beginning of time." 2. That, in the
Holy Scriptures, instead of history, we have "a heap of
fables; which can pretend to nothing but some inscrutable
truths, and therefore useless to mankind." 3. That, the
Scriptures are "full of additions, and interpolations, and
transpositions." 4. That, Noah "was still drunk when he
denounced a curse upon Canaan; for no man in his senses
could hold such language, or pass such a sentence."

A wiser man than Lord Bolingbroke once wrote :—

"The thing that hath been, it is that which shall be; and that which is
done, is that which shall be done; and there is no new thing under the
sun." (Ecclesiastes i. 9.)

In the infidel objections of Bolingbroke, the reader finds
the pith of all the infidel objections of the present day; and,
in order to refute them, nothing more is needed than to turn
to the manly defences of the Holy Bible written more than
a hundred years ago. Modern infidelity is the infidelity of
Bolingbroke and others, dished up, and served with newly-
invented garnishing, and a pretentiously learned flavour.
Hervey's treatise is free from all the ornate faultiness of his
"Meditations"; its style is flowing, clear, and forcible; and
its arguments fairly put and unanswerable. It would be
rendering useful service to republish it in the present alarming
prevalency of unbelief.

In the month of May, 1752, the livings of Weston-Favel
and Collingtree were rendered vacant by the death of
Hervey's father. The following extracts from letters to
Lady Frances Shirley refer to this event, and to other
matters.

"1732, *May* 19. I am upon the point to remove into Northamptonshire. It has pleased God to take my honoured father to Himself; so

---

[1] Life and Times of Countess of Huntingdon, vol. i., p. 191.

1752

Age 38

 that, I am obliged to depart from my present situation, and to take the living of Weston.[1]   O ! that I had strength of constitution, to watch over a flock, and feed them with the milk of the word !   But the will of the Lord is best.   He employs whom He will employ ; and whom He will, He lays aside.   Wise and righteous are all His ways.   'Tis very probable, I shall never have the pleasure of seeing your ladyship again, on this side the everlasting habitations.   My enfeebled state renders me like an aged tree, which must continue where it is fixed : to transplant it, or to remove it, is to kill it."

"*May* 23.   I am just arrived at Weston, after a pleasant journey, in an easy coach, and cool weather.   I am much fatigued, though we allowed two days for about seventy miles.   Thanks are due to your ladyship for making my Letter[2] acceptable to others, by approving it yourself, and honouring it with your recommendation.   I humbly bless God, if He pleases to give it favour in the eyes of others ; and should think it the highest privilege, if He would vouchsafe to render it at all serviceable to their best interests ; especially to such a distinguished and illustrious personage as the Princess of W——.   I assure you, my lady, I have not the least aversion to print any production of mine, in case better judges should think it might tend to maintain the honour of the Bible, or endear that inestimable book to mankind.   All I fear is, lest acute but irreligious minds should discover some weak sentiment ; should find some flaw in the argument ; and take occasion to wound the Redeemer, and vilify His truths, through my inadvertence.   Be so good, my lady, as to make my very respectful compliments acceptable to Dr. Hales,[3] and inform him of my suspicions.   If he would please to revise the little essay, and should think the 'Remarks' will stand the test of a rigorous examination, my scruples would be very much abated.   I believe, I durst undertake to vindicate all the observations, that are of a critical nature, with regard to the original language, or of an historic nature with regard to fact.   Whether I offend against the rules of polite and genteel demeanour, your ladyship is the best judge.   If your ladyship, or the Dr., should persist in your opinion, I wish you would be so good as to get the paper transcribed (no matter how close it is written) and transmitted to me in a frank ; for I have no copy of it, only in some incoherent minutes in shorthand.

"I know not what the Lord will do with me, or how I shall proceed.

---

[1] While in London Hervey had the offer of a tutorship in Jamaica. Writing to his father, he says,—"Dr. Nichols has made me an offer, which many young clergymen would covet :—to go over to Jamaica, to be tutor to a son of one of the most considerable persons in the island ; for which, I should be entitled immediately to £100 sterling a year, also meat, drink, washing, and lodging ; with an assurance of having, in a little time, a living of a hundred and fifty.   I am greatly obliged to the doctor, but have taken leave to decline accepting the proposal."

[2] His Pamphlet on Bolingbroke's " Study and Use of History."

[3] Probably the eminent Rev. Stephen Hales, D.D., of Teddington, Fellow of the Royal Society, a Member of the French Academy of Sciences, and Clerk of the Closet to the Princess Dowager of Wales.

My strength is so worn down, and my constitution so irreparably decayed, that it will be absolutely impossible for me to discharge my ministerial duty."

" *June* 13. Weston is near Northampton ; about two miles from the town ; pleasantly situated on an agreeable eminence. My house is quite retired ; so that we hear none of the tumultuous din of the world, and see nothing but the wonderful and charming works of the Creator. O ! that I may be enabled to improve this advantageous solitude! I did, on the day your ladyship mentions, ascend the pulpit ; and speak, for the space of half an hour, to my people. But with so much weakness! O ! 'tis well that the eternal God does not want strength of lungs, or delicacy of elocution ; but can do His great work of converting souls by the weakest, meanest instruments. If it was not so, I must absolutely despair of being successful in my labour, or serviceable in my office. I opened my commission to my new parishioners, from those words : ' Preach the gospel to every creature'; and gave them to understand, that, the end of my preaching amongst them, the design of my conversation with them, and the principal aim of my whole life would be, to bring them acquainted with the truth, and assist them in attaining the great salvation."

" *July* 3. Advised by my friends, importuned by my relations, and swayed by a concern for the circumstances of a mother and sister who live with me, I have been prevailed on to take a second benefice.[1] This obliges me to set out for Cambridge without delay, in order to be created Master of Arts. From thence, I proceed to London, to get a dispensation from the Archbishop, and the seals from the Lord Chancellor. On Wednesday night, I hope to be in town ; and, if I can get my business despatched by Saturday or Monday at the farthest, I may return soon enough to meet our Diocesan on his visitation at Northampton ; receive institution there ; and save myself the fatigue and expense of a journey to Peterborough. I was honoured with your ladyship's letter, just as I returned from visiting my people at Collingtree : the parish which I served, when I lived with my father, and of which I am going to be rector. It would have pleased you to have observed how glad the honest folks were to see their old curate. And why were they glad ? For no other reason, that I can conceive, but because I used to converse with them in private, just as I spoke to them from the pulpit; and endeavoured, at every interview, to set forward their eternal salvation. This, I find, is the grand secret, to win the affections of a flock. And in this, as in every other part of true Christianity, our interest and our duty are connected."

" *July* 11. I think your ladyship's objection was very just and weighty. I fancy it would be most advisable to send the little piece " (his Remarks

---

[1] The two livings of Weston-Favel and Collingtree were when worth about £180 a year. According to the " Clergy List," they are now worth £567 a year ; and the united population of the two villages is about 600. For several years, the Rev. Moses Brown was Hervey's curate at Collingtree.

1752
——
Age 38

T

on Bolingbroke) "abroad under my own name; as the acceptance, which my other Essays have found from the public, may promote the spread of this. And, I apprehend, my bookseller would give me something for the copy; which, at this juncture, would scarcely be consistent with prudence to neglect. The expense of taking my two livings is very great. It will cost me, I am told, six score pounds; and though, I believe, I have money enough in the bank, produced by my selling the property of my 'Meditations,' yet such a succour would be welcome and serviceable. Will your ladyship lend your name, either at full length or in initial letters, to dignify and recommend the performance? I humbly submit this proposal to your ladyship's determination: and shall be obliged, if you allow it; and shall acquiesce, if you reject it."

Hervey visited the metropolis, and, on his return to Weston-Favel, had a near escape from an untimely death. He writes :—

"*August* 2. Very early on Wednesday morning, I set out for North-ampton, in a new machine, called *The Berlin;* which holds four passengers, is drawn by a pair of horses, and driven in the manner of a post-chaise. On this side Newport, we came up with a stage-coach, and made an attempt to pass it. This the coachman perceiving, mended his pace; which provoked the driver of the *Berlin* to do the same, till they both lashed their horses into a full career; and were more like running a race, than conveying passengers. We very narrowly escaped falling foul on each other's wheels. I called out to the fellows; but to no purpose. Within the space of a minute or two, what I apprehended happened. My vehicle was overturned, and thrown with great violence on the ground. The coachman was tossed off his box, and lay bleeding in the road. There was only one person in the coach, and none but myself in the *Berlin;* yet, neither of us (so tender was the care of Divine Providence!) sustained any considerable hurt. I received only a slight bruise, and had the skin razed from my leg, where I might too reasonably have feared the misfortune of broken bones, dislocated limbs, or a fractured skull."

Hervey was now instituted, by the Bishop of Peterborough, in his second living, and opened his commission, among his new parishioners, by preaching from the text,—"To me, who am less than the least of all saints, is this grace given, that, I should preach among the Gentiles the unsearchable riches of Christ." He also sent to the press his "Remarks on Lord Bolingbroke's Letters," which, in the month of November, were published. He solicited Lady Frances Shirley to favour him with the criticisms of her friends; and, on December 5, 1752, wrote to her as follows :—

"I am much obliged to your Ladyship for taking the trouble of transmitting the sentiments of your critical acquaintance. If I live to write another letter, I will return my opinion with relation to them. This is designedly short; to correspond with my weak state of health. For I am again confined; though, blessed be God! not 'in durance vile.' I preached on Sunday; and renewed my cold; so that this morning I have lost my voice. What a dying life is mine! Every blast pierces me, and every cold crushes me. Blessed, for ever blessed be God! for a better life and happier state in the heavens. Where we shall be languid no more; and be ungrateful to Jesus no more; and sin against God no more."

To another friend, a few days later, he wrote :—

"*December* 14, 1752.—Your approbation of anything in my 'Remarks,' will give me singular satisfaction; yet, I should be no less obliged for your free thoughts, on what should have been added, expunged, or altered. Point out my blemishes, and supply my defects. Applause may be more soothing to my vanity; but such kind corrections will be more pleasing to my judgment, and more serviceable to our common cause. It is scarce probable, that, a second edition should be published, as the first was numerous; but, if there should be such a demand, I am sure, your animadversions would enrich and ennoble it. As an author, I would aim, singly aim at the glory of my Divine Master, and the furtherance of His everlasting Gospel. Nevertheless, I would, by no means, neglect the recommendations of a graceful composition. I would be glad to have the apples of gold, which are the truths of our holy religion, set in pictures of silver. Generally speaking, human nature must be pleased, in order to be profited. The wisest of men 'sought and found out acceptable words,' even when that which was written, was the truth of God."

In these extracts, the reader may find the reasons why Hervey became a pluralist. The thing cannot be commended; but, perhaps, in his case, it may be pardoned. He himself disliked it; but the circumstances of his widowed mother and fatherless sister, the importunity of his relatives, and the advice of his friends, overcame his righteous repugnance. At one time, he seems to have entertained the idea of giving one of the livings to his friend Dr. Stonehouse ;[1] but this was abandoned; and Hervey placed himself in the extremely objectionable position of holding two ecclesiastical benefices instead of only one. It is true, that, the united populations of Weston-Favel and Collingtree were not more than about six hundred souls; and that the income of the two livings was only about £180 a year; but the question is,

---

[1] Whitefield's "Letters." No. 916.

was it absolutely wrong, in every case, to become a pluralist? If it was not, Hervey was excusable, for, though £180 then was worth more than £600 now, the presentation to the two benefices was his own hereditary property, and, subject to the law of the land, he had a right to do as he liked with it. Still, the being a pluralist was an ugly fact. Churches have always objected to it. Even as early as the thirteenth century, at the Lateran council, holding more than one benefice was expressly forbidden, by a canon, under the penalty of deprivation ; the same canon, however, granting the pope a power to dispense with it in favour of persons of distinguished merit. The practical result was, there were so many found with a title to this merit, that the prohibition became useless. In this way, the holding of more benefices than one, became legal ; and such was the existing state of things in the time of Hervey. The law of the land created difficulties ; but they were far from being insuperable. Two certificates had to be obtained from the bishop of the Diocese, one for the Archbishop, and the other for the Lord Chancellor. Testimonials, also, had to be procured, from the neighbouring clergy, concerning the presentee's behaviour and conversation. He must also exhibit to the Archbishop, not only his letters of order of deacon and priest, but also a certificate of his having taken the degree of Master of Arts at the least, in one of the Universities of the realm. These and other preliminaries had to be observed ; after which, if the Archbishop was satisfied, the dispensation was granted (not by the pope as in former days, but), by the Faculty Office ; it was then confirmed under the broad seal of the Lord Chancellor ; and, finally, the affair was completed, by an application to the bishop of the diocese where the living was situated, for the presentee's admission and institution into his second cure of souls. Hervey had to pass through the whole of this worrying process ; and, beside other expenses, had to pay a stamp duty of £30 for every skin, or paper, or parchment, on which his dispensation was engrossed. No wonder, that, he speaks of it as having cost him "six score pounds." For five hundred years, or more, plurality of benefices had been an ecclesiastical disgrace ; and, though, perhaps, permissible in a case like Hervey's, it adds no lustre to his fame, and was not obtainable without handsome fees to the highest authorities of the English Church and State.

There is another fact, belonging to this period of Hervey's history, too curious to be omitted. Every one knows, that, Whitefield believed, that, the keeping of slaves was sanctioned by the Scriptures; that, hot countries could not be cultivated without negroes; and, that, the lives of numbers of white people had been destroyed in Georgia, and large amounts of money wasted, for want of negro labour. Holding such principles, Whitefield, in 1751, bought a number of slaves, partly to cultivate the land attached to his Orphan House, in Georgia: and partly to instruct them, and to make them Christians.[1] Strange to say, the gentle Hervey approved of this procedure; and having, during his residence in London, largely shared in Whitefield's hospitality, he gave to him, as a souvenir on leaving,—what? A slave! Hence the following :—

"When you please to demand, my brother will pay you £30, for the purchase of a Negro. And may the Lord Jesus Christ give you, or rather take for Himself, the precious soul of the poor slave!"

Whitefield readily acquiesced. His answer, referring to other matters as well as this, was as follows :—

"LONDON, *June* 9, 1752.

"MY VERY DEAR FRIEND,—I have received and read your manuscripts;[2] but for me to play the critic upon them, would be like holding up a candle to the sun. However, before I leave town, I will just mark a few places as you desire, and then send the manuscripts to your brother. I foretell their fate: nothing but your scenery can screen you. Self will never bear to die, though slain in so genteel a manner, without showing some resentment against its artful murderer.

"You are resolved not to die in my debt. I think to call your intended purchase *Weston*, and shall take care to remind him by whose means he was brought under the everlasting Gospel.

"O that Doctor Stonehouse may be brought out to preach it! If you do not take the other living" (Collingtree) "yourself, I think your giving it to the Doctor is a glorious scheme.

"Your brother has been so kind as to let me have the little mare again.

---

[1] Whitefield's "Works," vol. ii., p. 404.

[2] Probably "Theron and Aspasio," now in hand, though not published for three years afterwards. It could not be the "Remarks on Bolingbroke"; for there is no "scenery" in them.

My Master walked,—I ride, to preach the glorious Gospel. Whether riding or walking, Lord Jesus, let my whole heart be taken up with Thee!

"Adieu, my dearest sir, adieu. Cease not to pray for
"Ever yours whilst
"GEORGE WHITEFIELD."

One other letter from Whitefield may fitly close the year 1752. Whitefield had read Hervey's "Remarks on Bolingbroke," and now wished him to publish his "Theron and Aspasio."

"LONDON, *November* 14, 1752.

"MY VERY DEAR FRIEND,—"God will bless you for vindicating the honour of His sacred volumes in your last pamphlet, for which, as for all other unmerited favours, I most heartily thank you. I have just now read it, and doubt not of its being greatly blessed and owned, and going through many editions. I cannot discern any errata or inaccuracies in the composition. Surely, God hath raised my dear friend up, to let the polite world see how amiable are the doctrines of the Gospel. Why will you weary the world, and your friends, by delaying to publish your other long wished-for performance.[1] I shall be glad to peruse any of the Dialogues. The savour of the last is not of my mind. Pray let them see the light this winter. They will delight and warm many a heart.

"My dear, very dear friend, good-night. My kind respects await your mother and sister. My wife, who is quite an invalid, joins heartily with me, who am, my very dear sir, yours most affectionately in our common Lord,

"GEORGE WHITEFIELD."

Though so feeble and delicate, Hervey tried to preach twice every Sunday. His ministry also was popular and attractive, his churches being crowded to excess, and the windows sometimes removed, that, the people outside might hear. His style was familiar, and adapted to the congregations to whom he preached; and, of course, his sentiments were Calvinistical. "You have observed," said he, about this period of his history, "the walls on either side of the path leading to this church. They are covered, as you know, with ivy. Now, you may pluck off the leaves, and break off the branches, so that none of them shall be seen on the outside; but the roots of the plant have so worked themselves into the wall, that, it would be impossible entirely to eradicate them

---

[1] "Theron and Aspasio."

without taking down the wall, and not leaving one stone upon another. And so must this frail body be taken down; and then, and not till then, shall we get rid of the remains of a degenerate nature."[1]

Hervey's metaphor was striking; but metaphors are not arguments.

To employ his own expressions, Hervey began the year 1753 in "ill-health and weak spirits, which cramped his mind, and unnerved his hand." He was "sadly indisposed; languid and dispirited; out of humour with himself, and displeased with his own thoughts."

His "Theron and Aspasio" was now the chief and almost only occupation of his leisure hours. A part of the work was sent to Whitefield for revisal. Hence the following:—

"LONDON, *January* 27, 1753.

"MY VERY DEAR FRIEND,—I thank you a thousand times for the trouble you have been at, in revising my poor compositions, which, I am afraid, you have not treated with becoming severity.

"How many pardons shall I ask for mangling, and, I fear, murdering your dear 'Theron and Aspasio?' You will see by Monday's coach; which will bring a parcel directed for you. It contains one of your 'Dialogues,' and two more of my sermons; which I do not like very well myself, and, therefore, shall not wonder if you dislike them. If you think they will do for the public, pray return them immediately, because the other two go to the press next Monday. I have nothing to comfort me but this, 'that the Lord chooses the weak things of this world to confound the strong; and things, that are not, to bring to nought things that are. I think to sell all four sermons for sixpence. I write for the poor; you for the polite and noble. God will assuredly own and bless what you write.

"As yet, I have only had time to peruse one of your sweet 'Dialogues.' As fast as possible, I shall read the rest. I am more than paid for my trouble by reading them.

"The Lord be with your dear heart! Continue to pray for me. The Lord be with us! Grace! Grace!

"I am, dearest sir, in very great haste, but greater love,

"Yours, etc.,

"GEORGE WHITEFIELD."

Doddridge was dead, and beyond the reach of consultation; but Hervey now became acquainted with another eminent dissenter,—John Ryland, the well-known Baptist minister,—

---

[1] "Memorials of Rev. W. Bull," p. 8.

 who became the intimate friend of the Rector of Weston-Favel, and one of his most trusted advisers. In a letter, dated "February 3, 1753," Hervey sent to Ryland a rough outline of his "Theron and Aspasio," and said,

> "My piece is, as yet, only in embryo. Will you, dear sir, contribute your assistance to ripen the design, and bring it to the birth? With this view, I send you my four first dialogues. They are very incorrect, and shamefully blotted.[1] The first fault your pen will mend; the second your candour will excuse. But, instead of making any more apologies, give me leave to lay before you a plan of the whole scheme," etc. [2]

Hervey was almost fastidious in his literary tastes; and, hence, his habit of asking his friends to revise his manuscripts previous to their being printed. There can be no question, that, he went further, in this respect, than he need have done. Whitefield was a glorious evangelist; but made no pretensions to being a man of letters. Ryland was a strong-minded man; but not an accomplished scribe. The Countess of Huntingdon, in some respects, was one of the most remarkable women that ever lived; but polite literature was not the orbit in which she shone. And, yet, Hervey sought "friendly corrections" from the coroneted lady as well as from the great itinerant, and the Baptist minister. Hence, the following :—

> "Your ladyship is pleased to express a wish, that, I should proceed, without delay, in finishing my intended work. Be assured, your wishes, madam, have all the force of a command with me. I send you the first four ' Dialogues,' beseeching you to peruse them, not with the partiality of a friend, but the severity of a critic. The like request I have made of others, and have received their friendly corrections. I am deeply sensible of my own deficiencies, and, in order, therefore, to render my work, if possible, fit for public view—meet for the Master's use, I shall feel obliged by any corrections or improvements, which your pen may make. Your ladyship is at liberty to show the manuscript to whom you please. Your remarks, and those of your friends, may supply the sterility of my invention, and the poverty of my language. If you really approve of what I have sketched, I shall be encouraged to proceed in my work. May I not hope for the honour of dedicating it to your ladyship? It would give me singular pleasure to have any work of my pen patronised by the Countess of Huntingdon." [3]

---

[1] Hervey was remarkable for his beautiful handwriting.
[2] *Gospel Magazine,* 1774, p. 139.
[3] "Life and Times of Countess of Huntingdon," vol. i., p. 188.

Lady Huntingdon sympathized with the design of Hervey's book; claimed the assistance of all those whom she considered capable of suggesting improvements and useful hints; and transmitted their observations to the author; but declined the offered dedication.   Hervey writes:—

1753
——
Age 39

> "*July* 14, 1753.
>
> "MADAM,—Accept my thanks, for taking the trouble of perusing my very imperfect manuscript, and my grateful acknowledgments, for the improving touches and remarks you have made, as well as for those of your highly valuable friends and acquaintances. The corrections will be exceedingly beneficial to the work, and render it more acceptable to the public in general. But, I confess, I feel disappointed at your ladyship's declining to patronise the public attempt of my pen; nevertheless, your observations are so sensible and just, that, I cannot think of pressing the matter on your attention, further than to solicit your prayers for the success of the undertaking, and for the unworthy author."[1]

Writing, on the same subject, to Mr. Ryland, Hervey says:—

> "WESTON-FAVEL, *March* 17, 1753.
>
> "MY DEAR FRIEND,—I thank you, for the trouble of perusing my very imperfect manuscripts; and I desire Mr. Medley to accept my very grateful acknowledgments for the improving remarks he has made. I beg of him to proceed, and to use the same kind of severity with the other sketches. I am sensible, the pointing is inaccurate; and shall be much obliged for every correction in this particular. It will be no less beneficial to my piece, if he pleases to make free use of the pruning knife. Prolixity, upon such a subject, will infallibly create disgust, especially with the polite, for whose perusal and whose service, I would wish my attempt was properly calculated. I don't pretend, nor indeed do I wish, to write one *new* truth. The utmost of my aim is, to represent old doctrines in a pleasing light, and dress them in a fashionable or genteel manner."[2]

Such extracts as these are not without interest. They show, that, Hervey, unlike his friends Wesley and Whitefield, wrote not so much for the masses of the people as for the educated and genteel; and, that, he was intensely anxious to have his publications, in a literary point of view, as perfect as possible.

---

[1] "Life and Times of Countess of Huntingdon," vol. i., p. 190. The work was ultimately dedicated to Lady Frances Shirley.
[2] *Gospel Magazine*, 1774, p. 183.

It was in May, 1752, that, Hervey, in broken health, succeeded his father as Rector of Weston-Favel. Twelve months afterwards, he was called upon to preach, at the visitation of the Archdeacon of Peterborough, in All Saints Church, Northampton. Writing to Lady Frances Shirley, he says,—

"1753, *May* 10. I am now setting out for Northampton, where I am to preach the visitation sermon. I know not how I shall speak, so as to be heard, in that very large and lofty church. May the Lord God Omnipotent make His strength perfect, in my extreme weakness. O! for the eloquence of an Apollos, and the fervour of a Boanerges! I am quite ashamed of my poor, jejune, spiritless, composition; and I am no less ashamed of my unbelief, that, I dare not trust God for utterance; but, before an audience that is critical, forsooth must use my notes."

Hervey's text, on this occasion, was, "God forbid, that, I should glory," etc. (Gal. vi. 14); and the sermon was the first he published. Though not remarkable for either learning or argument, it was thoroughly evangelical and faithful; and, unless the belief and practice of the clergy there assembled were exceptional, it must have been somewhat startling. It was the sermon of a *Methodist;* and *Methodist sermons* then were seldom heard in the Established Church.

Preaching it was a duty; publishing it was an act of charity. Hence the following :—

"1753, *May* 19. I have lately been somewhat busied in preparing a sermon to be preached before the clergy, at our Archdeacon's visitation; and, to my weak nerves and languid spirits, a little business is a toil. A commentator, with whom I wish you may long be unacquainted, has taught me the meaning of Solomon's description, 'The grasshopper shall be a burden.' The sermon, though perfectly plain and artless, is in the press. It is printed for the relief of a poor afflicted child, as a short advertisement will inform the world. The person, to whose management it is consigned, has given orders for an impression of two thousand; besides a hundred and fifty, which I have bespoken for myself."

Printed sermons have seldom been popular; but the adventure, in this instance, succeeded. "I have no business going forward with the printer," wrote Hervey, in a letter to Lady Frances Shirley, on July 15, 1753.

"My last little essay would have remained in the obscurity of shorthand, if the father of the afflicted youth had not importuned me to send my sermon on a begging errand. I gave it him as a kind of lottery ticket, not without some hopes and many prayers, that it might meet with success, and come up a prize. Nor have I reason to repent ; for, though he printed two thousand, he tells me they are almost all sold."

An extract from another letter may be welcome. It refers, not only to this visitation sermon, but to Hervey's parochial labours.

"WESTON-FAVEL, *October* 28, 1753.

"I have, this afternoon, been preaching to a crowded audience. You would be surprised, and, I believe, every body wonders that I am able to officiate for myself. I am so weak that I can hardly walk to the end of my parish, though a small one ; and so tender, that I dare not visit my poor neighbours, for fear of catching cold in their bleak houses. Yet, I am enabled, on the Lord's-day, to catechise, and expound to my children in the morning, and to preach in the afternoon. Every Wednesday evening (hay-time and harvest only excepted) I read prayers, and give them a lecture-sermon in Weston church. This is the Lord's doing, or, as your favourite book expresses it, this is owing to 'the good hand of my God upon me.'

"God has been pleased to pity the poor youth, for whose relief the visitation-sermon, I preached at Northampton, was printed. An edition of two thousand is disposed of; and the manager, for the distressed object, is venturing upon another edition. See, dear sir, if God will bless, who can blast? If He will further, what can obstruct? A feather, a straw, if He pleases to command, shall be a polished shaft in His quiver. Trust not, therefore, in eloquence or argument, in depth of thought or beauty of style, all of which are confessedly wanting in the present case ; but 'trust ye in the Lord for ever, for in the Lord Jehovah is everlasting strength.'"

Another glimpse of Hervey, in the midst of his rustic congregations, is furnished by a letter written by one of Whitefield's preachers.

"Last Sabbath-day, I rode to hear Mr. Hervey at Collingtree ; and, to my great suprise as well as satisfaction, having never seen such a thing before in prayer-time, instead of singing psalms, they sung two of Dr. Watts' hymns, the clerk giving them out line by line. After prayer, without going out of the desk, the minister put off his surplice, and expounded the Second Lesson of the day. And then, without going up into the pulpit, he read Ephesians v. 25–27, and spoke from them very sweetly and clearly. He expounds every Wednesday night, at the same church ; preaches twice on the Sabbath ; catechizes the children ; and meets some people on Tuesdays and Thursdays, in or near the parish where his father preached."[1]

---

[1] "Life and Times of Countess of Huntingdon," vol. i., p. 192.

There was no high-church ritualism here; but a godly pastor making himself at home among his poor parishioners, and simply and earnestly trying to promote the spiritual and eternal welfare of them and of their children.

In his enfeebled health, the wonder is how Hervey managed to undertake so many of these rural services. And yet, while thus faithfully discharging his duties as a parish priest, he was, if not an extensive reader, a most diligent student of the holy Bible, and a conscientious cultivator of literary æsthetics. Wesley, when an old man, remarked,—

"I *could* even now write as floridly and rhetorically as even the admired Dr. B——; but, I dare not, because I seek the honour that cometh of God only. What is the praise of men to *me*, that have one foot in the grave, and am stepping into the land whence I shall not return. Therefore I dare no more write in a *fine style* than wear a fine coat. But were it otherwise, had I time to spare, I should still write as I do. I should purposely decline, what many admire, a highly ornamental style. I cannot admire French oratory; I despise it from my heart."

It was otherwise with Hervey. Of set purpose, he cultivated the "*fine style*" of writing. Wesley wrote for the *masses;* Hervey for the *élite* of human society.

"My writings," said he, "are not fit for ordinary people: I never give them to such persons, and dissuade this class of men from procuring them. O that they may be of some service to the more refined part of the world!"[1]

Wesley and Hervey were equally conscientious; and opinions will differ concerning the wisdom of their different decisions; though all will probably admit, that, if Wesley's writings had less of scholastic learning, sonorousness, and rhythm, they had vastly more point and power than those of his old Oxford friend. Still, both acted from the purest motive; and it is in such a light that their respective merits should be judged. In a letter to a friend, dated, "Weston-Favel, August 18, 1753, Hervey writes:—

"I wish you had taken minutes of what you saw most remarkable in your tour through Westmoreland and Cumberland. Described in your language, and embellished with your imagination, an account of these

---

[1] Letters to Lady F. Shirley, No. 106.

counties might be highly pleasing to all ; and, grafted with religious improvements, might be equally edifying. Such kind of writings suit the
present taste. We don't love close thinking. That is most likely to win
our approbation, which extenuates the fancy, without fatiguing the attention. Since this is the disposition of the age, let us endeavour to catch
men by guile ; turn even a foible to their advantage ; and bait the gospel
hook agreeably to the prevailing taste. In this sense, ' become all things
to all men.' "

Hervey was now possessed of a large and varied library ;
but, like Wesley, he was, to a great extent, " *homo unius
libri.*"

" My library," says he, " is composed of the books collected by my
father and grandfather ; among which there are multitudes, that I shall
continue a stranger to as long as I live, though they stand at my right
hand and my left every day. I want to be better acquainted with God's
holy word ; to have its inestimable truths lodged in my memory, its
heavenly doctrines impressed upon my heart ; that my tempers may take
their fashion from it ; that my private conversation may be seasoned with
it ; and my public ministrations enriched by it. Thus, dear sir, may the
word of Christ dwell in us richly ! I am, what people would call, a
moderate Calvinist ; but, I assure you, I can bear, I shall delight to
have, my notions sifted ; nor am I so attached to any favourite scheme,
but I can readily relinquish it, when Scripture and reason convince me it
is wrong."

Hervey's " Theron and Aspasio,"—by far the greatest
work of his short life,—was now nearly completed ; and his
time was chiefly occupied in putting it through the press.
All kinds of friends were consulted ; and their revisions and
emendations solicited. The book was too bulky, and yet
Hervey was at his wits' end to make it less. Postage of
proof-sheets was heavy ; and compositors and printers were
dilatory to a most worrying extent. The year throughout
was a trying one, especially to a valetudinarian like Hervey.
Brief extracts from his letters will best illustrate what we
mean.

" 1754, May 4." Writing to Mr. Ryland, Hervey says,—

" My bookseller tells me, it will be impossible to comprise my essay in
less than three volumes of the ' Meditations ' size. It is much against my
inclination to exceed the quantity of two volumes ; but, I believe, I must
submit, or else we shall cramp the design, and mutilate the plan." [1]

---

[1] Letters to Rev. J. Ryland. No. 6.

" May 20. I send two or three manuscripts, and beg of you to exercise the same frankness of admiration, and the same impartiality of censure upon them. My bookseller tells me, it cannot be comprised in less than three volumes. I have always had an aversion to so diffusive a work. Many will not have ability to purchase them ; many not have leisure to read them ; and to some, I fear, the very sight of three volumes would be like loads of meat to a squeamish stomach. Yet, I cannot contract the work, without omitting those parts which are intended to entertain the reader, keep.him in good humour, and allure or bribe him to go on. What would you advise ? I send ' Letters,' eight, nine, ten, and eleven ; and ' Dialogues,' fifteen and seventeen. Do, my dear sir, improve, polish, and enrich them. I am, this day, a prisoner in my chamber, and write in much pain. Blessed be God for that world, where all tears will be wiped away from our eyes, and there will be no more pain."

" May 30. I send herewith four of my ' Dialogues,' which I beg of you to examine with a kind severity. I do assure you, I can bear to receive censure from a friend, and will kiss the lips that administer it, especially when it is intended to preserve my attempts to further the glorious gospel from the contempt of the public. I will, ere long, send you, in a frank, a general view of my plan, which, in the execution, is become too prolix, and cannot be comprehended in less than three volumes, unless some judicious friend will help me to curtail and abridge. I am very unwilling to publish a work consisting of three volumes ; I apprehend this will obstruct the sale not a little."

" June 1." In a letter to Lady Frances Shirley, Hervey writes,—

" May I promise myself the benefit of your opinion concerning the publication of *three* volumes ? As you know the taste and temper of the polite world, I should be much obliged for your advice. And I beg you will not flatter my vanity ; but, if you think, that *three* volumes on a religious subject will be insupportable, be so kind as to tell me plainly. I would fain write what may be acceptable, in order to write what may be useful ; and, for my own part, I really am afraid, that, so large a work will be less likely to subserve such a design."

In another letter, to the same lady, a fortnight afterwards, Hervey wrote :—

" *June* 16. I have still another scruple, which respects not the gay and splendid world, but the mean and penurious. I would gladly have my books in those hands, which hold the plough, and ply the distaff, because these persons are as nearly related to the all-creating God, and as highly beloved by the ever-blessed Jesus, as those who wear a crown, or wield a sceptre. But these will hardly be able to purchase *three* volumes. I thank your ladyship for your kind offer, in reference to the princess ; but my work is so far from being ready to come abroad, that, it is not yet in the press. The necessary preliminaries, one of which is the number of the volumes, are not settled ; though, as to this particular, I begin to be pretty well satisfied."

" *June* 21. Before this arrives, I hope my 'Dialogues' will have received the free correction, and the friendly improvement of your pen. As, through my many and repeated infirmities, I had long discontinued and have often intermitted my intended work, I am informed, from London, that the abettors of the Socinian scheme have been pleased to triumph in my disappointment ; imagining that, through fear or inability, I had laid aside my design, and insinuating, that, I had changed my principles, or was conscious of the weakness of my cause. From these gentlemen, if my essay should appear in public, it may expect a severe examination, and probably a violent attack. I hope your friendship will anticipate their inveteracy, and remove those blemishes, which might give them a handle for censure, or a ground for insult. What is your opinion, as to publishing *three* volumes ? Mr. Moses Brown and another friend pronounce in the affirmative, though I am much afraid that this circumstance will clog the sale. There are several pieces that are a kind of excursion from the principal subject, calculated to relieve and entertain the reader, yet not without administering some spiritual benefit. A whole 'Dialogue' upon the wisdom, power, and goodness, displayed in the contrivance and formation of the human body. Two or three 'Letters,' pointing out the traces of the same grand and amiable attributes in the constitution of the earth, the air, and the ocean. These I am afraid to lop off, lest it should be like wiping the bloom from the plum, or taking the gold from the gingerbread. To you I say gingerbread, though I would not say so to the public, for I really think the taste of the present age is somewhat like the humour of children : their milk must be sugared, their wine spiced, and their necessary food garnished with flowers, and enriched with sweetmeats."

" *July* 8. I have had my bookseller's opinion with relation to the number of copies proper to be printed, at which I am somewhat surprised, and must desire your advice. He says 5000 in small, and 750 in large, octavo To this I have some objections. In the first place, the sale of such a prodigious quantity cannot be but hazardous, though, I must confess, I have no reason to distrust the goodness of that over-ruling Providence, to which I would humbly ascribe the acceptance of a preceding essay. This scruple, therefore, shall be set aside. But what think you of the following consideration? Errors and weaknesses, if such a number be printed at once, may never be corrected ; whereas, if we publish half the proposed number, and a second edition is demanded, there may be an opportunity of correcting mistakes, and re-touching inaccuracies. May I not hope to receive a few hints for a Preface, in which I am advised to declare, that, it is my firm resolution to enter no farther into the controversy ? with this view, that, in case the doctrines are attacked, other and abler champions may see a clear stage for their entrance."[1]

----

[1] Letters to Ryland, No. 7.

"*July* 13. Here are six 'Dialogues.' May God enable you to search them, as with a candle, and make them such as He will condescend to bless! I have dropped several objections and answers; yet, I fear, too many are still retained. A multiplicity of objects dissipates the attention either of the eye or mind. Are, what the painters call, the two unities preserved? one principal action and one grand point of view in each piece? Does Theron speak enough, or with such weight, and such a spice of the *sal Atticus*, as might suit his character? Here and there, a touch of wit or genteel satire in him, I think, would be grateful, especially in the first part, before he is brought to a conviction of his guilt?"
"You can scarcely imagine what a demand there is for the book, even before publication. It makes me rejoice with trembling. I now feel the loss of our valuable friend, Dr. Doddridge, to whose judgment I ever paid the highest deference. I expect you will tell me my manuscript is very prolix; but I designedly made it so, that my friends may judge what is proper to be omitted. It is easier you know, to expunge than to compose. I wish they would, with a leaden pencil, enclose in a parenthesis what they would have dropped. I hope to retrench one-fourth of the copy."

September 28. I have to request the honour of your name, to dignify and recommend my book, which has been, for a considerable time, committed to the press. It will, I believe, be entitled 'Theron and Aspasio; or, a Series of Dialogues and Letters, upon the most *Important* and *Interesting* Subjects.' The whole will constitute three volumes. It will, I apprehend, make its appearance about the time appointed for the meeting of the Parliament; and I know no person whose name will give the author more satisfaction, or be a higher recommendation to his performance, than your ladyship's."[1]

"*November* 24. You have highly obliged me, in permitting me to grace my work with your name. I have been, ever since I received your ladyship's letter, engaged to keep no less than eight hands constantly employed in printing, which has taken up all my time. Be so kind, madam, as to favour me with your advice, whether I should present the book to the princess.[2] I must, I apprehend, present it to the prince's preceptor,[3] because he is our diocesan, and treated me in a very genteel manner, when I received institution from him. This is the last frank I have. Could you, Madam, accommodate me with a fresh supply? At this juncture a few of those vehicles would be very welcome and serviceable."[4]

Again, a few days later, to the same lady, Hervey wrote:—

"To grant my request was obliging; to grant it so speedily was like yourself. My hands are still tied by the business of the press. You

---

[1] Letters to Lady F. Shirley, No. 69.
[2] The widow of Frederick, Prince of Wales.
[3] Dr. Thomas, Bishop of Peterborough.
[4] Letters to Lady F. Shirley, No. 70.

can hardly imagine what obstructions and mistakes happen in the process
of such a work, especially when the author is at a distance from the press.
I take it for granted your ladyship approves of my presenting the piece
to the princess, but would you have me attempt to put it into the hands
of the prince?[1] I question whether the bishop would think it a proper
book for his royal highness's collection.   I dare say Mr. Stone[2] (who, I am
told, is the principal director of the prince's conduct), would banish it, not
for a term of years, but, for ever ; and not to the American colonies, but
to the country of the Hottentots.   I dare not expect that the bishop himself will like it ; but, perhaps, he will dislike my practice, if I do not pay
him the compliment.   When he gave us a charge, at his last visitation,
he inveighed against enthusiasm on the one hand, and profaneness on
the other ; and some of our reverend brethren took notice, that, when
delivering himself on the former topic, he frequently threw his eye upon
my friend Hartley and me.   However, this I must say, he wrote me a very
handsome letter, when I presented him with the ' Remarks on Lord Bolingbroke ;' and, in a private letter, which I happened to see, expressed
no disapprobation concerning the ' Meditations.' "

"*December* 26.   I have a fresh obligation to your ladyship for pro-
. curing me the opinion of good Dr. Hales.[3] .I cannot but be pleased with
his approbation; but I cannot persuade myself, that, the bishop will
undertake to present the books, or even consent to his royal pupil's reading them.   In case he should present them, who knows in what manner
he may do it? Suppose he should shrug his shoulders, and say, ' An
ambitious and conceited clergyman of his diocese, by the importunity of
request, in a manner, forced him upon this office.   How ungraceful would
the affair appear, and how unsuitable to decorum of conduct! Upon the
whole, I am in a state of real perplexity.   I would not seem to slight the
Doctor's opinion, much less reject his solicitation; yet, I cannot prevail
upon myself to think, that, to execute the proposal would be the propriety
of action.   I hope, madam, you will give me your free advice, and help to
extricate me from this embarrassment, into which yourself, yes, you yourself, have led me.   For I should never have been known to such grand
personages, if you had not condescended to introduce me.   My name
had never been heard by a royal ear, if it had not received some credit
by your ladyship's notice."[4]

These extracts might be multiplied ; but the reader has
had sufficient for the purpose of showing the almost extreme
assiduity of Hervey in making his book correct and popular.
Among others, he consulted his old friend Wesley, who

---

[1] The Prince of Wales, afterwards George the Third.
[2] Andrew Stone, a proud, very able, and very mercenary man, and sub-
preceptor of the Prince of Wales.
[3] Dr. Hales was clerk of the closet to the Princess Dowager of Wales.
Letters to Lady F. Shirley, No. 73.

revised the first three "Dialogues," and "sent them back with a few inconsiderable corrections." Hervey replied, "You are not my friend, if you do not take more liberty with me." Wesley promised, that, he would; upon which the manuscripts were again revised; and alterations were made of a more important character.[1] Whether Wesley, on this occasion, had used the prerogatives of a *friend* to a greater extent than Hervey liked, is a matter which has never been explained; but it is quite certain, that, when Hervey's work was nearly ready for the public, Hervey and Wesley, by some means, had become alienated, and were no longer the warm-hearted friends they had been in former days. Writing to Lady Frances Shirley, under the date of January 9, 1755, Hervey says,—

" Mr. John Wesley takes me very roundly to task, on the score of pre-destination; at which I am much surprised. Because a reader, ten times less penetrating than he is, may easily see, that, this doctrine (be it true · or false) makes no part of my scheme; never comes under consideration; is purposely and carefully avoided. I cannot but fear he has some sinister design. Put the wolf's skin on the sheep, and the flock will shun him, the dogs will worry him. I do not charge such an artifice, but sometimes I cannot help forming a suspicion."

This is a mournful episode. From letters, already printed in the foregoing pages, it is manifest, that, Hervey, at one period, held Wesley in the highest affection and esteem ; and, that, this was mutual is evident from the fact, that, as recently as the year 1754, not only had Hervey twice over requested Wesley to revise his "Theron and Aspasio," but, Wesley (at the time an invalid like Hervey) had requested his friend to revise his "Notes on the New Testament." Hence the following :—

" WESTON-FAVEL, *June* 29, 1754.
"DEAR SIR,—I have read your ' Notes,' and have returned them by the Northampton carrier, and transmitted such observations as occur to my mind. I think, in general, you are too sparing of your remarks and improvements. Many expositions are too corpulent; your's are rather too lean. May the good hand of the Lord be with them and with their author! ' Bengelius ' is likewise returned, with thanks for the use of that valuable book. Please to present my affectionate respects to Mr. Charles,

---

[1] Wesley's " Works," vol. x., p. 305.

and desire him, if he has done with 'Vitringa,' to send it by the same conveyance as brings your parcel. Let me beg to be remembered in your prayers, and in his, that, I may not dishonour the relation of, dear sir, your brother and friend in Christ,

·" JAMES HERVEY." [1]

The two old Oxford friends were now estranged; and, mournful to relate, their friendship was not renewed till they met in heaven.   But more of this anon.

Hervey's " Theron and Aspasio " was advertised to be published on February 18, 1755; but he writes, " there are so many unexpected remoras, that, I dare not answer for its forthcoming, even at the expiration of ten days more."

A copy of the " large octavo edition " is before us, in three volumes; pp. 405, 464, and 446; with a dedication, as already intimated, " to the Right Honourable Lady Frances Shirley." [2] The following is a copy of " the Contents " :—

" Dialogue I. Character of the speakers.—On improving conversation.—Elegance and dignity of the Scriptures.

" Dialogue II. Walk through the gardens.—The beautiful frame and beneficial ordination of things.—Preparatory discourse on the Imputation of Christ's Righteousness.—Meaning of the terms settled.

" Dialogue III. Walk through a meadow.—Doctrine of Christ's satisfaction stated.— Considered as a Redemption Price, and as a Sacrifice for sin.—Variously typified under the Mosaic dispensation.

" Dialogue IV. Park and romantic mount. —Christ's death further considered, as the very punishment which our sins deserved.—Objections, ancient and modern, answered.—The whole summed up and improved.

" Dialogue V. Elegant arbour in the flower-garden.—Imputation of Christ's obedience.—Objections from reason canvassed.

" Dialogue VI. Gallery of pictures.—Library and its furniture.—A sordid taste in painting censured; a more graceful manner displayed.—Imputation of Christ's Righteousness resumed.—Objections from Scripture urged and refuted.

" Dialogue VII. Hay-making.—Pleasures of nature freely enjoyed.—Blessings of grace bestowed with equal freeness.—Theron's plan of acceptance with God; consists of sincerity, repentance, and good works, recommended by the merits of Christ.—This shown to be a false foundation.—No such thing as a good work, till we are accepted through the Redeemer.

---

[1] *Methodist Magazine*, 1847, p. 965.

[2] The work was published in two sizes: 3 vols., 8vo, 18s.; and 3 vols., 12mo, 9s.

"Dialogue VIII. Duelling.—Animadversions on the practice.—Spirituality and extent of the Divine law.—Infinite purity of God.

"Dialogue IX. Curious summer-house.—No relaxation of the Divine law, as to the precept or the penalty.—Its inflexible strictness, and principal ends.

"Dialogue X. Theron's last effort to demolish the evangelical scheme of justification.—Among other objections, more plausible and refined than the preceding, he strenuously insists, that, faith is our righteousness.—Review of the whole.

"Dialogue XI. Ruins of Babylon.—Fine passage from Mr. Howe.—Depravity and ruin of human nature, as they are represented in Scripture.—Applied, with a view to determine the yet dubious inquiry.

"Dialogue XII. Extremely hot day.—A solemn shady bower.—True method of deriving benefit from the classics.—The wonderful structure and economy of the human body.

"Dialogue XIII. Walk upon the terrace.—Depravity of human nature, laid open and proved from experience.—Uses of the doctrine, and its subserviency to the grand point.

"Dialogue XIV. Theron alone in the fields.—His soliloquy on the charms of rural nature.—His reflections on the past conferences.—Aspasio reinforces his arguments for the Imputation of Christ's Righteousness.—Recommends self-examination, the keeping of a diary, and prayer for the enlightening Spirit.—Departs, under an engagement to correspond by letter.

"Letter I. Aspasio opens the correspondence with some important articles of duty; designed to facilitate self-examination, and promote conviction of sin.

"Letter II. Theron, convinced of the iniquity of his life, and the evil of his heart, sees the necessity of a better righteousness than his own.—Desires a further explanation, and a fuller proof of the doctrine under debate.

"Letter III. Aspasio proves the point—from the Liturgy—the Articles—the Homilies of the Church of England—and the writings of the Fathers.

"Letter IV. Aspasio re-establishes the tenet, from the Scriptures of the Old Testament.

"Letter V. Aspasio relates a remarkable panic.—Terrors of the day of judgment.—Christ's Righteousness and its Imputation, largely demonstrated from the New Testament.

"Letter VI. Theron takes a cursory view of the habitable creation.—Traces the perfections of nature through the earth, air, and fire.—Admirable construction, and advantageous effects, of these elements.

"Letter VII. Aspasio takes occasion to display the no less admirable perfection of Christ's Righteousness.—Its Principle—Extent—Perseverance.

"Letter VIII. Aspasio describes a drought.—Majesty and beauty of the sun, after a night of rain.—The meritorious excellency of Christ's

Righteousness illustrated, from the magnificence of His works, and the
divinity of His person.

"Letter IX. Theron's account of the western cliffs—the wonders of the
ocean—and the benefits of navigation.

"Letter X. Aspasio enumerates the much richer benefits resulting
from the Imputation of Christ's Righteousness.—Shows their happy influence, on holiness of heart, and obedience of life.

"Letter XI. Aspasio exemplifies the last particular, in two very
memorable instances.—Especially in the conduct of Abraham offering up
his son Isaac.

"Letter XII. Aspasio touches upon union with Christ.—How described
in Scripture.—Its blessed and glorious effects.

"Dialogue XV. Aspasio revisits Theron.—Theron under anxiety of
spirit.—Partly to entertain, partly to comfort his friend, Aspasio enlarges
upon the bounty of the Creator, visible both in the animal and vegetable
world.—The new convert is slow of heart to believe.—Evangelical motives
to faith.

"Dialogue XVI. Harvest scene.—Philenor's gardens.—Statues.—Grove
of evergreens.—Nature of true faith.—Its sure foundation, and sovereign
supports.

"Dialogue XVII. A river voyage.—The diversified prospect.—Comparative happiness.—Advantages of peace.—A celebration of the Gospel
and its blessings, in a kind of rhapsody.—Christ's Righteousness applied,
to every case of distress, and every time of need."

Such is Hervey's own correct outline of his work. As the
reader will easily perceive, the book is a mixture of theological teaching and scenic painting, the latter being used, as
Hervey himself states, "to soften the asperities of argument."
His "views of nature" are employed, not as being essential
to the truths which he wished to teach, but rather, to grace
his book with ornament, and to render it more readable.
Whether this ought to be regarded as an excellence or
a blemish, Hervey leaves his readers· to determine. He
writes,—

· "The author confesses a very peculiar fondness for the amiable scenes
of creation. It is, therefore, not at all improbable, but his excursions on
this topic may be of the *diffusive* kind, and his descriptions somewhat
luxuriant. It is hoped, however, that, the benevolent reader will indulge
him in this favourite foible."

Hervey's work was one of great importance. Of his "luxuriant descriptions" nothing need be said, except, that, many
of them are quite equal to those in his "Meditations and

Contemplations." [1]   Nearly all of them, however, might have been entirely omitted without at all interfering with the principal doctrines which it was the object of Hervey to teach and vindicate.   They are excrescences, though beautiful,— oases in a doctrinal arena.   To many of Hervey's readers, they would be the most attractive sections of his book; to others, only intent on pursuing and mastering the author's argument, they would be embellished barriers, and would be skipped.

To Hervey's doctrines, considered as a whole, ortho- dox Christians can take no exception.   Wesley observed with perfect justness, "Most of the grand truths of Christi- anity are herein explained and proved with great strength and clearness." [2]   The *crux criticorum* was Hervey's peculiar views of what he called "the imputed righteousness of Christ." A few brief extracts will show what he meant.

"*Aspasio.* Justification is an act of God Almighty's grace; whereby He acquits His people from guilt, and accounts them righteous; for the sake of Christ's righteousness, which was wrought out for them, and is imputed to them.

"*Theron.* Two of your terms want some further explication.   What do you understand by *Christ's righteousness?*   And what is the meaning of *imputed?*

"*Aspasio.* By *Christ's righteousness*, I understand, *all* the various instances of His *active* and *passive* obedience; springing from the perfect holiness of His heart; continued through the whole progress of His life; and extending to the very last pang of His death.   By the word *imputed*, I would signify, that, this righteousness, though performed by our Lord, is *placed to our account;* is reckoned or adjudged by God as *our own.* Insomuch, that we may *plead* it, and *rely* on it, for the pardon of our sins; for adoption into His family; and for the enjoyment of life eternal."

Again: *Aspasio* says,—

"The nature of justification, and the nature of condemnation are two *opposites*, which will mutually illustrate each other.   What is implied in the condemnation of a sinner?   He forfeits eternal life, and is doomed to eternal death.   What is included in the justification of a sinner?   It

---

[1] Wesley writes:—"The twelfth dialogue is unexceptionable; and con- tains such an illustration of the wisdom of God in the structure of the human body, as, I believe, cannot be paralleled in either ancient or modern writers" (Wesley's "Works," vol. x., p. 314).

[2] Wesley's "Works," vol. x., p. 322.

supersedes his obligation to punishment, and invests him with a title to happiness. In order to the *first*, there must be a remission of sins. In order to the *second*, an imputation of righteousness. *Both* which are derived from Christ's mediation on our behalf; and *both* take place, when we are united to that Divine Head."

Theron answers,—

"This, I know, is the fine-spun theory of your systematic divines. But where is their *warrant* from Scripture? By what authority do they introduce such subtle distinctions?"

"*Aspasio.* I cannot think the distinction so subtle, or the theory so finely spun. To be released from the *damnatory* sentence, is one thing; to be treated as a *righteous* person, is evidently another. Absalom was pardoned, when he received a permission to remove from Geshur, and dwell at Jerusalem. But this was very different from the re-commencement of filial duty, and parental endearment. A rebel may be *exempted* from the capital punishment, which his traitorous practices deserve; without being *restored* to the dignity of his former state, or the rights of a loyal subject. In *Christianity* likewise, to be freed from the charge of guilt, and to be regarded as a righteous person, are two several blessings; really distinct in themselves, and often distinguished in Scripture."

Instances being adduced in proof of this, *Aspasio* continues,

"Let me produce one text more,—'I send thee to turn them from darkness to light, and from the power of Satan unto God; that, they may receive forgiveness of sins, and inheritance among them which are sanctified by faith that is in Me' (Acts xxvi. 18). Here Christ distinguishes between *remission of sins*, and the *inheritance of the saints;* between the *pardon* that delivers from hell, and the *justification* that entitles to heaven. So that the former does by no means constitute the latter; but is connected with it, as a link in the same sacred chain; or included in it, as part of the same glorious whole.

"*Theron.* Admitting your distinction to be just, is not the satisfaction, made by the death of Christ, sufficient of *itself* to obtain, both our full pardon, and our final happiness?

"*Aspasio.* Since my friend has started the question, I may venture, with all reverence to the divine counsels, to answer in the negative; it being necessary, that, the Redeemer of man should *obey*, as well as *suffer*, in their stead" (John x. 18; Matt. iii. 15; Rom. v. 17). "It should be considered, Whether Christ's sufferings were a complete satisfaction of the law? Complete they were with regard to the *penalty*, not with regard to the *precept*. A distinction obvious and important. From whence arises the following argument; which, for once, you will allow me to propose in the *logical* form. By what alone the law was not satisfied; by that alone sinners could not be justified: By Christ's sufferings alone, the law was not satisfied. Therefore, by Christ's sufferings alone, sinners could not be justified. But when we join the active with the passive obedience of our Lord,—the efficacy of the one, with the perfection of the other,—how does our justification stand firm, in the *fullest* sense of the word! We have *all* that the law demands, both for our exemption from the curse, and as a title to the blessing.

"*Theron.* But if we are justified by Christ's fulfilling the law, we are justified by works. So that, before you can strike out such a way of salvation, you must *contradict* yourself; and, what is more adventurous, you must abolish that fundamental principle of the Gospel; 'By the works of the law, shall no flesh be justified.'

"*Aspasio.* I grant it, *Theron.* We *are* justified by works. But whose? The works of Christ, not our own. And this is very far from contradicting ourselves; equally far is it from abolishing, what you call the *Gospel-principle.* Between the covenant of works, and the covenant of grace, this, I apprehend, is the difference: By the former, man was indispensably bound to obey, in his *own person.* By the latter, the obedience of *his surety* is accepted, instead of his own. The righteousness required by both, is, not *sincere,* but *complete;* not proportioned to the abilities of fallen man, but to the purity of the law, and the majesty of the Lawgiver. By this means, the glory of God as an awful sovereign, and the glory of His law as an inviolable system, are entirely preserved and illustriously displayed. The salvation of sinners, neither clashes with the truth, nor interferes with the justice of the supreme Legislator. On the contrary, it becomes a *faithful* and *just* procedure of the most High God, to justify *him that believeth on Jesus.*

"*Theron.* Farewell then to our own obedience. No more occasion for any holiness of life. Fine divinity truly! Should I not rather say? Downright Antinomianism!

"*Aspasio.* No, my friend; Christ came not to destroy the law, but to fulfil. He has fulfilled it to the very uttermost, in His own person. He has also merited for *us,* and conveys to *us,* those supplies of the Spirit, which alone can enable us to yield faithful and acceptable obedience.

"*Theron.* My principal objection is not satisfied. I was observing, that, according to *your* manner of stating the affair, salvation is no longer free, but founded upon works. They are the works of the law, though Christ performs them. To maintain that we are justified by these works, is to confound the difference between the law and the Gospel.

"*Aspasio.* Though we should admit your premises, we cannot acquiesce in your conclusion. The same righteousness, by which we are justified, is both legal and evangelical. *Legal,* in respect to *Christ,* who was made under the law, that He might obey all its commands. *Evangelical,* in respect to *us,* who work not ourselves, but believe in the great *fulfiller* of all righteousness. We are justified *by* works, if you look forward to our Surety. We are justified *without* works, if you cast a retrospective view on ourselves. The grand reason, which inclines some people to reject this comfortable doctrine, lies concealed, if not in an absolute disbelief of our Lord's eternal glory and Godhead, yet, in *unsettled* apprehensions of it, or an habitual *inattention* to it. If our Saviour was not really God, it would be a reasonable practice to disavow the imputation of His righteousness. Because, upon such a supposition, His obedience was no more than bounden duty; in which there could not be the least pretence to merit, and which could be profitable to none but Himself. Whereas, if we verily believe Him to be the Incarnate God, His submission to the law becomes an act of *voluntary* humiliation. Which circumstance, together with the *transcendent* dignity of His person, renders His obedience, not meritorious only, but inexpressibly and *infinitely* meritorious.

"*Theron.* But if Christ's righteousness, *His very* righteousness, be imputed; then, the true believers are altogether as righteous as Christ Himself. Whereas, if you maintain, that, His righteousness is imputed only *as to its effect*, you will keep clear of this rock.

"*Aspasio.* This, I fear, will be like keeping clear of *Scylla*, only to fall foul upon *Charybdis*. What are the effects of the Mediator's righteousness? Pardon of sin, justification of our persons, and the sanctification of our nature. Shall we say, these effects, these benefits, are imputed? To *talk* of their imputation, I think, is an affront to sound sense. All these benefits are not imputed, but imparted; they are not reckoned to us, but are really enjoyed by us. Yet it does by no means follow, that believers are altogether as righteous, as Christ; unless you can prove, that, to be the *receiver* is, in all respects, the same, as to be the *Author and Finisher*. The righteousness of Christ arises solely from Himself; the source of ours subsists in another. Christ's righteousness is originally and absolutely *His own;* whereas, it is made ours in a way of favour, and gracious imputation."

"*Theron.* But if Christ's perfect obedience be accounted ours, methinks, we should have no more need of *pardoning* mercy than Christ Himself.

"*Aspasio.* Yes; because *before* this imputation, we were sunk in guilt, and dead in sins. Because, *after* it, we are defective in our duty, and in many things offend.

"*Theron.* Does not this doctrine render the intercession of our Saviour *superfluous?* What occasion have *they* for an advocate with the Father, whose righteousness has neither blemish nor imperfection?

"*Aspasio.* They stand in need of an advocate, first, that they may be brought home to the *Repairer of their breaches*, and made partakers of His righteousness by a living faith. Next, that their faith may be preserved, notwithstanding all opposition, steadfast and immovable; or rather, may be carried on, victorious and triumphant, to the end.

"*Theron.* You say, ' Christ performed all that was conditionary' ; then He *repented* for us, and *believed* for us.

"*Aspasio.* Christ performed whatever was required by the covenant of works, both before it was violated, and after it had been transgressed. But neither *repentance* nor *faith* was comprehended in this institution. It was not therefore necessary, neither indeed was it possible, for our spotless and Divine Lord to repent of sin, or believe in a Saviour.

"*Theron.* However, from what you have advanced, *this* will unavoidably follow—That a man is to be justified, under the character of a notorious transgressor of the law; and justified under the character of a sinless observer of the law. And what is this, but a *glaring inconsistency ?*

"*Aspasio.* Not at all inconsistent, but absolutely needful, if we consider those distinct branches of the Divine law, the *preceptive* and the *penal.* Both which, in case of guilt already contracted, must necessarily be satisfied. Not at all inconsistent, if we take in the *two constituent parts* of justification, the acquittance from guilt, and a title to life. The former supposes us to be transgressors of the law; and such the highest saints in the world are. The latter requires us to be observers of the law; and such must the inheritors of heaven be. Much less is this inconsistent, if we consider believers in their *personal* and *relative* capacity; as they are in themselves, and as they are in their Surety. Notorious transgressors in themselves, they have a sinless obedience in Christ. The consciousness of *that,* will be an everlasting motive to humility; the belief of *this,* an inexhaustible source of joy."

In these extracts, the reader has, in Hervey's own words, a full account of his doctrine of the imputed righteousness of Christ. All must admit, his fairness in the putting of Theron's objections; most will doubt his successfulness in answering them. His theory, that, the death of Christ bought the sinner's pardon, and the righteousness of Christ procured for the sinner the privileges and rights of justification; or, to speak more precisely, of adoption into the family of God, was a speculative distinction, without Scriptural authority, and pregnant with antinomian heresy. He meant well; but he missed the mark. Wesley was right, when he said,—

"'The imputed righteousness of Christ' is a phrase not scriptural. It has done immense hurt. I have had abundant proof, that the frequent use of this unnecessary phrase, instead of 'furthering men's progress in vital holiness,' has made them satisfied without any holiness at all; yea, and encouraged them to work all uncleanness with greediness." [1]

Hervey's book created great commotion. It was both attacked and defended; and was turned to good purpose and to bad. Sandeman, in his "Letters on Theron and Aspasio," [2] both approved and disapproved. Cudworth, a dissenting minister, in his reply to Sandeman, [3] was a warm defender of his friend, the Church of England rector. Dr.

---

[1] Wesley's "Works," vol. x., p. 306.
[2] Published in two volumes, 8vo, in 1757.
[3] Published in 1760, pp. 224, octavo.

Witherspoon, "Minister of the Gospel in Beith," published a
pamphlet of 72 pages, in 1756, to show, that Hervey's doctrine of justification, by imputed righteousness, does not
weaken the obligations to holiness of life. Besides these,
other pamphlets were issued, on both sides of the dispute;
but the only one which Hervey himself answered, was a tract
by his old friend Wesley. This will be noticed hereafter.
Meanwhile, a selection from Hervey's voluminous correspondence will furnish the reader with glimpses of this period of
Hervey's history.

Lady Frances Shirley had given him a hint, that some one
wished to make a present to the author of "Theron and
Aspasio." He replied:—

WESTON-FAVEL, *February* 23, 1755.

"My thirst after books is very much allayed. I have bid adieu to the
curious and entertaining inventions of wit, or discoveries of science. My
principal attention is now devoted to the sacred oracles of inspiration.
These I should be glad to have in their noblest form and highest perfection; and, I find, there is now published a very fine edition of the Hebrew
Scriptures, by Father Houbigant. Such a present would be singularly
acceptable, and, I hope, it would be beneficial. I do not know the price:
though, I fear, it will be costly; as it consists of four tomes in folio, and
as Hebrew printing is uncommonly expensive." [1]

The next refers to the same subject, and to his being
thanked for a copy of his "Theron and Aspasio," by Her
Royal Highness the Princess of Wales.

"*March* 1. If what I mentioned be an improper proposal, you will have
such a kind regard to the unadvised writer, as to stifle and suppress his
project. My heart is not set on that or any other book. As I have the
Bible in its pure and sacred original, I can dispense with the circumstance
of a grand and pompous form.

"I have received a very friendly letter from the bishop; and Dr. Hales
has transmitted to me the thanks of her royal highness. Alas, madam!
what good does this do me? Or, if I were presented to a deanery, what
service would that do me when I stand at the great tribunal? Blessed
Jesus, let not my poor endeavours be rewarded with such chaff! Be Thou
glorified; let souls be edified; and then *they* who read, and *he* who wrote,
may one day rejoice together."

---

[1] Three weeks afterwards, Lady Frances Shirley herself sent this valuable work to Hervey, who described the present as "a magnificent and
beautiful set of books; the paper fine; the type grand; the binding rich;
the principal contents invaluable."

The demand for Hervey's book was such, that, though the first edition consisted of nearly six thousand copies, a second edition was almost immediately required. He writes to the Rev. John Ryland :—

"*March* 8. We have begun another edition, and ventured to print three thousand. Any remarks and improvements will be extremely welcome; but they must be communicated soon, otherwise, perhaps, they cannot take place; for it was proposed to begin upon each volume at once; and proceed, by means of several hands, and several presses, with great expedition.

"The Princess of Wales, and my other noble friends, were pleased to receive my books, in a very candid and obliging manner." [1]

Seven days later, he wrote again :—

"*March* 15. The author of the *London Magazine* has taken notice of 'Theron and Aspasio,' and, really, in a very respectful and honourable manner. My sentence in the *Gentleman's Magazine* is respited till next month. I know not whether the *Monthly Review* has taken me to task; but this I know, that, if God be for us, it matters not who is against us." [2]

Hervey perceived his book would be attacked on the ground, that, his doctrine of the imputed righteousness of Christ led to Antinomianism ; and he already entertained the idea of writing another work as a sort of appendix to his former one. Under the date of March 19, 1755, he observes :—

"I proposed to have closed the plan of 'Theron and Aspasio' with an explicit and pretty copious treatise on evangelical holiness or obedience; and to have shown my true believer in his dying moments. If your thoughts should happen to take such a turn, be so good as to suggest what you think the most advisable and advantageous way of managing this important point. This would most effectually stop the mouths of Arminians, and be the best security against the abuses of Antinomians. I could wish, if it were the Lord's will, that I might live to furnish out one more volume of this kind."

The sale of "Theron and Aspasio" proceeded with such rapidity, that, the second edition was made larger than Hervey and his publisher had originally agreed. Hence the following :—

"*April* 5. Our new edition goes on at a great rate. They have finished

---

[1] Letters to Ryland, No. 15.
[2] Ibid., No. 16.

very near half of each volume: and my publisher, presuming that I should have no objection, took the liberty of making the edition consist of 4,000, instead of 3,000, on which we had agreed. I suppose he was prompted to do this, by finding a call for the piece."[1]

In revising the work for this second edition, he earnestly asked the help, not only of John Ryland, the Baptist minister, but of William Cudworth, the minister of an Independent congregation, in Margaret Street, London. To the latter, he wrote as follows :—

"*April* 22. The doctrine, which you approve in my essay, and have clearly displayed and fully proved in your own writings, is not relished by everybody; no, not by many pious people. I take the liberty to send you a couple of letters containing objections.[2] I wish you would be so kind as to consider them, and, in your *concise* way, which I much admire, to make your remarks upon them. I am not shaken in my opinion by these attacks; but I should be glad to deliver it more clearly, and establish it more firmly, in another edition.

"I heartily wish you success in your projected work.[3] I assure you, it is my opinion, that, such a book, if well executed, will be one of the most valuable services to the present age. You will not, I hope, be too hasty. Mr. Wesley has huddled over his performance[4] in a most precipitate, and, therefore, most imperfect manner. One would think, his aim was, not to select the best and noblest passages, but to reprint those which came first to hand.

Cudworth responded to the request of Hervey; and the two henceforward became ardently attached and confiding friends. This, if it did not actually create, widened the breach between Hervey and his old adviser, Wesley. Ten

---

[1] Letters to Ryland, No. 17.

[2] Objections to Dialogue xvi. In other words, that, saving faith is "A real persuasion, that the blessed Jesus has shed His blood for *me*, and fulfilled all righteousness in *my stead*: that, through this great atonement and glorious obedience, He has purchased, even for my sinful soul, reconciliation with God, sanctifying grace, and all spiritual blessings"; and that, in the case of a man convinced of his sin and danger, this is the *only* requisite in order to the obtaining of pardon, and adoption into the family of God.

[3] "An intended collection of the most evangelical pieces from the beginning of the Reformation down to the present day."

[4] Wesley's "Christian Library, consisting of Extracts and Abridgments of the Choicest Pieces of Practical Divinity, which have been published in the English Tongue." In fifty-one volumes, 12mo; begun in 1749, and now being completed, in 1755. Hervey's critique is unjust, and indicates the alienation, which already existed between the two Oxford Methodists.

years before, Wesley and Cudworth had come into collision, by Wesley's publication of his two Dialogues "between an Antinomian and his friend;" partly written in answer to a "Dialogue" which Cudworth himself had published. Wesley, rightly or wrongly, accounted Cudworth an Antinomian, and spoke of him with a severity which he seldom used. Cudworth resented this; angry feelings were engendered; and, beyond a doubt, Hervey's affection and respect for Wesley were lamentably abated.

The year 1755 was a crisis in the history of the Societies, which had been founded by the labours of Wesley and his itinerant evangelists. At a Conference, held at Leeds, three days were spent in discussing the momentous question, whether the Methodists should separate from the Established Church. It was on this occasion, that, Charles Wesley composed and published his famous poetical "Epistle" to his brother. Hervey heard of this, and wrote as follows :—

"1755, *July* 5. I have just now read advertised in the magazine, the following book, 'An Epistle from Charles Wesley to John Wesley.' Has your ladyship seen or heard of it? If you have, be so good as to inform me of the design and contents. I hope, there is no hostility commenced between the brothers. I have no connection, nor correspondence with them, but should be sorry for such an event."[1]

Hervey had ceased to write to Wesley; but Wesley wrote to him. Hence the following :—

"WESTON, *August*, 1755.

"Pray return Mr. Wesley's letter. I find, by private intelligence, that, he has shown it in London; and has thought proper to animadvert upon me, by name, from his pulpit. I am inclined to take no notice either of his preaching or his writing.

"My good friend, Mr. Whitefield, is now at my house. He purposes to lift up his voice at Northampton, and proclaim the acceptable year of the Lord."[2]

Did Hervey get his "private intelligence" from Whitefield? Probably he did. It is a curious fact, that, at this very time, there was a misunderstanding between Wesley and Whitefield, respecting Methodist affairs at Norwich;[3] and, though

---

[1] Letters to Lady F. Shirley, No. 83.
[2] Letters to Ryland, No. 19.
[3] See Whitefield's "Works," vol. iii., p. 133.

there was no breach of friendship, it is not at all unlikely, that, this and cognate matters would be the subject of conversation at the meeting which Hervey mentions.

Whitefield was at Weston-Favel on August 30; and here he wrote several letters, remarking in one of them :—"Mr. Hervey is now writing another volume, upon Sançtification." This, of course, was the work which has been already named; but which was never published. Ten days after Whitefield's visit, Hervey described his plan, in a long letter, from which the following is an extract :—

"WESTON-FAVEL, *September* 10, 1755.

"MY DEAR FRIEND,—I esteem your letters as treasures. Though I destroy almost all I receive, every one of yours is preserved.

"The grasshopper is a burden to me. Every blast blows me down, or my continual indisposition and inconceivable languors pierce through me. I now hang a swelled face over my paper; occasioned only by taking the air yesterday in my chair, and finding a sharper atmosphere, than for many weeks I had been accustomed to. Pray for me, dear sir, that, established in Christ, and strong in His faith, I may be looking for, and hasting to the coming of the day of God; when this poor, enervated, crazy body, will be made like unto Christ's glorious body.

"I live with my mother and sister. Our method is, every morning at nine, when we breakfast, to read a verse or two from the Bible, and make it the subject of our conversation," etc., etc.

"I desire your opinion concerning the plan of my new work; which, with a weak hand and desponding heart, I have sketched out, though with very little hope of being enabled to execute.

"The *Plan* of the Supplement to *Theron* and *Aspasio.*

"Pleasure and happiness of Christ's religion (for I am of the same mind with Mr. Marshall, in his Treatise on Sanctification, namely, that, we must partake of the comforts of the Gospel, before we can practise the duties of the law).—Theron oppressed with fears, on account of his numerous sins.—Discouraged with doubts on account of his imperfect obedience.—The cordials of the Gospel re-administered, with some additional spirit and strength.—Objections to assurance of faith, stated, discussed, answered.—Vital holiness; its nature, necessity, excellency.— Its grand efficient, the blessed Spirit.—Its principal instrument, true faith; mixed with which, the Scriptures, the Lord's Supper, prayer, the divine promises, are powerful and effectual means; disunited from which, they are a dead letter and insignificant ordinances.—The evangelical principles of holiness, such as, ' I beseech you by the mercies of God'; 'Ye are bought with a price'; 'Ye are the temples of the living God'; etc.—All these privileges, though not hereditary, yet indefeasible; or the final perseverance of the believer.—Our friends part; renew their correspondence; Theron desires to glorify the God of his salvation, asks advice concerning the best method of family worship, educating children, instructing servants, edifying acquaintance.—On each of these particulars, Aspasio satisfies his inquiry, enlarges on the subject of education, especially of daughters; as that seems to be the most neglected, or the proper way of conducting it least understood.—Letter on the covenant of grace, comprising the substance, and being a kind of recapitulation, of the three foregoing volumes.—Aspasio seized with a sudden and fatal illness; his sentiments and behaviour in his last moments.

"If, dear sir, you see anything in this plan, that is improper; anything that is defective, supply it; and if any thoughts occur on any of the topics, be so kind as to suggest them."

Hervey, certainly, had great encouragement to continue the employment of his pen. The first edition of "Theron and Aspasio," as already stated, consisted of nearly six thousand copies; and the second of four thousand; and yet, within nine months from the time when the work was first published, a third edition issued from the press.

No wonder, that, the book obtained the attention of Hervey's old friend, Wesley. The first three of the Dialogues had been submitted to him, in manuscript, for his revision, and he had sent "some important alterations." Now he read the whole of Hervey's work, not only once, but twice, and says, "I wrote him my thoughts freely, but received no answer." This was probably the letter which Hervey mentions, in one of the foregoing pages, under the date of "August, 1755." In a little more than a year afterwards, Wesley wrote again; and this letter, he himself subsequently published; though, he says,—

"At the time I wrote, I had not the least thought of making it public. I only spoke my private thoughts, in a free, open manner, to a friend dear as a brother,—I had almost said, to a pupil,—to a son; for so near I still accounted him."

No doubt this second letter contained the substance of the former one. There is much in Hervey's book which Wesley heartily commends: the chief points of animadversion are two. (1) He begs that Hervey will lay aside the phrase "the imputed righteousness of Christ," adding, "it is not scriptural, it is not necessary, it has done immense hurt." Unprejudiced readers must allow that this position is impregnable. Many of Wesley's critiques are so brief as to be almost blunt, but

they serve to show that Hervey's interpretation of scriptural
texts, in support of his favourite idea of the Imputed Righteousness of Christ is, in many instances, at least, arbitrary
and incorrect; and, in all instances, insufficient for his purpose. To this part of Wesley's letter no exception ought to
have been taken. True, it destroys the pivot on which the
whole of Hervey's book is made to turn; but all that is said
is relevant, and there is nothing that is disrespectful. Wesley's
remarks were pointed, but not intended to be impolite. (2)
The other section of Wesley's criticisms, while correct in
sentiment, are perhaps hardly pertinent. Hervey, to some
extent, was undoubtedly a Calvinist; but he never taught, or
held the doctrines of unconditional election and reprobation.
Remembering this, Wesley was scarcely fair in such comments
as the following :—

"'The righteousness wrought out by Jesus Christ is wrought out for
all His people, to be the cause of their justification, and the purchase of
their salvation. The righteousness is the cause, and the purchase.' So
the death of Christ is not so much as named! 'For all His people.'
But what becomes of all other people? They must invariably perish for
ever. The die was cast or ever they were in being. The doctrine to pass
them by has—

"'Consigned their unborn souls to hell,
And damned them from their mother's womb.'

"I could sooner be a Turk, a deist, yea, an atheist, than I could believe
this. It is less absurd to deny the very existence of God, than to make
Him an almighty tyrant.

"'The whole world and all its seasons are rich with our Creator's
goodness. His tender mercies are over all His works.' Are they over the
bulk of mankind? Where is His goodness to the non-elect? How are
His tender mercies over them? His temporal blessings are given to
them. But are they blessings to them at all? Are they not all curses?
Does not God know they are? that, they will only increase their damnation? Does He not design they should? And this you call goodness!
This is tender mercy!

"'May we not discern pregnant proofs of goodness in each individual
object?' No; on your scheme, not a spark of it, in this world or the
next, to the far greater part of the work of His hands.

"'This is His tender complaint, They will not come unto me!' Nay,
that is not the case; they cannot. He Himself has decreed not to give
them that grace without which their coming is impossible.

"'The grand end which God proposes in all His favourable dispensations to fallen man is to demonstrate the sovereignty of His grace.'

 Not so : to impart happiness to His creatures is His grand end herein. Barely to demonstrate His sovereignty is a principle of action fit for the Great Turk, not the Most High God."

If Hervey had taught the doctrines of ultra-Calvinism, such strictures, though strongly worded, would not have been unjust. But the question is, did Hervey hold the tenets of unconditional election and reprobation ? If he did, Wesley was not unfair ; if otherwise, Wesley's remarks are not applicable. Hervey probably clung to the doctrine of election ; and, it may be said, this inevitably involves the doctrine of reprobation ; but there is no evidence that Hervey regarded it in such a light. On this subject, the man must be allowed to be his own exponent. In a letter, written to Lady Frances Shirley, immediately after Wesley had sent him his criticisims on "Theron and Aspasio," Hervey observes :—

WESTON, *November* 25, 1755.

" There is, doubtless, abundance to be said against Predestination. And abundance has been said, with great force of argument, for its support, and that by men of the most eminent learning and exalted piety. As this is the case, and as it is not necessary to faith and salvation either that we should embrace or that we should reject the doctrine, I think we may prudently and safely acquiesce in the advice of a great scholar and a great saint : 'Let a man go to the grammar-school of faith and holiness before he enters the university of election and predestination.' I am at the grammar-school ; and there, perhaps, I shall continue, till I hear the voice from heaven, saying, *Come up hither, and I will show thee* what thou couldest not comprehend in the regions below. Madam, shall I have the honour of your ladyship for a form-fellow? *You* shall be the head-scholar ; only be content to allow us your company, and do not leave us for a higher class. Let *us* study the glories of Christ's person, and the love of His heart ; let *us* contemplate His infinite satisfaction and everlasting righteousness. May the knowledge of these grand doctrines be revealed in our hearts by the blessed Spirit ! May the faith of these unspeakable privileges comfort our souls, purify our affections, and *work by love !* Then we shall, ere long, see every dark, mysterious point cleared up to our full satisfaction. We shall see, without a veil, the shining and adorable perfections of our God. We shall know His unsearchable counsels and wonderful ways, *even as we are known.*

" In the meantime, I would beg leave to decline all controversy. I can very freely converse or correspond with. persons who either adopt or discard Predestination ; provided, they will not drag in the litigated proposition, and force me to engage in disputation. But, if they are determined to obtrude the bone of contention, I had 'much rather remain alone and in silence ; for, I readily confess, that I am not master of the subject. Therefore it would be very unadvised in me to undertake either its establishment or refutation.

" I believe, I must desire your ladyship to return this letter, with your free remarks upon it, because I do not know but I shall be obliged to explain myself on this subject before the public. Because a person,[1] who makes a great figure in the religious world, has sent me some critical remarks and pretty keen censures on my late work, but inveighs particularly against my predestination principles ; at which I am somewhat surprised, because I have (whatever my sentiments are) studiously avoided this peculiarity ; I have but barely mentioned it, in the apostle's own words ; only in an incidental manner ; and without explaining, enlarging upon, or inculcating it."

On receiving Wesley's letter, Hervey wrote to his friend Ryland as follows :—

" 1756, *November* 29. Herewith, you have the grand attack from Mr. Wesley, of which I apprised you some time ago. Examine it closely ; return it speedily ; and, if you please, confute it effectually ; demolish the battery, and spike up the cannon. I have not answered in any shape, and, when I do answer with my pen, I propose nothing more than a general acknowledgment, and an inquiry, whether he proposes to print his animadversions."

Wesley's strictures were printed in 1758 ; and till then we must leave the subject.

The only pieces published by Hervey in 1756, were a " Recommendatory Letter," prefixed to his favourite book, " Marshall's Gospel Mystery of Sanctification "; and a " Preface " to " Jenks's Meditations," the latter of which was reprinted, in two volumes, by Hervey's expressed desire.[2] Besides these, however, he preached three sermons, which he subsequently committed to the press, with the titles,—" The

---

[1] Doubtless, Wesley.

[2] Whitefield, in a letter to Hervey, dated, December 9th, 1756, observes :—" Last night, Mr. M—— informed me, that, Mr. C——" (udworth ?) " showed him a pamphlet, wrote on purpose to prove the fundamental errors of my printed sermons, and that you had offered to preface it, but he chose you should not. That this is true, I as much believe, as that I am now at Rome. But I wish that my dear friend may not repent his connection and correspondence with some, when it is too late. This is my comfort, I have delivered my soul. Mr. R—— has sent me the two volumes of ' Jenks's Meditations,' and desires me to annex my recommendation to yours. I have answered, that, it will not be prudent, or beneficial to him, so to do. I fear they are too large to go off."

Time of Danger;" "The Means of Safety;" and "The Way of Holiness."[1]

Hervey's published sermons are few in number, principally because the sermons he preached were never written.

"I have never," said he, "since I was minister at Weston, used written notes; so that all my public Discourses are vanished into air; unless the blessed Spirit has left any traces of them, on the hearts of the hearers. And, though I have many Discourses, that were written before I discontinued the use of notes, they are all penned in short-hand, and are intelligible to none but the writer. I sometimes speak to my people an hour together; but I always blame myself for it. It detains the congregation too long. It renders the Discourse tiresome to be heard, and almost impossible to be remembered. This is one of the inconveniences attending the extempore method of preaching. We forget how the time passes away."[2]

The reason, why he wrote and published the three sermons above mentioned, he states in a letter to Lady Frances Shirley,—

"I am inclined," said he, "to print two or three Sermons, preached on the late *Fast-Days*. These, for some particular reason, I happened to take down in short-hand. As I have seen no Discourses, on this occasion, that were sufficiently *evangelical*, I have a strong desire, for the supply of this *one* defect *only*, to appear on the stage." "Here," he observed to Mr. Ryland, "I shall make a sacrifice of all my reputation (if I ever had any), with the elegant and polite; and let it go, freely let it go, if any honour may redound to the Lord our Righteousness."

At the time, England was at war with France; and many of the sermons preached on the day of national humiliation were published; but Hervey was not satisfied. He writes :—

"The author pretends to nothing refined or extraordinary; he affects neither brilliant thought, nor polished style; equally remote from nice criticism and profound learning, his Discourses are studiously *plain*, and brought down to the level of the meanest capacity. 'What then is his motive?' This is the very truth. In several of the sermons, published on this occasion, the *one thing needful* seems to be overlooked. Christ and His free grace,—Christ and His great salvation,—are either totally omitted, or but slightly touched. Till these doctrines are generally inculcated, the most eloquent harangues from the pulpit, or the most correct disserta-

---

[1] These Sermons were published in 1757; but preached in 1756.
[2] Letters to Lady F. Shirley, Nos. 91 and 95.

tions from the press, will be no better than a pointless arrow, and a broken bow."

Space forbids giving an outline of Hervey's sermons.[1] Suffice it to say, that, they are able and eloquent, and intensely earnest and faithful. If such were a fair specimen of his pulpit performances, Hervey's preaching must have been as remarkable as his writings; and, had he possessed Whitefield's voice and elocution, the effects would have been something marvellous. Mr. Ryland, who visited him at Weston-Favel twice a year, observes,—

"He loved simplicity in his *manner* of preaching. He had no complicated and perplexed conceptions; no crowd of thoughts to overwhelm his own understanding, or the conceptions of his hearers. In all his sermons, you might discern a clear and easy arrangement; nothing tedious; no long-winded periods; no perplexing parentheses; no tiresome circumlocutions; but everything adapted to the weakest memory of his auditors. He despised and avoided all boisterous noise,—all rude and violent vociferation in the pulpit. His subjects were always serious and sublime: they might well be ranged under three heads,—Ruin, Righteousness, and Regeneration. He always steered a middle course, between a haughty positivity, and a sceptical hesitation. He made it an invariable rule to be thoroughly convinced of the truth and importance of his subject, before he proceeded to state and defend it; but, when he was once in possession of a truth, he held it with the greatest fortitude and tenaciousness. He considered very minutely the state of all his hearers. He did not preach to a promiscuous auditory, as though they were all converted to Christ; nor did he treat true believers as though they were in an unregenerate state."

"He preached without notes," says his friend, Dr. Stonehouse, "excepting that he had before him a small leaf of paper, on which were written, in short-hand, the general heads and particulars of the sermon, which he sometimes looked at, and sometimes not. He was very regular in his plans, nor was he very long; from thirty to forty minutes was his usual time; rarely longer. His weakness rendering him, for several months before his death, incapable of speaking any length of time to his congregation, he shortened his discourses, and took a most useful method

---

[1] Hervey's Fast-Day Sermons had an enormous circulation. In a letter, dated August 5, 1758, he writes,—"Besides six thousand printed in London, an edition was printed in Scotland, which was speedily sold off. I was also desired, by a Society established for giving away religious books among the poor, to grant them leave to print an impression for this purpose. In Ireland they have been printed. Into Dutch they are translated; and a letter, from America, informs me, that, they have been reprinted there." All this was within two years of their first publication.

of inculcating his instructions. After he had expounded his text, and divided his sermon into two or three heads, he would speak briefly, and, at the conclusion of each head, enforce what he had said by a pertinent text of Scripture, desiring his congregation to turn to their Bibles, and double down that text. 'Now,' he added, 'my dear brethren if you forget my sermon, you cannot forget God's word in this text, unless you wilfully throw aside your Bibles. Show this to your children, or the absent part of your family, when you return home.' Then he gave a striking exhortation, and, at the end of it, another text for them to double down; so that they always had three texts, in order to their finding of which he paused in the pulpit for two or three minutes. This method had another good effect; it obliged the generality to bring their Bibles along with them, for those who were without Bibles lost the benefit of the texts, and were unemployed, while the great majority, who had theirs, were busy looking for the texts referred to in the sermon."

"My acquaintance with Mr. Hervey," writes the Rev. Dr. Haweis, "was only of one day. He was removing from his ministerial labours, just as I was ready to enter upon mine; and, being very desirous of seeing him before his departure to glory, I rode from Oxford to Weston-Favel, a distance of about fifty miles, for that purpose. I found him tall and much emaciated. His preaching was purely evangelical, and very similar to his writings, in beautiful comments on the Scriptures he quoted; but his manner of delivery, in the tone of voice and action, far from the elegance I expected. His church was very small; and, though full, was not remarkably crowded; but the people were very attentive to hear him."

These are mere glimpses of Hervey as a preacher; but they are of some importance, as being furnished by those who saw and heard him.

Hervey had become famous, and some of his friends wished for a formal recognition of the fact. The following refers to this, and also to Wesley's strictures on his "Theron and Aspasio" :—

"Now for the affair, relating to Mr. Ogilvie's proposal. Tell our amiable and benevolent friend, that, I am deeply sensible of his kindness; but I must beg of him to lay aside all thoughts of procuring for me so undeserved a distinction. I assure you, it would make me blush, and give me much uneasiness, to be addressed under the character of *doctor*. Never, no never, should I have taken as much as a *master's* degree, if I had not been obliged to it, in order to hold what we call ecclesiastical preferment. Preferment? Yes, if rightly understood, it is rightly so called. For what can be a more honourable or exalted office, than to labour for Christ? O that my brethren and I may always understand the word *preferment* in this truly precious and noble sense!

"It is a great uncertainty, whether I shall be enabled to add another

volume. I am told, a very formidable attack is going to be made upon
'Theron and Aspasio,' by a hand not well affected to the imputed
righteousness of our Lord, but remarkably zealous for the inherent
righteousness and *perfection* of man." [1]

In this world, no man basks in unclouded sunshine. Upon
the whole, the reviews of Hervey's "Theron and Aspasio,"
had been favourable; those of his later publications [2] had
been otherwise.

"Have a care," he wrote, in a letter, dated November 21, 1757, "Have
a care, you do not depreciate your works by inserting anything of mine.
My poor character is going to execution. The Reviewers have already
put the halter about its neck; if, therefore, you would obtain distinction,
or are a candidate for fame, stand clear and detached from such a contemptible scribbler."

Besides this, he suffered increasingly from enfeebled health.

"Incessant and insuperable languors," he wrote, "unfit me for every
business; render every enjoyment unrelishing; and, what is more deplorable, make my temper like the sore, inflamed, ulcerated flesh. Anything that comes unexpected, alarms me; anything that goes cross,
vexes me: I am sadly inclined to a peevish humour."

In another letter, belonging to the same period, he
writes :—

" I beg, I entreat you, if you value the honour of the Gospel, that, you
will dissuade those polite persons you mention, from coming to hear me
to-morrow. My spirits sink more and more. I am visited with some
returns of my hacking cough; perhaps I shall not be able to speak
at all. Such disagreeable circumstances will only expose me, and create
in them very unpleasing ideas of what I shall deliver. My imagination is
gone. I am sensible my sermons are flat, and my voice spiritless. The
poor country people love me tenderly, and, therefore, bear with my
infirmities; else, I should no longer attempt to preach, even before them.
I am now unfit to appear in the pulpit."

In the midst of all this, Hervey commenced the rebuilding
of his parsonage ; and, besides the vexations usually connected with such undertakings, he had to suffer the annoyance of the builder, with which he had contracted, decamping,
before the erection was completed, and exposing poor Hervey

---

[1] *Evangelical Magazine*, 1777, p. 73.
[2] "Marshall on Sanctification;" and "Jenks's Meditations."

to the worry of being dunned by the rogue's disappointed creditors.[1]

Hervey was more sensitive than he thought he was; and the combined circumstances just mentioned painfully affected him. In the excitement of his feelings, he began to prepare a shilling pamphlet, in reply to the *Critical Review,* which had designated Jenks's Meditations "ridiculous and enthusiastic." With greater vulgarity than refinement, they had been described "like hairs on the greasy coat of a groom, or like dish-water thrown down the kennel." Malevolence like this was too contemptible to be noticed; and, yet, Hervey put himself to considerable inconvenience in writing, " Ned Dry's Apology for the Critical Reviewers,"—a pamphlet which he intended to be a satirical castigation of his nameless opponents, as well as a vindication of Mr. Jenks and of himself. It was a mistake to notice anonymous revilers at all; and it was an additional mistake for Hervey to attempt to compose a satire. His mind was too exquisitely refined, and his soul too loving, to succeed in literary flagellation. He was himself in doubt respecting this, and wrote to Mr. Ryland as follows :—

"I have not had the pleasure of seeing the *Critical Review* for December; but, I find, from the advertisements in the public papers, that they take Mr. Jenks and his recommender to task. I am not disappointed; I expected no quarter from them.

"You would smile, and be a little surprised, if you were to see what employed my spare hours almost all last week. I never had such an inclination for buffoonery in all my life. It was occasioned by the unworthy and abusive treatment which the Reviewers bestow upon all the most valuable writers that appear in public; and, I verily think, if their insolence can be curbed, it must be done in obedience to that command of unerring wisdom, 'Answer a fool according to his folly.'"

Again ;—

"My friends, who have seen the piece, absolutely disapprove of it. Dr. Stonehouse says, it is a low, dull, spiritless thing ; that, I am no more fit for such kind of writing than a carrier's horse to run a race. He read it, he tells me, to some ingenious ladies, who have a regard for my character ; and they declared, they would come over to Weston, and would, upon their knees, (if it were needful,) solicit me not to publish it. Amidst such a diversity of opinions, how shall I determine ?"

---

[1] Letters to Ryland, Nos. 57 and 63.

Again ;—

"I have sent you Mr. Dry's apology; though it is written, it has been thrown aside. I have several doubts, whether my pen carries any edge, and whether the edge, if there is any, be like the saw, or the razor. Is it of the former kind? Then it will not answer my purpose, and will not gall and check the adversaries of Christ and His servants, but will give them occasion to triumph more extravagantly. I have also some doubt, whether this kind of writing suits my character, as a minister of Jesus Christ. Is it not the Εὐτραπελία which the apostle condemns and banishes from the conversation of Christians? The principal reason to justify such a manner of address is, that no other method seems to have the least probability of succeeding. All that is solid, these men will evade with a sneer; and all that is serious, they will turn into burlesque. Ridicule is the only vein in which they will bleed."

Nothing more need be added, except, that, though " Ned Dry's Apology for the Critical Reviewers," was written, it was never published.

Troubles often come in troops. In 1757, Mr. Robert Sandeman published his " Letters on Theron and Aspasio," in two volumes,—a work already noticed in the biography of Ingham. Concerning this, Hervey writes as follows :—

" WESTON-FAVEL, *August* 6, 1757.

" The author is a Scotchman, I presume, because the two volumes were printed at Edinburgh, and he gave orders for a set to be sent me from Edinburgh. He conceals his name, and none that I am· acquainted with are able to discover whose work it is. There are some strictures on my performance ; but by far the greatest part of the book is very wide from this mark. Some things are truly excellent; and some animadversions upon me are perfectly just; but others (if I mistake not) are unfair and disingenuous. The manner of writing is by no means despicable,—rather elegant and spirited, than coarse or dull. But there is such an implacable bitterness of spirit, and such an unchristian virulence of censure, against many of the best men that ever lived, and best authors that ever wrote, as much surprises and greatly offends me. I think I never saw a notion of faith more lax, nor an idea of grace more exalted, than in this book."

Sandeman's " Letters " created a great sensation ;[1] but

---

[1] The following are some of the publications to which Sandeman's book gave birth :—

1. A Sufficient Answer to the Author of the Letters on Theron and Aspasio. By J. Wesley.

2. Animadversions on the Letters on Theron and Aspasio.

Hervey had neither strength nor time to answer them. He was about to measure swords with an opponent far more noted than Mr. Sandeman, and left the latter in the hands of his friend, Mr. Cudworth, who, immediately after Hervey's death, issued " A defence of Theron and Aspasio against the Objections contained in a late Treatise, entitled ' Letters on Theron and Aspasio.' To which is prefixed, a series of Letters from Mr. Hervey to the author, authenticating this Defence with his entire approbation, and manifesting it to be the only one that can be presented to the public with that authority." pp. 224.

Perhaps the title was more ostentatious than facts would justify; but, still, there can be no doubt, that Hervey was perfectly cognisant of a correspondence between Cudworth and Sandeman, and, that, in the main, he approved of Cudworth's sentiments. Only three weeks before his death, he wrote to Cudworth as follows :—

"Excuse me for keeping your MS. so long. I have been extremely ill. This morning I have been up for four hours, and, in all that time, not able to look into a book, or hold up my head. I fully assent to your opinions ; and think you have proved the warrant of a sinner's application of Christ very satisfactorily. If I live, I should much desire a copy of this your correspondence, when you have revised and finished it. Or do you intend to print it ? "

Hervey now devoted his dying energies to the task of writing a reply to the animadversions of his old friend Wesley. Their friendship was beclouded ; and it is a mournful fact, that, the few last months of Hervey's lovely life were spent in fighting one, who, a quarter of a century before, had been the greatest of his human oracles. He writes,—

---

3. A Plain Account of Faith in Jesus Christ.
4. An Epistolary Correspondence, relating to the Letters on Theron and Aspasio.
5. The Law of Nature defended by Scripture.
6. The True Comer. By Colin Mackie.
7. Thoughts, on Letters to the Author of Theron and Aspasio.
8. An Inquiry into the Spirit and Tendency of Letters on Theron and Aspasio.
9. Palaemon's Creed, reviewed and examined : in two volumes. By David Wilson.
10. Nymphas to Sosipater, remarking on the Letters on Theron and Aspasio.

" 1758, *January* 3.

"Weak I am, very weak, and much out of order; insomuch, that I have not been able to go to church since Christmas. Mr. Wesley is angry with me, for speaking too much, and, as he thinks, too openly on the side of election and particular redemption. Pray favour me with your free opinion, and wherever you think he charges me justly, or I have expressed myself improperly, spare not to speak the naked truth. He has lately published a large book, price six shillings, stitched, on the doctrine of Original Sin; great part of which is an abridgment of Dr. Watts's Ruin and Recovery; and of another treatise, written by Mr. Hebden. In this, he takes occasion to quote two or three passages from Theron and Aspasio, one of which he thus introduces,—' To explain this a little further, in Mr. Hervey's words, By federal head I mean, that, as Adam was the first general representative (of *this kind*, says Aspasio, but Mr. Wesley makes him say) *of mankind*, Christ was,' etc. He goes on to the bottom of the page, then turns back to the upper part, and represents me as forming a conclusion in these words, ' All these expressions demonstrate, that, Adam, as well as Christ, was a representative of *all mankind;*[1] and, that, what he did, in this capacity, did not terminate in himself, but affected all whom he represented.' This is a very injurious representation. One sentence is a palpable misquotation. Would it be proper to take any notice of it ! I am sometimes apprehensive, that, he would draw me into a dispute about particular redemption. I know, he can say startling and horrid things on this subject; and this, perhaps, might be the most effectual method to prejudice people against my principal point.

Hervey's suspicion was unfounded and ungenerous ; but let it pass. His eyes, as far as Wesley was concerned, were now unfortunately jaundiced. Besides, he was, at present, extremely ill ; in fact, it was currently reported that he was dead. " I do not go out of my room," he wrote on January 21st, " till dinner time, and then it is rather to see my relations, than to take refreshment myself." And again, in another letter, dated the 12th of March, he states, that, he had " not been at church since Christmas." Still, he was not inactive. The following are extracts from his letters to Mr. Ryland.

" *Saturday Morning, January*, 1758. I am transcribing my intended answer to Mr. Wesley for the press, but find it difficult to preserve the

---

[1] Wesley says, " both the misplacing the commas, and the putting of ' mankind ' for ' this kind,' were the printer's fault, not mine ; a part of those numerous errors of the press, which were occasioned by my absence, from it, and the inaccuracy of the corrector " (Wesley's Works, vol. x. p. 332).

 decency of the gentleman, and the meekness of the Christian. There is so much unfair dealing running through my opponent's objections, and the most magisterial air all along supplies the place of argument. Pray for me, dear friend, that I may not betray the blessed cause, by the weakness of my reasoning, nor dishonour it by the badness of my temper. Whether I shall be able to finish this work, is apparently uncertain. My cough seizes me, in the night, like a lion; and leaves me, before the morning, weaker than a babe. It has so totally destroyed my small remainder of strength, that, I am quite unable to preach so much as once on the Lord's day. I am obliged to beg assistance, and am looking out for a curate, to take the whole business on his hand."

WESTON, *March*, 1758.

"I am transcribing, though very slowly, and with a most feeble hand, my remarks, 'on Mr. Wesley,' for the press. He urges no argument, either to establish his own opinion, or to overthrow mine; only denies the validity of my reasons."

It is a curious fact, that, Wesley's strictures on "Theron and Aspasio" had not yet been printed; so that, Hervey was employed in preparing an answer to what existed only in manuscript. Even as late as the 4th of March, 1758, Hervey, writing to a friend, observes :

"I have a long letter, containing two or three sheets, from Mr. Wesley. It consists of animadversions on my Dialogues and Letters. He wrote me one before, more stinging and sarcastic than this. I have taken no notice of either, being very unwilling to embark in controversy."

Perplexity is here. Wesley had written twice to Hervey, criticising "Theron and Aspasio." Hervey was obviously offended at Wesley's abruptness, and, as Hervey believed, dogmatism. Of course, remembering their former friendship, Wesley expected a reply; but, for some reason, Hervey, almost unexceptionally gentle and courteous, resolved to maintain a sort of sullen silence. As yet, Wesley's critique was not printed; it was simply a *private* letter. Hervey was apparently as unfit for controversy as he professed to be averse to it: in fact, he was actually dying; and, yet, the tremulous energies of the dying man were exerted to the utmost, in preparing an answer to Wesley's *private* letter, not to be sent to Wesley himself, but to be committed to the press. Why was this? If Wesley's letter was *wholly private*, why should Hervey answer it in *public?* He had a right to feel grieved, to be offended, and, if not discourteous, to refuse writing a reply; but was it fair that, without consulting Wesley, he should resolve to *publicly* answer a *private* communication, even though that communication was not in the most complaisant language? Wesley's second letter was dated, October 15, 1756, so that, Hervey had now had it in his possession for nearly a year and a half; and, as his correspondence proves, had shown it to several of his friends. Why did he, at the commencement of 1758, when his health had entirely failed, begin to answer a letter, which, for fifteen months, he had treated with silent sullenness? Was he instigated by Mr. Cudworth, who, at the same time, was in diligent correspondence with Mr. Sandeman? Or had Wesley been so annoyed, by Hervey's contemptuous silence, as to make his letter the subject of conversation among his friends, and Hervey having heard, that, what had been a private communication was now becoming the subject of public observation, was so extremely sensitive, and so afraid of tarnished honour, that, he unadvisedly resolved to print a public answer, and employed his dying days in writing it? It is impossible to answer these questions with certainty. Opinions will differ. Two holier men than Wesley and Hervey did not live ; but, by a most painful misunderstanding, they were now estranged. Which of them was blamable? Was either? or were both ?

Wesley disliked Hervey's doctrine of the imputed righteousness of Christ, and he told him so ;—a thing which, as a friend, he had a perfect right to do. If he erred at all, it was in using a brusque abruptness, the very opposite of the sort of style usually employed by Hervey, and which was undoubtedly somewhat grating to a sensitive mind like his. Still, even this may be excused. Wesley was without "learned leisure." Bearing in mind the incessant duties of his itinerant life, the wonder is, how he found time to write at all. Perforce of circumstances, as well as by deliberate choice, his style of writing was always concise, and frequently abrupt. Besides, in this instance, he was writing, not for the public, but privately to a friend.

"It is no wonder," says he, "that, several of my objections, as Mr. Hervey observes. 'appear more like notes and memorandums, than a just plea to the public.' It is true. They appear like what they are, like what they were originally intended for. I had no thought of ' a plea to the public ' when I wrote, but of ' notes and memorandums to a private man.' " [1]

One cannot but lament, that, they were not thus regarded. In such a case, an unseemly and unhappy controversy would have been avoided. For want of confidence, and a frank and friendly explanation, the two old and warm-hearted friends were alienated from each other. Hervey submitted Wesley's private letter to the inspection of friends who had no right to see it; Wesley, perhaps, yea probably, heard of this, and made it the subject of remark; Hervey, increasingly irritated, began to write an answer; and now Wesley, in an unlucky moment, published what, up to the present, had been a *private* letter. Hence the following, by Hervey, to a friend, perhaps Cudworth :—

"WESTON-FAVEL, *June* 23, 1758.

" I little thought, when I put Mr. Wesley's manuscript into your hand, that I should see it in print so soon. I took very little notice of it, and let it lie by me for several months, without giving it an attentive consideration. It seemed to me so palpably weak, dealing only in positive assertions and positive denials, that, I could not imagine he would adventure it into the world, without very great alterations. But it is now come abroad, just as you received it, in a two shillings' pamphlet, entitled, ' A Preservative from Unsettled Notions in Religion.' Of this pamphlet, what he has wrote against me, makes only a small part. Now then, the question is, Whether I shall attempt to answer it? Give me your opinion, as you have given me your assistance. Ill I have been, and ill I am ; torn almost to pieces by a cough in the night, which admits of no remedy; whatever is taken to assuage, exasperates it. Of all men living, that are not absolutely confined, surely I am the weakest. If by such weakness, the Lord Jesus will vouchsafe to glorify His name, how transparent, how effulgent, will be the glory of His power ! Blessed be the Lord, for setting our affections on a happier state! Blessed be His grace, for giving us some knowledge of Jesus, as the way to immortal mansions ! There we may be citizens; here only sojourners."

Hervey not only wrote his answer; but, unfortunately, he submitted it, for revision, to Mr. Cudworth, between whom and Wesley, for several years, Christian charity was nearly at zero. Most of Hervey's manuscript was sent to Cudworth during the three months, next succeeding the date of the foregoing letter.

---

[1] Wesley's " Works," vol. x. p. 305.

"I apprehend," writes Hervey, "that the piece will make a two-shilling pamphlet. I must entreat you to get time for the revisal of all of it. If you could suggest or insert anything to make it edifying and useful, 1 should be glad. Would it not be proper to print Mr. Wesley's letter, and prefix it to my answer?"

Hervey's reply to Wesley was completed ·in September. A month afterwards, he wrote as follows :—

WESTON, *October* 19, 1758.
"I am now so very ill, that, I scarce think I shall live to see the approaching Christmas. I spend almost all my time in reading and praying over the Bible. Indeed, indeed, you cannot conceive how the springs of life are relaxed and relaxing. 'What thou doest, do quickly,' is for me a proper admonition, as I am so apprehensive of my approaching dissolution."

Ill as he was, however, his mind was, at least, occasionally occupied with his controversial pamphlet, which, though written, was still under the revision of his friends. Five days after the date of the preceding extract, he says :—

"Let me repeat my thanks for the trouble you have taken, and for the assistance you have given me, in relation to my controversy with Mr. Wesley. He is so unfair in his quotations, and so magisterial in his manner, that, I find it no small difficulty to preserve the decency of the gentleman, and the meekness of the Christian, in my intended answer. May our Divine Master aid me in both these instances, or else not suffer me to write at all." [1]

A fortnight later, he wrote again :—

WESTON-FAVEL, *November* 7, 1758,
"I am now reduced to a state of infant weakness, and given over by my physician. My grand consolation is to meditate on Christ; and I am hourly repeating those heart-reviving lines of Dr. Young, in his Fourth Night.

"'This, only this, subdues the fear of death :—
And what is this? Survey the wondrous cure :
And, at each step, let higher wonder rise ! ·
Pardon for infinite offence !' etc.

"These amazingly comfortable lines, I dare say, you will treasure up in your heart; and, when you think of them, will think of me. Dear sir, pray for me, that, I may not disgrace my ministry, or dishonour the gos-

---

[1] *Gospel Magazine,* 1775, p. 255.

pel of my Master, in my last moments, by unbelief—base, provoking
unbelief. This probably is the last time you will ever hear from me: for,
indeed, it is with some difficulty I have written this; but I shall not fail
to remember you, in my intercession for my friends, at the throne of
Christ."

The following letter, though long, is too important to be
withheld :—

"LONDON, *November* 29, 1758.

"DEAR SIR,—A week or two ago, in my return from Norwich, I met
with Mr. Pierce of Bury, who informed me of a conversation, which he
had a few days before. Mr. Cudworth, he said, then told him, 'that, he
had prevailed on Mr. Hervey to write against me, who likewise, in what
he had written, referred to the book, which he (Mr. Cudworth) had lately
published.'

"Every one is welcome to write what he pleases concerning me. But
would it not be well for you to remember, that, before I published anything concerning you, I sent it to you in a private letter?—that, I waited
for an answer several months, but was not favoured with one line?—that,
when at length I published part of what I had sent you, I did it in the
most inoffensive manner possible; in the latter end of a larger work,
purely designed to *preserve* those in connection with me from being
tossed to and fro by various doctrines? What, therefore, I may fairly
expect from my friend, is, to mete to me with the same measure :—to send
to me first, in a private manner, any complaint he has against me;—to
wait as many months;—and, if I give you none, or no satisfactory answer,
then to lay the matter before the world, if you judge it will be to the
glory of God.

"But, whatever you do in this respect, one thing I request of you.
Give no countenance to that insolent, scurrilous, virulent libel, which
bears the name of William Cudworth. Indeed, how you can converse
with a man of his spirit, I cannot comprehend. O leave not your old
well-tried friends! The new is not comparable to them. I speak not
this because I am *afraid* of what any one can say or do to *me;* but I am
really concerned for *you.* An evil man has gained the ascendant over
you; and has persuaded a dying man, who had shunned it all his life,
to enter into controversy as he is stepping into eternity! Put off your
armour, my brother! You and I have no moments to spare. Let us
employ them all in promoting peace and good-will among men. And
may the peace of God keep your heart and mind in Christ Jesus! So
prays,   "Your affectionate brother and servant,

"J. WESLEY."[1]

This was Wesley's last letter to Hervey; the following,
written three weeks later, was Whitefield's :—

---

[1] *Arminian Magazine,* 1778, p. 136.

"LONDON, *December* 19, 1758.

"And is my dear friend indeed about to take his last flight? I dare not wish your return into this vale of tears; but our prayers are constantly ascending to the Father of our spirits, that, you may die in the embraces of a never-failing Jesus, and in all the fulness of an exalted faith. Oh when will my time come! I groan in this tabernacle, being burdened; and long to be clothed with my house from heaven.

"Farewell! My very dear friend, F-a-r-e-w-e-l-l! Yet a little while, and we shall meet,

> "'Where sin, and strife, and sorrow cease,
>   And all is love, and joy, and peace.'

"There Jesus will reward you for all the tokens of love which you have showed, for His great name's sake, to

"Yours most affectionately, in our common Lord,

"G. WHITEFIELD."

" P.S.—God comfort your mother and relations, and thousands and thousands more that will bewail your departure!" [1]

The following, it is believed, are Hervey's last letters,—the first to Mr. Cudworth; the second to Lady Frances Shirley:—

"*December* 15, 1758.

"DEAR MR. CUDWORTH,—I am so weak, I am scarce able to write my name.   "J. HERVEY."

"WESTON-FAVEL, *December* 16, 1758.

"MADAM,—I have received your ladyship's favour, and should have answered it before now; but I have been extremely ill, and still remain so bad, as to be obliged to make use of the pen of another, to inform your ladyship, that I am,

"Madam, your ladyship's most obliged, and most obedient, humble servant,

"J. HERVEY."

Nine days afterwards, Hervey was a corpse. To his curate, the Rev. Abraham Maddock, he observed,—

"O! how much Christ has done for me; and how little have I done for Him! If I preached even once a week, it was at last a burden to me. I have not visited the people of my parish as I ought to have done, I have not taken every opportunity of speaking for Christ. But, do not think, that, I am afraid to die; I assure you I am not. I know what my Saviour hath done for me, and I want to be gone."

On December 20th, being visited by his friend Dr. Stone-house, he remarked,—

---

[1] *New Spiritual Magazine*, 1783, p. 164.

"True, doctor, true; the only valuable treasures are in heaven. What would it avail me now to be Archbishop of Canterbury? Disease would show no respect to my mitre. The Gospel is offered to me, a poor country parson, the same as to his grace. Christ makes no difference between us. Oh! why then do ministers neglect the charge of so kind a Saviour, fawn upon the great, and hunt after worldly preferments with so much eagerness, to the disgrace of our orders? These, these are the things, not our poverty or obscurity, which render the clergy so justly contemptible to worldlings. No wonder, the service of our Church, grieved I am to say it, is become such a formal lifeless thing, since it is, alas! too generally executed by persons dead to godliness in all their conversation; whose indifferent religion, and worldly-minded behaviour proclaim the little regard they pay to the doctrines of the Lord, who bought them."

The day before his death, in walking across his room, he fainted, and, to all appearance was dead. On reviving, his brother William said, "We were afraid you were gone"; to which he answered, "I wish I were." And well he might, for, besides the utter exhaustion of his strength, his bones were so intensely sore, that, he shrank from the touch of his attendants, when it was necessary to alter his position; but, in the midst of weakness and of pain, he was unceasingly praising God for His boundless mercies, and never received even a piece of lemon to moisten his parched mouth, without uttering thanks.

On December 25, the day he died, he complained of a great inward conflict, and, as he sat in his easy chair, (for he was not able to lie in bed,) almost constantly had his eyes lifted towards heaven, and his hands clasped in prayer. "O let me spend," said he, "my last few moments in adoring our great Redeemer! 'Though my flesh and my heart fail me, yet, God is the strength of my heart, and my portion for ever.'" He then proceeded to expatiate on the words of St. Paul, "All things are yours,—life and death,—for ye are Christ's."

"Here," said he, "is the treasure of a Christian. Death is reckoned in this inventory. How thankful am I for death. It is the passage through which I pass to the Lord and giver of eternal life. It frees me from all this misery which I now endure, and which I am willing to endure, as long as God thinks fit. These light afflictions are but for a moment; and then comes an eternal weight of glory. O! welcome, welcome death! Thou mayest well be reckoned among the treasures of the Christian. To live is Christ, but to die is gain."

Being raised a little in his chair, he exclaimed, " Lord, now lettest Thou Thy servant depart in peace, according to Thy Word ; for mine eyes have seen Thy salvation." " Here," he continued, " is my cordial. What are all the cordials given to support the dying, in comparison of that which arises from the promises of salvation by Christ ? This, this supports me."

About three o'clock in the afternoon, he remarked, " The great conflict is over. Now all is done :" after which the only words he articulated intelligibly were, " Precious salvation." Between the hours of four and five on Christmas-Day, 1758, James Hervey tranquilly fell asleep, in the forty-fifth year of his age.

Three days afterwards, his body was buried under the Communion table of Weston-Favel Church, in the presence of a large congregation. By his own desire, the pall used, on the occasion, was that employed in covering the coffins of his poor parishioners. Deep was the distress of the assembled crowd. Some wept in silence; others sobbed ; and others were even more violently affected. The devout Rector was where " the wicked cease from troubling, and the weary are at rest."

Funeral sermons were preached, and printed, in London, by Romaine, the Lecturer of St. Dunstan's; and by Cudworth, the dissenting minister, in Margaret Street. Charles Wesley, also, poured out the affection of his lyric soul, in one of his glowing hymns, from which the following stanzas are extracted :—

> " He's gone ! the spotless soul is gone
>   Triumphant to his place above ;
> The prison walls are broken down,
>   The angels speed his swift remove,
> And, shouting, on their wings he flies,
> And *Hervey* rests in Paradise.
>
> " Redeemed by righteousness divine,
>   In God's own portraiture complete,
> With brighter rays ordained to shine,
>   He casts his crown at Jesu's feet,
> And hails Him sitting on the throne,
> For ever saved by grace alone.

  " Father, to us vouchsafe the grace
   Which brought our friend victorious through ;
  Let us his shining footsteps trace,
   Let us his steadfast faith pursue,
  Follow this follower of the Lamb,
  And conquer all through Jesu's name.

  In vain the Gnostic tempter tried,
   With guile, his upright heart to' ensnare ;
  His upright heart the fiend defied :
   No room for sin when Christ was there ;
  No need of *fancied* liberty,
  When Christ had made him truly free.

  " Free from the law of sin and death,
   Free from the Antinomian leaven,
  He led his Master's life beneath,
   And, labouring for the rest of heaven,
  By active love, and watchful prayer,
  He showed his heart already there.

  " How full of heaven his latest word !
   ' Thou bidd'st me now in peace depart ;
  For I have known my precious Lord,
   Have clasped Thee, Saviour, in my heart,
  My eyes Thy glorious joy have seen,'
  He spake, he died, and entered in."

The principal facts in Hervey's life have been narrated; and eulogy is not needed. His devout and loving piety has been amply illustrated in the numerous extracts from his letters. In learning, he was inferior to few. His acquaintance with the Latin authors was extensive; and it was one of his peculiarities, when he was called to tea, to bring with him his Hebrew Bible or Greek Testament, and lovingly instruct the members of his family, from the sacred text. His kindness to the poor was only bounded by his means. Private fortune he had none ; and, after the payment of his curate, his church emoluments were small ; but all the profits arising from the sale of his books,—no inconsiderable sum,—were devoted to the cause of charity; and one of his last directions was, that all future profits should be constantly applied to the same sacred purpose. As the master of a family, his example was worthy of imitation. Twice a day his domestics were summoned for holy worship. At nine every night, he spent about a quarter of an hour in expounding a text of

Scripture, and concluded with a prayer. At eight next morning, each of his servants was required to repeat the text of the previous evening, when he gave a summary of his exposition, and again engaged in prayer. As a friend, he was affectionate and faithful. "Though always ill," said Dr. Stonehouse, "Hervey was always cheerful." "I am always weak and ill," he himself remarked; "half dead while I live; yet my spirit rejoices in God my Saviour." His religion, however, led him to live a life of comparative retirement. The gentlemen of his neighbourhood showed him great respect; but he was seldom among their table guests; observing, "I can hardly name a polite family where the conversation ever turns on the things of God. I hear much frothy chit-chat; but not a word of Christ. And I am determined not to visit those companies where there is not room for my Master as well as for myself." ·

His ministerial duties were all performed with the greatest strictness. Few of his sermons have been printed,[1] for the simple reason, that, except in outline and in shorthand, few were written; but, in the·pulpit, he was always earnest, fervent, and affectionate, and often eloquent. He spake, because he believed and felt. Besides his Sunday preaching, he set up a week-night lecture; catechized the children; and, to the utmost of his ability, visited the homes of his parishioners. "Mr. Hervey," said the Rev. Henry Venn, "was the most extraordinary man I ever saw."[2] Probably there was a little of extravagance in this gushing eulogy; but there must have been distinguished excellence to prompt such a man as Venn to utter it. In the same way, the rapturous effusions of John Ryland must be received with caution; and likewise not a few of the hyperbolical en-

---

[1] Hervey's sermons, printed in his lifetime, were the following:—1. "The Cross of Christ, the Christian's Glory;" a Visitation Sermon. 2. "The Time of Danger." "The Means of Safety." And "The Way of Holiness;" three Fast-day Sermons. After his death, the following were published:—1. "The Ministry of Reconciliation." 2. "The Grounds of Christian Rejoicing." 3. "Salvation by Christ." 4. "Many made Righteous by the Obedience of One," two sermons. 5. "The Divinity of Christ," four sermons. 6. "On Repentance." 7. "Search the Scriptures." 8. "On Love to God," two sermons.

[2] Life of Venn, p. 332.

 comiums of Mr. Brown ; but we heartily endorse the judgment of the late Rev. David McNicol :—

"If Seneca is right in placing the praise of goodness above that of
greatness, Mr. Hervey has secured to himself, for ages, the noblest kind
of estimation. As a man, he was the delight of all who had the happiness
to be numbered among his acquaintance. Friendship in him was Christian love, softened with a tenderness peculiar to himself, and placed on a
select object ; a love accompanied by the most ingenuous confidence,
and exercised with unwearied honesty. In every other relation also of
the circle in which he moved, he was equally remarkable for his courtesy
and virtue."

Hervey was one of the most godly men of the age in
which he lived ; and certainly, he was one of the most
popular and successful authors. It is a curious fact, that, at
least, four of the Oxford Methodists were gifted with poetic
genius,—the two Wesleys, Gambold, and Hervey. In early
life, Hervey wrote several short poems, some of them
beautiful, and sent several of his hymns to his friend
Whitefield ; but, strangely enough, he ceased to cultivate
his talent, from a fear lest his poetry should feed the pride
and vanity of his heart. Throughout life, however, his love
of nature was that of an enthusiast ; and his " Meditations,"
especially, to a great extent, are poetry in prose. Devoutly
he blesses the Providence of God, for his well-used micro-
scope, which, in the gardens and fields about Weston-Favel,
he almost always took with him. He believed and intimated
that the discovery of so much of the wisdom, power, and
goodness of the great Creator, even in the minutest parts of
vegetable and animalcular creation, helped to attune his soul
to sing the song of the four-and-twenty elders, " Thou art
worthy, O Lord, to receive glory and honour and power ; for
Thou hast created all things, and for Thy pleasure they are
and were created."

"His character and career," observes a certain writer, "were a contrast
to those of Whitefield and of Wesley. He was essentially contemplative ;
they were eminently practical. His mission was to sanctify the senti-
mentalism of the day. In him, the breath of life did not blow, as in
Wesley, in a strong, steady, all-pervading current ; or, as in Whitefield,
like a rushing and resistless wind ; but in a gentle zephyr, toying with the
tresses of the trees, shaking the petals of the flowers and grasses of the
grave, yet the minister of convalescence and the messenger of peace."

Of course, opinions vary respecting Hervey's peculiar style; but the fact cannot be denied, that he became one of the most widely-read writers of his time. The young still read his "Meditations" with avidity; and many of the old remember the pleasure that his writings afforded them in their early days. With some degree of appropriateness, he has been designated the Melancthon of the Methodist Reformation. It is quite certain that the elaborated polish of Hervey's works secured them the attention of the upper circles of society, to a far greater extent than that attention was secured for the writings of Whitefield and Wesley. Hervey avowedly wrote for the *élite;* Whitefield and Wesley for the masses. Hervey's style is objectionable to those who cultivate a taste for the simple and chaste, in opposition to what is elaborate and grand; but, somehow, in Hervey's day, his books, as Whitefield said, "suited the taste of the polite." May it not be added, that, they also helped to refine the taste of Methodists? The polite read them because they were flowery; the Methodists, because they were savoury; and while, through their medium, the former looked at grace with less prejudice; the latter looked at nature with more delight.

The following, from the *North British Review*, is, perhaps, as just a critique on Hervey's writings as can be furnished :—

"Last century was the first in which pious people cared for style. The Puritans had apple-trees in their orchards, and savoury herbs in their kitchen-gardens, but kept no greenhouse, nor parterre; and, amongst evangelical authors, Hervey was about the first who made his style a study, and who sought, by planting flowers at the gate, to allure passengers into the garden. It is not, therefore, surprising that his ornaments should be more distinguished for profusion and brilliant hues than for simplicity and grace. Most people admire tulips and peonies and martegon-lilies, before they get on to love store-cups and mosses and ferns. We used to admire them ourselves, and felt that summer was not fully blown till we saw it sure and certain in these ample and exuberant flowers. Yes, and even now we feel that it would make a warmer June could we love peonies and martegons once more. Hervey was a man of taste equal to his age, and of a warmth and venturesomeness beyond it. He introduced the poetical and picturesque into religious literature, and became the Shenstone of theology. And, although he did what none had dared before him, the world was ready, and his success was rapid. The "Meditations" evangelized the natural sciences, and embowered the old divinity. There was philosophy in its right mind, and at the Saviour's feet; and the Lutheran dogma relieved from the academic gown, and keeping healthful holiday in shady woods and by the mountain stream. The tendency of his writing was to open the believer's eye in kindness and wonder on the works of God, and their effort was to attract to the Incarnate Mystery the heart surprised or softened by these works. We cannot, at the distance of a century, recall the fascination which surrounded them when newly published,—when no similar attempts had forestalled their freshness, and no imitations had blown their vigour into bombast. But we can trace their mellow influence still. We see, that, they have helped to make men of faith men of feeling, and men of piety men of taste. Over the bald and rugged places of systematic orthodoxy, they have trained the sweetest beauties of creation and softest graces of piety, and over its entire landscape have shed an illumination as genial as it is growthful and clear. If his ' Meditations ' be not purely classical, they are evangelical, and singularly adapted to the whole of man. Their cadence is in our popular preaching still, and may their spirit never quit our Christianity! It is the spirit of securest faith, and sunniest hope, and most seraphic love. And though it may be dangerous for young divines, like Samuel Parr, to copy their descriptive melody, it were a blessed ambition to emulate their author's large and lightsome piety,—his heart, ' open to the whole noon of nature,' and through all its brightness drinking the smile of a present God."

Here Hervey's Memoir ought to end ; but, unfortunately, posthumous facts must be added.

Already, it has been stated, that, the last days of the devout Rector of Weston-Favel were employed in writing his "Eleven Letters" in answer to Wesley's "Remarks on Theron and Aspasio." It is extremely disagreeable to tag to the end of a life so beautiful as Hervey's a controversial fracas which ought never to have happened, but fidelity forbids the unpleasant duty to be avoided. For more than a hundred years, partisans, on both sides, have discussed the question ; and, on both sides, not a little has been written which both Hervey and Wesley would wish to have blotted out. It would not be difficult to lengthen the unprofitable controversy by an analysis of Hervey's " Eleven Letters" (next to his " Theron and Aspasio," his ablest work), but the task is uninviting, and the subject shall be dismissed as briefly as possible.

Six years after Hervey's death, his "Eleven Letters" were surreptitiously published, 12mo, 288 pp., without the printer's name attached, and with nothing but a brief Preface, signed

"Philolethes," who acknowledged that the work now "found its way into the world, as it were, by stealth." A year afterwards, in 1765, an authentic edition was issued, with the following title—"Eleven Letters from the late Rev. Mr. Hervey, to the Rev. Mr. John Wesley; containing An Answer to that Gentleman's Remarks on Theron and Aspasio, Published from the Author's Manuscript, left in the possession of his Brother, Mr. Hervey. With a Preface, showing the Reason of their being now printed." 12mo, 297 pp.[1]

The Preface states, that, Hervey did not commence his reply to Wesley before Wesley published his private letter to Hervey, in his "Preservative against Unsettled Notions in Religion;" in other words, not until after June 23, 1758. This is an error; for, in a letter to the Rev. Mr. Ryland, dated "*January*, 1758, Hervey says he was even then 'transcribing his intended answer to Mr. Wesley for the press'" (see 315 page preceding).

Hervey's brother, in the Preface, proceeds to say :—

"When, in December, 1758, I was sent for to Weston, I asked him the evening before he died, 'what he would have done with the Letters to Mr. Wesley, whether he would have them published after his death?' He answered, 'By no means, because he had only transcribed about half of them fair for the press; but, as the corrections and alterations of the latter part were mostly in short-hand, it would be difficult to understand them, especially as some of the short-hand was entirely his own, and others could not make it out; therefore, he said, as it is not a finished piece, I desire you will think no more about it."

Mr. William Hervey adds :—

"As these were the last orders of my brother, I thought it right to obey them, and, therefore, I withstood the repeated solicitations of many of his friends, who wanted to have them printed. Notwithstanding the regard I had for the persons who solicited the publication, I could not be persuaded to print the Letters; and they never had appeared in public, with my consent, had not a surreptitious edition of them lately made its way from the press, and were I not under a firm persuasion that will be followed by more.

---

[1] The title of the surreptitious edition was, "Aspasio Vindicated, and the Scripture Doctrine of Imputed Righteousness Defended against the Objections and Animadversions of the Rev. Mr. John Wesley. In Eleven Letters, written and prepared for the Press, by the late Rev. Mr. J——s H——y, A.B."

"As this is the case, I think it my duty to the memory of my late brother to send forth as correct an edition as I possibly can, for as to that which has appeared (from what editor I know not) it is so faulty and incorrect, that, but little judgment can be formed from it, of the propriety and force of my brother's answers to Mr. Wesley.

"As to the unfairness of publishing my brother's Letters without my consent, and the injustice to his memory in sending so mangled a performance out under his name, they are too apparent to need any proof; and though, the editor, as I have been informed, gave away the whole impression, so that it is plain lucre was not the motive of his proceeding, and I would charitably hope he did it with a view of benefiting his readers, yet, it is so like doing evil that good may come, as, in my opinion, to be quite unjustifiable.

"I have one thing more to add, which is concerning the *seasonableness* of the following publication. It may, perhaps, be thought a needless revival of a dispute, which happened long ago, and which is now probably forgotten. In answer to which, I can assure the reader, that, though my brother died December 25, 1758, the controversy did by no means die with him, but still subsists in the daily publication and sale of Mr. Wesley's 'Preservative.' The controversy is, in the most effectual manner, daily and hourly kept alive by Mr. Wesley himself. This proves very sufficiently the *seasonableness*, and, as things have happened, the *expediency* of the present appearance of the following Letters in public."

Such was the substance of Mr. William Hervey's explanation or apology.

He says, he knew not who was the editor of the surreptitious edition of his brother's letters; and, in the absence of counter evidence, he is entitled to belief. It is somewhat staggering, however, that he had been informed, the editor "gave away the whole impression," without being told the donor's name; and also, that, as the proprietor of his brother's manuscript, he must have known in whose hands the manuscript had been placed since his brother's death. Mr. Cudworth is generally believed to have been the stealthy publisher; but, if he was, he was not alone. Mr. Ryland writes :—

"These letters were just upon the point of being suppressed, and lost to the Christian world for ever. Soon after Mr. Hervey's death, they were put into my hands for twelve or fourteen weeks. From a principle of foolish and false delicacy I did not take a copy of them, which I ought to have done. Happy for the Church, the manuscript fell into the hands of three of my friends, who had more sincerity, zeal, and courage than I had, and thus the manuscript was rescued from destruction, and the original copy at last brought to light."

Not many will coincide with Mr. Ryland's notions "of

foolish and false delicacy." Apart from the question, Hervey *versus* Wesley, the surreptitious publication of the book was a base, treacherous, nefarious deed. No wonder that the name of the editor was never authoritatively announced.

Mr. William Hervey complains, that, the edition was extremely "faulty and incorrect," and did not convey an adequate idea "of the propriety and force of his brother's Answers to Mr. Wesley." Fair play makes it imperative to say, that, intentionally or otherwise, this is far from being true. Any one who takes the trouble to compare the two editions will perceive, that, except in typographical corrections, the insertion of Hebrew words in Hebrew instead of English characters, the punctuation of sentences, and the addition of a quotation from St. Chrysostom in Greek, the authentic edition hardly differs a hair-breadth from the surreptitious one.

Mr. William Hervey's last reason, for the publication of his brother's manuscript, is not without force. Seven years before, Wesley had unwisely printed his " Remarks on Theron and Aspasio " in his " Preservative against Unsettled Notions in Religion." Notwithstanding Hervey's death, that book was still on sale ; and, thus, Hervey was continuously attacked without being able to answer for himself. Was this fair, and brotherly ? Perhaps, it was not enough to justify the avowed violation of Hervey's dying wish, and absolute command ; but does it not somewhat palliate the dishonour of the treacherous act, and, to some extent, relieve William Hervey of the odium which has been cast upon him ?

It is undeniable, that, Hervey's "Letters " contain severe, and apparently bitter recriminations against his old Oxford acquaintance ; but did he himself write them? Those, who are the friends of both the combatants, have doubted this, and have, at least, insinuated that their author was William Cudworth, Wesley's inveterate enemy. This might be so ; but it might be otherwise. It is true, that, the taunting reproaches in the " Eleven Letters " are not what might have been reasonably expected from a man of Hervey's loving and gentle spirit. His other writings are perfectly exempt from bitterness. He seemed incapable of wounding even an enemy, much more one who, in former days at least, had been a friend. Was his the hand, then, that wrote the reproaches in his "Letters"? Defenders regarded Cudworth as the culprit. There cannot be a doubt, that Cudworth was capable of this. He hated Wesley, and his style of writing, when he chose, was trenchant; but, after all, he might be innocent. The "Eleven Letters" were written during the last year of Hervey's life, when his illness, always serious, was greatly augmented, and not unlikely to affect his spirits. From his letters, already quoted, it is evident, his irritation against Wesley was such, that, he honestly confesses, he found it "no small difficulty to preserve the decency of the gentleman, and the meekness of the Christian in his intended Answer." Further, though naturally so loving and so gentle, his sensitiveness was excessive. And, once again, it must be borne in mind, that, with one or two exceptions, such as the attack in the *Critical Review*, his writings had evoked unmingled approbation,—religious, literary, and aristocratic circles all uniting in his praise; and, that this was not adapted to prepare him for the unceremonious animadversions sent to him by Wesley. God forbid! that, we should cast a speck, which does not belong to it, on a character so beautiful; but no man is exempt from errors; and, perhaps, the hints just dropped are worthy of attention.

The results were painful, and, in some respects, disastrous. Wesley himself was exceedingly annoyed. It was one of the *great* trials of his life. It engendered a polemical warfare which culminated in the great Calvinian controversy of 1770; a controversy which, on one side at least, grew in bitterness until the death of Toplady, in 1778. And, lastly, not to mention other direful effects, by the action of Dr. Erskine, who published Hervey's "Eleven Letters" in Scotland, and, not only so, but, in his Preface, made a violent attack on Wesley's doctrines, Methodism, across the Tweed, sustained an injury, not only deep, but of many years' duration.

It is a painful task to conclude the life of Hervey amid the din of war; but the facts are too important to be entirely omitted. The difference between the two Oxford Methodists was a mournful occurrence. Neither of them was perfect. Both are blamable. It was a misfortune, that, Wesley's animadversions were written in a style so blunt. It was a mistake in Hervey to allow his excessive sensitiveness to obtain such a mastery as to prevent his writing to his faithful friend for friendly explanation. It was a serious blunder for Wesley to publish his critique in his " Preservative against Unsettled Notions in Religion." And, finally, though Hervey's " Letters " are ably written, it was a great calamity, that, he died before he had given them a finishing revision ; and it was a huge breach of trust, as well as a grave impertinence, for any one to violate Hervey's most solemn wish, and to commit to the public press an uncompleted manuscript, whose publication Hervey, in dying accents, had prohibited.

REV. THOMAS BROUGHTON, M.A.,

THE FAITHFUL SECRETARY.

1735 THOMAS BROUGHTON was the son of English parents, who resided in Scotland. His father was Commissioner of Excise, at Edinburgh, and had sixteen children, born and baptized.

Even Mr. Broughton's descendants seem to know nothing of his early life. From Wesley, we learn, that he was a member of Exeter College, Oxford, and that he joined the Methodists in 1732.[1]

On leaving the University, he appears, first of all, to have officiated at Cowley, near Uxbridge; and, with such success, that, Sir John Harold remarks, in a letter to Wesley, "Several of Mr. Broughton's late parishioners at Cowley forget not the assembling of themselves together." In 1736, he became curate at the Tower of London; undertook to preach to the prisoners in Ludgate prison every Tuesday afternoon; and read prayers every night to a religious society at Wapping. By means of Whitefield, he was presented to St. Helen's, Bishopsgate Street Within; and, through faithfulness to his old Oxford friend, he lost it. The parishioners objected to Whitefield having the use of Broughton's pulpit. Broughton answered, "Through Mr. Whitefield's influence, I obtained the living of St. Helen's, and, if he insists upon it, he shall have my pulpit." Whitefield did insist, and Broughton lost his lectureship.

Like all the other Oxford Methodists, Broughton was ardently attached to Wesley. In the spring of 1735, when the venerable Rector of Epworth was at the point of death, he used his utmost endeavours, to secure the appointment of Wesley to the vacant rectory; but without effect. In the

---

[1] Wesley's Works, vol. viii., p. 334.

autumn of that year, Wesley went on his mission to Georgia; and Broughton wrote to him the following self-abasing letter, which has not before been published.

1735

" OXON, November 27, 1735.

" DEAR SIR,—God grant, that, this letter may find you happily arrived at the wished-for haven!

" O cross of Jesus! what a rock of offence art thou become to the greatest part of Christians! The Christians of the present times are ashamed of Christ; and thou, that art a teacher in Israel, art thou unlearning this sure, this important lesson,—'All that will live godly in Christ Jesus, shall suffer persecution'? You know I have. If I should say, that I have not shrunk from under the cross, I should be a liar. My own bad heart, and the observation I made of the agreeable life of my London friends, occasioned my first abatements in strictness of life and holiness of conversation. What pangs and agonies of heart, I felt at intervals! I laboured for peace; I panted after the love of God; but my heart grew foul, and became a cage of unclean thoughts, for want of mortification and self-denial. I embraced the doctrine of *imputed righteousness*, and had mean thoughts of works. Almost every day furnished me with new ideas of religion; but, alas! they all savoured too much, I doubt, of flesh and blood. Since my return from London, too, I have been amusing myself with pretty dreams of true religion; nor am I awake yet. Good God! art Thou as mighty to cast into hell NOW, as Thou wert seventeen hundred years ago? Did the first Christians cry mightily unto Thee to spare them, and did they see it *absolutely* necessary to work out their salvation with fear and trembling; and dare I, who have been a wretch, and most excessively wicked sinner, think to obtain heaven with less labour and sufferings? O! pray for me, that Satan may not sift me as wheat! I am a worm, and no man, tossed about with every blast of doctrine. Stablish, strengthen, settle me, O my God!

" Mr. Battely has committed his parish to my care. O! that I may feed his sheep, and be not a hireling! Mr. Salmon's heart is with you; but, he informs me, Mr. Clayton has convinced him, that, he ought to abide where he is, till his parents cease to forbid him going to Georgia. God will never suffer a supply of fit and able men to be wanting to take charge of his work in America.

" At Oxon, we hope to be stirring. The hand of the Lord will uphold our fainting steps. Cease not, dear brother, to pray for us, as we hope always to pray for you. Salute the brethren. We all salute you.

" I am, dear sir, your most obliged and affectionate brother in Christ,

" T. BROUGHTON."

This is far from being a bright and joyous letter; and yet it is conscientious and earnest. Like all the other Oxford Methodists, Broughton was seeking to be saved by his own

1737 good works. These were far from perfect ; and, hence, his abasement, anguish, and despondency.

In 1737, in the course of his official duty, as curate at the Tower of London, Broughton preached a sermon, which, by request of the commander of the garrison, was published, with the title,—

"The Christian Soldier; or, the Duties of a Religious Life recommended to the Army, from the Example of Cornelius." Text, Acts x. 1, 2.

In 1748, a second edition of this discourse was printed, with a Dedication to The Right Honourable Lord Viscount Ossulstone, in which, in reference to his style, Broughton says,—

"If your Lordship should think the Discourse, to the soldiers,[1] penned with too much emotion of heart, and warmth of expression,—if, as a spiritual watchman, the preacher has lifted up his voice as a trumpet, sounded an alarm, and uttered his words in thunder,—he would meekly desire to be understood with candour, as accommodating himself to the military genius and character, which disdain a cold, lifeless, and unpersuasive harangue. He has indeed used great plainness of speech ; and the rather, because no one has a more sincere regard for the profession, or a higher esteem for those excellent persons, who worthily fill the chief and most conspicuous posts in the army, than myself."

The following brief extracts from Broughton's sermon will furnish an idea of his fidelity, and honest-speaking zeal. Having described the character and conduct of Cornelius, he addressed his military audience as follows :—

"Cornelius was a devout man, and one that feared God. But are there many of you, my brethren, of this religious disposition ? Not to enumerate all the instances of piety and devotion, in which you are grossly and wholly defective, I will mention but a few.

"And, first, in point of *sobriety*. Alas! my friends, what strangers, nay, what enemies, are most of you to a sober, temperate way of life. How frequently do you, the meaner sort especially, through excess of liquor, *reel to and fro, and stagger, and lie in the streets like dead men!* How insatiable is your thirst after drink, as if the gratification of that appetite was a joy unspeakable and full of comfort! To this purpose, you assemble by troops in tippling-houses, where you destroy your health,

---

[1] The sermon was addressed to the second regiment of foot guards, who, to the beat of the drum, marched to the chapel, with the Commander of the garrison at their head.

and waste your money and time, in tumults, revellings, and drunkenness. In these houses, you often sit till midnight, and prevent the morning watch, not with hymns and psalms, as David did, but, with blasphemous rant and obscene songs.

"Again, your offences, in point of *chastity*, are very scandalous, and too notorious to be denied; insomuch, that, the bare sight of you is suspicious and painful to the modest part of the daughters of our land. Having eyes full of uncleanness and adultery, you wander after pernicious deceivers, and give yourselves loose to vile lusts and brutish affections. That I do not charge you wrongfully, in this respect, is too manifest, from the numerous and melancholy instances among you of putrefied bodies and rotten bones.

"Cornelius prayed to God always. But where, alas! shall we find this practice among you? Prayer seems to have been banished from the army, and cursing and swearing brought in, in its room. Most of you, I fear, live without prayer, and pass away days, months, and years, without bending your kness to the God who made you, to the Saviour that redeemed you, or to the Holy Ghost who alone can sanctify your souls, and fit you for heaven. Let me not seem uncharitable in this assertion: I speak truth, when I pass this censure on the most of you: for, if you did accustom yourselves to pray, the ears of good Christians would not be so often stunned with that horrible din of blasphemy, nor shocked with those dreadful oaths, curses, and ungodly speeches, which daily and hourly proceed out of your mouth. It is an unpleasant office, my friends, to reprove you in this public manner; but many of you can bear me witness, that, I have not spared private reproof, when, in my hearing, the name of God has been by you blasphemed. Oh! that the horrid practice of profane cursing and swearing was less frequent in the army! Is it, my friends, a military accomplishment to curse and swear? Do you imagine, that, it adds grace to your speech, or manliness to your looks? Or do you fancy, that, it resembles the roaring of a lion, and renders your presence terrible? Alas! vain men! no wise and good man looks upon a swearer to be a hero, or accounts him a courageous person, because he is a profane and wicked one."

The preacher uttering such reproofs as these was, to say the least, a courageous man,—a worthy brother of Wesley himself, who, four years afterwards, preached his withering sermon, on "The Almost Christian" before the Oxford University. Perhaps both were more pointed than pleasant; but in the time-serving age in which we live, the pulpit would be improved by a dash of that stern fidelity which was used by Wesley, Broughton, and the first Methodists. It is far easier to condemn sins, than to reprove sinners. It required greater heroism for Nathan to say to David, "Thou art the man," than to deliver Nathan's parable concerning the

1737   heinousness of David's sin; and for Elijah to say to Ahab, "Thou and thy father's house have troubled Israel," than to dwell on the general evils of idolatry. John the Baptist was, not rude, but, courageous, when, face to face, he told king Herod, "it was not lawful" for him to have his brother Philip's wife; and when, in a crowd of Pharisees and Sadducees, he exclaimed, "O generation of vipers, who hath warned you to flee from the wrath to come?" Who will accuse the Divine Redeemer of want of manners, in His fearful utterance, "Woe unto you, scribes and Pharisees, hypocrites! for ye are like unto whited sepulchres, which indeed appear beautiful outward, but are within full of dead men's bones, and of all uncleanness. Ye outwardly appear righteous unto men, but within are full of hypocrisy and iniquity. Ye serpents, ye generation of vipers, how can ye escape the damnation of hell?" Is such fidelity now common in the pulpits of England? Is it less necessary now than it used to be in the days of old? Are the congregations of the present day more educated and refined than David, Ahab, Herod, and the scribes and Pharisees? Have preachers improved upon the spirit and the courage of Nathan, Elijah, the Baptist, and Jesus Christ? And have they discovered a more effectual mode of addressing sinners? Is it not a fact, that, "Whatsoever things were written aforetime were written for our learning"? Is it better and safer to listen to those who "say to the seers, See not, and to the prophets, Prophesy not unto us right things, speak unto us smooth things, prophesy deceits"; or to listen to the voice of God Himself, "O son of man, I have set thee a watchman unto the house of Israel; therefore, thou shalt hear the word at my mouth, and warn them from me. When I say unto the wicked, O wicked man, thou shalt surely die: if thou dost not speak to warn the wicked from his way, that wicked man shall die in his iniquity; but his blood will I require at thine hand"?

This string of questions may be thought to indicate, that, the writer approves of the rough fidelity of the Oxford Methodists, and is far from satisfied with much of the preaching of the present day. Be it so. He has no wish to avoid the odium, if odium it be. Fine preaching has never effected great reformations. Preaching is often too polite to be

powerful. The pulpits of the age would be more successful
if filled by men like Wesley, Whitefield, and their friend
Broughton. A luxurious, self-indulgent generation needs,
not obsequiousness, but, unflinching honesty. Costly clothing,
and refined tastes do not turn sinners into saints; but is it
not a truth, that, in many instances, they frighten preachers
from a faithful, uncompromising discharge of duty? ·

Broughton belonged to another class. He fearlessly reproved the sinner, and as fearlessly told him of his danger.
Addressing his congregation of soldiers,—officers as well as
privates,—the bold preacher says,—

"Let the serious consideration of hell-torments constrain you to
repent, and live like the devout Cornelius. When the judgment is over,
and this last sad sentence passed, 'Depart from me, ye cursed, into everlasting fire,' the souls of the damned will immediately be thrust into a
'lake which burneth with fire and brimstone;' 'where the worm dieth not,
and the fire is not quenched.' In this doleful prison of darkness and
despair, condemned souls will be tormented with the devil and his angels;
and every part of them be racked with the sharpest agony. The *whorish
and adulterous eye* will then be put out in utter darkness. The *tongue*,
that was used to *cursing, swearing, and filthy talking*, will then be
scorched with tormenting flames, and be denied a drop of water to cool
its intolerable heat. The *body*, which used to be defiled with *drunkenness
and uncleanness*, will be burnt up as a firebrand. And, what is still worse,
though the pleasures of sin are but for a season, yet, the punishment of it
will be without end; for the smoke of the torment of the damned ascends
up (saith the Scripture) for ever and ever. The torments of hell are of a
never-ending duration; 'and who,' my friends, 'can dwell with everlasting
burnings?' O be wise, and consider these amazing truths, that, ye may
flee from the wrath to come. Bid, from this hour, a final farewell to
swearing, gaming, drunkenness, and uncleanness. Be sober, be chaste,
be temperate, keep holy the Sabbath-day, flee idleness and bad company.
Remember you are Christ's soldiers, and were listed under His banner at
your baptism. 'Turn ye, turn ye, from your evil ways.' The arms of
Divine mercy are still open to receive and embrace you. God willeth not
the death of sinners, but had rather they should repent and be saved.
Our Lord Jesus Christ is ready to own you, and wash you from your sins
in His own blood: and the Holy Ghost continually 'maketh intercession
for you, with groanings which cannot be uttered.'"

Such may be taken as a specimen of Broughton's preaching,
at all events at the commencement of his ministry.

After a five months' residence in Georgia, Charles Wesley
returned to England. Whitefield was ordained, by Bishop

 Benson, on the 20th of June 1736, and immediately commenced his marvellous career of preaching. At the Christmas following, when only twenty-two years of age, he was fully determined to join Wesley, Ingham, and Delamotte in America. Some of his friends, however, protested against this, and, among others, his friend Broughton, the result of which was, his departure was postponed until the beginning of the year 1738. The following was Broughton's letter on this occasion :—

"LONDON, January 28, 1737.

"DEAREST SIR,—My instruments are ready, and I am sat down to write to you ; but how shall I accost you? With what matter lengthen out my letter? Surely, I was never more at a loss than now how to address my friend. And yet, the springs of love, that issue from the fountain of my heart towards you, are not dried up. Methinks, I have the same affection and esteem for you as ever; but the *resolution* you have taken to leave your native country, and the melancholy consequences to the cause of religion, which are likely to ensue therefrom; together with the barren prospects of my inability to dissuade you from your hasty undertaking, at least, till you have taken the advice of a multitude of counsellors (in whom the wise man says there is safety),— all these things put together, besides the weight and variety of my own affairs, so entangle and distress me, that I know not what to communicate to you. But good Mr. Wogan [1] has expressed my sentiments to you in his own. His reasons against your going to Georgia are my reasons, and the reasons of several good men besides; particularly of Sir Erasmus Philips, who laid his commands upon me to dehort you if I could.

"Dear Mr. Whitefield, let me entreat you to examine the reasons. Surely, we ought to consider before we resolve, and to weigh things well before we proceed to put them into execution. Would you be glad to learn what are my objections against your going? Alas! I have many things to say unto you upon that head, but you cannot bear them now. All I would recommend to you at present, is not to harden yourself against what may be modestly and fairly alleged to your leaving England. Let not your friends be accounted your enemies, because they tell you the truth. Lastly, we all observe the golden rule of our Lord, 'Judge not according to the appearance, but judge righteous judgment.'

"My dear friend,—for you are so to me,—pardon my plain dealing,

---

[1] William Wogan was born in 1694; and, after being educated at Westminster and Oxford, entered the army. In 1718, he married Catherine Stanhope, of the family of the Earls of Chesterfield. He died at Ealing in 1758. He was a Millennarian, but attended the daily service of the Church of England, and advocated a strict attention to the Church's rubrics.—"Private Journal and Literary Remains of Dr. Byron."

and, if it deserves a worse name, yet, pardon it. I conclude my letter with an excellent collect of our Church on behalf of us both :—

"'O God, forasmuch as without Thee, we are not able to please Thee, mercifully grant that Thy Holy Spirit may, in all things, direct and rule our hearts, through Jesus Christ our Lord.'

"I am, dear sir, your affectionate brother,

"THOMAS BROUGHTON."[1]

"To the Rev. Mr. WHITEFIELD,
"At Mr. Grenville's, a Grocer, in Wine Street, at Bristol."

John Wesley arrived in England on February 1st, 1738. By repeated interviews with Peter Böhler, he was converted to Böhler's doctrines, 1. That, faith is "a sure trust and con- fidence which a man hath in God, that, through the merits of Christ, his sins are forgiven, and he reconciled to the favour of God. 2. That, the fruits of this faith are the witness of the Spirit, and the new birth. And, 3. That, this faith is given in a moment, and, that, instantaneously a man may be translated out of darkness into light, out of sin and fear into holiness and happiness. This, however, was an experience, which Wesley, as yet, had not realized; and, hence, he came to the conclusion, that, notwithstanding all his past piety and devotion, he was still without saving faith. Wesley asked his friend Böhler, whether, being destitute of faith, he "ought not to refrain from teaching others?" Böhler said, "No; do not hide in the earth the talent God hath given you." Accordingly, when Wesley, his brother Charles, and Brough- ton met, on April 25, in the house of Mr. Delamotte, at Blendon, the nature and fruits of faith became the subject of discussion. Wesley propounded his new ideas "clearly and fully;" and writes :—

"Mr. Broughton's great objection was, he could never think, that, I

1738

---

[1] A recent Bishop of the Church of England, on perusing this manu- script letter, wrote: "It is a very interesting document, and leads to many reflections. Mr. Broughton's day, and the day of his once friend Wesley, were more important in the history of our Church than many are willing to believe. They disturbed, but they taught; and they led others to think and teach. Whatever might be their errors, it was not for the careless and thoughtless and the ignorant to be their judges. It might be for the best that Whitefield would not take the advice in this letter; but the affectionate strain is peculiarly pleasing, and the pious union between two persons, who differed on some points, may be a lesson that need not be lost even in our own day."

had not faith, who had done and suffered such things. My brother was very angry, and told me, I did not know what mischief I had done by talking thus."

Charles Wesley's account of this important meeting, held at five o'clock in the morning, is more minute. He remarks :—

"1738, April 25. Soon after five, as we were met in our little chapel, Mrs. Delamotte came to us. We sang, and fell into a dispute whether conversion was gradual or instantaneous. My brother was very positive for the latter, and very shocking; and mentioned some late instances of gross sinners believing in a moment. I was much offended at his worse than unedifying discourse. Mrs. Delamotte left us abruptly. I stayed, and insisted, a man need not know when first he had faith. His obstinacy, in favouring the contrary opinion, drove me at last out of the room. Mr. Broughton was only not so much scandalized as myself. After dinner, he and my brother returned to town. I stayed behind, and read them the 'Life of Mr. Halyburton :' one instance, but only one, of instantaneous conversion.'

Strange to say, within three weeks after this religious fracas, Charles Wesley became a convert to the very opinions which had given him such huge offence; and began to pity and upbraid his friend Broughton for not thinking like himself. Accordingly he writes :—

"May 11. I was carried in a chair to Mr. Bray's" (the Moravian), "who is to supply Böhler's place. I found his sister" (Bray's) "in earnest pursuit of Christ; and his wife well inclined to conversion. I had not been here long, when Mr. Broughton called. I hoped to find him altered like myself; but, alas! his time is not yet come. As to M. Turner, he gave her up; 'but for you, M. Bray,' said he, 'I hope you are still in your senses, and not run mad after a faith which must be felt.' He went on contradicting and blaspheming. I thought it my duty to withstand him, and to confess my want of faith. 'God help you, poor man,' he replied; 'if I could think you have not faith, I am sure it would drive me to despair.'"

Charles Wesley was now as impassioned on the one side, as, three weeks before, he had been on the other. He and Broughton became estranged. Hence the following, in his journal :—

"1738, May 14. Several persons called to-day, and were convinced of unbelief. Some of them afterwards went to Mr. Broughton, and were soon made as easy as Satan and their own hearts could wish."

A week after this, Charles Wesley believed in Christ to the

saving of his soul ; and became increasingly anxious for his friend Broughton.   He writes :—

"May 27.   I was much assisted to intercede for poor Mr. Broughton, who continues the very life of all those that oppose the faith."

"July 11. Tuesday. Mr. Sparks, this morning, asked me whether I would preach for him at St. Helen's. I agreed to supply Mr. Broughton's place, who is now at Oxford, arming our friends against the faith. The pain in my side was very violent; but no sooner did I enter the coach than the pain left me, and I preached faith in Christ to a vast congregation, adding much extempore. After sermon, Mrs. Hind, with whom Mr. Broughton lodges, sent for me ; owned her agreement to the doctrine, and pressed me to come and talk with Mr. Broughton, who, she could not but believe, must himself agree to it."

At this period, Charles Wesley was intensely interested in the welfare of half a score of malefactors, under sentence of death, in Newgate prison, all of whom were executed at Tyburn, on the 19th of July. During the last nine days they had to live, besides other visits, and personal conversations with them, he preached to them at least six sermons, and twice administered to them the holy Sacrament. On the day of execution, he, and Broughton, and Mr. Sparks were at the prison as early as six o'clock.[1] At Tyburn, these three earnest ministers ascended the cart where, beneath the hideous gibbet, the ten poor wretches, with ropes round their necks, stood awaiting their ignominious end. Charles Wesley offered prayer, then Sparks, and then Broughton ; after which the cart was drawn away, and the lives of the miserable men were ended.

Charles Wesley believed that several of them had found peace with God ; and declared, that, the hour he spent beneath the Tyburn gallows "was the most blessed hour of his life." The alienation, however, between him and Broughton still continued. Three weeks afterwards, they met at Mrs. Hind's, and resumed their old disputes. The details of the interview are not recorded ; but Charles declares, that, Broughton acknowledged, he had never read the Homilies of the Established Church ; and adds, "he denied explicitly, that, we are saved by Christ's imputed righteousness ; and affirmed, that, works do justify, and have a share in making

---

[1] On this occasion, Broughton administered the Sacrament, and prayed.

1741

us righteous before God." The two were earnest and eager disputants ; but, to use Charles Wesley's words, they "parted good friends."

After this, we lose sight of Broughton until the year 1741, when he was chosen lecturer of Allhallows, Lombard Street ;[1] and when he also married.

The marriage was to have taken place early in the year; but had to be postponed, in consequence of the death of Mr. Capel (the young lady's father), only two days before the time primarily appointed. In a long letter, dated April 4, 1741, and addressed to Charles Morgan, Broughton gives full particulars of Mr. Capel's illness and decease, and relates, that, Mr. C. had been married twenty-five years, and was buried in a vault belonging to St. Peter's, Cornhill. He then remarks :—

"Immortal and unchangeable God! to what changes is poor, perishing mortality subjected to here below! To-day we live: to-morrow we die. The rising sun beholds us fresh and blooming in life: the setting, motionless, and pale, and sunk into the arms of death. Though in the secret counsels of a wise and gracious Providence, I do not doubt, yet, what a disagreeable turn this melancholy accident has given to my affairs! O, my more than brother! my virtuous and noble friend! let no earthly thing, not even the most endearing and lovely Miranda, be too much the object of your affections. Forgive the preacher. Our God is a jealous God. He is jealous of His love, which often causes Him to use mortifying means to wean us from the love of the creature.

"I can add no more on this too tender subject, except, that, the ever dear to me and devout Aspasia carries herself with inimitable discretion, meekness, nay, Christian cheerfulness and resignation, under this heavy stroke and unpleasant posture of affairs. We both salute you in the tenderest and most hearty manner ; and, with eager desires, look forward to the next happy month that promises us the blessing of seeing, and conversing with so choice, so beloved a friend. Be not afraid to step into the house of mourning. We will, for awhile, lay aside our garments of heaviness, and anoint ourselves with the oil of gladness, to welcome you on your arrival in England; and, by prayers and best wishes for your future happiness, we will add our mites to the crown of joy upon a certain affair that promises you an abundance of happiness.

"I am, my dear Theophilus,[2] your friend,

"THOMAS BROUGHTON."

It is a well-known fact, that, at this period, the vagaries of

---

[1] *Gentleman's Magazine*, 1741, p. 387.
[2] A pet name.

the Moravians created great excitement in the religious
world. Gambold openly joined the Brethren, as Ingham had
already done before him. Fickle Westley Hall was tainted
with their heresy; and even Charles Wesley, for a season,
was in danger of subsiding into their unscriptural *stillness*.
An effort was made to re-unite Wesley's London Societies
with the Moravians at Fetter Lane; and Wesley and Zinzendorf had a memorable conference in Gray's Inn public pro-
menade. Whitefield, also, for the time being, was so out of
favour with the Brotherhood, that James Hutton, who had
been his publisher, refused to have any further transactions
with him; and, to add to his annoyance, "the people of the
world," he says, "fled from him as from a viper," because of
his "injudicious and too severe expressions against Archbishop Tillotson, the author of the old Duty of Man."
Hooker, the mendacious editor of the *Weekly Miscellany*, in
his trenchant style, was attacking both Moravians and
Methodists indiscriminately; and a Mr. Hopson, one of the
twelve stewards of the Religious Societies, pronounced excommunication, from their fellowship, against all the members
who were guilty of the crime of hearing the Moravian
Brethren, or Wesley, or Whitefield preach.

In this miserable fracas, Broughton was not an uninterested
spectator. It is said, that, Mr. Hopson, just mentioned, was
instigated by the Bishop of London, and, that, his lordship
also entertained the idea of bringing the Moravian proceedings under the notice of Parliament. It is also alleged, that,
Broughton became one of his most active agents; and, that,
to accomplish the bishop's scheme of stamping out the
Moravian heresy, he availed himself of the services of Mr.
Bray, an ex-Moravian, who "made it his business to go
among the Brethren, construing all they did to suit his purpose, and then spreading calumnies concerning them." Be
that as it might, a pamphlet was printed, but not published,
against both the Methodists and Moravians, containing,
among other things, a letter, which Spangenberg had formerly addressed to Bray, and which was now made to
tell against the Brotherhood. With what correctness we
know not, the author of the "Memoirs of James Hutton"
writes,—

> "This pamphlet, which had been chiefly managed by Mr. Broughton, was not published, but industriously circulated among the Religious Societies in the metropolis. Broughton is charged with writing statements in it against the Brethren, altogether at variance with his personal knowledge and conviction, from fear lest the world should look upon him as one of the Brethren. Brother Gambold was deputed to visit him, and point out the consequences of such duplicity; and the result of Gambold's visit appears in the following memorandum of the 2nd of January, 1742: 'Mr. Broughton is much prejudiced against us, and he and Ziegenhagen' (chaplain at the court of George II.) 'lay their heads together to find fault, and the pamphlet, now printed, is read in all the Religious Societies in town.'"

No doubt there is some truth in this. Broughton was incapable of the cowardice and misrepresentation alleged against him; but there can be no question, that, he strongly disapproved of some of the doctrines and usages of the Moravians; and no fault can be found with him for this. Like all new religious movements, Moravianism was inexperienced, excitable, and, to some extent, erratic. Infancy cannot be expected to possess the perfection of manhood. With the best intentions, many of the Brethren said and did foolish things. Broughton censured this, and so also did his old friends, Wesley and Whitefield; but it is possible, that, he was desirous of going further than they. Wesley and Whitefield would have weeded Moravianism; Broughton and the Bishop of London would have totally uprooted it.

Nor is there anything in this to excite surprise. Broughton was full of religious zeal and intensely earnest; but he was a rigid Churchman, and, therefore, not in favour of sectarists. Besides, while firmly holding most of the leading doctrines of the Christian faith, he had a strong antipathy, as already seen, to those dogmas of the Brethren, which the Wesley brothers had been taught by Böhler. To what extent his opposition to Methodism and Moravianism was carried, it is impossible to determine. Neither can it be ascertained, whether he cherished his repugnance to Wesley's newly-found doctrines to the end of life. Charles Wesley, on visiting Newgate prison, in 1743, observes,—

> "I found the poor souls turned out of the way by Mr. Broughton. He told them, 'There is no knowing our sins forgiven; and, if any could expect it, not such wretches as they, but the good people, who had done

so and so.   As for *his* part, he had it not himself; therefore, it was plain they could not receive it.'"

And, again, in 1744, he writes, in his Journal :—

" November 11.   This evening, I heard of poor Mr. Broughton's zeal; but shall not persecute, after his example."
" November 28.   I put out of the Society all the disorderly walkers; who are, consequently, ready to make affidavit of whatever Mr. Broughton pleases."

There is obscurity in the last two extracts.   Both were written at Newcastle-on-Tyne ; and, yet, it is almost certain, that, Broughton was, not there, but, in London.   Probably letters from London had been received by Charles, during his northern tour ; but what he means by the "affidavits" and by Broughton's persecution, there is no evidence to show. On the old principle, that, where there is smoke there is fire, it may be safely inferred, that, though Charles Wesley, impulsive and impassioned, entertained an excessive prejudice against his old Oxford friend, Broughton was still in hostility to the doctrines and the action of the Methodists.

Did this continue to the end of life ?   We cannot tell. We hope not, and are encouraged in this by a fact which happened soon after the year 1750.   The Rev. Henry Venn is well known as having belonged to the party of evangelical clergymen, who sprang up in the days of Wesley, embracing the Revs. Samuel Walker, J. Jones, Dr. Conyers, W. Romaine, J. Berridge, and others who might be mentioned.   Mr. Venn commenced his earnest and useful ministry in 1750, by accepting the curacy of a Mr. Langley, who held the livings of St. Matthew, Friday Street, London, and of West Horsley, near Guildford, in Surrey.   It was his duty to serve the church in London during part of the summer months, and to reside the remainder of the year at Horsley.   In this employment he continued from 1750 to 1754, when he accepted the curacy of Clapham.   Such was his activity and zeal at Horsley, that, his family prayer was often attended by thirty or forty of his poorer neighbours ; and the number of communicants was increased, while he was curate, from twelve to sixty.   The neighbouring clergy stigmatized him as an enthusiast and a Methodist, which presupposes that, in spirit,

1743 doctrine, or behaviour, or all combined, he bore a likeness to
the branded sect. Up to the present, he was personally unknown to Wesley; but he had frequently been among his
auditors, and confesses, in a letter, dated March 21, 1754,
that, Wesley's words had often been " as thunder to his drowsy
soul." All this goes to prove, that, the sympathies of the
young curate were with Wesley and his friends; and, yet,
presuming that Broughton's antipathy to the recently risen
sect still existed, Venn was the means of conferring a substantial benefit on the man who opposed the principles
and party which he himself regarded with affectionate and
zealous approbation. The story, as related in the life of
Venn, is as follows:—

During the time that Mr. Venn held the curacy of Horsley,
Sir John Evelyn had the disposal of the living of Wotton,
in the same neighbourhood; a living then worth between
£200 and £300 a year, and at present worth double that
amount. Sir John was exceedingly anxious to obtain a
clergyman of exemplary character, and a man of knowledge
and learning. The squire of Horsley strongly recommended
Mr. Venn, and Sir John seemed ready to accept the recommendation of his friend; but Venn, who had long been
acquainted with Broughton, and had a high respect for his
virtues, judged him more in need of preferment than himself,
and wrote an anonymous letter to the patron, giving a full
and faithful account of Broughton's character, and urging his
appointment to the vacant Rectory. Sir John, after making
inquiry concerning Broughton, presented him; nor had
he ever reason to repent of following the advice of his
anonymous correspondent.[1]

If Broughton retained his objection to the doctrines of the
Methodists, is it likely, that Venn, himself a Methodist in
point of doctrine, would have recommended him for such
a post? Venn was well acquainted with him, and must have
known his sentiments, not only past but present. He had no
personal interests to serve. In fact, his act was one of gener-

---

[1] In the life of Venn, Broughton is called "Mr. *Bryan* Broughton,
Secretary to the Society for Promoting Christian Knowledge." This is a
mistake. There was a Mr. *Bryan* Broughton; but he was not the man
whom the author meant.

ous and rare disinterestedness.   He was full of youthful zeal, and ardent longings to promote the spread of Christian truth. Under such circumstances, is it rash to regard the action that he took as evidence that the views of Broughton, who, at the beginning of the Methodist movement, had opposed the Methodist doctrines, were now materially changed, and that, in his ministerial teachings, he was substantially in harmony with the Methodist clergy?   The reader must form his own opinion on the subject; but as Broughton has always been represented, not as a friend, but as a somewhat zealous opponent of the Methodists, it is hoped, that this seeming digression may not be deemed irrelevant.

To proceed.   In 1743, Broughton was appointed the Secretary of the Society for Promoting Christian Knowledge; an office which he held until his death in 1777.   For thirty-four years the secretarial duties of this Society were the principal employment of Broughton's life.   In the Society's house, first in Bartlett's Buildings, Holborn, and afterwards, in Hatton Garden, he spent five hours every day in the week, except on Saturdays and Sundays; and during these five hours, from 9 a.m., till 2 p.m., was accessible to all members and friends of the Society, who had business to transact.   Was his life mis-spent?   In answering this, some account of the Society itself is needful; and the following is chiefly taken from its own Reports.

It is a well-known fact, that, the useful and popular preaching of Horneck, Beveridge, and Smithies, led to the institution of the Society for the Reformation of Manners, in 1677.   Co-existent with this Society, were a large number of Christian brotherhoods, in London and throughout the kingdom, who held private meetings for religious fellowship, set up prayers in many of the city churches, and were most exemplary in their attendance at the monthly Sacrament, and at public services.   To some extent, these religious organizations were one; and yet they were distinct and separate.   The Society for the Reformation of Manners was intended to suppress vice in others; the religious societies were instituted principally to promote religion among themselves.   The Reformation Society was composed of members of the Church of England and of Dissenters unitedly; the religious societies did not admit Dissenters, and consisted entirely of the members of the Established Church.

Things proceeded thus, till about the end of 1698, when a few gentlemen, belonging to these fraternities, formed themselves into a Society "to promote the knowledge of true religion," on a more extensive scale than had been yet attempted ; and "in 1701, at their instance, a charter was obtained, from William III., whereby all the then subscribing members, with other persons of distinction in Church and State, were incorporated for the better carrying on of that branch of their designs, which related to the *Plantations, Colonies, and Factories* beyond the seas, belonging to the kingdom of England." This Society was henceforward known as "The Society for the Propagation of the Gospel in Foreign Parts."

The incorporation of this Society for foreign missions hardly satisfied the yearnings of many of its members, principally on the ground, that, the British plantations, colonies, and factories beyond the seas, were chiefly in America.

The American colonies were of great importance ; but others, besides them, needed sympathy and help. Hence, these godly and earnest workers in the cause of Christ, still continued to carry on, by distinct and separate efforts, other designs for the honour of God, and the good of the human race. The Society for the Propagation of the Gospel in Foreign Parts was chartered and designated on June 16, 1701. At the end of the same year, the parties making the distinct and separate efforts were called, "The Society for Promoting Christian Knowledge."

The original designs of the latter Society were two-fold. 1. "The dispersion, both at home and abroad, of Bibles, Prayer-Books, and Religious Tracts." 2. The promotion of "Charity Schools in all parts of the kingdom ; in which, besides receiving religious and useful instruction, the children of the poor might be inured to industry and labour, so as to make them, not only good Christians, but loyal and useful subjects of the realm, and willing, as well as fit, to be employed in trades and services, in husbandry, navigation, or any other business, that should be thought of most use and benefit to the public. With these views, the Society

printed and circulated a set of rules for the good order
and government of such schools,—rules which had been
approved by the archbishops and bishops, who directed that
the same should be observed within their respective dioceses."

" Besides these general designs, the Society undertook, in
1710, the management of such charities as might be put into
their hands, for the support and enlargement of the Protestant
Mission, then maintained by the King of Denmark, at Tranquebar, in the East Indies, for the conversion of the heathen
in those parts."   In the prosecution of this work, the Society
assisted the Missionaries, at Tranquebar, "with money, a
printing press, paper, and other necessaries."   In 1728, they
commenced a new mission, for the conversion of the native
population at Madras ; and, subsequently, another at Cudu-
lore, an English settlement near Fort St. David ; a third at
Calcutta ; and a fourth at Tirutschinapally, the capital of the
kingdom of Madurei, an inland country in East India.

In 1720, the Society extended their work to the Greek
Church in Palestine, Syria, Mesopotamia, Arabia,and Egypt ;
and, by a special fund, towards which King George I. contributed £500, printed, in Arabic, and, by means of correspondents in Russia, ultimately dispersed in the aforesaid
countries, 6000 Psalters, 10,000 New Testaments, and 5000
Catechetical Instructions, with an abidgment of the History
of the Bible annexed.

In 1725, when workhouses began to be instituted, for employing the poor and their children, the Society used its
influence to promote the extension of such establishments,
by publishing an account of those already in existence, and
by urging, that, "a particular regard ought always to be had
to such an education of poor children, as might, by bringing
them up in the faith, knowledge, and obedience of the Gospel,
prove the most effectual means to make them good men, and
useful to their country."

In 1732, the Society, hearing the melancholy account of
the sufferings of the Protestants in Saltzburg, issued two
publications on the subject, and raised a fund, out of which,
"besides many large remittances to Germany, they sent to
the colony of Georgia, in 1733, 1734, 1735, and 1741, four
transports, containing more than two hundred of those poor.

1743   persecuted Protestants; who, with two missionaries and a schoolmaster, were settled at Ebenezer, and there lived contented and comfortable."

This brief outline of the ordinary and special work of the Society brings us down to the time when Broughton was made Secretary. The following are extracts from the manuscript Minutes of the Board of Management:—

"Bartlett's Buildings. Tuesday, June 28, 1743. Agreed, that, the Rev. Mr. Thomas Broughton and Mr. Watts jointly perform the office of Secretary to this Society during pleasure.

"Agreed, that, Mr. Broughton come immediately to reside in the Society's house, and open, and give proper answers to, all letters concerning the Society," &c., &c.

"Tuesday, July 5th, 1743. Ordered, that, Mr. Broughton have twelve Addresses to Prisoners in Debt, and twelve Addresses to Prisoners for Crimes, out of the Society's store, for the use of poor prisoners.

"July 26, 1746. The Secretary having reported, that, the Highlanders, under confinement in the Tower, were desirous of religious books,—*Ordered*, that, Bibles, Testaments, Soldiers' Monitors, and Morning and Evening Prayers be sent them; and, that, the Secretary take care to have them distributed in a proper manner."

Here is added another field of usefulness,—that of benefiting indebted, criminal, and political prisoners. Remembering the interest which, for years past, Broughton had taken in the welfare of prison inmates, there can be little doubt, that, this proceeding of the Society was adopted at his suggestion. Broughton's sermon to Soldiers, in 1737, has been already mentioned. So far as can be ascertained, his only other publication was issued at the time referred to in the above extracts from the Society's Minute Book; and, as will be seen, it had its origin in his anxiety concerning prisons. Its title was as follows,—"A Serious and Affectionate Warning to Servants, more especially those of our Nobility and Gentry: occasioned by the shameful and untimely Death of Matthew Henderson; who was executed April 25, 1746, for the Murder of his Lady, Mrs. Dalrymple,[1]

---

[1] This was a most unaccountable and barbarous murder. The lady was the wife of Captain Dalrymple. The wretched youth had lived in the service of his master and mistress for the last five years. In the full confession that he made, he stated, he had no dislike to the unfortunate lady, and he murdered her, not from malice or for plunder, but solely at

With some Account of his Behaviour under Sentence of
Death. By Thomas Broughton, Lecturer of Allhallows,
Lombard Street, and late Fellow of Exeter College, Oxford. London. 1746." 47 pp. Broughton repeatedly visited
Matthew Henderson,—who was only nineteen years of
age,—in the murderer's cell, and expressed a hope, that,
he found peace with God. "His behaviour," says he, "at
the place of execution, was penitent and devout, and such
as moved the compassion of a great crowd of spectators,
who came to see him suffer." Two days before his death,
Henderson was also visited by Wesley, who wrote ;—

"April 23. At the earnest request of a friend," (was this Broughton?)
"I visited Matthew Henderson, condemned for murdering his mistress.
A real, deep work of God seemed to be already begun in his soul. Perhaps, by driving him too fast, Satan has driven him to God; to that
repentance which shall never be repented of."

Broughton's pamphlet,[2] on this melancholy occasion, is
characterized by great fidelity, and outspokenness; and, as
this is the last time, that, his authorship will be mentioned,
three extracts, bearing on questions that are still of profound
importance, may be acceptable :—

THE DANGER OF GREAT CITIES TO SERVANTS.—"As these great cities
entertain, so they ruin no small number of servants, who soon exchange
the simplicity of the country for the foppery of the town. Many of these,
if they brought a little religion with them hither, part with it soon, and
quickly arrive at more wickedness than, perhaps, they will ever get rid of.
Thus the town proves a school of corruption to them, wherein they learn
everything that is evil. Here they lose their good principles ; their morals
are stained; their heart grows bad; and they stand ready prepared for the
worst of crimes. With this wretched furniture of vices, how can they
make good servants? Nay, what can prevent their turning out very bad

the instigation of the devil. The details of the deed are too revolting to
be here recited. Suffice it to say, the murder was committed "of Wigmore
Street, Cavendish Square," on March 25, 1746; and, that, exactly a month
afterwards, "Matthew Henderson was carried in a cart from Newgate,
and executed at the end of New Bond Street. He went to the place of
execution in a white waistcoat, drawers, and stockings. Two clergymen,
one of the Church of England, and the other of the Church of Scotland,
prayed with him, in the cart, for a considerable time. His body was
carried from the gallows, and hung in irons, on a common, about five miles
from London, on the Edgware Road" (*London Magazine*, 1746).
  [2] A fourth edition of this pamphlet was published in 1763.

ones? They are under no religious restraint; who then will vouch for their veracity? They have cast off the fear of God; where then is their reverence for their master?"

ON DRUNKENNESS.—" No person addicted to this vice can answer for himself, but that, in his liquor, he may commit the most outrageous acts of violence. Being deprived of his reason, and the grace of God having forsaken him, he is ripe for the most daring crimes. If you suffer yourselves to be enflamed with drink, and overcome thereby, farewell every tender impression! every spark of humanity and gratitude! You are no longer a man, but a beast,—mad and furious, fierce, and ungovernable,—and no fitter to be trusted than a tiger."

ON LEWDNESS.—" You cannot be a companion of these merciless destroyers of soul and body without running into great expense. And, where will you find money to satisfy these ravenous harpies? How these abandoned wretches assemble, as it were, in troops, and, with more than masculine boldness, and no less than hellish assurance, assault the modesty of every one they meet! How, in contempt of the laws of God and their country, they attempt to decoy and ruin all such as have not grace and resolution to withstand them! These are the instruments of destruction to so many of our raw and unguarded youth, and cause numbers of them to bring down the grey hairs of their parents with sorrow to the grave. The neglect of severe discipline and painful correction, emboldens these transgressors to sin with a high hand, and even to act their abominations before the sun. Whence, our streets and alleys swarm with these execrable servants of the devil, who are continually carrying on a trade of sin; who make it their livelihood; and who subsist by the price of slaughtered souls."

But enough. We return to Broughton as Secretary of the Society for Promoting Christian Knowledge.

In 1740, Dr. Gibson, Bishop of London, issued a circular letter to the clergy of his diocese, lamenting "the decay of piety and religion, and the increase of sin and vice;" and strongly recommending them to patronize the Society for Promoting Christian Knowledge, in their work of printing and dispersing Religious Tracts. His Lordship urgently pleaded for the extensive circulation of such publications, on the ground, that, "being short, they were likely to be read; and, being plain, they were likely to be understood; and, being always at hand, and frequently perused, they would naturally make a deeper impression than instructions and admonitions, either from the pulpit, or by word of mouth."

To furnish an idea of the work of the Society in this department, it may be added, that, the Catalogue, when

Broughton became Secretary, embraced, besides Bibles, Psalters, New Testaments, and Prayer-Books—1. Small books and tracts on the Holy Scriptures. 2. On the Church Catechism. 3. On the Christian Religion, Doctrine, and Practice. 4. On the Sacraments and Church Service. 5. On Education and Schools. 6. On Devotion. 7. Miscellanies. 8. On Confirmation. 9. On Particular Duties. 10. On Common Vices. 11. On Charity Schools. 12. On Popery. And, finally, on Enthusiasm, under which heading were two publications only, namely, Bishop Gibson's " Caution against Enthusiasm," and " An Earnest and Affectionate Address to the Methodists." All the Bibles, books, and tracts were sold to the members of the Society at *cost price.* The number of the Society's publications were about 160. The Treasurers were the Rev. Dr. Denne, Archdeacon of Rochester, and Rector of St. Mary's, Lambeth ; William Tillard, Esq., Holborn ; and Benjamin Hoare, Esq., Fleet Street.

The number of Charity Schools, in London and Westminster, in 1744, were 136, containing 3119 boys and 1950 girls ; and, since their establishment, 15,250 boys had been apprenticed, sent to service, or to sea, or had been taken out by their respective friends. Of the girls, 1658 had been apprenticed, and 6162 had been employed in domestic service, etc.[1] Besides those in the metropolis, there were, throughout the kingdom, 1703 other charity schools, in which were educated, and " inured to industry and labour," 31,184 boys, and 4515 girls.

It must not be understood, that, these charity schools were supported by the Society for Promoting Christian Knowledge ;[2] but the Society had promoted their establishment ; and, to some extent, furnished them with books and

---

[1] The Society's Report, for 1763, contains a notice, " To all Farmers, Gardeners, and other Occupiers of Land in England," from the Trustees for the Charity Schools in St. Andrew's, Holborn, to the effect, that, they had been informed, the country was in need of labourers ; and that they were prepared " to bind Boys apprentices for seven years, to learn the art of husbandry ; and Girls for five years, to do household work ; and, that, they would give £5 with every boy, and £3 with every girl so apprenticed. The Boys had been taught reading, writing, and the first five rules of Arithmetic ; and the Girls to read and write, and " to do plain work."

[2] They were begun in 1688, and were all supported by private subscriptions. (Report of Society, for 1772.)

1743

tracts. Every year also, a sermon was preached, in London, under the auspices of the Society, at "the time of the yearly meeting of the children educated in the charity schools, in and about the cities of London and Westminster;" and all of these sermons (many of them exceedingly able) were published in the Society's Reports. That, such Schools were needed, there can be no question. The following description is taken from the sermon preached by the Rev. Glocester Ridley, LL.B., in 1757, and is alarmingly true of the "London Arabs" now existing. Speaking of the outcast children of the metropolis, the preacher represents them, as, "A brood of miserable wretches in themselves, and noxious vermin to society; a kind of rational brutes, but worse than savages, being equally beasts of prey, but more mischievous, from their use of reason and resemblance of human kind. They may be the care, the admiration, the triumph of Infidelity; but every generous heart must grieve to see reason so disordered and human nature so in ruins."

From what has been already written, an idea may be formed of the Society of which Broughton was the Secretary, from 1743 to 1777. It was a Bible, Prayer-Book, Religious Tract, Home and Foreign Mission, and Industrial Society, all in one. The present "British and Foreign Bible Society" was established in the year 1804; the "National Society for Promoting the Education of the Poor in the Principles of the Established Church," in 1811; the Religious Tract Society, in 1799; the Society for Promoting Christian Knowledge was long anterior to the oldest of these.

It had two kinds of members; 1. Those who gave annual subscriptions, lived in or near London, and were called *Residing* Members; 2. Corresponding Members, being persons, in Great Britain and Ireland, and other Protestant countries, who were chosen to correspond with the Society, on the state of religion in the places where they dwelt, to distribute the Society's publications, and to remit any occasional benefactions, which they or their friends might be pleased to contribute. No one, however, was elected a corresponding member, who was not "well affected to his Majesty King George and his Government, and to the Church of England as by law established;" and who was not "of a sober, and religious life and conversation, and of an humble, peaceable, and charitable disposition." The subscribing members were chiefly clergymen and bishops; including the following, who were often called Methodists, the Rev. Thomas Adam, Richard Conyers, Thomas Hartley, Henry Venn, and Vincent Perronet.[1] The last mentioned became a member as early as 1744. Among the few highly respectable lay-members, Sir John Thorold, an early friend of the Oxford Methodists, was the most munificent subscriber. The number of members altogether was, in 1767, upwards of 700; and the income, for that year, including a balance in hand, was £5580. In the same year, the Society sold, 3829 Bibles; 2281 New Testaments; 5416 Prayer-Books; 8902 other bound books; and 58,429 tracts. Of these, 1014 books and tracts were given to the Society, and 19,423 bought by it; the remainder, 58,420, were its own publications.

Such, then, was the Society of which Broughton was the chief manager. Its operations, comparatively speaking, might be small, but it had the honour of being the pioneer of some of the greatest movements of the present day. It distributed Bibles long before the British and Foreign Bible Society existed. The great Religious Tract Society was not formed until twenty-two years after Broughton's death. Its Foreign Missions were few in number, but were important and successful; one of its missionaries being the celebrated Schwartz, who, as early as 1772, had five native assistants, and was held in such high esteem, by the Hindoos, among whom he laboured, that, the Rajah of Tanjore made him tutor to his son. In the education of the children of the poor, the Society deserves the utmost commendation, for it promoted the work when all others neglected it; and not only gave the children useful and religious instruction, but "inured them to industry and labour," and prepared them to become useful subjects of the commonwealth.

Little is known of Broughton's pulpit labours; and, though his parishioners at Wotton numbered not more than about 600, if they had any pastoral visitation at all, their visitor must have been, not Broughton himself, but, a curate employed by him. Five days every week were spent in the

---

[1] The Rev. John Clayton, also, was a subscriber, of £2 2s. per annum.

1743

Society's House, in Hatton Garden; Saturday and Sunday, Broughton reserved for other duties. Some will doubt the propriety of his holding the Wotton living, when most of his time was devoted to work, which prevented him residing among his people; and that is a fair subject for discussion. All that we are disposed to say, is, that, Broughton was, unquestionably, a conscientious man, and, though liable to mistakes, there cannot be a doubt, he acted for the best. Broughton had a large family,—fifteen children altogether, five of whom died in infancy; and his official salary was small, the entire payment, by the Society, for "rent, taxes, and salaries" to himself and a "messenger," being, for the year 1767, not more than £290 8s. 9d. Was it surprising, that, with such a family and such a pittance, he was willing to accept preferment? It is true, when inducted into the Wotton living, he might have relinquished his secretarial office, and, perhaps, should have done; but, on the other hand, he, doubtless, felt that, as Secretary of the Society for Promoting Christian Knowledge, he had the opportunity of being far more extensively useful than he could be as a village clergyman, whose ministerial labours had to be confined to a population of six hundred souls. The two-fold position that he occupied is open to objection; but, without all the facts, for and against it, to pronounce a decisive judgment might be rash.

One thing is certain, Broughton's secretaryship was not a sinecure. The supervision of the missions in India and Georgia; the continuous printing and publishing of Bibles, books, and tracts; the charity schools' affairs; the publication of the annual Sermon and Report; and the correspondence with more than seven hundred subscribing and corresponding members, would find the Secretary quite enough of work, without the claims of Allhallows, Lombard Street, or the parishioners of Wotton, Surrey.

Two facts, connected with Broughton's term of office, are too important to be omitted.

In 1743, when Broughton became Secretary, Wales was almost without Bibles, and the poverty of vast numbers of the people was such, that, it was impossible for them to buy them. The Society for Promoting Christian Knowledge, becoming acquainted with this disgraceful fact, appealed to the public, without delay, for special contributions to publish a new edition of the Bible in the Welsh language, with the Common Prayer, and with the Psalms in Metre. The success of this appeal was such, that, the Society issued an edition, in 1748, of 15,000 copies; in 1752, a second edition of 15,000 Bibles, besides 5000 New Testaments, and as many Prayer-Books; and, in 1768, a third edition, with marginal references, of 20,000 copies. These copies of the Holy Scriptures were not given, but were sold at the lowest price possible.

Again: In 1763, it was ascertained, that, of the twenty thousand inhabitants of the Isle of Man, a very large majority were *entirely* ignorant of the English language; "and, yet, for many ages, the island had been without the Bible in the vulgar tongue, and congregations were necessitated to receive off-hand translations of the English Bible and Common Prayer, according to the different sense, attention, and ability of the officiating ministers." To remedy this fearful state of things, the Bishop of the Island began, in 1762, to collect subscriptions; and, in 1763, transferred the matter to the Society for Promoting Christian Knowledge. The result was, in 1768, the Society had printed in the Manx language, and distributed in the Isle of Man, 1000 copies of the four Gospels and of the Acts of the Apostles; 1500 Prayer-Books; 2000 Catechisms; and 1200 Christian Monitors. They were also proceeding with the translation and printing of the rest of the Holy Scriptures; the Apostolical Epistles being now, *for the first time*, translated into the native language of the island.

Little more remains to be narrated. On Sunday morning, December 21, 1777, in Hatton Garden, Broughton put on his ministerial robes, and, according to his wont, retired into his room till church-time. The bells were ringing, and he continued in his closet. They ceased, but he made no appearance. His friends entered, and found him on his knees,—dead.[1] An original portrait of him hangs in the Board

----

[1] Thomas Broughton, the Secretary of the Society for Promoting Christian Knowledge, and Thomas Broughton, Vicar of St. Mary Red-

¹⁷⁷⁷

Room of the Society for Promoting Christian Knowledge, 67, Lincoln's Inn Fields; from which the engraving, in the present volume, has been taken.

---

cliff, Bristol, and Prebendary of Sarum, have sometimes been mistakenly considered one and the same person. The latter, an eminent author, was son of the Rector of St. Andrew's, Holborn; and died, at Bristol, in 1774, at the age of 70. It is a curious fact, that, both the Thomas Broughtons died in the same month of the year, and on the same day of the month, and that the day was St. *Thomas's.*

OTHER OXFORD METHODISTS.

IT is difficult to determine the exact number, who, at one time or another, were Oxford Methodists. As early as the year 1733, four had left the brotherhood, three of the seceders being pupils of Wesley, and one under Clayton's care. Wesley writes :—

"I think, in the year 1735, we were fourteen or fifteen in number, all of one heart and of one mind."[1]

The "fourteen or fifteen" included the two Wesleys and Whitefield, Memoirs of whom have been designedly omitted in the present work. There were, also, Clayton, Ingham, Gambold, Hervey, and Broughton, with whom the reader has been made acquainted. Besides these, Robert Kirkham, Charles Morgan, William Smith, and Matthew Salmon, who have been briefly noticed, were, less or more, connected with them. Seven others, standing in the same relationship, must now be mentioned,—namely, Messrs. Boyce, Chapman, Kinchin, Hutchins, Atkinson, Whitelamb, and Hall. This is a greater number than that stated by Wesley; but it must be recollected, that, in 1735, Oxford Methodism was in the seventh year of its existence, and that some of its first members had then left the University.

REV. MR. BOYCE.

OF Mr. Boyce we know nothing, except that his father lived at Barton.[2] Did he subside into an ordinary country parish priest,—pious and plodding, but unenterprising and unknown? To say the least, it would be interesting to know his career, after he left Oxford. Will some one, better informed than the present writer, furnish what is lacking?

REV. WILLIAM CHAPMAN.

THE history of William Chapman also is wanting. He was ardently attached to the two Wesleys; but,

---

[1] Wesley's Works, vol. xiii., p. 288.   [2] Ibid., vol. xii., p. 6.

strangely enough, they never mention him. After their departure from Oxford, he was the nightly companion of Hervey; but, excepting the letter, dated "June 12, 1736," already given in Hervey's Memoir (page 208), we possess no epistolary correspondence between the two. Chapman, like all the other Oxford Methodists, was humble, earnest, and devout. The following, hitherto unpublished, letter affords ample evidence of this. It was addressed "To the Reverend Mr. John Wesley, at Savannah, in Georgia, America."

"Pembroke College, *September* 3, 1736.

"Reverend and dear Sir,—Your kind concern and repeated endeavours for my spiritual good, while at Oxford, will not suffer me to think, that, you have utterly lost all remembrance of me, though you have given me no testimony of your affection since your leaving England. What shall I conjecture this silence to be owing to? I will not inquire; but rather take it as a providential punishment and scourge, for my slow and slender proficiency under the blessed means I enjoyed of your's, and your dear brother's conversation.

"Too, too late, alas! do I see how dreadfully I was wanting to myself in not heartily embracing so glorious an opportunity of laying in a stock of spiritual courage, sufficient to have carried me victoriously on through a host of enemies. How does my base ingratitude to my Heavenly Benefactor, like a frightful spectre, present itself before me, for rejecting those kind offers of health and salvation! And for not disengaging myself from that bane of our spiritual progress,—*the fear of the world*,—which was always as fetters upon my feet, and manacles on my hands! O! through what a waste of uncomfortable, barren, and dry ground,—through what a wilderness of sorrows, perplexities, and distress, have I not been led, under the conduct of this delusive spirit; when the holy and loving Spirit of God would have led me into pleasant pastures, and refreshed my thirsty soul with the waters of comfort, and conducted me into those paths, which are pleasantness and peace. But, blessed be God! for the sense of these things, though, indeed, not till driven to it, by the pungency of the affliction, by the misery and torment of a divided state of heart, and the perpetual conflicts I endured. Blessed be the most high God! I am once again, I trust, in the strait and narrow way, that leadeth to the kingdom of heaven; from which that I may never stir a foot, till the cord of life is loosed, I dare say, you will not cease earnestly to request at the throne of grace.

"I am sorry, I deferred writing till it was too late to say more; though I cannot help telling you, before I conclude, that, I sit every evening with Mr. Hervey,—that great champion of the Lord of Hosts; and, that, I read, five times a week, to a Religious Society, in St. Ebbs' parish.

"Dear Sir, God Almighty prosper all your endeavours for the good of souls! Depend upon it, in due time, you will reap, and that abundantly, if you faint not.   My prayers are with you.   O ! that my body was there too, that, I might make up what I have lost, under such shining examples. Do, dear Sir, write me a long letter, by the first opportunity.   Adieu ! God and the Angels be with you !

"I am yours, my dear Brother, sincerely in Christ,

"W. CHAPMAN.

"My Lady Cocks and sisters are now in Oxford; and they desire their best services to you, and wish you good luck in the name of the Lord."

It is hoped, that, this fragment of the religious experience of the Oxford Methodists will not be unacceptable.   The men were intensely earnest and sincere, but not happy.

REV. CHARLES KINCHIN.

CHARLES KINCHIN, a Fellow of Corpus Christi College,[1] left Oxford about the same time the Wesleys did, and became Rector of Dummer, a small village of about four hundred inhabitants, with a benefice, at present, worth more than £400 a year.   Like a good Oxford Methodist, he visited from house to house, catechised the children, and had public prayers twice every day,—in the morning, before the people went to work, and, in the evening, after their return.

Towards the end of 1736, being likely to be chosen Dean of Corpus Christi College, he requested Whitefield to supply his place at Dummer, while he was absent on the business of the pending election.   Whitefield writes :—

"Mr. Kinchin's parish, consisting chiefly of poor and illiterate people, my proud heart, at first, could not well brook.   I would have given all the world for one of my Oxford friends, and mourned, for lack of them, like a dove.   But, upon giving myself to prayer, and reading Mr. Law's excellent character of *Ouranius*, in his *Serious Call to a Devout Life*, my mind was reconciled to such conversation as the place afforded me.   Mr. Kinchin loved his people, and was beloved by them.   I prosecuted his plan, and generally divided the day into three parts, eight hours for study and retirement, eight hours for sleep and meals, and eight hours for reading Prayers, catechising, and visiting the parish.   The profit I reaped, by these exercises, and conversing with the poor country people, was unspeakable. I soon began to be as much delighted with their artless conversation, as I had been formerly with the company of my Oxford friends; and frequently learnt as much by an afternoon's visit, as in a week's study."

---

[1] Wesley's Works, vol. i., p. 81.

Kinchin being elected Dean of Corpus Christi, was now frequently obliged to reside at Oxford ; but he still retained his rectory at Dummer, where Whitefield was succeeded by Hervey. The Dean, however, continued faithful to the principles of the Methodists, and, on the removal of Hervey, Whitefield, and others from the University, willingly took upon himself the spiritual charge of the Oxford prisoners. Charles Wesley on his return from Georgia, hastened to Oxford, where, in February, 1737, he met with his "old pupil, Robert Kirkham," "good Mr. Gambold," "poor languid Smith," and "Mr. Kinchin," whom, says he, "I found changed into a courageous soldier of Christ." A year afterwards, W. Seward, speaks of Kinchin *expounding* at Oxford, and of "forty gownsmen." being among his auditors.[1]

On March 15th, 1738, Wesley and Kinchin set out for Manchester, accompanied by Kinchin, and a Mr. Fox, who had been an inmate of Oxford prison. An extract from Wesley's Journal will help to illustrate the character, not of Wesley only, but, of Kinchin. Wesley writes :—

"1738. Tuesday, March 14. I set out," from Oxford, "for Manchester, with Mr. Kinchin, Fellow of Corpus Christi, and Mr. Fox, late a prisoner in the city prison. Between five and six, we called at Chapel-on-the-Heath ; where lived a poor man, sometime prisoner in the castle of Oxford. He was not at home ; but his wife came to us, to whom Mr. Kinchin spoke a few words, which so melted her heart, that she burst out into tears, and we went on rejoicing and praising God.

"About eight, it being rainy and very dark, we lost our way ; but, before nine, came to Shipston, having rode over, I know not how, a narrow foot-bridge, which lay across a deep ditch near the town. After supper, I read prayers to the people of the inn, and explained the Second Lesson ; I hope not in vain."

There is something beautiful in all this :—the two Oxford Methodists and an ex-prisoner, in a dark and rainy night, making the lanes ring with their praises to the Almighty, and, in the absence of a church, using a country inn, for

---

[1] Supplement to Whitefield's Answer to Bishop of London's Letter, p. 8.

reading the Church liturgy and expounding the word of God. Wesley proceeds :—

"The next day, we dined at Birmingham, and, soon after we left it, were reproved for our negligence there, in letting those, who attended us, go without either exhortation or instruction, by a severe shower of hail. At Hedgeford, about five, we endeavoured to be more faithful; and all who heard seemed serious and affected."

Here, again, is a useful lesson. As yet, neither Wesley nor Kinchin had found peace with God, by trustful faith in Christ. They were, if the reader likes the designation, *legalists*,—men seeking to be saved by their own good works. Be it so; but, in their conscientiousness with regard to duty, and in their earnest desire to be useful to their fellow-men, they set an example to Christian travellers, which is not generally followed. Wesley continues :—

"In the evening, we came to Stafford. The mistress of the house joined with us in family prayer. The next morning, one of the servants appeared deeply affected, as did the ostler, before we went. Soon after breakfast, stepping into the stable, I spake a few words to those who were there. A stranger, who heard me, said, 'Sir, I wish I was to travel with you;' and, when I went into the house, followed me, and began abruptly, 'Sir, I believe you are a good man, and I come to tell you a little of my life.' The tears stood in his eyes all the time he spoke; and we hoped not a word which was said to him was lost.

"At Newcastle, whither we came about ten, some, to whom we spoke at our inn, were very attentive; but a gay young woman waited on us, quite unconverted: however, we spoke on. When we went away, she fixed her eyes, and neither moved nor said one word, but appeared as much astonished as if she had seen one risen from the dead.

"Coming to Holms-Chapel about three, we were surprised at being shown into a room where a cloth and plates were laid. Soon after, two men came in to dinner. Mr. Kinchin told them, if they pleased, that gentleman would ask a blessing for them. They stared, and, as it were, consented; but sat still while I did it, one of them with his hat on. We began to speak on turning to God, and went on, though they appeared utterly regardless. After a while, their countenances changed, and one of them stole off his hat, and, laying it down behind him, said, all we said was true; but he had been a grievous sinner, and not considered it as he ought; but he was resolved, with God's help, now to turn to Him in earnest. We exhorted him and his companion, who now likewise drank in every word, to cry mightily to God, that, He would 'send them help from His holy place.'

"Being faint in the evening, I called at Altrincham, and there lit upon a Quaker, well skilled in, and therefore, as I soon found, sufficiently fond of controversy. After an hour spent therein, perhaps not in vain, I advised him to dispute as little as possible; but rather follow after holiness, and walk humbly with his God."

Men like Kinchin and Wesley will never be without adventures. This long three days' journey, in the wintry weather, was filled with incidents, by the earnest efforts of the travellers to be of service to those with whom they met. They were scholars, gentlemen, and philanthropists. Religion was all in all to them. They lived it; looked it; breathed it. Everywhere, in the humble home of the quondam prisoner, the town hotel, the country inn, and the ostler's stable,—among waiters, fellow-travellers, and disputatious Quakers,—they were equally about their Master's business. Would, that, in these days of unequalled locomotion, men of such a spirit and of such behaviour were multiplied!

Three days were spent in Manchester, one of them "entirely with Mr. Clayton, by whom," says Wesley, "and the rest of our friends here, we were much refreshed and strengthened." On the Sunday, both the Oxford Methodists "officiated at Salford Chapel"; and, on Monday, March 20th, they set out on their return to Oxford. Wesley writes:—

"Early in the morning, we left Manchester, taking with us Mr. Kinchin's brother, for whom we came, to be entered at Oxford. We were fully determined to lose no opportunity of awakening, instructing, or exhorting, any whom we might meet with on our journey. At Knutsford, where we first stopped, all we spake to thankfully received the word of exhortation. But, at Talk-on-the-Hill, where we dined, she with whom we were was so much of a gentlewoman, that, for near an hour, our labour seemed to be in vain. However, we spoke on. Upon a sudden, she looked as one just awakened out of sleep. Every word sunk into her heart. Nor have I seen so entire a change, both in the eyes, face, and manner of speaking, of any one in so short a time.

"About five, Mr. Kinchin riding by a man and woman double-horsed, the man said, 'Sir, you ought to thank God it is a fair day; for, if it rained, you would be sadly dirty with your little horse.' Mr. Kinchin answered, 'True; and we ought to thank God for our life, and health, and food, and raiment, and all things.' He then rode on, Mr. Fox following; the man said, 'Sir, my mistress would be glad to have some more talk with that gentleman.' We stayed, and when they came up began to search one another's hearts. They came to us again in the evening, at our inn at Stone, where I explained both to them and many of their acquaintance, who were come together, that great truth,—godliness hath the promise both of this life, and of that which is to come.

"Tuesday, March 21. Between nine and ten, we came to Hedgeford. Just then, one was giving an account of a young woman, who had dropped down dead there the day before. This gave us a fair occasion to exhort all that were present, 'so to number' their 'days,' that, they might apply their 'hearts unto wisdom.'

"In the afternoon, one overtook us, whom we soon found more inclined to speak than to hear. However, we spoke, and spared not. In the evening, we overtook a young man, a Quaker, who afterwards came to us, to our inn at Henley, whither he sent for the rest of his family, to join with us in prayer; to which I added, as usual, the exposition of the Second Lesson. Our other companion went with us a mile or two in the morning; and then not only spoke less than the day before, but took in good part a serious caution against talkativeness and vanity.

"An hour after, we were overtook by an elderly gentleman, who said he was going to enter his son at Oxford. We asked, 'At what college?' He said, he did not know; having no acquaintance there on whose recommendation he could depend. After some conversation, he expressed a deep sense of the providence of God; and told us, he knew God had cast us in his way, in answer to his prayer. In the evening, we reached Oxford, rejoicing in our having received so many fresh instances of that great truth, 'In all thy ways acknowledge Him, and He shall direct thy paths.'"

In a moral and religious sense, this episode in the lives of the two Oxford Methodists is pre-eminently picturesque. The two were of one mind and heart, and all their energies and time were devoted to the service of their great Master.

Four days were spent at Oxford, during which Wesley met Böhler, and was "amazed more and more, by the account he gave of the fruits of living faith,—the holiness and happiness which he affirmed to attend it." And, on Easter Monday, April 3rd, at Kinchin's desire, Wesley went with him to Dummer, where he remained, for him, the unusually lengthened period of a fortnight. Here they doubtless pondered Böhler's doctrines, and brought them to the test of Scripture; and here, perhaps, was held a meeting, which Wesley mentions, without giving the date and place of it.

"Soon after my return to England," he writes, "I had a meeting with Messrs. Ingham, Stonehouse, Hall, Hutchins, Kinchin, and a few other clergymen, who all appeared to be of one heart, as well as of one judgment, resolved to be Bible-Christians at all events; and, wherever they were, to preach, with all their might, plain old Bible Christianity."[1]

---

[1] Wesley's Works, vol. viii., p. 335.

Among others at Dummer, in whose religious interests Wesley took an active interest, was Kinchin's sister, who, three weeks after his departure, wrote to him, as follows :—

"You have been, I hope, an instrument, under God, of reclaiming me. I certainly was in a very unhappy state when you were here. God will recompense you for your prayers and kind offices. May my good God pour down the choicest of His blessings upon you, your mother, brothers, and sisters, and give us all grace, to strive and struggle against our sins. I beg you to join with me, in praying God to show forth His power in me. What a frail creature am I? I am afraid, I am sorely afraid, of falling back. What shall I do? What shall I do? O pray, I may put my whole trust in God, who is able and willing to help me." [1]

Kinchin himself also wrote to Wesley the following simple and humble letter :—

"*May* 2, 1738.

"REV. AND DEAR SIR,—My Lord and my God has made His servant a minister of the Gospel of His Son. He has committed to my care many immortal souls. And I am but a little child. I know not how to go out, or come in. Pray, therefore, earnestly for me, that, God would give His servant an understanding heart, to lead and instruct His people; that, I may discern between what is good and bad; for who is able to walk discreetly and uprightly before such a worldly-minded and refractory people? I beg the prayers and directions of my friends.

"My sister is much mended in health. She has received much benefit from you, under God, as to her spiritual concerns.

"Pray, write speedily to your sincere friend and servant,

"C. KINCHIN." [2]

Letters like these show the religious confidence and friendship which Kinchin and his sister cherished towards Wesley.

Kinchin, as yet, was only a penitent inquirer. In the month of August, 1738, Charles Wesley went to Oxford, and met him and Gambold, who, says he, " surprised me, by receiving my hard saying, that they had not faith. I was ashamed to see the great thankfulness, and child-like loving spirit of Mr. Kinchin, even before justification." They attended together a Society meeting, where C. Wesley read his sermon on, " The Scripture hath concluded all under sin." He writes,—

---

[1] *Methodist Magazine*, 1778, p. 177.
[2] Ibid., p. 176.

"I urged upon each my usual question, 'Do you deserve to be damned?' Mrs. Platt, with the utmost vehemence, cried out, 'Yes, I do, I do!' I prayed, that, if God saw there any contrite soul, He would fulfil His promise, of coming and making His abode with it. 'If Thou hast sent Thy Spirit to reprove any sinner of sin, in the name of Jesus Christ, I claim salvation for that sinner.' Again Mrs. Platt broke out into strong cries, but of joy, not sorrow, being quite overpowered with the love of Christ. I asked her, if she believed in Jesus. She answered in full assurance of faith. We sang and rejoiced over her (she still continued kneeling); but her voice was heard above ours. Mr. Kinchin asked, 'Have you forgiveness of sins?' 'I am perfectly assured I have.' 'Have you the earnest of the Spirit in your heart?' 'I have; I know I have: I feel it now within.' Her answers to these and the like questions, were expressive of the strongest confidence, to the great encouragement of all present." [1]

This, especially at the time, was a strange scene; and Kinchin was there as a listener and a learner. Soon after this, the two Wesleys and Whitefield were almost uniformly excluded from the pulpits of the Established Church. During the year 1739, Wesley himself was not allowed to preach in more than eight; and one of these was the pulpit of his friend Kinchin. In the month of March, when at Oxford, he wrote,—

"At my return to Mrs. Fox's, I found our dear brother Kinchin, just come from Dummer. We rejoiced, and gave thanks, and prayed, and took sweet counsel together; the result of which was, instead of setting out for London, as I designed, I set out for Dummer, there being no person to supply his church on Sunday."

Wesley, and his brother, and Whitefield were now, by force of circumstances, evangelistic itinerants; ordained clergymen, without churches, and yet preaching everywhere; and Kinchin was inclined to join them. It was, at this momentous period, that Hervey wrote to him the letter, dated, "April 18, 1739," an extract from which has been already given (see page 220). Whether that letter turned him from his purpose, there is no means of knowing. Any how, his decision, comparatively speaking, was of little consequence, for his work was nearly ended. In spirit, in aim, and in doctrine, however, he thoroughly sympathized with his outcast brethren, and, in time of need, sought their counsel and

---

[1] C. Wesley's Journal, vol. i., p. 129.

their prayers.   The following is an extract from a long letter addressed to Wesley, and hitherto unpublished.[1]

" DUMMER, *October* 9, 1739.

" MY DEAR BROTHER,—I am just setting out for Oxford, and thence, probably, for London, in order to print my sermon, on the Necessity and Work of the New Birth.   I have revised and enlarged it, have made a Preface, and also written a Dedication to the vice-chancellor, Dr. Mather, the Heads of Houses, with their Societies.   Mr. Hutchins has perused the whole.   I shall have him at Dummer while I am absent.   I asked the vice-Chancellor for the use of the University press; but his answer was, that, he could not consent to it.   I have written him a letter, desiring him to peruse the discourse, before he absolutely refuses the press; but he has made no reply.   I propose, therefore, to wait upon him at Oxford, to know whether he received my letter.   I also intend to ask Mr. Gambold and Mr. Wills to peruse my sermon.   If I had any opportunity, I would be glad for you to see it too.   I desire your prayers, and the prayers of your friends around you, that, God will bless my journey, and my design in publishing the discourse.

" We all join in love to you, and all around you; and constantly pray or you, and desire your prayers.   If you write within a week, direct to Mr. Fox's.

" Your unworthy brother,

" C. KINCHIN."

In a little more than two years after this, Kinchin entered into rest.   Wesley writes :—

" 1742.   January 4.   This day, I understand, poor Charles Kinchin died.

" Cui pudor, et justitia soror,
Incorrupta fides, nudaque veritas,
Quando ullum invenient parem ?"

This was high praise from a man like Wesley ; but it was not unmerited.

REV. RICHARD HUTCHINS, D.D.

IT has been already stated, that, Dr. Hutchins was Hervey's tutor.   We have no further information concerning him, ex-

---

[1] The remainder of the letter refers to some arrangements to render assistance to Mr. Fox, who accompanied Kinchin and Wesley to Manchester.   By Wesley's advice, he had settled at Oxford; and it was now proposed to subscribe £30, to pay his rent, and to establish him in business, as a vendor of " fowls, pigs, and cheeses."

cept the following, kindly supplied, from the Register of Lincoln College, Oxford, by the present Rector :—

" 1720. December 8. Richard Hutchins, B.A., was admitted to the rights and privileges of a Fellow of Lincoln College."

" 1739. November 6. Mr. Hutchins was chosen Sub-Rector."

" 1742. November 6. Mr. Hutchins was chosen Bursar and Librarian."

" 1755. July 9. Richard Hutchins, D.D., Fellow in one of the Founder's Fellowships for the Diocese of Lincoln, was, on this day, unanimously elected Rector of this College. And straightway a letter was drawn up, in the very words prescribed by the College Statutes, in order to its being sent to the Lord Bishop of Lincoln, sealed with the college seal, and subscribed by all the electors present, certifying their said election to his lordship, and praying him to admit to the Rectorship of this College the said Richard Hutchins, Sub-Rector."

" Dr. Richard Hutchins, our late worthy Rector, departed this life, on Friday, 10th August, 1781."

The only publication by Dr. Hutchins, which we have seen, is a Latin sermon, delivered at the time of his being made Doctor of Divinity, in 1747, and with the following title, — " Elucidatio Sexti Capitis Evangelii secundem Johannem, in solenni Praelectione habita in Schola Theologica Oxon, pro Gradu Doctoris in Theologia. A Ric. Hutchins, S. T. B. Colleg. Lincoln Socio., 1747," 8 vol. 51 pp. The sermon is learned and spiritual ; and the reader may infer what were the views and sympathies of its author, when it is stated, that, the third and *principal* division, is, that, the body and blood of Christ are communicated to the faithful in the Eucharist. In more respects than one, Dr. Hutchins continued an Oxford Methodist long after all his old friends had been dispersed.

REV. CHRISTOPHER ATKINSON.

IN the Parish Register of Thorp-Arch, near to Wetherby, in the county of York, there is the following entry, in Christopher Atkinson's own hand-writing :—

" The Rev. Christopher Atkinson, born in the parish of Windermere, Westmoreland, April, 1713, was inducted Vicar of Thorp-Arch and Walton, in July, 1749." [1]

---

[1] Another entry in the same Register is as follows :—" The parish

Here, for a quarter of a century, Mr. Atkinson lived and laboured. He and Ingham were not distant neighbours, and close at hand were flourishing societies of Methodists; and, yet, there is no evidence, that either Ingham, the Wesleys or Whitefield ever paid him visits. Why was this? It is impossible to tell. The two villages of Thorp-Arch and Walton were small, not containing a population of more than about three hundred each; but they were not remote from Otley, Leeds, and York, places which Wesley, at least, often visited.

Mr. Atkinson had a large family, and a church income hardly equal to his wants.[1] One of his sons, the Rev. Miles Atkinson, rose to considerable eminence. Besides being Vicar of Kippax, Lecturer of the parish church in Leeds, and Incumbent of St. Paul's, in that important town, he was the author of "Practical Sermons," in two octavo volumes, and had the honour of being sneered at by the half-infidel *Monthly Review* of the period in which he lived. The famous "Billy" Dawson was greatly benefited by his ministry and friendship in early life; and, in 1779, at Atkinson's request, Wesley preached in the parish church, at Leeds, to such a congregation as had seldom been assembled within its walls. In spirit and in doctrine, Miles Atkinson was thoroughly in harmony with the Methodists; and, from such a circumstance, perhaps, it may with safety be inferred, that, in this respect, he was walking in the footsteps of his father.

A happy death is generally the sequence of a holy and useful life; and such a death was that of Atkinson, the Oxford Methodist. The details are here given in the language of the son just mentioned. He visited him on the day of his decease, and thus writes :—

" My father walked out of doors to the very last, even in the morning of the day he died. I said to him, ' I hope, sir, your confidence is in

---

church of Thorp-Arch was rebuilt in 1756, and finished in 1762. William Sisset, Esq., gave the stone. The Rev. Mr. Atkinson gave fifteen guineas, and paid for the plastering. His mother, Mrs. Agnes Atkinson, gave the font. Lady Hastings gave five pounds for the pulpit. Mr. Sisset built his own and servants' seats, and gave the painting of the pews. The rest was done by the parishioners."

[1] Even now, the united value of the two livings is not more than about £400 a year.

the Lord Jesus Christ.' He answered, 'Entirely. I have no hope or confidence but in Him only. I am very sensible, that, I am, in myself, a poor, guilty, helpless sinner before God. I find, I have been guilty of every sin. There is not a commandment which I have not broken ; but the Lord Jesus Christ is my Saviour. His blood is sufficient for me. I rest upon His promises, and, (laying his head upon his breast and looking up) ' I feel the Spirit of God now supporting me.'

" Two of his twelve children had not arrived ; but, fearing his understanding might begin to fail, I asked him if he would like my mother and the rest of his children to be called up, that we might pray together, and receive his blessing. He immediately assented, and desired me to pray. The scene was very affecting. He seemed to be very fervent ; and, when the prayer was over, he tenderly and affectionately saluted us all, and invoked the blessing of God in Christ Jesus. Soon after, he spoke to me about the place in the churchyard, where he wished his body to be laid, and then said, ' Oh, son, I now feel the vanity of life. We often talk in health about its emptiness ; but this is the trying hour. I now experience it. My God ! what a condition should I now be in, if the business of eternity was unbegun !' And, then, he proceeded to speak of Christ and the happiness of heaven. His voice faltered ; but, at one time, I heard him say 'Come, Lord Jesus, come quickly ;' and, at another, ' I have finished my course, I have fought the good fight. Henceforth, there is laid up for me a crown of righteousness, which the Lord, the righteous Judge, will give me in that day.' He next addressed his chilren, and said, ' My dear children, whatever you have seen faulty in me, be careful to avoid ; if you have seen anything praiseworthy, that imitate and pursue. But, oh ! mind the one thing needful. Let God be your portion. Seek unto Him through the gracious Redeemer, and doubt not but He will provide for you what is necessary in this world. My dear wife, trust in God. O, my God, look down upon this my family, and let Thy blessing rest upon them ! Guide them by Thy blessed Spirit !'

" He continued praying, in a kind of feeble murmur until about the three last breaths he drew ; and then, at half-past four o'clock, on Monday afternoon, July 11, 1774, expired, aged sixty-one years, leaving behind him a wife and twelve children.

" His last words to one of his daughters were, ' My love, would you recall me from happiness ? ' "

Christopher Atkinson lies interred in the burial ground of Thorp-Arch church, of which he was the minister for five-and-twenty years.

REV. JOHN WHITELAMB.

JOHN WHITELAMB, the son of poor parents, was born in 1707, in the neighbourhood of Wroot, a small village of about three hundred inhabitants, in the county of Lincoln. The village stands upon an eminence, surrounded by 60,000 acres of land, which, in Whitelamb's days, were often flooded, rendering Wroot accessible only by boats. The land, also, even at the best of times, was fenny, moorish, swampy.

About the time of Whitelamb's birth, Henry Travis, Esq., of London, bequeathed three hundred and seventy-nine acres of land, for the endowment of three schools, at Wroot, Hatfield, and Thorne, in which children, male and female, were to be taught to read English, especially the Bible and Catechism, and to be well instructed in the principles of the Christian religion. The Archbishop of York was to be special visitor; the children were to be elected by the clergyman of each of the three respective parishes, and by his churchwardens; and on leaving school, and attaining the age of seventeen, each scholar was to be presented with a Bible and the "Whole Duty of Man." It was in the charity school, at Wroot, that Whitelamb received the rudiments of his education.

It is well known, that, Wesley's father was rector of both Epworth and Wroot, and that his greatest literary work was his "Dissertationes in Librum Jobi," a large-size folio book of 600 pages. Samuel Wesley was employed upon this remarkable production for more than five-and-twenty years. On leaving school, young Whitelamb became his amanuensis. For four years, he was occupied in transcribing the aged rector's Dissertations. He also designed its illustrations, several of which he also engraved.

While resident beneath the roof of Samuel Wesley, Whitelamb acquired a sufficient knowledge of the Greek and Latin languages, to enter Lincoln College, Oxford, where he was principally maintained by the Epworth Rector, and had Wesley for his tutor.

Samuel Wesley was a large-hearted man, to whom it was always a happiness to have the power of showing kindness to a fellow-creature. His own early life had been an almost friendless one. With an insatiable thirst for knowledge, he had to pursue it "under difficulties." Bitter experience had taught him the preciousness of a friend's assistance. These facts were quite sufficient to render the poor boy, from the Wroot Charity School, an object of affectionate regard; but there were others beside these. John Whitelamb was the son of one of Samuel Wesley's peasant parishioners; as an amanuensis, he had rendered the Rector important service for four long years; and, more than that, he had been the means of saving the Rector's life. In a letter, dated, "Epworth, September 5, 1728," Samuel Wesley writes :—

"God has given me two fair escapes for life within these few weeks. The first was when my old nag fell with me, trailed me in the stirrups by one foot, and trod upon the other, yet never hurt me.

"The other escape was much greater. On Monday week, at Burring-ham Ferry, we were driven down with a fierce stream and wind, and fell foul against a keel. Two of our horses were pitched overboard, and the boat was filled with water. I was just preparing to swim for life" (he was then sixty-six years of age), "when John Whitelamb's long legs and arms swarmed up into the keel, and lugged me in after him. My mare was swimming a quarter of an hour; but, at last, we all got safe to land. Help to praise Him who saves both man and beast."

Remembering all this, it will be felt, that, it was a grateful, as well as generous, act, for Samuel Wesley to send his youthful helper and deliverer to Lincoln College, Oxford.

Whitelamb's going to Oxford must have taken place soon after Samuel Wesley's providential deliverance from being drowned; for, five years after this, he had finished his collegiate education, and become the Rector's curate, and son-in-law.

Whitelamb was a steady student. "John Whitelamb," wrote Wesley, in 1731,—

" Reads one English, one Latin, and one Greek book alternately ; and never meddles with a new one, in any of the languages, till he has ended the old one. If he goes on as he has begun, I dare take upon me to say, that, by the time he has been here four or five years, there will not be such an one, of his standing, in Lincoln College, perhaps not in the University of Oxford."

Like his patrons, however, Whitelamb was very poor; and poverty always implies trials. The young gentlemen of Oxford, as a rule, had ample means, and could dress accordingly ; but Whitelamb, without a purse, had to submit to the indignity of wearing a worn-out college gown. Wesley, his tutor, pitied him, and yet had scarcely the ability to help him. Hence the following, to his brother Samuel, under the date of "November 17, 1731:"

"John Whitelamb wants a gown much, and I am not rich enough to buy him one at present. If you are willing that my twenty shillings (that were) should go toward that, I will add ten to them, and let it lie till I have tried my interest with my friends to make up the price of a new one."

No wonder that Susannah Wesley used to call Whitelamb "poor starveling Johnny." His position was a proud, and yet a painful one.

In 1733, Whitelamb became Samuel Wesley's curate, and, soon afterwards, married his daughter Mary. Whitelamb's wife was eleven years older than himself; and, through affliction in early life, and, probably, some mismanagement in her nurse, was of stunted growth, and considerably deformed ; but her face was exquisitely beautiful, and her amiable temper made her the delight and favourite of the whole of the Wesley family. In her elegy, written by her accomplished sister Mehetabel, and published in the *Gentleman's Magazine* for 1736, are the following lines :—

> "From earliest dawn of life, through Thee alone,
> The saint sublime, the finished Christian shone ;
> Yet would not grace one grain of pride allow,
> Or cry, ' Stand off, I'm holier than thou !'
> With business or devotion never cloyed,
> No moment of thy time passed unemployed,
> Nor was thy form unfair, (though Heaven confined
> To scanty limits thy exalted mind)."

> "Witness the brow, so faultless, open, clear,
> That none could ask if honesty was there :
> Witness the taintless lustre of thy skin,
> Bright emblem of the brighter soul within :
> That soul, which, easy, unaffected, mild,
> Through jetty eyes, with cheerful sweetness smiled.
> But, oh ! could fancy reach, or language speak
> The living beauties of thy lip and cheek,
> Where nature's pencil, leaving art no room,
> Touched to a miracle the vernal bloom,
> Lost though thou art in *Stella's* faithful line,
> Thy face, immortal as thy fame, should shine."

Such was John Whitelamb's wife. To provide for the newly-married pair, Samuel Wesley resigned to Whitelamb his rectory at Wroot. The village was sequestered, and the surrounding country, to a great extent, a swamp. The church, also, was extremely unpretending, and its walls composed of boulder stones which, in 1794, were used in paving Epworth streets. Still, there was a field for usefulness, and a benefice, which *now* is worth about £260 a year. Samuel Wesley's letter to the Lord Chancellor is so characteristic of both himself and his son-in-law, that its insertion is not irrelevant.

" January 14, 1734.

" MY LORD,—The small rectory of Wroot, in the diocese and county of Lincoln, is in the gift of the Lord Chancellor, and, more than seven years since, was conferred on Samuel Wesley, rector of Epworth. It lies in our low levels, and is often overflowed. During the time I have had it, the people have lost the fruits of the earth to that degree, that it has hardly brought me £50 per annum, *omnibus annis;* and, some years, not enough to pay my curate there his salary of £30 a year.

" This living, by your lordship's permission and favour, I would gladly resign to one Mr. John Whitelamb, born in the neighbourhood of Wroot, where his father and grandfather lived; when I took him from among the scholars of a charity school (founded by one Mr. Travers, an attorney), brought him to my house, and educated him there, where he was my amanuensis for four years, in transcribing my ' Dissertations on the Book of Job,' now well advanced in the press ; and was employed in drawing my maps and figures for it, as well as we could by the light of nature. After this, I sent him to Oxford, to my son John, Fellow of Lincoln College ; under whom he made such proficiency, that he was, the last summer, admitted, by the Bishop of Oxford, into deacon's orders, and became my curate at Epworth, while I came up to town to expedite the printing of my book.

" Since then, I gave my consent to his marrying one of my seven daughters, and they are married accordingly ; and, though I can spare little more with her, yet I would gladly give them a little glebe land at Wroot, where, I am sure, they will not want springs of water. But *they* love the place, though I can get nobody else to reside on it.

" If I do not flatter myself, he is indeed a valuable person, of uncommon brightness, learning, piety, and indefatigable industry ; always loyal to the king, zealous for the Church, and friendly to our dissenting brethren. For the truth of this character I will be answerable to God and man.

" If, therefore, your lordship will grant me the favour to let me resign my living unto him, and please to confer it on him, I shall always remain, your lordship's most bounden, most grateful, and most obedient servant, " SAMUEL WESLEY."

His lordship complied with this request, and, in the *Gentleman's Magazine* for the ensuing month, February, 1734, in the list of ecclesiastical preferments, was the following :—" Mr. Whitelamb to the rectory of Wroot, Lincolnshire."

Immediately after, Whitelamb and his wife removed to Wroot, and took "true pains among the people." Their parsonage is thus described by Samuel Wesley, junior :—

> " The house is good, and strong, and clean,
> Though there no battlements are seen,
> But humble roof of thatch, I ween,
>   Low rooms from rain to cover.
> Where, safe from poverty, (sore ill !)
> All may live happy if they will,
> As any that St. James's fill,
>   The Escurial, or the Louvre."

Their parishioners were sketched by Mehetabel Wesley, in the lines following :—

> " High births and virtue equally they scorn,
> As asses dull, on dunghills born ;
> Impervious as the stones, their heads are found,
> Their rage and hatred, steadfast as the ground."

The pictures are not attractive ; but, despite their thatched residence, and the boorishness of the people among whom they lived, Whitelamb and his wife were happy. Their union, however, was of brief duration. Within one short year of her marriage, the grave received all that was mortal of Mrs. Whitelamb and her infant child. She died in childbirth, at the end of October, 1734.

This was a terrible stroke to the young husband. For a season, he was inconsolable, and, to divert him from his trouble, his father-in-law brought him to the Epworth Rectory. This was just about the time when Oglethorpe returned from Georgia, whither he had gone with his first company of motley emigrants. Samuel Wesley, now within six months of his decease, took an intense interest in the Georgian colony, and declared that, if he had been ten years younger, he would gladly have devoted the remainder of his life and labours to the emigrants, and in acquiring the language of the Indians among whom they had to live. Among others who had gone to Georgia with Oglethorpe, and had returned with him, was John Lyndal, one of Samuel Wesley's parishioners, of whom the venerable Rector earnestly inquired whether the ministers who had migrated to the infant colony understood the Indian language, and could preach without interpreters. All this tended to turn poor Whitelamb's thoughts to Georgia ; and, five weeks after Mrs. Whitelamb's death, the Rector of Epworth wrote to General Oglethorpe as follows :—

" EPWORTH, *December* 7, 1734.

" DEAR SIR,—I cannot express how much I am obliged by your last kind and instructive letter concerning the affairs of Georgia. I could not read it without sighing, when I reflected on my own age and infirmities, which made such an expedition utterly impracticable for me. Yet, my mind worked hard about it ; and it is not impossible but Providence may have directed me to such an expedient as may prove more serviceable to your colony than I should ever have been."

Samuel Wesley then proceeds to give an account of the life of Whitelamb, and continues :—

"I consented to his marrying one of my daughters, there having been a long and intimate friendship between them. But neither he nor I were so happy as to have them live long together ; for she died in childbed of her first child. He was so inconsolable at her loss, that I was afraid he would soon have followed her ; to prevent which, I desired his company here at my own house, that he might have some amusement and business, by assisting me in my cure during my illness.

" It was then, sir, I received the favour of yours, and let him see it for diversion ; more especially, because John Lyndal and he had been fellow-parishioners and schoolfellows at Wroot, and had no little kindness one for the other. I made no great reflection on the thing at first ; but, soon after, I found he had thought often upon it ; was very desirous to go to Georgia himself ; and wrote the enclosed letter to me on the subject. As I knew not of any person more proper for such an undertaking, I thought the least I could do was to send the letter to your honour, who would be so very proper a judge of the affair ; and, if you approve, I shall not be wanting in my addresses to my Lord Bishop of London, or any other, to forward the matter as far as possible.

" As for his character, I shall take it upon myself to say, he is a good scholar, a sound Christian, and a good liver. He has a very happy memory, especially for languages, and a judgment and intelligence not inferior. My eldest son, at Tiverton, has some knowledge of him ; my two others, his tutor at Lincoln, and my third, of Christ Church, have been long and intimately acquainted with him ; and, I doubt not, they will give him, at least, as just a character as I have done.

"And here I shall drop the matter till I have the honour of hearing again from you, ever remaining your honour's most sincere and most obliged friend and servant,

" SAMUEL WESLEY."

Samuel Wesley died within five months after the date of this application to Oglethorpe; his son-in-law, John White-lamb, for some unknown reason, did not go to Georgia; but his sons John and Charles set sail for the recently founded colony on October 14, 1735.

Did Whitelamb miss the way of Providence in not becoming a Georgian missionary? Perhaps he did. At all events, the remaining thirty-four years of his life seem to have been of comparatively small importance to his fellow-men. While the two Wesleys, his brothers-in-law, and Whitefield, were preaching everywhere, and, with Christian heroism, were braving the most infernal and brutish persecutions; while Clayton, in Manchester, was living the active life of a Church of England Ritualist, and Ingham, in Yorkshire, was performing the part of a useful evangelist; while Gambold was restraining Moravian follies, and Broughton was doing his utmost to disperse Bibles, and religious books and tracts ;—poor, bereaved Whitelamb seems to have sunk down into a disconsolate and nearly useless widowerhood, and to have spent,—*wasted*, we had almost said,—his dreary life among the unappreciative dolts, so graphically described by his deceased wife's sister—Mehetabel. It is true, he had the care of about three hundred souls ; but, with his natural ability and collegiate education, he might, in addition to fulfilling his parochial duties, have rendered other service to the Church of Christ, and to mankind at large. At all events, his venerable patron did not sleep away his probationary being as his son-in-law, John Whitelamb, did.

It is a significant fact, that, though Whitelamb lived at Wroot nearly forty years after Wesley began his itinerant career, and though the visits of the latter, to Epworth and the neighbourhood, were numerous, he never, excepting once, and that during his first evangelistic tour to the north of England, came to Wroot. He writes :—

"1742, Sunday, June 13. At seven I preached at Haxey, on, 'What must I do to be saved?' Thence I went to Wroot, of which, as well as

Epworth, my father was rector for several years. Mr. Whitelamb offering me the church, I preached, in the morning, on, 'Ask, and it shall be given you ;' in the afternoon, on the difference between the righteousness of the law and the righteousness of faith. But the church could not contain the people, many of whom came from far ; and, I trust, not in vain. At six, I preached in Epworth churchyard to a vast multitude gathered together from all parts, on the beginning of our Lord's Sermon on the Mount. I continued among them for near three hours, and yet we scarce knew how to part."

It ought to be said, that, Wesley had been at Epworth and in the neighbourhood for the last eight days. He had preached from his father's tombstone, from, " The kingdom of God is not meat and drink ; but righteousness, and peace, and joy in the Holy Ghost ;" and again, from, " By grace are ye saved through faith ; " and a third time from, " Unto him that worketh not, but believeth on Him that justifieth the ungodly, his faith is counted to him for righteousness ;" and a fourth, either from the tombstone or in the street, on Friday, the 11th of June, on, " Ezekiel's vision of the resurrection of the dry bones ; " and a fifth, on the day before he went to Wroot, from the same subject as he took at the afternoon service in Whitelamb's church. His visit had occasioned immense excitement. During the sermon, on Friday, "lamentation and great mourning were heard ; God bowing the hearts of the people, so that, on every side, as with one accord, they lifted up their voice and wept aloud ;" and, on Saturday, he writes :—

" While I was speaking several dropped down as dead; and such a cry was heard of sinners groaning for the righteousness of faith as almost drowned my voice. But many of these soon lifted up their heads with joy, and broke out into thanksgiving, being assured that they now had the desire of their soul—the forgiveness of their sins."

Whitelamb was present at one, at least, of these Epworth services ; and, like others, was deeply impressed with the preacher's doctrines ; but, strangely enough, seems not to have spoken to him. Two days afterwards, however, he wrote to Wesley, and this, probably, occasioned the visit to Wroot just mentioned. His letter was as follows :—

" *June* 11, 1742.

" DEAR BROTHER,—I saw you at Epworth, on Tuesday evening. Fain would I have spoken to you, but that I am quite at a loss how to address or behave. Your way of thinking is so extraordinary,[1] that, your presence creates an awe, as if you were an inhabitant of another world. God grant you and your followers may always have entire liberty of conscience ! Will you not allow others the same ? Indeed, I cannot think as you do, any more than I can help honouring and loving you.

"Dear sir, will you credit me ? I retain the highest veneration for you. The sight of you moves me strangely. My heart overflows with gratitude. I feel, in a higher degree, all that tenderness and yearning of bowels with which I am affected towards every branch of Mr. Wesley's family. I cannot refrain from tears when I reflect, 'This is the man, who, at Oxford, was more than a father to me. This is he whom I have there heard expound, or dispute publicly, or preach at St. Mary's, with such applause. And Oh that I. should ever add, whom I have lately heard preach at Epworth !'[2]

"I am quite forgot. None of the family ever honours me with line ! Have I been ungrateful ? I appeal to sister Patty ; I appeal to Mr. Ellison,[3] whether I have or no. I have been passionate, fickle, a fool, but I hope I shall never be *ungrateful.*

"Dear sir, is it in my power to serve or oblige you in any way ? Glad I should be, that, you would make use of me. God open all our eyes, and lead us into truth, whatever it be.

"JOHN WHITELAMB."[4]

This is a curious letter. It is evident, that, there was, at least, a partial estrangement between Whitelamb and the Wesley family. Correspondence had ceased ; and, even when Wesley visited Epworth, and Whitelamb was one of his hearers, they parted without speaking. Why was this ? White-lamb did not believe in Wesley's doctrines ; but that is hardly sufficient to account for such a fact. Perhaps the reason may be found in Whitelamb's own confession, that, he had "been passionate, fickle, and a fool," though it is impossible to tell to what such words referred. In the melancholy state of mind in which he obviously was, the epithets might be a severer condemnation of himself than his spirit and behaviour had merited. Be that as it may, though Whitelamb lived for

---

[1] Wesley's text on this occasion, was, " Unto him that worketh not," etc. ; " the great truth," he writes, " so little understood in what is called a Christian country." Whitelamb evidently understood it not.

[2] Wesley adds, " on my father's tombstone."

[3] The rich farmer, who married Wesley's sister Susannah,—a brutal fellow, who was reduced to poverty, and ultimately lived on alms, which Wesley obtained for him, through Mr. Ebenezer Blackwell. The Rector of Epworth used to speak of him as " the *wen* of my family."

[4] *Arminian Magazine,* 1778, p. 184.

twenty-seven years after this, and though, with undeniable sincerity, he professes great gratitude for the past kindness of the Wesley family, and ardent and affectionate admiration of Wesley himself, this was the winding up of their friendly intercourse. Wesley says, with what correctness we know not, that, at "this time, and for some years afterwards," Whitelamb "did not believe the Christian Revelation;" but whether Wesley meant, that, Whitelamb was a disbeliever in the Bible as a whole, or only in those doctrines of the Bible which Wesley and his friends were daily preaching, it is impossible to say. If he meant the former, we incline to think there must have been some mistake; for, unless Whitelamb were the most arrant knave, he must, in such a case, have relinquished his high office of the Christian ministry. If Wesley meant the latter, his words are too strong, and it was an injustice to Whitelamb's character and memory to insert them in the *Arminian Magazine.*

Wesley's and Whitelamb's intercourse, at Wroot, seems to have been friendly and pleasant; but allowing the Arch-Methodist to preach in the humble pulpit of the little church gave great offence, and perhaps this was *one* of the reasons why Wesley ceased to visit him. The following letter, written within three months after Wesley's visit, is full of interest, and furnishes additional evidence, that, the young widower had been guilty of serious follies, and, as a consequence, had been eschewed by the Wesley family. It was addressed to Wesley's brother Charles.

WROOT, *September* 2, 1742.

"DEAR BROTHER,—I must make bold to give you that title. I was informed, that, you have entertained so hard an opinion of me as scarcely to hear me named with patience. This made me fear, the sight of me would not be agreeable. However, I have ventured to write, lest I should confirm that opinion by a behaviour that seems to show neglect and ingratitude.

"It is probably not in my power to alter your sentiments of me; but there is a day, which you and I expect, when it will appear, that, J. Whitelamb was never either ungrateful, or vicious; though, by the heat of youthful blood, and the want of experience of the world, he has been betrayed into very great follies.

"I had the happiness and honour (for I account it both) of seeing and conversing with my brother John, when he was last over. He behaved to me truly like himself. I found in him, what I have always experienced heretofore, the gentleman, the friend, the brother, the Christian.

"Dear sir, command me in anything, whereby I can show my regard to you, or the family; provided conscience be not concerned. Alas! that I should be forced to distinguish Mr. Wesley, from the preacher! My brother John demanded[1] my pulpit. By the authority of a tutor, and one to whom I have so great obligations, he has the disposal of whatever is mine. However, I find, by the outcry it caused, that it gives very great offence. I know not what measures may be taken against me, this triennial visitation; nor am I so solicitous about it, as I am uneasy that the interest of religion and the public peace should, in the least, suffer by my means.

"For, to be frank, I cannot but look upon your doctrines as of ill consequence. Consequence, I say; for, take them nakedly in themselves, and nothing seems more innocent, nay, good and holy. Suppose we grant, that, in you and the rest of the leaders, who are men of sense and discernment, what is called the seal and testimony of the Spirit, is something real; yet, I have great reason to think, that, in the generality of your followers, it is merely the effect of a heated fancy.

"So much for dispute; and I beg you will forgive me it. Oh that we could so have met, as that there should have been no contention, but in loving one another!

"I promised my tutor to write to him. Since then, I have had a dangerous illness. I am scarce well recovered; and, besides, it has left behind such a drowsy disposition, as I have not yet had resolution to conquer. I hope to fulfil my promise shortly. I have endeavoured to lay myself quite open to truth; and this (with shame I ought to say it) has cost me some pains. My dear mother Wesley, and poor sister Kezzy are gone.[2] God of the spirits of all flesh, grant us all to meet in a happy eternity!

"Dear brother, are you in earnest in what you teach? I cannot persuade any of my friends that you are. If you be, give me your prayers. If not, do not, as you have formerly done, ridicule me for being too religious. You little thought, when you laughed at me, for being shocked at your gay discourse, that you yourself should come to maintain the very notions which I had then.

"I am, your obliged and most affectionate brother,

"JOHN WHITELAMB."[3]

The last sentence of this letter is significant. John Whitelamb was religious before Charles Wesley was. When Charles was elected to Christ Church, in 1726, he was a sprightly,

---

[1] Wesley says, Whitelamb *offered* it.

[2] Mrs. Wesley died about six weeks before this letter was written. Kezziah Wesley died March 9, 1741, "full of thankfulness, resignation, and love."

[3] *Arminian Magazine*, 1778, p. 186.

rollicking young man, with more genius than grace. In 1728, or 1729, "he began to attend the weekly sacrament, and induced two or three other students to attend with him;" and this was really the beginning of the Methodist movement. It is a curious fact, that, this was the very time when Whitelamb went to Oxford. Was John Whitelamb, a young man of twenty-one, fresh from the religious atmosphere of the Epworth rectory, the means of reforming the sprightly Charles Wesley; and, in that indirect way, the means of Methodism being started? The question has never before been put; and it is one which, perhaps, cannot, with certainty, be answered.

Of the last twenty-seven years of Whitelamb's life we know nothing. More than a quarter of a century ago, an aged female, at Wroot, had a distinct recollection of him, and described him "as a person of retiring habits, and fond of solitude." She was present when he was suddenly seized, while on his way to perform divine service at the church, with the illness which shortly terminated in his death; and spoke of his funeral as having been attended by a considerable number of clergymen, who thus paid their last tribute of respect to a departed friend." [1]

Whitelamb died in the month of July, 1769; and, three months afterwards, Wesley wrote to Mrs. Woodhouse, of Epworth, as follows :—

"1769, October 4. How long is it since Mr. Whitelamb died? What disease did he die of? Did he lie ill for any time? Do you know any circumstances preceding or attending his death? Oh, why did he not die forty years ago, while he knew in whom he believed? Unsearchable are the counsels of God, and His ways past finding out.

"JOHN WESLEY." [2]

Wesley evidently knew nothing of the circumstances of Whitelamb's death; and his contrast in reference to the religious state of the deceased rector of Wroot "forty years ago" appears to be hardly generous. "Forty years ago" Methodism was just beginning; and it was not until

---

[1] *Methodist Magazine*, 1845, p. 151.
[2] Clarke's Wesley Family, vol. ii., p. 280.

nine years afterwards, that, Wesley himself attained the knowledge of being saved, not by good works, but, by faith in Christ.

In Wroot churchyard, a small stone, about two feet long and one foot broad, bears the following inscription :—

"In memory of John Whitelamb, Rector of this Parish thirty-five years. Buried 29th of July, 1769, aged 62 years. Worthy of imitation. This at the cost of Francis Wood, Esq., 1772."

REV. WESTLEY HALL.

IT is far from pleasant to conclude a book in darkness and in pollution ; but, in the present case, it cannot be avoided. In most flocks, there is, at least, one objectionable sheep ; and few are the brotherhoods without offenders. Among the patriarchs, Reuben, by sin, forfeited the rights of primogeniture and the priesthood ; and, among the apostles, Judas Iscariot was an infamous betrayer. History not only supplies examples, but hoists beacons. The former are useful, and the latter not unneeded. The story of the Oxford Methodists cannot be fully told without a reference to the sin and shame of Westley Hall. The subject is a nauseous one; but, it may help to enforce the apostolic admonition, founded upon the same kind of historic facts,—"Wherefore, let him that thinketh he standeth take heed lest he fall."

Of the origin of Westley Hall and his early life, we are ignorant.

At Lincoln College, Oxford, he was one of Wesley's pupils, and was a man of agreeable person, pleasing manners, and good property. The time of his joining the Methodist brotherhood is not known ; but Susanna Wesley, writing to her son John, on October 25, 1732, observes :—

"I heartily join with your small Society in all their pious and charitable actions, which are intended for God's glory ; and am glad to hear that Mr. Clayton and Mr. Hall have met with desired success. You do well to wait on the Bishop ; though, if he be a good man, I cannot think it in the power of any one to prejudice him against you. Your arguments against horse-races do certainly conclude against masquerades, balls, plays, operas, and all such light and vain diversions, which, whether the gay people of the world will own it or no, do strongly confirm and strengthen the lust of the flesh, the lust of the eye, and the pride of life ; all of which we must renounce, or renounce our God and hope of eternal salvation. I will not say, it is impossible for a person to have any sense of religion, who frequents those vile assemblies ; but I never, throughout the course of my long life, knew so much as one serious Christian that did ; nor can I see how a lover of God can have any relish for such vain amusements."[1]

Hall seems to have been ordained as early as the year 1734. Hence, in another letter, dated March 30, 1734, Wesley's mother, after referring to the religious practices of the Oxford Methodists and other matters, says,—

" I cannot think Mr. Hall does well in refusing an opportunity of doing so much service to religion, as he certainly might do, if he accepted the living he is about to refuse. Surely, there never was more need of orthodox, sober divines in our Lord's vineyard, than there is now ; and why a man of his extraordinary piety, and love to souls, should decline the service in this critical juncture, I cannot conceive. But this is none of my business."[2]

These extracts furnish the reader with a glimpse of Hall at Oxford. Wesley himself testifies that, while at the University, Hall "was holy and unblamable in all manner of conversation." In what his "*extraordinary* piety " consisted, we are not informed ; but it is a curious fact, that, he, of all men, made ostentatious professions of his having the gift mentioned by the Divine Redeemer (Matt. xix. 10–12).[3] This reads oddly in connection with the following extract from one of Wesley's letters :—

" 1784, August 31. Many years ago, Mr. Hall, then strong in faith, believed God called him to marry my youngest sister. He told her so. She fully believed him, and none could convince one or the other to the contrary. I talked with her about it; but she had ' so often made it matter of prayer, that, she could not be deceived.' In a week, he dropped her, courted her elder sister, and, as soon as was convenient, married her."[4]

What is the history of this strange transaction ? Martha Wesley was born in 1707 ; Kezziah, her sister, in 1710.

---

[1] Clarke's Wesley Family, vol. ii., p. 102.
[2] *Methodist Magazine*, 1845, p. 37.
[3] Wesley's Works, vol. ii., p. 75.   [4] Ibid., vol. xii., p. 453.

About the year 1734, Westley Hall met Martha at her uncle's house in London, proposed to marry her, and, without the knowledge of her parents, or her brothers, was accepted. He then accompanied John and Charles to Epworth, and there saw Kezziah, grew enamoured of her, courted, and obtained her consent, and that of the family in general, to marry him ; all of them being ignorant of his pre-engagement with Martha. Returning to London, Hall renewed his addresses to " poor Patty," who was completely unconscious of what had transpired at Epworth. She wrote to her mother, stating, that for some time past, she had been betrothed to Hall. Kezziah, on learning this, renounced all claim to him. The mother wrote to Martha, assuring her, "that, if she obtained the consent of her uncle, there was no obstacle" to the marriage. The uncle raised no objection ; gave Martha a dowry of £500 ; and the wedding was completed.

Such, in outline, is the account given by Dr. Adam Clarke. It is not without difficulties. Knowing all the facts, Mrs. Wesley's approbation is unaccountable, except on the ground, that, now and for years afterwards, she held a high opinion of Hall's piety and character. Charles Wesley, at the time, was excessively indignant, and wrote to Martha a poetical epistle full of terrible invective ; and yet, soon afterwards, when the Wesleys were about to embark for Georgia, it was arranged that Hall should attend them, indicating, that, some sort of a reconciliation had taken place between Charles and Hall. The following are selections from Charles's poem :—

> "When he, who long in virtue's paths had trod,
> Deaf to the voice of conscience and of God,
> Drops the fair mask, proves traitor to his vow,
> And thou the temptress, and the tempted thou,—
> Prepare thee then to meet the infernal war,
> And dare beyond what woman knows to dare ;
> Guard each avenue to thy fluttering heart,
> And act the sister's and the Christian's part."
>
> *   *   *   *   *   *
>
> Trembling, I hear his horrid vows renewed,
> I see him come, by *Delia's* groans pursued.
> Poor injured Delia ! all her groans are vain ;
> Or he denies, or, listening, mocks her pain.
> What, though her eyes with ceaseless tears o'erflow,
> Her bosom heave with agonizing woe ;

What, though the horror of his falsehood near
Tear up her faith, and plunge her in despair;
Yet can he think (so blind to heaven's decree,
And the sure fate of cursed apostasy),
Soon as he tells the secret of his breast,
And puts the angel off—and stands confessed,
When love, and grief, and shame, and anguish meet,
To make his crimes and *Delia's* wrongs complete,
That, then the injured maid will cease to grieve,
Behold him in a sister's arms, and live !
Mistaken wretch—by thy unkindness hurled
From ease, from love, from thee, and from the world;
Soon must she land on that immortal shore,
Where falsehood never can torment her more :
There all her sufferings and her sorrows cease,
Nor saints turn devils there to vex her peace !"

Poor jilted Kezziah took the matter more calmly. In a letter to her brother John, dated June 16, 1734, not long before Martha's marriage, she observed,—

"I intended not to write till I could give you an account of Mr. Hall's affair; but it is needless, because, I believe, he won't do anything without your approbation. I am entirely of your opinion, that, we ought to 'endeavour after perfect resignation'; and I have learned to practise this duty in one particular, which, I think, is of the greatest importance in life, namely, marriage. I am as indifferent as it is lawful for any person to be, whether I ever change my state or not; because, I think a single life is the more excellent way; and there are also several reasons why I rather desire to continue as I am. One is, because, I desire to be entirely disengaged from the world; but the chief is, I am so well apprized of the great duty a wife owes to her husband, that, I think it is almost impossible she should ever discharge it as she ought. But I can scarce say, I have the liberty of choosing: for my relations are continually soliciting me to marry. I shall endeavour to be as resigned and cheerful as possible to whatever God is pleased to ordain for me."

Comment on the above facts would not be difficult; but the reader must form his own opinion on all the parties concerned in this mournful business. We only add a copy of verses printed in the *Gentleman's Magazine*, for September, 1735, p. 551,—verses portraying a nuptial life, the very opposite of that which awaited the unfortunately wedded couple.

"ON THE MARRIAGE OF MR. WESTLEY HALL TO MISS PATTY WESLEY.

" Hymen, light thy purest flame,
  Every sacred rite prepare;
Never to thy altar came
  A more pious, faithful pair.

" Thee, dispensing mighty pleasure,
  Rashly sensual minds invoke;
Only those partake thy treasure
  Paired in Virtue's easy yoke.

" Such are *Hall* and *Wesley* joining,
  Kindred souls with plighting hands,
Each to each entire resigning,
  One become by nuptial bands.

" Happy union, which destroys
  Half the ills of life below;
But the current of our joys
  Makes with double vigour flow.

" Sympathising friends abate
  The severer strokes of fate;
Happy hours still happier prove
  When they smile on those we love.

" Joys to vulgar minds unknown
  Shall their daily converse crown;
Easy slumbers, pure delights,
  Bless their ever peaceful nights.

" Oh Lucina, sacred power,
  Here employ thy grateful care;
Smiling on the genial hour,
  Give an offspring wise and fair!

" That, when the zealous sire shall charm no more
Th' attentive audience with his sacred lore,
Those lips in silence closed, whose heavenly skill
Could raptures with persuasive words instil;
A *son* may in the important work engage,
And with his precepts mend the future age:
That, when the accomplished mother, snatched by fate,
No more shall grace the matrimonial state;
No more exhibit, in her virtuous life,
The bright exemplar of a perfect wife;
A *daughter*, blest with each maternal grace,
May shine the pattern of the female race!"

As already related (see pp. 65–67), it was fully arranged, that, a month after the appearance of this epithalamium, Westley Hall and his newly-wedded wife should accompany the Wesleys to Georgia; and, that, at the last moment, Hall declined to go, on the ground, that, his uncle and his mother had engaged to obtain for him an English benefice. The man, in more respects than one, was double-minded. In unstableness, as well as incontinency, he was Reuben *redivivus*.

The church appointment, secured for Hall, seems to have been the office of curate, at Wootton-Rivers, a small village of about four hundred inhabitants, in the county of Wilts. Here he took, not only his wife, but, strangely enough, Kezziah Wesley, with whose affections he had so basely trifled. The two sisters were evidently reconciled; but their brother Samuel, a keen judge of character, regarded Hall with feelings of suspicion and dislike. Hence the following extract from one of Samuel's letters, dated, "Blundell's School, Tiverton, Devon, September 29, 1736," and addressed to his brother Charles in Georgia :—

"Brother Hall's is a black story. There was no great likelihood of his being a favourite with me: his tongue is too smooth for my roughness, and rather inclines me to suspect than believe. Indeed, I little suspected the horrid truth; but, finding him on the reserve, I thought, he was something like Rivington, and feared me as a jester; which is a sure sign either of guilt on the one hand, or pride on the other. It is certainly true of that marriage; it will not, and it cannot come to good. He is now at a curacy in Wiltshire, near Marlborough. I have no correspondence with Kez.: I did design it after reading yours; but the hearing, that, she is gone to live with Patty and her husband made me drop my design."

It was certainly a strange,—an almost unaccountable thing, for Kezziah Wesley to become domiciled with such a man. It is true, her venerable father had died just about the time of the ill-fated marriage, leaving both her mother and herself without a home; but the mother had found a welcome in the house of her son Samuel; who was also wishful to have Kezziah beneath his roof, if his brother John would continue to allow her £50 a year.[1] Why, then, did she go to Westley

---

[1] Clarke's Wesley Family, vol. ii., p. 184.

Hall's?   Samuel Wesley strongly disapproved of this; and
so also did his brother Charles.   Hence the following, from
Charles's Journal, written only three days after his return
from Georgia :—

> "1736, December 6.   I spent an hour at my uncle's, equally welcome
> and unexpected.   They informed me, my brother Hall was gone to a
> curacy, very melancholy, and impatient at the mention of Georgia; and
> that my sister Kezzy was gone to live with him.
> "Serpentes avibus geminentur, tigribus agnæ."

Hall was a hawk among the doves of the Wesley family.
There was dislike, and there was also a reasonable suspicion.
A sort of truce existed; but it was hollow and uncertain.
Samuel Wesley regarded Hall as a smooth-tongued hypo-
crite, and evidently thought his sister Kezziah had made a
great mistake in making the house of Hall her domicile.
Charles Wesley was equally dissatisfied, as is evident from
his Latin quotation; and, yet, ten weeks after writing thus,
he went to Hall's himself, as a friendly visitor, and spent a
week with the reverend *coquet*, and with his "sisters, Patt
and Kez."[1]   Indeed, a few months afterwards, Mrs. Wesley,
the widow, who had taken up her residence at the house of
her son Samuel, at Tiverton, removed to Hall's at Wootton-
Rivers, where, on August 5, 1737, she wrote :—

> "Mr. Hall and his wife are very good to me.   He behaves like a
> gentleman and a Christian; and my daughter with as much duty and
> tenderness as can be expressed."[2]

Shortly after this, Westley Hall seems to have removed to
Salisbury.   Hence the following entry in Charles Wesley's
Journal :—

> "1737, December 29.   I supped in Salisbury, at my brother Hall's."

In 1739, he came to London.   In a letter, to her son
Samuel, dated "March 8, 1739, Mrs. Wesley writes :—

> "I have been informed, that, Mr. Hall intends to remove his family to
> London, hath taken a house, and I must (if it please God I live) go with
> them."[3]

---

[1] C. Wesley's Journal, vol. i., p. 69.
[2] Clarke's Wesley Family, vol. ii., p. 106.   [3] Ibid., p. 110.

Here he associated with Wesley and his brother, and, like them, was soon involved in the Moravian squabbles. A "famous French Prophetess," of the name of Lavington, sprang up among them, who, at one of their meetings, on June 7, 1739, asked, "Can a man attain perfection here?" Charles Wesley answered, "No." The Prophetess began groaning. Charles turned and said, "If you have anything to speak, speak it." She lifted up her voice, like the lady on the tripod, and cried out vehemently, "Look for perfection; I say, absolute perfection!" Charles writes :—

"I was minded to rebuke her; but God gave me uncommon recollection, and command of spirit, so that, I sat quiet, and replied not. I offered, at last, to sing, which she allowed, but did not join. Bray pressed me to stay, and hear her pray. They knelt; I stood. She prayed most pompously. I durst not say, Amen. She concluded with a horrible, hellish laugh; and showed violent displeasure against our baptized Quaker, saying, 'God had showed her, He would destroy all outward things."

On the three following days, Charles Wesley took the depositions of certain parties, "concerning her lewd life and conversation;" read the account to the Society; and warned his friends against her. On June 12th, at another of their meetings, she again appeared. Charles remarks :—

"She flew upon us like a tigress; tried to outface me; and insisted, that, she was immediately inspired. I prayed. She cried, 'The devil was in me. I was a fool, a blockhead, a blind leader of the blind.' She roared outrageously; said, it was the lion in her. (True; but not the Lion of Judah.) She *would* come to the Society in spite of me: if not, they would all go down. I asked, 'Who is on God's side? Who for the old Prophets rather than the new? Let them follow me.' They followed me into the preaching room. I prayed, and expounded the lesson with extraordinary power."

The next day, the two Wesleys, with their brother-in-law, Westley Hall, met the Society, and discussed "the Prophetess's affair." Charles Wesley says,—

"Bray and Bowers were much humbled. All agreed to disown the prophetess. Brother Hall proposed expelling Shaw and Wolf. We consented, *nem. con.*, that, their names should be erased out of the Society-book, because they disowned themselves members of the Church of England."

Thus we find Westley Hall employed in silencing the profanities of a half-crazed woman, and expelling men from a religious society, because they would not acknowledge themselves to be members of the Established Church.

It is not known in what church Hall officiated during his residence in London; but there is one circumstance connected with his ministry while here, too interesting to be omitted. At this period, the great themes of the preaching and of the conversation of Wesley and his brother were their newly found doctrines of Justification by Faith only, the Witness of the Spirit, and the New Birth. For many a long year, Susannah Wesley had been one of the most Christian women then living; but her sons' doctrine of the Witness of the Spirit was one of which she had scarcely ever heard. Now, however, at the age of seventy, and only three years before her death, she obtained the blessing for herself, and obtained it under the ministry of Westley Hall. Wesley writes :—

"1739, September 3. I talked largely with my mother, who told me, that, till a short time since, she had scarce heard such a thing mentioned as the having God's Spirit bearing witness with our spirit: much less did she imagine, that, this was the common privilege of all true believers. 'Therefore,' said she, 'I never durst ask it for myself. But two or three weeks ago, while my son Hall was pronouncing those words, in delivering the cup to me,—The blood of our Lord Jesus Christ, which was given for thee,—the words struck my heart, and I knew, God, for Christ's sake, had forgiven me all my sins.'"

Westley Hall, though a clergyman of the Established Church, continued to attend the Moravian meetings; and, to his credit, it ought to be recorded, that, for a time at least, he withstood the Moravian heresies. Charles Wesley writes :—

"1740, May 14. I found Mr. Hall at Fetter Lane, asking them, whether they would try their spirits by the Word, or the Word by their spirits. I enforced the question, which they strove to evade. Rabbi Hutton[1] forbade their answering me. I warned the few remaining brethren to beware of the leaven of *stillness;* showed them the delusion of those who had cast off the ordinances, and confined the faith to *themselves only;* I foretold the dreadful consequences of their enthusiasm; set the case of Gregor before their eyes; besought, entreated, conjured them not to renounce the means, or deny the Lord that bought them; read a letter

---

[1] James Hutton, the publisher,—an early friend of the Wesleys, and one of the principal Moravians in England.

from one who had been strongly tempted to leave off the Sacrament, but, in receiving, was powerfully convinced that her dissuader was the devil. Hodges, Hall, and Howel Harris confirmed my words. Others were hereby emboldened to bear their testimony to the divine ordinances. By the strength of the Lord, we have stood between the living and the dead; and the plague, we trust, is stayed."

Fickleness was one of Westley Hall's characteristic faults. Within a twelvemonth after this resistance of the Moravian *stillness*, he himself adopted it, and argued against the two Wesleys, that, "silent prayer, and quiet waiting for God, was the only possible way to attain living, saving faith." [1]

Still, Hall and the Wesley brothers continued to be on friendly terms; so much so, that, when Whitefield and Wesley quarrelled respecting the doctrine of "Free Grace," and Whitefield declared his intention to attack Wesley and his brother wherever he went, Westley Hall assumed the office of peace-maker, waited upon Whitefield, and reminded him of a promise, he had made, " that, whatever his private opinion was, he would never publicly preach against " them.[2] This, however, was not of long duration. At the close of 1739, Wesley took possession of "The Foundry," which he fitted up as a place for preaching and the meetings of his London Society. Here, he, also, opened a day-school for the children of the poor; and, over the band-room, there were apartments, occupied by his mother and himself. Here, the Stewards and Leaders met to receive and distribute money, and to manage the general affairs of the London Methodists. Westley Hall seems to have held some sort of office at the Foundry; and he began, during Wesley's absence in the north, to be treacherous to Wesley himself, as, seven years before, he had been to Wesley's sister Kezziah. Wesley writes :—

" 1742, Sunday, October 31. Several of the leaders desired to have an hour's conversation with me. I found, they were greatly perplexed about 'want of management, ill-husbandry, encouraging idleness, improper distribution of money,' 'being imposed upon by fair pretences,' and 'men who talked well, but had no grace in their hearts.' I asked, who those

---

[1] Wesley's Works, vol. i., p. 279.
[2] Ibid., p. 286.

men were; but that they could not tell. Who encouraged idleness; when and how; what money had been improperly distributed; by whom, and to whom; in what instances I had been imposed upon (as I presumed they meant *me*); and what were the particulars of that ill-husbandry and mismanagement of which they complained. They stared at one another as men in amaze. I began to be amazed too, not being able to imagine what was the matter, till one dropped a word, by which all came out. They had been talking with Mr. Hall, who had started so many objections against all I said or did, that, they were in the utmost consternation, till the fire thus broke out, which then at once vanished away."

Wesley's mother had died in the Foundry three months previous to this disclosure; and Wesley had invited Hall and his wife (who had been bereaved of several children) to take up their residence in his own humble dwelling. The following letter, addressed to Mrs. Hall, refers to this and other matters.

"NEWCASTLE-UPON-TYNE, *Nov.* 17, 1742.

"DEAR SISTER,—I believe the death of your children is a great instance of the goodness of God towards you. You have often mentioned to me how much of your time they took up. Now that time is restored to you, and you have nothing to do but to serve the Lord without carefulness and without distraction, till you are sanctified in body, soul, and spirit.

' As soon as I saw Mr. Hall, I invited him to stay at the Foundry; but he desired I would have him excused. There is a strange inconsistency in his tempers and sentiments with regard to me. The *still brethren*[1] have gradually infused into him as much as they could of their own contempt of me and my brother, and dislike of our whole method of proceeding, which is as different from theirs as light from darkness. Nay, they have blunderingly taught him to find fault even with my economy and want of management both of my family and society. Whereas, I know this is the peculiar talent which God has given me, wherein (by His grace) I am not behind the very chiefest of them. Notwithstanding this, there remains in him something of his old regard for me, which he had at Oxford; and, by-and-by, it will prevail. He will find out these wretched men, and the clouds will flee away.

"My belief is, that, the present design of God, is to visit the poor desolate Church of England; and, that, therefore, neither deluded Mr. Gambold, nor any who leave it, will prosper. O pray for the peace of Jerusalem. 'They shall prosper that love thee.'

"Mr. Hall has paid me for the books. I don't want any money of you;

---

[1] The Moravians.

your love is sufficient. But write, as often and as largely as you can, to your affectionate friend and brother,

" JOHN WESLEY." [1]

Not long after this, "poor Moravianized Mr. Hall," as Charles Wesley calls him, seems to have removed to Salisbury, and there to have occupied a chapel, and set up a Society of his own, which his wife refused to join. Charles Wesley writes :—

" 1743, August 11. From ten to two, I got with my sister Hall in Salisbury. She stands alone. Every soul of her husband's Society has forsaken the ordinances of God; for which reason she refuses to belong to it."

Westley Hall was now an avowed Dissenter. His wife objected to leave the Church of her venerable father. Her husband's disciples jeered her ; and, before long, her husband himself committed against her the most cruel wrongs. Another extract from Charles Wesley's Journal will be useful. On his way from London to Bristol, he wrote :—

" 1745, June 19. Three miles on this side Salisbury, a *still* sister came out to meet, and try her skill upon, me. But, alas ! it was labour lost ! I knew the *happy sinner*, and all her paces. I found my sister as a rock in the midst of waves. Mr. Hall's Society had all left the Church, and mocked and persecuted her for not leaving it. Many pressed me to preach ; but I answered them, ' My heart was not *free* to it.' At four, I set out with my sister ; and reached Bristol in the afternoon of the next day."

Six months after this, Hall, not satisfied with his dissenting success at Salisbury, used his utmost endeavours to make converts of the two Wesley brothers. To John Wesley he wrote a long letter, earnestly pressing him and his brother "to renounce the Church of England." Hall's letter is lost ; but Wesley's answer exists, and is too important to be omitted. It exhibits the ground taken by Hall, and shows the position and difficulties of some, at least, of the Oxford Methodists.

" *December* 30, 1745.

" DEAR BROTHER,—Now you act the part of a friend. It has long been our desire, that you would speak freely. And we will do the same. What we know not yet, may God reveal to us !

---

[1] Clarke's Wesley Family, vol. ii., p. 338.

"You think, First, that, we undertake to *defend* some things, which are not *defensible* by the *Word of God.* You instance three: on each of which we will explain ourselves as clearly as we can.

" 1. 'That, the *validity* of our *ministry* depends on a *succession* supposed to be from the Apostles, and a *commission* derived from the Pope of *Rome,* and his *successors* or *dependents.*'

" We believe, it would not be right for us to *administer,* either Baptism or the Lord's Supper, unless we had a *commission* so to do from those Bishops, whom we apprehend to be in a *succession* from the Apostles. And, yet, we allow, these Bishops are the successors of those, who are dependent on the Bishop of *Rome.* But, we would be glad to know, on what reasons you believe this to be inconsistent with the Word of God.

"2. 'That, there is an *outward Priesthood,* and consequently an *outward Sacrifice,* ordained and offered by the Bishop of *Rome,* and his *successors* or *dependents,* in the Church of *England,* as *vicars* and vicegerents of Christ.'

"We believe there is and always was, in *every* Christian Church (whether dependent on the Bishop of *Rome* or not) an *outward Priesthood* ordained by Jesus Christ, and an *outward Sacrifice* offered therein, by men authorized to act, as *Ambassadors of Christ, and Stewards of the mysteries of God.* On what grounds do you believe, that, Christ has abolished that *Priesthood or Sacrifice ?*

"3. ' That, this *Papal Hierarchy* and *Prelacy,* which still continues in the Church of England, is of *Apostolical Institution,* and authorized thereby; though not by the *written Word.*'

"We believe, that, the threefold order of ministers, (which you seem to mean by *Papal Hierarchy* and *Prelacy,*) is not only authorized by its *Apostolical Institution,* but also by the *written Word.* Yet, we are willing to hear and weigh whatever reasons induce you to believe to the contrary.

"You think, Secondly, ' That, we ourselves give up some things as *indefensible,* which are defended by the same law and *authority,* that establish the things above mentioned: such as are many of the *Laws, Customs,* and *Practices* of the *Ecclesiastical Courts.*'

"We allow, 1. That, those *Laws, Customs,* and *Practices* are really *indefensible ;* 2. That, there are Acts of Parliament, in *defence* of them; and also of the threefold order. But, will you show us, how it follows, either, 1. that, those things and these stand or fall together? Or, 2. that, we cannot *sincerely plead for* the one, though we *give up* the other? Do you not here quite overlook one circumstance, which might be a key to our whole behaviour? Namely, that, we no more look upon those *filthy abuses,* which *adhere* to our Church, as *parts* of the building; than we look upon any *filth* which may *adhere* to the walls of *Westminster Abbey,* as a part of that structure.

"You think, Thirdly, ' That, there are other things which we *defend* and *practise,* in *open contradiction* to the *Orders* of the Church of *England.* And this you judge to be a *just exception* against the *sincerity* of our *professions* to adhere to it.'

"Compare what we *profess* with what we *practise*, and you will possibly be of another judgment. We profess, 1. That, we will obey all the laws of that Church, (such we allow the Rubrics to be, but not the Customs of the Ecclesiastical Courts,) so far as we can with a safe conscience. 2. That, we will obey, with the same restriction, the Bishops, as executors of those *laws*. But their bare *will*, distinct from those *laws*, we do not *profess* to obey at all. Now point out, What is there in our *practice*, which is an *open contradiction* to these *professions ?*

"Is *Field-Preaching ?* Not at all. It is contrary to no law, which we *profess* to obey.

"The allowing *Lay-Preachers ?* We are not clear, that, this is contrary to any *such law*. But, if it is, this is one of the exempt cases; one wherein we cannot obey with a safe conscience. Therefore, (be it right or wrong on other accounts,) it is however no just exception against our sincerity.

"The *Rules* and *Directions* given to our *Societies ?* which, you say, is a discipline *utterly forbidden* by the *Bishops*. When and where did any Bishop *forbid* this ? And if any did, by what *law ?* We know not either the man who ever *did* forbid, or the law by which he *could* forbid it.

"The allowing *persons* (for we require none) to *communicate* at the chapel, in contradiction, (you think,) to *all those Rubrics*, which require *all* to attend *always*, on their own *parish* church and *pastor*, and to receive *only* at his table ?

"Which Rubrics are those ? We cannot find them. And, till these are produced, all that is so frequently said of *parochial* unity, etc., is merely *gratis dictum*. Consequently, neither is this any just exception against the sincerity of any of our professions.

"JOHN WESLEY."[1]

This long, but sententiously expressed letter is of considerable importance. It contains the arguments employed by Hall to induce Wesley and his brother to renounce their connection with the Church of England; and it shows, that, notwithstanding the novel steps that Wesley had taken during the last half a dozen years, he still, in some respects, belonged to the High-Church clergy, and believed in the popish figment of apostolical succession, and could talk of the "*outward Sacrifice*" offered in the Church.

Hall failed to convert Wesley to his Dissenting principles ; and equally failed to persuade him to abandon out-door preaching, the employment of lay-evangelists, and the administration of the sacraments in unconsecrated chapels. The two old friends were not yet finally separated ; but they

---

[1] Wesley's Journal, 1st edition.

had no confidence in each other.　A few months after the date of the above letter, Wesley wrote as follows :—

"1746.　July 20.　I set out for Salisbury, where, to my utter amazement, Mr. Hall desired me to preach.　Was his motive only, to grace his own cause?　Or rather, was this the last gasp of expiring love?"

The last gasp of expiring love it proved.　In a little more than a year afterwards, Hall infamously deserted his wife and family.　From a letter, published in the *Gentleman's Magazine*, and dated " Salisbury,- October 30, 1747," we learn, that, " by an uncommon appearance of sanctity, joined with indefatigable labour in field and house preaching," he had drawn " multitudes of the meaner sort, both of Dissenters and the Established Church, to attend him.　And, though he had continually advanced the grossest absurdities, both in his preaching and writings,[1] yet, he so bewitched his followers, that, his words had greater weight with them than the words of Christ and His Apostles."　The writer continues,—

" Last Wednesday, he took formal leave of his corrupted flock, and had the impudence to justify his infamous conduct from the case of Elkanah, (1 Sam. i. 1, 2), which he largely expounded.　On Friday morning, he set out for London, having first stripped his wife, (a virtuous woman by whom he has had several children,) of all her childbed linen, and whatever he could readily convert into money, leaving her in the deepest distress.　The fire of jealousy has broken out in many families, where *wives* or *daughters* were his followers."

At the time of this disgraceful occurrence, Charles Wesley was in Ireland ; but John, with as little delay as possible, hastened to the desolate home of his forsaken sister, where he wrote :—

" From the concurrent account of many witnesses, who spoke no more than they personally knew, I now learned as much as is hitherto brought to light concerning the fall of poor Mr. Hall.　Twelve years ago, he was, without all question, filled with faith and the love of God.　He was a pattern of humility, meekness, seriousness, and, above all, of self-

---

[1] It is difficult to say what is meant by the word " writings."　Does it refer to some newspaper correspondence?　Or to published sermons, tracts, or pamphlets?　I have never met with anything published by Westley Hall himself; or heard of anything except a poetical epistle to his son, mentioned hereafter; and his sermon, preached at Salisbury, in defence of polygamy.

denial; so that, in all England, I knew not his fellow. It were easy to point out the several steps, whereby he fell from his steadfastness; even till he fell into a course of adultery, yea, and avowed it in the face of the sun!"

Wesley wrote to the miserable delinquent the following long, faithful, and Christian letter, in which "the several steps, whereby he fell from his steadfastness" are enumerated.

"LONDON, *December* 22, 1747.

"DEAR BROTHER,—1. When you were at Oxford with me, fourteen or fifteen years ago, you were holy and unblamable in all manner of conversation. I greatly rejoiced in the grace of God, which was given unto you, which was often a blessing to my own soul. Yet, even then, you had frequently starts of thought, which were not of God, though they at first appeared so to be. But you were humble and teachable: you were easily convinced, and those imaginations vanished away.

"2. More than twelve years ago, you told me, God had revealed it to you, that you should marry my youngest sister. I was much surprised, being well assured that you were able to receive our Lord's saying, (so you had continually testified,) and to be an 'eunuch for the kingdom of heaven's sake.' But, you vehemently affirmed, the thing was of God; you were certain it was His will. God had made it plain to you, that, you must marry, and, that, she was the very person. You asked, and gained her consent, and fixed the circumstances relating thereto.

"3. Hence, I date your fall. Here were several faults in one. You leaned altogether to your own understanding, not consulting either me, who was then the guide of your soul, or the parents of your intended wife, till you had settled the whole affair. And while you followed the voice of nature, you said it was the voice of God.

"4. In a few days, you had a counter revelation, that, you were not to marry her, but her sister. This last error was far worse than the first. But, you were now quite above conviction. So, in spite of her poor, astonished parent, of her brothers, of all your vows and promises, you shortly after jilted the younger, and married the elder sister. The other, who had honoured you as an angel from heaven, and still loved you much too well, (for you had stolen her heart from the God of her youth,) refused to be comforted. She fell into a lingering illness, which terminated in her death. And doth not her blood still cry unto God from the earth? Surely it is upon *your* head.

"5. Till this time, you were a pattern of lowliness, meekness, serious-ness, and continual advertence to the presence of God; and, above all, of self-denial of every kind, and of suffering all things with joyfulness. But there was now a worm at the root of the gourd. Yet, it did not presently wither away; but, for two years or more, after your marriage, you behaved nearly the same as before.

"Then anger and surliness began to appear, particularly toward your wife. But it was not long before you were sensible of this, and you seemed to have conquered it.

"6. You went up to London ten years ago. After this, you began to speak on any head; not with your usual diffidence and self-abasement, but with a kind of confidence in your own judgment, and an air of self-sufficiency. A natural consequence was, the treating with more sharpness and contempt those who opposed either your judgment or practice.

"7. You came to live at London. You then, for a season, appeared to gain ground again. You acted in concert with my brother and me; heard our advice, and sometimes followed it. But, this continued only till you contracted a fresh acquaintance with some of the Brethren of Fetter Lane. Henceforward, you were quite shut up to us; we had no manner of influence over you. You were more and more prejudiced against us, and would receive nothing which we said.

"8. About six years ago, you removed to Salisbury, and began a society there. For a year or two, you went with them to church and sacrament, and simply preached faith working by love. God was with you, and they increased both in number, and in the knowledge and love of God.

"About four years since, you broke off all friendship with us. You would not so much as make use of our hymns, either in public or private; but laid them quite aside, and took the German Hymn-book in their stead.

"You would not willingly suffer any of your people to read anything which we wrote. You angrily caught one of my sermons out of your servant's hand, saying, you would have no such books read in your house. In much the same manner, you spoke to Mrs. Whitemarsh, when you found her reading one of the "Appeals." So that, as far as in you lay, you fixed a great gulf between us and you, which remains to this day, notwithstanding a few steps lately made towards a re-union.

"About the same time, you left off going to church, as well as to the sacrament. Your followers very soon trod in your steps; and, not content with neglecting the ordinances of God, they began, after your example, to *despise* them, and all that continued to use them, speaking with equal contempt of the public service, of private prayer, of baptism, and of the Lord's Supper.

"From this time, also, you began to espouse and teach many uncommon opinions: as, that, there is no resurrection of the body; that, there is no general judgment to come; and, that, there is no hell, no worm that never dieth, no fire that never shall be quenched.

"9. Your seriousness and advertence to the presence of God, now, declined daily. You could talk on anything or nothing, just as others did. You could break a jest, or laugh at it heartily; and, as for fasting, abstinence, and self-denial, you, with the Moravians, trampled it under foot.

In an interjected note, Wesley says,—

In the following paragraphs, I recited to him the things he had done with regard to more than one, or two, or three women, concluding thus:—

"And now you know not that you have done anything amiss! You can eat and drink and be merry! You are every day engaged with variety of company, and frequent the coffee houses! Alas, my brother, what is this? How are you above measure hardened by the deceitfulness of sin? Do you remember the story of Santon Barsisa? I pray God, your last end may not be like his! Oh, how you have grieved the Spirit of God! Return to Him with weeping, fasting, and mourning. You are in the very belly of hell; only the pit hath not shut its mouth upon you. Arise, thou sleeper, and call upon thy God! Perhaps, He may yet be found. Because He still bears with *me*, I cannot despair for *you*. But you have not a moment to lose. May God, this instant, strike you to the heart, that you may feel His wrath abiding on you, and have no rest in your bones, by reason of your sin, till all your iniquities are done away."

"JOHN WESLEY."

What success attended Wesley's honest letter? Hall had left his wife at the end of October, 1747. Three months afterwards, he had returned to Salisbury; and Wesley, on his way to Bristol, resolved to call on him. He writes:—

"1748. *January* 26.

"Mr. Hall, having heard I was coming, had given strict orders, that no one should let me in. The inner door he had locked himself, and, I suppose, taken away the key. Yet, when I knocked at the outer gate, which was locked also, William Sims opened the wicket. I walked straight in. A girl stood in the gateway, but turned as soon as she 'saw me. I followed close at her heels, and went in after her at a back door. I asked the maid, 'Where is Mr. Hall?' She said, 'In the parlour,' and went in to him. I followed her, and found him sitting with my sister, but he presently rose and went up-stairs. He then sent William Sims down, and bid him, 'Tell my brother he has no business in my house.' After a few minutes, I went to a house in the town, and my sister came to me. In about an hour, she returned home; but he sent word to the gate, she might go to the place whence she came. I met a little company, gathered up out of the wreck, both in the evening, and at five in the morning, and exhorted them to go on in the Bible way, and not to be wise above that is written."

Having thus failed in his attempt to reason with Westley Hall, and having tried to be of use to a mere handful of the best of the faithless man's followers, Wesley, two days afterwards, went on his way to Bristol.

Things grew worse and worse. Hall's first female victim was a young woman, employed in his house as a seamstress. Other infidelities followed; until, at length, his much-enduring wife was driven from him. The man became a professed polygamist. Life at home became intolerable to "poor Patty;" and, even when she fled from the husband, who had become a monster and a brute, again and again she and her brothers were harassed by his following her. The following are extracts from her brother Charles's Journal :—

"1750. *August* 13.—I met my sister Hall in the churchyard," (Bristol) "and carried her to the room. I had begun preaching, when Mr. Hall walked up the room, and through the desk, and carried her off with him. I was somewhat disturbed; yet went on.

"*August* 15.—He came up again, calling me by my name. I fled, and he pursued ; but could not find me in my lurking place.

"1751. *June* 4.—Instead of proceeding in Ezekiel, I expounded" (at Bristol) "Hebrew x. 34 : 'Now the just shall live by faith; but, if he draw back, my soul shall have no pleasure in him.' I saw the reason with Mr. Hall. He came up toward the desk. Mr. Hamilton stopped him. I gave out a hymn. He sang louder than us all. I spoke sharply of his apostasy, and prayed earnestly for him ; desired their prayers for me, lest, after preaching to others, I myself, also, should be a castaway. He walked away, turned back, threatened. The people were all in tears, and agony of prayer."

There is something horrible in such a scene as this. Westley Hall was "now a settled Deist ;"[1] and, yet, here we find him, with stentorian lustiness, and in mockery, singing, in the midst of a disturbed congregation, one of Charles Wesley's Christian hymns. The man seemed to be abandoned by his God, and left to his own corrupted passions. He is said to have thrown off all restraint, and all regard to decency. He publicly and privately recommended polygamy, as conformable to nature, preached in its defence, and practised as he preached. For years, he lived the life of an adventurer, and a profligate ; acting sometimes as a physician, sometimes as a priest, or figured away with his sword, cane, and scarlet cloak ; assuming any character, according to his humour, or the convenience of the day.[2]

His wife had borne him ten children, nine of whom had been interred at Salisbury. One of them,—Wesley Hall,— still survived, and was being educated at the expense of his uncles, John and Charles. At the age of fourteen, the

---

[1] Wesley's Works, vol. ii., p. 214.
[2] Dove's Wesley Family.

worse than fatherless boy was seized with small-pox, and died. Dr. Adam Clarke says, he had seen "a folio printed sheet, evidently the publication of Mr. Hall;" entitled, "The Art of Happiness; or, the Right use of Reason : an Epistle to Wesley Hall, Junior." "The whole," writes the Doctor, "is a miserable Deistical address, strongly advising his son to follow the dictates of his own nature, as the best way of fulfilling the purposes of his Creator!"

The following are the opening lines :—

> "My son, my son, if e'er a parent's voice
> Has power to warn, let this direct thy choice ;
> Take reason's path, and mad opinions leave,—
> Reason is truth that never can deceive."

Declaiming against superstition and bigotry, and, perhaps, shooting a shaft against the boy's uncles,—the two Wesleys,— the profligate poet writes :—

> "Inspired with frantic, false, fanatic zeal,
> See, with what rage, they threat damnation,—hell,
> To all who fair expose the wretched lies,
> The frauds, the follies, falsehood, forgeries,
> Of Romish fathers, councils, canons, schools,
> Impostors' orders, monks' and madmen's rules."

Love, the universal passion, is eulogized as follows :—

> "By thee inspired, we learn each tuneful art,
> To raise the passions, or improve the heart ;
> The mystic union of the sounding strings,
> The wondrous commerce of the secret springs,
> Whence social joy, and sympathetic pain,
> And friendship's force, and love's eternal reign.
> *******
> With all the mighty charms by heaven designed,
> To raise the bliss of every godlike mind,
> In love concentring, from that image bright,
> The fairest mirror of th' Eternal light."

"He concludes," says Dr. Clarke, "his ungodly advices to his godly son, in these words :—

> "Instructed thus, may'st thou a temple raise,
> More glorious far than that of ancient days ;
> The work of wisdom, and of virtue fair,
> With strength and beauty built beyond compare ;

> By reason's perfect rule, and nature's scale,
> Which God's whole order may to man reveal ;
> Where all things tend, and whence they all began,
> Of His machinery the wondrous plan."

The date of the death of the last of Hall's legitimate offspring has not been recorded ; but his memory was embalmed, and his father's gibbeted, by his uncle, Charles Wesley, in a poetical pamphlet, entitled " Funeral Hymns," published in 1759, pp. 70. The tenth of these hymns is devoted entirely to the son, and is exquisitely beautiful ; the eleventh is a withering invective against the apostate father. The following is a copy :—

> " Rest, happy saint, with God secure,
>   Lodged in the bosom of the Lamb ;
> Thy joy is full, thy state is sure,
>   Through all eternity the same ;
> The heavenly doors have shut thee in,
> The mighty gulf is fixed between.

> " Thy God forbade the son to bear
>   The father's wickedness below :
> And O ! thou canst not suffer there
>   His foul reproach, his guilty woe,
> His fearful doom thou canst not feel,
> Or fall, like him, from heaven to hell.

> " That tender sense of infant grace,
>   (Extinct in him,) which dwelt in thee,
> Nor sin, nor Satan can efface :
>   From pain and grief for ever free,
> Thou canst not now his fall deplore,
> Or pray for one that prays no more.

> " Yet may thy last expiring prayer,
>   For a lost parent's soul, prevail,
> And move the God of love to spare,
>   To' arrest him, at the mouth of hell :
> O God of love, Thine ear incline,
> And save a soul that once was Thine !

> " Thou didst his heaven-born spirit draw,
>   Thou didst his child-like heart inspire,
> And fill with love's profoundest awe ;
>   Though now inflamed with hellish fire,
> He dares Thy favourite Son blaspheme,
> And hates the God that died for him.

" Commissioned by the dying God,
      Blessed with a powerful ministry,
  The world he pointed to Thy blood,
      And turned whole multitudes to Thee ;
  Others he saved, himself a prey
  To hell, an hopeless castaway.

" Murderer of souls, Thou knowest, he lives.
      (Poor souls for whom Thyself hast died,)
  His dreadful punishment receives,
      And bears the mark of sullen pride ;
  And furious lusts his bosom tear,
  And the dire worm of sad despair.

" Condemned, like haggard Cain, to rove,
      By Satan and himself pursued,
  Apostate from redeeming love,
      Abandoned to the curse of God ;
  Thou hear'st the vagabond complain,
  Loud howling, while he bites his chain.

" But O, Thou righteous God, how long
      Shall Thy vindictive anger last ?
  Canst Thou not yet forgive the wrong,
      Bid all his penal woes be past ?
  All power, all mercy as Thou art,
  O break his adamantine heart !

" Before the yawning cavern close
      Its mouth on its devoted prey,
  Thou, who hast died to save Thy foes,
      Thy death's omnipotence display ;
  And snatch from that eternal fire,
  And let him in Thy arms expire."

It would be an odious task to relate all the details of
Westley Hall's sad apostasy. Suffice to say, that he, at
length, went off to the West Indies with one of his concu-
bines, lived there with her till she died, and then returned
to England, where, professing penitential sorrow, he was cordially received by his incomparable wife, who showed him
every Christian attention till his death, which took place at
Bristol, on January 3, 1776 ; some of his last words being, "I
have injured an angel ! an angel that never reproached me !"
Wesley writes :—

" 1776, January 2—Tuesday. I set out early" from London, "and came
just time enough not to see, but to bury poor Mr. Hall, my brother-in-

law, who died on Wednesday morning, I trust, in peace ; for God had given him deep repentance. Such another monument of Divine mercy, considering how low he had fallen, and from what height of holiness, I have not seen, no, not in seventy years ! I had designed to visit him in the morning ; but he did not stay for my coming. It is enough, if, after all his wanderings, we meet again in Abraham's bosom."

"*Requiescat in pace!*" And yet, justice demands that a word more be added. The fact cannot be denied, that, in many instances, the faults of husbands may be traced to the tempers, frailties, and follies of their wives. A bad wife often makes a good husband bad. Was this the fact in the case of Westley Hall ? Did the man who, at Oxford, was so pre-eminently holy, become a licentious infidel through the misbehaviour of his wife ? This is not a memoir of " Patty " Hall ; but to be entirely silent concerning her might create suspicion, that, she was not unblamable in her connubial life. Hence, even at the expense of returning to the dung-hill of Westley Hall's disgusting wickedness, a few more facts must be stated.

Assuming Martha Wesley to have been aware, that, Westley Hall had proposed marriage to her sister Kezziah, and had jilted her, it was a huge, seriously censurable imprudence for her to become his wife ; but that being said, there is not another fact to be told against her. What was her behaviour to one of the worst of husbands ?

The seduction of the seamstress has been already mentioned. Mrs. Hall knew nothing of her husband's criminality till the poor girl actually fell in labour. Hall had gone from home ; his wife instantly ordered her other servants to call in a doctor. The servants refused. She remonstrated with them on their inhumanity. They completed her surprise by telling her the seamstress was in labour through her criminal connection with their master. The poor wife was terribly wounded ; but the life of her husband's paramour was in danger. The servants refused to stir, and she herself had to bring in a midwife. Her purse contained six pounds. Five of these she gave to a neighbour to look after the adulterous young mother ; with the other pound, she went off to seek her worthless husband, who had designedly gone to London ; mildly told him what had happened, and actually persuaded him to return to Salisbury as soon as the young woman and her child could be removed to another dwelling.

Another instance must be given. One day, Hall had the shameful inhumanity to bring home one of his illegitimate infants, and to order his wife to take charge of it. Will it be believed, that "Patty" actually brought out her cradle, placed the bastard babe in it, and continued to perform for it all that its helplessness required!

Was the woman demented? or a good-tempered silly fool, without any self-respect, and without the least idea of what was due unto herself? Not so; but just the opposite. As a proof of this, the following may be given :—

While nursing the illegitimate child just mentioned, her own charming boy, Wesley Hall, displeased his father, who had as little government of his temper as of his passions. In a rage, the father thrust his son into a dark closet, and locked him up. The poor boy was terrified to distraction. His mother, with her usual calmness, desired her husband to release the child. He refused. She entreated; but he was resolute. "Sir," said she, at length thoroughly aroused; "Sir, thank the grace of God, that, while *my* child is thus cruelly treated, suffering to distraction a punishment he has not merited, I had not turned *your* babe out of the cradle; but now I *demand*, that you will immediately unlock the closet and release the child, or, if you refuse, I myself will do it." The miserable poltroon succumbed, and the little prisoner regained his liberty. There was more in this than female firmness. Caitiff as he was, Hall had exercised the authority of a father, and his wife did her utmost not to set aside that authority; wishing, with true philosophy, that the lips which had pronounced the sentence might pronounce also its repeal. The woman, taking and maintaining this position, was the very opposite of a senseless, insipid household drudge, without either mind or manners, a very slave to some selfish brute who unfortunately rules over her.

If "Patty" Wesley,—we are reluctant to call her "Patty" Hall,—erred at all, it was on the side of fidelity to her worthless husband, and of kindness to his wretched mistresses. "How could you give money to your husband's concubine?" asked her brother Charles "I knew," she answered, "that *I* could obtain what I wanted from many ; but she, poor hapless creature, could not. *Pity* is due to the wicked, the good claim *esteem.* Besides, I did not act as a *woman*, but as a *Christian.*"

Notwithstanding all her bad treatment, this incomparable wife was never heard to speak of her husband but with kindness. Two extracts from her letters will show both her feelings and good sense, under circumstances the most trying to a female mind :—

"Being convinced, that, I cannot possibly oblige you any longer, by anything I can say or do, I have determined to rid you of so useless a burden, as soon as it shall please God to give me an opportunity. If you have so much humanity left for a wife, who has lived so many years with you, as to allow anything toward a maintenance, I will thank you."

"I conjure you to tell what fatal delusion could make me offend a person whom, of all creatures upon earth, I desired most to please. I shall be exceedingly obliged to you, if you will be so good as to satisfy me in this particular. But, be that as it may, whether you think fit to grant or deny my request, one thing I must inform you of, which is, that, I never can, so long as I am in my senses, wilfully bring any evil upon you. No, death itself does not appear so shocking to me, as endeavouring to lay you under any other obligation than those of conscience and honour. For which reason, I design to put myself again absolutely in your power. If you make a kind use of that power, I shall thank God and you. If not, the time is very short that I can stay on this side the grave ; and in the same sentiments that I have lived, I trust, it will be given me to die."

It is hardly necessary to give further details of this memorable woman. Enough has been said, to show, that, Westley Hall's infamous behaviour was not owing to the character or conduct of his wife. We only add an extract from a manuscript, now before us, written by her niece, Miss Sarah Wesley, with whom she lived on the most loving and confidential terms. Miss Wesley, daughter of Charles, observes :—

"Dr. Johnson was an early friend of hers ; to her my father owed his acquaintance with the Doctor, and I, the honour of his favour. I used to accompany her to Bolt Court, and had the privilege of hearing their discourse.

"Her whole character was eminent for magnanimity and tenderness. When her unfortunate husband contended for the lawfulness of polygamy, and acted on his erroneous principles, in all her expostulations, she never lost her command of language, or gave him a reproachful word.

"She was particularly distinguished with favour, by my grandmother, for her docile and tranquil spirit; and her brothers and sisters nick-named her the patient *Grisele.* Such was her attachment to my uncle John, that, if she was in any pain or trouble in her infant days, the sight of him would instantly cheer her. I never heard of so strong an affection, which lasted toward him through life. My grandmother once entered the room, where the children were in high glee and frolic, and said, 'Ah, you will all, one day, be more thoughtful, as you grow in years.' Martha replied, 'Shall I be more thoughtful?' 'No,' said her mother. Indeed, by all that I have heard, she was born a philosopher, and preferred her mother's chamber to sports or recreations, which naturally endeared her to the parent, whom she almost idolized.

"Were I to relate the instances of her kindness to me, I could fill a book. No parent's love could exceed hers. It was a joyful day whenever I was to spend it with her. Even my brothers looked forward with delightful anticipation, when her weekly visit was to be paid us (for one day of the week was appropriated by my father to receive her). Her conversation so far resembled my uncle's, that, children idolized her; and her memory, to the last, supplied the place of books. She had the best of our poets by heart; and her mode of giving advice was so gentle, that offence could not be taken. Her compassion and charity to the poor were such, that, my father used to say, it was needless to give anything to Pat for her own comfort; she always gave it away to some beggar, and forgot herself.

"I was with her at her death. Composed and tranquil, she reasoned about every pain, as occasioning it, with the same serenity she would have spoken of common things. She had no disease, but the springs of life were worn out. A little before her departure, she called me to her bedside, and said, 'You have heard me wish for assurance,' (of happiness, she meant), 'I have it now. Shout!' and died!"

Mrs. Hall was the last survivor of the Wesley family,—her father, mother, brothers, and sisters having all died before her. In the *Gentleman's Magazine* for 1791, there is the following obituary notice.

"1791. *July* 12, in the City Road, in her eighty-fourth year, Mrs. Martha Hall, widow of the Rev. Mr. H., and last surviving sister of the Rev. John and Charles Wesley. She was equally distinguished by piety, understanding, and sweetness of temper. Her sympathy for the wretched, and her bounty, even to the worthless, will eternize her memory in better worlds than this."

Her remains are interred in the same vault as those of her brother John, in the burial ground of his chapel, in City Road, London.

Our story of the Oxford Methodists is ended.

ADDENDUM.

By an oversight, the following letter was not inserted in Hervey's memoir. It ought to have found a place at page 220. When Wesley became an out-door preacher, in 1739, Hervey wrote him a letter of remonstrance, to which he replied as follows :—

"As to your advice, that, I should settle in college, I have no business there, having now no office, and no pupils. And whether the other branch of your proposal be expedient, namely, to accept of a cure of souls, it will be time enough to consider when one is offered to me. But, in the meantime, you think, I ought to be still, because, otherwise, I shall invade another's office. You, accordingly, ask, How is it, that, I assemble Christians who are none of my charge, to sing psalms, and pray, and hear the Scriptures expounded ; and think it hard to justify this in other men's parishes, upon catholic principles.

"Permit me to speak plainly. If, by 'catholic principles,' you mean any other than scriptural, they weigh nothing with me ; I allow no other rule, whether of faith or practice, than the Holy Scriptures. But, on scriptural principles, I do not think it hard to justify what I do. God, in Scripture, commands me, according to my power, to instruct the ignorant, reform the wicked, confirm the virtuous. Man forbids me to do this in another's parish ; that is, in effect, not to do it at all ; seeing I have now no parish of my own, nor probably ever shall. Whom then shall I hear ? God or man ? '*If it be just to obey man rather than God, judge ye.*' '*A dispensation of the Gospel is committed to me, and woe is me, if I preach not the Gospel.*' But where shall I preach it, upon the principles you mention? Not in any of the *Christian* parts, at least, of the habitable earth ; for all these are, after a sort, divided into parishes.

"Suffer me to tell you my principles in this matter. I look upon *all the world as my parish;* thus far I mean, that, in whatever part of it I am, I judge it meet, right, and my bounden duty, to declare unto all, that are willing to hear, the glad tidings of salvation. This is the work, which I know, God has called me to ; and sure I am, that His blessing attends it. Great encouragement have I, therefore, to be faithful in fulfilling the work He hath given me to do. His servant I am; and, as such, am employed according to the plain direction of His word,—'*as I have opportunity, doing good to all men.*' And His providence clearly concurs with His word ; which has disengaged me from all things else, that I might singly attend on this very thing, '*and go about doing good.*'

"If you ask, 'How can this be ? How can one do good, of whom *men say all manner of evil?*' I will put you in mind, (though you once knew this, yea, and much established me in that great truth,) the more evil men say of me for my Lord's sake, the more good He will do by me. That it is for His sake, I know, and He knoweth, and the event agreeth thereto; for He mightily confirms the word I speak, by the Holy Ghost, given unto them that hear them. I fear you have herein made shipwreck of the faith. I fear, '*Satan, transformed into an angel of light,*' hath assaulted you, and prevailed also. I fear, that offspring of hell, worldly or mystic prudence, has drawn you away from the simplicity of the Gospel. How else could you ever conceive, that, the being reviled, and '*hated of all men,*' should make us less fit for our Master's service? How else could you ever think of '*saving yourself and them that hear you,*' without being *the filth and offscouring of the world*'?

"To this hour, is this Scripture true. And I therein rejoice, yea, and will rejoice. Blessed be God, I enjoy the reproach of Christ! O may you also be vile, exceeding vile for His sake! God forbid that you hould ever be other than generally scandalous; I had almost said universally. If any man tell you, there is a new way of following Christ ' he is a liar, and the truth is not in him.'

" JOHN WESLEY."

INDEX OF NAMES.

Mr. Tyerman's work was fairly called for, both by the fact that no life of Wesley had been published for forty years, and because Southey's, the only one tolerably written as a literary performance, is the production of a writer who was not himself a member of the Society, who in few points of character resembled the subject of his memoir, and possessed no sources of information which were not already before the world. Mr. Tyerman is a Wesleyan minister, and his materials, both printed and in manuscript, have been accumulating for seventeen years. He has made most diligent use of them; and his history, in regard to its facts, is incomparably more full than any that preceded it.—*Saturday Review*, London.

The time had fairly come for a new and original life of Wesley, embodying, as such a work must, a history of the forming period of Methodism. * * * The changes wrought by the lapse of time have prepared the way for fuller, fairer, and more appreciative examination and statement of the subject, and it is well that the execution of that task has devolved upon one so competent. Mr. Tyerman is thoroughly a Wesleyan, and yet he is able to discuss the subject taken in hand with judicial calmness. A ripe scholar—having made Methodist history a specialty—and a practiced writer, he possessed peculiar fitness for that kind of work, and viewing his subject from so great a distance of time, and in the softened light of a hundred years ago, he was better situated than any of his predecessors in the same field to see the subject in its true relations and circumstances. He has been charged with injustice to the good name of Wesley, but to us it seems quite otherwise. Time and its changes have removed the halo in which it was once encircled and its real character hidden. Some of this false glory having passed away, its unreality is recognized; but as all true greatness appears greatest when set in the clearest light, so nowhere else are the character and the works of Wesley shown to so great advantage as in these pages. We have read the work with real pleasure, and we trust it will meet with a large sale, and be widely read by both Methodists and others.—*N. Y. Christian Advocate.*

Full of interest as this work will be for Wesleyans, it will also prove most truly so for the philosophic observer of religious movements.—*Westminster Review*, London.

Mr. Tyerman is master of much valuable material that no early biographer or critic has made use of.—*Examiner*, London.

The life is one of intense and varied interest. Not a page can we open without our attention being riveted. There is no doubt that this will be recognized henceforth as the standard life of the great preacher, and we are thankful that such a book has been written by one fully capable of understanding and describing its religious influences.—*Christian Work.*

A most interesting and real picture of John Wesley as he was, of the times in which he lived, and of the remarkable movements and scenes in which he bore so prominent a part. There is much in this volume to interest Christians of all denominations.—*Lutheran Observer.*

The writer is in every way fitted to the task. Himself a Wesleyan minister, and in full sympathy with the life and work of the subject of his memoir, it was to him a labor of love and delight. He also enjoyed better facilities than any of his predecessors for the prosecution of the work. His materials, both written and printed, had been accumulating for nearly twenty years, and he has availed himself of them with no common degree of diligence and skill. His work is not only admirable from a literary point of view, but, in regard to its facts, is so full and in every way authenticated with such painstaking scrutiny as to be incomparably superior to any of the former biographies of Wesley. It is not a work for Methodists alone, nor one in which the religious world only will be interested. John Wesley was no ordinary man. Intellectually far above the average standing of the ministry, of naturally broad and liberal views, still further enlarged by education and experience with the world, he excited a wider and more lasting influence upon the religious thought of England and America than any other man of his time. His name will always be held in grateful remembrance by all who honor worth and sincerity, and who see in a life devoted to the advancement of the highest interest of mankind—to the elevation and enlightenment of the poor, the lowly, and degraded—something that demands admiration, without regard to the dividing lines of the sects.—*N. Y. Evening Post.*

Its author eschews irrelevant controversy and unprofitable speculations, and confines himself to the facts and incidents in the eventful life of the great preacher, and to his views, sentiments, doctrines, and herculean labors. It is a work which not only Methodists will desire to read, but which will be eagerly sought for by all who can appreciate and admire the self-sacrifice and unswerving devotion of one of the most earnest, fearless, and successful defenders of the faith whose name has passed into modern history.—*Albany Evening Journal.*

For those who wish to know every fact that can be known of Wesley's life, this biography will probably supersede all others.—*Athenæum*, London.

The preparation of this biography has evidently been a labor of love with Mr. Tyerman, but he has to a commendable degree avoided the besetting sin of biographers—excessive eulogy—and his work is such a record of Wesley's life as not only Methodists but the public at large will be willing to accept without reservation. Few men have lived in modern times who have better deserved attention at the hands of the historian than Wesley, for the religious reform movement of which he was the head was the most important that has ever taken place.—*Philadelphia Evening Telegraph.*

Mr. Tyerman's book is by far the most valuable life of Wesley. Its thoroughness, frankness, fearlessness, simplicity; bold, yet self-distrusting discrimination; its loving, yet not blind appreciation of the subject; its patient, painstaking, one would think exhaustive, collection of data and weighing of evidence; its gathering into a focus all the scattered rays of information about Wesley and his work; all this makes one profoundly grateful to Mr. Tyerman. The leading minds of other denominations will welcome this as distinctly the best life of Wesley ever issued; and Methodists will recognize the gracious wisdom of Providence in setting Mr. Tyerman apart for this work.—*City Road Magazine*, London.

Mr. Tyerman has compiled a biography that an examination of the first volume convinces us is infinitely the best yet published, and that promises to be accepted as the standard one. It is very circumstantial, and very calmly and justly appreciative, the greatest care being manifested to present the whole truth and to abstain from any thing like mere eulogy of his subject. Many hitherto unpublished letters of Wesley are given, and in other directions the work has unusual interest.—*Philadelphia Inquirer.*

Seventeen years of patient labor, the careful study of an immense mass of unpublished original manuscript letters and documents, fidelity to his subject, with an impartiality of judgment that is frequently seen in his strictures upon Wesley's language and actions, and an enthusiastic love for the venerated man, are among the author's qualifications for his work. So far as possible he has followed the plan which has made Dr. Hanna's life of Thomas Chalmers a model of biography. Wesley, for the most part, is here his own biographer. The author, with skill, and in a lucid style, has arranged the facts and shaped the story, without regard to the philosophy of it. * * * We have been fascinated over his interesting pages, not only with his photographic views of his hero, but with his equally faithful representations of Whitefield and the compeers of these two great ministers of Christ.—*Christian Intelligencer*, N. Y.

An extremely able and interesting life of John Wesley. It is complete and accurate, written in an agreeable style, full of those reminiscences illustrative of slight traits of character which form the great charm of a biography; a striking and faithful picture of a remarkable man.—*English Independent.*

The best biography of the great leader of modern active Christianity.—*Freeman.*

Mr. Tyerman, as his last, and we think his best biographer, has produced a record highly honorable to his subject, fresh and lively in style, copious in information, discriminating and candid in its tone, and worthy of a first rank as a biographical history of early Methodism.—*Methodist New Connexion Magazine.*

The verdict of his numerous readers will be that he has admirably succeeded; henceforth his production will be pre-eminently *the* Life of Wesley, and we question whether it will ever be superseded or rivaled by any subsequent biography, certainly not for the amplitude of its information or the impartiality or faithfulness with which facts are given. So fully and vividly is the spiritual and moral condition of the country during Wesley's lifetime depicted in these pages, that the reader finds the work a most excellent general religious history of the nation for the period, and for this purpose it will have great value as a book of reference.—*Methodist Quarterly*, London.

Mr. Tyerman especially deserves well of the general public, because his Methodist reverence for the subject of his narrative does not induce him to keep back or cover up any thing. An honest and thorough biography, dealing with naked facts, and chiefly leaving the reader to his own impressions, is a rare thing in religious history; but this, in the main, Mr. Tyerman has given.—*Chicago Evening Journal.*

Mr. Tyerman has earned a debt of gratitude from his readers by the faithful, painstaking light which he throws on the man and his time, and it may fairly be said that this, the fifth life of Wesley which has been published, is the first which presents him to us both justly and fully.—*Christian Register.*

There are few biographies more minute, careful, and impartial than "Tyerman's Wesley." There is no influence nor incident which in any way had to do with the great preacher's character and opinions that Mr. Tyerman does not describe with faithful sincerity. The work is not alone a life of Wesley—every relative and friend and disciple is given such generous mention that it seems a perfect nest of biographies, and it is at the same time a profuse and thorough history of the foundation and first forty years of Methodism. * * * He is at no pains to hide John Wesley's faults and foibles: he gives us a definite picture of the man exactly as he was. * * * There could not be a more accurate record of Wesley's noble life and unselfish labors, of his innumerable publications and most important sermons. The literature of Methodism has no more judicious and valuable work than this.— *N. Y. Tribune.*

He is not an eulogist, but a biographer, and he gives us Wesley as he lived, and hence his work is entitled to the high praise that is due to impartiality. No one desires to read of an ideal Wesley, but to have the real man reproduced, and Mr. Tyerman has reproduced his hero.—*Boston Traveller.*

There is a conscientious honesty in the portraiture of his hero which wins our regard for the author too.—*Christian Standard.*

We regard this as an invaluable contribution to Church history. * * * We believe the author has given us a history worthy of confidence, as he has certainly given it in a pleasing style.—*Methodist Protestant*, Baltimore.

The style is pleasant, easy, and intelligible.—*Boston Journal.*

Mr. Tyerman's work will henceforth be regarded as the standard life of Wesley.—*Evangelical Magazine.*

No novel can excel this work for sustained interest.—*Central Advocate.*

This is the most complete, and will doubtless prove the most satisfactory biography of Wesley yet written. It is the result of diligent research and much painstaking, extending through twenty of the best years of a man's life. Mr. Tyerman, the biographer, has been living amid favorable circumstances to do this, which has been to him a work of love. He writes *con amore*, yet free from the blinding influence of prejudice. It is to be expected that he would have his own predilections, and if he did not have them his work would not be worthy of public notice; but the severest criticism will fail, we think, to detect any miscoloring of essential facts, however it may estimate personal opinion of the man or events in his life. * * * The book is more than a valuable, almost indispensable, accession to the literature of the Methodist Church; it is a part of the theological treasures of the age. —*College Courant.*

It deserves the praise, not only of being the fullest biography of Wesley, but also of being eminently painstaking, veracious, and trustworthy.—*Edinburgh Review.*

It is full, fair, and written with an enthusiasm that the reader can hardly help sharing, as he is brought by the force of the author into close acquaintance with one of the remarkable religious leaders of the world. * * * One can not arise from a perusal of this book without feeling an increased admiration for the noble, courageous, patient saint; and the devout reader will be moved with a heartfelt gratitude to God for the life and example of such a man. The book should be read not only by all Methodists, but by every one who is interested either in accounts of moral heroism and greatness of soul, or who would trace the rise of a great form of religious thought and its development through the magnetic enthusiasm of a gifted and unselfish nature.—*Louisville Courier Journal.*

The best way to make a biography interesting is to permit its hero, as far as possible, to tell his own story. This plan has been adopted by Mr. Tyerman with notable success, and has resulted in the production of a work alike instructive and entertaining.—*Brooklyn Union.*

* * * It is as interesting as a novel, and as refreshing as a kindling sermon. To those who do not sympathize with Methodism, but who are interested in the career and experience of an eminent religious genius and reformer, the book presents strong attractions.— *Boston Globe.*

PUBLISHED BY HARPER & BROTHERS, NEW YORK.

VALUABLE & INTERESTING WORKS

FOR PUBLIC AND PRIVATE LIBRARIES,

PUBLISHED BY HARPER & BROTHERS, NEW YORK.

☞ *For a full List of Books suitable for Libraries, see* HARPER & BROTHERS' TRADE-LIST *and* CATALOGUE, *which may be had gratuitously on application to the Publishers personally, or by letter enclosing Six Cents.*

☞ HARPER & BROTHERS *will send any of the following works by mail, postage prepaid, to any part of the United States, on receipt of the price.*

FLAMMARION'S ATMOSPHERE. The Atmosphere. Translated from the French of CAMILLE FLAMMARION. Edited by JAMES GLAISHER, F.R.S., Superintendent of the Magnetical and Meteorological Department of the Royal Observatory at Greenwich. With 10 Chromo-Lithographs and 86 Woodcuts. 8vo, Cloth.

HUDSON'S HISTORY OF JOURNALISM. Journalism in the United States, from 1690 to 1872. By FREDERIC HUDSON. Crown 8vo, Cloth, $5 00.

PIKE'S SUB-TROPICAL RAMBLES. Sub-Tropical Rambles in the Land of the Aphanapteryx. By NICHOLAS PIKE, U. S. Consul, Port Louis, Mauritius. Profusely Illustrated from the Author's own Sketches; containing also Maps and Valuable Meteorological Charts. 8vo, Cloth, $3 50.

TYERMAN'S OXFORD METHODISTS. The Oxford Methodists: Memoirs of the Rev. Messrs. Clayton, Ingham, Gambold, Hervey, and Broughton, with Biographical Notices of others. By the Rev. L. TYERMAN, Author of "Life and Times of the Rev. John Wesley," &c. Crown 8vo, Cloth, $2 50.

TRISTRAM'S THE LAND OF MOAB. The Result of Travels and Discoveries on the East Side of the Dead Sea and the Jordan. By H. B. TRISTRAM, M.A., LL.D., F.R.S., Master of the Greatham Hospital, and Honorary Canon of Durham. With New Map and Illustrations. Crown 8vo, Cloth, $2 50.

SANTO DOMINGO, Past and Present: with a Glance at Hayti. By SAMUEL HAZARD. Maps and Illustrations. Crown 8vo, Cloth, $3 50.

LIFE OF ALFRED COOKMAN. The Life of the Rev. Alfred Cookman; with some Account of his Father, the Rev. George Grimston Cookman. By HENRY B. RIDGAWAY, D.D. With an Introduction by Bishop FOSTER, LL.D. Portrait on Steel. 12mo, Cloth, $2 00.

HERVEY'S CHRISTIAN RHETORIC. A System of Christian Rhetoric, for the Use of Preachers and Other Speakers. By GEORGE WINFRED HERVEY, M.A., Author of "Rhetoric of Conversation," &c. 8vo, Cloth.

CASTELAR'S OLD ROME AND NEW ITALY. Old Rome and New Italy. By EMILIO CASTELAR. Translated by Mrs. ARTHUR ARNOLD. 12mo, Cloth, $1 75.

THE TREATY OF WASHINGTON: Its Negotiation, Execution, and the Discussions Relating Thereto. By CALEB CUSHING. Crown 8vo, Cloth, $2 00.

PRIME'S I GO A-FISHING. I Go a-Fishing. By W. C. PRIME. Crown 8vo, Cloth, Beveled Edges, $2 50.

HALLOCK'S FISHING TOURIST. The Fishing Tourist: Angler's Guide and Reference Book. By CHARLES HALLOCK, Secretary of the "Blooming-Grove Park Association." Illustrations. Crown 8vo, Cloth, $2 00.

SCOTT'S AMERICAN FISHING. Fishing in American Waters. By GENIO C. SCOTT. With 170 Illustrations. Crown 8vo, Cloth, $3 50.

ANNUAL RECORD OF SCIENCE AND INDUSTRY FOR 1872. Edited by Prof. SPENCER F. BAIRD, of the Smithsonian Institution, with the Assistance of Eminent Men of Science. 12mo, over 700 pp., Cloth, $2 00. (Uniform with the *Annual Record of Science and Industry for* 1871. 12mo, Cloth, $2 00.)

COL. FORNEY'S ANECDOTES OF PUBLIC MEN. Anecdotes of Public Men. By JOHN W. FORNEY. 12mo, Cloth, $2 00.

MISS BEECHER'S HOUSEKEEPER AND HEALTHKEEPER: Containing Five Hundred Recipes for Economical and Healthful Cooking; also, many Directions for securing Health and Happiness. Approved by Physicians of all Classes. Illustrations. 12mo, Cloth, $1 50.

FARM BALLADS. By WILL CARLETON. Handsomely Illustrated. Square 8vo, Ornamental Cloth, $2 00; Gilt Edges, $2 50.

POETS OF THE NINETEENTH CENTURY. The Poets of the Nineteenth Century. Selected and Edited by the Rev. Robert Aris Willmott. With English and American Additions, arranged by Evert A. Duyckinck, Editor of "Cyclopædia of American Literature." Comprising Selections from the Greatest Authors of the Age. Superbly Illustrated with 141 Engravings from Designs by the most Eminent Artists. In elegant small 4to form, printed on Superfine Tinted Paper, richly bound in extra Cloth, Beveled, Gilt Edges, $5 00; Half Calf, $5 50; Full Turkey Morocco, $9 00.

THE REVISION OF THE ENGLISH VERSION OF THE NEW TESTAMENT. With an Introduction by the Rev. P. Schaff, D.D. 618 pp., Crown 8vo, Cloth, $3 00.

This work embraces in one volume:

I. ON A FRESH REVISION OF THE ENGLISH NEW TESTAMENT. By J. B. Lightfoot, D.D., Canon of St. Paul's, and Hulsean Professor of Divinity, Cambridge. Second Edition, Revised. 196 pp.

II. ON THE AUTHORIZED VERSION OF THE NEW TESTAMENT in Connection with some Recent Proposals for its Revision. By Richard Chenevix Trench, D.D., Archbishop of Dublin. 194 pp.

III. CONSIDERATIONS ON THE REVISION OF THE ENGLISH VERSION OF THE NEW TESTAMENT. By J. C. Ellicott, D.D., Bishop of Gloucester and Bristol. 178 pp.

NORDHOFF'S CALIFORNIA. California: For Health, Pleasure, and Residence. A Book for Travelers and Settlers. Illustrated. 8vo, Paper, $2 00; Cloth, $2 50.

MOTLEY'S DUTCH REPUBLIC. The Rise of the Dutch Republic. By John Lothrop Motley, LL.D., D.C.L. With a Portrait of William of Orange. 3 vols., 8vo, Cloth, $10 50.

MOTLEY'S UNITED NETHERLAND'S. History of the United Netherlands: from the Death of William the Silent to the Twelve Years' Truce—1609. With a full View of the English-Dutch Struggle against Spain, and of the Origin and Destruction of the Spanish Armada. By John Lothrop Motley, LL.D., D.C.L. Portraits. 4 vols., 8vo, Cloth, $14 00.

NAPOLEON'S LIFE OF CÆSAR. The History of Julius Cæsar. By His late Imperial Majesty Napoleon III. Two Volumes ready. Library Edition, 8vo, Cloth, $3 50 per vol.

Maps to Vols. I. and II. sold separately. Price $1 50 each, NET.

HAYDN'S DICTIONARY OF DATES, relating to all Ages and Nations. For Universal Reference. Edited by Benjamin Vincent, Assistant Secretary and Keeper of the Library of the Royal Institution of Great Britain; and Revised for the Use of American Readers. 8vo, Cloth, $5 00; Sheep, $6 00.

MACGREGOR'S ROB ROY ON THE JORDAN. The Rob Roy on the Jordan, Nile, Red Sea, and Gennesareth, &c. A Canoe Cruise in Palestine and Egypt, and the Waters of Damascus. By J. Macgregor, M.A. With Maps and Illustrations. Crown 8vo, Cloth, $2 50.

WALLACE'S MALAY ARCHIPELAGO. The Malay Archipelago: the Land of the Orang-Utan and the Bird of Paradise. A Narrative of Travel, 1854–1862. With Studies of Man and Nature. By Alfred Russel Wallace. With Ten Maps and Fifty-one Elegant Illustrations. Crown 8vo, Cloth, $2 50.

WHYMPER'S ALASKA. Travel and Adventure in the Territory of Alaska, formerly Russian America—now Ceded to the United States—and in various other parts of the North Pacific. By Frederick Whymper. With Map and Illustrations. Crown 8vo, Cloth, $2 50.

ORTON'S ANDES AND THE AMAZON. The Andes and the Amazon; or, Across the Continent of South America. By James Orton, M.A., Professor of Natural History in Vassar College, Poughkeepsie, N. Y., and Corresponding Member of the Academy of Natural Sciences, Philadelphia. With a New Map of Equatorial America and numerous Illustrations. Crown 8vo, Cloth, $2 00.

WINCHELL'S SKETCHES OF CREATION. Sketches of Creation: a Popular View of some of the Grand Conclusions of the Sciences in reference to the History of Matter and of Life. Together with a Statement of the Intimations of Science respecting the Primordial Condition and the Ultimate Destiny of the Earth and the Solar System. By Alexander Winchell, LL.D., Professor of Geology, Zoology, and Botany in the University of Michigan, and Director of the State Geological Survey. With Illustrations. 12mo, Cloth, $2 00.

WHITE'S MASSACRE OF ST. BARTHOLOMEW. The Massacre of St. Bartholomew: Preceded by a History of the Religious Wars in the Reign of Charles IX. By Henry White, M.A. With Illustrations. 8vo, Cloth, $1 75.

LOSSING'S FIELD-BOOK OF THE REVOLUTION. Pictorial Field-Book of the Revolution; or, Illustrations, by Pen and Pencil, of the History, Biography, Scenery, Relics, and Traditions of the War for Independence. By BENSON J. LOSSING. 2 vols., 8vo, Cloth, $14 00; Sheep, $15 00; Half Calf, $18 00; Full Turkey Morocco, $22 00.

LOSSING'S FIELD-BOOK OF THE WAR OF 1812. Pictorial Field-Book of the War of 1812; or, Illustrations, by Pen and Pencil, of the History, Biography, Scenery, Relics, and Traditions of the Last War for American Independence. By BENSON J. LOSSING. With several hundred Engravings on Wood, by Lossing and Barritt, chiefly from Original Sketches by the Author. 1088 pages, 8vo, Cloth, $7 00; Sheep, $8 50; Half Calf, $10 00.

ALFORD'S GREEK TESTAMENT. The Greek Testament: with a critically revised Text; a Digest of Various Readings; Marginal References to Verbal and Idiomatic Usage; Prolegomena; and a Critical and Exegetical Commentary. For the Use of Theological Students and Ministers. By HENRY ALFORD, D.D., Dean of Canterbury. Vol. I., containing the Four Gospels. 944 pages, 8vo, Cloth, $6 00; Sheep, $6 50.

ABBOTT'S FREDERICK THE GREAT. The History of Frederick the Second, called Frederick the Great. By JOHN S. C. ABBOTT. Elegantly Illustrated. 8vo, Cloth, $5 00.

ABBOTT'S HISTORY OF THE FRENCH REVOLUTION. The French Revolution of 1789, as viewed in the Light of Republican Institutions. By JOHN S. C. ABBOTT. With 100 Engravings. 8vo, Cloth, $5 00.

ABBOTT'S NAPOLEON BONAPARTE. The History of Napoleon Bonaparte. By JOHN S. C. ABBOTT. With Maps, Woodcuts, and Portraits on Steel. 2 vols., 8vo, Cloth, $10 00.

ABBOTT'S NAPOLEON AT ST. HELENA; or, Interesting Anecdotes and Remarkable Conversations of the Emperor during the Five and a Half Years of his Captivity. Collected from the Memorials of Las Casas, O'Meara, Montholon, Antommarchi, and others. By JOHN S. C. ABBOTT. With Illustrations. 8vo, Cloth, $5 00.

ADDISON'S COMPLETE WORKS. The Works of Joseph Addison, embracing the whole of the "Spectator." Complete in 3 vols., 8vo, Cloth, $6 00.

ALCOCK'S JAPAN. The Capital of the Tycoon: a Narrative of a Three Years' Residence in Japan. By Sir RUTHERFORD ALCOCK, K.C.B., Her Majesty's Envoy Extraordinary and Minister Plenipotentiary in Japan. With Maps and Engravings. 2 vols., 12mo, Cloth, $3 50.

ALISON'S HISTORY OF EUROPE. FIRST SERIES: From the Commencement of the French Revolution, in 1789, to the Restoration of the Bourbons, in 1815. [In addition to the Notes on Chapter LXXVI., which correct the errors of the original work concerning the United States, a copious Analytical Index has been appended to this American edition.] SECOND SERIES: From the Fall of Napoleon, in 1815, to the Accession of Louis Napoleon, in 1852. 8 vols., 8vo, Cloth, $16 00.

BALDWIN'S PRE-HISTORIC NATIONS. Pre-Historic Nations; or, Inquiries concerning some of the Great Peoples and Civilizations of Antiquity, and their Probable Relation to a still Older Civilization of the Ethiopians or Cushites of Arabia. By JOHN D. BALDWIN, Member of the American Oriental Society. 12mo, Cloth, $1 75.

BARTH'S NORTH AND CENTRAL AFRICA. Travels and Discoveries in North and Central Africa: being a Journal of an Expedition undertaken under the Auspices of H. B. M.'s Government, in the Years 1849–1855. By HENRY BARTH, Ph.D., D.C.L. Illustrated. 3 vols., 8vo, Cloth, $12 00.

HENRY WARD BEECHER'S SERMONS. Sermons by HENRY WARD BEECHER, Plymouth Church, Brooklyn. Selected from Published and Unpublished Discourses, and Revised by their Author. With Steel Portrait. Complete in 2 vols., 8vo, Cloth, $5 00.

LYMAN BEECHER'S AUTOBIOGRAPHY, &c. Autobiography, Correspondence, &c., of Lyman Beecher, D.D. Edited by his Son, CHARLES BEECHER. With Three Steel Portraits, and Engravings on Wood. In 2 vols., 12mo, Cloth, $5 00.

BOSWELL'S JOHNSON. The Life of Samuel Johnson, LL.D. Including a Journey to the Hebrides. By JAMES BOSWELL, Esq. A New Edition, with numerous Additions and Notes. By JOHN WILSON CROKER, LL.D., F.R.S. Portrait of Boswell. 2 vols., 8vo, Cloth, $4 00.

DRAPER'S CIVIL WAR. History of the American Civil War. By JOHN W. DRAPER, M.D., LL.D., Professor of Chemistry and Physiology in the University of New York. In Three Vols. 8vo, Cloth, $3 50 per vol.

DRAPER'S INTELLECTUAL DEVELOPMENT OF EUROPE. A History of the Intellectual Development of Europe. By JOHN W. DRAPER, M.D., LL.D., Professor of Chemistry and Physiology in the University of New York. 8vo, Cloth, $5 00.

DRAPER'S AMERICAN CIVIL POLICY. Thoughts on the Future Civil Policy of America. By JOHN W. DRAPER, M.D., LL.D., Professor of Chemistry and Physiology in the University of New York. Crown 8vo, Cloth, $2 50.

DU CHAILLU'S AFRICA. Explorations and Adventures in Equatorial Africa with Accounts of the Manners and Customs of the People, and of the Chase of the Gorilla, the Crocodile, Leopard, Elephant, Hippopotamus, and other Animals. By PAUL B. DU CHAILLU. Numerous Illustrations. 8vo, Cloth, $5 00.

BELLOWS'S OLD WORLD. The Old World in its New Face: Impressions of Europe in 1867–1868. By HENRY W. BELLOWS. 2 vols., 12mo, Cloth, $3 50.

BRODHEAD'S HISTORY OF NEW YORK. History of the State of New York. By JOHN ROMEYN BRODHEAD. 1609–1691. 2 vols. 8vo, Cloth, $3 00 per vol.

BROUGHAM'S AUTOBIOGRAPHY. Life and Times of HENRY, LORD BROUGHAM. Written by Himself. In Three Volumes. 12mo, Cloth, $2 00 per vol.

BULWER'S PROSE WORKS. Miscellaneous Prose Works of Edward Bulwer, Lord Lytton. 2 vols., 12mo, Cloth, $3 50.

BULWER'S HORACE. The Odes and Epodes of Horace. A Metrical Translation into English. With Introduction and Commentaries. By LORD LYTTON. With Latin Text from the Editions of Orelli, Macleane, and Yonge. 12mo, Cloth, $1 75.

BULWER'S KING ARTHUR. A Poem. By EARL LYTTON. New Edition. 12mo, Cloth, $1 75.

BURNS'S LIFE AND WORKS. The Life and Works of Robert Burns. Edited by ROBERT CHAMBERS. 4 vols., 12mo, Cloth, $6 00.

REINDEER, DOGS, AND SNOW-SHOES. A Journal of Siberian Travel and Explorations made in the Years 1865–'67. By RICHARD J. BUSH, late of the Russo-American Telegraph Expedition. Illustrated. Crown 8vo, Cloth, $3 00.

CARLYLE'S FREDERICK THE GREAT. History of Friedrich II., called Frederick the Great. By THOMAS CARLYLE. Portraits, Maps, Plans, &c. 6 vols., 12mo, Cloth, $12 00.

CARLYLE'S FRENCH REVOLUTION. History of the French Revolution. Newly Revised by the Author, with Index, &c. 2 vols., 12mo, Cloth, $3 50.

CARLYLE'S OLIVER CROMWELL. Letters and Speeches of Oliver Cromwell. With Elucidations and Connecting Narrative. 2 vols., 12mo, Cloth, $3 50.

CHALMERS'S POSTHUMOUS WORKS. The Posthumous Works of Dr. Chalmers. Edited by his Son-in-Law, Rev. WILLIAM HANNA, LL.D. Complete in 9 vols., 12mo, Cloth, $13 50.

COLERIDGE'S COMPLETE WORKS. The Complete Works of Samuel Taylor Coleridge. With an Introductory Essay upon his Philosophical and Theological Opinions. Edited by Professor SHEDD. Complete in Seven Vols. With a fine Portrait. Small 8vo, Cloth, $10 50.

DOOLITTLE'S CHINA. Social Life of the Chinese: with some Account of their Religious, Governmental, Educational, and Business Customs and Opinions. With special but not exclusive Reference to Fuhchau. By Rev. JUSTUS DOOLITTLE, Fourteen Years Member of the Fuhchau Mission of the American Board. Illustrated with more than 150 characteristic Engravings on Wood. 2 vols., 12mo, Cloth, $5 00.

GIBBON'S ROME. History of the Decline and Fall of the Roman Empire. By EDWARD GIBBON. With Notes by Rev. H. H. MILMAN and M. GUIZOT. A new cheap Edition. To which is added a complete Index of the whole Work, and a Portrait of the Author. 6 vols., 12mo, Cloth, $9 00.

HAZEN'S SCHOOL AND ARMY IN GERMANY AND FRANCE. The School and the Army in Germany and France, with a Diary of Siege Life at Versailles. By Brevet Major-General W. B. HAZEN, U.S.A., Colonel Sixth Infantry. Crown 8vo, Cloth, $2 50.

www.ingramcontent.com/pod-product-compliance
Lightning Source LLC
Chambersburg PA
CBHW020900130726
47900CB00014B/1309